Phoenix Rising

Anunnaki Wars, Volume 1

C.S. Wade

Published by Platinum Oak, 2020.

PHOENIX RISING

First edition. July 1, 2020.

Copyright © 2020 C.S. Wade.

ISBN: 978-1733775724

Written by C.S. Wade.

This is for my two grown daughters who have pushed me to write. My long time love and abiding activity through good and bad. To my beautiful seven grandkids with love. I wish your lives filled with nothing but love and happiness. Adversity can lead to better things if you allow it to. And to any who stood by and supported me in all my endeavors. To one who will always be my friend Thane Gilmore. To all my friends I have in the game of Guild Wars and all the WvW's in Yaks Bend. To those in the guilds of Eye, PoV, Doom, Foul and Waar. I have laughed and cursed while filling interminable nightse nights battling against all odds. Both wins and losses help keep me sane and not to take myself seriously.

Phoenix Rising
Anunnaki Wars

C.S. Wade

Platinum Oak Publishing
All rights reserved.
ISBN- 978-1-7337757-2-4[1]
Cover Images by Shutterstock
Cover Art by Nejron Photo
Cover Lettering by Fivver: hmd gfx

---

1. https://www.myidentifiers.com/

title_registration?isbn=978-1-7337757-2-4&icon_type=Assigned

DEDICATION

THIS IS FOR MY TWO grown daughters who have pushed me to write. My long-time love and abiding activity through good and bad. To my beautiful seven grandkids with love. I wish your lives were filled with nothing but love and happiness. Adversity can lead to better things if you allow it to. And to any who stood by and supported me in all my endeavors. To one who will always be my friend Thane Gilmore. To all my friends I have in the game of Guild Wars and all the WvW's in Yaks Bend. To those in the guilds of Eye, PoV, Doom, Foul and Waar. I have laughed and cursed while filling long nights battling against all odds. Both wins and losses help keep me sane and not to take myself seriously.

Prologue

Three Sars after War of the Gods.
GGS 03 in the third spiral arm of the outer rim.

KLAXONS SCREAMED OUT warnings as the ship's Ai avatar Nari called out. "Incoming. Unidentified source. Condition Red, repeat Condition Red. All hands. Emergency stations," Nari raced towards the refitted ex-war cruiser's bridge.

When the broadcast sounded, Commander Prince Aidan, reviewing the latest Galactic Gate's deployment on the outer bridge landing, lunged for the closest chair, feet away, too late.

A deafening detonation and a crackling sizzle as plasma flashed across the starboard side of the ship, ripping open the hull along the pathway. Bulkheads, gear, unprotected technicians, and extensive sections of the outer skin sucked away by the rapacious vacuum before the blast emergency shielding engaged.

Aidan pinwheeled off the upper command landing walkway to the lower cargo hold, skidding along the floor before slamming against the bay doors. The impact tearing the breath from his lungs. A searing, blinding pain engulfed him.

The screech of gravity engines reverberated in pace with the detonations, attempting to compensate for the instant destabilization of the cruiser.

Equipment and goods not anchored became dangerous projectiles. Debris flying around missed the isomorphic form of Nari as he melted to the floor. His gelatinous body reforming on the upper war-scarred bridge. The strident notes of warning Klaxons shrill as emergency alarms shrieked throughout the passageways.

Agony stabbed Aidan as he righted himself and saw Nari reappearing above, heading to the control bridge. Bright overhead lighting turned red, submerging the deck in a primal radiance. He clenched his teeth, sucked in a breath, and dragged himself to a sitting position. Excruciating pain exploded throughout his body as he threw back his head, as an uncontrolled hiss of breath escaped from him.

A Sigil of an obsidian black phoenix at the center of his chest's uniform rippled as if alive. He felt broken bones joining and mangled flesh coming together as his bionanites embedded in the suit mended his body, allowing him to get back on his feet. Once the bionanites repaired his injuries to non-life threatening, they injected him with enhancing drugs and painkillers.

"Prince Aidan, are you capable of commanding? Your bios are not registering the status of your injuries."

It took Aidan a moment to catch his breath as the meds took effect. "I'll survive," he drew deep breaths as the pain dulled. He pulled himself to a standing position with the gravity rails next to the launch bay doors; twenty stories tall. With a flick of his wrist, the holo'haptic control panel appeared. Aidan spent precious minutes trying to bring the controls online. He needed to assess the starboard hulls damage. Four tries later, along with fluent cursing, the controls were still non-responsive as sweat poured across his face as the bay temperature rose.

"Starboard side bridge bay systems nonfunctional. I can't synchronize to primary controls. Give me an idea who or what hit us?" Aidan asked, moving toward the antigrav tube lift.

"No readout of hostiles or non-hostiles in the locality. No sub-hyper wave or rupture., nor a warp signature bow wave located." Nari reported.

Focking techs. During this mission, they claimed the power needed was in the gate placement and charging systems. They stripped essential defensive systems. Should've listened to my gut.

"Check for tachyon signatures. I'd bet their stealth'd."

"No tachyons in the area within forty-two light sars."

"So, no information on who shot us. Or where they are?"

"Affirmative, Commander."

"Why attack? A bow shot would force us to comply. Whoever did this is after something. The ship's old, poor girl's not worth much, even pirates' ships are a step up," Aidan said, while Nari remained silent on the subject.

Last Stance, the battlecruiser's name an irony lost on no one on board, when the council refitted her for this mission to deploy the Gates. Technology discovered toward the end of the war, which would allow faster travel throughout the galaxy. A thought came to him, sending a chill Razing down his spine.

The Gate.

"They can't tell we have a Galactic Gate on board, can they? Verify our last Gate is in storage bay O."

"Checking now," a moment later Nari responded, "readouts from storage deck O offline."

"Which scanner officer scheduled for duty when hit?"

"Duty logs show Officer Carna scheduled, yet physical log reveals no one standing the station during the assault."

"Locate Carna, my uniform's internal heads-up holo is nonfunctioning."

The gibberish of tech's panicked inquiries across the emergency comm's a hysterical background of noise which overrode Nari's answer.

"Shut those techs up."

The cacophony from the emergency channel died. Pushed to a secondary channel.

"Bring online our light artillery cannons and set them for automatic fire, deploy seekers, maybe they can find what hit us. Our regular sensors too damaged to detect anything. Keep your eyes clear for a ship. In the meantime, I need a sitrep for crew and ship."

"Acknowledged Commander. Sitrep as follows. Starboard side M-deck has an explosive decompression breach. Status of twenty-six crew members; unknown because of damaged systems in sector. M-deck received a direct strike, along the starboard side, from a plasma energy weapon. Signature: unknown origins. Seventy crew injured. Minor to

6

severe damage. However, they appear capable of standing their stations. Seven others suffered life-threatening damage, med drones moved them to the life tenders bay, forty-eight without damage."

Damage. Funny how Ai's view Elohim's injuries.

"Breech sealed temporarily by emergency blast shields." Moments passed before Nari continued. "Eighty-seven confirmed dead in the surrounding debris field."

That statement struck him like a shockwave. Guilt tore at him. He closed his eyes and took a deep breath. Eighty-seven souls lost; he cursed the gods and daemons, struck the bulkhead next to him, hard. The pain cleared his head. He needed to focus on the living crew's safety, still he would not leave the dead here in the galaxy's wilderness outer rim without proper burial.

"Make every effort to retrieve those bodies."

"Anyone close to the damaged decks able to do a visual and broadcast back?"

His voice giving away none of his earlier feelings.

"Negative. Explosions cut crew members off, or they are at critical posts."

"I'll do it," Aidan said. "I'll use the repair tunnel. Check for any damage in sectors I need to pass through."

"Commander, those sections are clear, yet the emergency blast shielding is enveloping the shaft at M-deck. The scanners show no further information. If there is an energy failure—-."

Aidan cut him off, "Understood. However, someone must do it, and I'm available. I need you on the bridge. When done, I'll head back. Keep trying to find the sheating ship. Whoever hit us must be out there. Close. We're dinner to the predator. Move us to the upper atmosphere of the gas giant. The planet will scramble our signal enough to hide us while we make repairs. Our shields should hold."

"Negative. We have thrusters only; our impulse and Warp engines are offline."

Drog. "Override command, work on engines. We need them back online."

He signed off and headed to the tube. When he arrived at M-deck, the void stared back at him. A monstrous opening of glimmering stars, the rainbow shimmer of shielding extended from section twenty to thirty-five.

Internal walls showed gaping spots where fluids and sparks flowed. Helc, only enough drones to patch the hull. He reported his findings to Nari and descended to the Galactic Gate Bay. Sweat trickled down his sides. I can't lose this gate; they'll bring me before the council. The gate's existence; classified.

"Arrived storage O-deck."

As soon as he verified the gate secured and safe, he let his breath out. Thank the gods.

"Heading to bridge."

Another detonation jerked him off his feet. Before he could rise, a blue-white form, intense arcs of lightning flashing around its body, flowed through the door. Shaped vaguely Elohim. Aidan put his hand above his eyes to shield them from the blinding light. Seconds later, another form of indistinguishable angry red lava and flowing black shadows arrived. Its form changing constantly. The first lashed out with a bolt of plasma, entangling both together.

They're fighting.

Bright blue plasma lightning tore into the black shadows as fire rolled across the brilliance of the other. The two joined as if grappling, and crashed through the floor, leaving a black smoking hole. He shook his head, closed his eyes, then opened them. The black scorched hole still there. He opened his mouth to speak, overridden by his comm's emergency priority signal.

"Internal breech N-Deck. Venting atmosphere. Fires and explosions, spreading from primary breech location. Commander, the tunnels in your sector are no longer viable for passage. You must take the passageways."

"Shift all deflective shielding to protective emergency blast shields. We're not going anywhere soon. Send a repair crew to seal the breech. Now."

Ryakin unsure if the automatic systems worked as he stood. "Check for intruders, I think, I... just check. Crew members are to report any unusual sightings."

"No intruders, commander on internal scanners. Though unable to verify information due to damaged sensors. Did you see intruders, Commander?"

He kept what occurred to himself, for now. "Not sure. Hit my head. Things got blurry for a moment."

Nari paused before proceeding with updates. "All repair drones working to seal M-deck, no available drones for N-deck."

"On it."

He recognized Daedni's voice, his cousin and the ship's female astrophysicist officer. The cruiser shuddered violently once more.

"I can take the fire suppression teams from I deck and rig a temporary seal."

Just like her rushing to danger to save others. "Where are the fire crews for N-deck Nari?"

"Dead or sustained severe damage and are in the life tender bay."

"Go ahead, Lieutenant. If the repair takes longer than twenty minutes, leave emergency shielding in place. We might need to land planetside. Those shields will allow us to make an atmospheric entry."

He worked his way upward from the storage bays and passageways.

Forced along a maze-like path, he worked past fires, toxic smoke, and blocked passages. The tortured ship shuddered and screeched as he tried to reach a lift, still working. Along the way, he found five technicians, confused, lost, and panicked. Two levels later, they arrived at a spot next to escape pods where he left them. Now he moved faster.

"Gravity engine failure." Nari broadcast across ship wide comms. Klaxons changed tone with the newest warning. He floated upward as his uniform morphed into full battle armor. The nanites sensing conditions required atmospheric protection.

"Yeah, got it," he said under his breath. The battle armor nanites switched the bottom of his boots to magnetic, snapping him back to the floor. He sucked in his breath as pain shot through him. The jarring impact aggravating his earlier injuries, still healing. Moments later, he reached a cargo bay where a green light on the lift displayed the control panel operational.

As he stepped into the chamber, a crackling roar of fire broke out through the wall to his left and the holo'haptic control panel blinked out. Strident fire warning Klaxons blared throughout the chamber as the entrance door sealed behind him. Smoke burned his eyes, blinding him as the caustic odor of electrical systems burning choked him before his helmet snapped and locked shut over his head.

His battle armor's heads-up display or HUD went to thermals showing fire tearing through the internal systems. A lightning storm crackled along the walls, jumping from one piece of vital equipment to another.

The automatic fire suppression kicked in. Coating everything, including him, in white powdery foam. Smoke filled the chamber as his HUD, working for the moment, went from thermal to x-ray, showing the smoke removal system damaged.

Klaxons once more wailed warnings as he ran for the lift, just making it as the lift doors slammed shut as a ball of fire raced towards him. He watched through the transparent metasteel doors as it sucked the furious fire out into the void through the bay doors. Three levels up, the lift stopped between floors, forcing him to climb the emergency ladder the rest of the way. Once out, he realized the control panel in this bay was functional. Quick before the panel failed, he called out as he moved towards it, "view screen outer starboard hull. Full side."

The solid walls became translucent. His stomach roiled, and he swallowed hard. Starshine lit portions of the cruiser's hull as sparkling confetti wreckage spread through the vacuum of deepspace in an ever-expanding field. Bodies floated silently past, contorted in death before disappearing. An olive-green planet rose to fill the screen. The ship was in a slow roll. Drog. He realized the last explosion broke the anchors loose.

"Kick in port side thrusters. Now," he yelled, sprinting for the lift. "Whatever hit us last time took out our anchors. We're spinning towards the planet's atmosphere."

"Aware of situation Commander." Nari cut through the chatter of reports coming in on the status of the ship from critical stations.

"Locate officers." Aidan's battle suit's HUD worked this time.

10

Showed his officers spread across the ship. Stress levels and health off to the side of his helmet. It glitched for a second, then cleared.

Two officers, Frea and Agg, suffered minor injuries. Eti's injuries appeared severe, though not life threatening with the injection of bionanites. He was arguing with a drone, refusing to go to the life tender bay and leave his station.

He turned his attention to the ship's status. Damage information scrolled across the screen on the wall panel. What little data readout showed did not augur well for the crippled cruiser, the information a cascade of failing or destroyed systems.

The HUD glitch of earlier cleared. Four of his ranking officers, Sabsian, Ricmaia, Javalid and Carna, the scanner officer derelict in her duty earlier, showed their location on E-deck. Not their duty stations. Drog, sheat, he swore.

"Commander to officers on E-deck, return to your stations."

In blatant disregard for protocol Sabsian, Aidan's second in command answered without acknowledging his rank.

"We are evacuating. On my orders. We're not dying because of your incompetence."

A howl of screeching metal came through the comms, "Hear that. Your ship's being torn apart. An enemy got within striking distance without discovery." The pop and whoosh of escape pod doors opening came through loud on Aidan's comms.

"This is a peacetime mission. They removed any classified detection equipment and weapons. You're aware of that."

Silence greeted him. "This is a direct order. Stand your stations."

"The ship's coming apart. Be smart, save the crew. Abandon ship. Us, we're leaving now." Sabsian jeered.

Sabsian created headaches and delayed schedules for him more than once. His instinct to throw him out of an airlock took all his willpower to overcome. Peacetime adhered to different rules. Ryakin wished he ignored the rules.

"Don't worry. I shall inform the council about your commanding abilities... or lack thereof," Sabsian said over the laughter. Then got in one last blow. "This time your mother can't save you."

Sabsian would not listen. He tried appealing to the others, "Ri——."

Nari cut in once more. "Commander, we are level. Can't maintain this for long. Too late to evade the planet's gravity well; it is already too strong. The cruiser's engines are still offline, along with the forward and rear thrusters, and the hyperskip engine. Lower wing thrusters appear online, but power to the hydraulics to extend them possibly damaged. M-deck included parts of the extension struts. Readouts malfunctioning throughout. I have no report on the condition of the hydraulic machinery."

The overhead Klaxons tone became a deep bass sound rising to a high pitch before repeating. "Failure of life support system in one hour fifteen minutes."

That changed circumstances drastically.

He turned his attention to the most immediate problem. The wing hydraulics. "Agg, Frea, I need you to go to M-deck and inspect the automatic extensions for the wing. If damaged, check the manual pump controls. They might still be intact. I need those wings out."

Aidan strode through the bay, heading towards the green light, a beacon shining in the smoke-filled bay chamber. The lift took him straight up without further problems. At least one thing works.

Nari could not control the crippled ship no matter how advanced an Ai. Shorthanded with the loss of four bridge officers and the others managing critical systems. He decided on the action he intended to take to save his crew.

"What's our chance of reaching the planet's surface intact?" Aidan said as he stepped through the doors. The automatic doors closed, opened, and closed, each time with a hiss. "Engage blast emergency door. It clanged shut behind him."

"Sixty-eight percent chance failure to reach the surface intact."

"Any tricks running through those circuits of yours to pull us out?"

He threw himself into his chair and looked over the controls. Too few.

"Advise evacuation," Nari said.

"Agreed; sound evacuation now."

"Abandon ship. Repeat. Abandon ship."

Sabsian was right. Fock, he hated the fact he agreed with his second's assessment.

He hit the switch on the interface control. "Deploying distress beacons. Now." The shaking increased. The equipment on the floors and walls rattled and banged as the deck responded to the vibrations. Ship-wide systems failing fast. Too many red lights flashed and blinked before him. Critical sections missing in the holo'haptic panels. Showing internal physical sectors broken.

"What's not damaged?" he said under his breath. "Ignore remark," he interjected before Nari listed them. "Manual override."

Physical control handles, and gyroscopic ship's equipment extended. When he grabbed the handles, they yanked out of his hands. The added strength of his armor did not help. The second time he held on. Still, took all his strength, supplemented with his armors, to keep the ship level. Necessary or the pods exiting smashed into the sides.

His officer's stations, empty chairs in a half circle along the forward walls taunted him with failure.

"Sabsian and three others left earlier. There are Agg, Eti, Frea, and Daedni, all taking care of critical problems."

Nari nodded, "Aware. Distress beacons transmitting, Commander."

Aidan held tight to the bucking controls. For the next twenty minutes, they fought the damaged cruiser, trying to keep the ship level in the upper exosphere of the planet. Eons passed as his muscles screamed with the strain. The vibrations becoming more violent every minute. Off to the sides, bright red-orange thrusters turned icy pink. Their electromagnetic engines kicked in, showing them far enough away to escape without harm.

"Daedni and seventeen others still on board at N-deck. Agg and Frea still attempting to extend the wings. Two minutes till Lieutenant Daedni's group seals the breech." Nari said.

"Forget the breach, cousin. I want everyone to escape pods. Now. That's an order."

"Yes, sir," Daedni answered.

"Agg, Frea, abandon ship. Forget the struts."

"Yes, sir. Heading to pods now."

13

Minutes later, the pink dots of the escape pods showed on his viewscreen. Relief washed over him. They made it.

"Handoff the control codes. Calculate you have ten minutes to escape," Nari said.

Aidan figured Nari would estimate the ratio of dead to Aidan's guilt. Aidan knew Nari would analyze correctly, that Aidan would fight to save everyone calculated by past behavior. Nari's calculations would be correct. This left Aidan only one choice. Force Nari to comply with his next order. Nari, the crew's best chance for survival, he more than anyone understood how ingenious Nari was in a tight spot.

"Nari, direct protocol three eight five seven: Ordered as follows. Get my crew to safety. Protect them at all costs," he said. While not taking his eyes off the trajectory readout before him as he kept the dying cruiser as level as possible.

Aidan sensed the moment Nari froze as conflicting programming raged through his circuits. The ghost of Nari's first prime programming rose in protest.

Originally, he was Prince Aidan's assigned childhood protector. He fulfilled that position for far more sars than as his battle Ai. A Battle Ai's priority demanded unquestioned obedience to a Commander's orders.

"Now, Nari." The second command overrode Nari's stalled programming. Forced him to transfer his program into the Ai's designated escape pod on C-deck. The external body design Murian. Internal electromagnetic circuitry and hydraulic tubing, steel and composite ceramics, and a primary control center. The positron processing brain located where any Murian's was in his head. Once the transmission finished, Nari transferred his control functions of the ship over to the computer.

"I——"

Aidan cut him off as he punched the firing sequence, not trusting Nari to do so. The explosive anchor bolts blew, and the pod blasted away.

"Manual control protocol transferred," a strange, modulated female voice said, lacking something subtle; something Nari's voice imparted.

The wall to Aidan's left exploded. Coolant, fuel, and replicator fluid poured into the air, forming globules of gelatinous liquid. Air hoses ruptured around him. Pure oxygen poured into the cabin. Their hoses writhing and twisting violently, hissing noise emanated from them. A thrashing hose knocked him to the floor. He struggled back into the chair. His muscles strained as sweat poured down his forehead. He gained his seat as furious fire licked across the forward viewscreen. The trajectory of the ex-cruiser far too steep. Last Stance became a flaming star, shooting across the heavens of the infant planet.

Time stilled as each detail sharpened; clarified, and he found himself in a sea of silence.

Images flashed through his mind's eye of his childhood. His mother and father. Nari protecting him from childhood disasters. Daedni and others, both friends and enemies, played before him, as the ship shuddered unnoticed in raging violence around him. Liolies, his mate's ethereal charms, a mischievous smile glimmering in his mind's eye. The pain of not seeing his mate one last time forced his mind to shy away. Turned his mind to the receding trails of electromagnetic thrusters till they appeared as only a twinkle of light against the blackness of the void.

His attention snapped back as his restraints wrenched him hard against the chair. An assault of sound engulfed him. Screeching metal, hissing gas and the crackling of intense heat as plasma flashed through the chairs, gyroscopic equipment and controls, screamed as his hands burned.

Fire exploded across the viewscreen as a sudden, intense blue-white light saturated the bridge. The bitter taste of fear and defeat ripped through him. Yet still he battled the burning cruiser for control, refusing to give up and die.

A form coalesced before him. Agonizing pain blossomed, blocking out all else. The inky hands of darkness pulled him into its swirling void as the sound of receding screaming faded to nothing.

Chapter 1

GGS 335890 Goem 1st.
Kieran Kingdom Present Turn - Star of Hope viewing.
Ki's Trade Lane: Five skips out–Lady Jynnalt Zu'Airal

LOVE WILL DESTROY AN empire... Or raise one up as the Phoenix rises and the galaxy burns.

Prophecy? Cautionary tale? Or a line from a poignant poem, written by an anonymous Malkuth six hundred sars ago, as scholars claim.

Whispers and rumors amongst the commoners and secret sects asserted a separate opinion, claiming it's one of the sacred texts. In Particular, the Book of Queens. The only book the Temple forbid the public. Long ago claimed a book of Apocrypha within the Temple.

Why? Why grant access only to those of the highest rank within the Temple and only female priestess?

The pinprick of light grew, capturing her attention before bursting to full glory. The cool darkness of the viewing platform closed around her as she stood soaking in the blossoming image of the star.

Soft, haunting music filled the chamber. Time stilled. For a split-second, an odd sensation overcame her, as if she were everything... and nothing.

The noise of shuffling feet and the quiet rustle of clothing snapped her back to this moment. Murmured voices, accompanied by oohs and ahs intruding, reminded her strangers surrounded her. Strangers Her Highness, Lady Tesiskel, her mother, called friends. Friends met less than two turns ago. Politically influential or enormously wealthy.

Moments later, the Star of Hope settled into a brilliance far greater than the surrounding stars. Heaviness gripped her as her fingers absentmindedly stroked the thin, almost invisible, delicate golden torque around her throat. Reflected on the fact the star's exquisite image, its dying throes immortalized.

The morbid memory dredged up another line. Life and death balances at the edge of a void. *By the luminous ones.* Her brow furrowed. *Where did she remember the line from?*

The star reached its full grandeur moments later. The chamber lights increased enough to perceive those around her. Though they still stood somewhat in shadow. She glanced over at Eshin and wondered what she thought of this absorption the galaxies' Elohim species have for a long-dead star. How they worshiped the light, and the charred system once warmed by its radiance, now dust and legend.

Glaegrar's notorious skeptics and yet claimed to be mystics. A paradox, but she learned long ago not to try to figure out her nani. Most accused Eshin of falsehood when she informed them she was a Glaegrar. Their species interacted little with others except for their envoys during the Council of Nine.

Eshin, stout and short, came to the middle of her waist. Burnished red skin, huge slanted golden eyes, her cheeks with three protruding bone points accenting the top line of her cheekbones. She painted the bone points' colors with whatever took her fancy. Long, thick, rich black hair braided with golden metal bands along its length every few inches.

A thin chain with diamond-shaped gold metal spaced evenly apart and a blue-green gem in the middle of her forehead adorned her head. Eshin's smile showed the sharp teeth of a carnivorous predator.

She wore a purple sleeveless tunic to her midriff. The collar's edge pointed out with broad flowing pants of the same color. Her belt matching her headpiece and sandals. The only part of her outfit which changed from turn to turn was the color of her cheekbone points.

"Society, nasty sort." Eshin's tone indicated she found them distasteful. "Your mother *would* count them as friends."

Jynnalt glanced around the chamber, noticing them scattered

throughout the guests, standoffish as if passing judgment. She counted twenty-five Society members attending the event. Five of their Priests present with the other members gave her a creepy sense, as if they were judging them for crimes they might have committed.

Society members wore distinctive plain brown robes, flowing loose pants with hooded cowls pulled over their heads, their faces in the shadowy recess. Their only concession to style; sarc skin, black boots, and belt. She turned away from Eshin and surreptitiously glanced around for her mother, wanting to stay out of her sight. She admired the elegant chamber of the officers' hall. The Anunnaki prized style and elegance over plain necessity. Grace and artful splendor over unadorned utilitarian. No matter the practical use. Bulkheads and beams decorated with symbols, images, and designs favored throughout the empire. Did not matter if a warship or civilian yacht.

Doorways to public areas metacrystals far harder than any recognized metal. Yet, when power was applied to the metacrystals, the metal became translucent. Bulkhead doors to the private zone's made of normal metasteel. Passageways lined with a curved beam ribbing flowed from floor to ceiling. Clawed feet at floor level and the heads of fierce mythological creatures met overhead in defiance.

The door next to her whooshed open, showing bioluminous lighting strips along the outer wall. Holographic torches of fire lit the passageway. The time past the eighteenth hour of the night. The moist dark green of oxygen-producing stilken material covering the ceilings and upper walls for passive oxygen production. Which reminded her. She promised to take her brother to view the phytoplankton grown in the deep levels of the ship in massive tanks. He was less interested in visiting where they made the chemical production of oxygen used as a backup to the natural systems for emergencies.

A Susiute entered with its spouse. Both squat, broad-bodied with bright pink skin, small eyes, and short snouts. Her mother abhorred them, claimed they were crass. Worse to most Elohim, including her, was the nauseating odor which followed them wherever they went. She tried not to gag as they passed. The couple dressed in hideous clashing colors and adorned in so much jewelry; they clattered as they walked.

"Why did your mother invite them? She despises them." Eshin said, as she wrinkled her nose at the waft of sickening odor as they moved past.

"To show how cosmopolitan she is." Jynnalt shrugged. "I do not understand how she thinks." Bored, her mind wandered to her earlier thoughts. Her father held a fascination for the Phoenix poem. Or had. He died when she was twelve sars, leaving her at the mercy of her ambitious rank conscious mother whenever she was home from the fleet academy.

The cloying scent of her mother's perfume floated her way, announcing her presence like a suffocating blanket. She tried to drop her hand from her torque, though not fast enough, as her mother gave her hand a sharp stinging slap.

"How many times must I tell you playing with your torque in public is vulgar? Appears your mind is elsewhere, or you're bored with the company." She hissed in her ear, lacking the honeyed tones reserved for her male friends.

Jynnalt turned towards her mother to apologize and realized she already left to greet a wealthy guest across the chamber.

A tall Elohim entered. Oddly, she sensed he was familiar and frowned. Stared after him as he strode across the chamber as if on a mission. Dressed like a Society member, yet she sensed he was not one. *Strange?*

Loud conversation and shrill, brash female laughter entered the chamber from the passageway upon his heels, crashed upon the serene setting with abandon. Jynnalt winced before the door slid shut and silenced the noise, glancing towards her mother. Thank the gods. Her mother appeared not to note the intrusion upon the scene. No doubt Jynnalt's fault in her mother's eyes. She let her breath out.

Her mother harangued her for the slightest lack of etiquette. Jynnalt's only relief came when she escaped to the academy. Did not matter if she committed the transgression or not. Before the party ended, she figured her mother's list of crimes against her would be lengthy. Her offenses heinous, whether she did nothing more than stand in one place.

Without thinking, she once more stroked her torque. Her mother across the chamber shot her a tight frown. She dropped her hand.

Air controllers set to a pleasant coolness for the guest's comfort did not help as sweat poured down her sides. Three more months, and she would no longer be under her mother's control. An eon seemed to stretch before her. *If* she made her seventeenth first breath sars. Of late, she seemed clumsy. Before they left Kiestrial, Caltac' her combat sensial saved her from two accidents, Eshin another. Both claimed someone was trying to kill her. She doubted that; she was clumsy at times.

Earlier, her mother and Knight Commander Elgar fought for the fifth time. Knight Elgar saying, his brusque voice dripping with censure, "the shipwrights did not design the flagship of the Arch Dukian for upscale parties. She is a proud warship with accredited battles. None of those pretentious False Reality tournament wins. These Inner Kingdoms are so proud of winning. You should be happy I diverted our course to allow you to watch the blossoming of the Star of Hope in this sector. You put us behind schedule by five full turns," He said. Then attempted to ignore her.

When he continued to refuse her mother's request, she threatened to send a pulse to the Queen. Elgar threw up his hands and gave in, admitting fighting battles easier; at least he understood the rules. They now sat five skips out from Ki's Kingdom's trade lanes, anchored at the best spot in the sector to view the star's light emerge. After they arrived, her mother made the rounds of other ships in the vicinity. All waiting to witness the star's light emerge. She made recent friends amongst the cruise liners, luxury pleasure barges, and expensive private star yachts.

Jynnalt informed by her house's Blooded De Rank, the royal barge of Tc arrived and anchored next to them. Yet her mother did not extend an invitation. Not wise in her opinion to snub their Queen's contracted in-laws. No chance in *helc* her mother was unaware King Rualui and his wife, Queen Jena, arrived for the viewing. If their Blooded De Rank was aware, they arrived her mother was conscious of the fact, as well.

The civilians and crew females grumbled with disappointment when Prince Ryakin did not arrive with his brother. Informed, he was on festival maneuvers at Nibiru's Capital System. Every female within hearing whispering about him.

She frowned. What game was mother playing, or was she? Jynnalt thought about this before she figured her mother feared they would refuse her offer. Which would mortify her if they declined her invitation. Society's blooded matrons would gossip and flay her reputation like voracious locus across a ripe field of grains during the festival if they refused.

Ninety-eight guests arrived the turn before the actual event. This forced the ranking Knights to bunk with the lower Master Guild officers and crews to accommodate her guests.

The fleet guild liaison notified Elgar he filed a complaint against the house. Worse, her mother added insult to injury by commandeering the officer's viewing platform and feasthall. To Jynnalt's mortification, her mother then banished the officers as if they tainted her guest. She complained the whole time to everyone about the Knights, officers and crew as lacking proper discipline and manners. Jynnalt tried to explain Cineuian was not a court pleasure barge. Her mother ignored her pleas.

She realized she missed the camaraderie from her training turns at Ki's fleet academy. Missed the exuberance and carefree feelings of time spent with fellow trainees. The normal easy-going conversations of tactics or a burst of laughter at jokes or pranks they played on each other absent.

The sporadic bits of laughter here and there sounded forced, phony, contrived. Stifling her. The chamber lit in low-level lighting hid their true selves from those around them.

Classical music by one of the great and long-deceased Temple's Master, a soothing sound throughout the chamber. As opposed to the growling harsher, hard in your face beats most fleet members preferred. Sometimes including herself. Being honest, she admitted to herself she loved the classical Malkuth music but kept the fact to herself in the academy.

Skyta, one of her companions standing behind her next to a pillar, spoke loud enough for Jynnalt to overhear the conversation.

"Did you know the High Temple refuses to sanction the Society Order? They claim they are not a religion. They designated them as a political order. Prohibiting them certain rights, like entry to preach in empires."

A gasp of sound from the other reached Jynnalt before Skyta rushed on in a conspiratorial whisper.

"Princess Tesiskel has the excellent sense to ignore their stupid decrees."

Jynnalt stiffened, and asked Eshin, "does my mother know the High Temple disapproves of the Society?"

In alarm, she peered around the chamber. The Society members now missing. She glanced around, seeing the seating pillows of rich natural colors and waist-high refreshment tables scattered throughout the chamber. Loaded with honeyed mead from the golden plains of the Sagust system, wines, and alcoholic drinks from the far reaches of the galaxy. Ripe succulent fruits arranged beside tall pitchers of drinks, the skins bright orange, deep reds, yellows, and greens.

A Grasisidea walked by, towering over her, long strides heading straight for the table with the honeyed mead of its home system. The click of its chitin exoskeleton making her shudder. She avoided them. They stared at her as if she might make a delicious meal.

What was her mother thinking? Eshin earlier pointed out the discrepancies from her mother's normal behavior, combined with Skyta's conversation, made her wonder. She straightened and paid more attention to the guest.

The stranger she spotted earlier stood by a Phursian. A species with a spotted muscular build and red bumpy skin and small horns on its head. The Phursian talking to a Jianian's who's distinctive gray-green head, fur, and blue and yellow striped body, unmistakable amongst the others present.

Odd, she now viewed more species her mother disliked. The Jianian stared her way with a sudden twist of his head. His sizable beaked nose and small beady eyes reminding her more of a raptor than the Elohim species he belonged to before he turned back to the Phursian.

"Eshin, did you know the Temple does not sanction the Society?"

"Did you keep your head in a black hole while at the academy? Of course, I was aware of the fact. So is every single thinking species of the galaxy."

Chagrined by Eshin's remark, she went back to searching for the

Society members. She preferred to ignore any parts of the galaxy, which might include her mother's influence. Eshin's expression said she understood.

Three pillared archways separated the chamber leading into the officers' feast hall. Long tables set with the best dishes and cutlery aboard adorned with fancy glow globes, which floated inches off the white table. The covering found in what far-flung storage bay escaped her.

Behind her, whoever Skyta was talking with whispered, "I'm told they swear their members to secrecy. Those who break their vows disappear, never seen again."

"*Helc*," Skyta said loud enough for all around to understand, her tone irate, "rumor and lies to discourage anyone from joining. I'd bet spread by the Priestesses of the Temple themselves. They want to keep their stranglehold on the citizens."

Jynnalt spun and faced them. "Enough. You shall not be disrespectful of the Temple. Not in my hearing. I excuse you from your duties this evening, Skyta," she said, as her chest heaved. Her eyes narrowed as she glared at them both.

She froze at the chilly sound of her mother's calm voice behind her.

"You cannot dismiss your companion. For any reason. You lack the authority. Worse, you've made yourself the center of attention."

Jynnalt glanced around; her voice must have carried to every corner of the chamber. Everyone was looking her direction.

"I will speak with you later, Lady Airal." The threat clear.

The smirk of triumph on Skyta's face familiar. Anything she stated now to defend herself would make the rebuke harsher.

Skyta would gain pleasure if her mother punished her further. She intended to deny her the satisfaction. She clenched her jaw and lifted her head.

The expression on her mother's face left her in no doubt she would pay for this transgression. Later. She did not care.

A deep voice interjected behind her.

"It would be a shame not to introduce such a lovely lady. I've overheard a lot about you. Top of your class at the academy."

She doubted this male cared a wit to meet her. More likely trying to impress her mother. Which showed he lacked a true understanding of their relationship. Jynnalt recognized with full clarity who he was, her mother's latest lover. Jynnalt overheard the gossip at the academy, amazed how fast a malicious rumor traveled. The galactic pulse appeared slow in comparison.

"Lady Jynnalt Zu'Airal heir to the title of Arch Duchianess, I would like to introduce Sabas Iana of the Merchant Guilds." Her mother cocked her head sideways, looking up at him from under her eyelashes. Laughed, a soft lilting sound so appealing to the males always crowded around her. Tesiskel placed her hand on his shoulder, light yet possessive, leaving Jynnalt no doubt the rumors true, at least in this case.

Jynnalt felt coarse next to her mother. She towered over her. Her mother, along with her younger sister, both delicate yet curvy forms reached her shoulders, both considered exceptional beauties throughout the empire.

Her form tall, long and toned from her time at the academy. She found her sister or mother in any crowd by looking where the males gathered as if collector insects vying for a flower's pollen.

Jynnalt thought about the fact she was everything they were not. Her hair a mix of fiery oranges and reds, curly and unruly. Offset by odd light moss green eyes and pale skin, which favored her father's side of the family. Unlike her mother and sister's soft lavender blue skin.

At least Sabas stood an inch taller than her, so she did not have to tilt her head downward to converse with him.

The second Eshin's deep throaty voice sounded next to her; she grasped this evening became a disaster.

"I see Tesiskel. He fits your type. Handsome, wealthy, arrogant, and not worth the skin he stands in." Her brazen contempt laced every word. Her mother gasped.

Jynnalt tensed, she forgot Eshin stood beside her. Her mother's response not long in coming.

"Sabas, I wish to have a word with Lady Airal."

He bowed his head before turning towards the refreshment table. Not before a spark of rage flash through his eyes. Looking back towards Tesiskel, he asked, "Would you care for a drink?"

The anger no longer present. Did she imagine it?

"Yes, a white wine from the Zuicaiacn system. From my father's winery and the best on the table." Smiling, she turned back to Jynnalt, "a word." Her tone did not match the smile plastered on her face. Jynnalt understood well what that entailed as her mother stalked closer to the viewing wall.

Jynnalt on her heels thinking quick blurted, "Mother, do you understand the High Temple does not approve of the Society Order? Why invite them with your other guest, they will bring trouble to our house." She hoped the question might distract her from the lecture on bringing Eshin to the viewing.

The shock on her mother's face reassured her. At least her mother did not realize the matter of the Society's illegality. Her father told her once her mother lacked intelligence. Cunning her strongest strength. He also explained she paid little attention to the finer details of tradition or laws when the situation suited her. Jynnalt thought of what he asserted and figured this was one of those times.

"I will enquire about why this occurred."

Her mother tilted her head as if thinking before staring her straight in the eye. "Why Commander Elgar did not inform me of this when I submitted the list, I can't imagine. Unless he meant to punish me for going over his head." A frown crossed her mother's face as she appeared to concentrate.

"There were other important issues on Commander Elgar's mind. Other than your event."

"Does not matter. He is responsible. I will inform the authorities if any ask questions about their presence aboard. Best if we avoid them finding out, though. For everyone involved, and the honor of our house."

Her mother's expression neutral, but Jynnalt understood what she implied. Jynnalt realized, as usual, she would make sure the blame did not fall on her. Hot anger at her mother for blaming her father's longtime friend rose, and she stiffened, ready to defend him.

"I——."

Her mother interrupted her; her voice soft, "Jynnalt, I can tell you don't approve of my decisions since your father's passing being raised as you were. These back-lane border kingdoms have strange ideas about females. Your father was the worst offender. I am trying to teach you things females of the inner empire's civilized kingdoms learn young." Her mother reached upward and slipped an errant strand of Jynnalt's' unruly hair back into place. "Remember, you must attend the imperial courts, and I do not wish for you to embarrass yourself."

"I know."

She stared at the floor. *How does mother always make me feel ungrateful?* Still, the moment of tenderness softened her anger. The rustle of servers moving around, placing platters on the table as rich aromas of meats, spices, and sauces worked its way on the air throughout the chamber. Guests glanced their direction, then back to the long table.

The moment passed as soon as her mother's voice hardened, saying, "I demand you punish Eshin. What a nasty troll your father hired to raise you. She insulted my guest." Her mouth twisted in anger.

It amazed Jynnalt how fast her mother's demeanor changed. One reason she never was comfortable in her presence.

"Send her back to her quarters. Her place is looking after your brother and sister, at least until I can replace her. Not mingling with her betters."

Jynnalt's back stiffened as she laid eyes upon Duurua, a festival child her mother took in as a babe. She treated him more like a family member than she did Jynnalt.

"Yes, mother." Brief answers best she learned from experience. "Ah, I believe your guests are waiting for you to lead them to dinner." This the only thing she thought of to divert her attention away from the matter of Eshin.

"Take care of what I told you and think a bit before discarding my advice. You need to understand your place. And who you interact within a social setting is of foremost importance. Now, I must attend to my guests." Tesiskel patted her hand. An awkward moment for them both, then rushed away.

Jynnalt's appetite at some point slipped away without her noticing as she mulled over everything from this evening.

Eshin materialized next to her, causing Jynnalt to flinch. "Gods, warn me before you appear out of thin air."

"Don't worry, I'm going. I overheard the entire thing. Nasty troll, eh? And the likes of her claiming to fire me. I informed your mother I will leave the house's employment on your next first breath turn."

Scuffling chairs, indistinct murmurs of guest talking, and the tinkle of cutlery and dishes punctuated with her mother's sparkling conversation filled the chamber. A peel of laughter, never heard while her father lived from her mother, skittered across her tattered nerves. Her mood soured further. "I believe I am ready to retire. Will you walk with me to my quarters?"

"If you leave this early, without permission, your mother will become incised."

"Does it matter? At least there will be no further crimes for me to commit against her guests."

As they left, she observed the stranger again. He stood off to the side, with what appeared a chalice of wine, facing the feasthall and diners as if waiting for something. Yep, not a Society member. Their order forbid mind-affecting drinks or drugs.

A quick push from behind got her moving again. "Child, it's impolite to stare. I taught you better."

Jynnalt gave a cheeky smile at Eshin. Her admonishments never stung the same as her mother's. Her nani both praised and criticized, taking away the sting of the latter. On the way to her quarters, they talked on trivial subjects, avoiding the minefield between them. Mother.

After Eshin left for the guild server's quarters, she sat in front of her family's holo mural on her viewing wall, watching past happier times. The holo's slid by. Showing times at the beach when her father taught them to swim. Or at their summer fortress, Razing the wind on their war beasts. Laughing and competing on the dangerous winding trails dressed as commoners while she and her sister's hair flowed out behind them. Her brother rode further behind, crying out for them to ride slower, trying to catch up with them. Or when her father took them into the forest to teach them how to survive and live off the land.

She clutched at the laughter and the mystical tales of older, more gracious times. How her father spun stories for them. His hugs when she hurt herself or failed at something, his praise when she accomplished a goal or mastered a skill. Then she remembered the screaming and fighting which occurred whenever they arrived back at their ancestral fortress. The sound of her mother yelling at him for taking the children with him on these outings spoiled her enjoyment of the scenes.

Grief and agony at the loss of her father when she was only twelve sars rose, a rippled echo from her past, one she thought long buried. The poem's sadness and thoughts of the dead star left her in a strange mood.

Restlessness seized her, and she took a walk to one of the lower decks in search of food. Lost in memories, she wandered deep in thought. She must have passed by feasthalls without noticing. The familiar fleet routine and sounds around her soothing.

She found herself in power plant three, a restricted sector, without realizing how she arrived. She stopped at the sound of a demanding voice around the corner.

"What are you doing down here?"

A voice identified himself as Master Guild officer Johien.

"I swear I got this cleared to give them a tour. They are interested in buying two hundred power plants from Ki's mechanic and energy guild. Informed, we make the best for the best tithe. I only showed them readouts."

"I need to verify this information. Follow me." Footsteps and voices moved away, heading towards the security station. Her implanted cybernetics, because of her rank, gave her full access anywhere on the ship. To the security enforcers' scanners, she was technically invisible.

The drone sentries logged her presence but did not inform security. Her rank gave her access to the highest classified areas. If Knight Elgar or another ranking Knight required her location, Cineuian would notify them where to find her.

She preferred not to announce her presence and turned to go, not wanting to interfere with security. Eshin would skin her hide if she caught her being sneaky. She always proclaimed, "weak characters skulk around watching others." Before pointing to Skyta.

A movement to her left caught her attention. Stepping back, she sensed she should stay hidden. She stared hard, seeing the vague outline of a male outfitted in Society attire. A moment later, the form stepped out from behind the pylon.

The Stranger from earlier glanced her direction before stepping back into the shadows. A flash of light blinded her. Seconds passed before her eyesight cleared. The intruder now gone. She notified the sentry officer, who then locked the sector. A frantic search ensued while others carefully checked the last few hours' security holo's but found nothing. No flash of light she claimed to see.

It showed her looking in the direction. She saw herself flinch, but nothing more. Cineuian notified the sentry of the other intruders right away. Which security stopped and questioned, though accompanied by a Master guild officer. Commander Elgar notified by security they found no other intruders in their computer's logs. Nor did the holo's show any others in the passageways.

Before long, they all stared at her, as if she were crazy, and she decided she might be better off dropping the topic and head back to her quarters.

Certain a lack of food caused her to imagine things.

"Cineuian, what Feasthall is open?"

"Upper deck-three corridor twenty-three number seventeen. Feasthall is always open."

Chapter 2

335890 GGS Goem 1st
Nibiru System:
Nitiru Planet Imperial Fleet Base–Prince Ryakin Da'Tc

RYAKIN STOOD LOOKING out from the control tower of Tc's upper observation deck of the launch bay. The base comprised six levels, the lowest two levels: the barracks for the TCNPs seventy-ninth solar fleet. Tc kingdom's tribute to the Imperial Anunnaki Emperor's defense forces of Nibiru's capital system.

They scattered nine kingdoms, four wardens, and the Emperor's Imperial bases across the planet Nitiru. The Anunnaki Empires fleet bases in mountain ranges or dormant volcanoes. They reserved Nitiru's seventh planet in the Nibiru System for fleet and Area Control fourteen operations. The Ministry of fourteen's bases, hidden unlike the others, classified to even the upper ranks, even they were unaware of their exact locations.

Tc's base cut in the steep sides of the Treiligra stratocone volcano, the fifth largest on Nitiru. The base encompassed thirty-two standards deep by fifteen standards long, comprising one hundred and six double levels midway up the mountain's flank.

High in the command tower, Ryakin looked upon the gleaming black shuttles which sat to the right of the take-off zone. Five rows across, ten rows deep of graceful swept-back wings on long widebodies. Mid center sat deepspace fighters, similar in body style yet sleeker, deadlier, and menacing. To the far left sat rows of whirlwinds, their upper round fan blades folded closed against their sides. To him, they resembled the giant dragonflies of this planet rather than a mechanical beast.

"Just once, can we take advantage of our rank?" Ustrix said as he ambled into the tower chamber, yawning. His eyes bloodshot, yet he still projected the image of a professional fleet officer. His uniform squared away properly and every hair and whisker in place. "Every reasonable commander and Executive Commander are sound asleep. They will enjoy a leisurely morning and a midturn meal before they even think of heading for their shuttles."

Ustrix yawned. Bigger this time. "Last night's entertainment went well with everyone but you. The others enjoyed the pleasure of females and gambling."

Ryakin did not miss the not-so-subtle dig.

Ustrix stepped up to the viewing wall, watching the controlled, frantic movement in the lower launch bay. "We should do it again sometime. Next time you might join us in the festivities."

"Next time will be never. The contract is a standard lifetime one. Same as any Royal or Imperial one," he said and moved to the tower operators.

"Request Anunnaki Imperial command for permission to launch." Ryakin asked the tower control operator.

Seconds later, they received an affirmative response.

"Notify Igigi control of the launch of TCNPs seventy-ninth, Sigil and Silks of the Nemesis inbound shuttles to fleet docking station. Inform standby crews to bring Nemesis online from standby mode. Start Impulse engine sequence and prepare for full boarding crew."

As soon as they received the go signal from the Igigi, he commanded, "Commence launch now."

He walked back over to Ustrix and examined the activity below, now more chaotic with the launch command in effect.

"The party got out of control. We are lucky Rualui's pulse, combined with forty plat talons, smoothed things over. My head is still pounding. The thought of food makes my stomach turn. I can do without entertainment like that for the next twenty sars."

"Don't be a dragon's aras. The boys and I got to view you out from under that iron control you show the galaxy," Ustrix said, his eyes gleaming. "My opinion, the party was worth every bit of tithe it cost me. Did you and Duac have a pleasant talk?" Ustrix asked, changing the subject.

Ryakin realized he was fishing for information. He rubbed his forehead before responding. "None of your business."

Ustrix's shoulders shook as he tried hard to hold back his laughter. "Don't worry, looking at you, no one ever would accuse you of being anything other than a professional officer, and soon to be a Queen's consort. I'm sure Duac will vouch for your behavior."

Ryakin chuckled. "In your parlance means boring. I do not understand the humor of drinking far more than prudent and acting an arse for others to laugh at."

A red light flashed at the far launch tube as Ryakin's head throbbed in time with the warning light. The front shuttle of row one's loading gate clanged shut behind the ship. A grating tone blared across the bay. The activity on the floor by service crews increased. Ryakin winced again, rubbing his forehead harder.

"Outer view screen," Ryakin said. The window screen blurred for a moment, then changed to the outside, showing the volcano's flank and an enormous gate opening. The shuttle sped up through the tube, gaining velocity from the rail launcher. Fuel engines kicked in seconds before the shuttle left the tube, accelerating to proper flight speed.

Three thousand standards above the ground, the twin red eyes of the powerful thrust from the exhaust pushed the ship upward towards the heavens. The shuttle disappeared into the eastern rising star, bathed in fiery streaks of golden red and orange. Engineering and life tender crews on board the shuttle heading to Nemesis docked at Royal Tc slot seventy-nine. The loading and take off repeated throughout the morning as the star rose high above and the turn aged into mid-turn.

The last group headed out to the loading station, along with Ryakin and Ustrix. As they arrived, their pilots boarded the command shuttle and started the preflight checks before cleared by the tower and rolled on the lift platform.

Both Ustrix and Ryakin, waiting for the preflight checks to finish, stood next to their shuttle platform. Hit hard from behind, Ryakin crashed into Ustrix, almost taking them both to the floor before he got his balance and stopped his forward momentum. Ustrix not so lucky ended on his aras.

Ryakin glimpsed the offender retreating as he weaved in and out of the officers lining the outside corridor.

Two security officers yelled out *"halt,"* before Razing after the offender. Seconds later, an exit door slammed, the sound reverberating throughout the bay, followed by another, fainter in the distant hallway.

Ryakin touched the back of his ear, activating his cyberware communications; "I want a lock-down to all exits from the barracks corridors. Unknown intruder wearing a Tc house uniform. Spotted, leaving launch bay one, heading toward lower barracks. Security in pursuit. Base priority alert. Repeat Base priority alert."

"He's an intruder?"

Ustrix frowned as he picked himself up off the floor, glancing the direction the male fled. "He's wearing a Tc uniform, the sigil and silks badge Tc's."

Ryakin snapped, "I don't care what *focking* uniform he wore. No warrior under my command wears a uniform that disheveled. Believe me, and I got an excellent view of the boots. The boots, not fleet issued; but civilian. The intruder grabbed a uniform out of someone's locker to gain access to the launch bay. When he's found I want the name on the uniform, then inform MGO4 Tiliaran which fleet member was derelict in their duty. They left their locker unsecured."

Security informed Ryakin they found the intruder in an air shaft. Dead, his biological resurrection spirit meh chip destroyed by an unknown poison and his Dna signature scrambled. They informed him they needed the temple's guardians to examine the body if they hoped to extract a signature.

Ryakin once more brushed the back of his ear, "Approve transfer of the body to the High temple for further investigation."

Turning to Ustrix, he said, "someone went to a lot of trouble to stop us finding out who that citizen was." Once more he touched the back of his ear, "Security, I want any information discovered forwarded to me as soon as you get an answer from the Temple."

Their shuttle rolled off the lift and onto the platform. Ryakin and Ustrix boarded and took their seats, fastening in as the hatch hissed shut and latched with a metallic thunk.

"Notify your brother." Ustrix said.

Ryakin looked out the viewer, noticing more security guarding the doors. Eight officers with massive, well-trained Shishi felis canis at their side now patrolled the launch chamber. Other security officers and crews gave them a broad berth.

"Not till I obtain answers. Besides, he took Jena to view the Star of Hope blossoming. As soon as the event is over, they will skip back for the opening festival ceremonies." Ryakin ran his fingers through his hair and tried to force himself to relax. "I will not be the one to cut short their rare chance at a vacation."

Ustrix, his friend since they entered the warrior's academy at seven, sars sympathized. Both second sons who lost their fathers in less-than-ideal circumstances. Both raised by caring, loving older brothers.

Ustrix responsible sometimes, yet a scoundrel most of the time. Like most blooded ranking officers, he lived with one foot in the rarefied air of the aristocratic ranking and one foot in the fleet. More worried about entertainment, pleasure-seeking, and gambling than duties, which to Ustrix ranked a distant fourth.

"I have a lot to prepare. First the False Reality battle games, along with this last-minute patrol the emperor ordered. The reavers are raiding closer to the inner borders with each turn."

Ustrix frowned. "I did not get any message on the matter of reavers."

"The council thought best to limit the information, not wanting to create panic during the festival." Ryakin looked at the paperwork list on his consol. "I'm short on time, as it is to prepare for my signing ceremony. Which cuts my time to spend with my bride to seven turns before I rush off to attend the FR battle games at the Galactic Interstellar Alliance. It's been thirty sars since Tc made the last round of games at GIA. I don't intend to disappoint my brother by being late. You know that would disqualify our fleet. I'm hoping to use this patrol to run a few simulations to prepare."

"And where exactly does your bride fit in all this hectic activity?"

"I said I intend to go over my signing speech to my bride at the same time I work on my strategy for the games. Mulling over my future will waste valuable time right now."

Ustrix laughed, "You keep your nose to the grinder and in a few sars, you will be the dullest officer I know."

"Maybe, but I will have an acceptable wife. A career I enjoy and believe in, and satisfaction knowing I've done the best I can with my life."

Ryakin went back to working on the holo computer interface before him, trying to ignore Ustrix.

"You're the best commander in Tc's fleet. You studied the combatants well enough to beat them without thinking. Lighten up; let others investigate this matter. Your fleet officers are competent. Enjoy life a little. Don't wait for later. Don't allow your duty to rule you to the point you lose sight of the things you value; family, friends, and loved ones. Duty carries a whip you don't want used to often."

This a constant reoccurring theme with Ustrix since graduating from the academy and receiving their assignments.

Ryakin's jaw tightens once more at this conversation. Leaning back, he stretched, trying to relax and flicked his hand towards the interface panel; it blinked out.

Ustrix was smart. Brilliant, even. Yet lacked drive, which leaned towards lazy. Ryakin knew why the warrior's council never assigned him a command in his brother's fleet. The sad truth: Ustrix assigned to his Executive Command because Ryakin made a personal request and vouched for his behavior and performance. Ustrix left unaware of those facts.

"Both my marriage and a win at the FR game right now are important to my brother and vital to Tc. You are aware of the economic condition my father left Tc. At least yours only caused a scandal. Rualui worked hard these last few sars. He deserves for things to go right. For a change. I will not add more problems while he is trying to spend a few turns with his wife. Someone illegally entered the base under my

35

command, making this my responsibility, not my brothers. Rualui has enough to deal with."

"And the fact your uncle put an expensive bet on your team winning." The sarcasm in Ustrix's voice unmistakable.

"You're the last person who should *bitkh* about another's gambling."

Before Ustrix could respond, the pilot announced, "Prepare for launch."

The whine of the engines reached a fever pitch as the shuttle rocked back-and-forth, straining for release from the launching anchors. The light in the tunnel turned from red to blue and the shuttle shot forward, Razing along the acceleration rails. As the shuttle exited the tube, a blast of fiery turbulence escaped in its wake. The unique seating reduced the effects of the g-forces and kept them from being crushed into their seats. Minutes later, distant stars twinkled outside their viewers. They passed out of the atmosphere into the black ionosphere, heading toward deepspace. The docking station a far-off pinprick of twinkling light in the distance.

Sometime later, they heard the pilot communicating with the docking station in the background. Still five hours out before they docked. He sensed Ustrix wanted to say more. Ryakin cut him off, saying, "I'm happy with this contract with Queen Jildius. We suit each other. We spent a pleasant enough time together, separating on suitable terms. She's attractive, though not a beauty. Still, my opinion is we can't sign the contract soon enough. Besides, my brother is upgrading Tc's fleet and needs the influx of tithe to help pay the overall cost."

"Pretty and pleasant are not words to describe a female you will spend the rest of your life with. What about fire? Passion? Love?"

Ustrix's hands dramatically waved around, emphasizing his words. "What about Lady Wiante? You courted her for sars. I thought you would offer for her. Both her house, and she appeared very receptive to an alliance with Tc's royal house."

Ryakin changed the subject to Ustrix's love life. "Like you and the last what, five, no wait, six times you thought yourself in love, believed you found your mate. Your family's matchmakers pull their hair out, trying to keep up with your predilections. If you are not careful, your brother will enforce his prerogative and pick your mate to advance your house. *As he should.* Your mother spoils you. Your brother should stop that."

"Really, would you like to tell my mother her idea of marriage or love is wrong?"

He thought about Ustrix's formidable mother and laughed, shaking his head. "I doubt even I have that much courage."

Ustrix grinned, "Neither does my brother, or I, for that matter. One of her greatest pleasures is spoiling me," he said, his grin backing up his statement.

"Go to sleep Ustrix, earlier you *bitkhij* about your lack of sleep. Let me get back to work," Ryakin said, sensing the tension between them dissipate.

"Fine, I will dream of females who lack morals with ethereal charms and widespread... arms." Ustrix burst out laughing. "The expression just now on your face. Hilarious. Hmm, maybe you are the one with a dirty mind, Ryakin." Ustrix smirked at him as he leaned the chair as far back as possible and seconds later snored loudly.

Two hours later, Ryakin finished his reports. Happy, he produced three to four FR simulations for the crew to work on during their patrol duty. Reviewed their patrol routes and memorized them. Looking over at Ustrix sleeping, he decided it was not a terrible idea. His head still pounded as he leaned back in his chair and fell into a light sleep. Sometime later, a bang followed by a soft thump brought him awake as the pilot announced their arrival at the docking station.

Chapter 3

335890 GGS Goem 6th.
Trade Lane Tower Exit: Nibiru System–Lady Jynnalt

DISORIENTATED AND CONFUSED, she thought she was dreaming. The throbbing in her head attested to the reality of the situation.

"What the *helc*," she cursed under her breath. Something warm and sticky trickled down the side of her face. She touched the throbbing spot and found an open gash, and winced. When she pulled back her hand, her fingertips coated in blood made her stomach roil and the room spin.

She drew several deep breaths and focused on the brilliant colors in the ornate rug. The room stopped spinning. Her stomach still queasy, she used her desk as leverage to stand. Her mural holo, crazy colors and mixed flashes of static.

What happened? Sweat formed on her forehead and upper lip as she stared at her uniform nanite cabinet. It appeared as if down a long tunnel far away.

"*Action stations*! *Action stations*! This is not a drill. Repeat. This is not a drill." *Think I figured that out myself.*

"Passengers to assigned emergency pods. Instructions on interior doors. All-access to ship's computers locked to crew members."

"Cineuian report."

No response. A second later she called out once more, "Cineuian Report."

No answer. She worked her way along the wall to the front of her nanite uniform cabinet. "Bridge?"

"All bridge officer's presence required in DCIC." *Strange, not Cineuian's voice.* A standard female computer voice.

"Acknowledged. EC Officer Airal heading to bridge. ETA five minutes."

Jynnalt stepped into the nanite uniform booth and turned as the door slid shut. Seconds later, the door opened, and she stepped out dressed in her battle uniform. She grabbed her rank pin attached to the side of the container and slapped the pin on just below her left collarbone. The same Heraldic colors and Sigil as her uniform, purple of the Arch Dukian's background with the Sigil of two abyss black Phoenixes, a crown centered between them. After an injection of pain meds, the drone sent her vitals to the Life Tender Bay, which cleared her for duty.

The floor trembled and bucked. She stumbled, then caught her footing.

The throbbing in her head decreased, and minutes later, the pain receded.

Whatever happened was playing havoc with their gravity field systems. They were definitely out of sync. One minute her body heavy as a stone, the next light as a feather.

As she reached her door, the female computer voice announced. "Doors on manual. Repeat doors on manual."

"Great," she said under her breath.

"Emergency power to essential grav lift tubes only. Access denied to all others."

She struggled with the door panel for a moment and discover the hydraulic handle frozen, forcing her to pull out the manual pump lever. Six arduous pumps later, the door opened enough for her to squeeze out to the hallway.

Red pulsing lights of the emergency system drenched the hall, Klaxon's now mercifully silent. The flow of directed chaos as crew members rushed to their stations forced her along towards the nearest lift.

Moments later, she stepped into the anti-grav tube; the scanner checking her Sigil authentication pin on her uniform. Her heart raced as her panic rose once the doors closed.

Two officers saluted with a bow of their heads. She nodded back. One sporting a black eye, the other a head injury.

"Call a life tender drone once you reach your stations and tend to those injuries. Soon."

"Yes," EC, they said in unison.

Minutes later, after the last crew members stepped off and raced away to their stations, the tube stopped. A bell chimed, announcing the bridge. She took a deep breath. Too many minutes in the crowded lift left her on the verge of hyperventilating. Something she barely learned to control in the academy, almost washing out her first sar.

The calm, controlled atmosphere of the bridge strengthened her. Commander Elgar and the Knight Officers stood in DCIC, huddled over the holo'haptic command table. Elgar and the others intent upon the isomorphic three-dimensional holo projections of deepspace outside the ship.

The bridge officers focused on their jobs, cocooned in the lights of their console interfaces. Various officers called out information in crisp professional tones. Their hands moving with practiced ease across haptic controls, trying to regain input from the static and quick flashes of vague images. Not an excellent sign. The Dagger of Cineuian, a state-of-the-art dreadnought. The first bio-neural nanite cells for faster control and command across the ship and other benefits, combined with a top-of-the-line deepspace scanner whisps and sensor systems. She boasted the most advanced entang communications in the empire.

A life tender drone detached from a station against the wall and approached Jynnalt. Ran a quick scan, sprayed rejuvenating skin where needed, and gave her another shot of painkiller before moving back to the drone cradle.

She headed straight to the DCIC; Officers bowed their heads towards her as they moved to make room.

Elgar remarked, still paying attention to the battle map holo displayed before them. "Little longer than five minutes."

"The door on manual took longer to open than expected. The hydraulic pump froze."

Elgar grunted before going back to what he was discussing. "The skip from the trade lane tower to the exit beacon landed us in the middle of a something, maybe an anomaly of some sort."

"Powerful enough to cripple Cineuian." Elgar indicated a place on the map, "this put the center of whatever this thing is here, off our lower port-side. We pulled away, but not before the *droging* thing did substantial damage to our hull and sensors."

The engineering Knight broke into the conversation. "The Ai's higher functions shut down and is not responding to the wake-up codes. We believe the Ai is protecting itself. I assigned my best techs to the job. They discovered the bio-neural fluid non-responsive. Damaged in some manner yet to determine. They are replacing what they can." The Knight shrugged. "My engineers need a few hours to clean out the damaged cells and regenerate fresh ones from in storage. It will require some systems to stay shut down. There's a limited amount of replacement cell."

The signal Knight chimed in, "shipwide cyberware is offline. We need at least the command deck for the officers and Knights. We only kept manual computer controls and wireless. However, the wireless is iffy."

"I'll try but helm, navigation and life support come first."

The Knight next to Elgar spoke. "From what we can tell, this storm, for reference, is distorting our sensors and signals. The plasma lighting took out the port-side hull's sensors before the scanners got a full read-out. Our database mentions nothing of this nature listed for this sector. At least not at this time."

Another Knight spoke up, "our consoles show the skip and warp engines erratic. This might have affected them. We are running diagnostics."

"It is paramount you tell me the conditions of those engines soon." Elgar said, a concerned expression on his face.

One of the bridge officers, a female, said, "sending information received as we exited skip. Now."

A flick of the hand from the officer and the information appeared, floating above the holo-field as a ghostly image.

The engineering Knight spoke once more, an intent expression on his face. "Interesting. These show a gravitational pull equal to a small black hole before they blinked out. Never heard of any storm capable of that."

Jynnalt spoke, "we can't gather further information till the outer hull regeneration finishes. I recommend we shut down non-essential area's life support to speed up the process."

"Agreed. Notify all personnel to evacuate to essential areas until further announcement. As soon as the area's cleared of personnel, shut down and transfer power to hull regeneration tubes," Elgar said.

"Any communications from the Tower?" Jynnalt asked.

"None. Our transmission is not getting through, or we are not receiving," the Knight signal officer said, before turning his attention back to his interface.

"I need visuals of our surroundings," Elgar gazed at the little information available to him. "Any suggestions on our best course of action?"

Jynnalt moved closer to the holo map before saying. "Send out a Ghoster. Their electronics' the highest shielding. They can use their emergency manual backup thrusters to maneuver. That should keep the pilots in control."

Elgar acknowledged the idea and relayed the order to port-side lower launch bay ten. "Launch Ghoster twenty-seven, one pilot and one navigation co-pilot. Sight check anomaly. Acquire images and information readouts, if possible. Sending blind, without backup from home. Manual control thrusters only. Keep within recovery range."

"Bay ten acknowledge. Out."

"Anyone run into something like this before? Speak up." Elgar said, as heads shook.

"Helm keep putting distance between us and the anomaly till we acquire further information. Notify me when the Ghoster returns or the technicians finish repairs. I want every tech working, do whatever's necessary, even if not in the manual," his tone firm. "Engage drift thrusters three quarters and move us forty thousand standards back towards the Tower. Move us out of this soup, so we can contact someone, anyone. Use ion thrusters. There is no information on how the hydrogen thrusters might affect whatever this is. I prefer not to blow ourselves to shards."

The subtle vibration underfoot increased as their massive ion drift thrusters engaged.

"EC Airal and I will be in my ready chamber."

Moments later, the door whooshed shut behind her. Elgar headed straight to the sizable chair on the other side of the desk. Jynnalt moved to the other chair and waited for him to say what was on his mind.

Elgar cracked his knuckles, staring off into the distance for a bit. Then gazed at her, a thoughtful frown on his face.

"Hectic for your first turn on the command deck, yet you managed yourself well. Your father would be proud. Take some advice from an old hand. This crew is the best Ki's fleet offers. Never ask, give praise when deserved and no matter someone's rank, understand who can complete whatever mission you give them. Believe in them and they will follow you to *helc* and back."

He stood and went over to one of the built-in wall cabinets, reached to the back, pushed hard, then withdrew a tall-necked dark bottle.

"Rilaitio alcohol? I thought it's illegal," she said, staring as if he held a venomous insect.

"Yep, I won't tell if you don't. Your father always kept four or five bottles on hand. His supplier kept selling to me after... he died. I take a drink now and then. You appear like you can use one."

"Only a small one." She reached out and took the glass Elgar held her direction gingerly before he sat.

"Thanks," she sniffed the glass. Her eyes watered, and her nose wrinkled from the pungent odor. She rolled the glass through her palms.

"Why did the Igigi in the Tower fail to warn us the skip exit beacon was hazardous, or notify us there was a problem in the sector?" She asked, placing the glass on the desk.

He took a sip. "Whew, I forgot how potent this stuff is." He held the whiskey to the light and swirled it around as he stared thoughtfully at the rich golden-brown liquid, before glancing over at her.

"I wondered the same thing. Until we send a signal out, we won't receive any answers. Speculation won't help," he said, before changing the subject. "So, how did it feel?" He sat back waiting, drink in hand, then added, "first time on the bridge as EC?"

Elgar was her father's longtime friend and her guardian. Per her father's specific request. She hesitated, "different from the False Reality simulated games. This... electric. Intense. I could sense the crackle of tension from the crew as if a storm underlay the calm. FR is never like that. If that makes any sense," she bit her lip, picked up her glass and stared into the liquid, not sure what he would say.

"If you couldn't tell the difference, you'd disappoint me. Many Knights and officers can't. A shame, as this leads to poor decisions during actual battles. Real-life possesses consequences. FR games do not. Your mind instinctively should know the difference. Trust your gut reaction and act accordingly. A mistake in the physical universe will cost you and your crew. Profoundly. Sometimes permanently."

She braved a drink. Volcanic fire poured down her throat. She choked and coughed as her eyes watered, and she tried to catch her breath while Elgar chuckled on the other side of the desk.

"I told you it's strong. Sip it. You don't gulp this whiskey."

Elgar, a gruff, plain-speaking, intelligent commoner, rose through the ranks during the Great War. Death's Avatar passed him over for the ranking blooded who fell before the scythe.

If you were smart, you recognized the spark of intelligence in his eyes. Savvy, quick thinking and fearless, he took command of the ship Raptor when the ranking officers and knights perished. Took out by a direct hit to the bridge when the shields failed. He rallied the lower crew and turned the battle in the favor of the Kierian Kingdom. Her father rewarded him by giving him a knighthood. Afterward, he rose through the ranks without further advantage.

Her father told her Elgar never forgot his humble beginnings, no matter how high he climbed. Jynnalt found him kind, warm, and open-hearted, with little tolerance for those lacking in morals, lazy or slothful.

He was the House of Arial's most experienced fleet commander and highly decorated. She knew enough to listen when he spoke. Elgar healthy, his body trim, fit into his uniform with no alterations for age. Clean-shaven per fleet regulations, his hair short and neat, coppery red with light gray at his temples.

After another sip, he looked Jynnalt in the eye. "Decisions, which can cost lives, are hard to make. A leader learns to live with what he demands of his crew." A haunted expression flashed through his eyes. "Or those decisions will destroy them."

Has he? She changed the subject. "Did you know mother left with her friend Sabas and took the household with her?"

Elgar took another sip of his drink, before he glanced her way, "yes, she informed me before she left of what she thought of my command, including my knights and officers."

A moment passed before he added, "she would drive me and the crew insane if still onboard. I can picture her on the bridge, hysterical, creating havoc. Believe me, I would drug her and lock her in an escape pod. To *helc* with the consequences," he said, slamming back the drink before leaning back in his chair. "Did Eshin leave with your brother and sister?"

"Yes," nothing more need be said.

For the next couple of hours, they waited for the Ghoster to return. Or the hull to regenerate. They talked about her father and caught up with one another.

The signal officer's voice came over Elgar's comm's, "Commander, the Ghoster landed. Images relayed to DCIC."

"Acknowledged."

Both he and Jynnalt headed to the bridge.

A miasma of gases, gravimetric waves, and a boiling storm of heated plasma roiled just outside the Ghoster. Immense flashes of lightning blinded the bridge crew and encircled the massive, seething cauldron of volatile atmosphere.

He shook his head and straightened. "If I didn't know better, I would think daemons sent it. One second, all is normal. The next this," he gave a slight nod toward the three-dimensional image.

"*Chaos daemons,* the environmental controls are fluctuating. One minute we're freezing, the next we are being cooked for dinner," the signal Knight said, wiping sweat from his brow. The lights flickered. "*Helc*, add power problems to the list." He stared at the engineering Knight as if their predicament his fault.

Both the Ghoster officers arrived to discuss what they noted while out there. "The miasma in this area is impregnable," the co-pilot said. "We tried to leave deepspace whisps, but the storm destroyed them within seconds of launching."

One of the Knights spoke up, "We're still too close. We can't extend our scanners without damaging them till the hull rejuvenates. This leaves us blind for now."

Elgar nodded his head and glanced over to another station. "Comm's status from Igigi contact?"

"Nothing, no signal, Commander. I hailed on all frequencies."

"Forget the long-range entang comm's go-to short-range radio."

"Did. No response, Commander."

"Keep trying."

"Yes, Commander," the comm's officer turned back to his station, "Igigi - Igigi- Igigi, this is The Dagger of Cineuian DGC Ki 5981. Requesting contact Igigi–Igigi, 74,800,000 standards 180 Degrees Trade Lane Exit Tower skip beacon. Anunnaki Empire Nibiru System Encountered UNKNOWN STORM ANOMALY. Full Fleet crewed along with one hundred and seventy-eight non-Fleet aboard. Minor Injuries. We have sensor damage, our Ai matrix non-functioning, power plant, and gravimetric systems fluctuating. Assistance requested from Nibiru system control tower for Evac of non - essential crew and civilians. Over."

Time passed as they waited for an answer. Nothing. Not a single response.

"Hull regeneration completed. Whisps deployed, sensors extended." The engineering Knight reported.

"Commander, a gravimetric wave is building within the storm. The wave will reach us in forty minutes."

Seconds later, the fuzzy outline of their dreadnought appeared on the holo as the sensors came online. Jynnalt glanced up from the command-and-control, "look," her brows furrowed, not waiting for an answer. She stared at the image. A vague outline emerged, and she asked the sensor officer to enlarge the image. Elgar nodded his head toward the officer. After tense moments, she pointed again in excitement, "there. There it is again," she glanced over at Elgar and knew he realized what she detected by the shocked expression on his face. A planetoid the size of one of Nibiru's smallest moons sat at the center of the raging storm off their port. Blurry, yet easy enough to classify.

"*Drog, Helc, Sheat,*" Elgar swore.

They all understood this was not a storm, but a rogue of immense power. The havoc on their systems came from formidable radiation, emp pulses from the rogue planetoid.

"Why the *helc* was there no warning at the gate? Why is the Igigi not moving the exit beacon to a safer location for exiting ships?" She wondered out loud.

"Overlay the projected path of the planetoid and Nibiru's system," Elgar ordered. Her heart stopped. The rogue would tear through the system, hitting Nibiru Proper, the Anunnaki empire's capital planet. "We must warn them of the danger."

"If we move far enough away, can we spare power to send an extensive range entang message to Nibiru's planetary Igigi's platform?" Elgar requested of his signal officer.

The signal Knight thought a moment, "We can, if far enough away."

"How much further away to send?" Jynnalt said.

Elgar answered before the Knight could, saying, "the facts are more about how fast and as opposed to how far we can move. Thrusters aren't fast enough. We can't engage the deflector's this close so no go on warp. Too much interference. At least not this close," he said, intent upon the data flow before him. "The only news I like is the hyper skip and warp engines are working, so if we move the ship away fast enough, we can warp."

The helm Knight spoke for the first time. "We need to energize the hull plating to full power. Next, polarize the hull and extend our shields in a sizeable field to protect us from the emps pulsing out in waves blanketing the sector. That's an enormous amount of power, and we can't rely on getting enough. We need to leave enough power for our essential systems."

"I see an idea floating around in your head. Let's hear what you're thinking." Elgar said.

"If we could harness the plasma lighting on the exterior, it should give us enough additional power."

The engineering Knight broke in, "it would blow every relay and node throughout the ship and possibly damage the bio-cells in her neural net we replaced."

She stared off over his head, eyes narrowed as she walked, gazing at the projection before her, thinking. Realized what she was doing and stopped. Every eye upon her.

"Nibiru possesses one of the older emergency beacons if I remember right from my training," she cocked her head, staring at him.

"And?"

She heard the tension in his voice as she said, "The academic's insistence on all those tedious emergency skip procedures."

"Yes..." His face lit with comprehension.

"This is a dreadnought; those drills aren't for capital ships. The disruptive spatial waves in a system do too much damage."

"My team did, in an FR competition. Once. With minimal disruption. Besides, nowhere near as much damage as this rogue will cause."

"In an FR simulator where physicality is not real." Elgar reminded her.

"Yes, however, it *is* probable my training Ai said the maneuver would work. The timing must be exact."

"You realize the Ai is unavailable."

"Helm and Navigation with the main computer can do the computations. At the academy, you know they don't allow us an Ai during the actual competitions. They only allow them prior to the games for planning."

She waited. When he said nothing, she rushed on, "we can plot a skip manually to the emergency beacon from here. The problem, a long skip's power requirement, is prohibitive. If we can control the plasma energy by directing the power flow to the skip engines, we overcome the problem."

Elgar peered at the engineering Knight. Who, even though he appeared skeptical, was nodding in the affirmative, his eyes narrowed in thought.

He stared back at Jynnalt, "training Ai's are notorious for not taking into consideration real-life complications. Their solutions are not always workable in the physical realm," he said, pausing a moment, rubbing at the back of his neck, "*however*, it could work," he conceded.

"We can stay here. This is the safest course, but we would leave Nibiru Proper at the mercy of this beast. Understand, making the skip will pose a risk to the crew and those aboard," Elgar said.

She waited. This their only option, in her opinion.

Elgar nodded, "Comm's, skip, navigation and helm officers to DCIC."

As soon as they arrived, Elgar explained the situation and asked if they could perform a manual skip to the old civilian emergency beacon.

The Skip officer responded. "It's all about the timing."

"During my academy turns, I plotted spot on every time," the navigation officer said.

"Can you do that from here?"

"I never—-."

Elgar interrupted him. "I did not ask if you did. I asked if you could. Give me an honest assessment."

"Outside the rogue's emp pulses, yes, inside this mess, the odds are not good."

The skip Knight commander broke in. "The rogue is putting out enough emp pulses to damage the gyrostatic equipment if we bring them online. Under normal circumstances, normally outer deflectors worked. We need to redirect at least some power there."

The skip officer watching the information flow got excited. "If we use our warp engines, we might move the nose far enough outside the EMP's pulses. I need warp eight to bypass the normal spin up procedures to jump straight to skip. Still, iffy to bring out the warp rings without at least one deflector." He glanced over at the helm officer.

"I believe we're far enough away to deploy the rings."

"Good. Otherwise, a no go. The skips gyrostatic system in the nose is extremely sensitive. Once clear," he shrugged, "no guarantees. I won't be sure till the nose is out there."

Elgar called out to the bridge officers on deck. "Commence deployment of warp rings. Send aft shield power to forward deflector."

Moments later, the ship's computer warned, "Commencing to deploy warp rings. Stated Yellow."

He informed the Navigation officer, "I need you to plot to the emergency beacon without Ai assistance. Can you do this? Don't lie to me, son."

The Navigation officer responded. "I believe I can." he stood taller, his voice firm, a professional from the top of his head to the bottom of his battle boots.

The Helm officer nodded Elgar's direction, "if the nav officer can lock on to the coordinates and engineering gets me the power. I'll get us there."

Ship's computer warned, "Stated Green. Rings deployed forward; deflector activated."

Like well-trained bridge officers in the Kierian's fleet, they did not turn away from a challenge.

If she were wrong, it would end in death. *At least I won't have to face anyone.* She berated herself for the thought as soon as the thought ran through her head.

"Comms prepare an emergency warning message. When we exit, send it, no delays. No matter what happens. Concentrate on getting that message out. Trillions of lives are at stake."

The comm's officer nodded and started working on the message.

"Everything is on you when we exit." Elgar said.

He turned to the crew. "Prepare for an emergency skip from warp."

The computer warning system sent out the command, "Actions Station. Set condition Red. Repeat condition Red."

"All passengers and non-essential personnel to your assigned emergency escape pods."

He moved over to Jynnalt. "Strap in."

She glanced up at his worried tone.

"We're in for a heck of a wild ride." He said, heading to his seat and strapping in himself.

"Engineering Knight, turn off hull plasma shields and open conduits to engines." Sparks and flares raced along the equipment as officers jerked away from their console's panels.

"Engineering, I need that energy flow controlled." Seconds later, the arcing stopped. "Helm, aft thrusters' ten points every five minutes. At impulse ten, siphon one quarter power over to deflectors three quarters to warp engines."

The ship shook hard, sluggish at first before gaining speed. The vibrations increased as the grip of the rogue held tight. Seconds later, they lurched forward, jerking Jynnalt hard against her harness.

"Impulse one,"

The ship bucked as it picked up momentum. Moments passed as the nauseating vibrations settled to normal. The helm counted out their impulse speed.

Navigation called out, "Threshold in three minutes, two minutes, one minute."

Her hands shook. Nausea rose in her throat as she watched the Navigation officer. His stare intent, concentrating on the screen as if nothing else mattered but those numbers counting down on his consol. The tension on the bridge rose. A split second too late at their jobs, and they ended in disaster.

Elgar waited for the navigations officer's call out, ordering. "On my Mark warp."

Helm called out, "Condition Blue. Repeat Condition Blue for warp."

"Power to all forward deflectors."

"Clearing threshold in 5-4-3-2-1."

"Mark." Elgar commanded.

"Warp engine engaged," the helms officer said.

They raced along the leading edge of the wave. Building warp speed as they rode the shock wave.

"I have a lock. Lock engaged." The navigation officer said seconds later.

"All stations stand by to execute skip on my mark."

"Mark."

The helm officer spun them in to skip. The shockwave behind pushed them through chaos space with the additional combined plasma energy at an unheard-of speed.

For a moment, they all stretched, then snapped back to normal.

Chapter 4

335890 Goem 6th.
Nibiru Proper: City of Agade–Prince Ea Con'Ru

EA PULSED MASTER APILSIN as rose gold rays of dawn bathed Agade, turning the white-capped mountain a deep golden patina. He breathed deep and let the serenity from the sheer glow of the scene envelop him as he stood looking out from his balcony.

A smile came unbidden to his lips as he thought of last night's escapades. He and his misbegotten friends, as his father called them, enjoyed.

Guilds shut down any non-essential jobs to allow members to enjoy the festival. Critical guild members got shorter work cycles. The Astrometric guilds considered secondary lab's noncritical, so Ea knew the lab's empty. He counted on the time alone to recuperate and recover as he worked on his chaos theory. The intense concentration science demanded shut out everything, calmed his mind, gave him a deep sense of peace.

His appreciation for Master Apilsin, his mentor, arose from the fact he did not have to explain himself. As he walked out the door, his private pulse buzzed and, thinking it might be Master Apilsin, answered.

A male dressed in robes fashionable enough for blooded society but subdued and tasteful appeared on the full-size holo-pad.

"Father," beads of sweat popped out on his forehead, "I was on my way out," Ea said. *Drog. Why right this minute? It's as if he spies on my every move.*

"Excellent. You are to come to my study. My vyzier sent a skyskimmer for you."

"I have my own. Why send one of yours?" he asked.

"To make sure you appear. This time."

The door chime sounded behind him. "Your ride has arrived." The pulse blinked out.

His stomach queasy and his legs weak. He answered the door. *Did he know about last evening's debauchery?* He couldn't think of an excuse not to go. *Drog. Drog. Drog.*

Less than fifteen minutes later, he joined his father, who sat in his studies chair as if a throne. A stern expression upon his face. Ea glanced around. No chairs. His heart raced. Definite lecture.

Two agonizing hours later, he left.

Straight for the lower guild sector in Agade, the capital city of Nibiru Proper.

Throughout the Galactic Interstellar Alliance or GIA. Agade was the largest city, proclaimed one of eight jewels of the galaxy.

All are welcome.

Declared by the Council of Nine or CON, the most cosmopolitan city accommodating all species and races.

The city provided False Reality, or FR, for non-oxygen breathers to enjoy their planet's delights.

Agade rose from the lower plains of the commoner's tent sector, up through the foothills of the guilds and concubines to the upper reaches of Agade's mountainside.

There the blooded houses perched high above the rest.

The city during starlight, obsidian black, gray, and brownstones and metacrete. Common stone offset with whites, reds, and golds of rare marble. Most buildings built out of imported sandstone facade with carved artful scenes of daily activity along them.

The landscaping guild used the natural land and the artful placement of plants, walkways, and statues to create a wonderland of beauty. Sky-high power ziggurats. Delicate official buildings, with mythical creatures reaching for the heavens, peeked out over the tree canopies.

To the delight of visitors, the city came alive during the dark of night. Subtle bioluminous lighting from trees to walkways and statues made an ethereal vista. Swirls of artistic shapes of blues, yellows, red and greens glowed on columns, statues, and pathways. Patterns, glyphs, and art formed directions for those lost. In the morning's starlight, the natural colors of the landscape once more prevailed, no hint of the colors locked within.

Ea left the upper city through a needle gate for the lower guild section. The entrance gates packed this time of the morning. Besides, friends of his were leaving by the outer gate, and for the moment he preferred to avoid them. He took the scenic pathway. It would take far longer to walk, but he needed time to think.

Master Apilsin could wait. Ea's needs more pressing. Head down, arms clasped behind his back, his lips tight, he followed his favorite route to the lab's park.

Ea ignored the colorful rustling trees or the grasses with fluffy white tops and other more exotic plants imported from around the galaxy by the Rider merchants. Swaying to the slightest breeze, the flowers released their scents, luscious and inviting, creating a heady, sweet aroma.

Even the flowery scents did not soothe him. Focused on the earlier lecture, his father's voice ringing through his head with a litany of accusations.

Too flamboyant, I don't think so, Ea glanced down at the somber red and purple stripes of his robes. His cloak, thrown over his left forearm, for now, too hot to wear, threaded with the rich patina of Orichalcum in golden splendor with the Sigil of the house of Ru's colors showing. Plain gilded silver sandals finished his assembly. Flamboyant. He shook his head. His ensemble barely acceptable by the turn's standards. Father only believed in wearing the house colors. In ancient times, the law declared blooded houses wore only their house's colors, now more tradition than law. *Boriiinng*.

The walkway shimmered as his delicate and fashionable sandals caused him discomfort from the burning heat of the stone pathway. Added discomfort to all his woes.

Next accusation by his father. *He ran with the wrong crowds.* Who did he expect me to run around with? As the son of a concubine, his friends were sons of concubines.

The roar of a waterfall around the bend matched his chaotic thoughts. Ea born to his father's favorite concubine, his eldest male offspring. His father's official wife, Antu, so far having forgotten to present him with a child. Let alone a male trueborn heir during their marriage of twenty-two sars. The fault laid at her pillows as Anu produced thirty children so far with his various concubines, all female, except for Ea and his younger twin brother.

Did he gamble too heavily? Maybe. Sweat trickled along his sides and down his face as unbearable heat plagued him. No worse than other heirs of high-ranking blood houses. He shook his head once more, braver out here than when standing before his father in his private study.

A Phursian accompanied by a Jianian hurried past. Neither stopped to chat. Both appeared miserable from what must be furnace-like heat to them. Their natural habitats cold climates. An unusual sight as both species avoided planets this hot.

Ea rounded the bend as the thunder of the waterfall overwhelmed his thoughts. An enchanting rainbow arched across the waterfall mist, delighting him. He shivered after the heat of the pathway, the cool spray wafting over him causing the thin linen of his robes to cling to his skin.

Cool air after an hour turned cold as he stood watching the roiling pool and the blissful colorful fish swimming beneath the waterfall, dreading the roasting heat of the open pathway.

He sighed, then moved back into the heat of the turn. Ambled along past, colorful ornamental shade trees spaced esthetically. Ea's damp clothing made the heat bearable. His thoughts again turned to the lashing his father doled out. Did he spend more time in the pleasure houses than others? He snorted, the cheerful babble of the running stream Razing beside the pathway to the enormous pond to his right softened the sound. Not as much as other titled heirs. Why does he never talk about my standing with the guild? What about my accolades on the theoretical duality of the universe proclaimed within the two gods and their avatars battles?

A loud splash broke his concentration as ripples spread across the pond. The sparkling twinkle of golden light shimmered on the surface, transfixing him where the fish jumped moments earlier. The faint incessant buzz of the dragonflies and pollen collectors going about their work soothing.

Father never pays attention to the pollen collectors, yet the garden would not bloom without them. He views guild workers the same. They don't exist. Somehow, without effort, everything appears at the snap of his fingers. Did he ever think about how it got there? What difference would he make if he spent more time on political entertainments to keep their houses standing amongst the others? Seriously, our standing.

His last accusation struck Ea as ridiculous.

Emperor Lahamu produced no legal heir for the last twelve sars, leaving his father, the official Cupbearer, as next in line. Other than the throne, where would their house rise? Prince Anu, the only legal heir. No one challenged those rights.

Everyone sought house Ru's entertainments, not the other way around. Besides, the events the greater blooded and ranking houses threw left him bored with a pounding headache the next star rise. Gossip abounded, which he might have enjoyed, but for the background wailing of bards who the upper ranking females chose for their soirees and galas, grated on his nerves.

Ea found the music ponderous and too dark for his taste. Tales of death and dying, of lost empires and heinous deeds. Why not upbeat stuff with a fast beat now and then? Or even something a little more sensual?

One time, standing next to a holo'ed bard pad, the unthinkable happened. He turned towards the pad as he took a bite of his capailla's on flatbread, a delicacy of certain fish eggs from Straiousgious he loved. Now face to face with the re-creation of a scene of a long-ago blooded councilor stabbed in the eye. Vivid holographic blood sprayed outwards. His stomach heaved and his capailla spewed all over a formidable Dowager Duchianess and her insipid daughter.

That cost his father too many plat talons. Which father forced him to work off over a whole soul-wrenching sar in his employment. After that, Ea ever careful to never stand next to the holoprojector during an ongoing show. The dancing worse. Stilted steps side by side with perfect form, and gods forbid no touching, so sedate you may as well hold a conversation. He shuddered.

Not to mention the house's matchmakers. They perched like vultures upon the upper balconies. Avid and alert, leaning over the railings as they noted each touch of a hand or Gods forbid dances which amounted to over one an hour. Each sar that passed without his father producing a trueborn heir, the more calculating the gleam in the matchmaker's eyes as they consider him marriage material for their employer's daughters. Even more so as sars passed and the Emperor and Empress did not produce a child. After his father, Ea stood as the heir apparent to the Anunnaki throne.

For now, there were still half-sisters of Prince Anu's of breedable age. Other than his wife, Antu.

Each step he took on the pathway, the trapped sensation increased.

Caught between the glittery halls of wealth, privilege, and power or the bland, solid, studious yet comfortable life of the guild. This is where non-heirs of the blooded presided alongside commoners. Or the more prestigious warrior guilds. One he refused to enter.

In the guilds, he mingled with the ambitious, intelligent commoners climbing out of the arduous, demanding life they were born within or the non-heirs of the titled stepping down from one of overwhelming privilege.

Why does father not understand I'm protecting myself from future disappointment? Ea would cease to be acceptable to the blooded houses if his father produced a trueborn heir.

The second Antu presented Anu, a male son, Ea, would be persona non grata to the wealthy and influential society. Obscurity henceforth. A male born to a concubine held little value. No longer required to attend functions for their houses, which truthfully, he would not mind.

His income diminished to what he earned through the guild and his talents. The thought filled him with hollowness at the loss. The cost of his visits to the pleasure houses, his clothing, and gambling expenses significantly diminished.

Raucous cries of crows interrupted his thoughts. Then the stench reached him. He gagged as he got closer to a set of screening bushes. He covered his nose and rushed past the offensive scent.

As soon as possible, he would notify the groundkeeper's guild on his way back home an animal died in the park. Worse, guild workers did not remove the carcass fast enough. *How Revolting.* Five minutes later, he realized he stood before the door of the lab.

Looking around at first, he missed Master Apilsin walking towards him. Short, squat, heavy of bone, with long curly light golden-brown hair. His hair tied back with a mahogany brown ribbon matching his eyes.

The impression of most was drabness and somber reflection. Laugh wrinkles and a quick twinkle in his eyes along with silver streaks at his temples belayed the first impression. Master Apilsin, though older, still lively in gait. A keen intellect laced with humor twinkled in his eyes, and an intellect Ea respected.

The repair sequencer no longer able to correct all his cellular damage.

Age came to even those with full access to life units and resurrection cloning vats. Commoner's can gain access to the former, but not the latter. Masters in the guilds given access to both. Apilsin declined the vat. His coppery bronze skin and brown eyes marked him as one from a younger, hotter star system.

Ea, a foot taller with elegant slender bones, shining silvery hair exquisitely curled and groomed, stood out like a dandy next to him.

The pin above Master Apilsin's left breast proclaimed his rank, guild, and master's level. Six blue stars in a circle of Orichalcum rich gold gleamed against the deep brown of the cloak thrown over his arm. It dawned on Ea; Master Apilsin might one day be up on the wall as he glanced towards the past masters rendered with skillful style. A glowing depiction of them lighting the corridor. A means for those seeking the labs to see in the dark without the aid of the harsh light of glow globes.

As if he read Ea's mind as he unlocked the door Master Apilsin said, "Looking for a spot on the wall for me are you," he chuckled, "I am not in any hurry to light some amorous young Lord's way to a tryst with a female of dubious morals, yet. Especially as I shall no longer be able to enjoy such delights myself."

Ea burst out laughing till tears ran down his face, and he fought to catch his breath. "I was not thinking in quite those terms. Leave it to you to see my thought from a far more ah.... physical point of view."

Apilsin, looking pensive, glanced over at Ea. His eyes narrowed, staring at him as they both walked into the astrometric lab.

"It's not like you to be working during festival times. From your demeanor, someone gave you a rough time this star rise. My guess, your father or a female?" He let the question hang in the air between them.

Ea shrugged eloquently, "Father." After moments of silence dragged on, Ea stated, "I got slightly deeper into debt than I could cover. The note came due earlier than my allowance. Father, well.... he covered the amount, or I'd be in court again for dereliction of debt and dishonest gambling fraud."

Ea found he could not look Master Apilsin in the eye and wandered back to a darker area of the chamber. To avoid any deeper scrutiny, he dropped his cloak over the back of a chair as if completing their conversation.

Apilsin silent in the background. But Ea sensed he watched him as he halfheartedly wandered the chamber after his quick admission.

"You are canny, Ea, yet you lack the wisdom to use your cleverness. Why not be more... discreet? I'm sure your father would overlook these... indiscretions. You want to please him, it shows, yet you flaunt your activities in his face. Activities, you know, he disapproves. I would bet my best wine when he was younger and full of himself. He enjoyed the same pursuits with his friends. All young males do. Did you ever hear a word of indiscretions?"

Ea shook his head. "I wholeheartedly doubt he did."

"Why?" Apilsin asked. "It is more likely he was discreet, something it would not harm you to learn. It would also not be out of line for your father to expect an apology as he paid the bill while letting you off with only a lecture."

Ea, thinking, ran his fingers across the ghostly, haptic astrometric control panels. He felt the familiar whisper of a touch, just enough feedback to let him know he hit a key without thinking. "I believe I will stay here hiding, like a rodent, not wanting spied by the felis, that being father. At least for this turn. I'm tired of his lectures and fault finding. He says I shame our blood's reputation and standing at court." Ea snorted, "as if it matters."

Stopping before an interface without seeing it, he remarked, "father suggested I might want to forgo this sars hot festival and concentrate on more important things. What exactly the nebulous, important thing entailed he did not specify. If I were trueborn, father would forgive me anything," Ea rushed on, "I see this happen all the time. Spoiled from the moment they're born. I, concubine born, only seen by father when something displeases him."

"Ea, you're too smart to believe your remark. Your father realizes you exist, and the fact your concubine born, I doubt matters. You are his son."

Apilsin moved towards the door yet stopped just short of the auto control mechanism. Ea sensed he waited for something. Silence filled the chamber until he could not stand it anymore, blurting out.

"I worked hard to earn my position in the guild, unlike other commissioned blooded. Three turns ago you decried the fact I was a potential title holder, so denied full membership. For now. Half of me is in the guild and a half in the blooded's rarefied atmosphere. I'm a placeholder in two places."

Ea's frown deepened. The familiar stir of anger and resentment arose. He worked hard to reach the top position in the fields he had. "Not once has father praised my accomplishments. Not the smallest positive remark," he said, his fingers trailing the edge of the console.

"Let me try to have fun with my friends and wham. Father swoops in and admonishes me as if I am still a child hiding behind mother's robes in the city of the concubines."

The remark led to other, less pleasant thoughts. Ea shuddered, pushing the black memories back where they belonged in his consciousness, memories best left buried in bottomless gloomy spaces. At least father protected me from the obvious perils of what occurred in the city, unlike others of his friends.

Almost forgetting Apilsin's presence in the room, listening to his ranting. He stopped, staring at the interface without seeing it, avoiding looking at him.

"Answer me honestly. Do you really think your father would be any different with a trueborn heir?"

Ea, ambivalent for a moment as he stopped to think about the question. If he was honest, he did not doubt for a moment his father would be any more lenient. In fact, he suspected if trueborn, his father might be harsher. Still, the dressing down stung. He avoided the question; not wanting to admit the truth. He turned the discussion in a different direction.

"I am nothing like my father. He believes in the old ways. Ritualized etiquette," Ea frowned, "what use in our modern galaxy. Old-fashioned ideas from ancient warrior classes ignored by the fashionable in these civilized times."

"Ea, has it never occurred to you rules, culture, and traditions dominate all classes?" His tone stern. "Feeling sorry for yourself won't change a thing other than making the situation worse. Self-pity is for those of weak character."

Before he came up with an answer, an interface light furiously blinking caught his attention. Ea realized the interface was Nibiru's inner systems emergency sensors.

He forgot about the conversation and moved towards it. He sensed something wrong yet did not understand what the something might entail. Teased at the back of his brain like an insect buzzing in the corner. Tugged and pulled. Without thinking, he input his codes, then realized they did not work.

"Master Apilsin, the computer is not accepting my codes. Try yours. I think there is an emergency at the system's beacon." He felt rather than saw him move up beside him. Not taking his eyes off the blinking light, he moved over to give Apilsin room.

Ea, looking around, realized this was the only light blinking. There should have been more flashing warning lights as soon as an emergency beacon activated. That is what bothered him. Yet they appeared normal, as if nothing untoward occurred. This was a monitoring station, so did not directly help to notify the proper authorities of an emergency. But the station recorded the events for future review by the proper personnel. His unease increased.

Moving over to the recording holo meh, he checked to see if it was on. The recording holo was running. He detected a frown upon Apilsin's face as his fingers flashed across the panel of the console Ea pointed out, worrying him.

"The entire warning system planetwide is down," Apilsin said as his fingers flew over the inputs. "It was deliberate. Whoever did this must have forgotten or did not know this station needs a master's input code to disable the beacon warning function. No one can remotely disable this recording station. Or they did not bother figuring no civilian guild member would be here. This is atrocious," Master Apilsin said under his breath. From his tone, Ea realized he was more than worried, which scared him.

"I'm getting a terrible sense about this."

Ea barely heard him as he muttered the last under his breath.

"Okay, the system will restart in two minutes. Two minutes afterward the computer will be back on-line," Apilsin said.

Those four minutes an eon.

"There."

The anger in his mentor's voice clear. The chamber came alive with bright red flashing lights and a cacophony of harsh discordant sound. Ea's unease fell straight into dread.

Chapter 5

335890 GGS Goem 6th.
Nibiru System: Emergency Beacon: The Dagger of Cineuian—Lady
Jynnalt

THE SHIP SHIMMERED around her, blurred for a microsecond before becoming solid. Collision sirens screamed out warnings.

"Starboard thrusters. Now!" Elgar yelled. Their view screens, outer sensors even damaged, showed the ever-enlarging ship charging straight at them.

An illusion. They jumped out of skip in the other ship's flight path. The impact causing the dreadnought to jerk hard, lights flickered before plunging the bridge into darkness.

Seconds later, the emergency backup power came on. Elgar lay unconscious, thrown to the floor; his straps broken.

A life tender drone responding was already halfway to him. Jynnalt unbuckled and rushed to his side. Her chest tight. Please, please let him be okay, she prayed. Confused by how his straps failed as she rushed to check his condition. He was still breathing, thank the gods. She stood. Realized she was in command and took a deep breath. Seconds later, a life tender drone loaded Elgar in a repair unit and removed him from the bridge. Everyone on the bridge waited for her command. Before she gathered herself, the ship rocked with a sudden violent movement. She stumbled and grabbed the command chair and held on till the ship stopped dancing under her feet. Hull breach klaxons roared to life, *gods, and daemons what now.*

The computer voice announced in a calm tone, "starboard section fifty in full decompression."

The viewscreen showed their artificial atmosphere hemorrhaging into space as the hole widened, taking everything not anchored out with it. Spewed internal guts from the sector and twenty crew members into space in the blink of an eye.

The computer notified across ship-wide comms. "Warning. Internal explosion deck fifty aft. Power plant five critical overload. Ruptured hydrogen lines in decks twenty-five to fifty. Fires advancing to other decks. Emergency crews and spiderdrones en route." The computer warning system fell silent.

"Shutdown all volatile fuel lines to those decks, she called out without thinking." A memory came to her, stopped her in her tracks, demanded her attention. The Society members during the turn of the Star of Hope viewing. She remembered the Society Priest's escorted by Master guild officer Johien to power plant five and seven. Security caught them at five.

Security discovered the pass Master Johien used to gain access to the restricted area forged. A turn later, he committed suicide in his cell.

A red light on the engineering officer's board turned blue, catching her attention. "Hull breach contained."

It hit her. Sabotage. Both power plants located where, if they blew, would do the most damage.

How long before seven goes critical?

"Engineer jettison power plant seven's core. Now!" The officer hesitated, then followed her order.

"Flank speed starboard. Tractor that battleship and dragged them with us." The helm officer responded in an instant.

"Keep us between the core and the battleship. Get me distance from the coming shock wave. The dreadnought can survive the hit. The battleship can't."

Two minutes later, her hunch proved correct.

"Ejected core going critical."

"Brace for Impact." She called over comms, strapping in herself.

"Ten minutes till explosion," her scanner officer said. Impact Klaxons shriek to life.

335890 GGS Goem 6th.
Nibiru System: Emergency Beacon: - Prince Ryakin

THE DARKNESS ABOVE Natiture, the gas giant in Nibiru's system, blossomed with a speck of white to an ever-expanding jagged circle. Streaks of lightning emanated throughout the area. The chaotic rippling of a skip displacement window forming revealed in the holo projection. Ryakin moved to DCIC, followed by Ustrix as soon as the faintest glimmer of light appeared.

"Move in closer to assist with evacuations in case the ship's beyond saving. Fireteams standby." He said, watching the event horizon widen as they approached.

"Prepare grappling tractors. Let's make sure we do this as we train. Stay tight. When the Igigi send the tug to tow them to the shipwright's docks, we'll pull off and transport the ship's crew and citizens to Cary's Travelers Station."

"Just your luck. They'll hail you a hero for saving the gorking hide from some idiotic captain of a star pleasure barge before your contract ceremony."

Intent upon watching the exit window, Ryakin said, "If I give you the credit, will that make you happy?"

Ustrix laughed, "Won't matter, you can do no wrong. Somehow, they would still give you credit."

Seconds later, Ryakin could not believe his eyes. A dreadnought exploded out of skip like a missile aimed straight for them. For a split second, everything appeared to stretch before snapping back to true size once the aft end exited the skip window.

Nemesis, the ships Ai started Collision alarms. The discordant sound jarring. "Starboard side thrusters flank speed," Ryakin commanded.

Nemesis responded faster than the helm officer, turning away; not fast enough. The grinding screech as ships slid along the hulls, bone wrenching.

Ryakin flew into the air, suspended there, before violently slammed down to the bridge; hard. Skidding and rolling until stopped by the lower stairwell to the antigrav lift tube.

Stunned, he lay there for a moment, trying to catch his breath before rising unsteadily to his feet with the help of the nearby railing. He stumbled to his command chair, wiping blood free from his eyes, a long gash across his brow. His uniform suit protecting him from severe injury. He growled under his breath, "*fock*, I will have someone's danglers over this."

Ustrix picked himself up and shook his head, spitting blood, saliva, and a tooth out. Those appeared to be his only injuries. Ryakin saw his bridge officers working with controlled yet desperate movements as reports poured in from the lower decks. The rage, anger, and fear coursing through him showed on their faces. Yet as a well-trained crew, they went about their jobs with efficient, if frantic, precision.

"*Fock. By the Dark One.* Whoever is in command of that Dreadnought will pay as soon as I get my hands on them," Ryakin said. *Bitkhjing* to no one in particular. He strode past Ustrix, still spitting blood from his mouth, his face flushed, his nostrils flared. He gave Ryakin a quick nod. Ustrix heard him over the sirens, still screaming out warnings.

"Nemesis silence the sirens. Relay information to the interfaces of the officers in charge of their division, with information critical to the ship's safety."

"Acknowledged." A deep baritone voice answered.

"Nemesis, location of Dreadnought, ident and commander?"

"The ship's, ident, Dagger of Cineuian Dreadnaught Ki 5981, Commander Knight Elgar. The ship is no longer in danger and sustained minimal damage. I detected a trailing gravity shock wave before the skip window closed. The Dagger of Cineuian is two thousand standards off our starboard at one hundred degrees by one hundred fifty degrees upper."

He's worried about the *Droging* Dreadnought.

"It sustained no hull breach from contact with us. A more damaging internal explosion from its power plant five, one minute afterward caused a significant decompression breach. The power plant went critical. Unknown cause. They turned as they exited. This decreased damage to us by forty-seven percent. The Ai of the dreadnought is nonfunctioning or in protected mode, while the ship is active."

Ryakin did not give a *flying fock* about the dreadnoughts Ai. "Scan their computer if their Ai's offline, it can't block you. Hack them and find out what happened. I want to know why they made an illegal skip in system with a capital ship. And Nemesis, I want a report on my ship, not the *sheating dreadnought*."

"Damage to ship is minimal. Emergency spiderdrones extinguished fires where fuel hoses ruptured on deck fourteen's lower hydroponics' atmosphere production. Breached hull self-healed before enlarging beyond repair. Loss of three hydroponic units. Oxygen production still maintained shipside at 99.0134 percent. Oxygen within acceptable range. No major damage reported from life collection drones. All systems functional. Commander, if we sustained severe damage, I would report that first."

Did the Ai scold me? He shook off the odd sensation.

"Comm's, I want a face to face with the Commander of the dreadnought. What the *helc* are they teaching their Knights in their warrior's"

Ryakin, his anger under control, prepared to speak to the dreadnought's commander. He doubted their conversation would be pleasant.

He turned towards Ustrix in DCIC, "what in the god's name is going on over there?"

An image of a red-haired female answered, cutting him off, "we ejected power plants seven port side. It's going critical. Prepare your crew. We are tractoring your ship now."

A sharp jerk and the floor came up to meet him. The viewscreen winked out, and the sensation of being towed at a speed not recommended in any training classes he knew made his stomach queasy.

To keep Nemesis from being torn apart, he was quick to take the pressure off the hull. "Engage aft starboard thruster. Match speed to the dreadnought." Both he and Ustrix dived for their command chairs and strapped in at the same time.

Seconds later he called out, "Full impulse."

The Dreadnaught maneuvered between them and the exploding power plant, taking the brunt of the explosive shock wave.

The shockwave hit hard on the only unprotected part of the ship, starboard aft. Like a giant hand spun them around and slammed them into the lower port side of the dreadnought.

Earsplitting horns blasted the bridge. Their harnesses would leave bruises. "Damage report."

"Starboard side; a gash of eighty-two feet long and ten feet thick at the central midline. Decompression of outer sector nine breach, inner blast doors sealed and holding."

"Explosions and internal fires caused a cascade of system failures and non-critical fluctuations throughout sector nine. Fire suppression spiderdrones will not contain sector fires without venting to the void. Venting now. Sixty-seven percent of adjacent sectors decompressed. Life support, doors, and gravity systems are malfunctioning mid-level. Skip engines three, seven and five fluctuating. Cores to power plants three and four ejected to avoid overloads. Three life support power plants burning their ejection mechanism malfunctioning. Emergency crews are working to contain or release the manual locking mechanism and eject the power plants. Estimated control in approximately twenty minutes. Power for core systems rerouted to back-up and recovery. All holding steady."

"Incoming." Nemesis said.

Five skip windows opened. Colossal Malkuth galactic explorer ships shot out of exit windows. At the proper distance and locations. One headed straight for them. Tractor'd both damaged ships and skipped with them in tow. Seconds later, they exited just outside the system closest to the repair docks. The Malkuth ship, released them as if contaminated, skipped out.

"Fury transferred us to the repair docks. The Dagger of Cineuian is four hundred standards off our port, upper longitude degree one five-six by vertical degree five-six point three. The debris from the accident, including crew members, deposited alongside. Outer mid-sensors malfunctioning, no information available on crew members in the void. No contact with The Dagger of Cineuian."

"Malkuth always have something up their sleeves. How did five of their largest explorer's happened to be in the Phoenix sector?" He asked as he stared at the blank viewscreen. "They rarely visit this sector. They might be why the dreadnought skipped illegally." Ustrix said. "Perhaps the dreadnought has done something illegal?"

"Who?" Ryakin said, scowling. "I will discover why soon enough."

Ustrix muttered under his breath as a trickle of blood ran down his chin. "I know they saved our proverbial aras back there, and believe me, I'm grateful. But you would think if they took us to the dance, they might have stopped to give us a kiss."

"Did we need further help?" Nemesis asked.

"No...," Ustrix said with an elaborate shrug.

"Your remark makes little sense. We are not dancing. Fury had no nefarious reason for being in this sector. They are allies, not enemies."

"If I thought an Ai had emotions, I would say you offended Nemesis with your remarks, Ustrix," Ryakin said. While staring at the blue blinking light showing the Ai in active mode.

"Fury apologized. He clarified there was no time for an explanation. He informed me he has a greater responsibility to deal with than us. Trusted me to take care of the situation."

Strange, can't miss the sense of pride in Nemesis's voice.

"Fury huh, did he, by chance, explain the oh so much greater problem?" Ustrix said, wiping more blood from his mouth. His sarcasm lost on Nemesis. A life drone made its way over to him, gave him a shot, and rolled away. Seconds later, he stopped bleeding, and the cuts healed.

"No," Nemesis tone final.

Ryakin motioned Ustrix back to DCIC. "Stop irritating Nemesis. We need to prepare for the shipwrights to take control and make sure they remove our injured to the life center at Cary. The accommodations for the next few turns at the Station will be hectic, and no doubt packed."

Before tugging Nemesis to the dock's, shipwrights sealed the outer skin. Temporary for now, giving the hull time to heal.

Officers' irate curses reached Ryakin each time they lost contact with their crews below deck. They struggled to reroute through different channels, to regain contact and restore power where necessary. The flow of information to the bridge needed for preparation on the shutdown and handover was difficult with all the damage. Nemesis inundated with demands no longer in speaking mode.

Chapter 6

335890 GGS Goem 6th.
Astrometric Labs: Agade city–Prince Ea

EA MOVED OVER TO THE Drum Spatial Placement System interface, most called DSPS. A holo blossomed in front of them, showing a deepspace dreadnought and a solar battleship too close at the emergency beacon. The readout displayed a ship-to-ship collision ten minutes earlier. Apilsin turned towards Ea, the same shock on Apilsin's face as his.

Ea ran the holo image back to the start. A full-sized battle dreadnought, and a royal battleship collided, before moving away from each other at the emergency skip beacon. *When was the last in system crash?* Ea racked his brain. Not since the Igigi took over handling traffic over five hundred sars ago.

"Identity of the ship's involvement in the collision?" Master Apilsin asked in a sharp command as he moved over to the interface.

"Royal Inner Battleship, class V, Imperial Commander Knight Ryakin Da'Tc ident Nemesis Tc 856413. The second ship is a Dukian's Outer Dreadnought, class Lican, commanded by Knight Elgar of Ki ident Dagger of Cineuian Ki 5981," a flat monotone computer voice said.

"Weird," Apilsin motioned Ea over to the interface where he stood, "no communications from the Igigi control platform."

He put in his code, his fingers nimble, danced across the feedback keys.

The chamber suffocating as sweat trickled down Ea's sides, the cooling equipment he realized offline. Bad for computers. While Apilsin worked, he went to restart the blowers.

When he rejoined his mentor, he realized the situation was calamitous. Apilsin between typing furiously combined with word commands frowned, grumbled, typed again, hit the command key waiting between each time. Watching. To Ea, it felt like forever. Nothing. Not a single frequency response displayed across the screen. Apilsin tried others.

"Ea notify the Igigi of what is happening. They appear unaware of what is occurring. Peculiar. I will try to communicate with the ships."

Ea went to the interface Apilsin pointed out to him. As he reached it, an emergency beeping pulse and red flashing light came to life. He snatched his hand away as if a deadly silken sat there causing his heart to race over his fright, his hands trembling as he punched in his codes.

He tried three more times. No access kept blinking across the screen. "Apilsin, I can't bring up this interface. My codes are still not working."

Apilsin walked over, punched in his codes. A direct emergency priority one message from The Dagger of Cineuian scrolled across the screen. Entag priority.

Apilsin headed straight to the back wall. Right before he would slam into the wall, a hidden door whooshed open, and he passed through to the inner chamber. Ea tried to follow, but wall snapped shut in his face. Now he stood facing the back wall with no door and no access. He paced outside for a minute or two. The door reappeared and Master Apilsin called out, "I gave you an emergency clearance for entrance and full access," Apilsin said in explanation. "It uses an advanced combination of stealth and holo'haptic projection feedback. It looks and feels solid."

Ea entered, impressed by the door to the chamber. The chamber smaller than the outer yet packed with more equipment. Amazed, he was unaware of this area when he spent so much time in the lab.

"What the *Helc*," Ea swore as the message scrolled across the screen. Incoming planetoid. Twenty-one hours, thirty-three minutes before the rogue planetoid arrives at the outer system edge. The plotted path will bring Nibiru Proper into direct contact.

Approximate size one hundred sixteen standards at the equator, check sensors for an incoming light signal, normal communications not responding, Igigi not responding, inter-deepspace channels not responding. Entag channels open with no response. Jamming signals suspected. Evacuate planet. Repeat. Evacuate planet.

The readout hit Ea, as if kicked in the stomach, "Dagger of Cineuian Ki 5981." The message repeating on a loop.

"Do you believe what this message says?" Ea asked as he glanced over at Master Apilsin. Somewhere deep inside he was praying to the gods his mentor would declare this a nasty prank and dispel the building terror coiled within him.

Apilsin's brows furrowed, deep in thought, Ea wise enough to remain quiet. Ea interrupted him once in the fourteen sars he was his mentor. The glower he received, along with the sharp retort from his mild-tempered mentor, something he avoided afterward.

"Ea," Apilsin said, his tone setting off alarms in his head, "if this is correct, and we are being jammed, the Igigi might not have received this message. We classify encrypted fleet entag frequency so that even the Igigi cannot decrypt our fleet messages. Entag is the only signal capable of bypassing system jamming. The first step of a surprise attack is to cut off communications for a surprise attack. A festival is a perfect time. The civilian guilds and fleets on skeleton crews."

"Still, no matter how exhausted, there are still civilians and fleet personnel on duty," Ea said, his voice quivering.

Apilsin shook his head, "from what I've been able to discover. Someone sabotaged the civilian interface to show a normal flow of signals. The problem is, they are false. They're broadcast from somewhere here on Nibiru Proper. The exact location on the planet I can't determine. I set a program to track the signal output. So far, nothing. This implies a sophisticated attack. Problematic. This takes someone with the highest access codes. Five, to be exact. I am one of the five."

Ea's terror racketed up another inch, making him feel sick.

"They monitor those frequencies at nine other fleet stations. I checked them. None are responding. I can't turn them on from this remote station. Under normal conditions, they have three fleet members with specific clearance in this chamber; except festival, when they assign only one."

Ea looked around the chamber. Only the two of them present.

"The fleet member stationed here is absent. Dereliction of duty would send them before the warrior's courts. They do not just forget their duty or abandon their station without cause. The warrior is a victim or a traitor," Apilsin said, looking towards the wall's hidden entrance.

"Crows," Ea blurted out as he remembered them close to the lab. "Down the pathway, crows fought over something on the ground. The smell of death gagged me. I hurried past. You don't think...." Ea said, as he trailed off to nothing. The thought too horrible to contemplate.

"We need to find out. Show me." Master Apilsin followed him out and up the pathway. They found the crows still fighting amongst their selves over whatever was on the ground.

"I will wait here." Ea knees weak. He held his arm over his nose. If the crows were fighting over the missing fleet member, he preferred to avoid the sight.

Master Apilsin's face when he returned told Ea the answer. A dull, distant, booming sound caught his attention. A storm appeared to be gathering in the northwest as cold gusts of wind now ruffled his thin robes, causing him to shiver. Ominous black-gray clouds piled higher each second. The clouds lit with random flashes of gold or vivid blue. His face turned pallid and his hands clammy as his fear rose. A louder, distant boom came once more. He flinched.

Ea frowned. *Weather*. The Igigi, who controlled system traffic and security, also controlled the weather systems. Yesterturn their information pulse said they set mild, pleasant weather for outdoor entertainments in Agade. They moved the storm out over the plains, southwest of Agade and other major cities for the festival. This storm front was moving *towards* Agade.

Apilsin glanced the direction Ea stared. A thoughtful frown crossed his face. "The Igigi are not responding to normal hails. Someone shut our systems down." He met Ea with a level look, "by someone aware I scheduled no civilian to work at this station. Someone high enough in rank cognizant of the restricted access chamber and that only one fleet warrior assigned instead of the normal three."

"We need to reach the Igigi, other than the emperor; they govern the systems complete emergency control relays. They are part of whatever is happening, or they are in trouble."

"Only Igigi can access their systems. Can anyone even step on their platforms without the Temple elite Protectorate blasting them to vapor?" Ea asked. He found the Igigi disquieting. Odd rough gray skin with slight lumps and bumps if you stood close enough to see them. Enormous almond-shaped black eyes without pupils. Eyes which reminded him of chaos denizen to the Dark God. They barely reached to his hips, and their heads appeared too big for their bodies. He shuddered. No one knew if Igigi are related to insect species, but they reminded him of one. They are one of the two most enigmatic species in the galaxy. The other, the Glaegrar's.

Apilsin stirred and hurried back towards the lab, forcing Ea to hustle to keep up with him, not wanting to find himself alone in the park.

"I have a buddy amongst the Igigi, strange little fellow, but he showed me a trick to reach his communications station. This signal bypasses the normal comms. Uses the background universe frequencies to hide within. Smart. And sneaky. The two of us enjoy arguing over theories about exotic dark matter, and the dark energy currents the Sailors use." Apilsin said as Ea watched him move over to the first interface and punch in whatever codes and program he and this friendly Igigi arranged.

Seconds passed as the holo showed static, then a horrific scene solidified before them. Ea's blood ran cold.

An Igigi still sitting in his chair. Head down as if resting, a pool of mahogany brown blood flowed sluggishly across the table to drip off the edge from a gaping head wound. Ea was no expert, but the wound resembled gauss rifle damage, yet oddly, the edges smooth like an energy weapon. He could not tell which type of weapon inflicted the damage.

"Now we understand why they're not responding." The tone of sadness in Apilsin's voice mingled with an underlying rage. Something Ea never heard before from his mentor.

"The Igigi are not available to run the systems or responded to hails or message as they are all dead."

Ea could see more bodies strewn about the enormous chamber. Inky pools forming around them with gaping holes in various parts of their bodies. Expanding pools, splashes, and streaks of blood on the walls attested to the violence of the attack. Shrill whistles sounded, yet there was no living presence capable of hearing to respond.

"I would say an attack is imminent. How the dreadnought made the skip in system is beyond me. They risked their lives to make sure the message got to us. We must make sure their effort is not in vain. Your father, as heir to the throne, can convince the Emperor of the danger."

Ea shook his head, "he won't listen. You realize what he thinks of me. He believes I'm wild and out of control. He will believe it's a prank."

"Ea, stop and think." The sharpness in Apilsin's voice a slap, one he needed. "I won't get past the lowest palace guards without a Royal or Imperial writ of attendance. You're aware of those facts. My authority only extends as far as the guild. You must convince your father," Apilsin rushed to the other chamber, then came back out and handed Ea a meh.

"Show him this. He is not stupid. He will know what to do."

"If you leave now, you should be able to reach him before he leaves for the start of mid-morn entertainments. I bet you walked here; you always do when upset."

Ea nodded. His mentor astonished him with how well he understood him.

"My private skyskimmer is just around the corner, take it and hurry. Convince your father this is not a prank. At all costs."

Ea shoved the recorded meh holo in his cloak pocket, flung the cloak across his chest and on the right side, and snapped it tight. The chill wind rising from the incoming storm now required its use.

Apilsin moved to an interface and opened a pulse channel to the Imperial Guild Headquarters. Ea, hurrying so fast towards the door while looking back, ran smack into the Ministry of Science Guild master, Thoozkin.

"Gods sorry. I did not realize you were there." He helped Master Thoozkin rise as he rushed an apology.

"Ea, you need to hurry. If you don't leave now, you will miss your appointment." Apilsin pointed toward the door. "Thanks for stopping by."

Ea stepped towards Master Apilsin, "but...."

"Ea, I need to talk privately with Master Thoozkin."

At least he was not leaving him alone in case whoever killed the fleet guard came back. Ea rushed out the door and down the corridor to where the skyskimmer sat, repeating the startup codes given to him. As he reached the end of the corridor, the sound of voices echoed behind him, and he glanced the direction of the lab. Two blooded males, around his age, walked into the lab. He sensed something familiar about them, yet could not quite place them. Eventually, it would come to him, he was sure.

Now they're three citizens to keep Master Apilsin safe. Relief washed through him. A moment later he saw the skimmer two steps ahead, ran and jumped on before Razing away. The recorded meh in his cloak pocket a burning weight. The only thing he concentrated on as he raced toward his father's fortress was how to make him listen.

Chapter 7

THE SOOTHING DARKNESS of the bridge, backlit by the array of lights from the consoles, showed the dark form of the Temple guardian as he paced. Ikath jumped at this recon and infiltration mission to investigate peculiar activity connecting the planet Plainausor of the kingdom Ithora to the Anunnaki empire.

Ikath obsessed with what happened to his parents and little sister. He wanted justice for them and peace for himself. Every spare moment available, he followed the smallest leads, without the Temple's blessing. Why kidnap yet not murder his brother and him before dumping them on the brutal streets of Jias in the system of Plainausor, of the Council of Nine's Guild Alliance's Kingdom of Ithora, a manufacturing system, baffled him. Wealthy merchants ran an illegal and dynamic underground slave brokerage in the Caspis sector. Too many nights to count dreams and visions haunted him, lurid and elusive, yet upon waking slipped away like a fast-flowing stream. Afterward, restlessness and frustration overwhelmed him.

GIA, which the Merchant Guild Alliance's kingdom of Ithora fell under, outlawed slavery over five hundred sars ago. No self-respecting citizen on Plainausor owned slaves. But in the seedier underground warrens, they're more colorful and wealthy criminal merchants brokered slave sales for other kingdoms and empires. Selling or buying them under other alliances, which allowed the practice. Ikath, viewed as reprehensible, unconscionable, holding nothing but disdain for those who kept slaves or took part in the merchandizing of sentient species.

Ikath followed threads of information and rumors from Plainausor straight to this planet. Somehow the connection to the unrest in the Temple and the galactic rise of the reavers linked to criminal slavers. Somehow this connected to wealthy blooded houses in the Anunnaki Empire. For now, he was unsure how. Somehow, all this connected to the rise of civil strife in far too many empires. At least, from what he discovered so far in his informal investigation.

The High priestess, in charge of these investigations, aware of his personal ties to this case, yet looked the other way. Once you joined the Temple, your past deeds washed away in the waters of life, allowing one to start with a pure history. That the date of your rebirth as a Temple member.

No one, no matter rank, station or past criminal life, allowed to keep anything, not even their clothes, as they passed through the entrance gate as a supplicant. If accepted, they must earn their way. No one from any station of life given exclusive treatment or raised above another without earning the privilege. The first seven sars learning the temple ways, and hard, grueling work in the fields or production centers.

The Temple's Highest Priestess received access to information to their life before acceptance. No other. She, the one who decided on their placement because of their past life. To make sure prior problems or obligations did not interfere with life in the Temple.

The laws of the Temple harsh and demanding. Work hard, follow the rules. For most, the chance to rise to prominent positions enticing along with the individual freedoms afforded Temple members. The negative side. The Temple did not hand out second chances after the first seven sars. Nor did they forgive, if you broke their laws, the judgment of the High Priestess finally and beyond appeal.

This mission ranked at the highest classified level and was volunteer only. Minimal survival rates for the Guardian who accepted. The plus side, every temple resource available, no questions asked. The Guardian who agreed to take the mission assigned a Ghost Walker. Which was to assist him, when necessary, yet strangely never seen by the Guardian?

He needed this mission. He did not care about the risks. So far, the few disjointed pieces of evidence he found about the mystery surrounding his family pointed here, to this wealthy outer rim empire.

Five sars earlier, against his and his brothers' objections, the temple closed the investigation in their family's murder. He needed one small shred of evidence to take to the Temple with proof of someone, anyone involved with what happened. He could use the information to demand the temple reopen a formal investigation.

The case declared frozen by the Temple High Priestess of the Guardians. She claimed during these time's wasting resources to pursue the case further without fresh leads foolish.

This ship hosted an Ai, Ikath displeased they assigned him one for this mission. Like most in the galaxy, except for fleet members, he was uncomfortable with their use. The war five hundred sars in the past by Ai's on biological life forms a raw sore amongst many. Throughout the galaxy, the devastating war brought sentient biological life to the edge of extinction. This is the history taught in all galactic CON alliance training classes.

Empires and kingdoms kept excellent records; space faring races boasted of long memories. Distrust of Ai's ran deep amongst most galactic species. They almost lost the war. A sudden, inexplicable surrender of the Ai's at the height of their moment of victory left the galaxy scholars in confusion. Why? To this turn, a riddle left unanswered.

He stopped pacing for a moment to check the status of the Anunnaki blooded's arrivals for their traditional hot festival. "Ai, give me the status of the arrivals."

"All but one arrived and docked. Forty-four dreadnoughts of the greater nobles are in orbit in the outer system. The lesser nobles and peers have a combined total of eighty-two deep battleships, battlecruisers, destroyers, frigates per their ranks in their kingdoms. All non-fleet members and house blooded already shuttled down to Nibiru Proper. One Greater outer blooded family has not arrived."

Annoyance overcame him. "Ai, who is arriving late?"

Ikath paced, waiting for the answer. A second passed.

The Ai spoke once more, "an outer kingdom greater noble of Ki, The Dagger of Cineuian. A deepspace Dreadnought, blood house Airal, the heir to the Arch Duchianess, is on board with family. Her mother, Regent, since she was twelve. She is now the Dow——."

"*Enough*, I asked which ship is late, not a family history. Nor some long-winded explanation."

Silence. Pacing now, he became lost in thought about those terrifying times on the streets for his brother and him.

His memory blank of how his brother and he arrived at Plainausor because of his age. Or the proceeding events before arriving. He and his brother chased down rumors of a group of anarchists led by his uncle, murdered his father, mother, and little sister, yet the inquiry came up empty. His uncle still free and attending to his official duties within the empire. Many puzzled about why they only kidnapped his eldest brother and himself. Behind the scenes, rumors circulated about all kinds of reasons amongst the populace. Three of the loyal Councilors speculated his uncle intended to rule through his brother but kept those thoughts to themselves.

Burned into his memory were the three long sars of starvation or beatings when caught stealing food. Remembered the horrific races through streets when slave catchers came searching for orphans to sell in illegal private sales. He still felt the filth and damp of the underground train tunnels where they made their home. Freezing cold or oven-like heat of the two seasons of Plainausor seared upon his spirit.

Somehow, against the odds, his older brother kept them alive. Believed someone would find them. He remembered his brother telling him fearsome people called Ghost Walkers were looking for them.

To him, four sars old when kidnapped, his prior life a fabled dream which faded with each turn, till dust in his memory blowing away in the winds of survival.

He thought about the time his brother got sick and almost died. The memory swamped him, overwhelmed him. His breath froze, and his heart hammered. The ship's walls closed in around him. The sound of his pounding heart overwhelmed everything else, his throat tightening as terror and fear clawed at him. Frantic, he reached for the necklace around his throat and rubbed the bluish green stone between his fingers, slowly regaining control as his breathing calmed.

Loud beeping broke into his thoughts. One of the targeted citizens he was investigating was meeting someone in a garden area. A place they thought immune to listening devices. They were wrong. The Temple's equipment far more impressive than the Council of Nine.

"Ai turn up the volume and record," he said as he sat.

Sound blasted him. He slapped the palms of his hands tight against his ears as he yelled, "What the *Sheat? Turn* it down."

Silence reigned. "What in the two God's. Are you too dumb to understand not to blow someone's ears out? The simplest computer is not that stupid," he said, clenching his jaw.

"You did not specify how loud, nor how quiet. You requested the volume turned up. Recording now in process. And for your information, a computer has no ability to think. I thought they taught your that in your first sars training."

The airlock engagement warning light lit up, catching his attention. He reached for his stunner baton handle hanging from his belt. Flicking his wrist, he extended the end two-and-a-half times its length and moved towards the bridge airlock hatchway. He stood with his back to the wall; the stunner held close against his leg, ready to whip out and stun whoever entered.

"Can you identify who? How many?" Ikath whispered, sweat pouring along his sides. Not now, not yet, ran through his mind.

The ship while in orbit stealth'd. *Could the stealth engine be faulty?* This Ai appeared defective. If he survived, he would request the Temple do a diagnostic. And repair or send this thing for scrap. *Droging* Ai never correctly obeyed a single order he gave so far this mission.

Next thing he knew, he was staring at a pair of boots in nanite gray from the floor level. Blood pounded in his ears and a million stinging needles assailed his senses as sensation rushed back into his limbs, causing him to grit his teeth.

"Riurrel, how are you doing?" A voice said above and to his right.

Followed by footsteps moving towards the cockpit pilot's chair. "I am betting he was about to attack me as I came through the door?" The voice, a pleasant deep bass, inquired.

Who does that? Talk to an Ai as if they're equal. His brows moved into a frown as his muscles relaxed from the stunner. He knew who stunned him. The *droging* Ai. Full blast from his ship's own protective mechanism. A mechanism designed to safeguard the Guardian. Unbelievable. *Now,* the Ai is complaining to the intruder.

"*Look what he did to me.* He made my beautiful crytinmetal floors, worn and broken. Left exposed access panels everywhere. SPILLED oil on my intake and outtake valves and BURNT it."

This *droging* Ai is angry over that.

"He scattered hoses across the floor, *creating this mess.* I am surprised with all his pacing; he does not trip and fall over them. He tore my seating. MY SEATING. He smeared deepspace dust and ion particles all over my hull. Explosive deepspace dust. *Look at me.* I am as filthy as a station hopper's ship. I am not presentable. At any decent docks, I am embarrassed to show my hull. And he treats me like I am an idiot. Calls me *the Ai.* They told him my name when they assigned him to me. Wonder how he would like me to call him *the Elohim* all the time. Do I? No. I am polite and use his name."

A burning bolt of prickling raced through his body as the stunner effect wore off. This male appeared familiar to the Ai. The Temple must have sent him. He decided it's about time he spoke and discover who, and why, this citizen was here. He also wanted to know how he accessed his ship.

Ikath heard the command chair swivel and footsteps come his way as the boots came back into view. "It appears the stunner you hit him with is wearing off. Our friend will want answers."

"*He is not my friend.* The Temple assigned my mission to him."

He suffered enough of this machine, referring to him in this manner. "It is not your mission. It is *mine.* I am undercover and need to appear in need of tithe. This ship is too expensive to pass muster for the part. I burned the oil to keep the ship from *appearing like* someone smeared the nasty stuff on for effect. I neutralized the deepspace dust and ion and I can replace your *droging* seat covers and access panels."

The stranger chuckled. "Riurrel, give him a chance. I don't believe he did all that to harm you. His cover is as a freelance transporter and fixer. A ship of your quality someone in his position should not be able to afford. You want this mission to succeed. Don't you?" The silence wore on for moments before the Ai answered.

"Yes," a long stubborn pause ensued before the Ai spoke, "can you please assign someone else?"

"I am sorry I can't. There are important reasons the High Priestess picked him. I need you to cooperate to make sure you accomplish your mission. Both of you together could save billions of lives."

The coaxing sound in the stranger's voice made Ikath wince. "Seriously, it's a droging machine."

"Hey, I am right here, and a living entity. How would you feel if I treated you as if you didn't exist? Hmm."

Ikath, all at once, could move rather than just speak. Rolled to his side and rose to his still unsteady feet. Before walking over and dropping into the co-pilot's chair. Silence reigned for seconds before he said, "You're an intelligent machine, a tool, not a living biological species." He turned towards the stranger saying, "I believe you know my Ai well."

A small, though painful, electric shock bit into his ankle from the floor.

"*Drog, helc, shea—-*"

"I am not yours. And I am a living being."

Ikath was not pushing his luck by arguing. He preferred not to get shocked again. There was something wrong with this Ai.

"Riurrel, my *NAME* is Riurrel, Elohim."

"*Okay*," yet the Ai hit him with another stinging bite on his other ankle. "*By the gods and daemons, stop that.*" A stronger stinging bite of electricity hit both his ankles, causing him to jump out of the seat.

"Riurrel, stop. Play nice." The stranger said. The sound of his voice once more caught Ikath's attention. Somehow, familiar. Something, a second passed, yet what eluded him, sank back into the recess of his mind, out of reach. Ikath forced his mind back to the situation at hand.

"Did the temple send you?" Ikath asked, curious because he was still five turns from his required check-in to his handler.

"Not exactly. I set a tracker on an individual I believe involved with the Society. He has connections with those you are investigating here. While you were otherwise engaged on the floor, I uploaded the information to Riurrel. I ran into a slight problem, in the form of an anomalous rogue planetoid, which will arrive in the system soon. The rogue, if left unchecked, can destroy Nibiru Proper. So, I'm needed elsewhere. A Malkuth deep explorer picked up a distress call from an incoming dreadnought, notified others close enough to lend aid. All five arrived while you were out. One rescued the dreadnought and the battleship, a story for a different time, while the others set up to destroy as much of the planetoid as possible."

"What do you expect me to do? Don't say leave, I can't. I am just getting the information I need."

"Listen, no matter what they do, the Malkuth estimates in five hours enormous pieces of the planetoid will crash down into Nibiru Proper. Their only choice is to destroy the planetoid, leaving shattered pieces which will careen through the system. The hardest hit will be Agade and the plains below the city and out as far as the Sartianous Sea. The disaster will be the worst the Anunnaki Empire experienced since its inception."

Ikath stared. This would ruin all his arduous work. If his suspects died, he lost the information. And the first genuine lead he found so far in what happened to his family. "Wait, you said you have a tracker on a person of interest in the investigation. Are they still planet-bound?" Ikath asked.

"Yes. I need you to follow up for me. Keep tracking this person. Listen, if you show up at the right moment and offer to evacuate them off planet; say to one of the safe orbiting stations deemed out of the trajectory of the most dangerous pieces. I doubt they'll turn you down. Best to head to a pleasure and entertainment station, where you can secure a pass showing you off the planet before the event. Try the Carouser station. I have a contact to help you at The Windward Frigate feasthall."

The stranger waited, staring as if to unnerve him. Then, as if satisfied, he turned back towards the console before standing to leave.

"I gave Riurrel direct access to the High Priestess. His identification marks any report for her eyes only. Traitors will not consider an Ai's indent for reports with important information. Talk to no one else. I suspect this suspect might have connections within the Temple. I have somewhere else to be for now. Something of greater importance, or I would do this myself. I leave you to figure out how to rescue this person. Also, if me, I'd rescue anyone else with him. They are part of this conspiracy somehow. If you accomplish your goal with this group, you're not stuck listening to conversations from orbit. And you will get a bigger picture, and far more information."

The stranger rose and bowed his head slightly in Ikath's direction in respect before he moved towards the airlock. "Riurrel, remember he is important to you completing your mission." The stranger said, his tone stern for the first time.

Ikath looked at the empty pilot seat. Wondering if he sat, if the thing might shock him again.

He turned to ask the stranger his name, hit by a flash of light, when his eyesight cleared the citizen; gone.

Ghost Walker. Must be. *Spooky how they disappear the way they do. Thought the rumors were used to scare those they hunted.* Ikath spent sars in the Temple, this his first supposed face-to-face meeting with one. He now understood why a Ghost Walker struck fear in the minds of those they hunted. The stranger must be the Ghost Walker assigned to him.

Ikath realized he never got a good glimpse of the Walker. Dressed in Society robes made of cloth with an odd shimmer. The hood kept his face hidden in shadow. The boots. He got a good long view of the boots. They were not Society styled either. Strange runic symbols carved into them, but you would not see them if you were not two inches away, like laying stunned on the floor.

"Riurrel. We need to talk."

"So *now* you know my name."

87

Chapter 8

335890 GGS Goem 6th.
Nibiru Proper: City of Agade Concubine sector–Guardian Ikath

IKATH FOLLOWED THE worn ancient stone roadway to the ornate gate at the concubine's city, the gate itself a garish red with a fleshy pink lotus flower at the center. The symbolism he doubted lost on most visitors.

To the northwest, a storm of boiling black clouds full of angry streaks of lightning approached fast. The loud crash of thunder reverberated and shook the ground. *Are the Igigi playing farsar up there, too involved with their game to worry about the weather controls?* The wind since he landed no longer a gentle breeze playing with his clothing, now grasping and angry, pushing him along, whipping his cloak around him.

Arriving at the gate, he discovered no guards, the gate ajar enough for someone to slip through to the inner concubine sanctuary city. *Why is the target still here?* The evacuation warnings sounding loud, jarring on his nerves.

His cyberware connection to the Ai allowed him communication without detection by normal security measures. The technology of the ship, far more advanced than any he'd used before. He'd give this Ai that.

Earlier he located the one the Ghost Walker put the tracker on within the upper Imperial concubine city. The houses in that area larger, the private fencing higher and adorned with fancy crenellation at the top depicted artful carvings of daily life. Hidden behind them were elegant gardens surrounding vast storied mansions.

He arrived at the one the tracker showed his target located. The outer gate and mansion's front door stood open. The interior as expensively chic as the wealthiest blooded of any empire. From the shadows where he stood, it appeared as if someone threw clothes and furniture around, piling them on the floor. Someone desperate and panicked, looking for something important. The walls speckled and splashed with an inky color; he shook his head; he never understood how the blooded considered something a five sar old could paint art.

The sound of arguing burst from the mansion. Others must be inside with the target. *How many?* He changed his vision to thermal. Four citizens in the mansion and one in the garden. One of them moved towards the back of the building and upward. The tracker showed him as the target. Three others at the front door arguing amongst themselves.

The one with the tracking device joined the other three minutes later. He increased his hearing. Impressed with the tech, better than anything he worked with in the past. Or the emergency enforcers left their stations and were no longer manning the illegal tech suppression equipment.

They stepped out on the portico. "When do we find out how our tithe got spent?" The speaker wore a guild master's pin, level six orichalcum. From this angle, he could see a slight part of the embossed guild designation. His cyberware recording. Later, the Ai could re-triangulate from the edges. The one he was tracking held up a strange ornate box before taking out a white, glowing jewel of unknown composition by his readings.

"Ikath, the jewel is exhibiting unusual energy. I cannot identify the type. *Strange.* My database does not list the material of the box, or the jewel's composition. The box either contains or shields the energy of the jewel when inside. My database is extensive yet lists both items as unknown."

To Ikath the Ai sounded both annoyed and *perplexed*. Minutes later, the Ai broke in again.

"Inbound meteorites twenty minutes from impact. One has a ninety-two percent chance to be a direct hit to the concubine's city terminal, also I moved earlier to a different and safer location."

"You should have notified me before you moved," Ikath retorted, his tone sharp. "Where are you now?"

"I am three blocks from your location to your left, in the largest garden. The gate is open, so you have access. Or I could go back. You can explain to the temple what happened, and why you let me get destroyed. First, though, I will pulse your command to me."

Ikath ignored the remark saying, "you broke the law. This is a restricted area. You're forbidden to disobey the law. Under any circumstances." Ikath said, frowning, concerned at the flagrant disregard by an Ai of his legal code.

"No one challenged me, and there are no restricted area notifications broadcasting, so I broke no laws."

The Ai's tone indignant, *droging* thing almost sounds alive. He reminded himself what this ship really was, an advanced machine that could work a logical algorithm joined to speech and behavior patterns.

"You're telling me there are no restricted area beacons" He worried whether the Ai could lie. The *droging* thing appeared capable of about anything at this point.

"Yes."

Ikath tense said, "I would have told you to move if you bothered to inform me."

"So, you admit I am right. Did you forget my name is Riurrel? *Remember.*"

He ignored the remark. "Focus on the energy source from the jewel. We might have to give those four a lift. I need to know if that thing is dangerous," Ikath said, not taking his eyes off the somewhat hypnotic jewel held up to the storm's light. He changed his vision through his cyberware too far-sight and zoomed in closer. *What is it?* What energy class is this which this highly advanced Ai can't find the information in his database? Worse, he appeared mystified by the jewel and the container box.

The glacial white jewel, when held up to the light, produced iridescent patterns that flashed across the surface, getting faster by the second. Now, zoomed in, Ikath realized something resembling blood dripped from the hand of the one holding it high above his head.

"Riurrel, what composition is the liquid dripping from the hand of the one holding the jewel?"

"Blood."

His focus changed to the others, hypnotized by the changing patterns across the jewel's surface. Unconcerned by the horrific sight of the blood's slow drips splashing on the floor at their feet.

"With this," he said, addressing those behind him as a small misty cloud swirled, rising upward. "This is how I prove my family's rights to the throne." The four, mesmerized, stared at the jewel.

Movement caught his eye, the garden gate of the mansion opening slowly, careful. A male peeked out, glanced around, before slipping out to the street. He appeared dressed like a lesser ranking blooded. *Drog.* Concentrating on the others. He forgot about the one in the garden. A sloppy mistake.

Ikath pulled his cloak hood over his face and stepped further back in the alleyway's shadow. Using his cyberware, he stealthed, blending with the wall. His clothing, another unique item assigned to him for this mission. When energy is applied, the material bent light around the item it enfolded. The only drawback. Movement by him could negate the result and create a weird watery effect. Those who are observant noticed. Fast.

Seconds later the wind picked up, snatching napkins and a tablecloth out an open window, and sent them pinwheeling wildly along the street. Colorful cloth and garbage wrapped around trees and bushes, plucked free to once more fly high into the air before coming down and rushing along the ground.

Sweat popped out on his forehead. If a tablecloth blew against the cloak, it would expose him. He held his breath till they blew harmlessly past.

His focus moved back to the stranger on the road rushing towards the front gate of the mansion. From the garden, he just exited. *Strange.*

As he reached the outer gate of the mansion, he called out.

"Prince Alalus, we must hurry." His voice startling the four out of their weird trance.

"A late arrival ruined everything. Somehow, they got a warning out.

The city is pandemonium, full of terrified citizens. It's impossible to get around. I've been hunting everywhere for you."

Interesting.

"Yes," the Ai sounded in his head, "he does not care about their welfare from his mental readouts, they aggravate him. I believe he was looking for something, most likely the jewel."

Ikath wished he did not need the Ai, or he'd turn off his cyberware connection. It was distracting having the Ai in his head, reading his surface thoughts.

The stranger spoke again, this time the sound of urgency in his voice real. "We need to go. We can't be planetside when those meteorites hit. Put that jewel away," he said, as if noticing what one held in his hand while motioning for them to follow. "There's a ship at the terminal prepared to lift off waiting for us."

A pile of clothes on the floor moved, and Ikath stared. He realized to his horror they were bodies, glanced back at what he thought was art. Recognized it was not what he first assumed, but blood splattered across the walls. Ikath glanced at their clothing before he realized their sandals and toga hems covered in blood. They ignored the bodies at their feet as if they were nothing more than what Ikath originally thought they were. Piled up *clothes.*

His attention moved back to the one with the jewel and the strange ornate box. An embossed winged creature curled around the box with fierce claws for clasps. Lovingly, he caressed the jewel before placing the gleaming white jewel inside and closing the lid. As soon as the lid snapped shut, the winged creature disappeared, now a faint etching with no visible seams.

The one called Prince Alalus, who he was tracking for the Walker, slipped the box into his cloak. With an expert flick of his wrist threw his cloak across his shoulders, snapped the clasp, and glanced back inside the house. "What a shame."

Ikath not sure if he was referring to the potential loss of the house, or the dead littered on the floor in grotesque piles. Ikath's jaw tightened.

The wind increased as the turn darkened, the storm's fury moving faster than he expected. The howling wind blowing through the empty streets forced him to increase his sound, followed by the feedback he was exceeding the safety levels. He ignored the warning.

"What in the *helc* are you four doing here? I told you to head straight to the terminal. I wasted time looking for you," the stranger said as he tried to hurry them along the street.

"Jabutia and I helped Master Thoozkin with a slight problem. Okinisha came here with Prince Alalus to retrieve his family's heirloom. All ended well," the one speaking said as he put his cloak on and adjusted his clothes before looking up with a satisfied grin. Another conspirator complained about the ruination of his best sandals. "they're covered in blood, which never comes out. I will have to throw them away." He said as he fussed with his cloak.

The stranger snapped, "Then why are you wearing them on this turn of all turns? More comfortable and utilitarian clothing, a better choice for this situation."

"Just like one of lower rank to lack understanding. One is never in public at less than their best. It sets the wrong impression. What if I'm required to appear on an official pulse? I should present myself as calm and in control during a time of crisis."

The stranger now hustled them out the gate to the roadway. "I shall follow your wisdom in those matters. Later."

The acerbity in the stranger's voice, loud and clear. Ikath would have laughed if the situation was not so dire. The fact those four who the stranger herded ahead of him were oblivious to the sarcasm amazed him.

"Your clothing is a mess." The one who complained earlier frowning said, "the company we keep is also as important." He stared pointedly at the one hustling them off to the terminal.

Their voices receded into the distance. Ikath rushed through the alleyways, looking for something of value in the houses. In one house, he found what he wanted. A small safe with brilliant jewels hanging out, as if someone grabbed a handful before rushing to the terminal.

A looter made a suitable cover story. They should believe it. Doubted, they'd turn him into the enforcers. He grabbed a fistful of jewels from the safe and stuffed them into his cloak pockets. He made sure the jewels peeked out as his cloak whipped around him in the wind.

"You're *stealing*. Temple rules forbid stealing. I will put the information in my report. And you thought to question *my* integrity earlier."

Great, an Ai with misplaced morals combined with no idea how to run an undercover operation. "You do that. Or you might help me uncover what they are doing. Our mission: remember, or you can keep on complaining."

"*Ikath incoming.*" The Ai's warning accompanied a massive detonation overhead.

Slammed to the ground. *That will leave bruises.* He rose, demanding, "Report."

"I'm undamaged, except for one of my support legs. It's scratched. A *long deep* scratch. You will need to fix this as soon as possible," the Ai said before his tone changed. "Ikath, there are two damaged children on the second floor, the farthest back corner in the house the others left."

"Any other life signs? Check by the doorway. I thought something move there earlier."

A second later. "No."

"Understood," the movement earlier, the death throes of one on the floor. "Locate the five who left here and keep me informed of their whereabouts." He ran back down the street and into the mansion. The enormous wanton killing inside turned his stomach. Frantic, he searched for and found twins, threw both unconscious children over his shoulders and ran back across to the alleyway. Followed the Ai's directions to his location. He arrived at the ship and ran up the ramp, rushing through to the lower cabin quarters. Deposited both children in his own quarters' bed. A small emergency life drone entered. Life drone? Again, surprised. Unaware, the ship came equipped with one. *Live to learn.* He ran out, back on mission.

"Where are they... *Riurrel?*" *This droging Ai might cooperate more if I used its name.*

"Four on the ground damaged from the earlier blast, one not damaged, standing, still in the same location when the explosion hit."

"Twenty minutes passed since the blast. Why aren't they moving? Are they dead, injured?" He backtracked to be a little behind them, then exited the alley and headed up the road.

As he got closer, Riurrel informed him. "One damaged beyond repair. His meh chip destroyed when his head impacted with enough velocity to burst his skull open like a ripe fruit smashed on the ground."

"Thanks for the graphic's, Riurrel," Ikath said, with no pity. He surmised they somehow took a hand in this disaster. He reaped from the field he sowed.

"How else to explain his damaged condition?"

The Ai sounded puzzled, so he let it go. He approached the four while staying at the sides of houses as if trying to sneak past.

The ones still alive rose, looking dazed. They turned towards the terminal where they were heading. The one from the garden spoke into a communication device, shaking his head. Black smoke rose skyward. Dispersed by the storm's winds. Glanced at the well-dressed body at his feet. A flash of lightning freezing the tableau with raw clarity.

In the harsh, unforgiving light, Ikath spotted the body. Blood and brains splashed across the road as bad as Riurrel's description. The cloak identified him. The male who worried about dressing for the public would not attend any pulse interviews at this turn or any other. Another shutter flash of lightning froze them once more in a harsh tableau. Followed by a thunderous boom as the ground rumbled in response to the assault from the sky.

Lightning's bright imprint left an afterimage in the dark. *Doubt they missed seeing me.*

"You there. We need help. The meteorite's blast overhead earlier killed one of our friends."

Ikath pretended to freeze. Then plodded towards their group. The stranger took no time to glimpse the flash of jewels in his cloak.

"I couldn't care less why you are here. If you help us out, we can make it worth your while. We'll pay you more tithe than you have stashed in your cloak."

Ikath played dumb, pretending he did not understand what he referenced. The wind increased, forcing him to brace against it. He watched the others, dazed, wander down the road, the frigate's upper hull high above the garden wall. How could anyone miss a frigate parked in a garden sticking high above the fence beyond him? He waited. Seconds passed. *Come on, are you blind?*

The stranger spotted him watching the others.

Both cloak's whipping and snapping as the wind grew in force. The stranger stepped closer to make sure Ikath overheard him through the shrieking wind. "I know your type. Fast exit out in case a job goes bad. So, how are you getting out?"

He bought his cover.

One called out, "Hey, a ship. In the garden over there." Pointing to where Riurrel sat.

"That's your exit out, isn't it?" He demanded.

"Yes," Ikath said, forcing a look of resignation on his face.

"Listen, I can fly anything. I have no time to overcome your ships, lockouts. Besides, these idiots need looking after. I swear. I will pay you well as soon as we're off the planet and in a safe orbital station."

"Okay, but if you double-cross me, I will make sure you pay. One way or another." Ikath moved up the street next to the one who saw the ship before heading through the garden gate.

They followed, rushing up the ramp. The howling wind now screaming around them.

"Will this thing fly? The hull is filthy and looks as if the thing belongs in a junkyard." The one named Prince Alalus yelled above the wind as the ramp retracted and the door clanged shut. "By the gods," his voice close to hysteria, "the seats back here torn. Disgusting. Is there nowhere else to sit?"

"The floor," Ikath said as he raced towards the cockpit before jumping in the command chair. Not surprised as the stranger took the co-pilot seat. "Thought you needed to supervise them."

"Yeah, here close enough. I might kill one or two if I sit back there. My name is Riciad, yours?" His tone casual, as if not in the middle of a disaster.

"Ikath," he said, intent upon the controls. He reached forward, pulling up both the haptic holo feedback stick and handle. Punched the ignition to the vertical takeoff thrusters and held on tight as they rose, ignoring safety checks.

A powerful gust of wind caught the frigate and Riurrel lurched port side. One of the front landing gear struts retracting clipped the wall and sheared off. A flaming meteorite plowed past. An explosive burst hit the well-tended garden, leaving a smoking hole. Searing Riurrel's hull and spraying dirt and debris on the underside, the pressure wave blasting them upward and away from the ground. The wall crushed rubble.

Ikath thanked the gods for the gust of wind and prayed to make it through the mass of meteorites now streaking around them. Getting out alive under the circumstances might be harder than Ikath thought.

"Well, we shall have a rather exciting landing and exit from the ship," Riciad said, amusement in his voice, the sheared off landing leg light flashing. "If we survive."

Ikath swore he heard a slight hint of laughter, as if he found the entire ordeal funny.

He fought against the wind to gain altitude. The turbulence bad enough to force them downward, at times, making manual flight tricky. The sky added to their problems as a sudden downpour of rain hammered the ship and blurred the viewer's vision. Ikath felt they were doing a crazy dance to the dictates of the storm and its partner, the meteors.

Several times, Ikath yanked the frigate this way or that out of the path of incoming dangers. Derogatory yelling about his flying abilities reached him from those in the passenger cabin. He'd downgraded the inertial dampeners from the efficient ones equipped on the ship for effect of being broke.

He ignored them, concentrating hard on flying. A flash of lightning showed an inbound meteor to his port, and he banked hard, going into a spin before pulling out.

What the helc is Riurrel doing? Obviously, the Ai did not feel the need to help. Pouting now? He figured he was making a point of not helping. An inexpensive ship would not have a sophisticated Ai. He would have words later about the proper time to sulk.

Halfway out of the meteorites zone he spotted a weird-looking ring glowing on Riciad's finger, his left hand held over it. Riciad spotted Ikath looking and gave a sheepish grin. "Nervous habit."

He does not appear nervous. Unlike himself. A flash of lightning exposed an incoming meteorite and Ikath banked hard, missing by a hair's breadth. The ship's computer, maybe a class five for the quality of the ship.

"Computer, find a less dangerous trajectory."

Ikath took a second to read the flight path and change direction. Still touch and go as he dodged incoming meteorites. But once out of the leading edge, his shields managed the smaller ones.

He observed Riciad move his hand away from the glowing ring. Now the ring's gem appeared like a normal Bloodstone. No glow. Must be some type of body tech. Ikath held back a smile as yells of pain came his way from the cabin. "This *sheating* ship is electrocuting us."

Ikath glanced back. "Must be the storm. I'll look at the grounding wires once we land." Sometimes having a temperamental Ai had benefits.

Ikath informed Riciad they'd dock at the Carouser Traveler's pleasure station. "The emergency broadcast lists the station as safe, out of the path of the meteorites. It's a better choice than Cary's Travelers Station, which keeps meticulous records." Watching to see how Riciad reacted.

"Not a terrible idea. Head there."

He set the ship to autopilot and pretending to snooze, ignoring the others. He thought about how to stay connected with this enigmatic blooded. Sensed Riciad his ticket to complete his mission. When they arrived, tithe exchanged hands with corrupt officials, registering his party as arriving one turn earlier.

As Riciad was walking away, he turned towards him. "I'm impressed. Honest. I wondered a few times if we'd get out alive. Took a bit of fancy flying. If you look at your accounts, you'll see my appreciation. And the fact I kept my word. Someone with your flying abilities might come in handy in my line of work. Now and then. Any way I can reach you if I need, you're... help again." He looked Ikath in the eye. "*If* you are discreet and stay out of trouble. I'd advise you to tell no one of this... *adventure.*"

"Not my business. Who goes where or why. I admit I need some tithe and a credit line to get established and gain a sponsor." He took a step as if to leave and stopped, as if remembering something. "I transport things, clean up messes. I don't do murders or assist with murders. Ever. Brings too much heat from local enforcers and temple guardians. A Ghost Walker tracking me is not something I ever want to experience? What about you?"

"No."

"Me either. I'd like to keep it that way. Talk to the feasthall owner of The Windward Frigate if you want any future services. He'll be able to reach me." Ikath left, walking towards the cheap pod section of the station, his boots clanking on the cheap metal walkway. No expensive chamber for him.

Once settled in the cubical pod, he opened the account. Sat back in surprise at the amount deposited. Then he remembered the talk he wanted to have with the Ai.

"Riurrel, just what the *helc* were you doing during our flight off-planet? Were you turn dreaming in the middle of a deadly storm?" He could not keep the mockery from his voice. "Afraid you would *crash us*? I might have used at least a little assistance. It was touch and go a few times back there."

"Someone jammed me, locked me out for most of the flight. The scariest thing. Ever. No one should be able to lock me out of my systems. My sensors worked; I knew what *was happening*. Yet, nothing responded from navigation or helm. By the way, why did you get so close to those meteorites? I swear my programming froze each time. For seconds. I was sure you would run me straight into one. I need to give you lessons in *avoidance flying*. My hull's scorched and scraped and dented in *eighteen* spots. That reminds me. I set up repairs with the docking station. And a complete cleaning inside and out. And some necessary parts replaced."

Ikath speculated once more if this Ai might be capable of lying.

A chime from the repair station caught his attention, and he glanced back at his account. The repairs took half of what Riciad paid him. So much for a little extra tithe to smooth palms for information. Then it hit him. How did he access the account? Ikath locked him out.

Sighed wondering if he could afford Riurrel. Wished once more the Temple assigned him a more run of the stars ship.

Chapter 9

335890 GGS Goem 6th.
Public Travelers Station: Narti–Lady Jynnalt.

THREE HOURS AFTER THE Dagger of Cineuian docked, pulled in by tugs to the outer capital docking and repair station of the Imperial Shipwright guild, Jynnalt disembarked. The wounded and dead removed first while the crew assisted with proper shutdown procedures, as this was a civilian dock. Fleet ships, not their normal customer.

She took the mag-lift train connected to the Traveler station as Cineuian's shuttles were inaccessible behind the damaged bay doors. Transparent metasteel encircled the high-speed mag-lift. The onyx black of deepspace ablaze with twinkling stars above her while the station in the distance increased to the size of a small moon. They pulled into the interior entrance of the dis-embarkment platform to pandemonium.

Once they arrived, they came face to face with the chaos of the planetside evacuation. Under normal traffic and conditions, Narti's Traveler Station rating a solid ninety-two. From the chaos as they entered the arrival gate from the platform, she'd never guessed their rating to be that high. Jynnalt, worried about her family, verified her mother and the rest of her household arrived at the station as soon as possible. Her mother, as usual, met friends here before heading planetside. They never left the station, thank the gods.

She then left to check on Elgar. The med center chaotic bustling as life tenders and drones rushed past, not stopping to inquire after her or her injuries.

Door scanners sent her vital's to the droid station. Apparently, she did not warrant attention from what the scan told them. The flow of injured arrived in a steady stream. She tried to stay out of the way; she walked over to an information panel and checked for Elgar's name. The list of injured long and growing by the second, though not because of the incoming meteorites but by panicky citizens as they fought to evacuate off-planet. Twenty minutes later, she found him listed at center ten, sedated in a repair tank unit. No vatting necessary. Full recovery; ten turns. No visitors allowed.

After that, she went back to the repair dock where The Dagger of Cineuian sat docked. Stepped off the mag-lift to the sound of an irate voice yelling at the dock techs. She glanced over and recognized the commander of the battleship she collided with earlier. He did not see her, so she hurried off into the office area for those working on Cineuian, not brave enough to face his criticism.

She arrived as the repair techs fought to open one of the shuttle bays. Doing nothing while every available pilot worked frantically to evacuate citizens made her stomach churn. She needed to do something. Citizens endangered ate at her, especially children. As she entered the shipwright's office, her blood house's Sigil pin pinged out her identification. The master shipwright rose, nodding in deference, yet wasting no time to relay the information gained so far.

"Your Ladyship, someone tampered with the Dreadnoughts Ai's code. When this occurred, we are not sure. My master engineers informed me they found a shutdown code and other codes they don't understand. They removed them, sending them to Ministry Nine AC nine for investigation, then rebooted the system. The Ai passed all checks afterward. We are running additional checks in case we missed something. It was necessary to bring in a Temple code expert."

"Did you get one of the shuttle bays open yet? I want to help with the evacuation."

A deep voice, one she recognized, spoke behind her. "Not without us. Your turns of ditching your paladins long gone. Did you think in this crush you lost us? When you stepped off the fleet's ship, you became our responsibility. You are three months from your seventeenth breath turn. You're stuck with us. *Forever.*"

Drat, with everything happening, she forgot her newly assigned paladins would meet her at the Travelers station to take the shuttle with her to Nibiru Proper. From this, turn forward at least nine paladins in tow, sometimes more, when she was off fleet duty. At least they stayed out of sight. Most of the time. Cer Tavas, familiar to her for the last thirteen sars, her Command Paladin. He transferred into her father's service a sar before he died. He, like Elgar, stayed in touch, and over time became a mentor.

The only choice given to a ranking blooded of who was in their paladin's service was the choice of who commanded. She picked Cer Tavas. He assigned the rest.

"I did not intend to ditch you... I forgot," she said as she glanced at the dreadnought dwarfing the station's repair dock. "A lot happened this turn."

"Agreed. The docks informed us Elgar became injured during the skip and you brought in the Dagger of Cineuian. And got the warning out."

"The warning still might be too late. Now they need every available pilot to help with the evacuation. Every non- capital ship and shuttle utilized. Near misses and crashes are adding to the confusion and difficulties of the evacuation. I am getting one of Cineuian's shuttles and going to help." Even she recognized she was belligerent. Forced herself to relax. Her paladins could not stop her. However, Tavas could argue against her wishes, and if she ignored him, he might file a complaint to his guild. If she received an injury or died by ignoring him, the complaint absolved him of wrongdoing.

"Sorry, we have assigned every shuttle we have on hand. Your dreadnought's a tough nut to crack. We are still trying to open the bay doors." The master shipwright said as soon as he overheard what she told Tavas.

He pointed to the young male by the battleship she avoided earlier. "That indignant Knight can't locate a shuttle either. Demanding something we don't have won't make it appear."

"He's the commander of the damaged battleship, at least from what I overheard. He can use his ship's battle bridge. It's better than a shuttle, bigger and safer with shields and defensive capabilities which can blast through smaller incoming meteorites civilian shuttles can't avoid. I spotted his paladins not far away, heading his direction. They also train paladins as pilots. Think about the capital ships in fleet orbital docks and don't forget those stationed on Nitiru. You can use the emergency command override to commandeer them for the evacuation."

The master's face lit, never having dealt with an emergency of this scale. "Perfect. Safer and stronger. For an unknown reason, the Igigi are not giving any traffic assist. I am sure the council will investigate later. For now, there is nothing we can do. Every pilot is flying without guidance, for landing and takeoff planetside. I will notify emergency headquarters to send more command pilots this way to fly the battle bridges."

He yelled out to the techs on the dock, making her wince.

"Go tell Prince Ryakin he can use his battle bridge in place of a shuttle. Remind him to wait until we release the clamps before he blows the bolts. If you don't, he'll tear them off. His brother and family are not on the listed arrivals."

She grasped his anger now, not at her. The sense of powerlessness when not able to save those you love. Something she well understood. This the same sense of panic and horror as her father died. The memory as she hugged him tight as he lay on the ground foaming at the mouth spasming in his death throes swamped her for a second.

"Your paladins can fill in for the crew," the shipwright asked, satisfied when Tavas nodded.

The master shipwright walked to his desk and cleared them to enter and take control of the battle bridge. The tech's worked as fast as possible on the clamps. A dreadnought, no simple task as they designed the battle bridge to only blow the bolts under conditions when the ship was unsalvageable. It took six hours. The solar battleship took only one. She viewed the battle bridge of the battleship Nemesis break loose and go to Impulse five straight from drift six, headed towards Nibiru Proper. Praying he finds his family safe.

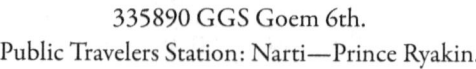

RYAKIN ANGRY AND FRUSTRATED for not thinking about utilizing the battle bridge in these circumstances. A paladin pointed out the obvious. *A paladin*. Why the fact a paladin, not a fleet officer or crew member, thought of the plan offended him, he was not sure. But it did. He pulsed Ustrix. He needed him for this.

Ustrix responded while in the background his family loaded on to their house's private yacht, the guild workers on a bigger solar barge. "Did you find a shuttle?"

"No, something better. Nemesis battle bridge."

"Smart thinking, shields, weapons, more space."

"I didn't. Some paladin came up with the idea."

"Ah... paladin. Are you certain?"

"Yes, and worse. When I inquired who gave the suggestion, the shipwright informed me it was the paladin of the female commander of the Dreadnought in their repair bay. The one who skipped the very same dreadnought on top of us. Then attempted to blow us up with a critical power core overload."

"She saved us from the full brunt of that explosion. Without the help of her ships, Ai. On a dreadnought that's impressive. Give her a break. She was trying to save Nibiru and seven trillion citizens in-system. She impressed me, harnessing the plasma and the shockwave to give them enough power to skip that far."

"I know. Still stings. Nemesis is out of commission in sleep mode while on the repair docks. Let's change the subject. The master shipwright informed me the fastest way for you to get here was to ask one of the tug pilots for a ride. He already cleared you as a passenger. Tubes are over-packed, and five have broken, stranding thousands. The techs have started work on the battlebridge's clamps. You don't have long, thirty minutes at most." Ryakin said, shutting off the comm. The pulse glitchy because of the colossal energy weapons discharged from the Malkuth explorer ships. And emps from nuclear missiles fired from the in-system Traveler's Stations, destroying sizeable incoming pieces to protect themselves.

For now, the ship's systems and scanners were offline. His paladins onboard worked frantically through the safety checks. Frustrated, he drummed his fingers on the command chair's gel cyberware connections control and noticed the expressions on his paladin's faces. Tight, worried. Yet professional, not saying a word. He realized they're as worried about their families as he was about his. The youngest paladin looking at his private pulse constantly. Married three months. Sick worry on his face.

Ryakin spoke, "As soon as Ustrix arrives will leave. I intend to rescue *all* our families."

A relief crossed their faces. Twenty minutes later, a tug came straight at them before pivoting to a perfect point stop thirty yards away. Then coasted to the airlock connection. A slight bump and the connection hoses locked. The airlock light flashed red, seconds later turned steady blue.

Ustrix arrived. He was the best pilot in the Inner Kingdoms. Not shy about letting everyone understand that fact, either. The Inner Kingdom's academy trainers claimed they'd never seen better.

Full viewscreen on. From the top of the consoles to the ceiling became translucent in a half circle around the bridge lining the outer wall. As soon as Ustrix boarded, Narti's station controller came over the comm's.

Ryakin followed instructions for takeoff. The ship shuddered as the explosive bolts released and they shot out the outer gate of the dock. Once clear in open deepspace, his tension eased a little.

Halfway to Nibiru Proper, his house's private comm chirped. His brother Rualui's holo full of static, yet the visual clear enough. The rest of his tension drained away. He breathed easier. His brother was alive. Bags under his eyes and a shadow of a beard on his face, so unlike him. Rualui abhorred those who lacked proper cleanliness or affected a messy appearance so popular, believed pandering to fashion gross vanity.

"We evacuated most of Agade and outlying areas. Shields are on backup power, the primary power disrupted by the emps from explosions above ground level. So, until they have a meteorite on a direct path, the shields are on standby. Between the bigger meteorites, they must disengage to conserve power. I authorized food and water from our private stores. That gives them enough supplies to last six months."

"What about Jena? Is she with you?"

"Jena is in Haelitica out on the plains. She was visiting her family while here. For now, they have no incoming. They can shelter in the nearby deep caves until we can evacuate them. I'm heading to the city as soon as done here to join her."

The static increased, and Ryakin missed the next couple of things his brother said before the pulsed cleared again.

"Ugallu has not pulsed me or Master Seneschal Tendao. The pulse planetside comes and goes. I tried to reach him with no luck. With what is happening, I am worried. Have you heard from him?"

"No, though I am surprised by your sudden concern for his welfare."

"He is family. I may not agree with him, but I still care. Besides, he is under the throne's responsibility. Which is me."

Over Rualui's shoulders, Ryakin viewed a small incoming meteorite. The scanner showed three more following the same path. His brother glanced back, then said, "Have to go."

The pulse blinked out, the holo now gone. "Full scanner view; Agade and surrounding areas," Ryakin commanded as he flew towards the city terminal.

The viewscreen showed a meteorite, a roaring ball of fire trailing black smoke as it smashed through the thick atmosphere. Once the meteor reached the level of the Fire mountains forest, it crashed through the upper treetops, leaving a trail of destruction. The forest burst into flames, a wrath of fire reaching for the sky. Three others followed behind the first. Huge black billowing plumage obscuring the ground. He descended in a sharp dive, trying to gain a lower altitude below the smoke.

Collision alarms sounded, his heartbeat pounding as a rush of adrenaline hit. He banked sharply, missing an outbound ship. He took a deep breath and his pulse calmed as he cleared the shuttle. Inches away from their outer shields.

Seconds later, he spotted the city's major terminal. Terror-stricken citizens fought for a seat on the outbound shuttles as fear and panic spread. Looping around, he kept looking for somewhere to land till his brother's signal disappeared.

The instruments glitchy from the emp's. Even the fleet's battle-hardened ship's equipment hard pressed at times to pick up anything. Twenty seconds later, a beep and the scanners once more locked on his brother's personal pulse. The signal moving fast towards Haelitica, on the other side of Fire Mountain. He must be on a mag-lift tube train.

Ryakin changed direction, passing over Agade's southern public terminal as he headed toward Fire Mountain. The open terminal loading zones packed with citizens evacuating. A sizeable fragment passing over the top of the ship towards the plains ahead of them, a chilling sight. The crowds shoved and pushed in panic towards the shuttles.

They climbed towards the peak of the mountain. Ryakin swerved, missing a small fast-moving meteorite as they came over the peak. A screaming screech from the undercarriage shielding when scraped along one peak from the maneuver.

"How about I pilot," Ustrix asked, "and you work navigation." Stark terror on Ryakin's paladin's faces and the pleading look from Ustrix caused him to relent, rather than let his fear rule him. If he crashed, his family suffered. Ryakin sent primary control to Ustrix's chair. Relief so profound on their faces, he started to say something, then decided might be best to leave his thoughts unsaid.

The great forest on the northern flank of hardwoods a raging fire out of control. A major township, four villages, and a small commoner's tent city wiped out of existence. Vanished in a blink of an eye from explosive detonations of meteorites above ground. Thick black smoke rose skyward, blanketing the area, forcing Ustrix to change to instrumentation flight. Dangerous, as they were not reliable yet forced to, as he could not rely on viewer visuals.

As they flew past a small township, seven ships prepared to close their doors as pandemonium broke out. Panic swept through those below in a rippling tide, spreading as those in the back pushed and shoved those waiting to board ahead of them. In seconds, anarchy escalated out of control. Knocking anyone out of the way. Climbing over any that fell. Not noticing if they injured or killed those underfoot.

One of his paladins called out, "your lordship, look over there. Our families." The oldest female, the wife of Jahar, his commanding paladin, appeared to be keeping them together. "I sent a pulse but never found out if the signal went through," he said. His tone expressing his relief.

Nine of their families stood outside the crush of the mob surrounding the loading ships. Their body language spoke of desperation as they looked around. The mothers, with a fierce hold on their children, prepared to fend off any who might threaten them.

"Get as close as possible," Ryakin said, then looked over at the paladins. "Load them fast. As soon as we are close to the ground, that mob will rush us. Be ready. Your families will have to jump for the ramp as we can't land. Too risky."

Ustrix maneuvered the ship with the ramp away from the chaos of the terminal. So far, panic benefited them. No one realized they were lowering closer to the ground.

The paladins stood by as the door opened, and the ramp lowered, five feet from the ground and swaying wildly. Ustrix labored to steady the ship. Tricky under the best of circumstances. The paladins yelled out to attract their attention. As soon as they spotted their husbands or fathers, they raced their direction. The adults threw the children up on the ramp. When the children were aboard, the wives jumped on, the youngest wives helping the elders before following up the ramp.

Those at the edges of the terminal realized the ship was low enough to board and raced towards them. Five males pulled the youngest wife off the ramp, trying to access the ship. Others rushed their direction. The paladins holding them off. The junior wife pushed further away, unable to fight her way back towards the ramp.

"Go head to our house's fortress. I'll pick the two of you up when we come to evacuate. We won't leave you behind. Just be waiting when we arrive."

The paladin nodded, gratitude shining in his eyes before jumping to join his wife. Ryakin noted he grabbed her and fought his way out of the forming crowd, soon lost in the crush. They slammed the ramp door closed and rose. A minute later Ryakin saw him commandeer a skimmer, and he and his wife disappeared fast over the hill.

The enforcers lost control of the loading areas. Now, even they fought for a spot on one of the seven ships.

A flash of light blinded them as the viewscreen turned dazzling white. Ryakin shielded his eyes from the blinding intensity. Moments later, the viewscreen cleared, showing a mushroom fireball rising high into the sky. Northwest in the Bursa's Sea direction.

The ground groaned as if a giant woke beneath and seconds later swelled towards the bottom of the ship. Ustrix forced the ship upward to avoid the ground, impacting the undercarriage shielding. The ground slammed down before swelling higher. Inches between them and disaster.

Two ships full, ready for takeoff, crashed on their sides, exploding. Shrapnel burst outward, tearing through thousands who moments before fought to enter them. Like a wave, those still alive raced away as deadly debris rained down on them.

The other ship's outer skins damaged from the blast, unable to become airborne. A blown off door bounced off their outer shield. Ustrix shot higher out of the deadly rain of wreckage.

A shockwave of super-heated air and dirt slammed into their shields. Ustrix used every ounce of skill to keep them skyborne as they spun out of control. Moments passed as they held on, spinning planetside. Ustrix gained control and pulled up before they slammed into the ground, then shot skyward.

Nothing beneath them survived. Ryakin prayed for his paladin and wife far enough away.

Darkness descended on the scene of destruction. Swirling dust and debris blocked out the light.

The battlebridge, unlike the civilian shuttles designed and built to withstand severe conditions. Their shields held while the civilians disintegrated in seconds as their power cores overloaded, exploding. The need to find his brother and family intensified, beat at him after what occurred.

"Ustrix, head to Haelitica. There is nothing we can do here."

They arrived, flying five feet above the houses. Flew over emergency crews working at a fever pace, putting out fires and locating citizens buried under debris from collapsed buildings and walls. A ground shake hit the city from the earlier enormous meteorite strike in the Bursa Sea.

The impact annihilated a chain of volcanic islands. Bursa's shallow sea vaporized for a hundred standards in all directions. Now a steaming caldron. Every living thing instantly boiled in the sea and surrounding air.

Ship's scanners showed an image of a giant Tsunami heading for the shoreline. Rualui's pulse chirped once more on Ryakin's comm's, and he got a lock. The signal moving up a steep hill away from the shore. Ryakin realized from his instruments those on foot would never make it. They needed to reach them fast. "Ustrix, head straight in on the signal or the wave will catch them."

They found his brother, aiding his struggling pregnant wife, along with a substantial group. They were running towards the top of the hill, trying to beat the wave Razing towards them. Ustrix landed uphill not too far ahead, the ramp lowered by the time the group reached the ship. Within seconds the ship's alarms systems kicked on, notifying of overload as they jumped aboard.

"Shut those alarms off."

We will either all survive, or we die here. He need not say it aloud. Everyone's face reflected his thought. The last boarded minutes ahead of the roiling wave bearing down on them.

"Get us out of here. *Now.*"

For a moment, Ryakin was not sure they would rise before the Tsunami reached them. The ship rocking as it struggled against the extra weight, but once more the formidable engines and shields saved them. Ustrix used a fancy trick, using the shields to give a powerful push away from the ground. They rose like a clumsy torpid flyer. But they rose. Just out of the furious water's reach. An hour later, they passed from the upper atmosphere to deepspace. Notified by Master Seneschal Tendao when headed for the fortress, to find the residents already evacuated.

Informed them, one of his young Paladins arrived with his wife and evacuated along with the others.

Now just a matter of waiting for landing clearance. Hundreds of other shuttles and non-capital fleet ships in holding patterns outside Narti's station. They discussed heading to Cary. Upon requested course change informed Cary beyond capacity. Wait time for landing; turns. Ryakin stayed in line for Narti.

Ryakin would never forget the sight of the wall of water Razing towards them. Nor the fact they were only feet away from the raging fury of the Tsunami water that washed beneath them. Using the shields for an extra lift by Ustrix, brilliant.

335890 GGS Goem 6th.
Public Travelers Station: Narti–Lady Jynnalt

"THIS IS STCS TO TWO three niner seven niner. Disengage restraining clamps in ten minutes." The voice of the Narti Control Station operator called out. Even during the chaotic evacuation emergency, the voice calm, controlled.

"Acknowledged, two three niner seven niner," Jynnalt said as her paladins waited for the five tugs to move away before the clamps released.

She swallowed and took a deep breath, trying to settle her roiling stomach and shaking hands as the need to pee overwhelmed her. *By the Dark One stop. You've trained for this at least a thousand times, concentrate. Focus.* She stared straight ahead. *Relax.* Caltac', her personal, sensial combat trainer's voice sounded in her head. She glanced over at Tavas, acting as copilot. The red lighting casting an eerie glow on his face as he concentrated on his gauges. She scrutinized him as he made a few adjustments. She, like others in her academy class, only piloted the battle bridge in FR simulations. This turn she learned quick enough the difference between the two.

"It gets easier with time," Tavas remarked without looking her way.

She frowned, *Drog.* She stared at her gauges. "You sound like Caltac," she mumbled under her breath.

"What did you say?"

"Nothing," she ducked her head closer to the gages as if concentrating on them. Out of the corner of her eye, she saw the ghost of a smile cross his face as he went about his own checks.

"We're all nervous the first time. Concentrate on your job, nothing else. Besides, your marks as a pilot showed you top of your class. Lady Razin, the only one higher," he said as he continued getting ready to disengage. Moments later, she realized her hands shook less, and she forgot about having to pee.

"Check engines two three niner seven niner."

She throttled the engines to E one and monitored her gauges while listening to the roar of the hydrogen fuel engines. The ship bucked and strained against the launch bolts holding it in place. The tingle of excitement overcame her. Drowned her earlier fear. She loved flying. The battle bridge of The Dagger of Cineuian would be the largest ship she ever physically piloted.

The other paladins checked their gauges and beeped all clear signals. She throttled the engine back a little. STCS came on comms again.

"Shields required. Its goanna be a rough ride down. Meteorites will be incoming for the next five turns. Eyes open. No entry platform handoff. Unknown ground control. You will be on manual going in."

"Affirmative, niner seven niner," she shortened the call sign to the last numbers, as no others on this frequency were using those idents.

"Imperial critical zones pinging illegal to land and a shoot on sight if ignored."

"Affirmative, niner seven niner," she stuck to the strict protocol, even though this was a civilian deepspace control operator.

"Sending flight path to entry window; Now," STCS informed her. A microsecond passed before the information arrived.

"Received; niner seven niner," she said as she gripped the throttle handle and the directional stick a little tighter. Her safety harness tightened.

"Prepare for launch on mark."

"Affirmative," she throttled to E two as the explosive engines thundered, fighting harder against the restraining bolts.

"Three... Two... One... Mark." The restraining bolts blew open, and the ship shot forward, forcing them back into their gel padding. She pushed the throttle to E six wide open. Seconds later, they shot out and away from the Narti station. The amount of traffic around the station making maneuvering tricky.

Fifteen minutes later STCS came across the comm's, "Cleared from STCS. Service terminated. Squawk GCS."

"Affirmative." Jynnalt responded, changing her transponder code to Nibiru's civilian ground control of three four two two.

"Frequency change approved," STCS called out. The comm went silent. No response from Nibiru's ground control. Now on their own. The paladins and her silent as they concentrated on their instruments. Twice, they barely missed colliding with incoming ships flown by incompetent civilians. Five times, the staccato of the auto fire of the griffins blasted huge bolides to small granules around them as they flew towards the chaotic evacuation planetside.

Chapter 10

DEAD. MURDERED. The Temple and Igigi defenses destroyed. An armored body of a Temple Protectorate warrior lay across the control panels, sprawled in death. He raised his eyes from the bodies and walked towards the control panel. All this his fault. He allowed the past to blind him. On the Dagger of Cineuian, when tracking the formidable weapon now heading for the Anunnaki Empires capital, he hesitated. Lost the chance to stop the weapon.

He should have controlled his emotions when he spotted the female. She looked so much like his dead wife; the sight hit him like a gut punch. If he paid more attention to what he was trying to recover and not gotten distracted, this disaster would not have happened. Find and destroy the control device. Try to discover who's behind the weapon. Simple task.

The attackers on the platforms weapon's able to defeat the Protectorate's best defenses, and their superior nanite armor. The attackers' weapons signatures Murian.

Another strange circumstance about this contrived disaster. How did the intruders disable the Igigi's advanced weapons systems? *How?* This era not technologically capable of the feat.

The Igigi designed in a distant time with specific internal biological programming. Most galaxy denizens of this era unaware of their true abilities, or the fact they were self-replicating created biological Ai clones. No one would want them in orbit if they realized their capabilities. So, they left their clientele in a state of blissful ignorance.

The Temple provided warriors and weapons, which the Igigi's used as their first line of defense.

Well trained using the most sophisticated equipment of these times, they fought to the last warrior, yet fell before the ruthless attack. A brutal end. Precise headshots, through their meh chip, made their end final. The putrescence odor of rotting flesh from the decaying bodies combined with the gruesome sight chilling. After all this time, and all the battles fought, he wondered why death affected him still. The sense of intense horror and sorrow at the same time.

As he walked through the station, he found no living being. Not one. His steps grew heavier and slower as he moved towards the control chamber. The Igigi on this station old friends.

The clacking echoes of his boots on the black polished metacrystal stone floor the only sound.

Visual images and code flowed across the walls from floor to ceiling. The images rising to the surface, between the technical station's traffic control information or weather mapping, before fading away. Recordings of all incoming and outgoing traffic of the client's system. Vital information mixed with the Igigi's normal life aboard the platform.

The recorded meh's of the Igigi who lived and worked here. A testament to their owner's life. Memories a sacred art.

Icy silence met the echoes of his footsteps with the stillness of a tomb.

"I am sorry," Vith whispered. His tone spoke of respect, sadness, and sorrow. "The Igigi always respectful towards me when we visited. I liked them."

To most citizens, Vith appeared like any other sizable deepspace luxury star yacht. An expensive toy owned by a wealthy citizen.

In truth, Vith was an advanced heavy battlecruiser designed and built by him on his private homeworld. Far more sophisticated than any fleet ships in weaponry, tracking, communications, and stealth equipment in this galaxy and time. He designed a limited number for the Temple, though without the advanced weapons Vith boasted. Especially a very temperamental one, second to none in the galaxy. Only Vith more advanced.

He knew what this weapon unleashed upon the Anunnaki Empire was. Seen the use of this weapon during the Murian war. By one species only. A species defeated. Pushed back to their galaxy. He understood withdrawing to his sanctuary homeworld once more, no longer a choice. His soul cried out against abandoning the living to the horror of this enemy.

He heard the rumors of the rise of a strange order called the Society. The Council of Nine, uneasy with the information the Rider's gave them, sent the Holiest High Temple Priestess to ask for his help. She informed him of the whispers of unsanctioned weapons and engineered riots backed by financial manipulations in once peaceful empires creating chaos. Ships and Travelers Stations attacked in protected Trade Lanes and sectors. The Council of Nine sent Ghost Walkers to investigate after the Temple Guardians investigating were murdered. This left CON and the high Temple unable so far to discover who or what was behind the unrest. Not Ghost Walker's normal type of mission, but CON and the Temple were desperate.

The Council of Nine, or CON, as most referred to them, formed after the last Great War three hundred sars ago against the Sabations. Peace ruled. Prosperity became the norm instead of the exception under their combined alliances. Once more, he retired to his world on the outer rim, far removed from civilization. Till the High Priestess showed up with this urgent appeal. Embroiling him in the galaxy's turmoil once more, forcing him to put aside his search for answers.

The information the High Priestess gave him led to a suspect, which he tagged with an advanced tracker. Seemed he was only a low-level minion of the Society. Till the suspect contracted for a rumored unfamiliar weapon. Eight turns later, Vith's equipment picked up the artificial gravity shock wave when the planetoid phased. He double-checked the signature, hoping to convince himself the event was a natural occurrence rather than an artificial one. The frequency signal necessary to power the phase-shift weapon distinctive. He tracked the signal; to the sector where galactic citizens gathered to view the Star of

Hope's light as it appeared. Under normal circumstances, he avoided the Star of Hope event. Unpleasant memories haunted him, to say the least.

The planetoid though not far away. Hidden in the void of deepspace for now.

During the original war, that became the downfall of this weapon. The inability to disguise its signature. Along with the range and the fact this was a suicide weapon, each step requiring an operator. It did not work on remote switches. To set the final trajectory, the operator must be in the location and stay until the rogue planetoid arrived. Thus, killing them most of the time.

He tracked the signal to a Kieran dreadnought called The Dagger of Cineuian from the Anunnaki Empire. A ship he was intimately familiar with and one he preferred to avoid. A blend of happy and sorrowful memories overwhelmed him when he realized where the suspected fanatic went.

When he arrived, the trail went cold. The weapons control device must be in sleep mode, for now, the planetoid sitting in the distance in sub chaotic space. The technology of these times unable to detect the anomaly until armed.

Whoever controlled the device entered the ship soon after he or she arrived.

The Regent of the young Duchianess invited attending patrons to see the Star of Hope. This allowed him to infiltrate the Dagger of Cineuian's viewing platform, permitted him to mingle unnoticed with so many unknown citizens aboard. Whoever controlled the device must be close. Once he gained the device, he would need to exit fast. The only means fast enough, a Seer ring.

The problem. He used the ring on his home world. However, he needed five galactic turns to reach home using Vith's technologically advanced engines. Not allowing him time to complete his mission. The closest ring, the galactic High Temple, two skips away. He could quantum shift, board the ship, find the device, and exit back to the High Temple through the ring. The ship being stationary benefited him. Quantum shifts notoriously dangerous on moving locations.

He would have to risk entering the High Temple at GIA. Use his battle suit to phase-shift past the Priestesses guarding the chamber.

Their holy rules only allowed three of the High Priestess within the temple's inner sanctum. The Ring chamber. He preferred not to explain his presence. He'd have to work fast. Rings made a soft, whooshing sound when activated. The drawback to this phase shifting, one hundred and eight hours to the second, and the ring brought him back, whether he wanted to. The other powers of the rings denied him.

He followed two Society members, who joined up with one of the fleet's power plant technicians. At which point the female showed up, and he hesitated. *What the helc. Why was she there? Could she be a conspirator?* Was she meeting with the traitor? Everything inside him rebelled at the idea.

Precious seconds away from recovering the device and discovering who was using it, and he wavered. At which moment she noticed him and called out to security, forcing him to step back through the ring early. This should not have happened. He should not have allowed his feelings for one long dead to rule his actions. He vanished before her in a flash of blue light. That did not worry him. A quantum shift does not appear on holo's devices as they occur at the sub chaotic level. Though biological systems overwhelmed by the intense Chaos, pressure interpreted the sensation as blinding light.

He sent a distress signal once he discovered where the planetoid anomaly headed after leaving the Dagger of Cineuian. Two of the Malkuth's largest explorers' ships, Fury and Radiant Enforcer, picked up the distress signal. They notified three others in the Phoenix sector to assist them in stopping the disaster.

The High Temple ring unavailable for the next five galactic turns, which forced him to take the Galactic Gates. Vith's advanced skip engines gave him an advantage, but still he raced to reach the Anunnaki Empires Igigi platform before the planetoid.

As they arrived, Vith notified him of a lack of life signs on the platform. *Impossible.* He needed the Igigi to help stop the disaster unleashed upon the Anunnaki.

Vith notified him Riurrel was in orbit around Nibiru Proper with a Temple Guardian on board. The criminal he was tracking met with those the Guardian surveilled from orbit.

He passed the investigation to the Temple Guardian. He needed the one he tracked alive, needed his connections to the Society. And answers about the female. Shocked at first when he realized who the Temple Guardian was. He requested Riurrel keep him safe. The Igigi platform now, though, demanded his attention.

Now hours later, as he walked through the platform, it was a cathedral of death and left him powerless, as the weight of eons of events pressed upon him. He rounded a corner and the inner chamber doors stood open before him, showers of sparks arching in the interior as consoles and lights blinked haphazardly on and off. The odor of burning power conduits filled the air. He hesitated outside the doors to the cavernous control chamber.

What he witnessed from where he stood was the bodies of small gray Igigi's twisted and sprawled littering the floor and along the outer ring of the consoles. Hundreds of bodies in the massive circular chamber. Inky pools beneath them, spreading out from where each fell. Splattered blood and gore across the walls and equipment. Isosoleies, the platform's commander, sat before the largest control console.

His head and arm lay as if taking a nap. Cloudy black eyes looking towards the door and a pool of the Igigi's blood spreading across the controls told Aidan life no longer inhabited the form. Sorrow tugged hard, and his eyes watered for a second. Then he took a deep breath and stepped into the chamber.

He moved to the control console and removed the body from the chair and respectfully laid him on the floor by the others. Sat down and brought up the last three turns recordings.

He pulled up the internal recordings of the attack on the station. Depressed yet determined to discover information. The attackers were good. Too good.

Vith informed him he detected burst from phase-shifting armor residue signatures throughout the platform. The defenders had no chance as the enemy shifted around, slaughtering them as they appeared and disappeared. They rushed through the Igigi, killing them without the slightest fight. *How?* The Igigi have ancient and formidable weapons and warning systems besides those provided by the Temple. *How did the attackers overcome the Igigi systems? More important, how did they know about them in the first place?*

He turned off the recorded discordant sounds of the holo after the first few agonized screams of anguish and pain as they died.

Someone murdered the Igigi and the Temple Protectorate warriors. With extinct technology. Somehow, somewhere, someone discovered a cache of potent weapons and armor from the ancient Murian times. Whoever found the cache appeared to want to bring down CON. They appeared willing to tear the galaxy apart to do so.

He pulsed the Igigi headquarters. Downloaded the platforms recorded meh holo's information to Vith and sat waiting for the files to transfer. For later investigation and review. Maybe he could find a clue about where they acquired the technology. Over time, he found ten caches of ancient weapon technology and transferred them to his world or sealed them from prying eyes. He would double-check the sealed one's first.

For the next twenty hours, he sat unmoving as the scene of destruction played out on the screens before him.

Helpless, as the pieces of the destroyed planetoid wreaked havoc as they crashed through the system. Smashing into Nibiru Proper or the smaller worlds. The Malkuth's collective power destroyed the planetoid halfway to the system. Then worked with feverous desperation to decrease the size of every fragment possible.

He sent Vith to aid them. Even with him helping, the Malkuth only able to diminish the damage. Only break them down to non-planetary or world killers. Nibiru Proper still took heavy damage from the impact of so many meteorites of assorted sizes.

His breathing sped up, his lips a taut white line as ships crashed into each other and panic took hold of the citizens. The death toll rising by the second. The meteorites becoming bright blossom of fire as they raced towards the ground and destruction. Blazing showers of death.

Without thinking, he slammed his fist on the damaged, useless controls before him. Observed as ships on the ground never get airborne, thousands of smaller fragments punching holes through them as effective as any fleet fighter's griffin cannons.

He forced himself to witness the destruction as darkness descended over the planet. Over time, tons of dust thrown into the sky and seized by the upper winds, air currents which obscured his vision. Engulfed the planet below, hiding the ongoing destruction from the prying sky eyes in orbit, still recording on the Igigi platform.

How long he sat there? Frozen as the scene unfolded before him, he was not sure. Vith startled him sometime later with the information he could do nothing more and the transfer from the platform finished.

Time for them to leave. He stood and took one last look around before moving to the back wall and opened a hidden panel. Input the proper codes to the Igigi's home system. Set the platform's engines on a delay timer. This gave him time to put distance between him and the time vortex. Kept him from getting sucked in as the platform formed the entag location bubble. From a safe distance, he waited as space and time folded around the platform. Moments later, the platform vanished as if it had never existed.

He repeated the same scene at the Igigi Trade Lane tower. Attacked in the same manner. At the tower, he put the bodies on their standby ship to return them home.

A white-hot fire burned in him. He would discover who did this.

Chapter 11

KING RUALUI, WITH HIS Queen Jena, accompanied by Ustrix, entered through the ornate outer double doors. Lady Airal and her mother close on their heels. The blustery wind blowing a slush of black and gray ashy whitefall in the chamber before the doors closed. The causeways glow globe's dim yellow lights glimpsed as others entered. Coated in pernicious ash since the disaster. For months now, the Imperial maintenance guilds fought a never-ending battle to keep them clean of ash and dirt.

The entering guests handed over both their outer cloaks and under cloaks to the guild servers waiting by the entrance. Another change because of the disaster. Outer cloaks of a thick plain waterproof material a new necessity. Cleaned and dried before retrieved by the patrons as they left the entertainments. If anyone went outside for long, they wore them. Otherwise, their clothes became ruined beyond repair.

Prince Ea wandered over for an introduction to Lady Airal, soon to be the new Queen of Ki. His curiosity pied. Stories and tales circulated about her amongst the ranking; some good, worst.

Six months earlier Queen Jildius of Ki, along with her royal house's heirs, died in the worst historical disaster to hit the Anunnaki empire. This wiped out her bloodline in one fell swoop. Other blooded houses reached deep into their bloodlines to replace titleholders and heirs, who died during that month of harrowing terror.

Afterward, the blood house of Airal ascended to the royal throne of Ki. Princess Tesiskel, Lady Airal's mother, he remembered by vague rumors swirling through the court. Whispered innuendo, she was the lover of the late Emperor Durua. The gossip titillating enough for him to remember all these sars later.

The scandal depraved enough, her father and their house members demanded she, an Imperial princess, contracted with all haste to an outer border Arch Dukian. Which forced her out of Imperial society and out of sight. The rank high enough for an Imperial Princess, but an outer border one, carrying far lesser prestige than an inner title for her punishment.

Whispers circulated for months of a male child born to her. A child that Emperor Durua secretly repudiated in favor of his adopted son. Emperor Lahamu. That, though, a whole different story.

If speculations about Princess Tesiskel bore a child true, he would now be a citizen of the Temple. Or holding a position in a ranking house unrelated to her blood, placed anonymously.

As he approached, he overheard her complaining loud and scathingly about Prince Ryakin's' manners.

Gossip rampant, King Rualui and the Kierian council agreed to honor the contracted marriage drawn up between the two kingdoms. If true, tradition demanded Lady Airal stay at Prince Ryakin's side during the first festival opening event they attended together. Whispers of an announcement imminent. No Prince Ryakin present spoke volumes. Could the rumor mills be wrong? For once? The Emperor and Empress themselves late. Leaving Prince Ryakin still time to arrive. His speculations answered as Ea walked close enough to overhear the conversation amongst their group.

"If he cared the least bit for his soon to be brides' house, he would be here. I will not wait, embarrassed by your house's lack of manners. If Prince Ryakin is not here by the time the Emperor and Empress arrive, or the Blooded De Rank starts the announcements of the precedence of titles. I will take my ranking position inline rather than wait here."

Princess Tesiskel stared at Lady Airal as if this was her fault. Ea stood to the side, ignored by those in the group as the drama played out.

"King Rualui, I will speak to my father about this breach of etiquette on your house's part," Tesiskel said, her eyes narrowing. "I know you are waiting for his approval for new fleet ships. Paid for upon the official signing by Ki, because of this marriage contract." She said as a small, vicious smile flashed across her face. Her head high, she stared at King Rualui.

"I'm sure Prince Ryakin got held up for an excellent reason." Queen Jena stared right back at her; her arms linked through her husband's.

Lady Airal's cheeks turn red, and she looked everywhere but at her mother. Each time the ornate outer doors opened, and the Imperial guild staff let a guest inside, a gust of freezing wind invaded, swirling about those in the lobby. The rush of air ruffling clothes and causing patrons to shiver as they rushed from lavish barges to the doors. Laughter and curses rode in on the wind, along with grayish-whitefall melting into puddles on the polished white marble floor.

Each time, Lady Airal glanced towards the doors. Hopeful, which turned to stark disappointment when the one entering was not Prince Ryakin.

Heart-rending for Ea to observe. At this moment, it was hard for him to see the courageous female. The one who risked all to warn Nibiru Proper then later joined the evacuations' efforts fighting to save citizens of all ranks and classes. Bards now writing songs and poems about the events of the disaster included her as the heroine. Reports claimed she risked herself and her paladins to save commoners, blooded, and ranking guild members alike. The female before him appeared timid. Edgy.

Ea loved females, big, little, petite, and not so petite. He considered himself an admirer of the female form. Though she did not fit the ideal of fashion of the inner kingdoms, to him she was stunning, her coloring vivid to his jaded eye. Still, he liked his... acquaintances of the opposite sex to have fire and sass. This female displayed none. She stood as tall as Ea. Statuesque, with molten thick red hair covering her ears, cascaded loosely over her shoulders with natural waves and curls down to her hips. Glowing translucent skin and the oddest colored eyes, moss green, emphasized by their almond shape and long dark brown lashes.

All set in a square face with high cheekbones. Her lips were a little too lush for his tastes. Other than the oddity of her green eyes, she resembled any other border kingdom female, whether blooded or commoner. Ea found the idea easy to imagine border females as trained warriors, as rumors claimed. Females in the outer borders allowed to hold the ruling title of a house. He, for one, believed not such a terrible idea. In his experience, ranking females hid their intelligence and capabilities in the inner kingdoms, not so amongst the commoners and guilds. He always thought his mother unique. Till he met commoners assessed to a guild, or those born and raised within them. That is where he learned the truth.

Most considered outer border females brash, their manner intimidating. Inner Kingdoms, the epitome of fashion. Haughty in their superiority over others. Polite with a hint of sarcasm. Their skin beguilingly soft lavender or ravishing dark blue, shining silver or ebony black straight hair, framing soft oval faces. Heavy-lidded felis shaped eyes of enchanting pink or deep mysterious red. Small svelte willowy shapes on delicate frames reaching to most Imperial inner kingdoms male's shoulders. And those so beguiling pointy ears.

The group standing behind them broke into raucous laughter, catching Ea's attention. A male with his back to them spoke loud enough for those around to overhear.

"I heard his father demanded a friend of his son's aid him with a little help from behind with...." The male made a lewd hip movement back and forth. The females in his group gasped and tittered.

Princess Tesiskel's face froze, her lips tight. He realized she thought they were referring to her father.

He knew the rumors well enough, but for someone to be crass enough to speak of them in her hearing, unpleasant manners, to say the least. The vindictiveness of a lower blooded, in his opinion.

The ill-mannered male spoke again. "After three daughters and a son, both his father and wife died in a tragic accident. This left him able to marry his long-time friend and lover," the speaker whispered. Loud enough for Prince Ea and surrounding parties to listen.

Ea cleared his throat. "It amazes me how petty some who should know better can be," he said, staring at the speaker. The male at least displayed the grace of contrite embarrassment to excuse himself and move off. Seconds later, the male waved down someone in the waiting crush at the entrance as guild servers rushed forward to collect their cloaks.

He noticed Lady Airal appeared confused about why the conversation upset her mother. He watched her gaze at her mother's stiff face, staring straight ahead, bright red spots on her cheeks. Then glanced around, spotting the male who spoke earlier as he disappeared off into the crowd. *Helc*, she does not know about her grandfather. Her mother should have spoken to her before she exposed her to those to crass for polite society.

The huge double doors opened, and the Blooded De Rank hit the gong, announcing the Emperor and Empress seated.

"Lady Airal, don't stay long. You promised to visit your Great uncle, Lord Khy, on the morns turn. You have always been a favorite of his." She reached forward and patted her daughters' shoulder. "Why, by the Luminous One I can't fathom." The remark contrasting her actions. "You made the promise, and you shall keep your word," Princess Tesiskel said before rushing off, keeping her earlier promise as she abandoned her eldest daughter to strangers.

Lady Airal's cheeks reddened as her mother hustled to where her father and her family stood. Queen Jena placed a gentle hand on her arm.

"I am sure there is a reason for his not arriving this evening."

Lady Airal nodded, her eyes shining, holding her head high.

"I will not announce Tc and Ki agreed to honor the contract this evening. You understand this is best," King Rualui said.

Ea cleared his throat. "Might I get an introduction to this stunning creature by your side?"

Ea happy to see the slightest smile flit across Lady Airal's face, though her eyes shined bright with unshed tears. Moments later he heard his name called by the Blooded De Rank, bowed his head with proper politeness, then hurried away.

PHOENIX RISING

335891 GGS Kinto 28th.
Niuard system private world Imperial House of Zu: Caretakers:
Society Order–Lady Jynnalt

THE DAWN'S SKY OF DARK lavender showed a hint of red along the horizon as they landed at the outer terminal. Four hours later, the sky bright with starshine and towering grayish-white clouds passing overhead, they still waited for clearance to exit the ship. Jynnalt bored stood at the open ramp doorway. She shivered as the bright morning light shined across the ice on the terminal's stones, not yet cleared away. Whitefall, three feet deep, covered the natural lay of the ground. The reflected light blinding without darkening eyewear. Once landed, government officials informed them they could not disembark till an inspection team came aboard to check for contraband. *Contraband? Did they not receive our transponder codes stating this star yacht represents the Imperial house of Zu and the Royal house of Airal?*

The officials finally arrived. Two hours later, after they searched every nook and cranny of the ship. The searchers discovered three innocuous items. They declared these illegal contrabands and confiscated them. One of them, her favorite hairbrush, given her on her eleventh first breath turns of wever's bristles. They told her she could receive the items back if she applied to the Niuard illegal goods division and paid a fine. The fine dependent on the item or items. A malicious grin crossed a Society member's face as he remarked, "any item made from the wever is in the highest expense category." One male, Jynnalt thought to be the leader, said, "We allow no private transportation within city limits. Public tube or walking only. You're to park your private hover barge outside the city in the provided parking spots. For a cost, from there you can walk till you reach the city public tubes."

The Society Priest took the items and left. Jynnalt stalked over to the pulse pad. Her mood did not improve when she informed her mother only to have her censure her.

"Did you not bother checking the status of the world and its laws before leaving? Like any blooded with half a brain. Your grandfather awarded the Society Order as the caretakers of Niuard. They have strict rules which your grandfather respects. You would think you would stay abreast of your family's holdings."

Why? They don't bother with our holding's, why would I with theirs? She kept that tidbit to herself.

"Your grandfather is keeping a close eye on how well the Society as caretakers are doing. He is considering allowing them to take over other private family holdings. The higher production and lower crime since their administration have impressed him. Behave yourself and do not shame your family while there."

Her mother shut down the pulse with finality.

What about the hereditary caretakers and their rights? She turned back towards the others, "I don't care what she says its robbery, by all the daemons and luminous ones. They should put out warning beacons with a list of what they allow or not allow. *Before* anyone enters their sphere of influence. I wonder how many returned after having items confiscated. I won't ever come back." She stormed towards the exit, "relative or not. He can visit me at Ki. Gods and daemons curse them," she said to no one in particular. "I will pay whatever the cost to get my hairbrush back." She said as she glanced over at Lady Iacha, remembering why she was here.

Thoughts of the past four months, arguments over the Queenship and how she prayed to the gods for someone, anyone found alive in the bloodline ahead of her. She became stressed as time passed while she waited. The record keepers of the Book of Blood searching to find a single heir above Jynnalt. She argued before the throne constantly during this time to keep her position as Arch Dukianess. A title she trained for was comfortable with and confident of her ability to perform her duties. She resented this invasive intrusion in her life, and her family's.

It devastated her when informed by Emperor Lahamu, the title of Arch Dukianess of Ki, awarded this morn to Lady Racin Edan'Airal. She legally ascended to the title in a private ceremony with the Temple officiating, making it final. never told her this was about to happen, nor invite her to the ceremony. The sense of betrayal by her closet friend since they were both five sars old cut deep.

Jynnalt gave in, entrapped by the lack of heirs from the late Queen's line, and losing her hereditary title. She would not leave her family in the limbo of a non-titled house. And powerless.

It meant she would marry Prince Ryakin, who despised her. *Not her fault* he moved in so close to the *droging* beacon. Still, the test of the Phoenix Armor stood between her and the Queenship. If she passed, the official appointment as Queen of Ki followed a month later, officiated by the Temple's High Priestess. This meant she was free till Goem first of ninety-one.

As soon as they declared her the new heiress to the throne of Ki, the Empress assigned her companions after a heated exchange between them.

Jynnalt disagreed with the Empress and her views of a female's place. The Empress believed Jynnalt should bow to her husband's wishes in matters of ruling Ki and showed how eminently displeased with Jynnalt's forceful opinions.

"My husband will be a consort, not a King. Ki does not allow a King. Males are no more intelligent than females, nor wiser about ruling. Etiquette should not determine who rules or how. I can do the best for my citizen's without playing word games or following every single court intrigue. Or my consorts' demand. A decision planned for betterment of everyone serves best, no matter who makes the eventual decision."

Empress Lahmu sucked in her breath, shocked. "Your Kingdom's citizen's wellbeing depends on how much you understand the politics of your kingdom, Empire, GIA and CON from turn-to-turn. Believe me, they change with the slightest whims within the courts. Males have a better grasp of these things."

After their disagreement, Empress Lahmu assigned her the leading expert on proper social behavior. Lady Iacha. Empress Lahmu understood no matter the circumstances, Lady Iacha would be a hard but fair teacher. The Empress tasked her with teaching Lady Airal the social observances a Queen needed to understand. That was far more important than actual decision making, the Empress claimed many times. Jynnalt did not agree, becoming frustrated.

Lady Iacha reminded her of her mother, too critical. Though she admitted, like Eshin, she praised her when she did something correctly.

This making her soften her view of her a little. How the *helc* could proper manners and who's who and who's in power now be harder to understand and keep up with than battle tactics and combat? Which she excelled. Yet, she admitted to herself; she failed miserably at politics.

She turned her thoughts to why she was here. For this thin sliver of time, she could do as she pleased. No longer obligated to any duties, Jynnalt's status officially in limbo for now. She intended to enjoy her free time, something of a luxury for her.

Her thoughts jerked back to now as Lady Iacha told the companions to retrieve their cloaks. They were exiting when twelve enforcers accompanied by more Society members met them at the top of the ramp.

"Our priest notified us you have paladins and others who carry weapons with you. We allow no weapons worldside on Niuard. No one, not paladins or protectors, may." The gaunt, skeleton faced Society member stared at Caltac' as he said this. "You can either surrender the weapons to us or lock them away in your ship's armory." Seconds passed as the tension rose.

Caltac broke in saying, "I am here to view the ruins," he handed over a temple writ, "this lady and her entourage were kind enough to offer me a——."

"We do not acknowledge the Temple's authority here."

"I beg to differ, Lady Airal, soon to be *Queen* Airal's, status *always* allows her to keep her paladins *armed* within the Anunnaki Empire's Sphere of Influence," Tavas said. Shooting a challenging stare towards the Society officials.

Iacha stood straighter, glancing at Jynnalt. "Lady Airal, it is your responsibility to maintain control of your paladin's or anyone else in your party," she said. Arranging her cloak, a disapproving frown upon her face. "We are in the inner boundaries of the Imperial Empire. Are you expecting an attack here? Remember, we are not in the wilds of Ki."

Jynnalt felt the heat rise in her face and her jaw tighten, then realized Iacha was staring at the group of enforcers. She grasped their hands were tightening on their weapons, intent looks on their faces, their stance aggressive. Iacha silently warning her of the danger of allowing this to escalate. She took the hint.

Iacha said, her tone reprimanding and scolding, "Lady Airal, may I remind you, you function as an emissary every place you go. Be gracious, and they will remember. Ignore their customs and laws, and they will also remember those actions. Besides, you can file a formal complaint *later*." She stared the Society member straight in the eye. "I will report these affairs to the Temple and the Empress."

Caltac' scrutinized Jynnalt. She knew he would do as she asked. She hesitated, then nodded his direction, and he disarmed along with the rest.

"Wise choice. Now I am prepared to leave as soon as these officials finish." Lady Iacha said, staring at Jynnalt's paladins and her sensial, a stern expression on her face.

Twenty minutes later, the weapons were all placed in the armory. A Society member put a lock on the door along with a seal. "When you're ready to lift off, we will remove the seal. Not before."

The one who appeared most senior amongst them presented a handsome face. Yet with a cruel look in his eye. He walked over to the star yacht's disguised weapons battery and placed an unusual device on the controls. The device snapped tight against the console's panel, and a red baleful eye pulsed.

"No weapons other than those approved by the Society allowed worldside, including ship's weaponry. Her Captiva and crew's faces showed their discomfort with the disarmament of the ship."

Her tension rose along with the slightest fluttery sensation in her stomach. Most citizens or officials could not tell the difference between a pleasure star yacht and a refitted heavy battlecruiser from Ki, with all the fleet hardware still functional. He did. Who *is* he?

With that done, the Society member and enforcers left. Her sense of freedom, fun shopping and riding the back hills on her uncle's famous war beasts vanished. Replaced by a growing sense of dread.

"Let's hurry. I want to leave as soon as possible."

Her paladin's expression as uneasy as she felt.

Along the way, they passed a huge, bloated canid on the roadway to Niuard's largest city, Tinial. Covered by rats, insects and hundreds of black carrion flyers which lived on any temperate world or planet.

Low-flying luxury barges, skyskimmers, and public repulser runners raced past. Disturbing the insects and carrion flyers which rose in an angry black cloud before settling back down on the gruesome sight.

Dead, anything carried disease. Along a heavily traveled transportation route, inexcusable and unsanitary. Caltac' once told her some empires were too poor or too corrupt to support a state of cleanliness for their citizens. Most of the latter rather than the former.

They took their barge in as far as allowed before walking the rest of the way. Paying an exorbitant fee to park. The fee, she was sure, went directly to the Society Order's coffers. Leaving them still twenty-five leagues to travel as Lord Khy's estate sat at the outer edges of the merchant's area.

When they entered the city, they spotted citizens with desperate expressions in plain drab clothes of browns and grays rushing to unknown destinations. How they did not run into others, she was not sure as they kept their eyes on the ground. The only color, it seemed, were visitors like themselves. Everything around them depressing. Subdued. The sounds in the merchant's sector, a murmur of quiet voices. Not the normal ruckus of merchants hawking their wares of merchandise throughout the galaxy. The replicator's surfaces sitting next to the kiosk, dull and worn.

When the citizens made eye contact with Society members or Enforcers, they looked back down, pretending to work. Odd. Fear not something seen in the Anunnaki empire amongst the guilds or commoners. She glanced over at Caltac'. His eyes narrowed with a speculative expression at the Society members patrolling the market. Accompanied by hard looking Enforcers.

The last time she was here, the immense wealth of the world on display in festive colors dazzling everywhere. Merchant's kiosks covered in canopies of bright stripes billowing with each puff of wind. The air filled with loud popping noises. The blinding glints from the myriad replicator unit sitting next to gaudy textiles, or the glint of alluring intricately shaped jewelry with expensive stones, or colorful household goods. Guild members and commoners alike in bright, elegant clothing strolling from stall-to-stall shopping. Loud merchants hawking wares over laughter and conversations. Children with pets running around playing under parents' watchful eyes as they begged for a treat or item from indulgent parents. She remembered those mischievous, hopeful eyes.

Now, the streets stood practically empty except for outsiders, Society, and Enforcers along with a few scurrying citizens, the only ones present on the thoroughfare. Elevated numbers of enforcers and Society members with an indifferent expression on their faces everywhere she glanced. Too many. If things were peaceful, implied by the removal of their weapons, why so many Enforcers?

The very atmosphere a pall grating on her already thinly stretched nerves. The streets and alleys crowded with shabby merchants selling household goods for any price. Their haggling spoke of an undertone of desperation. As they passed through the food markets, little food appeared available in the kiosk's outer shelves and not a single replicator insight.

The underground public runner areas no different from the ones above. Few travelers except outsiders. They exited near their destination in the commoner's market section. What foodstuff sat out far too overpriced. Stunned, she stared at the cost in shock. While starving canis, all ribs and bones roamed the streets, snatching at the citizen's hands if they held the smallest piece of food. One threatened a threadbare, unattended child. A merchant nearby hit the beast with a hand-fashioned cudgel, then glanced around as if afraid. He appeared worried his act would bring undue attention. He slipped back into the booth he tended, ignoring the child. Shocked, she tried to go after her to check on her wellbeing. Caltac' kept her from doing so with a firm grip on her arm and a shake of his head as the child vanished into an alley.

In the street ahead, three Society members and about twenty Enforcers encircled a group of pure white toga clad Malkuth. A sign they were scholars. One Society member stood with his hand held out to the male before him. Tavas gave her a shove as she slowed. Lady Iacha gave him a disapproving stare before turning to Jynnalt. "You should file a complaint with your paladin's guild for roughness," she said. Loud enough for him to hear, "*however*, he is correct. It's impolite to stop and stare or involve yourself when officials are managing a situation not under your authority." She scolded, quiet unease in her tone.

Ten minutes later, they arrived at Lord Khy's estate. The gates stood open with no paladins on guard. Tents and crude shacks littered the once artfully tended grounds as far as she could see. Ragged children played or sat and stared, quiet. Subdued. Outside hovels.

They reached the mansion after a depressing walk through this impromptu shack town. Strange citizens, not guild workers, as they displayed no guild badges, wandered through the mansion. Filth everywhere.

A male came rushing down the stairs to greet them. "I was waiting for you. Your uncle took a bad turn. I needed to attend to him, leaving me unable to meet with you at the station. You understand."

"We just arrived," Lady Iacha said before asking in as polite a voice as possible. "Who are all these... citizens?"

"They live here under the newest laws passed by the Society Caretakers. No one can own something privately which all may not partake. To Jynnalt, the sing-song tone sounded like a brainwashed passage from a cult. Her unease turned to anger at the condition of Lord Khy's once immaculate estate.

"Still, why is the mansion filthy, the grounds not cared for?" Jynnalt asked, her tone sharp. "Does no one know how to clean?"

"Your remark is offensive. I will report this to the Society officials."

"Do you know who you are addressing?" Lady Iacha asked, not hiding her disapproval.

"Yes, a citizen. Like the rest of us on Niuard. Nor do I care. The Society told me to expect visitors for," jerking his head toward the stairs, "him."

Lady Iacha made a noise in the back of her throat, then said. "Please, we would like to visit her uncle and leave. We will not bother you for long."

"We will see who is in trouble once I report what we found here to the emperor," Jynnalt said under her breath. Unable to let go his attitude and what she witnessed.

As they entered the small chamber, Lord Khy sat uninterested in his surroundings. She gave him a quick smile, watching for his reaction. The last time she met him was ten sars ago. Her memory of him as a kind old male who laughed all the time. One who allowed her to take one of his famous war beasts and go for a long, exhilarating ride. His private tithe came from the sale of his foals, raised, and trained by his stable. Many a house of the Anunnaki and elsewhere boasted of his war beasts' bloodlines in their stables.

Then, as if his faculties came back, he spoke, "you're the perfect likeness of your mother. I met her once when she and her brother came to court with their family. Beautiful lady. Gracious and kind, the outer borders have the purest stock," he said, his breath misty in the freezing air. "Breeding always shows."

The chamber so icy none of the ladies removed their cloaks, their breaths steaming in the air. Not even Lady Iacha, who normally considered wearing a cloak inside impolite. Lord Khy, in thin clothing, sat shivering.

"Khy, this is your great-niece. You are thinking of someone else."

Jynnalt aghast at his causal reference toward her uncle.

The life tender moved towards Lord Khy aggressively. She frowned, and he detected her displeasure.

"I'm sorry. Memory lapses after the last vatting is common for him. He mixes up those who come to visit him. Even his brother-in-law, your grandfather, and his benefactor."

So, this piece of sheat knows who I am, contrary to his earlier statement.

"The other turn he referred to him as the Lord of Nothing. He stammered it out because he could not remember the actual title. A shame when the memory goes. The Society claims it is a kindness once they reach a certain number of vattings. Best to let them go. A blessing for all concerned."

Her cheeks burned, and she wanted to strike the obnoxious smile off his face. She stood straighter, staring hard at him. Her jaw clenched tight, trying to hold her temper in check as her breath quickened.

"Wouldn't you agree?" He asked, staring at her uncle as if he wanted to kill him. As if her agreement would somehow permit him to do so.

"No. And anyone," she stepped within an inch of his face,

"attempting to do so will incur my wrath. Something I assure you; you do not want to experience."

Lady Iacha moved over to a holo'projection wall showing Lord Khy's most prized war beasts he bred, raised, and trained. Elohim Warrior, Mystic Relic, and Furious, the three most famous and the largest frames on the wall. Jynnalt realized Lady Iacha did so to distract from the blunt threat by Jynnalt, which lacked any finesse.

"I loved the war beasts I bought in the past from this stable. It would interest me to see them once more. There might be a foal that interest me to buy before we leave. I can send my herdsmen to come back and pick the foal up when ready to wean."

"They are all gone. Sent to the butchers," the Society life tender said nonchalantly, as if the creature's demise, each worth a fortune by any wealthy standards, did not matter.

Lady Iacha's mouth fell open, most likely for the first time in her life, so shocked by the remark before stammering out, "you must be mistaken. Those war beasts are the pride of the house of Zu."

"No one may own anything of value they can't share with everyone. There are two million citizens. How do you share ten thousand war beasts amongst them? The Society declared it necessary to slaughter them to add to the food stores. No citizen starves on Niuard. The Society demands fairness for all. They show those to selfish to share the proper way. Besides, riding is a frivolous pastime of the idle wealthy," he said, the sneering tone brazen.

"No one starves in Ki, yet no citizen, lives like this." Jynnalt said the temperature unnoticed as heat burned through her. She gazed at the life tender. Her face stony. The other ladies moved closer to the door apprehensively. Spooked by the life tender's mad gleam in his eyes and the strange litany which did not match the reality of what they witnessed since arriving.

Lord Khy spoke, his voice loud, the underlying rage hard to miss.

"My brother-in-law allowed these criminals to murder my war beasts. He came personally and oversaw the actual killing. Slashed the throat of Furious right in front of me. His blood splashed across me as he thrashed and pawed desperately for air. I could not watch any longer. Wished I could kill my brother-law where he stood. I opposed my sister's marriage. Others in the family, not just me, realized what an Araikia slime slug he was. Yet, most refused to listen. Lusting after his eventual title. He has done nothing but brought dishonor to our house. I lay foul murder at his feet."

The life tender's face an enraged expression raised his hand and stepped towards him, "Don't you speak of your brother-in-law that way. You only live well because of him. I shall report your disrespect," he said as Lord Khy flinched away.

Caltac' grabbed his wrist, stopping his forward movement.

"How dare you touch me!"

Caltac' said nothing, the loud crack of bone snapping followed by a howl of agony from the Society life tender Caltac's response.

For the first time, Jynnalt saw Lady Iacha's, eyes flash with anger, not at Caltac', but the life tender. Her tone dripped venom, "live well," outrage in her voice clear. "His clothing is squalid and thin, the temperature of his chamber freezing, and he is far too gaunt, implying you do not feed him enough. That's abuse, not living well. We are leaving. I have seen enough," Lady Iacha told him as she stepped towards the door. "How disgraceful to think of hitting someone old and helpless. Believe me, the Empress, no less shall hear about this." She motioned for the others to leave and for Caltac' to release the life tender.

Jynnalt silent, her heart a drumbeat pounding in her ears, her throat dry as she sucked in air, her rage growing by the second. She did not realize she was storming along the roadway that led to the city causeway. She paid little attention to her surroundings, her mind on everything she learned this turn. Till she ran smack into Caltac'.

"Stop." He pointed down the road. A crowd formed at the gate during the time they were inside. "Give me all the tithe you have on you. None of you stopped to shop. It should be enough."

For a second, she eyed the group and hesitated, spoiling for a fight. Till she saw the look on Caltac' and her paladin's faces. Now she spotted children and females mixed with the group and changed her mind. She, her companions, and Lady Iacha handed over their chit's. All total, the amount loaded on them came to over ten plat talons. A minor fortune.

When they got close to the gate, Caltac' threw the chits as far away as possible. Those few who stood their ground Caltac' and her paladins moved. Violent and swift. Then hustled their charges down the street before more crowds formed. They reached the outer city's public tube without further incident.

Caltac', Tavas and the other paladins grabbed their arms, stopping them before they stepped on the platform, heading to the underground station. Shook their heads. Lady Iacha silent, glanced around, fear on her face. Jynnalt sensed the surrounding wrongness as she tried to figure out what made them so cautious. Then it hit her. No Society or Enforcers insight. Anywhere. Unkempt merchants stepped out from behind their sad kiosk's staring around, puzzled.

Overhead, the throaty roar of incoming atmos fighters reached them at the same time. The merchants stayed where they stood, still uncertain what was happening.

Caltac' grabbed Jynnalt, dragging her into the underground tunnel to the tubes. The paladins did the same to her female companions, hustling them fast behind them. Moments after they raced inside the tunnel, it shook under them, knocking them off their feet. A shower of metastone dust and dirt covering them. Quick Caltac' yanked Jynnalt back to her feet. The paladins rose, grabbed the other females, pushing them ahead as they chased after the two, Razing further into the tunnels.

Chapter 12

335891 GGS Kinto 28th.
Blood House of Ib: Emperor Lahamu: Imperial Greater Council
Agade–Prince Ryakin

THE STAR SAT LOW ON the horizon, bathing Agade, Fire Mountain, and the lower plains' bloody crimson as the night came swiftly this time of the sar. The peaks shrouded dark lavender as faint stars twinkled above, heralding the death of the turn.

Ryakin arrived later than he expected as earlier. He stopped to congratulate Duac over his appointment to the Nicaialy Destiny as the Executive Commander. He rushed to an open seat, after properly asking for permission to enter the Greater Council as a guest from the chamber scribe. His brother held the floor as he sat.

"Ideological promises to the disenfranchised and criminals by those with malice and ulterior motives forge acts of sedition. You know what I refer to."

The chamber erupted with stomping feet and nodding heads. Ryakin noticed others looking around, eyes narrowed, lips taut. Prince Satoric's anger at the speech obvious. Rualui made an enemy this turn. A formidable one. His brother held up his hand for silence, and the noise abated except for the subtle rustle of clothing.

Ryakin sat quietly, observing the proceedings. Listening. Watching the reactions of council members. He was here because he wanted a private word with his brother afterward. In fact, this his first time attending one of the Greater council meetings. Not being a member, he preferred to spend his time in more useful pursuits. Unlike those who hang out, trying to garner attention from the elite and influential. Here he witnessed his brother for the first time as a statesman. Not a family member. A discomforting sense of dislocation gripped him.

Rualui spoke once more when the chamber quieted. "After the horrors mount of starvation, loss of privileges, property and wealth, they appeal to CON. Abused by those in the upper echelon who absorb the wealth of their Empire. They are no better than parasites. The Council of Nine sends in the Temple warriors to restore the Empire. What they agreed to so willingly requires spilled blood to take back. Those who brought ruin and misery to once-thriving governments," Rualui said, moving away from the central speaker stand, "never once considered the wellbeing of their citizens."

Ryakin watched him walk with slow dignity towards the raised dais seating. Three levels high in a half circle shape. The double council throne chair for the Emperor and Empress behind him at the opposite end of the chamber.

"The sad truth," Rualui said as he paced before them, "the promised utopia never arrives. Those who made promises never meant to fulfill them. Smoke and mirrors to steal wealth from citizens by appealing to their sense of decency. By the time they realize they're conned, it's too late. Their rights gone, and their privileges no longer exist." He said, pausing as he gazed at the council members.

"Political warfare against the average citizen. They use an empire's citizens against themselves," Rualui said. "If they win," he paused before going on, "a wave of blood, mass sacrifices, and swift retribution to those who opposed them. Who will be the ones to pay the price? *The innocent. The valiant*, who stood against them, those who the power hungry condemn. This proven time after appalling time, throughout the galaxies' empires ever since the last Great War three hundred sars ago."

"If you do nothing, these predators, who call themselves the Society Order, will take full advantage. They already have. Do not ignore them because you believe them weak. A minor cult. Their power is growing within our empire... and throughout the galaxy. We need to investigate and take proper measures to ensure we do not become one of those failed empires. Those needing rescue by the *Temple*," he said, moving back to his seat conceding the floor over to the council elder.

Prince Satoric requested the floor, and Emperor Lahamu nodded. The elder yielded the floor.

"I find King Rualui to be an impressive orator. He entertains well with broad and sweeping generalizations. Did you catch at the end where he admitted we need to investigate the Society Order?" he asked, walking with his hands behind his back before those in the chamber. "Meaning he knows nothing about them. Or how they might govern. I, with the approval of this council, as an experiment, allowed my blood house of Zu's private holdings of Niuard world caretaken by the Society Order. Not as a titled citizen, as they do not view governance in that manner, but by the Order's beliefs. I wanted to prove their ability to govern private holdings."

Rualui stood. "Private holdings must follow the laws of the empire. I have witnessed the avalanche of complaints arriving each turn to the Second Ministries AC nine. Far exceeding the normal amount sent by the usual malcontents and rabble."

"Please be seated. Prince Satoric has the floor. You may ask for the floor once he is through." The elder reproached, frowning in Rualui's direction.

Prince Satoric countered, "Any alternative system of change is hard for many to accept. They want the old ways, whether in their best interest. Once they adjust, they will accept the administration and settle. We must give the Society Order enough time for the citizens to adjust to their circumstances. Or we do them an injustice. The reference to those empires the Temple rescued mentioned by King Rualui had nothing to do with The Society Order."

"Different names for the same governance do not change facts," Rualui said, responding to Prince Satoric's statement.

Emperor Lahamu stood before the elder could reprimand his brother again, "the debate is now closed. We will take a vote."

For the next half hour, the council stayed in the voting chambers. Ryakin sat thinking how to frame the discussion he wanted about his soon to be bride with his brother. He wanted to debate the wisdom of the contract. This soon to be Queen no longer the quiet, acceptable Queen Jildius. This wild female Jynnalt, who trouble seems to follow everywhere, would bring ruin upon their house. If she passed the test of Queenship in Ki on the eighteenth of Droe. Someone he forgot for now who once told him it was an archaic test. Eleven died in the attempt to prove their worth since the Kingdom's inception. Ryakin would bet his last gold talon that was nonsense spread to give the new Queen unquestioning authority at the start of her rulership. Superstitions appealed little to him. He imaged the smoke and mirror tests were dramatic and awe-inspiring, or they failed their purpose; to legitimize a new Queen.

His relief was immense when the council reentered. The scribe handed the sealed votes to the Alder. Sitting still and thinking was not Ryakin's biggest pastime, he forced himself to stop drumming his fingers on his chair. The Alder stepped forward with the results, but before he could say a word, Emperor Lahamu's Vyzier rushed over to him and handed him a communique. Everyone froze, waiting to hear what occurred important enough to interrupt a Greater Council meeting.

Seconds later, Emperor Lahamu stood. A frown upon his face. "We will remove the votes unsealed and destroy them. This matter referred to the council's schedule for next week's agenda. The world under discussion is under attack. I want to know by whom. And why? Soon. I adjourn this council for the turn. I want the solar fleets sent to control the situation." He and the Empress left the chamber, allowing no further arguments or remarks. Prince Satoric tried to demand the floor, though ignored as the emperor left the chamber. The council members rushed out behind him. Ryakin spotted his brother in the hall speaking with Emperor Lahamu moments later and waited for the emperor to leave. Rualui waved Ryakin over to his side. Before Ryakin could say anything, his brother spoke.

"I was about to send my paladins to find you. Take the seventy-ninth fleet to Niuard. I need proof of what is occurring. Emperor Lahamu gave permission moments ago for me to send you. Also, before you leave, please notify Princess Tesiskel, her daughter may be in danger. Tell her if possible, you will bring her home. Safe and whole."

"I should have known. If there is a disaster happening somewhere, she will be in the mix. She's a jinx."

Rualui gave him a stern look. "She left this morning to visit her great uncle. At the request of her mother. And you want to blame her?"

"I was joking. Still, everywhere she goes, something happens. So, the talk I wanted, I guess, will wait."

"Yes, you need to hurry. Prince Satoric assigned Knight Commander Aikoina to take the twenty-seventh to resolve whatever problem arose. More like to cover-up. He can't afford this vote to go against him. The Greater Council would demand he removed the Society Order and restore the hereditary caretakers. He paid a fortune to remove them to start with and expected the Society over-time to cover his losses. If the council voted against the Society and favored of the Caretakers, it'd force him to remove them. Financially, he and his house ruined if this occurred."

"You always know the right thing to say to motivate me," he said while his brother walked with him towards the private skyskimmers parking terminal. "Aikoina demanded they dismiss me from the academy, supposedly for cheating, because my team beat his is something I never forgot nor forgave. I sense you discovered this fact."

"This is serious. Academy rivalries were not on my mind when I mentioned him. I am trying to point out the fallacy of not thinking this is important," Rualui said, stopping in front of Ryakin.

"Prince Satoric is in a rush to cover up whatever is occurring. I can't allow that to happen. Aikoina is his top commander. Why do you think he is sending him? The vote went against the investigation. He needs to make sure they cover any wrongdoing up before a re-vote. Most of the council cannot see the dangers of the Society Order. They feel I'm paranoid. Claim Prince Satoric's can do with his house's private world as he pleases. Prince Satoric claims the Caretakers willingly gave up their positions and agreed to allow the Society to administer the world instead."

Ryakin realized how angry his brother was when he spoke again.

"Niuard caretakers complained to the council, claimed he forced them out by coercion. This is the first move to disenfranchise the hereditary caretakers across the empire."

"Prince Satoric threatened them. He informed them if they don't take the tithe offered to relinquish their hereditary rights, he'd remove them, anyway. In which case they'd end up with nothing."

"Most of the council think the way to control the Society Order is to not allow them to administer your house's holdings." Rualui turned to his brother. "We can't let the vote be in his favor. Think of this in military terms. This will give them a beachhead into our empire. The ability to affect our politics."

"Since when am I part of your we? I'm not so sure they aren't right. Ugallu thinks the Greater council and Kingdom's need to stay out of the other houses' businesses."

"Yes, he told me the other turn. He believes I meddle where I should not. I told him I do what is best for our kingdom's citizens and the empire." Rualui said before falling silent.

They parted ways when they reached the terminal. His brother hurrying off, his paladins rushing to keep him insight.

Ryakin arrived ten minutes later at the private landing pad to the blood house of Airal's fortress. Now on Fleet Duty, his paladins no longer trailed him. Not having paladins until he contracted to the Queen of Ki to become her consort, he was uncomfortable with them following him everywhere. Thankful fleet rules did not allow paladins to accompany ranking members while they were actively on duty. He noted Prince Satoric's official luxury barge parked in the Kieran enclave. The crews stood ready to leave and the soft hum of the running engine informed him he did not intend to stay long. Ryakin figured he came to tell Tesiskel the news and debated leaving. But he promised his brother, so he would make this quick. First, he alerted the seventy-ninth to prepare for launch and notify the standby crew for loading. Ryakin still needed to discover which pleasure house Ustrix might be frolicking. For now, he answered none of his pulses.

He walked up the hallway towards Tesiskel's assigned quarters. No guild protectors stood guard or workers rushing about their business in the halls. His instincts went to high alert.

He walked to the outer door of the anti-chamber, which stood open. No females or guild members in attendance in here either. He stepped back out. The sharp sound of a slap from the outer garden to his right caught his attention. He stepped that direction to intervene but then heard Prince Satoric.

"If you ruined my plans, daughter, you'll pay. Do you understand?"

"You promised to take care of my problem, yet nothing happens. I did something myself and relieved you of the necessity. I thought this would please you."

The pleading tone pitiful, yet he sensed an undertone of hatred.

"I sent three assassins, supposedly the best. They never returned. In the meantime, I hired others. Have patience. I shall resolve the situation. I meant what I said. Do not interfere or try to take matters into your hands again. I can still recall you home. While there, we can discuss the situation. Someplace you found... unpleasant in the past. Your actions might cost me far more than I can afford."

"No. Please, by the gods, no. I swear I will not interfere again." The pleading tone desperate.

"I am glad you understand my point. Now I must leave to deal with this mess."

Footsteps headed his way, and he ducked behind the column as someone stormed past into the interior chamber, the steps fading off into the distance. He backed out. The humming pitch of the barge out front changed, and he recognized it was preparing to debark. In a rush of air, the barge disappeared over the courtyard wall. He overheard another male voice heading to the interior.

"Why can't the *bitkhij* just die? Like anyone else would by now. She is costing us far too much."

He thought it best not to leave just then and froze. He moved towards the garden gate to the hall and backtracked to chime the door; in case someone spotted his skyskimmer parked outside and wondered about why later. A movement caught his eye, and he stood still once more. After moments passed, and nothing happened, he relaxed. *A flyer or tree rodent, most likely.*

He left the garden and circled back to the front and chimed the door.

Tesiskel answered, not a companion or guild worker, a large red mark across her cheek and her eyes glassy as if crying. *So, her father slapped her.*

He passed along the message his brother sent him to deliver. She thanked him; her manner cold then closed the door with no further interaction. *She does not seem too concerned about her daughter. Maybe she feels Jynnalt's safe at her Great Uncles. Or is more worried about her problems, which is likely.* Disquiet rose within him at the lack of caring she displayed. Before he stepped away on the other side of the door, a male voice called out. "Mother, did grandfathered come back?"

Must be Jynnalt's brother. After what he learned this turn, he decided there was more urgency to speak to his brother regarding annulling the marriage contract. *This is the most dysfunctional family I've ever met.*

Ustrix pulsed him as he got to his skyskimmer. Ryakin informed him to meet him in Nemesis. On the way, he tried to figure out what he overheard and what it meant. This event at Niuard sounded like his brother claimed, more than just a stirring of nebula's dust. Ustrix finally pulsed back, already heading to board having heard the news.

Ryakin now commanded Tc's newest dreadnought. Nemesis Ai core transferred on Ryakin's request, and his programming elevated when they scrapped the solar battleship. Twelve other battle dreadnoughts of the seventy-ninth fleet rendezvoused at Tc's starbase, Veista, at the edge of the system. An hour later, they warped out en route to Niuard.

As they came out of skip, they met with resistance from a skeleton ragtag squadron. They dispatched them fast. His signal officer informed him one ship got a message out. Within another fifteen minutes, they would know the answer to what the message consisted.

335891 GGS Kinto 29th.
Niuard world: Forest and Ruins–Lady Jynnalt

THE SAVAGE LEAPED TOWARDS her, a glint of light along a long-wicked blade held before him. Tavas killed him before he reached her by rupturing his throat with a crushing kick. They may not have weapons, but they still wore armor, and each paladin excelled in hand-to-hand combat. He took the handgun; the attacker disdained using, to his detriment, from his belt. She grabbed the wicked-looking knife the reaver intended to gut her with from the ground next to him. She tucked it into her belt.

One female screamed during the attack before covering her mouth, realizing too late she gave away their location to the others hunting them. The youngest companion pulled her away from the dead body and pushed her up the hill.

A second attacker rushed out from the trees along the path. Stabbed the youngest in the temple before she realized he was there. Silent she crumpled to the ground. The one who screamed seconds earlier now screaming, unhinged and hysterical. Her screaming stopped with abruptness as she fell with his blade through her eye. Before Jynnalt could react, the reaver melted back into the trees.

The distant staccato booming of gauss guns and the sizzle of plasma rifles coincided with bright flashes of orange or streaks of blue, white. Sulfur and ozone made their way on the wind.

The dark of night lit with the burning fire of the city and Lord Khy's estate. Even this far away, the fire cast eerie shadows throughout the forest. Screams and angry voices in a strange language came from a distance somewhere behind them. Caltac' covering their retreat, with devastating results to the reavers who crossed his path. The hunters became the hunted. She prayed to the gods to protect Caltac'.

The rumors he was a disgraced Ghost Walker seemed more likely these last few hours as they fought their way through the forest towards the ruins. The Temple Protectorates could not match his skill. He was fast, too fast to follow his brutal assault. He disappeared in a blink of an eye. Shocked, she realized she never could beat him in training. In an actual fight outside their training matches, she never would.

One Malkuth male who joined them earlier with others still alive. He as hapless as her companions. The others died protecting him. She thought he might be a high-ranking scholar.

To the left of her group, flashes from gauss and plasma rifles erupted, followed by screams and crashing underbrush. Others trying to flee the city. Found by reavers in the bright light of the silvery moons. The gas giant overhead reflected off fresh whitefall. She turned to go to their aid.

Tavas grabbed her arm. "They're dead. You can't help them."

"You don't know that," she said as undulating calls of victory rang out. Giving truth to his words. The sting of defeat filled her as she rushed up the path after the others.

Seconds later, five reavers rushed in from the right. The last priestess carrying the relic turned to fight. Jynnalt killed one with the knife she grabbed earlier. The razor-sharp edge connected at the lower extremity of the ribs, grated across bone, and sank to the handguard.

The attacker grunted, falling backward, yanking the knife out of her hand, rolled over, sat up, and pawed at the knife hilt. He gave an emphatic tug, and it slid out. A second later, a stream of thick purple blood erupted from his mouth. The reaver appeared puzzled as he fell to his side, dead.

Two others advanced toward Tavas and Keif, both attackers going for their handguns. Her paladins were on them before they finish drawing. Seconds later, she overheard the sickening crack of bone as the attackers fell to the ground, glassy eyes staring upward. The priestess killed the one she fought as the last ran back into the trees and into the shadowy gloom.

The wind blew a gust of thick grey smoke throughout the forest, diminishing her vision and making her eyes water. A bitter burned odor of electrical power conduits burning, mixed with the odor of wood, cloth, and flesh arrived with the smoke. Originating from the burning city below. She choked with a sputtering cough.

Quick they raced to catch up to the others far ahead. Lady Iacha in the rear. Jynnalt and the priestess surprised as the last of the five reaver's rush out, tackling them both.

The reaver, priestess, and Jynnalt fell in a tangle of limbs. Something puffed in her face as she slammed into the side of a gnarled, ancient cedar tree. A rich rotten scent of earth and leaves mingled with a potent cinnamon odor. A queer tight sensation gripped her stomach, and her mouth watered with nausea.

Rolling to her side, she realized ash from the Priestess's relic covered her face and body, and she inhaled an enormous quantity. She spotted the priestess and the reaver sprawled together in death. Tavas and Keif yanked her to her feet.

She felt woozy and everything spun around her. Confused, she glanced around for Caltac' till she remembered he was somewhere behind in the forest.

The temple priestesses died protecting the relic. Strange what the Temple viewed as valuable. An ancient, brittle bag of skin full of ash. A small amount spilled across the ground, mixed in with the roots of the ancient cedar and the cooling blood of the priestess.

An overwhelming urge grabbed her. Frantic, she gathered up what ash she could, putting it back in the pouch, then attaching the brittle bag to her belt. *Safekeeping for the Temple if any of us survive.* The odds grim any of them would see the turns next rising.

She took a deep breath, icy air clearing her head. Caltac' caught up with them. "We can stop and rest here."

He spotted the Priestess, the hilt of a knife sticking out of her temple, and moved over to kneel beside her. He murmured words of the prayer of passage to the next life. The vivid sight of blood stark against the whitefall reminded her of when they met hours ago.

Her party tried to get to their ship but forced back by overwhelming numbers. Six of her paladins died protecting them as they retreated. Taken out by gauss and plasma rifles and a strange energy weapon which paralyzed the warriors, leaving them incapable of fighting back.

They retreated to a dead-end alley after their disastrous attempt to reach their ship. Caltac' leading them off the main causeway. The Malkuth group she spotted earlier making the same wrong turn and becoming trapped with them.

As soon as Caltac' reached the wall, he ran his hands over it in a strange pattern. The wall vanished. It was something she understood existed but never till now encountered, a holo'isomorphic wall which appeared and felt real. This one replicated a worn stone wall.

A Priestess and three Protectorates stood on the other side. The wall hid a secret tunnel. The Priestess clutched at a pouch on her belt until she saw they were not attackers, but others fleeing the violence.

They moved into the tunnel. Something rank wrapped around her senses, as if decaying bodies lay within the tunnel gagged her, forcing her to cover her mouth and nose with the edge of her cloak. "Gods, what is that stench?"

Ignoring Jynnalt's remark, the Priestess waved them down the tunnel as three invaders rounded the corner, running towards them, firing. Plasma bolts sizzled past her head, burning groves in the wall next to her.

The reaver's hugged the rotting wood of the passage, firing at the three Temple Protectorates and Caltac'. They stayed back to cover the others retreat as they raced into the depths of the black maw. Within moments, the firing stopped and the sound of running footsteps reached her. Relief flooded her when she saw Caltac' and the Temple Protectorates. Minutes passed of total darkness, of following the sound of footsteps ahead, the floor treacherous and steep. Twice she slid and almost fell. Ten minutes later, floating glow globes burst to life. She breathed easier. Not far ahead, a stone wall brought the tunnel to a dead end.

The priestess stepped forward, and as Caltac' did earlier, ran her hand over the wall in a pattern and it vanished. She rushed up and out of the exit. A gust of freezing air whistled into where they stood. The Temple Protectorates rushed past and caught up with the Priestess, vanishing into the woods following a small pathway.

"At least we're not trapped down here," one of the Malkuth said before following the others out. She agreed with the sentiment, glad to leave the tunnel.

Lady Iacha motioned Jynnalt ahead. She shook her head. "You take my companions first; we can cover your exit."

"That's outrageous nor proper."

"At the moment, I don't care. Now move. If you stand here arguing, we all die."

Lady Iacha, with a huff, herded the other females before her, muttering under her breath the entire time. They exited into the upper surrounding forest, Razing for the trail where the others disappeared. She rode this trail once before when they visited. This one headed to the high ruins above.

At first, they made rapid time unhindered. Following the Priestess and her protectorates, Caltac' told them to stay with the others and disappeared towards their back trail but did not explain why.

Several minutes later, the roar of atmos craft flashed overhead, dropping hunting parties of reavers to cut off escaping citizens in the mountain forest. From then on, they fought their way upward, heading steadily towards the ruins.

Whitefall started four hours after they left the tunnel, adding to their problems as exhaustion set in from the constant fighting to get this far. The wind, raw and wet, blowing strands of her hair in complete disarray around her. The strands clung to her face and body, making her shiver. Her face ached, frozen from the icy wind, as the temperature plunged, and twilight approached. Glad they were finally beyond the lower smoke-filled forest. The storm not having reached the upper forest yet. The gas giant the world circled cast pewter, silvery light, along with the two bright moons as clouds scudded fast overhead, heading south. She shivered with each gust of wind. Thankful at least for the winter cloak she wore.

Once night fell, they moved faster, yet still two hours away from their destination.

A loud crack of a branch to her right startled her, jerking her mind back to the here and now, as a small, furry, long-eared creature raced past her. She gazed around at those left of her party, the Malkuth and the Priestess group. Now the only ones left of their party were Caltac', three of her paladins, Lady Ithaca, and one Malkuth, a scholar, not a warrior. They paid a heavy price to get this far. At least they made the reaver's pay. Attrition though took its toll.

She sat back, accepting the water passed to her by Tavas, and drank. Jynnalt did not realize how thirsty she was till the water touched her lips.

The only light in the forest was flashes from Gauss guns and plasma bolts from reaver's rifles. Screams wafted their way on the freezing wind from citizens who escape the city, hunted and killed by roving bands of reavers. She gazed towards the far-distant city and Lord Khy's estate, now only an orange glow on the horizon.

"From the scent upon the air, this storm will become a blizzard covering the entire mountain soon. At the rate we are moving, the storm will worsen about the time we reach the ruins. We need to push ahead faster," the only surviving Malkuth said.

Caltac' nodded agreement. High above, the heavens erupted with streaks of fire and explosions expanding outward against the backdrop of twinkling stars.

"I believe the fleet has arrived. Now it's a matter of surviving long enough for the fleet warriors to reach us," Tavas said.

Hours later, they boarded Nemesis. Found by Tc's elite Apax warriors and Ryakin when they entered the ruins. Her refitted cruiser a smoking ruin, her crew dead, leaving her no choice but to accept his offer of a lift back to Agade.

Just her luck, Ryakin rescued her.

Chapter 13

335891 GGS Cava 8th.
Nibiru Proper Agade: commoners city–Guardian Ikath

LORD RICIAD CONTACTED Ikath, demanding he accompanied him to the commoner's city to pick up an important item. The star lowering upon Fire mountains as they arrived at the lower outer gate. The atmosphere serene. For a split-second, time stopped as if the universe stood still. The creatures of the garden park silent. Riciad's and his footsteps recrimination against the moment as they followed the stone pathway to the commoner's city. Awash in a golden patina. The star sank deeper. Rosy gold colors morphed to angry crimson, saturating the land a bloody hue. Ikath watched shadows grow longer as starlight gave way to twilight.

They came upon a small crowd listening to a Society Order's so-called Priest at one of the outer merchant's squares. Lord Riciad stopped, leaving him no recourse but to linger. He found the ideas the Society advocated distasteful. They promoted false information, implying the poorest abused by the highest. Outside of criminal enterprises, Ikath recognized those deserving of help got help. At least throughout GIA and the Temple, he could not speak for elsewhere.

Ikath, cloaked and hooded in coarse cloth of various simple browns and tans, stood next to Lord Riciad. Both their postures relaxed, dressed similarly to the surrounding commoners. He leaned against the stone door frame; his arms crossed over his chest. His eyes hooded, observing the crowd.

"Why are enforcers looking the other way? I thought after what occurred on Niuard, the Greater Council voted the Society Order as disruptive. Thought they denied them skip entrance to the empire or residence systems," Ikath said, looking around, puzzled at the lack of enforces. Normally this time of evening enforcers patrolled around the feasthalls and public squares as drinking created rowdier crowds.

"Besides, I listened to their speeches elsewhere, and their ideas lack logic. To make a society of equivalence, someone somewhere must arbitrate who gets what and when."

Without looking towards him, Lord Riciad said, "such a terrible thing? I have seen societies where the strongest take what they want first, all other's regulated to the dregs left over. Wouldn't the empire the Society endorses be better?"

"Maybe," he said, wondering where this might lead. *Why'd they stopped here*? His eyes tightened, and he stared at the Society Priest spewing rhetoric. He thought they were here to pick something up for him to transport to an outer GIA location.

"I have seen those types of empires and kingdoms. Brutal. Savage. Lacking any hint of civilized behavior. The argument lacks validity when those circumstances do not exist, when Empire's laws are fairly enforced to protect the various classes. Ever abuses? *Absolutely*. In that case, you fix the problems. Not destroy the entire system," he said as he flung his hand with contempt toward the Society Priest. "They don't want a fair empire, they want power, control and their boots on the necks of the citizens. No thanks, I'll pass."

Lord Riciad looked at him with the intentness of a predator, watching its prey right before striking. Ikath paid no attention now to the speech, his full attention on his surroundings.

Ikath observed most citizens ignored the illegal speaker, not bothering to stop and listen, shoulders turned away as they rushed past. The hour late and their work over, they wanted drinks and time with friends. Besides, who needed trouble? Must be the reason the Society priest strategically located himself across from the Quondell, the most popular feasthall in this merchant quadrant. The tent flaps and sides open to allow airflow, the season warmer than usual, the turn longer, the workload's greater during this time. The open tent flaps allowed citizens inside to overhear the Priest. For now. After the mead flowed freely and more arrived to relax, the atmosphere would become boisterous, drowning out everything else. "Why do you believe what they teach would not work?" Lord Riciad asked, his tone more demanding.

"Simple, the arbitrators of the goods and privileges, in this case, the Society Order, become the elite. Every society has elites, the only difference, *who* control the wealth and power of an empire. Who gets to be the elites? I guarantee it won't be those holding power this turn. It will be the Priest of the Society Order. I have seen their so-called book of faith. Dark. Grim. Demands everything of the faithful yet gives little in return. Instead of a vibrant economy, you have stagnation and extensive poverty of the masses. The Priest's meanwhile live in obscene luxury. The populace deluded at first by the Society dangling the idea they will somehow receive all they desire. They won't. What they attain is slavery based upon the harsh rules of *their* religion. The sad truth. Their lives become worse. *Far worse.* I have seen rulership of that type. Sleight of hand and illusions by those who rule with an iron fist while telling them it's a silken weaver's glove. No, thank you."

"Ah, you think for yourself. I'm curious. What do you think of the Temple and its faith?"

Ikath shrugged. "They stay out of my life; I don't argue with their teachings. The Society though, does not allow the slightest disagreement with their book of faith. You either follow every law, if not, you're punished in the same harsh manner for a minor infraction as for a greater one. Fanatic's usher in blood, death, and destruction. Read the passages on ownership of anything. Their book claims all wealth belongs to the Order to distribute to the deserving. Who determines who is deserving? They determine who deserves what goods, food, and even how much essential water, by how well they obey their holy scriptures. They claim only the most faithful deserve rewards. I'm not stupid enough to fall for their lies. I've read their books. Scary stuff. I will take a pass on their honeyed words, which leads to a harsh reality."

"Do you believe what the Temple tells you? Follow the rules they set?

Have no problem with the fact I have more wealth and privilege than, say, you?"

Ikath's instincts reared its head. "Why all these questions? You told me my life and problems are my business, remember? Besides, rules are restrictive," he said, forcing hostility into his voice, turning as if to leave. The Temple his lifesaver, keeping him afloat. What he held sacred. What he must hide from prying eyes.

"Calm yourself. I was only curious about your thoughts. Not prying. Keep your secrets. At least, I learned a little more about you. Pragmaticism rules your head. Something I value, and no emotional ties to the Temple. As to the Society," he shrugged, "I wanted to determine for myself if they will be trouble for the empire. Now that I am on the council."

Ikath relaxed slightly.

"He is lying. A scan of his brain shows deceit. Be careful," Riurrel said through their cyber connection, sounding concerned.

Ikath's nostrils flared, and he compressed his lips. "What do you think his intent is? Is he trying to tie me to the Temple?" he asked Riurrel?

"Really? Unbelievable. I am not a mind reader. Your job is to discover intent. I gave you the facts. Remember your long, tedious, and boring lecture you gave me a while back for offering an opinion?"

Ikath ignored his snarky remark. He now wondered if this trip to pick something up in the commoner's city hid a more nefarious reason. Before Riurrel remarked further, Lord Riciad spoke.

"Rumors are rampant about this Society Order. At least in council chambers by King Rualui, who many believe is too cautious. At least those who bother to show up anymore for the greater council. King Rualui claims they rile the commoners to acts of violence with lies and untruths. Claims they spread dissent and hatred of the blood houses."

"What happened?" Ikath asked, even though already aware of the answer.

"Those on the greater council denied the motion. They said King Rualui dramatized various events to achieve his agenda. Prince Satoric convinced them to vote to lift the ban after another six months."

The longer the Society Priest spoke, the more heated the accusations. Deliberate rants against blood houses and high-ranking guild members. Accusing them of starving children and the commoners and lower guild workers with exorbitant taxes. Claiming the ranking hand out cruel and unlawful judgments against their loved ones, forcing them to go begging for food in the streets. The speaker even blamed the blooded houses and guilds for the lack of crops and debilitating heat because they refuse to negotiate for the services of the Igigi. Ikath looked around, seeing none of the poverty and discontent spoken of by the rogue Priest. He traveled extensively throughout the empire and did not ascertain these conditions anywhere else either.

Strange, the speaker absolved Prince Satoric and his inner group, including Prince Alalus, under investigation by him for the Ghost Walker of wrongdoing. That caught his attention. Why absolve them. They held the greatest wealth other than the throne. He paid more attention as Lord Riciad showed no inclination to move.

The Society, using false rhetoric, twisting information and circumstance to fit a narrative, why is no one calling them out on the misinformation? Ikath well aware the blooded sent foods and supplies to help since the disaster. He saw their Sigil and Silks stamped on food and goods sitting on the docks preparing to load onboard the ships and sent to those regions the hardest hit. The Society priest did not report those facts.

Ikath recorded through his Cyber connection to Riurrel a holo of the speech. Riurrel, for once, silent, thank the gods, leaving Ikath able to focus on his surroundings. Other than the helpful hint earlier, Ikath cognizant Riurrel was pouting, denied an expensive upgrade. Once more. Ikath suspected Riurrel of scheming on how to gain the upgrade since he locked Riurrel out of his Temple account. It wouldn't matter, he was not getting the upgrade no matter how long he pouted. Riurrel already cost him a minor fortune in upkeep.

The tempo of the rhetoric increased with each word the speaker spoke. Ikath figured the rally now approaching its actual purpose. The speaker gesturing while standing on a small packing container as his compatriots mingled with the crowd handing out holo leaflets. Hard to view their faces hidden in the recessed darkness of their hoods. Hidden from the golden light of the glow globs and softer bioluminous lighting as twilight darkened into night.

"You guild workers, who wait on them in their private fortresses, where they gorge themselves and ignore your desperation, slit their throats while they sleep. If you can't bring yourself to do this to protect your children..." Here the Society priest paused for effect. "Let in others who will and walk away, don't look back."

"We will bring their systems to their knees and take what should be yours. What you worked for." He pointed out at the crowd. "Afterwards, those that are working inside for the cause do as much damage as you can till you receive a signal, then set fire to everything as you leave. The rest of you listen to the broadsheet. It will direct you to where you can gather to protest. That will be your part. Show up, and someone will give you food and goods to take back home afterward. We only ask you to show up. The ones inside the fortresses take nothing with you. You are not thieves. When you have set the fires, run as fast as you can for the merchant's docking facilities. We will provide ships to take you and your families off planet to safety out of their corrupt reach."

We shall protect you until we gain control of the empire. Several in the crowd went from being restless to outright belligerent, demanding destruction of the blooded houses. Ikath noticed a few commoners placed tithe in the basket before melting away, uncomfortable with the subject.

"Riurrel, are those native Nibiru commoners the disruptive ones?" Seconds later, the answer as he thought.

"No. They are from planets of comparable size, gravity, and close chemical composition. This allows for a similar appearance."

"I understand the why. Your purpose in explaining maybe to imply I am lacking in intelligence."

"I am trying to be thorough, so you will realize my value."

"Still not getting that upgrade."

"Worth a try."

Ikath caught the shrug in his voice.

Looking at Lord Riciad he said, "the ships will not be available if they ever rile the commoners to the violence they demand."

Lord Riciad glanced at him and agreed. "No, I do not believe, if they fall for this rhetoric, no ships will be there to carry them to safety. Fanatics need their martyrs. Rabble-rousing leaders always determine they are too valuable to the cause to fulfill that specific position."

Ikath caught the pure contempt in Lord Riciad's tone before he said, "still, someone will use any uprising to ascend to greater power. Convenient for those left out of the rant we overheard; I'd bet."

The speaker, done with his rhetoric, melted off in the crowd along with the other hooded Society priest. The crowd dispersed with muttered conversations as those who listened moved towards the feasthalls.

A moment passed while they stood in the black shadows of the night looking out on the square, now empty. A brief time later, guild bards arrived and set up for the evening's entertainments. Colorful covered stalls around the outer edge left the square open for the holo shows. Live theater entertainment in one corner. Food vendors hawking exotic cuisines not served in the feasthalls battled with the music of the bards and theater, adding to the noise.

"Where's the food and goods sent by the houses disappearing? I am aware they're sending help. I saw the boxes sitting at the docks marked with the houses Sigils and Silks for the commoner's cities?"

"Tithe is an influential incentive for some low-level journey transportation worker who feels wronged. A slight change in paperwork at the last moment and the loads conveniently sent elsewhere. They ask no questions." He looked straight at him. "I believe you have done a few of those runs yourself now and then."

Ikath's face heated. He realized the fact he was guilty as charged, nor did he bother checking the legality of the goods. All to play the part for his cover. Shame filled him. He vowed to be more careful about what he hauled from now on. He'd not contribute to starving the commoners. For any reason.

The bright twinkle of silvery stars blazed in the black vault overhead, as the two stood shrouded in darkness. Those in the square lit by soft bioluminous plants placed with great care for the proper subdued night lighting and the rich golden light of spaced glow globes. The feasthalls now fully enclosed against the night. An occasional opening and closing of the tent flaps threw light across where they stood. A crashing ruckus of loud voices, singing and laughter flowed out until the tent flap fell back in place.

"I do not understand what many of my fellow council members think. Those of us new to our titles shunned by those who held their titles prior or were direct heirs before the disaster."

The remark caught his attention. "Riurrel, when we first met Riciad, I remember the others referred to him as titled?"

"Yes, something you want me to investigate?"

"Yes, check out when he ascended to his title. Tell me as soon as you have the answer."

Casually fishing for information, he said, "rumors are rampant throughout the empire. Someone murdered the Igigi at the exit tower and the Nibiru platform before the disaster. Some claim someone murdered them to prevent them from giving warning or aid. Someone told me you are on the investigative counsel," he said.

"Some council members believe someone engineered a crisis to take advantage of the situation. And are now making the condition worse to gain control. *If* someone did, they would have to be high ranking enough to aid them in seizing power. Besides, can you think of any who can gain access to the Igigi platforms with Temple Protectorates as their defenders and the Igigi defenses?"

"Did he say Igigi defenses?" Riurrel asked, his tone suspicious.

"Yes, is there a problem?"

"No," Riurrel said, yet to Ikath he sounded as if he was hiding something.

No matter how much he coaxed Riurrel, he behaved as if the remark and his reaction were unimportant. Ikath sensed otherwise and intended to discover why. Now, though, not the time.

The night hour grew late, yet Lord Riciad stood silent in the dark next to him, watching the square come alive. Citizens ambling in the evening's pleasant atmosphere joined with the boisterousness of the feasthall spilling out each time the tent flap opened.

Then, just as suddenly, Lord Riciad spoke. "After meeting Prince Satoric and his group of ambitious, but indolent pleasure seekers, can you believe the rumors they put together something of this magnitude? I will say they are cunning, but if what others hint at is true, this took intelligence to plan. *If* you believe the rumors. I think a natural event occurred, and some blooded or high-ranking guild members took full advantage. The Igigi missed the mark and won't admit their mistake. So, they start a ridiculous rumor, to spread doubt about their incompetence, which is what we on the special counsel are investigating. Not a supposed attack upon them prior to the event."

One of the small silvery holo proclamations leaflets blew their way and Ikath picked it up. Riurrel piped in as he touched it.

"That broadsheet will self-destruct in thirty-six hours. I made a copy. Sent the self-destruct code for review by the Temple Guardians. Before you lecture me, I used the proper means and encapsulated the message with a warning."

It aggravated him when Riurrel popped into his head with no warning. His attention wrenched back to Lord Riciad when he spoke.

"Let's image what the fanciful rumormongers think happened. Prince Satoric and his cronies would be the only ones aiding those in need." He laughed, a soft musical sound which, to Ikath, had an undertone of menace. "And the empire like a starbaked Rital sitting in a pond overheating when the star is high overhead, too late realize they are cooking and perish. Ingenious, would you not say? *If*, they orchestrated the entire thing."

Not sure whether that required an answer from him, he kept silent. Thinking about the remarks the Society priest said earlier. When he hinted at that very thing. Half an hour passed as both listened to a strolling bard singing a song. A favorite throughout the empire, his anti-grav tithe cup floating waist-high next to him, a misty cloud beneath from the super-cooled nitrogen.

"I believe I reconsidered my stance on the Society. Next time a vote comes up, I will vote against them. They are genuine believers. Fanatics. Harmful to themselves more than others. It amazes me time on end when intelligent beings can so easily be duped. They bring about their own destruction by other's far more cunning but not always more intelligent," Lord Riciad said. A hint of laughter in his tone, as if some obscene joke.

"Fanatics can be a dangerous weapon. I hope, if someone is using them, they remember a wild beast will still bite those who feed them," Ikath said. He wondered if the package they came to retrieve would arrive soon.

"Wisely said, my friend. Wisely said." Lord Riciad straightened. "This begins to bore me. Besides, the item we came for arrived earlier."

A burly male commoner bumped into Lord Riciad half an hour ago, apologized, then walked away. He must have been the drop, and he missed it, as his thoughts were elsewhere. Not good.

Riurrel broke in, "I notified the proper authorities through an anonymous channel of the Society priest and his speech. The Temple informed me minutes ago a guardian is here, besides you. They're aware of the situation."

Ikath's attention, caught by Lord Riciad as he looked inside a small bag, grinned broadly, his white teeth easy to view in the dark. Straightened before striding back the way they came without another word, forcing him to scramble to catch up with him. Leaving Ikath once more wondering who Lord Riciad was. One thing he knew. He was not a lowly blooded house male far from succession who got lucky through a disaster. Then accepted within turns of his ascending to said title into the highest spheres of influence.

Yet, from what Ikath learned from his investigations. No one appeared aware of him until recently. What scared Ikath? Who Lord Riciad might really be? Why no recent information about him? As if he popped out of thin air.

Chapter 14

335891 GGS Goem 5th.
Nibiru Proper Agade Ki's Royal Fortification's–Queen Jynnalt

THE QUIET OF THE FORTRESS left her restless, unable to sleep. She stood at her balcony railing, staring up at the vast expanse of brilliant stars against the deep black of the celestial vault over Agade. The disaster forced sudden, unwanted changes to her life. Changes proving to be a trying exercise in court relationships for her, Prince Ryakin, at the top of the list.

Her impressions of Nibiru Proper; a cosmopolitan planet with no substance. She wished over time her opinion would change. The behavior of those in the empire's capital bewildered her and left her in a constant state of shock at the blooded and upper ranking guild master's behavior. She now understood why her father and other blooded houses of the outer kingdoms came to the capital only when tradition or the emperor demanded.

Whispers at court, loud enough for her to hear, followed wherever she went. They called her abrasive, confrontational, haughty. Skyta made it worse by passing around false information to her newfound friends. None of it favorable to Jynnalt. To her, the Imperial court appeared frivolous, immoral, and perverse. The door chimed as Eshin entered. Her signature the only one allowed unlimited access to Jynnalt's private chambers.

"I figured I would find you out here on your balcony."

"I couldn't sleep. What is wrong with me, Eshin? I can't adjust to the court. Every time I try, I fail, or a disaster follows, or I say something, and they look at me as if I am some newly discovered poisonous fungus."

"You're outspoken," Eshin laid a hand on her arm. "Unwilling to follow someone or something because it's popular. Those with no sense of self. Fear those who do. Be proud of who you are, where you come from, what your kingdom stands for. Never change to appease the mob of popularity."

"Easy to say, harder to live by. All my companions are now Lady Razine's," she said, and snorted. "Still, she got Skyta, which is akin to a curse, something I would not wish upon anyone. I like Lady Iacha, but sometimes she embarrasses me when she defends me ever since Niuard, and she is *old*. Since the attack, everyone the Empress asks to attend me declines. They whisper I'm a jinx. I feel as if I am floating in the void without a star to guide me."

"Not in Ki. You need to get the legalities wrapped up and go home where you belong. Do not get misled. Ki stands for faith, honor, and duty. Facts I, your father, and your mentors taught you since you started talking. They are values worth keeping. The Phoenix armor would not accept one it found lacking. In Ki's extensive history, eleven failed. They died horrible deaths, suffocated and burned to a crisp in the armor."

Jynnalt shivered at the thought that might have been her fate.

"The armor accepted you. Have the same faith in yourself. The citizens of Ki, no matter who might say otherwise, will obey only you till your death. Be as strong for them. The Kingdom is your responsibility now."

A comfortable silence fell between them. Eshin, a dark shadow next to her. As she stared into the velvety black vault full of fiery stars, reminding her of the legendary phoenix and its connection to the armor. She relived her terror as she approached the container with the armor and the four ferocious guardians for the test of Queenship. In fact, she almost declined, which was any heir's right.

Kierian myth claimed the armor belonged to the last Phoenix Queen of legend. It stood in a case guarded by statues of resting Phoenix's. Fierce and intimidating beast, three stories high, dominating the middle of the huge royal courtyard open to the public.

Legend held the four guardians would devour any who sought to steal or destroy the armor. Fact or fantasy, who knew? Yet, for over a thousand sars, the armor still stood in the morning light. If the Reigning Queen was alive, the armor remained iridescent black and standing. When the Queen became injured or ill, the armor turned gray. When she died, the armor fell into a heap of ash and stayed ash until it accepted a new Queen.

Stories Jynnalt grew up hearing about the armor ran through her head at the turn of the bonding. She balked, almost refused. Then she heard her mother's laughter at that critical moment, resounding across the silent courtyard. That was the genuine reason she stepped into the container. To prove her mother wrong. To stop her sense of shame, of what, she was not sure. It shamed her to realize she did not do it because she wanted to be Queen. She did it to prove her mother wrong.

The guardians, tall and imposing. For a second when she looked up, she thought they moved, bowed closer to observe her. Weighed her worthiness. The moment passed. *It must be an optical illusion created by the clever way someone built them.* She hesitated a second before stepping in when the clear metal container door opened as if inviting her. She forced herself to move her foot forward and step inside, weak and nauseated as her hands shook before facing out towards those gathered to witness the event.

Nothing happened. She stared at the crowd as they grew restless. Then the ash moved like a living thing, climbing up her limbs from her feet. Slow at first, then faster and faster till it formed over her. Powdery ash invaded her, pouring into her nose, the sense of suffocating overwhelming. Panicked, she tried to leave, yet her limbs would not respond to her command to step out of the booth. Terror gripped her; it was rejecting her.

Her heart raced, and she forced herself to inhale deeply. Ash entered her lungs. Instead of suffocating, a surge of power raced through her limbs. Her breathing eased, and the ash reversed itself back to a pile at her feet. She'd passed the first test.

The door opened, and she stepped out to kneel before the guardian and give a prayer to the gods. Time passed and once more, the packed crowds in the square and on the walls became restless. A sigh of relief, not just from her but the crowd, as the first stirring of ash rose, forming into the Phoenix armor. Now standing witness to her Queenship, a silent sentinel within the container. Only then did the officials and Kierian Temple Priestess proclaim her Queen.

She almost fell over in relief. Now, no matter what else happened, whether the Anunnaki emperor or GIA or the Council of Nine approved her Queenship, the citizens of Ki would accept no other.

"Thinking about the Phoenix Armor." The question startled her out of her thoughts. She forgot Eshin stood next to her. It was a statement, not a question, as if Eshin read her mind.

"There's a reason they train Kierian youths in the sword's art. Why Kierian sword masters still forge metal swords and knives in secret. The forge fires as hot as a dragon's breath by a process known only to Kierian masters. Ki's swords unmatched in quality, even in these technological times." Eshin said.

Jynnalt thought about the one presented to her by her father on her eleventh, first breath turn. Remembered the sword's rich smoky mirror finish. One edge blunt and thick, the other with faint, perceptible wavy lines with a laser-sharp edge. With the lightest touch, it cut deep. Flawless. Everything about it fit her now, though not at eleven. It amazed her how they forged it when she was a child, yet fit her perfectly as an adult. But the Queen of Ki could not demand their secrets. The swords, so well balanced, a novice was dangerous with one.

Men's swords were longer and heavier than females. Both swords, though equal in their ability to inflict terror and death when wielded by the professionally trained in ancient times.

Trained by Caltac' as soon as she stood up and walked, she was no novice. She loved the dance of the swords and participated in the competition during the Kierian festival, and every sar since she turned twelve, she won.

Eshin spoke once more. "Why do you think Kiestrial still produces swords by masters who train for a lifetime? They are no longer useful on the battlefield, not against modern nanite armor with protective low energy shields. Or why do the sword guilds of Kiestrial not lack for orders? Ki's swords prized amongst the wealthiest families and nobles throughout the galaxy. Did you ever wonder why? Tradition and ceremony carry more weight than you might imagine. Think about why your father insisted you train with the best sensial available for hire."

"I am not sure what you mean."

Eshin harrumphed. "Quality. A solid foundation. An anchor. That's what tradition is, to remind you of what has value and to ignore supposedly grand ideas, no matter how appealing. Some things are timeless. As true this turn as in the times of the Phoenix Queens."

The temple, like the outer kingdoms, adhered to the tradition of the art of the sword. Ghost Walkers to this turn still use them under certain circumstances. In fact, the sight of their swords at their backs intimidates the most hardened criminal.

"Eshin, do you ever wonder if you chose the right path for yourself?" Jynnalt asked, staring once more at the inky black of twinkling stars. A sense of dread at what the dawn's turn would bring.

"If you worry only about your needs, you will always find disappointment in life. Family, friends, faith, and your kingdom form the basis of happiness. Life is about challenges. If you turn away and demand an easier life, you will never realize what you're capable of achieving. Besides, who wants a boring life?"

"I never got to hold the title of Arch Dukianess. Why did the house of Airal have to descend from our Original Queen Listiria? Why was Queen Jildius reckless enough to load every single potential heir of her bloodline all in one place? The royal barge," she said, knowing Eshin would not miss the frustration in her voice. Now Lady Razin, her best friend and longtime companion, ascended as the next bloodline holder.

"Why do I resent Razin?" she asked, blurting it out. Her face hot, sick as shame engulfed her.

Eshin's voice was gentle, not what she expected after her outburst. "Deep down you understand Racin did not steal what did not belong to her. As Queen, you cannot hold the title, nor the hereditary lands and property of the Arch Dukian."

"It tears at me. Racin and her family took possession of my home. I now must ask to enter, to go where once I played and swam on beaches. Where I rode through forests on war beast, no longer mine," she said. She thought about places where she and the companions giggled about boys and whispered secrets with each other. Where she trained her entire life to hold a title, she now never would.

"What hurts the worst, the mausoleums of my ancestors, where father lays in sacred ground, no longer am I allowed free access.". She bit her lower lip as her eyes blurred, her fingers dancing across the thin torq around her neck. She realized what she was doing and dropped her hand. The torq a part of her. In all her memory she wore it. The torq was never too large, nor too tight. Why no one understood? No one remembered where it came from or when.

"I'm a stranger now in the home I grew up in. Everything has changed. The Sigils and Silks packed and sent to the Queen's palace. A far more splendid building, but a building I have no connection with," she said, the tone of her voice flat.

"When I was there for the Queenship test, I wandered around and got lost. The elegant, pillared chambers and arched doorways with fancy filigree edging everywhere are beautiful, but so is Airal's ancestral fortress, in its own way. Father would walk around with me telling stories of the mystical beast embossed into the stonework and statues, or the long-ago battles carved within the wood." Her voice wistful. "I recognize every nook and cranny." Her fingers danced across the torq once more.

"The palace is full of long corridors, with hundreds of doors, doors leading to areas I have no clue who they belonged to. What office they might fulfill. The place is like a giant fish viewing tank and just as intrusive. The sense the smallest swipe and it would come crashing down, left me gasping for air."

Eshin, as usual, waiting for her to finish before saying, "I came here to talk to you about several things. These issues are yours to resolve. The reason I came is to tell you I made two requests of Razin. The first is for her to transfer the Dagger of Cineuian to the throne to become the royal flagship. In return, you gave her the Star Runner, the late Queen's royal dreadnought," Eshin said, showing not the slightest shame at claiming the request came from Jynnalt. "The second is you get to keep your highest ranked Paladins and Caltac'. I am aware of how unsettled you are without familiar faces around you. Razin, with her normal grace and understanding, has agreed."

Jynnalt tilted her head, her shoulders slumped. Her hair fell forward, covering the side of her face. "How do I resolve being bitterly ashamed of my selfish attitude, yet I am consumed with burning anger? I find I cannot overcome the thoughts; I now hold towards Razin?" Her throat tightened, and heat burned in her face as she thought about it. The sparkle of stars above withheld whatever secrets they might impart. Not Eshin.

"You became possessive of anything associated with your father after he died. You refused to let the slightest thing change since the death of your father. In your mind, they have now taken all those things you held valuable away from you. You understand there is no malice or intent of harm by Razin's, or on her family's part."

Jynnalt looked over at her. "I hate change. What is wrong with things staying the same?"

"The very essence of life *is change*. You need to let your grief go, or it will consume you. You still search for who murdered your father, and why. I'm afraid if you discover those answers, they might destroy you. It would profoundly grieve your father if that happened. Let the past go. Accept your future. If you do, you will discover once more your friendship with Razin. You must choose whether you will remain in the past or grab your future with both hands. I leave you with your decision. You recognize deep in your heart what is the right choice." She patted her hand, moved to leave, before turning back towards her. "I almost forgot. The replicator in my chambers claims the Cithian tea is no longer available. Someone forgot to reorder it." Without another word, she turned and left.

Tomorrow, all would officially change for her. She would stand before a High Priestess of The Holy Seer Temple of Radiance. At the Anunnaki Empires division, on their tithed homeworld within the Nibiru system. A long-honored tradition. Also, necessary to have the title recognized throughout the Galactic Interstellar Alliance and the Council of Nine.

Jynnalt felt torn. What decision should she make on the morrow? She agonized between her wants and what her sense of duty demanded? She accepted the Queenship of Ki. That placed a burden upon every decision she made. Her first reaction upon learning she would become Queen bordered on abject panic. This marriage was another unexpected obligation, the contract marriage to Prince Ryakin, who disliked her knowing nothing about her confusing.

He brought his ship to close to the beacon. Nor did she order the attack on Niuard. Once, recently, she saw him in the company of a delicate female. One who, if you said boo to, would fall over, who hung on every word a male expounded. Yet, these males flocked around her. He snubbed her when she saw him in the other female's company, and she sensed his friend's made fun of her. Standing off and laughing aloud before looking her direction. She and her original companions stood out like oaks amongst the delicate flowers of the females of the inner kingdoms. Now she stood alone. Though the Empress said she was sending companions for tomorrow's event.

Racin told her she was being too sensitive, which added to her evolving resentment towards her. In the past, Racin normally jumped to her defense. Now she's more concerned with her new position than being her friend. Racin even inherited Jynnalt's companions. Leaving Jynnalt surrounded by females, she lacked comparable moral grounds. At least until the fateful attack on Niuard. Females now avoided wanting to stand as her companion, though it could advance their marriage prospects spectacularly. Now she stood alone in a crowded sea of ranking blooded.

Jynnalt determined to do the right thing. Yet, conflicted. The contract sealed by the kingdom of Ki and Tc. Tc enforced their claim as no actual specific name appeared on the contract. Only the terminology stating the Queen of Ki. Both Kingdom's councils agreed. Ki would pay a heavy penalty if she rejected the marriage contract. Her first function as Queen would place a financially burdened on the Kierian citizens.

Her thoughts wavered back and forth as the night progressed. A terrible battle raged for hours within her mind as she stared at the stars burning in the velvet black vault above.

The thoughts about how her father sacrificed his wants, so those he swore his oath stayed protected and prospered. A ranking blooded's duty, her father told her, must rise above their own needs. Honor demanded a blooded always does what's right for the benefit of the house and those they serve, not for themselves, as he explained to her once. "Your choices define you and those you're sworn to oversee. I would not you children," he ran his hand over her head, "my greatest happiness in life if I did not marry your mother. A sacrifice can produce great happiness. You must make the first to receive the second."

He moved away to his bookshelf. Real metal leaf books. "I enjoy many friends and hobbies which fulfill me. I'm happy, satisfied with my life. Besides, with three children, your mother and I can avoid each other within reason."

Once she convinced herself to sign the contract of marriage, during the next turns official events, peace-filled her. She collapsed into her pillows; sound asleep as soon as she lay her head on the pillow.

Chapter 15

RYAKIN STALKED INTO his brother's chamber, throwing his cloak over the chair as he flung himself down. Yanked the chalice full of mead from the server's hand, splashing the liquid on his newest over doublet and shirt, before tossing the rest back. Then motioned the server for a refill. Rualui nodded towards the guild server as he sat back in his chair, linking his hands over his stomach.

"Rather late, is it not? I expected you earlier."

Ryakin familiar with the tone. It meant a lecture, and he'd bet this marriage contract the key aspect. He wanted to discuss the matter as well. His resentment rose. Rualui preachy over responsibility and honor. Ryakin believed in those virtues yet believed his brother tougher on him because of their father's failings. He learned over the sars to beat his brother to whatever the lecture might entail. Go on the offensive. Land the first punch.

"How is this female, Jynnalt, ever to rule as wealthy a kingdom as Ki? Many allege her manners are worse than a commoner. She blurts out whatever enters her head. Rumor claims she behaved in a manner unfitting an Arch Duchianess, let alone a Queen, at the opening festival ceremony?"

His brother remained silent, watching him, forcing him to keep talking. Ryakin stood and leaned forward on the front of the desk his brother sat behind. "She embarrassed our house and Jena's."

Ryakin thought his brother would defend his wife instinctively. Though a normal arranged marriage, contracted when they were children, his brother loved his wife with a passion rare amongst the titled. He did not rise to the bait, so Ryakin rushed on. "I heard before she even entered the court entertainments, she acted like a herd beast before the butcher's knife."

His brother held up a hand, stopping his tirade. "Because of your tardiness." Rualui stared at Ryakin for a moment before continuing. "Something happened while we waited for you to arrive. The wretched incident put her mother in a foul mood. Speaking of lacking in the social graces. What was so important you could not show up for the opening ceremonies? I specifically asked you to accompany her and her relatives. I wanted to announce the fulfillment of the original contract with Ki. Did you deliberately show disrespect, or were you just thoughtless? I'm hoping it's the latter."

He realized if he told his brother he was with their uncle, a fight would ensue. Rualui did not approve of their uncle and his companions. Influential friends who could enrich Tc far more than a wealthy outer border Queen. No matter how prosperous.

Ryakin enjoyed Lady Wiante and her gentle nature and acceptable social demeanor. Who wanted a wild, uncouth jinx for a wife? No sane male, he knew. Lady Wiante suggested, more than once after the disaster when Queen Jildius died, Tc should demand a release from the earlier contract.

"First, why did you not inform me you would use the event to announce the old contract between Ki's Queen and myself still valid? Second, If I'd been aware. I would have been on time."

"My vyzier informed me he notified you through the official fleet channels. He showed me the acknowledgement receipt."

Ryakin's eyes narrowed. His brother never lied. But he never received the message either. One more thing to investigate in his growing list of late. For now, he would keep this to himself.

"I went to the Cary Travelers station's feasthall, the Crafty Rebel. A bard my classmates and I are fond of promoted as playing there," he said.

Thankfully true, his colleagues were present for the show. He left out the fact his uncle and associates were also present. If only his brother did not feel such contempt for his uncle, he would see the truth. Rualui thought Ugallu and his friend's ideas dangerous, which might bring ruin to their house and Kingdom.

So, for now, Ryakin thought it best to hedge the facts. His brother relaxed back in his seat. So Ryakin hammered home his point.

"Others informed me she treated the newest Arch Duchianess as if she were diseased? Someone told me they are best friends. Gods forbid, how she would act if you were an enemy. Worse, the hand she placed on my arm when we were first introduced was sweating. Disgusting," he walked over and got another drink from the refreshment table before he started back on his complaints. "She spoke to people she should not while ignoring several important matrons, who believe me, are already spreading tales of her lack of manners."

His brother seemed to listen, so he went on, "her mother reproached her about her conversation's subjects over three times and warned her there are topics not suitable for polite company. At one point, she stuttered an answer when the Empress asked her a question. Later, she did not acknowledge Lady Wiante when presented to her, so busy talking about her heroic deeds during the disaster. The next turn one of her companion's and a matron her mother is friends with informed me."

His brother fiddled with his drink, sitting on the table before him, not looking at him but his liquor.

"Lucky for us, the Empress thought her endearing and chastised, those horrified by her actions. Her own mother mortified by her conduct. Princess Tesiskel implied to Lady Wiante, Lady Airal is tactless and self-centered, believes the galaxy revolves around her needs. What kind of person is she when her own parent is ashamed of her conduct? It humiliated me each time someone approached with tales of her conduct. Believe me, the death of Queen Jildius a disaster for the Kingdom of Ki."

When he stood to get a drink after his rushed rant, he recognized the anger on his brother's face.

"Maybe the fault lies with the mother and not the daughter. Jena dislikes Princess Tesiskel with a loathing I have rarely seen her display towards another. Did you consider Lady Airal might not understand the finer points of court protocol? Remember, they crowned her in Ki less than three months ago before arriving here for the official crowning by the Emperor and The Temple. Right after the catastrophe, she spent her time helping Agade and the commoners get back on their feet." Rualui said, his gait still stiff from his injury. The injury he suffered while aiding one of his lesser blooded during the emergency still healing, walked over to the glass wall holding his collections of recorded meh's. The subjects covered everything from myths and fables to history, math, science, and engineering, along with some others of pure entertainment meant to idle away boring hours. He doubted his brother expected much idle time.

Rualui ordered his most recent meh to play. The ruins of the capital after the last meteorite hit flared to life, floor to ceiling, where the wall became a three-dimensional projector.

Red and brown dust swirled to the dance of the wind, as if rushing to claim the city for its own. Burning buildings, vague outlines through the haze of ash and smoke-filled background. Jagged-saw-toothed buildings glimpsed for a second before disappearing as if the wind wanted to hide the damage from prying eyes.

"This is where you're soon to be bride spent her first couple of months. She helped the needy, making sure food deliveries got to starving commoners. Imperial commoners who she's not obligated to help. Brought in life tenders from anywhere and everywhere to aid those who were in need, no matter their rank," his brother said, a hard edge to his tone. "She did not attend entertainments and theater with the rest of the female blooded who went about their daily affairs little affected by the disaster. From the shocked looked on your face, you did not even bother to check on her whereabouts and speaks volumes about your character."

The harshness coming from his brother stung, even if true. Ryakin sat with crossed arms and stared at the images. He refused to meet his brother's eyes. Not sure now what to think.

"Jena brought this to my attention when I forbid her to do the same. Believe me, I argued long and hard with her, winning the argument only because she is carrying our first child." He took a drink before continuing. "Jena's impressed by Jynnalt. Not a simple thing to accomplish, as you know. Jena detests the inner high-ranking females; thinks they are lazy and self-indulgent. Believes, they should learn a little humility. You're soon to be bride did not flinch from arduous work. Or talking to commoners to discover their needs," his brother said. He limped back to his chair and sat, taking a deep drink from his chalice. "A quality of far more value in a Queen to my thinking than well-trained etiquette."

Ryakin eyed the chalice and wondered if Jena medicated the mead. He did not question for one second. She would do so, especially if his brother avoided the life tenders. The wound should have healed before now. He would talk to Jena if his brother's limp did not heal over the next fortnight. In public, none would suspect his brother in pain, as he hid the fact well. Ryakin bet with all the overtaxed repair units used for the disaster, his brother doubtless refused to use one when he thought there were others with worse injuries.

Rualui began once settled, "They did not train her to be a Queen. The outer border kingdoms expect their Arch Dukianess or Dukians, depending on whom the heir is, to be their defenders. Their Kingdom's Fleets, turn after turn, fight against bandits, pirates, and reavers. Inner Kingdoms Fleets fight in FR battles and brag about their skills. I'm telling you, they'd not last long against the border fleets. That is why they demand they leave court affairs to their Queen, her consort, and the councils of the kingdom." Ryakin saw him shift in his chair, trying to get comfortable. "In no one's wildest thoughts did anyone suspect she'd become Queen. Too many ahead of her in the line of succession. Give her a chance to adjust. They taught her battle strategies, tactics, and survival, which is far less complex than the intrigue of courtly arts with its layers of subtle innuendo and backstabbing politics. She will settle with the proper support from her councilors and advisors. And her Consort," his brother said, as he stared him straight in the eye.

"It takes more than settling. You need intelligence, courage, and astuteness to rule. You taught me that, remember? Father never settled to his title, proving even those born to a position cannot always gain the required abilities. Look how father left Tc and our house."

Rualui rose from his chair and leaned forward. With great care, he placed his chalice on the desk. Ryakin knew he was only that deliberate when angry and attempting to keep from lashing out.

"Do not speak of father that way. You do not know all the facts, nor did you spend time with him. You were too young. You do not understand what and why our father died or how the Kingdom ended up in this situation after his death."

Ryakin realized his brother thought he overstepped, again. Decided it wisest to discuss something else.

His brother always insinuated there was more to the story, yet never elaborated. He figured this the only way his brother could defend their father, who he adored and loved. Ryakin pitied him in this one area where he could not recognize the facts before him. Hoping one turn, his brother would see the truth like everyone else.

Ryakin changed the discussion. "Ugallu, claims with the death of Queen Jildius the contract is void. Ki's council should annul the contract as well as Tc."

Rualui walked back over to the refreshment table. Ryakin understood he did it to calm himself. He studied him as he poured more mead. Aware his brother intended to drop the subject, and he relaxed. Ryakin hated fighting with him.

"Our uncle," Rualui enumerated each word, "does not always have our families or Tc's best interest at heart. One turn you will understand. For now, I am asking you to make peace with your soon to be bride and the newest Queen of Ki. I believe she's more intelligent and courageous than your aware. Stop listening to gossips. Show your support and take a hand in helping to guide her about court etiquette. Help her become a Queen." Rualui said, sitting back and getting comfortable once again. "However, that is not the reason I called you here. You jumped to the conclusion it's about your upcoming contract ceremony. I leave the decision to you; I trust you will make the right one. I just ask you not be hasty in your decision."

His brother an expert at guilt. He ignored everything he said. Just dropped the decision on his head, knowing he would do as his brother asked. *Drog* him.

"I wanted to be the one to tell you something you won't like. I did not want you to discover this from a passing gossiper. Like your friend Ustrix, who has an uncanny way of discovering something even if encrypted and classified seconds after sealed." Ryakin laughed, and the tension eased between them.

"Never have figured out how he does it, nor have the others, and we all tried to pry his methods out of him." Ryakin stretched, needing to move, sensing he would not like what his brother wanted to tell him.

"I've ordered Ugallu to the Galactic Interstellar Alliance council as an envoy to the Eithincore Empire for Tc. We need more Orichalcum. They offer the cheapest for the new fleet ships, so I can build as soon as you honor the contract with Ki, and they deliver the first payment. Ryakin, this contract to Ki's Queen is of vital importance to Tc. Father had no time before he died—-"

Cutting him off, Ryakin walked back towards him. "I am sure you meant to say committed suicide."

The brothers standing inches apart when the door opened.

"Am I interrupting something?" She looked from one to the other.

"No. We are discussing family matters. The normal disagreement," Rualui said as he sat once more.

"With the normal impasse, I see," she said, moving to his brothers' side.

He observed his brother relax in her presence and forced himself to sit down and pick up his chalice, taking a deep drink. Rualui moved to the refreshment table once more, yet left his mead chalice there, filling a different one with crystal clear water before coming back and sitting. Jena, on the arm of his chair, stroked his hair. Ryakin grasped the fact he craved the closeness of his brother and wife's marriage.

"The second reason I required your presence, I need a favor. An old friend of the family came asking for help. He wants an introduction to Lady Airal once she is crowned. You met him once before, the Rider Kiah Sian. I discussed the matter with Queen Jildius after she arrived, but" he shrugged his shoulders, "With everything that occurred, I forgot to discuss the matter with Lady Airal. Kiah arrived this morning. I informed him you could make the introductions. I already secured his appearance at the contract ceremony with the Temple. This is important. Important enough, he will add Tc to his galactic pod's route if he gains what he needs."

The implications staggering to Ryakin. A galactic pod brought untold wealth to a kingdom or empire. All benefited. From the highest to the lowest.

"What is he wanting? Why can't Tc provide what he is looking for?" Ryakin said.

"Because of the way they pass along the leadership of their pod. This leaves Kiah with no legal heir."

Ryakin thought a moment before saying, "The last time I met Kiah, he told me he has three sons and five daughters. You're telling me he has no heir amongst them?" His brows drew down as he looked at his brother. "Unless I am thinking of the wrong person.'"

"No, you are thinking correctly. However, only a male with the Rider's gene, who can also impress a Sailor can inherit the pod. His sons are carriers of the gene, but testing proved they cannot impress, which removed them from leading the pod. Three of his daughters have the gene, however, females only impress female Sailors. The adopted male will eventually marry one of his daughters per their laws. This keeps the pod's bloodlines within the leadership's succession. Kiah, legally, by rider law, can adopt any child with the gene and the ability to impress and make him his heir. Ki's small pod, servicing the empire, shows an extraordinary impression rate amongst their offspring. He believes there is a shot at finding a male child with the gene."

"So why not just ask the Kierian pod Riders if they will allow him to adopt one of theirs?" Ryakin asked curiously.

"Pods are very cagey about their children. If any are born with the gene, they need them for their own pods. They will rarely hand over their children to an outside pod, no matter how prestigious. Would you give up a child to another house so they could have an heir? This is the quandary for him. However, they might consider the request if the Queen of Ki asked. Not, I might add, if she demands it, then they would refuse, make sure she understands. Still, they respect the Queens of Ki. Unusual amongst Riders, to say the least. She might at least give him a chance to present his case. That is all he is asking. An introduction through the Queen to her local Riders," Rualui said.

His brother never sought a favor before, so it inclined Ryakin to do this, particularly as this seemed such a simple thing. As soon as he realized he agreed to do as his brother asked, it also meant he would fulfill the contract. *Drog,* how does his brother always maneuver him so easily?

"Are you staying for a late dinner? I can have it served in our private quarters," Jena asked as she rose from the arm of the chair.

"No, I am about to leave," Ryakin said, grabbing his cloak from the chair. "When is our uncle supposed to be back?" he asked as he flung his cloak over his shoulder, the night now turning cold. The warmth of the earlier turn long past. The chill of evening descended as the wind increased.

"Depending on how fast he accomplishes the goal, maybe a sar or two."

Ryakin stiffened. He always got that his brother was not fond of their uncle, though he never explained why. This went beyond not agreeing on most subjects. This action appeared vindictive on his brothers' part. He suspected his brother resented how close he and his uncle were.

As if reading his thoughts, his brother said, "you need time to find your own way, not the direction our uncle keeps trying to push you. Please, for me, for our kingdom, try to make this marriage work. Give her time to learn and grow," Rualui said, standing. Jena giving him her support by wrapping her arm around his waist casually.

"I will do this. But not for you. I will do what is necessary for Tc. Something father, who you defend so fiercely, never did."

With that said, he took his leave. Once outside, he strode towards his fleet quarters, his mood foul. Passing the palatial home of the Arch Dukian Lord Seilinia Avilus'Aos he ran into Lady Wiante, leaving the entertainments. He decided instead to take her offer to join her in making the late social rounds of the evening. First, she suggested they head to her quarters to replace her over-cloak as the one she wore damaged by careless service personnel.

Chapter 16

DAWN BROKE ACROSS THE horizon as they landed at the water dock of the Temple world, sitting below the equator on the island of Pyricanth. The automatic holo drone shuttle pilot came over the speakers, "Destination reached, transferring control to High Temple dock command. Most never paid attention to whether a live or drone pilot controlled their shuttles or barges."

The pilot blinked out as the Temple controls took over, leaving Jynnalt uneasy. One of her quirks, she kept to herself, a dislike of automated drones' pilot.

"I prefer a live pilot, no matter how excellent these *droging* drones fly," Racin complained to no one in particular. When they landed the shuttle, the door opened to heavy white fog engulfing the bay. The jungle canopy peeking out of the mists eerie as if floating on the mist, hiding the lush forest beneath. Dark, jagged-edged mountains rose high into the sky on either side of the bay. The early dawn's hazy fog leaving the rising star, frosted and ethereal.

On the beach, fog swirled and flowed, the normal stifling heat of the turn still cool. She got a peek at a river flowing into the bay. Dark black sands glistened under the silvery fog as it slid back, exposing what lay underneath. The encompassing moisture heavy with every breath. In the distance, a massive volcanic mountain named Arichicile, which this world was famous, towered high above the land, dark green jungle dressing its flanks. The white-capped crown still evident during the season of heat.

Lady Racin standing behind her said, "it has a strange appeal."

Before Jynnalt could answer, Ryakin's shuttle arrived, Silks and Sigils flashing on the hull. Landing in a flourish, spraying water across Racin and her in the ramp's doorway and the Temple Priestesses on the wharf.

"He got a live pilot. No drone flies like that," Racin said. A hint of resentment in her voice and admiration for the pilot's skill as droplets of water ran down her cloak unnoticed.

Jynnalt said nothing, afraid her cursing might insult the Temple Priestess. She kept her head up, ignoring the fact the shuttle landing drenched her and Razin.

The other shuttle's landing ramp lowered and Ryakin stepped out. Not bothering to see if the flashy landing caused damage to his soon to be bride and her party.

The attending priestess motioned for Jynnalt and her party to disembark. Screaming and hooting calls floated across the treetops, which reached long shadowy fingers towards the beach. Strange undulating eerie sounds followed by quick coughing grunts and barking noises came from within the verdant jungle. A broad gray magnetic crystalline stone track led from the landing wharf into the emerald canopy of trees.

Ryakin's party, by tradition, loaded in the front repulser barge, a long rectangular box, the bottoms highly magnetic, sat grounded in a cleared area farther in from the bay. More barges than Jynnalt saw anyplace outside the markets. When she and her party entered the one reserved for her, the barge rose inches off the ground and the walls turned translucent, allowing her to view the outer landscape.

For an hour they traveled, coasting along the negatively charged track, climbing along the mountain trail, following a twisting, torturous path. Cool, filtered, recycled air hid the oppressive heat of the jungle from the occupants. The thick interlaced overhead canopy of the trees strangled out the smallest attempt of starlight to find its way to the jungle floor. Heavy undergrowth moved and shook as creatures stalked beside them. The subtle bioluminous lighting from the barge's bright beacons in the gloomy jungle. Their entourage reminded her of the giant glow centipedes from her home in Kestrel. Or what once was home.

The higher the path rose, the farther apart the trees grew. Here and there, strange stones mixed with enormous, scattered boulders and stunted trees as the jungle thinned. They crested a ridge and starlight blinded her for a second.

Beneath them, a broad valley opened before her, ordered and peaceful, patchwork squares of waving cereal crops, colorful vegetable gardens and orchard trees lay spread before her. The lower hills growing rows upon rows of Vining plants in perfect lines on the sides of the mountain. Terraced lands higher up comprised rice paddies and grain crops. The imposing mountain rose high into the clouds straight ahead, its immense upper flanks covered in a swirling mist from hot springs scattered on its flanks. Massive dark stone fortifications crowned the craggy heights.

Grazing herds of animals and riding beasts' insignificant dots in the distant open meadows of soft rolling hills and lush green grasses.

From this vantage, the homes appeared as if a child's toys. Long, clear buildings with a riot of colors sat beside them. At the highest end of the valley, a giant ziggurat rose. Behind it, a rainbow misted waterfall tumbled to the river behind. The river emerged in front of the ziggurat and bisected the valley in a long silvery rope along a winding path. Three-quarters of the way across the valley, the river curved to the left, hidden from her sight. Starlight shimmered off several immense lakes and ponds sustained by estuaries. Thunderous sounds of an unseen waterfall to her left. The sound loud inside the barge. The track dropped towards the valley and followed along the river's edge, bordered with cultivated trees, leaving the jungle behind. The view created a sense of peace, reminding her of home. Her father and she loved the valley and foothills below their fortress. They both stood many times on the high walls in silence as the star sank beneath the horizon, bathing the land in a radiant golden patina.

A rustle of clothing and whispered voices broke her sense of peace, reminding her of why she was here. Ryakin's lead barge started on the twisty road cut into the side of the ridge. Once they reached the bottom, the road leveled. Trees hung heavy with fruits and nuts as workers collected their bounty to put in tall, weaved baskets beside them. Her brow furrowed until she remembered the Temple forbid any metal or composite machinery to process their food. They used various herdbeast to work the land along with wooden and stone sharpened equipment or obsidian scythes and blades. Even their fishing boats were wooden with sails or oars. Metals were for war. Something the Temple excelled at when called upon to defend their followers and the faithful. Metals were also for deepspace items and ships.

As they floated past those working in the field, they paid no attention to them, intent upon their work. Temporary quarters were ready and set up for them by a young priestess when they arrived. A half-hour later, Jynnalt stood, heat sick from the oppressive warmth streaming into her assigned quarters. Her stomach churned, and dizziness assailed her. Starlight coming from round tall windows cast shadowed crosses on the floor. The sensation she was drowning with each breath she took gripped her.

Her guild servers searched in vain for the chamber's controls. Not finding them, the oldest one rushed off in search of one of the lower priestesses to discover how they could get cool air into Jynnalt's quarters. The server came back with an angry expression on her face.

"That priestess had the nerve. Told me minor discomfort wouldn't kill us."

Jynnalt realized they were all staring at her while she was prostrate on the plush couch and stood. She thought she would die as sweat poured down her sides and back. The scorching breeze coming in through the chamber's open door from the hallway's worse, not better. She swayed on her feet, feeling sick as her stomach roiled. She kept gulping air and bent forward, trying to keep from passing out.

One of the other guild servers rushed in through the doorway.

"Down the hallway is a courtyard with an enormous water fountain. Cool and comfortable, with benches spread throughout.

Minutes later, following the attendant, she turned toward the courtyard. A blast of a refreshing breeze of cool air hit her. Her stomach settled; her head cleared. Sighs of relief and delight came from the guild servers and her party, their arms full of what they needed to prepare her.

Razine blurted, "I shall kill anyone who tries to remove me from here before the ceremony." And plopped herself on a bench, a huge smile on her face, her eyes closed with pleasure.

Hours later, a priestess found them and informed them Jynnalt needed to head to the ceremony's platform. Twenty minutes afterward, Jynnalt stood before the assembled guests and representatives. The high priestess of the Anunnaki Temple crowned her while her attendants, and the GIA and Council of Nine's official's witnesses the event.

A scorching breeze ruffled her colorful robes, tugged at her tortuously braided hair. The high priestess placed a thin filigree crown, shaped like two Phoenix's with their wings spread wrapping around her head. Wingtips meeting at the base of her skull and the center of her forehead. Their head and beaks entwined at the top of her head. A small blood-red jewel hung down from the tips of the wings to sit in the middle of her forehead. Her torq throb as soon as the priestess placed the crown upon her.

Now came the sealing of the marriage contract. The part she dreaded.

As Ryakin joined her, a fierce burst of blistering wind blew across the platform. Searing her skin as if from a sword maker's kiln door when opened, and she swayed on her feet. The High Priestess, oblivious, asked, "if you consent to this contract, holdout your left hand for the mixing of blood."

Silence descended. Fear crept to the surface. The hiss of whispers thunderous. Ryakin's lips tighten, yet she stood frozen, incapable of saying anything, or move her left hand with the marriage tattoos, towards the Priestess.

Ryakin did something she never expected. He leaned forward, smiled a heartwarming smile, reaching all the way to his appealing sky-blue eyes and whispered, "Don't worry, I'm terrified as well."

Startled, the corners of her mouth turned up, and she pressed them together to keep from bursting out laughing. The remark so unexpected coming from him.

She turned towards the High Priestess, held out her hand to her, which she nicked, and Jynnalt's blood flowed across her palm. The Priestess turned towards Ryakin. Asking him if he consented?

He handed her his hand. The Priestess cut his palm, then placed both their hands together, binding them with a cloth. "With this, the mingling of your blood, you both swear to honor the contract as negotiated in good faith?"

"Yes," she answered, followed by Ryakin's agreement. The Priestess declared them joined.

Hours later, they signed the official meh's and got them recorded in all the legal libraries. Another priestess led them to a massive outdoor courtyard with viewing platforms around the edges. At the four corners were massive ornate marble pillars. Actual flames danced on top of the pillars and a bright bonfire blazed in the center of the square, lending a hypnotic and strangely primitive impression. Friends and guests, forbidden by tradition to attend the official ceremony, now join the entertainments in the courtyard.

Jynnalt amazed how chilly the air was as the star settled behind the horizon after the torturous heat earlier in the turn. Purple and green waving lights in the sky from the world's magnetic pole reflected off the snowcapped top of the volcano. The temperature must drop fast because of the high altitude, she thought, as she wandered over to a viewing platform of black granite. She climbed the stairs and gazed across the valley as Ryakin moved to join his friends and family. Her mother enjoying gossiping with the Ladies of his house, amusing them with anecdotes of uncouth outer border kingdoms, and customs.

Ryakin stood in the middle of his friends, ignoring her once more. She should have realized his kindness during the ceremony a trick. He wanted to make her accept him. Worried she would back out, and the orichalcum talons promised to his brother, King of Tc, to build a new fleet would slip through their fingers.

From houses, white smoke drifted skyward. The faintest scent of sweet woods upon the air. She closed her eyes and inhaled while standing before this bucolic scene while shadows lengthened and deepened to darkness, claiming the valley from the starlight of the turn. She stood watching as luminous lights bloomed inside buildings and along walkways, crisscrossing the valley, defiant of the night. The sight enchanting to Jynnalt. She turned towards the sounds of footsteps and recognized a friend of Ryakin's, though she could not remember his name. Accompanied by a Rider she did not know walking towards her. She caught the tail end of their conversation as they got closer.

"They say they are investigating the rumors," the Rider said. He had light blue skin and was short by galactic standards. Her first impression deep laugh lines in a craggy face and eyes full of kindness. When he looked up at her, he gave her an impression of someone full of humor. Yet in the flickering firelight, she acknowledged she could be wrong. A long-hooked nose and curly long yellow-white hair pulled back at the nape of his neck hinted towards him being a citizen of Ercinia or a similar star system.

The male's voice reminded her of her father, not in timber but in the quiet, measured tone. Riders wore simple clothes from the common hempumulus plant. Pants tucked inside knee-high herdbeast skin boots, and an overshirt stopping mid-thigh cinched by a braided herdbeast skin belt at his waist. The runic symbol of his pod embossed on the bulky belt buckle. Unpretentious. The normal array of extensive weapons Riders normally wore not allowed on Temple grounds. As they got closer, she detected he wore a Rider's badge, confirming her thoughts. Not any badge, but a galactic pod leaders' badge.

In Kiestrial, Ki's capital systems, the small local pod dressed the same. Riders give up their birth homes, allegiance once accepted, hence the same style of clothing across the galaxy. Ki's pod's migratory route did not range far out of Anunnaki Empire. Their Riders spent time at Kestrel and the Duchy of Airal. They claimed the Duchy provided the best hospitality in the empire, something her house prided itself on.

She remembered Ryakin's friend's name as he stepped forward, Ustrix, who bowed his head with respect

"I would like to introduce Kiah Tis Sian. Of the inner galactic pod Cloaking Shadows, Rider of Mercurial, the pod's leader.

Kiah bowed his head with proper deference before looking her straight in the eye. "Your Highness, your hair is like a fiery waterfall. I spotted you when you arrived earlier this morning." The heat rose in her cheeks, and she looked down at her hands. The sound of her mother's voice moving towards them replaced the warmth with a cold stiffness.

"Yes, and hard to tame, thick wiry and knots at the slightest provocation. And her eyes, such a weird green color. I swear, sometimes I don't believe she's, my child. Unlike her sister, whose hair is like the softest silk, and the purest white. I don't even have to put a rinse on to help her keep her hair color. Her eyes are the softest lovely pink of Agade's sky at star rise. Not to mention, my youngest daughter's delicate size." Tesiskel, standing next to Jynnalt, reached up and laid her hand on her shoulder, emphasizing her tall, gangly frame compared to her mother's petite one.

"You love your children no matter what their faults, wouldn't you agree?" She looked at Kiah and smiled sweetly, a smile which normally melted males to her bidding.

From the expression on Kiah's face, Jynnalt suspected he wasn't falling for it. *Good for him.* Before he could counter with a remark, Ryakin strolled up and joined their gathering, saying, "I find her perfect." He stared straight at her, and the heat from Kiah's earlier comment become fire as a flutter tripped across her stomach. Her eyebrows scrunched together. *Helc, why'd he say that?*

Jynnalt observed her mother's face go from an enchanting smile to a frigid one. The smile fixed, her eyes blazing. Jynnalt became apprehensive, knowing the outcome. Few targets of her mother's anger argued back. Including her. She swallowed and stared at the ground. She found herself the focus of the destructive aftermath too many times since her father died, and tried not to make it worse. Though truthfully, she failed at the effort more than succeeded.

"How very enlightened of you Ryakin," Tesiskel said in a tone Jynnalt understood well. She turned back to the scenery of fiery stars above and the lights in the valley.

Her mother's voice soft and melodious, underlain with steel. "Who would view their bride in a negative light on their joining turn?" She shrugged as if ridiculing what he said. "She is lucky to have such a gallant husband," laying a hand on Ryakin's arm. "We make do with what we have."

Jynnalt sensed her mother's eyes upon her and, as if to spite her, her mother said, "I hope you can break some of her worst habits. I could not. Her father spoiled her for far too long... before he died."

Jynnalt overheard Kiah tell Ustrix he would like to meet the other ranking blooded present. He stated he wanted to form contracts with many of them if all went as he hoped. Soon afterward, I will join my pod in orbit. My mate tells me the pod's restless at the time spent in this system.

As Kiah and Ustrix moved down the stairs, their voices carried to those standing on the platform. "I was unaware mothers of the Anunnaki Empire ate their young. Queen Airal should not tolerate that behavior. To do so makes her appear weak."

Ustrix's answer floated up to them. "When Tesiskel's husband died, she reverted to her birth title of Imperial Princess. By not remarrying, she keeps her birth title. Ki, as an outer border kingdom, has less political importance in the empire, though very wealthy. Technically, her mother exceeds her rank as an Imperial princess," whatever else he said lost in the crush of blooded well-wishers. Jynnalt glanced sideways and discerned her mother's autocratic expression as she nodded her direction. *Drog*, she is making sure I understand my place, Queen or not.

A priestess announced the food served. The guests and officials moved towards the tables, brought in while they were speaking, laden with aromatic meats of all varieties and in rich sauces made with spices from across the galaxies' Temple lands. Fresh fruits and vegetables, grown on the Temple lands, overflowing. They served wines of various vintages with dinner. There were also exotic hard alcohols, that few drank in strange distinctive bottles from far off empires or kingdoms.

The conversation settled down to households and children or FR games and politics. Till the Temple Priestess and Priest put on a traditional holo theater, about first joining's. Afterward, drinks and formal dancing ensued. Of which King Rualui and his wife, as the highest-ranking blooded present, took the floor by themselves until they completed the first formal round of the dance. The last dance reserved for only Ryakin and Jynnalt.

Tesiskel excused herself and left with a small group of her friends halfway through the festivities. Her mother leaving before the last dance, shocking to the others present. Whispered voices and glances shot her direction as if she herself broke some unspoken rule.

She ignored them, something she was excellent at doing of late. Still, the relief of tension intense as she scrutinized her mother and friends leave, laughing and joking amongst themselves. Shame seared through Jynnalt, like a virus that returns when she least expects.

Towards the end of the entertainment, most broke off into small, more intimate groups. Leaving Jynnalt standing by herself for several moments, till approached again by the male Rider Kiah.

"Would you like a walk in the gardens? I noted how intent you were upon the view earlier."

Jynnalt glanced to where Prince Ryakin stood, a grin on his face at something someone in his group said.

"I asked permission to approach you for a walk, besides your Paladins will be with us, I assume," he said. Glancing back at the nine paladins located spread throughout the small crowd standing around the dance floor.

"I find your customs concerning females strange. Female Riders make their own choices and believe me, no one dares to tell them what to do. Nor do they have males following them around to protect them," he chuckled. "I pity anyone who might think they are helpless." He said. He led her down towards the steps at the far back, leading to the garden. The soft sounds of a burbling creek blended with serenading cricidades and other night insects.

The gas giant this world orbited lit the two moons overhead. "They call this area the garden of life." The twinkle of moonlight glinted off the fast-flowing creek. "There," he pointed, "flow's the waters of life. The Tree of life located higher up the mountain inside the fortress of the Temple."

"I'm not helpless either." Jynnalt blurted in response to his earlier statement. "And I'm well-trained in personal and fleet combat. Tradition demands sacrifices from everyone. Though annoying, I must admit." Jynnalt inclined her head in his direction. "I believe you have more than complaints about my culture to talk with me about, or that you craved my company for a walk." Jynnalt said as she moved over to a glowing white flower and inhaled, its scent sweet and intoxicating.

"You are like Rider females, right to the point which I find refreshing after time spent in your society," he said as Jynnalt turned back to him.

"I will also get straight to the point. I need an heir."

Jynnalt's paladins moved up close, almost crowding her. "Ah," she tried not to frown but failed, tried to think of something witty to say, but words stuck in her throat.

"No, no, no, I believe I stated that incorrectly," he rushed on, "as you know, I am a Rider. We cannot pass on the leadership of the pod to an heir without the gene, yet the heir must also be capable of impressing a Solar Sailor. Past the age of one sar, scans can reveal if they have the gene and can impress. If we do not produce a child with the proper abilities, we may adopt one." He talked faster, realizing he still had not corrected the first impression, afraid he would be interrupted, and she would leave before he got to make his request. "Under normal circumstances, we can find a child in our own pod with the gene. For reasons I don't have time to state, impossible for now. The other option is to find a pod willing to allow an outside pod to adopt one of theirs with the gene and the ability to impress."

Jynnalt relaxed. This was something she understood, as the Anunnaki pods, in the Kestrel's system, spent time at her past home, she understood their strange ways and laws. "I see. Ki's pod. You want to make an offer to ally with them for an heir. Why not just approached their leader instead of me? Why this request outside the pod?"

"Other Riders informed me your late father, and you built a history of excellent relations with the local pod and its leaders. Added to the fact you are now Queen of Ki, which the Anunnaki pods esteem. I hoped if you asked, respectfully, for an introduction for me, the pod might consider my plight."

Jynnalt heard a touch of desperation in his tone. "I will not order them to aid you." She stopped before him, looking him in the eye, "I will not endanger Ki's excellent relations with our pod for a stranger."

"I am just asking for an introduction. And a polite request on your part, they consider my request.

"I *might* accommodate your request, however, let me think for a

191

moment," Jynnalt said.

He walked silently beside her. She realized he ignored her status as queen. Yet found she was unoffended. Oddly, this made her feel normal. That sensation missing for a long time. She disregarded his breech of etiquette.

What does it hurt to ask? As long as he does not demand they give up a child with the gene.

She stopped, turning towards him. "I shall send your request tomorrow to the pod leader and make your offer. It is up to them if they receive you or not. Make no demands, though. I will ban you from Ki if you do. Understand?" To Jynnalt, if he was honest, his request could do no harm. Still, she wanted him to understand how seriously she took her duties to those of Ki, including the pod's well-being. The Queens of Ki swear a sacred oath to protect them and their breeding grounds.

He bowed his head in reverence, "It is gratifying to see a sovereign view Riders with such respect. Now, may I ask another question? This one more personal." Jynnalt nodded her head. She liked his frankness and open style.

"Why do you allow your mother to speak to you in such a manner?" He stopped under the outer edge of the canopy of the single massive tree in the garden. Twisted gnarled branches reached out covering the garden creek, which encircled it before passing on down the slight hill.

Jynnalt stiffened. No one ever dared to speak about her mother in such a way. Except Eshin. She relaxed. Those of other spheres of influence lacked understanding of the remarkable bonds of family by those in the border kingdoms.

"She is my mother. Respect for the family an important tradition of my culture." A funny expression passed over his face before he bowed once again and excused himself. As he walked away, she caught what he muttered to himself, "do without that kind of respect."

Her mother seemed abusive towards her, to outsiders, but she knew she only wanted the best for her. Tesiskel never adapted to border society, which in her mind, Jynnalt symbolized having none of her mother's features. She resembled her father's family except for the color of her eyes.

Abrasive, cynical and judgmental, she was still Jynnalt's mother. Jynnalt's mood brooding now, she resolved to stroll through the garden for a while before heading back. Well-meaning or not, it still ached deep down where she refused to look about her mother's behavior towards her.

A voice came out of nowhere. Jynnalt gasped and jerked back. Her heel caught a slight rock, and she stumbled, arms flailing. A hand flashed out faster than she could see, grabbed her with an iron grip, keeping her from falling. The shadowy form moved into the moonlight.

He appeared like a Malkuth, though clothed in black from head to toe. Long, loose flowing robes, belted in what she recognized as a nanite material. What she thought was a full skirt; she realized split into pants when he stepped forward. Silver and gold bands, with a raised embossed emblem she did not recognize on a Sigil pin. She noted the unusual tattoo's peeking out on both wrists under his long loose sleeves. What the symbols meant eluded her. A cloak made of a strange glimmering appearance; the color onyx black rippled around his form in the slight breeze. The hood of his cloak over his head, making it impossible for Jynnalt to see his face other than his eyes, burning a mercurial silver.

Tavas grabbed for his plasma staff at his back and stopped. No staff. This, the second time her paladin denied his ability to carry his rifle or plasma staff when needed.

He moved in closer to the unknown male. "I would release her. Now."

Jynnalt understood Tavas' viewed this stranger as a threat by his stance, prepared for a fight.

The shadowy form pulled Jynnalt to a stable position, before releasing her and removing his hood, revealing himself to her Paladins. Jynnalt viewed Tavas glance up towards the platform where the guests and Ryakin stood out of hearing. He stepped between her and the stranger.

Jynnalt knew only one full-blooded Malkuth, her trainer Caltac', a supposed ex-Temple Ghost Walker. This male reminded her of him.

"Who... Who are you?" Jynnalt managed? The male turned casually away from Tavas and inclined his head in respect. There were the lightest lines at the corners of his eyes. His face elegant, the skin translucent with faint scars on his left cheekbone and a slash which went from the upper right scalp disappearing into his robe. His hair, silvery-white, braided in small sections, pulled tight on his head, banded with a complicatedly entwined metal ring. All joined in one large braid at the back of his neck, the length reaching almost to the floor.

"I am identified, young queen, as N'lari amongst the Malkuth." he said, and shrugged as a sardonic smile flashed across his face before disappearing.

Jynnalt wondered if she imagined it. "I belong to nowhere at the moment, though I have worked for the Temple in many capacities," Jynnalt noted the stranger stood a head taller than her.

"Do not fear, I am no enemy of yours." He shifted his gaze to stare at Tavas; "I only seek refuge in these times of trouble." Though he whispered, his voice carried a tone of command without him even trying. Silence descended as if waiting for her reaction, broken by the hooting of a night flyer somewhere close.

Tavas stiffened, though few races interacted with the Malkuth on a turn-to-turn basis. They have contact with them in several ways. Some more pleasant than others. Everyone heard the whispered legends of the various sects within the Malkuth. Especially a sect called the Keepers. They claimed to be Keepers of the Rings. Most of the tales revolved around one called N'lari and his followers.

"You.... You... cannot be he; all know he is dead, along with those who followed him in battle that turn," Jynnalt said in a shocked voice. "My father told me tales about N'lari and his followers. During the last battle at the system of Cineuian, they alone turned the tide in the Nine's favor. He told me about their bravery and self-sacrifice against the Sabations. All, even the Malkuth, claim N'lari and his followers vanished, chasing after the last fleeing Sabation ships into the deep void. Never seen again."

"They do not know everything in the galaxy, child. I knew your father, using a... different name, I admit. The priestess here can confirm my identity if you doubt my words."

Jynnalt nodded towards Tavas. He came back ten minutes later and whispered in her ear.

"He does not lie," he said, and stepped back.

"If all you seek is refuge, I grant it, within the borders of Ki, which is as far as my authority extends. The Temple has a greater reach. Have they denied you?" Her hand trembled a little. Besides her father's stories, she read about him in her warrior's academy. She soaked up every word, and every meh in the on-campus library she could discover about him and his followers. Overwhelmed by his presence.

"I fear I must also ask that you allow me to use technology outlawed and add me to your paladin's ranks for the time being."

Tavas stepped forward, "your highness...." before he could finish, Jynnalt cut him off answering.

"Yes."

N'lari touched his belt on its side and changed before their eyes, becoming smaller with pale red eyes. Now he wore the uniform of her paladins. The scars on his face, still there.

Advanced glamor technology. For a moment Jynnalt wondered if she made a mistake, then remembered who he was.

"It'd be best if we spoke no more of this."

Jynnalt agreed and made them all swear to silence. They returned to the entertainment, plus one extra paladin. The gong for the last dance reverberated across the courtyard, and she stepped into Ryakin's arms. Her breath caught in her throat as his arms encircled her. A strange emotion burned through her as he pulled her tight against him. Lightning raced through her in the strangest sensation, making her weak. She remembered nothing of the dance except the expression in his eyes before she realized they were parting to a smattering of clapping and stomping feet. Being held by him ended far too soon for her. Afterward, they all headed back to their respective barges and shuttles for home.

Chapter 17

RYAKIN AND HIS BROTHER stood in the garden, having left the females to fend for themselves as they got fresh air and privacy to talk. The last of the three moons rose above the horizon, frosted silvery-white behind thin misty clouds from the sudden earlier storm. Ryakin appreciated the weather far more without the Igigi controlling every minor facet. The storms wilder, starshine, brighter.

"Did you know Jynnalt's never set foot outside the fortress during festival? Except for some archaic sword competition, held each sar. Even after her rite of womanhood. Her Nani explained the matter, so I might understand the ah... status of Jynnalt's knowledge of the marriage pillows. Not, I might add, her mother, which I found strange," Ryakin said. He studied the heruo smoke rising from the pipes of those in the garden. There would be more than the normal number of occupants in cleansing units on the morrow. "She explained, the upper rank's outer border kingdoms frown upon certain practices of festival. Though she admitted their commoners allowed the claiming dance."

"I know what the border kingdom's views are of the festival's ah... more primitive aspects. To some, this makes them appear not as *enlightened* as ours," Rualui said with a shrug. Still, many of our females, my wife included, chose not to enjoy that feature of the festival. There were no problems on mine and Jena's first night because of a lack of knowledge on her part.

"At what point did you think to inform me of that fact about their customs?" Ryakin slammed back his Altecia whiskey, placing the chalice on the tray as a server wandered past. The sharp, smoky flavor burned as the whiskey slid down his throat.

Rualui slapped his forehead. "Oh right, I forgot to tell you to read the contract before signing. Sorry about that." A hint of disgust in his tone. "At your age, I figured you might have done research on your brides' home, customs and laws," motioning for another chalice of mead before the waiter wandered back inside the chamber. "Nothing changed, not one word or agreement, as written when the contract was for Queen Jildius. If you did not care, then why should you now?"

Without missing a beat, Ryakin shot back, "because now I might face a hysterical female on her first night. Queen Jildius had a matter-of-fact manner about her that suited me. Regardless of whether she attended festivals, she did not put me in mind of a timid rodent."

"Yestereve, you did not appear to dislike her. In fact, I thought you found her appealing. I witnessed your reaction when you danced. And hers."

"She has an appealing countenance, I will give her that, and she fit rather well when we danced. Neither fact makes her as good a match as Jildius or many others who, over time, requested a connection to our house."

"My advice. Go slow. From the gossip my wife overheard, you are proficient enough in the pillows. I'm sure you will figure things out," Rualui said, with a raised eyebrow, challenging him to deny the fact.

Ryakin grimaced at the remark. Yet, he stayed silent. Deigning not to answer.

"Besides, trust her nani Eshin. She is wise and will talk with Jynnalt, in place of her mother. Most likely, she already has. As for Jynnalt's suitability, the house of Airal is a venerated and honorable house. In fact, her house is one of the founding houses of Ki. I do not consider any outer kingdoms nor their houses lesser than ours, or any others," he said, placing his chalice upon the stone baluster of the balcony. "What amazes me is we are so arrogant we ignore information about the outer kingdoms. Label them barbaric. As if they are not part of the Empire," he said. The ever-increasing numbers of inky shadows slinking off into the gardens caused him to shake his head.

"I think I shall join the ladies. Jena would scold me if she knew I was out here long enough to inhale any heruo particles floating in the air. I don't doubt she'd make me waste time in a cleansing unit."

Ryakin gaze at his brother's hasty retreat towards the patio doors. Rualui reached the doorway and turned. "I still believe your assessment of your recent bride is inaccurate. I've told you this before. She is not some timid rodent. Which I believe you will discover. Stop listening to gossip by those with malicious intent. Try paying more attention to her," Rualui said before striding off to his wife and their intimate circle of friends.

"Doubt it," he said under his breath as his brother walked through the portico's open doors. *Reminds me, I need to replace her paladins. Soon. As her consort, I have that right whether she agrees.*

Staring off without seeing the garden before him, he reflected on her narration of what happened on Niuard.

She insisted the attack was a full-scale assault. By a race she did not recognize, her translator struggled to interpret the language, returning an error tone every ten words for every single word it deciphered. Claimed they were not outlaws or pirates. They were reavers. Ugallu pulsed his support of the Society Order to Ryakin turns after the incidence. For a moment, he wondered if he might have joined before dismissing the idea.

The Society wasted no time calling her a liar, their enforcers testifying forty or fifty outlaws and pirates attacked. They claimed; disgruntled dissidents took advantage of the chaos. Informed the Imperial investigators, they were the ones who set the city and her uncle's estate on fire and looted the merchants.

Still, the council, backed by Emperor Lahamu, voted to rescind the Society's skip rights to the Anunnaki Empire. Once again.

Every Caretaker worthy of their rank or fleet member knows it does not take a significant force to wreak havoc on a small world. When he arrived with the fleet, all they found were roving outlaws worldside, which they dispatched in no time. They found no forces in the surrounding forest. Rualui sent Ryakin to question the locals because the council ignored their testimonies. The citizens' stories backed Jynnalt's, claiming those who attacked were not normal outlaws or bandits. This information left Ryakin in a quandary. What was the truth? Could Jynnalt and her paladins become confused by the chaos of battle? He wondered? After a moment's thought, he realized she might but her paladins. For now, these questions would have to wait until he gained more information.

Jynnalt, her paladins, her sensial Caltac', Lady Iacha and one lone Malkuth scholar and around one thousand merchants and citizens, the dissenting voices to the Society's account. Worse, she would not stop speaking of the event. Becoming an embarrassment.

There was a fact not released to the public that made him uneasy. One hundred thousand citizens still unaccounted on Niuard. The Society claimed they could not verify the numbers because dissidents set ablaze their official records office. Prince Satoric informed everyone the problem would straighten itself out. Still, something of that magnitude dismissed so cavalierly with no further investigation made him uneasy.

Ryakin changed drinks to the Carellian Whiskey imported from Ugallu's moon distillery. He needed something a little stronger as he thought about what he discovered so far. Ustrix walked over to join him twenty minutes later. Half an hour later, after more whiskey and friendly conversation as others joined them on the patio, he realized he could not hide out here any longer. Time for him to make his appearance. Ustrix followed him back to the entertainments. Minutes later, both waylaid by Tristian, one of their longtime friends, coming off his kingdom's Nibiru patrol duty. This was Da's kingdom's fleet rotation to patrol the empire's local trade lanes with the Imperial fleet. Tristian waved and headed their direction.

"I was late getting here because I checked the pleasure palaces and gambling chambers looking for Ustrix. Then one of the crew mentioned its Ryakin's first public appearance with his bride, figured he roped you in as the rest of us are otherwise engaged with duties. Decided I would come to see this hideous creature for myself." He said, looking around for said bride. "I heard she's as ugly as a canis, sharp of tongued and yet, afraid of her own shadow. Please tell me they blindfolded you for the ceremony. So, I won't have to think you gave in without a fight," he said, getting a laugh out of both Ryakin and Ustrix.

"Well, prior to introductions to my bride, let's make the proper rounds before the matrons bar us from future events," Ryakin said. "First, though, I am getting something else to drink. The whiskey went straight to my head. Not good when dealing with dragons, you know, the matrons who lie in wait to consume the unwary."

No server was close by, so he headed for the refreshment tables. As he walked away, he overheard Ustrix saying, "that's fine with me if the matrons ban me from these boring events."

Tristian heartily agreed. Ryakin grinned. Blooded fleet members notorious for not wanting to attend high ranking social events. Yet demanded by their houses to do so, to gain political advancement in the fleet. Peace time demanded such as they received no accommodations or war medals. Politic's ruled. As Ryakin approached with his drink, he overheard Ustrix remarking to Tristian.

"Better than end up a boring old warrior who wished he lived more, followed duty less."

"Just who would you be talking about?" Ryakin asked. Use to jabs from his friends, he tolerated them with good humor.

"Who us?" Ustrix winked at Tristian, "we were talking about the old married folks here." As he casually glanced around the chamber before settling back on Ryakin, "Oh wait, I forgot you joined them."

Ryakin laughed adding. "Don't worry, your turn is coming. I shall with good cheer be there for you." Out of the corner of his eye, he caught Jynnalt staring at him. As soon as she realized he noticed, she glanced away.

"So, you don't feel too bad Tristian, Ustrix resisted attending, leaving me no choice but to resort to guilt. I reminded him of the last time I bailed the two of you out of trouble. He'd been looking forward to a night of pleasure and gambling, but allowed me to drag him along. Don't worry, I'm retiring early, leaving you two able to go carousing before long.

They made the rounds at a slow pace until they stopped at a sizeable group of males. The females scattered elsewhere, discussing clothes, upcoming social events, and invariably gossiping about everyone and everything.

His attention caught when a Knight of the Grand Temple of Radiance he admired spoke. Cer Hjiall Gneist earned his title the hard way, not born of a blooded house. Brash, outspoken, with a long scar down one side of his face, which he refused to have removed. Short, cropped hair like any fleet member, though he no longer wore a battle nanite uniform. Many viewed him as a relic from a different time. The only reason he was here was Emperor Lahamu enjoyed his company and always sent him an invitation. His instinctive and innovative battle tactics from the Great War no longer viewed as effective within the warrior's council because of advances in technology. Ryakin thought otherwise.

"Someone is orchestrating these events. Attacks have increased throughout the Council of Nine's protected empires. They are trying to destabilize the fragile peace the nine-alliances worked hard to achieve after the Great War. The warrior's council believe the Society Order implicated in many of the attacks yet has no solid proof."

A blooded Knight Valierous, the lowest ranking Knight in the group, in gaudy colors of the finest material, frowned, shaking his head. He ogled an ethereal female in gauzy clothing as she floated past, before looking back saying. "What about the attack last month? Unnerving how swift the attack occurred and then ended. Our fleet could not respond fast enough. By the time we arrived, the attack was over. The world of Nios in flames in the Merchant Guilds Alliance. In one turn. I swear. My sister's best friend arrived hours afterward when she went to visit a friend. The sight horrified her as her barge orbited. Her Captiva sent out a message and then left. He did not want to hang around. Some claim the Society was negotiating for a contract a week prior, which the Caretaker and Govingshin Cer Fayjete refused. The Caretakers pointed to the Society, implying revenge on their part to extort them into handing over the world to administer."

A Saques, his Sigil pin, the houses of Bele, spoke. "In a briefing in the last turn at the war council, the Society came up for discussion. The Council of Nine believes they're behind the rise of criminal acts throughout the galaxy. To me, this implies they were the attackers. Retribution and extortion when Caretakers and controlling house refuse their offers."

Another interjected, wearing the Sigil pin of a Sarl, of the blood house of Spahn. "Rumor claims Ghost Walkers are investigating. An unusual and drastic measure by CON, backed by the Temple, which shows how worried they are over these events. The war council notified the fleets they are to turn over any information we hear or receive related to them. The fact, not one operative from any empire discovered a central organizational system for the Society, is also troubling."

Another, a Knight Grand Cross of the Stars, the third son of the Tita Dukian of the blood house of Tanean, said, "there are a lot of random facts. Bits and pieces of stories, when all put together, make no sense. We still have no solid information about the attack on Niuard. My uncle on the council claims the commoners and guild citizens have voiced concern over the situation. System accidents are high, and the weather is uncertain, some places out of control. Inner system security, now filled by the Imperial fleet, to cover the lack of the Igigi's services spreading our system fleets thin. This takes them from their protective duties. Leaving the system open to infiltration from outlaws and pirates along the empire's civilian and guild inter-system travel lanes. The guilds posting higher than normal losses. And civilian abductions of wealthy guild and commoner merchants for ransom, along with the theft of their star yachts. Many want the Igigi contracted once more, so the fleet can respond in time to distress calls."

The Knight Valierous spoke. "Bandits, outlaws, and pirates. The Society is innocent of all these conspiracy charges. Stop listening to drunks in commoner's feasthalls. Or raving females. Review the facts of the attack, ignore the crazy border female's hysterical report. Are you going to believe her over well-trained enforcers? She and her paladins made the charge against the Society because of their ineffectiveness in protecting her companions, who died, daughters of high ranking blooded," the implication clear.

Ryakin stood outside the group, listening with polite boredom till he this latest Knight spoke. Tristian and Ustrix off to the side. A fiery flash of anger rose as his breath quickened, surprising him by his reaction at the accusations and disrespect to his bride. His knuckles whitened around his chalice.

"I believe you are speaking of *my wife*." He said, stepping into the gathered circle of males, his voice silky smooth, staring at the one who spoke.

"I meant no disrespect. Rumors say she abandoned her companions to die, hiding out in the ruins with her paladins. Lady Iacha won't say anything against her because she is too well mannered. I——."

The sound of Ryakin's fist connecting with the face of the knight satisfying. The other staggered backward from the blow. For a second, the sound reverberated throughout the chamber. Silence descended as the guests looked around for the disturbance. When no further violence occurred, and staff headed the direction of the disruption, they went back to what they were doing. Though whispers were louder, and patrons surreptitiously stared their way.

"My Apax warriors and I found her. She *droging* did not abandon her companions. The evidence clear, they fought every step of the way to those ruins. They hid because of overwhelming numbers," he ground out, "the *Society* forced her and her paladins to disarm. They almost died because of the idiotic rules of this Order you are defending, as Niuard's administrators. Let me throw you on a battlefield with no weapons and see how long you survive," he said as he stepped closer to the other. "I would advise you to take back what you said and never speak my wife's name; ever."

The sight of the Knight's bleeding nose and lip satisfying. "Or you will answer. *To me*," he said, realizing the irony as he was thinking those thoughts earlier, somehow coming from another they infuriated him.

The male bowed his head, dripping blood in his embroidered pocket cloth, mumbled an apology, then stalked away. Ryakin memorized him as he headed towards Prince Satoric's enlarging circle across the room.

After a while, he could not avoid joining up with his new relatives by law. Ustrix and Tristian trailing behind.

"Thought we might get some actual action back there. Believe me, it would be the talk of the festivals for sars afterward," Ustrix said before adding, "he's a notorious gossip. The more malicious or salacious, the more he spreads the tale. Embellishing the story, not against his moral code. He will make sure to smear you now." Ustrix said quiet enough not to be overheard by any other than the three of them.

The impassioned voice of Prince Satoric impossible to miss as they approached the group.

"He is incapable. Citizens suffer, and the emperor does nothing. He allows CON and GIA to rule us, from their patronizing far off distance. Worse, they follow the Temple and the Malkuth's lead."

To his shock and dismay, three of the knights in the circle, including the one he punched earlier, were nodding their heads in agreement. In his mind, subversion, no less, spoken so openly, disquieting. The rest stiffened, their expressions disapproving, moving away before Prince Satoric continued with his complaints against Emperor Lahamu.

"Shipments of platinum talons have disappeared. Rumor hints Emperor Lahamu never sent them, and the commoners, starving, are desperate enough to threaten to revolt. That's not happened since the uprising over six hundred sars ago."

"You must try the Eliasian wine," a voice said from his left, one he recognized, musical, challenging.

Ryakin stiffened. Before turning to face Lady Wiante. Tall, slender, in an erotic sheer gown sparkling with diamond dust, with designs barely covering her more intimate feminine qualities. Soft blue hair with highlights caught the flickering light of the golden glow globes, trailing in lazy abundance over her shoulders. Her skin the lightest lavender.

A true native of Nibiru Proper. Her wide-set eyes a soft red. She sipped from a graceful crystalline chalice, smiling at him over the rim. He wondered how, in such a brief time, she lost her appeal. "Lady Wiante," he said, his voice neutral, not wanting another scene. Once enough for the night's entertainment.

He thought about the distasteful scene from the other turn. His brother breaking off the negotiations with Lady Wiante's house, claiming Ugallu, his uncle, did not have the legal rights to negotiate, infuriated them. They knew they required King Rualui's acceptance, yet, assured by Lord Ugallu Zu*Tc, they would receive his approval advanced the contract through the matchmakers. The idea Lady Wiante and Lord Ryakin appeared well suited did not hurt the matchmaker's confidence about the contract, either. This all rushed into after the Queen of Ki died.

He realized, too late, they were manipulating him. Setting his teeth on edge.

The attempt to force his hand by Lady Wiante occurred the evening he left his brother's house. He ran into her on the way to his quarters. The events of the evening changed his mind about breaking off the contract with Jynnalt. Now he spotted Ugallu's handy work in the sorry affair.

His brother was right, Tc would profit from the contract with Ki. He, more than his brother, knew how desperately they needed new fleet ships. In a way, Ryakin relieved to follow his brother's request. Still, he would have preferred a less controversial bride.

Ryakin frowned, waiting for the actual reason she approached him, trying to gain control over his anger. She leaned her body against his, her voice a husky whisper.

"I wanted you to know. My father forced me the other turn to try to trick you," she looked up from under her eyelashes. "He feels cheated because your brother refused to honor the contract agreed upon by your uncle. He thought if you compromised me, it would nullify the contract, at least by the Kieran council. They're notorious prudes." She moved at that moment, her breast rubbing seductively along his side.

Ryakin stepped back enough to make his point. "My uncle was wrong not to consult my brother. And worse, to imply Rualui approved. After your family's behavior, I would agree, he was correct to disavow the whole sorry affair."

"True, my father, along with your uncle, acted badly, but he was desperate. And your uncle encouraged him. You see that, don't you? I would like to keep your friendship. The idea pains me to have lost your affection over a misunderstanding."

Leaning towards her, he whispered in her ear, "I am sorry your father forced you to attempt to have my contract annulled. I am now married and prefer to forget the whole miserable incident. It would be best if you did also, as to friendship, I'm leaving soon for Ki. You might need to make new friends." Ryakin said tersely, dismissing her as he straightened.

She turned away, then stopped and bowed her head. "Queen Jynnalt," she lowered her eyes and stammered, "I.... I.... am sorry, I did not see you there. I was having a private..." she peeked coyly at Ryakin, her eyelashes fanning her cheekbones, "word with your husband. We're old friends, almost married ourselves," she said.

"Lady Wiante, I am sure my husband has many friends here. I hope he will make other more *respectable* friends in Ki," she said, turning towards Ryakin, then back towards Lady Wiante saying. "Oh, and Lady Wiante almost does not count, in case they did not teach you that." With that said, she stepped next to Ryakin, slipped her arm through his, staring straight ahead. Her cheeks flushed, head held high and her eyes bright. Ryakin felt a strange rush of pride at how she managed the situation. Yet, wondered if he should be insulted regarding her remark about his friends. He suspected Lady Wiante's timing engineered to humiliate Jynnalt. He regarded the soft sway of Lady Wiante's hips as she left, amazed how quick his ardor for her cooled.

A gong sounded, and the music stopped. Imperial Vizier Osmelron on the Emperor's balcony stated that Emperor Lahamu required their attention for several announcements. Those below bowed their heads for several seconds when the emperor appeared at the railing.

"The Chakian ambassador brought news with him from the Council of Nine and the Galactic Interstellar Alliances council. This is in direct relation to the Citrea treaty. They demand, and we concurred, to find a peaceful solution between our empires. We have agreed to suspend fleet exercises along the border of the Citrea kingdom."

Emperor Lahamu stared explicitly at Prince Satoric. "Altercations with the Citrea military fleet within their territory will cease."

Silence descended as Prince Satoric and Emperor Lahamu stared at each other. A chill settled upon the chamber. Till Emperor Lahamu spoke again. "The second announcement is the Empress is carrying an heir. She is well past the dangerous time of the possibility of a miscarriage. We shall retire to our estates in a less turbulent system until her time of travail. I now release you back to this evening's entertainment." The crowds below bowed once more. When they looked upward, Emperor Lahamu was no longer present. The curtains closed.

Throughout the chambers were smiles, excited voices and rapidly whispered comments. Fits of giggles from the younger females broke out amongst them. The older members more subdued gave happy toasts. An heir. At last. The worry over a probable civil war, even with a legitimate Cupbearer, no longer a possibility.

Younger couples filed back on the dance floor in high spirits. The lights dimmed. The music started, a few of the older couples danced, many though preferring to discuss the facts revealed this evening by the announcements.

Prince Ea, missing in action for most of the night, joined Ryakin's brother and his wife's small group. A stranger wearing the colors of Tc, a steel headband with three small pearls, placed him as a Caiscou, his Sigil pin the blood house of Ligish. Someone trailing along behind him in Merchant Guild clothing.

Ryakin's brother introduced him as Lord Riciad Zabu'Ligish. The man's features a mask of polite serenity, Ryakin sensed something dangerous lurked beneath the surface. To a fleet member trained in sizing up an opponent, he exuded the air of a predator. Lord Riciad reacted to Jynnalt's presence with an intense stare, as if unnerved, yet trying not to show the fact. Ryakin moved next to him and whispered, "Do you have a problem with my bride?" his blood still boiling from the earlier encounter with the Knight.

"I was admiring her, as any male would," he rushed on, "but that is not why I was staring. She reminds me of someone from my distant past, is all." He looked down at the red wine in his chalice before looking straight at Ryakin. "One who died. Forgive me if I offended you." Lord Riciad said before turning to talk with Prince Alalus, who joined them.

Moments later he turned to Ryakin's brother, "Your Highness, may I introduce Ikath Kilorian, one I am endorsing, for a guild position with Tc. At a rank that befits his experience and training."

Ikath bowed, yet said nothing. Ryakin took an instant liking to him.

"He is skilled in the transportation of goods and personnel. I wanted to present him before the normal crush of the turn-to-turn business makes it next to impossible." Lord Riciad said.

To Ryakin, the tone sounded sly, sneaky, setting his teeth on edge. He chided himself, admitting he used entertainment to advance his goals, as did others.

Ustrix and Tristan took their leave and headed out. They claimed they still could get into the best-rated pleasure house before the doors closed. *If* they left this minute. They were already pulsing their reservations as they went for their cloaks.

Jynnalt said. "The issue is complex. Someone is deliberately driving the actions of the reavers. I believe to make us lose faith in the Alliances. The unusual exorbitant amount of occurrence of these events in various sectors makes it harder for the Alliance to respond to them all. I, for one, prefer to stay within the umbrella of the alliance. In normal times, they give us protected galactic trade, along established trade routes, which I remind you they control through the Igigi. And which is the foremost reason for alliances. The Temple and CON are discussing how to stop the reavers now that they have an idea of the numbers and types of attacks."

"Yet, they still seem incapable of providing the protections they promised, or perform their sworn duties," Prince Satoric said. "Including our Emperor." Gasps met this statement as he stared back at his granddaughter, Jynnalt.

So, the knight from the earlier group got his ideas from Jynnalt's grandfather.

Jynnalt stared right back, a defiant glint in her eyes, then demanded, "Show me proof, not rhetoric."

"So, my granddaughter is not the idiot her mother proclaims. Your mother always lacked any wit. I should not have relied upon her observations. After your father died, I should have challenged his final and ridicules protection order." He gazed around at those gathered. "Imagine, allowing a commoner, no matter how high he has risen in the Fleet, to manage the hereditary title of an Arch Duchiness's. Even if an Outer Border Kingdom. And worse for our emperor to uphold the decree." He sneered. "I should have brought you here anyway for your training. Instead of leaving you in the hands of crass border trainers."

From the expression on Jynnalt's face, she understood he insulted her and her kingdom. Ryakin thought about speaking up in her defense, then stopped as she straightens and lifted her head as her eyes narrowed. He relaxed, ready to go to her defense but waiting to see if she would need help. He followed his brother's advice, determined to get to know his bride before passing judgment.

"My father left instructions on my training. I doubt you could provide mentors as excellent or qualified in the fields. I needed tutoring to fulfill my duties.

"I think she is correct in that assessment." Emperor Lahamu and his Empress moved into their circle. Everyone bowed their heads and made room for them. "My wife wished to congratulate her highness on her Queenship and marriage before we retired."

Empress Lahumu slid her arm through Jynnalt's and motioned for Ryakin to join them. "Indulge me, walk with me. My husband would like a private word with Prince Satoric," the Empress said. The rest of those in the circle melted away at the announcement.

Others fell back before them as they meandered around the chamber. Prince Ryakin, this might offend, but I will say it anyway. Males are children in adults' bodies.

Jynnalt broke out laughing before responding, all eyes turning their direction. She did not care. "I heard the same from my Nani Eshin many times."

"And I also, too, many times from my mother. I believe all females think the same," Ryakin said with a rakish grin.

Empress Lahumu smiled back, "your charming company is always welcome at court. Your mother is wise. I enjoy our talks when she visits." She turned back to Jynnalt, saying, "remember this if nothing else. Do not equate your first time to how it will always be. Please give yourself time to adjust. Do not force your feelings, let them develop naturally." The Empress strolled them back to where they started, talking now about all the latest gossip circulating.

Ryakin realized Prince Satoric left while the Empress paraded them through the chamber, showing her approval. Emperor Lahamu Ryakin observed with an unpleasant dignity upon his face, glancing at the empty space Prince Satoric's occupied earlier. When they stopped before him congratulated them with kindness. Moments later, the Imperial couple left, followed shortly by Ryakin and Jynnalt.

Later that night, he sat watching Jynnalt sleep. Confused, he realized; she affected him like no other female he met in his lifetime. During one turn, his view of her changed drastically. Why? That he did not understand. She responded to his advances with abandon. Other females did, so why the impression this time so different?

In fact, he slowed her down so she would not be too sore the next morning. Nor did she complain at the sharp burst of pain of her first breeding, which did little to deter her passion, he discovered.

His brother was right. She surprised him several times this turn. He stared at her for a second, shook his head, then stretched, weary from the night's exertions. Falling into their sleeping pillows beside her, he covered himself with the luxurious fur cover. Seconds later, he was sound asleep. Happier than in a long time, wondering if he'd found what his brother possessed in his marriage.

Chapter 18

335892 GGS Kinto 16th
Ki' Queen's Roost Palace. –Queen Jynnalt

KALMIA'S PRIVATE OFFICE the exact opposite of her stark anti-chamber. Jynnalt gazed around, incredulous. Clutter filled every nook and cranny. *It's a wonder she ever finds anything.* Meh disks and pens filled holding vases to overflowing, while the vases themselves balanced tenuously on tables or even each other. Overcrowded chairs and tables, along with stacks of waist-high priceless metal sheaf books.

A maze of tight narrow pathways, the only open space. Glow globes floated throughout the chamber, palm-held holo viewers and projectors scattered around the chamber as if thoughtlessly dropped. Mounted on a heavy stand outside on the terrace was an astrophysics telescope with all the bells and whistles. Early morning's golden light glinted off a sophisticated silver metal neural net stationary robotic head and bust on the opposite side.

Jynnalt realized the eyes followed Kalmia's every move. She shuddered before looking elsewhere. Real-time holo navigations charts covered walls; each in a different spectrum of energy or colors. Nebula's, and constellations, trade routes and Galactic gates. Seven charts showed the Solar Sailor's pods migration patterns from the least to the greatest. Jynnalt recognized Kiah's pod route and hoped he found what he was looking for. One chart showed ancient acceleration gates. Millions. Odd. Her academy teacher for beacon skips and gate training informed the class all the acceleration gates destroyed by CON and the Temple. Along with all their navigation locations after the war. She wondered if these were just estimations on Kalmia's part. Maybe she found a relic from when the acceleration gates were in use.

Jynnalt wandered over and touched the Kestrel's system, her earlier home, now Lady Razin's. The map changed, enlarging showing the star and system. The empire information bards holo's running in the background, filling the chamber with quiet noise, the actual words too soft to make out.

Kalmia's desk alone, piled high with unknown charts and meh's recorders, with some balanced on the edge of the desk. Strangely, other charts, on pounded sheets of thin unknown metals, with strange symbols and unreadable ancient runic marks, caught Jynnalt's attention.

No space-faring galactic empire or kingdom uses any form of the once prevalent metal books. At least not for the last five thousand sars. The only ones left reside in private collection's, like her father's, or those preserved in the High temples scattered throughout the galaxy. Handheld books made of the thinnest metal stamped with words or images. Primitive but effective for storing information, which is the basis for archaic civilization to rise to space-faring travelers.

Kalmia spoke up behind Jynnalt, making her flinch. "I pounded the metal sheets myself," she shrugged, "a hobby."

"The markings?" Jynnalt asked as she walked over to look closer.

"Copied from ancient texts preserved at the Holy Seer of Radiance Temple's Great Library at Silsatisus or from Temple walls, I visited when able. Whenever I go to GIA's council for assorted reasons, if possible, I hop over to the library. I spend a turn or two looking for information on the Murians. There are times I copy the lesser-known legends into these books. The work I do requires I travel a lot, which allows me to visit the ruins of older temples and copy their legends," she said before changing the subject. "Follow me," Kalmia said, waiting for Ryakin to catch up before opening a cleverly hidden door. Well-worn stairs went downward to a maze of underground passageways before they entered a disastrous litter of... storage, a grander replica of the chamber they'd left.

As they entered, Kalmia picked up the conversation from earlier.

"Your father was a remarkable person. Many times, he helped with my research at the temple. We all mourned his loss. Did he tell you he was a part of our group?

"Group?"

"Yes, amateur historian's, many of us are attempting to prove the Murians were not mythical beings. Nor did our ancestors make them up to teach moral or socially acceptable behavior. Or explain away natural events like storms, lightning, or volcanos. The scholars say they used fear of punishment or anticipation of reward from the gods after death to enforce laws," she said as she dug through vases full of mysterious items, causing them to wobble and threaten to crash to the ground. "We disagree."

Before Jynnalt answered, she rushed on, "our group believes they are the founding bloodlines of all Elohim. Stories and legends always have a kernel of truth. We believe Murians, not the Malkuth, created the Galactic Gates and trade lanes, tamed the Solar Sailors, or created them. Our analyst believes the Igigi are biological Ai clones designed to build, maintain, and control those systems. The exception is the Sailors, they need riders with unique Dna signatures and abilities. We have not figured out why. Yet."

Ryakin called out, "Hey, where are you guys? I'm lost somewhere back here in the maze of stacks."

Jynnalt figured something interesting caught his attention, causing him to fall behind.

"If true, what happened to them? How did the Malkuth become the guardians of their technology?" Jynnalt said, figuring Ryakin would work his way towards them.

"Believe me," Kalmia raised her voice, so Ryakin could hear her from wherever he was, "we all want to know. The Malkuth keep their secrets with help, I might add, from the Temple. Many believe the Books of the Temple are history. Not mystical. They tell of actual events from ancient turns, which over time became myths and parable."

Jynnalt figured Ryakin's thinking would head straight to the fact the Malkuth did not manufacture the Galactic Gates, or the trade lane technology. She understood he would wonder how they maintain control over them. Ryakin ever the pragmatist she learned since their marriage. Jynnalt's' thoughts wander to the last eight months since she and Ryakin arrived at Kiestrial. A response to stop her from thinking about the enclosed space. Dutifully, she followed Kalmia from stack to stack, barely paying attention to her ramblings. Once she lost sight of Kalmia and rushed to catch up to keep from being abandoned in this maze. Afraid if lost, it would take turns before anyone found her. A sheen of sweat on her forehead as the surrounding stacks closed in on her. Getting narrower and narrower. The high vaulted ceiling the only thing keeping her from hyperventilating.

Over the last eight months since they landed in the Capital city of Kishira and moved into the Queen's Roost Palace, she and Ryakin took the time to learn about each other. Both loved riding war beasts. Dawn, with a lack of obligations, allowed them time to ride, laugh, talk, and plan their future as they rode through bucolic carefully cultivated gardens. Or race through the wild majestic forest below the palace in the mountainous terrain of the Adsullata Fire mountains, named after the rare trees flourishing on its flanks. Both appeared equal in hand-to-hand combat and weapons practicing in semi-secret as the Queen's council disapproved, informing her to leave physical fighting to her blooded.

Racin and Ustrix, permanent guests since they arrived, though Jynnalt avoided Racin she did not send her away either, outdid them both in flying any craft either flew. This grew to fierce competition and heavy betting throughout the palace citizens.

At first, she recognized the fact it disconcerted Ryakin to have a female so physically capable, particularly in fighting. So, she backed off, letting him win, choosing not to hurt their growing friendship. Especially in the ancient art of sword fighting, in which she excelled. N'lari, now a permanent member of her command paladins and a friend, advised her against this. Informed her, Ryakin was not the type to accept a false win. He proved to be right. Ryakin exploded one turn, throwing down his sword, telling her if she allowed him to win, she insulted him. Ryakin a fierce yet honest competitor.

Afterward, she held back nothing, showing her actual ability as her skill improved under both Caltac' and N'lari's tutelage. A fleeting time afterward. He laughed, shook his head, and agreed with her. Jynnalt's sword skills appeared far better than his. In fleet matters, she proved better at the overall strategy. Ryakin more adaptive at instantaneous field tactical decisions. Together they made an unbeatable team at the FR war games, scoring the highest this sar in the empire. Jynnalt understood their titles would not allow them to take part further than regional battles. The Greater council would never approve. Their participation a breech in Ki's view of FR battle games. To them they were first sar training for the warrior's fleet. Beyond this, a frivolous pursuit best done on idle time. Which Ki's fleet lacked.

Ryakin, highly competitive, upset when informed of the fact as he was looking forward to advancing to the alliance games. Ki dropped out, leaving Iallful in the lead. Without Ryakin commanding, Tc fell to fifth place but still qualified for the GIA games.

She never forgot the morning he told her he no longer doubted her word about Niuard. Which led them to discuss why Prince Satoric and the Society lied about the event. What did they gain? What are they hiding?

Over time, she told him her deepest thoughts and fears, and he in return gave her confidence and a sense of her worth, faith in herself and her decisions outside of the fleet and battles. For the first time, she regained something she lost when someone murdered her father. She regained a sense of herself. Her fire, her willpower.

Kalmia called her name twice before she realized and turned her attention back to her.

"Ryakin informed me you're carrying a child, a son. He informed me you're making the announcement this Starfall in the public feasthall. And that you also will announce you're leaving the next morn for the Imperial court and the hot festival?"

Jynnalt paused a moment before answering. Pregnancy still an unfamiliar sensation. "Yes," she said, changing the subject as an odd sensation gripped her. Back to something Kalmia seemed fond of talking about.

"Why a lack of knowledge of the Murians if they were real? Other than tales the commoners tell, or cryptic poems from the Temple books, or scenes carved into sacred temple walls?"

"That is a mystery your father and I, and others like us, are trying to discover. So far, we have been able to glean a catastrophic event precipitated by the disappearance of the ancients. What? Why? How come? That is the unknown. The temples and some ruins throughout the galaxy hold pieces of the puzzle, yet not the full story. Your father found a mention of a Last Stance, but the reference to the event makes no sense." She said, moving to another pile and dug through as she talked.

"Your father believed the first civilizations we have records of, little as it is, are the ancestors of the Malkuth." She moved once more to a different pile. "In fact, he had a vast library, one his sister, you aunt, given to her upon her marriage, as a contract gift by the Glargrar. One he gained later upon her death. I believe the books he read, the reason he joined our group. After his sister's death, he became one of our leading members, poring over resources, helping with personnel, and putting a lot of time into the project."

"I never realized he was so involved with religion. I understood his favorite poem was Phoenix Rising, but I thought he liked the sentiment the poem evokes."

"No, your father believed it was a key to an important event and a prophecy."

Kalmia stood in triumph. "Here the bugger is. Thought you could hide, ha-ha, I am craftier than that."

It startled Jynnalt, Kalmia's strange exchange with the meh recording she now held. She watched her stride over to a holoprojector, inserting it into the proper slot. She gazed around for Ryakin, lost some place in the rear of the enormous chamber she followed Kalmia through. Curious why Kalmia did not tag the meh's for easy recall later when a loud discordant bell rang.

Kalmia clicked something on her belt and a strange glimmer of an aura envelop her. A viewer popped open, showing Kalmia's neat anti-chamber. Only Kalmia was in it. Jynnalt did a double-take before realizing the form a holo-projection. It did not show the actual chamber they stood in now. Kalmia walked to the office door; the feedback system good enough to sense a presence. The door opened. Jynnalt spotted

Ustrix.

"Yes," Kalmia said to Ustrix.

"Queen Jynnalt and Prince Ryakin's Blooded Da Rank informed me they left for here earlier. I need to speak to Prince Ryakin about something private. Are they here?"

The next thing Kalmia said shocked Jynnalt. "The Blooded Da Rank misinformed you. Or maybe they decided not to come for whatever reason. Either way, I have not seen them. I have a lot of work and must take my leave." She bowed her head, then shut the door.

Before the door shut in Ustrix's face, Jynnalt saw him staring open-mouthed, not use to rude offhanded manners.

Jynnalt flushed, and her eyes narrowed. "Why did you lie to Ryakin's friend about our presence here?" She said as she stepped back, operatives well-trained in combat, not only information collection, and Kalmia once worked in the field. Ryakin, she was sure, would also have seen or heard the exchange.

"Don't get your hackles up. I did not bring you down here to do away with you, and the technology you saw is not unique to Ki's Ministry fourteen. All fourteen's Ministries use this advanced tech. Sitting Royals are aware. Now both you and Ryakin know," Kalmia said, as if the technology was no big deal. "Besides, I did not rise to this position by killing off Ki's Queens, but by keeping them alive and informed of threats. I need to send something of significant importance to the Imperial's Ministry fourteen and I want no one outside this chamber knowing the fact." Ryakin appeared beside her, and a rush of relief raced through her.

"This," she pointed to the holoprojector with the meh, "my operatives along with others collected over a sar. Several of my agents lost their lives getting the information to us," Kalmia said as her voice hardened. She turned on the holoprojector.

Horrific images of destroyed towns, shipyards, and docks, smoking ruins, torched hovercraft, and the masts of wrecked watercraft peeked out, then disappeared as waves washed over them. Towns, blackened pits where homes and office buildings once stood, ominous black stains splashed across the few pitted and lopsided walls still standing along fissured roadways.

"These at one time bustling ports or cities." Kalmia interjected as the holo changed, showing Travelers stations or Fleet bases. Now nothing more than trillions of sparkling pieces of reflective floating debris. Skip scavengers flitting in amongst the wreckage. As each scene flickered across the viewer, their names and spheres of influence listed beneath them.

Shocked, Jynnalt sensed Ryakin next to her and his rising anger. Kalmia's voice startled her when she spoke, having forgotten about her wrapped up in the horror of the scenes.

"The trouble started seventy sars ago. Every few months an incident occurred, raids on pleasure barges, small Travelers Stations attacked. The citizens either murdered or vanished. We think they took them to sell as slaves. Smaller fleet ships on patrol also disappeared. Most attributed this to an increase in the slaver's activity. They like to stay out of the watchful eyes of the Council of Nine. They might have thought they were being spied upon. I worked on those types of cases when I was in the field. The numbers have escalated within the CON alliances, larger Travelers Worlds, and automatic deepspace shipwright yards. The attacks are swift, appalling, and devastating. Investigations found no survivors."

Jynnalt broke in, "There must be at least a survivor somewhere in seventy sars," she said as Ryakin agreed with her.

"None," Kalmia's voice was emphatic, then she hesitated. "I take that back; some did, but the stories are so bizarre no one listened. The Temple is listening now. However, we did not account for all the citizens either. At one shipwright's deep repair yard, over four hundred citizens out of seven hundred and fifty-nine missing. This is the same each time. Destruction of the places attacked, combined with high fatalities and missing citizens, sound familiar?"

"We never had a reported attack on a world within an influential CON empire. The agency believes Niuard is the first, but Jynnalt and her party as well as the commoners' escape left them exposed. This time they left survivors. Believe me, the council has examined your testimony down to every detail. It's unnerved CON and their alliances. Those attacked did not set their shieldwalls. We believe someone betrayed them from within. No distress signal sent either. Which begs the question, why? Except in Niuard. Most of the time Riders discover the destruction when they arrive for trade in a system, or patrols if fleet bases or Traveler's station attacked."

"They recently changed their tactics to include storage moons where only automated Ai's protect valuable production. Watch."

A scene of eerie stillness. The typical hum of robotic drones traveling between buildings with parts and materials unmoving. Silent. Smoke like a thick mist hugging the ground, shrouding the production plant. All controlled by the guilds manufacturing Ai's. Or protective security Ai's armed with sophisticated sensors, high-end rail ditcher mortars with armor-piercing laser's, high energy kinetic and sonic cannons. The defensives systems destroyed, the doors to the buildings hanging at odd angles.

Kalmia spoke up again as soon as the devastation on the viewer finished, "over ten moon production facilities, found in the last few months in the same condition. We have not figured out how they defeated the Ai security. Financially, the theft of the newest ship pattern buffers, and pattern production parts, are a heavy loss to those houses guilds or merchants who owned them in Ki."

"Why is this information not more common, at least amongst the fleet or greater councils?" Jynnalt asked, staring at the frozen image on the viewer.

"Up till now, most of the attacks happened against unprotected systems not belonging to any of the nine alliances."

"Is this common knowledge, at least, within your Ministry or similar organizations within GIA and CON?" Ryakin asked as he glanced at Kalmia. "I'm guessing," he thrust his chin towards the viewer, "this is the reason you want no one aware of why we are here."

"Correct," Kalmia then stepped on a holo-pad on the floor before touching a jewel on her bracelet she always wore. A 3D holo flared to life. The holo showed two males. Both wore simple tunics and robes, austere, unassuming, with the neutral coloring of browns, tans, and grays of the Societies' Order. What they discussed disquieting. Without naming names, their conversation about prominent level blooded guild members, merchants, and judges in various sectors of empires who collaborated with them. Secret members. Traitors. Part of whatever it was their working to accomplish. Everything seemed nebulous. Vague. The sense of danger and treachery came through loud and clear as a sonic shockwave. They were watching holos of meetings and gatherings. Some holos showed four or five citizens, or other areas with bigger gatherings. All conversations revolved around destroying CON and its most formidable and wealthy empires. The Anunnaki Empire appears at the top of their list. Though not the most influential or wealthy, which made little sense.

"How does this involve Ki? This falls under CON and the Temple's jurisdiction," Jynnalt said. Her brow furrowed as she stared at the last frozen image of a form hidden deep in the shadows wearing the Society's Orders distinctive cloak.

Kalmia hit a switch, and the holo restarted. Now three males were discussing the Anunnaki Empire, the largest one saying. "Our first attack on the empire failed because of several unfortunate events which our masters did not foresee. Higher-up's now want us to facilitate the murder of the Emperor and Empress before the heir is born. This should create enough chaos and disruption to their government, allowing our agents in place to coordinate with others."

As the conversation proceeded, her mouth fell slack and her eyes widened. The longer she listened, the hotter her face became as her breathing increase to the point of hyperventilating.

From what those on the tape said, they even now control many high-ranking blooded, some guild masters, others well-placed Imperial whisper fourteen operatives. Towards the end they discussed their supposed failure to inflict enough damage to destroy the seat of power of the Anunnaki Empire. Her eyes narrowed. Fifty million lost lives and untold animals and over ten sars worth of food production estimated, destroyed.

One of the Society members remarked, "at least we got rid of some targets." both chuckled. The third one emphasized the alternative plan appeared flawless to him. Charge those who are innocent of any wrong after the fact, laying the suspicions preceding the murder. How certain parties would benefit should the heir not be born. Later, others recall those remarks with a little help. One of them moved out of sight, reentering the frame with a heruo pipe in his hand.

"Ignorant commoners are the linchpin of the plan. Convince them the Society is working for them. Stir them to violence, allowing our operatives to move into place without opposition. If we keep screaming from the rooftops, enough will fall for the deception and support us. Once they are defenseless, we can enslave them. How I would love to see their faces when that occurs. Both laughed at that remark. Most of the commoners and some ranking blooded and guild members will keep quiet and keep their heads down, not wanting attacked as dissidents. See, the master's plan is perfect. Control of the mobs and fear of speaking against us will hand the empire to us without a battle."

Jynnalt's blood ran cold at the remark. The image froze at that second.

"This next part is where Ki comes in," Kalmia said, "And, before you ask, no, I don't have information or evidence who." She restarted the viewer.

"How in the daemon's name did our two operatives in Ki allow such a massive screw up in the first place? If those two had done their job, the Society would already control the Anunnaki Empire."

Dropping his voice to a whisper, one said, "are you crazy? One of those operators is our master's mistress. Don't get caught talking like that around any others. Losing your head would be the least thing to worry about. I've heard he keeps a vat in his dungeons so the tortures can go on forever if he wishes. Or at least till they are insane. No mind left. You don't want a visit there, I guarantee." The holo disappeared.

"Where are the whisper operatives who attained these holo's now? Jynnalt spoke slow, each word enunciated. I want to interview them," she said as she moved closer to Ryakin. Her eyes glittering.

"Dead. These holos, we received, full of static. We cleaned them to gain this much clarity. One holo arrived set to an automatic timer to send. One video we caught an assassin murdering our operative. We got the murder on video but no other information," she said, pausing. "We are not sure if the assassin was aware they recorded the murder, or they deliberately sent us a warning. Believe me, the manner of death was gruesome."

Ryakin cut in. "What are you wanting us to do?"

"I need you to make sure this person," the holo-projection changed to an unassuming female, "is on your royal travel roster as a member of your personal server's guild. That will keep her from having to go through the normal entry terminal for guild workers. The Imperial Ministry Fourteen's Master Zioria is expecting her and this meh. That is all you must do." She reached down and turned off the holo-projection.

"I will make sure she gets to Nibiru Proper and her destination."

Kalmia stepped close to her and Ryakin. "Listen, do nothing other than request the royal writ for my operative. Stay away and let her do her job. I can tell you're angry. I informed you of the situation, per law, and asked you to perform a small, though vital, task. Unusual, I admit, but too many died for this information. Think about your kingdom's citizens. They can't afford to lose another Queen so soon. It would demoralize the Kierian citizens, and give these criminals, and whoever is behind this, the upper hand."

"She is correct. You, as Queen, are too important to Ki. Leave this to those trained for these things. I recognize the stubborn expression but leave this alone." Ryakin said.

After a moment, she relaxed, looking at Kalmia. "I am holding you to your word. You will take care of this. Now I believe we should leave, or our paladins will search the entire palace and grounds for us if we are much later."

"Don't worry, I took care of that. However, you are right, we've been here long enough. Follow me. We will leave through a different exit."

They came to a small door leading to a private nook well hidden behind boulders and evergreen trees. Kalmia asked if they wanted her to send for a hoverbarge? Jynnalt preferred to walk. Wanting to discuss with Ryakin what they learned today while in the isolated, restricted access of the royal park.

The palace was fifty times bigger than originally designed, a triumph of engineering. The facade of graceful looking columns which held up peaked ornate roofs covering patio's, raised balconies and porches deep enough for furniture to be outside in any weather. Radiant heat from the floors for the cold season or cooling mists during the hot season made the porches comfortable. The Kierian palace carved deep into the mountain and relied on geothermal energy for heat and power.

A gentle breeze blew now and then through the garden, followed by the soft rustle of green leaves. The turns' temperature pleasant as warm starlight of the mid-afternoon caressed her skin. The sky a clear turquoise, the star a golden orb above. Fliers fluttered through trees decked in bright, warm colors as insects buzzed along pathways lined with border hedges, moving from flower to flower. Beckoned by enticing sweet scents. The royal garden ran three standards long and two standards broad on the high plateau, the palace cut from the Adsullata Fire Mountain overlooking Kishira, Ki's capital city. The palace sat back against the face of the mountain, cutting deep into its bowels. As Jynnalt walked with Ryakin in the park, her long, elegant skirt and matching top, covered in sheer stilken over dress, swirled around her in the gentle breeze. She shivered from the coolness on her exposed waist after the stifling heat of the chamber.

"Your Highnesses," Tavas, along with Caltac' and ten others, approached. "You informed the guild you wanted private time with each other this morning. However, you are cutting it close to attend the council. Should we delay or inform them you will be on schedule?" He said, though curious, but too well-trained to mention the royal couple's breach of security by not allowing them access to their location.

"We will be ready soon. I have a minor detail to take care of, Ryakin stated."

Tavas touched the back of his ear, "inform the council they will arrive shortly."

She and Ryakin moved towards the side gate to the palace patio, their paladins following at a discreet distance.

Chapter 19

JYNNALT STARED AT BLADES of lush grass, her ears ringing, her head throbbing as a fire burned from her upper ribcage across to her right hip.

Twice she tried to rise to her knees, the first attempt failing. As soon as she put pressure on her left arm, agonizing pain ripped through her. Dizziness engulfed her, and once more she found herself staring at blades of grass.

The thunder of her breath blocked out all other sounds. Pain roared through her, consumed her, a liquid warmth of wetness spread across her side, soaking her clothes.

A voice in her head ordered, *get up or die*. She obeyed, blindly. Concentrating, she pulled her knees under her, holding her left arm close to her body. The slightest movement made her suck in her breath as a guttural moan escaped her lips. She stopped. Waited for the dizziness to pass this time, her breathing ragged and harsh.

Yelling, screams, and slapping sounds intruded on her consciousness. A grunt to her far left caught her attention, the sound confusing. A giant insect whizzed past, followed by a thunking noise. More buzzed past, burrowing in the ground, spraying dirt in her face. One struck next to her hand, and a rush of adrenaline flooded her system. Not insects. Projectiles. She got to her feet and staggered behind the nearest tree, a massive old oak.

The sight before her a horror of bodies. A hundred feet away from her, eight of the Emperor's Eagle paladins. Crumpled and laying at odd angles on the ground, not moving. Emperor Lahamu farther away, trying to crawl towards safety, while seven of his paladins fought furiously, trying to protect him. Off to her left, five of her paladins, twenty feet away, lifeless glassy eyes staring toward the stars blazing overhead. One attacker going around finishing them beyond vatting. There would be no witnesses.

Movement to her right caught her attention. Seconds passed before her eyes adjusted to the light. A merchant, one of those showing rugs when she arrived earlier. Ten rugs rolled out next to the pavilion before the Emperor and Empress. Three merchants discussing their quality with the master guild of ministry nine as others helped them roll out the exquisite rugs. She ignored the throbbing in her head, needing to think.

A server took them over to a trestle table and left them with refreshment, saying the Emperor and Empress would see them after the merchants left. Jynnalt perceived the goods were excellent quality with exotic weaves from the Chisia empire. The emperor indulging the Empress, whose belly was huge with child.

A male who appeared to be a merchant unaware of her hiding behind the tree close to him. He unrolled a rug and out spilled kinetic handguns, swords, and a sonic personnel canon. As he squatted near her, she moved his direction, focusing on his back. She tried to move fast, yet pain sapped her strength, slowing her. She focused on her need for a weapon. Without one little chance, she'd survive the night.

Someone grabbed her from behind and without thinking she whipped back her uninjured arm, heard a grunt, and stumbled forward, instantly released.

"Tavas, it's Tavas," a voice said harshly in her ear, as she gasped. Peered back, Tavas stood there covered in blood. She reached a trembling hand out, and he grabbed it, pulling her after him. Away from the needed weapons. She pulled back. This time, he yanked her forward and a gasp of pain escaped as agony gripped her in a vise.

"I have to get you to safety." He pulled her harder after him.

She pulled back once more, though as weak as she was, she did not resist him for long.

Tavas stopped, and she fell against him, "listen, something jammed our comm's. For now, they're focused on the Eagle warriors."

Still, she fought him, prying at his hand to release her. A sharp, stinging slap got her to focus before Tavas yanked her forward again. Away from the fighting, she glanced back and recognized four of her paladins following, covering their retreat. They kept themselves between her and the attackers.

The largest one moved forward and spoke low, "The emperor is dead, the last of the Eagles are giving their lives so the Empress and heir can escape."

Jynnalt glanced in that direction. Ten Eagle paladins fought valiantly, while four others herded the Empress towards a side gate before the assassins cut them off, forcing them back toward the killing ground.

Tavas pulled her after him once more. "We need to leave. Now. They're focused on the Empress. We cannot help her; her Eagle warriors will have to save her. Think of your child." Not waiting for an answer, he pulled her towards an outer side gate hidden in the shadows. She moved as fast as she could, the acrimonious taste of helplessness at abandoning the sovereign to her fate, and fear for her child a conflicting fire within. Yet, a fierce emotion to protect her child gripped her. Weakened by her wounds, her strength ebbed with each step. She needed a life tender. Soon.

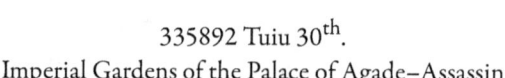

335892 Tuiu 30th.
Imperial Gardens of the Palace of Agade–Assassin

A TALL, STRIKING FIGURE stepped out of the deep shadows of the covered veranda. From here, he directed the events unfolding. The client's requested three primary targets. Wealthy enough to have guards, but not high-ranking enough to involve the Temple.

Instructions said no witnesses. Standard request, though he would charge extra for each additional body. They claimed they could delay the local enforcers for a half hour before they responded. Still, the problems this job presented concerned him.

He required twenty-three of the best assassins from the clan, a dangerous amount to be loitering planetside. Neither he nor the clan comfortable with those numbers. This one job alone would allow him to retire. Able to buy the minor world close to the outer rim, swayed his decision to take the job.

One sitting outside any sphere of influence. His fifteen children scattered throughout the galaxy under aliases to keep them and himself safe needed a proper home. He intended to provide one with the best tutors and an enormous mansion.

A target added an hour before they left for the job angered him. He almost refused. Once more, the added tithe swayed his decision. A red-haired female. They required the newest target's body removed from the scene, along with at least four protectors.

Too bad, she's exquisite. Ran through his mind as he managed his men.

The last communique listed more changes. Changes at the last moment, risky. His nerves over this job increased with each added element. Originally, he planned the attack to happen three turns from now, *not* planetside. Too many enforcers and planetary detection systems.

He organized the assassination to happen on Narti, one of the system's larger Traveler Station. Their Emperor intended to sponsor a theater event for the date, a gift for his Queen. His reputation such as he hired the highest-ranking bards within the empire. Citizens fought for an invitation to attend not only for the political advantage but the event itself. That would have been perfect. The crowded venue provided easy access and quick escape avenues. When in the crush of a crowd or the dark of a theater, his assassins struck with swift precision and melted away unseen.

The lack of an Igigi platform because of a disaster tipped his decision to go ahead with the job. And a substantial addition of tithe. Half, as usual, paid upfront to his account.

Still, too many variables planetside. Even without Igigi, they would have scanners and trackers. Murder of any ranking citizens did not sit well with empires. Incidents like those made for unwelcome pulse flashes from the news bards, making the natives restless and brought too much attention to criminal activity.

Minutes into the job, he sensed something amiss. Unease crept in, not familiar sensation. These guards appeared too well trained for paid protectors. In fact, not just trained well, but displaying exceptional skill. More than half of the assassins he brought planetside lay dead. He called for additional help, which arrived in minutes. Before arriving, he put crew members on standby, thinking more about a quick escape than any actual problems with the job. Failure not an option. Never happened before, not within his clan. Not in all his time in business.

The thought crossed his mind to pull out. Leave the job undone. However, an assassin does not go far if he cannot complete jobs.

He did not run when things got tough. That's how he became the head of an assassins' clan. How he molded them to become the most sought after in the galaxy.

He needed this job. He planned to retire before the Avatar of Death came, hunting him with his scythe. The time arrived for him to disappear. He survived longer than most and preferred to retire and enjoy a pleasant life.

His reputation taking a hit bothered his vanity. Nor would he give up the tithe. Poor, not a familiar sensation. Besides, the clan would disown him. He shuddered. An assassin without a clan, a pitiful creature.

He lost track of the red-haired wench. After scanning the area, he found her. She and the last of her guards moving away from the killing field.

The red head and her fighters heading towards the outer wall, which puzzled him. Why head to a dead end? Could they intend to hoist her over the wall? He scanned the area with his night vision. The assassin looked for a spot somewhere for them to climb over. Then he sighted a small semi-hidden gate covered by brushes and short ornamental trees.

Impressive. No panic. He enjoyed watching the red-haired wenches' guards; formidable fighters, every single one. The others in fancier gear, not shabby but too technical and formal in their techniques. The quality of these fighters worried him. Not about his men defeating them, but that such supposed low-level ranking bought fighters of this superior quality caused him to frown. His clan's assassins, the finest in the galaxy. This job should have wrapped up minutes after starting. Yet, the fighting far from ending.

He brought his most valued fighters. In overwhelming numbers. Because of being planetside, he hoped to finish and leave shortly. No matter how excellent the fighters are, greater numbers and sophisticated high-tech weaponry win. Attrition a far crueler mistress than luck.

Shame the client wanted them all dead. These fighters impressed him. He'd been in the business for a long time and the demand for decent ring arena slaves high. Added to the odd request to remove the red-haired wench and four of her protector's bodies troubling. Not his concern, though still curious about the strange request. He did not question clients. If they adhered to his rules, he followed theirs. Assassins worked off reputation.

The Assassin called eight of his men to break off from the other fight. Directed them to stop the red-haired wench's group before they reached the wall.

"Use swords. They're too close to the outer wall. Our clients disabled the vibration detectors and burst energy sniffers in the garden. The kinetic roar of weapons will alert the surrounding enclaves. Reports of those coming from an outer garden will have the enforcers rushing here in all haste."

His focused returned to the group clustered around the white-haired pregnant female as her protectors fought his assassins. Their numbers decreasing, still too slow, but desperation setting in from their reaction times. Desperate meant the fights almost finished. Normally, paid guards abandoned their client at this point. These fought harder, step by bloody step, towards a small alcove. *Perhaps they sensed turning to run would not save them.*

Twenty minutes more of fighting. His eyes narrowed, and he shook his head. Realized the information given to him faulty. "Back off and use the sonic cannon," he said through comm's designed by the assassin's league, "this has gone on for too long. Move fast. The blast will set the outer detectors off.

One assassin put a long tube to his shoulder and fired. A high whine became an earth-shattering roar within seconds. The shock wave leveling everything around it, including the three guards outside the alcove as the ground rumbled in response to the assault.

"Quick. We're behind schedule."

— § —

335892 Tuiu 30th.
Imperial Gardens of the Palace of Agade, -
Queen Jynnalt's Paladins.

— § —

THEY ALMOST REACHED the gate when eight attackers rushed them from the side. Silver moonlight glinted off the edge of sword blades. The oldest paladin, Abdi, yelled, shoving Queen Jynnalt to the ground, saving her life. A long knife went straight through his heart. Abdi crumpling as he fell to the ground dead beside the Queen spurred the rest of them to fight harder. Relief flashed through Tavas when she scrambled to her feet.

Minutes passed as they shoved Queen Jynnalt this way and that between them as they fought to keep her in the middle. Several times, one or another shoved her to the ground, then yanked her back to her feet, then shoved her back down.

The attacks stopped. Tavas spotted nine bodies on the ground, three paladins still stood, covered in blood and gore. Some theirs. Movement at the pavilion pulled his attention in that direction.

The sound of Jynnalt's gasp when she stared behind them before turning away made him glance back. Three males dressed as ranking Anunnaki blooded stood over the body of Emperor Lahamu. The sight of the emperor lying dead shocked Tavas. Something slammed hard into him, sending him flying as darkness took him.

PHOENIX RISING

HE GLANCED OVER TO where the other eight went to finish the red-hair wench and her protectors. He expected to see the targets dead. Instead, the last of his assassin fell. Thinking fast, he yelled into his comm's for the one with the cannon to turn towards the group close to the wall. Hit them now. She and her guards too close to the gate and the possibility they might escape elevated. He calculated the distance. Sonic cannons are a short-range weapon. It might not pack a killing punch, but the shock would take them down. When they blew through the air, landing hard and not rising, he turned his attention back to the cleanup, satisfied.

Three strange figures moving around the chief target sprawled on the ground caught the Assassin's attention. He whirled at the creak of sound behind him. His plasma handheld pointing at a stranger entering through a small gate.

"I would not use that if you desire the rest of your payment. And please ignore the three over by the body. They are verifying the job's done."

The assassin called out on his comm's "Ignore those three. Get back to the cleanup. You've got fifteen minutes." His crew completed the task efficiently in five, ready to leave on the disguised hovercraft. He did one last check of the grounds, nodded their direction. A minute later, they exited through the merchant's needle gate out into the causeway toward the private dock assigned to them to land.

"I see you accomplished the job. Truth is, I thought for a moment, you might not achieve the goal. I'm impressed. You're as excellent as your reputation. And your clan. Still, a few almost got away. I thought I would have to interfere, take matters into my own hands. Would have cost you, and your clan." He motioned, and several males dressed in Society robes stepped into the light.

The Society order gave him the creeps. Reminded him of grotesques blood-sucking insects on unsavory planets he visited, not in appearances but in attitude. Cold, vicious. Uncaring.

"Check the grounds. Leave just enough evidence to point to the Queen," the stranger said, as he turned towards him. "I am giving you thirty minutes to leave the atmosphere. Ten minutes afterward, every fleet ship in the Anunnaki Empire will hunt you down." The shadowy figure paused. "you aided the Queen of Ki to murder the Emperor and Empress of the Anunnaki Empire."

"Queen of Ki? Emperor and Empress?" His voice wavered. Shock flashed through his gut as he looked to where the male body laid surrounded by the fallen fighters.

"Yes," the stranger said, "the red-haired female is the Queen of Ki. The other two targets, the Emperor and Empress of the Anunnaki Empire. Oh, and I thought you should know, I placed a tracker on your ship. I would advise you not to dump those bodies before you're far enough away. Or I will send in an anonymous tip. The tip will claim you double-crossed the Queen, killing her after she paid you. You won't find the tracker, I assure you. Don't waste the little time I gave you looking." The client's voice pleasant and conversational, so at odds with his words.

A flash of white teeth in a sardonic smile caused a dark chill to pass through him. The stranger called over his comm's, "in forty minutes send enforcers to arrest Prince Ryakin, King Rualui, and Prince Anu. Lockdown their fleets and Paladins barracks before you serve the arrest writ. Arrest none of their families. Let's not allow sympathy to build up for them." When he finished, the stranger said, "You may leave now." He made a shooing motion as if he was dismissing a child or servant. "Oh, and if you did not figure this out so far, my associates will not take kindly to your being anywhere near this empire. *Ever*."

The assassin left fast, wanting the *helc* away from this daemon possessed citizen. Forty minutes later, it took all his skills and tricks to evade the ships closing in on them.

He headed to the cargo bay once safely away. His clan took a tremendous hit with twenty lost in this fiasco. Their reputation would never recover. They assassinated not only a Queen but an Emperor and

Empress. The greater sin, a pregnant Empress. Not good. In fact, a disaster. The Temple Ghost Walkers would roust all the clans as they hunted for them. With tithe that good, he should have investigated further. The others on board put the bodies of his clan's assassins, who died in the airlock, before shooting them into deepspace as they passed by a gas giant. Assassins recognized this as their likely end, accepted their fate. For a fleeting moment, he thought he would avoid this fate.

He moved to the last five rugs to dispose of their bodies. A moan came from one. He moved over and untied the rug. Shocked for a second, he realized the female still alive. Quickly he checked the others and found them also breathing, but unconscious. The cannon too far away for a killing strike, like he thought. About to slit their throats, he stopped. He and his clan deserved more tithe, double-crossed by the clients, a plan formed in his mind for revenge. And insurance.

Three turns later, he met up with a Free Solar Federation slaver to make the exchange. The extra tithe earned added to the original job. Which he promptly split amongst himself and his men, conveniently leaving out who they assassinated. For now, let them enjoy their earnings.

Then he ordered them to head to one of their clan's paid hideouts. They would not stay long. This place shared by the galaxy's undesirables. No one talked to strangers and the illicit members of the galaxy relaxed their guard within the station, not worried about enforcers or guardians.

He would explain to his crew before they left the hideout why they could not go back to the clan and needed to scatter as far from each other as possible.

The Temple would soon send Ghost Walkers to hunt them. Hence, why his clan avoided certain jobs. Too late now.

Two turns later, when loaded up and ready to leave, he stayed a little longer than he intended at the local pleasure house. He enjoyed the delights of one of the more expensive ladies as a treat to himself.

Afterward, he headed to his ship. Time to buy the world on the outer rim system and round up his children. Time to live an enjoyable life and get out of reach of the Ghost Walkers.

Halfway up the plank, his ship detonated in a fiery explosion. Debris rained down upon the dock, killing any standing close to the blast.

The explosion took out the plank he stood on. Blown under a support pylon for the dock, he lost consciousness. When he came around later, he knew his injuries severe. Overheard two pirates talking.

"He's lucky he's dead. The head boss would have taken his danglers for bringing this trouble. The boss convinced those two Ghost Walkers those they came looking for died in an accidental explosion while docked. They looked around, then left. One stared straight at me as if he read my mind. I swear. I wanted to crawl out of my skin and hide."

Every single crewmember on board, ready to leave when the bomb blew. He checked his account, figuring he needed a fast vessel. He felt gut kicked on top of all his other pains. His account bone dry, not a single gereh left. Frantic, he searched all his accounts; drained. How did they know about all his accounts? Swearing, he laid there raging for hours.

Reaching for the hidden stash of talons, when he finally ran out of energy, in a secret pocket, from the coins he received in the sale of those five. On him still when he went to the pleasure house. His heart pounded, afraid those vanished in the explosion. Sighed in relief at the solid feel of coins. A small fortune, by any standards.

Eight turns later, he sat at one of his hideouts; he utilized when the heat got too intense for his normal haunts drinking rage building. His clan destroyed. Everyone murdered. He thought through everything which occurred. They'd made their first mistake. Leaving him alive by not double-checking the Dna signatures in the blast area. Never, ever go after an assassin and fail. He would find a way to make every one of them pay.

Yet, he needed a plan and more tithe, along with a changed identity. He held one ace in the hole. He alone capable of identifying one client. A high-ranking Society Priest. Hidden amongst them as one of their own.

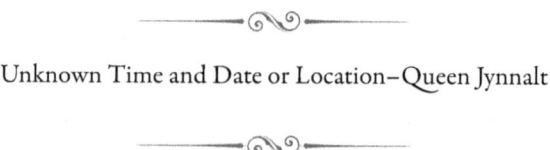

Unknown Time and Date or Location–Queen Jynnalt

A THUNDEROUS SOUND roused her. Barely conscious, she

recognized the slamming of a hatch door. Seconds later, another slammed farther away. Jynnalt's ravenous thirst gnawed at her. Her tongue stuck to the roof of her mouth, and she worked at getting it loose so she could call out.

"Water. Please." Her voice broke, cracked and whispery, the sound shocking. Jynnalt looked around, tried to discover her whereabouts. Around her, black forms hunched over, or lay upon the floor, the soft sounds of a child crying, somewhere close, accompanied by pitiful noises, reached her.

Others here. Others hurt. Like her?

No one came to her pitiful pleas. She attempted to rise from a nest of clothes she was lying on. *Clothes?* Where the *helc* am I?

Pain hit, hard. As if acid burned through her and darkness claimed her.

Desperate thirst roused her. She moved slower, trying to rise, stopping each time pain rose, threatening to engulf her. She failed and laid back down. The piles of rags upon the floor within her vision covered bodies, making her question if they were still breathing.

A rustling sound reached her as someone moved next to her, yet too weak to turn her head in that direction. Hurt many times through the sars when at the academy, Jynnalt's trainers advised her that making yourself get up and move around is best for a quick recovery. Best if you did not linger in the repair unit. Here, powerless to even turn her head.

A voice whispered in her ear, familiar to her, somehow. Exhausted, she let the thought go.

"I have water for you, but you must take tiny sips," the voice said in a stern tone. For the next few minutes, which seemed like hours, he dripped water into her mouth from a rag. "Enough for now."

Desperate for more, she tried to grab the rag and pull it back towards her mouth and failed.

"Do you think you can sit up?" The hopeful tone made her want to please him.

"I.... not sure. I can try." The sound of her voice still shocking.

He leaned over and slid his arm under her shoulders. "my name is Kendo. I will be as gentle as possible. Take it slow and easy sitting up.

Okay,"

Jynnalt nodded. The slight gesture caused pain to thunder through her head.

"There is no rush." The worry in his voice puzzled her. He lifted her to a sitting position. The movement ignited a shock of stabbing, burning pain in Jynnalt's side, stomach, and back. He stopped at the harsh intake of her breath, giving her a moment to collect herself.

"Are you all right?"

Minutes passed before she answered. "Yes, give me a moment." Her voice a bare croaking whisper. She glanced up at him and for a split second, the worried face of her father superimposed itself upon the stranger. Once during a trip, Jynnalt caught a rare illness, and her father never left her side. Even feverish as a child, she knew his face reflected what was in his eyes, fear, and agony.

An urge to comfort him made her reach out with a weak hand and place it upon his face. "Father, don't worry," she whispered as darkness took her.

Chapter 20

335892 GGS Elec 28th.
A slave ship: Location–Unknown—Elder Kendo Listria of the Malkuth

THE REDONE TRANSPORT appeared to have once been a high altitude drop battleship. They stuffed him in the ship's underbelly, along with other prisoners. Stacks of pods as far up as he could see into the darkness above. Kendo had seen designs of this sort during his studies of the Great War. Sabation designs. Anti-gravity drop-pods where warriors stood stacked rows upon rows before unleashed upon a planet like a plague of raining locust.

Their captors appeared to be working their way across the galaxy. He asked prisoners as they arrived, their species, if he did not recognize them, which empire they came from, and where the attack occurred. To him, as he gathered the information, it appeared as if they were navigating in a zigzag pattern across the galaxy.

Outlaws attacked the ship he was traveling on in a concerted effort. Five different consortiums acting together unusual. He recognized a few brands' the outlaw cartels burned in their follower's arms. They murdered every crew member who fought against them. Next, all the high ranking Malkuth and their protectors on board. Before murdering them, they scanned them, shaking their heads, moving to the next.

They tortured the civilians yet did not find what they wanted, *him*. The advanced glamor tech far beyond the abilities of the outlaws and empires scanners. His own body's energy powered the technology. If alive, the device protected him. It did not change his outer looks, other than fool simplistic facial recognition. The technology changed his Dna signature to mimic a registered low-level scholar of the Malkuth Empire.

Afterward, they took the forty scholars' captives for their trouble and expense, including him. Scholars amongst slavers sell for prime tithe on the market. Star traveling empires of mid-tech civilization still allowed the practice. They paid maximum tithe to acquire them.

Later, the outlaws met up with slave merchants and sold them off lane. The slave's new owners armor a weird mix of captured pieces from across the galaxy's empires. Their lack of a single form of standard armor implied outlaws, yet they appeared militant. Organized. With a formalized hierarchy.

From what he figured out, they moved outside the trade lanes, attacking private yachts and merchant ships with live crews, ignoring auto-piloted Ai ships. They hit small run-down Travelers Stations and empires, fleet's repair docks, and a few smaller worlds outside protection of CON. Their attacks swift, brutal, and merciless. They loaded any ships not damaged in the attack on to massive escort battleships traveling with them. Before long Kendo came to the belief, they were reavers, not outlaws or pirates.

Someone in CON must feed them information on where and when to attack to avoid patrols. An insider would have information on ships, stations, or worlds to strike. Even more important, they would have access to overcome high-level advanced security on the targets they went after.

Distinct vibrations and rumbling sounds underfoot informed him they started their run along the acceleration gate to create a warp bubble bow wave. They used skip engines twice. *Why not use them all the time?* A few times they used back lane Star Gates. They must have a means of fooling the Igigi operating them. Or the Igigi corrupted with bribes. A concerning factor. There was one advantage to using these ancient acceleration gates. They have the smallest frequency footprint, capable of hiding them from scanning empire patrols as they entered warp.

His trainers claimed the Great War was the last time they used these gates. Afterward, the Malkuth presented the galaxy members in CON plans to build the short skip engines. This allowed them to maneuverer outside the trade lanes and Galactic Gates controlled by the Igigi and the Temple. The locations of the acceleration gates no longer listed on any nav charts. The Council of Nine claimed they destroyed them. This belied the facts.

CON lied. To what purpose?

The reavers discovered their locations and now use them to move around undetected. They appeared in good working order. Because the frequency footprint of the gates is almost nil, a patrol would need to be next to the vicinity for scanners to detect their use. This explained how the reavers kept out of sight and struck without warning.

When they went to drift, battleships, cruisers, and dreadnoughts airlocked with them and disgorged more captured prisoners. Shoved into the hold of this massive ancient transport. Their captors disposed of the dead by ejecting them into gas giants.

When they moved him from one ship to another, he got a glimpse of their hulls. Scarred like an old warrior from too many battles and held together by welding and rivets, an outdated process for the last three hundred sars.

A female, wearing clothes, now rags, only a wealthy citizen of most empires afforded, dumped into the hold after one of their stops. Followed moments later by four males, manacled, and thrown in after her. All covered head to toe in bruises and scabbed over cuts. He saw a long foul slash from shoulder to hip across the front of the female and a gash across her forehead; her back from her heels to her neck, a deep black and yellow with festering pus.

Three turns later, he got a decent look at the males and recognized them from the attack on Niuard. The Ghost Walker not amongst them. Kendo wondered if he died in their defense in whatever misadventure brought them here.

He thought back on the response from the Temple Priestess. After the attack, when he asked about the one called Caltac', they informed him the citizen in question was not a Ghost Walker. Kendo was not stupid; he recognized one when he witnessed them fighting. Their unique style unmistakable. Kendo's curiosity piqued about why the

Priestess lied.

Their only concern at that time: the relic. He told them about the Protectorate's deaths. How they fought to protect the Priestess. Explained how she died. The ash spilled across the ground, mingling with her blood. He gave them the location from memory. Afterward, he was not sure what happened to the relic.

Now, in weird synchronicity, the female, and her paladins, shared the same fate as he. Under less-than-optimal circumstances. This time, instead of hunted. Prisoners.

The paladins took turns forcing water down her throat, making sure she was on her side all the time. They tried to keep the pressure off her back and the injury on her front. Her hair a stiff, matted mess of dried blood. Biological nanites hard pressed to repair injuries that extensive. He figured she would be dead by the next turn or two. Sadden by the amount of death seen in his lifetime of late.

This time, he learned their names. Tavas, Keif, Tiarn, and Aidral. He overheard the female's name during their desperate flight from the city on Niuard, Jynnalt.

Kendo wondered if the attack on Niuard staged to capture him. By whom or why, an unknown part of an unsolvable puzzle. For now. He lacked enough information. He strongly suspected this dealt with the past. So, he turned his attention to the female.

Over time, the female improved. She could stand and eat without help. What lay ahead, he could not say. One thing he was sure of, only the strongest would survive.

A sudden bumping and jolting startled those in the hold. The paladin Tavas called out to those within hearing,

"We are entering an atmosphere, not being attacked. Do not panic. Pass it along."

The captives, terrified, calmed at that information; the entry was rough but no longer frightening. Moments later, the hull reacted to the atmosphere, turning from solid metal to opaque than clear. *Strange.* Kendo looked around at the captives who uneasy to start with panicked, a few injured others as they tried to plaster themselves along the walls. The four paladins in loud firm voices informed them the floor was metacrystal, which calmed them once more. Loud moans of pain from those trampled seconds before filled the air.

Looking down, he saw the smooth surface of golden plains, Thick dark green timbered areas covered the upper half of a vast continent cut in half by a volcanic mountain range. Oxygen-producing plants, *thank the gods*. Both poles, white lands of thick ice covering whole continents. To his lower left, a desert of rich browns, tans and yellow strata on stark plateaus and mesas rose out of the painted desert edging along worn mountain ranges.

To the lower left, a curving ring of stratovolcanoes rose proudly, hemming in a vast expanse of grassland. Whitefall halfway down their flanks. Smoke rose lazily from three of the largest. Massive rivers crisscrossed throughout the plains, converging to become one gigantic waterfall.

As the transport came in lower, a steep-sided canyon appeared carved miles deep by a river. A slow, lazy river with soft windblown ripples curved in a winding pattern, other times a boiling mass of white water on long straight stretches.

The crack on the planet appeared to go for hundreds of miles toward what he thought might be south. The ship banked sharply, removing the canyon from view, straightened, headed toward a plateau. Strange symbols carved into the stone lined with flashing landing lights. Other ships came in next to them. Each homing in on a specific symbol. He tensed. His gut queasy. To him, they seemed to come in too steep and fast as the ground rushed up at him. He glanced over at the paladins; they did not blink an eye, unconcerned. *Bravado or do they know something I don't.*

Right as he thought they would crash, they leveled fast, the nose tipped almost straight up. Powerful thrusters on the bottom of the hull flared to life, jolted him hard. The gargantuan ship slowed. Lowering towards the lights flashing on the ground.

They landed with a bone-jarring bounce on the flat rock of the plateau. The metal struts let off an ear-shattering hiss to those in the hold as the hydraulics took the immense weight of the ship. Once the transport landed the height from the bottom of the hold to the plateau, still twenty stories above the rocky floor. Moments afterward, the pilots powered down the engines. The incessant sounds now replaced by the crackle and popping of cooling composite metals of engine casings.

Guards entered, forcing them all to one side. One yanked Jynnalt to her feet, her condition making her slow to respond to his command. Kendo heard her hissed intake of breath, but not a word or groan passed her lips. The guards moving the prisoners in front of the pods from above, strapped them in and shut the capsule pod door. The floor opened on one side, with loud groans and hissing. Once open, grinding noises filled the air and the pods' lowered towards the ground, jerking and swinging. They repeated the cycle until those from the hold stood on the stone plateau. Two stars peeked over the eastern horizon, rising.

Their captors patrolled, monitoring them. Although dressed in a mix of armor from throughout the galaxy, the weapons were top grade. Their arrogant stances served well to intimidate most, prompting compliance from the debarking prisoners. Their authority absolute. Kendo doubted any here would outright challenge them, not even his recent friends.

The scorching heat from cooling engines blew their way, adding to their misery. The early morning blazing hot. He gagged on the overpowering ozone from the reentry ion engines. With the prisoners unloaded, one who appeared in command walked to a spot, squatted, punched in a code on the rock floor. Up rose a big round tube. He punched in another code on the side, and a door slid open.

They loaded the prisoner's group by group in the lift and lowered them to the canyon floor by antigrav tubes. All the ships across the plateau doing the same with their cargo of prisoners. Once those from his ship's hold arrived below, they set off in a forced march through the canyon. *Odd*, the guards rode beast's, not mechanical transports. They sat high above on the huge, humped creatures, looking down on the captives.

While they marched along the causeway, lighter than air transports floated serenely by overhead. The sky was full of them, heading various directions. Some close enough to see passengers along the outer walkways enjoying the scenery, yet not close enough to see which species they might be.

Lashes from the guard's whip burned, drawing blood, along with hand gestures and yanks on their restraints, conveyed what their captors demanded. Forcing them to follow the long, winding pathway. Turn after turn, leading them away from the high plateau. They trekked along the canyon pathway till they exited on to a stone metacrete road. Flat white sands of the desert on either side. To him, the road seemed out of place and appeared to lead nowhere.

They walked for hours under the two blistering stars. Thirst made Kendo desperate, reminding him that Jynnalt, weaker, must be in terrible condition. Dehydrated, she needed water soon. *It will be a waste of my efforts to keep her alive on the ship if she dies now.* For a second, he thought he saw a flash of tattoos on the left side of her face, shoulder, and arm. Next second, nothing. No tattoos. Was he hallucinating?

The sophisticated and pretentious tones of a Dalagian from the Merchant Guilds Alliance reached him, unfiltered through his translator, which appeared to not work. "Water," the prisoner begged in galactic, "please, I need water." The captive, a dark, blue-skinned male, short and blocky in body, pointed at the water bag then himself.

Kendo scrutinized with suspicion the cunning expressions and gestures one guard made towards the other's before they erupted in guttural laughter. A cruel smile on the guard's lips as he took one of the water bags from the saddle on the beast. He stood before the Dalagian and drank long, deep gulps. Smiled, then poured the water out on the sand, his smile increasing as the liquid in a shimmering stream puddled before quickly disappearing.

The Dalagian lunged for the bag, yanking it out of the guard's hands, tilted his head back and drank deep gulps. In a blink, the guard whipped out a razor-sharp obsidian blade, which sliced the prisoner's throat open. Kendo could see the white of bone the knife cut so deep. Blood sprayed across the guard, and Jynnalt standing next to the prisoner. Blood ran down her arm and side in bright rivulets of dark brown.

The paladins flinched. If free, the guard would be dead.

Jynnalt swayed on her feet. Heat sickness left her unaware, half of her side sprayed with blood as rivulets ran down her face, and he realized her chances of surviving slim. The prisoners stood shocked, nauseous, fear showing in their eyes. The other guards, laughing, strolled over and helped take the restraints from the still twitching body. Picking the body up by the hands and feet, they moved to the edge of the road. They swung three times and released, throwing it as far away as possible. Weird why the *helc* did they not just carry the body off the causeway. Seconds later, Kendo comprehended the reason.

The sand around the body erupted with bizarre carnivorous insects. They sprayed a fluid, dissolving the body and bones, then sucked the liquid up through long tubes protruding from what he thought must be their head. Without thinking, Kendo stepped closer to the center of the road. He realized the guards studied them with an intent focus. Less than five minutes passed, and the insects finished, leaving nothing of the body. Seconds later, they disappeared in the sand. The guards stood boldly at the edge of the road, implying the roadway itself safe. He relaxed. Ten minutes later, they were on the march again.

Forced to keep going, no matter their condition, the prisoners staggered forward. Yet no one made the mistake of asking for water. Two more died of heatstroke, pulling down the group as they fell. The bodies disposed of in the same manner. Kendo shocked at his sense of relief for the rest because of a death. Berated himself, *do not become an animal. Do not sink into depravity*, he chanted to himself. None of them astonished now when the insects erupted to consume the dead.

Kendo understood Jynnalt was moving on autopilot. He did not believe she would survive the journey to their destination.

One time, the wind hit him and the others hard enough to throw them off their feet. Their chains and the strength of the Paladins braced against the onslaught, the only thing keeping them on the road. The wall of dust left them coated in a fine white powdery sand. When the winds calmed, the guard's clothing was clean, not a speck on them. *Shields.* They have personal shields, Kendo realized. *How did I miss that?* He clenched his fist.

They were laughing at us, while protected from the heat and dust, with plenty of water. Something stirred deep within him. Clawed to get out. He'd battled this beast before and learned how to control it. Breathing deep, he closed his eyes as his temple throbbed. Slowed his breath till the rage calmed. As the turn wore on, one star chasing after the other, moving from east to west high in the sky. Desperation turned to indifference. Kendo aware of only each monumental step forward.

The surrounding sands shimmered with heat, as illusions of water in the far distance urged the column on towards a nonexistent reward. Time ceased for him. His surroundings disappeared in a blur of color. Kendo's lips cracked. His body bruised with dried bloody welts from the whips of the guards. The clothes he wore covered in fine white dust from head to toe from the windborne swirling sand. His thoughts on one thing, and one thing only, putting one foot after another as he staggered along the causeway.

Kendo stopped when he felt hard tugs on his restraints. Both stars a bloated deep burning red covering half the horizon, the air pregnant with heat. When he looked back, Jynnalt, her eyes glazed and vacant, was still standing. Her body's resilience astonished him.

335892 GGS Elec 28th.
Nibiru Proper Agade–Prince Ea

A PULSE FROM AN UNKNOWN channel popped up on Ea's private comm's. He and Ustrix were enjoying dinner at an early hour together at a popular feasthall. The Dragon's Breath, before heading out for a night in the pleasure halls and gambling establishments together. They developed a comfortable friendship since the troubles broke out, each in their own way dealt with the difficulties of uncertainties their families faced.

The message read, gather your family members. Tell none of your full-time guild servers. Call your paladins to duty on your estate compound. Expel *all* servers, no exceptions. Lock yourself inside your hall's inner compound walls. Lock and barricade the outer gates once the servers leave. Fill everything you can with water to control fire. Do this now. Waste no time. Trust no one.

The pulse terrified him. He re-read the information again, showing the pulse to Ustrix.

Ustrix's private pulse chirped. He received a duplicate of Ea's pulse. Both looked at each other. No signature except for an R. Nothing else.

"What would it hurt to follow the instructions? We might appear foolish in the morn, allowing our newest friends a merry laugh at our expense? If this is a prank. In these times, might not hurt to be cautious, though would you not agree?" Ustrix asked.

"Let's head to our skimmers. We can talk along the way." Ea, now wishing he did not talk Ustrix into parking so far away to walk the distance for exercise. As they started out, he pulsed his vyzier.

"Isimud, I want you to check on the family. Make sure they are okay. Make a story up if you must. I'll be arriving soon," he said as Ustrix, and he reviewed the pulse again as they reached the skimmers. Ea gazed around, feeling the surroundings surreal. Everything around them ordinary. Nothing unusual. The feasthall servers their normal polite selves. Ea, deep in thought, jumped when Ustrix spoke next to him.

"What do you think? Real. Or a hoax that will have us both looking foolish in the morn?"

Ea observed his shaking hands as if they did not belong to him. Glanced at Ustrix to see if he noticed. "How is it possible? They are about to go on a rampage yet appear so unconcerned. Treat everyone politely." Still, he sensed the truth of the message in his pulse handheld. Shamed at the sound of fear in his voice. Knew Ustrix courteously ignored the fear in his voice.

Ustrix shaking his head said, "I believe the pulse to be true. Rumors have floated around for the last few turns that some are advocating violence against the blood houses. Our Minister of fourteen discussed the subject two turns ago with my brother. I thought yours would have." Ustrix walked faster, "our whisper operatives investigations uncovered a concerted effort to starve the commoners. In fact, I meant to bring the subject up after dinner. Thought bringing this up in poor taste before we ate."

"Maybe we *should* have discussed this first. And why now? Ea realized he sounded gruffer than he meant. His hands trembled harder than before.

"Our investigations revealed no food or goods are getting through from most of the houses. The exceptions being Prince Satoric, and two of the other Wardens, and the highest five sitting council members. The commoners are starving, is why."

Ea stared at Ustrix as if he missed something vital. "My house has sent help. In fact, I have even raided father's account to make sure enough supplies got sent to those beholden to our blood." Disbelief in Ea's voice. Viewed every server as they walked past as an attacker. "Do they not believe the enforces would act? Or the fleet? This all makes no sense," he said, thinking aloud, bewildered.

"You're not starving, or watching your families' children die a slow, painful death. Whoever is behind this, is using everything possible to break the commoner's bonds with the blood houses *and* the temple," Ustrix said, straddling his skimmer, which purred to life.

"What are you talking about?"

"They're accusing not only the blood houses and the Malkuth of ignoring the commoner's desperate plight, but they include the temple in their accusations. Think. First the disaster. Then the emperor murdered, which further destabilized the political situation, right when they announced an heir to be born to the public. Now food and goods diverted. Someone is trying to bring down the empire. From within. Someone high up. More like many high up officials. Traitors, with outside help. They're manipulating the commoners and guild citizens."

The Wardens came to mind, at least three. If what Ustrix said was true, their shipments of goods and food the only ones getting through. He kept that to himself, as you never knew who might be listening. Speaking against the Three Wardens not healthy. Especially him.

"The Society has increased its presence throughout the empire. First claiming to be here at the request of several guilds, making their writ's legitimate. Yet, their...."

Ea interrupted him. "I thought the Greater council declared the Society skip barred after the events at Niuard."

"I see you have not been paying attention to the Great Council. Three of the Wardens nullified the earlier ruling quietly two turns after the murder of the emperor. If what my brother's whisper operatives are saying, whoever is doing this is counting on starvation and fear overcoming their normal reason and decency. The Society has convinced a sizable enough number they are telling the truth. We both understand they twist their truth to make their accusations sound grave enough. They point to the supposed cruelty of the blooded and their neglect of the commoners."

"Cruelty! What the *droging helc* are they talking about?"

Ustrix glanced over at Ea now sitting on his skimmer, "there are rumors of mass arrest. Citizens disappearing in the darkness of night. Entire families, some claim. Denial of basic life services. Our operatives tried to verify the claims of missing commoners, found none. The courts no more overtaxed this season of cold and it's normal cyclic increase in criminal activity. Life tender stations from the largest city buildings to the smallest report with proof, all citizens treated fair. And in a reasonable time, no matter station or title."

"So, misinformation about the blooded, spread with malice, to add to the lack of food and goods. This reeks of an organized incitement of the citizens." He called back Isimud. "Call our paladins, every one of them, even those off duty. Once they arrive, have them remove every single server no matter their rank or time working for our house," Ea ready to leave turned towards Ustrix. "Do you think we can trust the paladins?"

"Yes, at least I believe so. Whoever sent this told us to bring them to our house's enclaves. Besides, there have been no rumors about unrest amongst them. At least, none of my brother's whisper's uncovered."

Ea pulsed his vyzier once more. "Isimud, say whatever you have to. I don't care what, just get every family member home, understood?" Ea said, logging off without waiting for an answer.

"I'm calling my father. If I were you, I would call your brother. If this is an actual threat, I will not leave my father to perish at the misguided hands of starving, desperate people."

Ea's pulse buzzed loud and menacing, making them both jump at the sound. A holo of his father appeared.

"I have been trying to reach you. For the last few hours, I tried your private line. I have something important——" The line went dead.

Ea heard fear in his father's voice before the holo shut down. Something he'd never heard before. Both gave the other a worried look.

"My father fears nothing, at least not before now." Ea said

Neither spoke. Seconds later, they sped off towards their respective houses.

Twenty minutes later, Ea stood explaining the situation to Isimud as he showed him the pulse. "Be quick. I don't believe there's much time. Fill every single item that can hold water, including the old water tower. If this is real, we cannot rely on the enforcers or the fire tenders for help. This will overwhelm their services."

Ea stopped before rushing off to prepare the family.

"The warning came thirty minutes ago."

Isimud listened, not saying a word. Before Ea closed the connection, he saw him rush out of the chamber, talking on his official pulse as he left.

Hours later, Ea, his clothes singed and scorched in places, stank of smoke and a ripe sour body odor. Desperation and terror held him in its grip as he fought to keep the embers from the compound's outer fires from landing on the major buildings. Capable of sending them up in a blaze. A heavy coppery odor arrived with the wind and blended with the overpowering scent of smoke. An odor he was unaccustomed to smelling wafting over the high walls for the last hour. A smell that filled him with a sick, soul-shredding fear.

This night of horror forever forged in his mind; he swore never to forget. Screams erupted at the gates close by. The scattered staccato sounds of projectile weapons and the sizzling sound, along with blue flashes from plasma rifles, assaulted his senses. The sharp tang of ozone odor mingled with the acidic scent of fire heavy in the air. Twenty minutes later, explosions rocked the city, silencing the wail of sirens.

News bards relayed information, which was not much, through public channels, till the power failed, most likely sabotaged. Ea and his family aghast as fires burned at blooded family compounds till the feeds failed.

The normal soothing light of bioluminous felt oddly bizarre in their family's enclave in the outer gardens, their only light. The background fires from *helc* on the outside of their wall, casting a bright glow.

They turned to their private pulse holo's for information from other citizens when the public pulse failed. What they received, horrifying. The chaos of running, screaming citizens. Children, females, and males, shot, stabbed or beat to death as they raced for safety, banging on doors that did not open, murdered by the mobs in the streets.

Once the shock of what he viewed made him stop breathing, his knee's weak and his bowls roiled. A mother and her three children, one a babe in arms, begging at a gate before the mob hacked them to pieces. Their blood splashed across the wall and her assailants before running in rivulets across the stones of the causeway.

Ea reached out to turn off the pulse, but his mother, Nammu, stopped him. "Don't, if you can't. But we need to keep this on. We must prepare. I recognized the gate where that happened. The main mob is still a distance away."

She turned towards the mothers, "take the children, go to the kitchen, and gather water and food enough for several hours, also get blankets and warm clothes. The cellars are cold. Kialian and three paladins will help you. I am sorry, but they cannot stay with you. They must come back here to stand defense on the walls."

One junior mother cried as she wrapped her arms around her daughter of three sars. Nammu looked at her with both exasperation and understanding before saying.

"The cellar is impervious to fire and has many hiding places. Find them, and no matter what you hear outside, stay quiet."

The mother nodded, sniffed, dried her tears on her skirt before following the others.

For the next couple of hours, they took in anyone banging on their doors. Ea would not allow his house, or himself, to give in to the terror. To descend into barbarism by ignoring the pleas of those outside. Deep down, he understood he might be the one trapped outside or someone he loved.

Five of his family somewhere out there in all this chaos. He prayed to the gods someone let them in if they banged on their doors.

The mob reached their enclave less than twenty minutes later. He thought he would be deaf for turns from the sounds of the projectile rifles firing and blinded from the brilliant blue plasma bursts. Three paladins went down, and their house life tender drones rushed into action, placing them in med units and removing them from the assault.

Glass jars full of combustible fluids flew over the wall. Setting trees, bushes, and the surrounding grasses not already scorched on fire, adding to the earlier ones now under control. The outer garden area a roaring inferno. Ignoring his pitiful attempts to defeat the blaze, Ea sprinted towards the buildings. Everyone fought the fire, even the paladins abandon the walls to help.

The crackling roar of the inferno overriding the yells of the mob outside. Once they got the fire under control, he realized the mob had moved on. They must have figured the fire would finish them. That and not wanting to continue to face their paladin's deadly weapons. Their house better prepared for the onslaught. The chanting and screams now, faint sounds blowing on the wind. Embers burned here and there, but the conflagration was under control.

Screaming and running feet headed back towards their gate. Ea recoiled in horror. The assault upon his psyche crushing at the wave of sound heading back in their direction, his mind registering the fact the angry mob not yet finished with them.

His stomach roiled and his mouth watered with nausea. Not again. Amazed, his paladins jumped back up on the wall, prepared once more to fight as the horizon of Agade lightened with the first hint of dawn.

The shriek of atmos engines assaulted his senses, drowning out the screaming mob. Ea forced himself to walk up the stairs to the top of the wall next to his paladins. The longest walk of his life. His paladins prepared to die to defend the house. They swore an oath; he would do no less. He swallowed hard and grabbed a rifle off the ground from one of the earlier fallen paladins.

The incessant chatter of atmos griffins reached him from far down the street. Screaming, pushing commoners, who earlier murdered citizens in cold blood, now ran for their lives, terror on their faces as they rounded the causeways corner.

Now banging on doors, begging entrance. At the enclaves, they earlier tried to burn to the ground. Desperate to get out of the deadly hail of bullets and streaks of plasma fire. The causeway turned into a carnal killing ground of blood, guts, and writhing bodies.

Reaper whirlwinds, and local ground forces atmos fighters, flashed past just above the height of the walls, firing hundreds of rounds a second. Followed by missile-armed atmos fighters. The Paladin standing beside him grabbed him and threw them both off the wall. Others dived for the ground at the same time. The impact knocked the breath out of him and blinded him for a moment. Backwash from the craft flattened those in the streets who survived the barrage. Thumping sounds of whirling blades above sleek black bodies and white underbellies flashed past. Ea helped to his feet by the Paladin. Dusting himself off, he watched the atmos craft receding in the distance. The sight gave him vicious delight. Followed seconds later by the thought he should be ashamed, yet honest enough to admit he felt no sympathy for the rioters.

Bursts of white-hot tracer rounds lit the causeway in brilliant streaks of light further off. Ea climbed the stairs back to the top. The sight of blood splattered walls, from bullets which tore through unprotected bodies ripping them apart, gouged out chunks of stone from walls, embedded in shattered bodies, adding to the horror.

Ea numb. The sight should have sickened him. Yet lacked the ability to pull up the slightest bit of empathy. He realized somewhere in the back of his head he wanted them to die, to suffer for all they had done this turn.

Chapter 21

LAVENDER-GRAY LIGHT peeked over the horizon of Fire Mountain. Lower sections of the city still shrouded in darkness as stars twinkled overhead. Sizable crowds gathered outside the three commoners' massive gates into Agade proper.

For now, the gates stood locked. Scheduled to open in two hours at the normal time. Each minute that passed, the crowds below increased. After a half-hour, the crowds far beyond the normal size. Twelve stories up, the Lieutenant enforcer heard yelling from the restless commoners below.

"*Focking* murders, dragon daemons, traitors, usurpers." Voice enhancers increased the volume and the distance the sound traveled.

One turned, speaking to the crowds. "Prince Anu and his lying festival spawn from the outer border Kingdom tried to usurp the throne. We must make sure all Prince Anu's bootlickers and conspirators get exposed and punished." His voice, enhanced, carried across the crowds.

Well, that's a recent one. The implication Queen Jynnalt is the illegitimate offspring of Prince Anu.

The same speaker raised one fist high, pumping it as the crowds chanted. "Traitors... traitors... traitors." The speaker stopped for a moment for effect. "We must Punish the transgressors," he said.

The crowd yelled out, "yes," each time to his inflammatory rhetoric.

The statements made by the speaker increased the commoner's chanting; both in volume and anger. After the riots earlier in the month, unease took hold of him. The speaker was trying to incite the crowd.

The enforcers on the upper walls, seeing the size and disposition of the commoners gathering, called for reinforcements from the Imperial ground fleet's stationed outside the city. One of the troop sergeants who arrived as back up stood next to him. He kept glancing towards the west as a flash of lightning streaked across the sky. The illumination highlighted dark raging storm clouds moving fast. The Lieutenant glanced the same direction. *A storm is coming.* He examined the crowd below, noticing mixed throughout them the distinctive robes and cloaks of the Society. They weaved in and out amongst the citizens, handing out holo meh's broadsheets.

When visiting his family in the commoner's city, he overheard Society Priest's encouraging impressionable young adults to speak out against the blooded. Worse, they encouraged lawlessness and rioting. Claimed the blooded made laws unfair to commoners and guild members. Their so-called Priest encouraged those lacking morals to act in a manner forbidden in the Books. This created more work for Agade enforcers. Thankfully, none of his clan appeared to participate in the earlier riots. Other Enforcers he talked with said the same of their clans. He quietly investigated how none of Nibiru's commoners seemed involved, yet the three Wardens pointed the blame on them.

A message arrived that under no circumstances were the gates to open. Announcer drones flew over the crowds, ordering them to disperse.

"Any refusing will have lethal force used against them."

Next, they deployed holo recording drones over the walls for later identification and arrest of the instigators if the crowds turned violent.

The dissidents shaking fist while yelling out traitors, others ineffectually throwing rocks at the drones. Ground troops moved to cannon placements. As soon as the drones went over the walls, those below in Society robes melted away into shadowed side streets. He sent one in stealth mode to follow the last Society member slinking away. Ordered the drone to report the findings back to him. He turned back to focus on the crowds at the wall.

The wind picked up, and the storm gathered strength, moving in quick. The cool dawn temperature plummeted, becoming icy cold as tempestuous ominous clouds covered the rising star, plunged them back into darkness. Minutes later, he monitored the crowds as they melted away. The first driving flakes of whitefall mixed with ice crystals landed on his uniform. The snapping crack of his cloak to the voracious wind warned of the ferocity of the incoming storm. This the first time he thanked the gods since the disaster for the lack of the Igigi platform and its weather control system.

High on the imposing outer walkway, the First Lieutenant scrutinized the feasthalls tent glow in the distance with warm, inviting lights. The shimmer of environmental shields of the tents flared each time in response to the howling wind.

He let go of his gauss rifle slung across his chest to blow into his hands, warming them. Hopefully, his commander would call him back to the station soon as the disruptive mob no longer a threat. He glanced up and down the outer wall, not seeing a single citizen.

Winter made for idle hands and free time amongst the commoners. The time they gathered to tell tales. Discuss marriage for their children with the other clans. Determines who plants, or harvest which grounds. Whose clan will work the forest or fishing come spring. They only enter the city proper to barter their tithe goods.

This time of the sar, in feasthalls and tents, political discussions abounded. Feasthall owners called in enforcers to control drunken fights over political differences. Sobriety the following turn after a night in a cell and the cost of reparations to the feasthall's owners. Along with a quick stint before a judge brought about a return to sanity.

335892 Caldr 29th.
Nibiru Proper Terminal Agade - Main Agade Terminal

IN THE BLOODED CITY sector terminal, they dealt with a

dissimilar problem. The vast city terminal a chaos of blaring horns from personal hovercraft and booming private repulser yacht's klaxons. Combined with the shrill notes from small private atmos-yachts and lower peerage hover barges. Smaller, more maneuverable, and faster skyskimmers weaved in and out, looking to grab the first available spot to park before others. Tempers flared, and fistfights broke out, snarling traffic further as their craft blocked those behind. The crash and scree of crytinmetal on crytinmetal filled the air as fender benders became too many for enforcers to oversee. They sent a flash message to all vehicles that if involved in a non-injury accident, they should send the holo's from their pilot's meh's for review by enforcers later. Flashing red and orange lights from emergency craft came and went. Life tender drones treated on-the-spot injuries, or if needing critical care, flew off with the citizens to life centers. One of the ranking enforcers called for backup. Denied. They informed him they needed every available enforcer not at the terminal to be at the commoner's gates of the city wall.

335892 GGS Caldr 29th.
Nibiru Proper Agade High Court–Prince Ryakin

THE ENFORCERS FLEW Ryakin with the other accused in on a heavily guarded Imperial prison transport along with his brother and various Tc and Ki guild members. Forty commoners chained in the lower deck. The mountains, a black outline on the horizon, edged in red as the star's first rays tried to claim the summit. Minutes later, the light disappeared, obscured by black boiling clouds.

In the riot's confusion earlier in the month, Prince Anu vanished. Many speculated he might be dead. Rumors circulated that high ranking blooded did not want him to go to trial. Afraid Prince Anu might win, handing him the Empire. They didn't care about his innocence or guilt. They wanted him out-of-the-way so they could make a claim for the throne.

Whispers amongst the blooded abounded the true wrongdoers

could not afford to lose control. They would face the executioner's box if exposed, or if any investigations into what occurred within the empire became known. Bets in the gambling house as to the likely culprits put the odds-on favorite as Prince Satoric. Others betting on the consortium of the wardens together. Some bet on the Society. A few bets came in that Prince Anu, the house of Airal and the King of Tc, the culprits they stood accused of being. Very few.

Ryakin squinted as the dawn's light burned his eyes, not having seen starlight for the last six months. They kept him in isolation, except for those times when they took him out of his cell to question him.

If bloody skin where fingernails once grew, swollen lips, black eyes, and deep bruises covering his body along with torn, burned flesh counted as questioning. He glanced around at the others and realized all in as terrible shape as himself. His brother worse. He realized when he glanced at him and regarded his condition. His jaw tightened, his hands shaking at the sight. Rage at his brother's and the others treatment.

Grief at the loss of Jynnalt ate at him, filled a dark empty spot since the murder of the Emperor and the Empresses' strange disappearance.

With Jynnalt dead, he weighed lying. Nothing could harm her now. But he could save the others, just as innocent as himself and Jynnalt. Ryakin could inform the court when asked to speak that only he and Jynnalt committed the crime. He'd claim they acted to increase the tithe of the Kingdom. And to increase their influence at the Greater council. Prince Anu and his brother ignorant of their plans. His declaration of guilt would put an immense black hole in framing the others and keep the throne out of their greedy hands.

His confession and death would absolve the others of wrongdoing. Snatching victory from the actual culprits hiding in the shadows, believing they won. From the executioner's box, he could strike a blow at the conspirators. A strange sense of renewal and strength rose within him.

They flew in over the crowds. To Ryakin's view, the upper city streets full to overflowing of citizens jammed into one causeway, the one of Justice, like ants rushing to a food source.

Square buildings along the way, four to ten stories tall and connected with slate stone roofs, lined the road. A crush of blooded passing under the Arch of Justice as they entered the opening entrance on foot, something they'd never done before. Amazed, many didn't drop dead as they passed underneath the archway. Justice not their strongest qualities from what he endured this past fortnight. Once through, the area widened to a forty-acre open-air stone-paved courtyard surrounded by the empire's ten massive pure white colonnaded Courts in a half circle.

Seconds later, the prison transport landed in the back of the cordoned off-court terminal parking. The court buildings each sat upon an enormous stone foundation. The largest building of the ten, the Imperial Court. Twenty-two pure white marble steps rose from the lower courtyard to the vast covered portico patio. An extensive line of enforcers protected the walkway to the court, making sure the prisoners survived to attend their trial. Whoever engineered the murder of Emperor Lahamu saved that honor for this public farce. Followed by a swift execution of their pawns. Sealing their control over the empire unchallenged.

He and the others pushed, pummeled, and dragged up the stairs by the guards. On the way, he spotted the execution booth of judgment, already set up in the courtyard's center. A chill raced through him, and his knees went weak. He reached for his earlier rage, straightening as once more the emotion rose within him. He ignored the sharp stab of pain, layered over the dull throb, his constant companion since the first time they questioned him.

For the last six months, he barely endured. The only thing that saved him was repeating a litany of nonsense in his head, blocking everything out. Now he changed the litany from nonsense to a sense of action. *I will not cower. Before they execute me, I will stare out at the crowd, head high, I will not be on my knees begging, dragged to the booth. I will deny them their win. I will beat them.*

He glanced again at the booth. Ominous. Final. Debilitating fear seized him. He swallowed, took a deep breath. *Use your fear, don't let it use you.* The thought, combined with his abiding faith, allowed him to walk forward with a measured step. His back straight, his head high, praying Prince Anu would make those who falsely accused them pay.

Ryakin passed Prince Alalus, Riciad, and Prince Jaui, his uncle's friends, and realized his uncle stood with them and not the family. All smug and self-satisfied. He glared at his uncle as he passed. Something hot and searing grew within him, something he never felt before this turn. Betrayal. Hatred. Now he realized everything his brother tried to warn him about their uncle true. Selfish and uncaring, only seeing his wants and needs above the families. Or their house.

Adjudicators Guild members sat enclosed at security-control booths. Between them, Ryakin saw the shimmer of force fields. The center walkway to the Adsullata Fire tree's massive wooden doors, adorned with horrendous scenes of ancient judgments carved into inlaid sandstone.

The accused, and their defending scribes, the accuser's scribes, and the judges the only ones to pass through those doors. All others, including guild workers or blooded spectators, family members, and witnesses, filtered through semi-hidden doors of normal size off to each side. Tall, elegant pillars held up the triangular roof above. Every blooded house, from a greater to a lesser rank, and the peerage was here to view the trial. The lower-ranking forced to stand outside watching on the five-story-tall holo's scattered everywhere throughout the courtyard of the events inside.

Six agonizing months in darkness allowed him time to think about what occurred. Whoever did this needed someone to take the blame, and who better than those who held the power they desired? He prayed by the two gods and the Luminous Ones that when Jynnalt died, her death swift and merciful. He couldn't bear to think of her in agony.

His torturer informed him the young female they requested a royal writ for murdered hours before the Emperor by Jynnalt. The guard taunted him as he explained the young female carried vital information for the Imperial Emperor's Minister of fourteen, Master Zioria. Evidence against Jynnalt, himself, and the other conspirator's she uncovered while in their service. The meh missing, the investigating enforcers assumed Jynnalt absconded with the incriminating proof. For six months, he wondered if Kalmia set them up or if an innocent pawn herself. He found the idea hard to comprehend. Kalmia the best in Ki's kingdom both in the field and as head of her division. But no one is infallible.

They told Ryakin they arrested him moments after a passing patrol of enforcers discovered the bodies. Two of his paladins trying to defend him, along with six enforcers, died before he got his paladins to surrender.

Whoever did this designed the murder of the Emperor and Empress, carrying the heir, to inflict the most damage on the empire and create anarchy amongst the blooded houses.

He doubted the Empress, or the heir, still lived. However, claiming the Empress lived gave the real criminals time to ward off Prince Anu receiving the crown. Long enough for the conspirators to accuse him of the murder, aided by the royals of Tc and Ki.

One turn, he overheard the guards talking as they walked away after dumping him in his cell.

"Wonder if Prince Anu is as strong as this one and his brother. Once they discover where, he ran to ground. Bet he won't keep his mouth shut for long. He'll disclose the information mark my words. Imperialist canids." he spit on the floor, just missing the others shoe. "Soft. Those types always are. They will get the punishment they deserve. I knew, as soon as the emperor announced the Empress with child, Prince Anu would make a move. Look how he paraded around all the time acting like the thrones already his. Once the Emperor announced the Empress pregnant with an heir, everything changed. Prince Anu no longer a hair's breath away from the throne. No need to hunt for the motive."

The other guard spoke up. "Yeah, Prince Satoric is right. They allow too much power to the cupbearer. He intends for that to change. Even if they are a true heir, which Prince Anu is not."

Ryakin could not learn more because they moved out of hearing. If, as the guards said, they accused Prince Anu, the throne now opens to a power grab. An event that might precipitate a civil war. Whoever planned this took out their most formidable opponents before the first shots fired. Prince Anu the legal heir while the Empress was missing, and the rulers of Tc and Ki stood accused of the crimes. An inner kingdom with a powerful influence in the council, and a wealthy border kingdom. Once Jynnalt and he signed the marriage contract, their influence in both inner and outer kingdoms difficult to defeat. This left only the weaker kingdoms standing against whoever did this. This travesty gave them the ability to dangle the rulership before any potential heirs of Tc and Ki as a reward for their support. With the true title holders out of the way, this left a vacuum until they gained control of the Anunnaki fleets and the throne.

Those on trial today, casualties in a war they never knew they were fighting. An angry snap of a cloak, loud as rifle fire, jolted his attention back. The wind picked up fast as a freezing blast of air hit him and fluffy gray whitefall fell on his shoulders. This swift change of weather reminded him of how much Nibiru Proper changed after the disaster.

Standing beside the dark edge of one pillar stood a tall, imposing figure. The shadows obscured his face as they passed. He tried to gaze backward, slowing down before a shove from behind made him stumble. When he glanced again, the figure no longer stood there. Minutes later, head high, he walked into the packed court chamber.

Objections and uproars of outrage abounded, even from those believing them guilty. Prince Satoric, now the highest-ranking official of the empire, calmed everyone down, explaining the guards in their fanatical zeal did this without permission. We arrested them this morn, and they're awaiting their own trial. We did not have time to put them in the repair units before the trial. The explanation settled the blooded in the tiers, but those in the gallery in the far back remained restless, voices still buzzing with outrage.

Ryakin ignored them. He intended to pay strict attention, so when he gave his false confession, he would not leave un-answered any contrived evidence pointing to others.

The trial started with the commoners and guild members who already confessed. Their confessions played back to those present, ignoring the fact torture used to gain the information. Nothing in any confession specifically pointed to any other accused. No names, no identifying signatures, meaning not enough evidence to include other's involvement except for the fact employed by the accused houses. However, even so, damaging enough to make one wonder about the guilt of those standing trial this turn. Those who confessed judged quick and removed from the court, sent to the outer courtyard for execution.

Screams and begging from the galley where their families sat disrupted the court. Enforcers sent to extract them.

They called a brief recess between the commoner's trial and the royals and blooded. Few left their seats, worried they would lose them if they got up for refreshments sold from the kiosk's outside.

When the court convened, Prince Satoric nodded, and the lights dimmed. The holo projection grid in the center between the accused and the judges burst into life. The holo, full of static, making most scenes next to impossible to see anything occurring except for movement and blurry colors. Ryakin wondered how they thought this holo meh proved anything from that fateful evening. Though what little viewable recorded showed beyond a doubt, Jynnalt was present. That she and her paladins fought with someone.

Prince Satoric, after the holo shut off, stepped forward with a flourish, addressing the gallery and gathered witnesses.

"Queen Jynnalt Tc*Airal, we believe from what evidence we gathered used an unknown jammer technology. We suspect she expected the jammer to block the security holo's of the Imperial Garden. However, our enforcers proved capable of retrieving some of the criminal action." He held up a small device for those in the court to see. "We discovered Jynnalt's signature on this jammer," he said, pointing to the item. Silence fell for a few seconds before he commenced again. "We retrieved this from her quarters. The earlier murder of a young female in the employ of the Kierian Ministry fourteen section AC one. She notified Master Zioria, the overseer of the Imperial Ministry fourteen, she received evidence which she only trusted to hand over to him.

The court wonders why she did not hand this information over to Mistress Kalmia to deliver to Master Zioria? For now, this is a question for a different court. And the proper channels. But I digress."

He walked before the council as he spoke. "Master Zioria expected to receive a security holo from a junior whisper agent working for him in KI. We cannot reveal more of the reason she was investigating as we categorize this investigation as secret. We never found the meh. Rather convenient for whoever it would expose. Queen Jynnalt's Vyzier claimed under questioning to have no knowledge of the whisper agent. He informed those who questioned him that Queen Jynnalt herself attained the royal writ for the female. He died later of an infection he caught while in prison, so cannot testify here this turn."

A hiss of breath flashed across the courtroom. Kierans aware the Queen's Vyzier, young and healthy.

Others nodded in the gallery as they listened to the evidence, which did not bode well for the accused. Prince Satoric explained they did not understand what happened to the Empress, or two of her paladins, as they found no DNA signatures at the crime scene. "Think about that for a second. The Empress and Queen Jynnalt missing. What is the motive if not ransom? Or a way to control the empire through the heir later?"

Prince Iltasadum stood. "I believe you made the case *against* Queen Jynnalt and Ki being involved. The Queen of the wealthiest border kingdom does not need extra tithe. You have not shown a single piece of evidence to motive," he said.

Many chortled in the court chamber as the wealth of Ki far exceeded many an inner kingdom.

"Yes, but if they helped Prince Anu remove the threat to his ascension to the throne, he would be indebted to them. These three conspirators could combine their votes and sway the council however they wanted. Increasing their power at the expense of the citizens and lesser blooded." Prince Satoric said as he glared at Ryakin. "Time for those accused to declare their position and give evidence of what they claim," Prince Satoric said without taking his eyes off Ryakin. "The court calls upon..." he stared at the accused before him.

Me, call me. Ryakin glowered back at Prince Satoric.

"King Rualui, you are to give your statement as to truth or falsehood of the court's claims. Does any here stand in his defense?" The rustle of clothing loud in the silence which descended upon the court chamber.

"Then—-.

The central doors of justice crashed open, the explosive sound vibrated through the floors and seats, rattling the chamber's tiers of justice. Gasps and twisting bodies as everyone attempted to discover what caused the commotion and who might dare to enter illegally through the doors of Justice.

The High Priestess attended by two acolytes three steps behind her and an envoy from the Galactic Interstellar Alliance stood outlined in the doorway. A freezing wind blew in with them, whipping their clothes tight around them. Yet the Anunnaki High Priestess stood as if unaffected, her staff of authority held with long familiarity. She walked with slow dignity to the tiered judge's section at the front, past the prisoners, without one glance in their direction.

In a ringing tone, she declared, "I stand for all. Including those who gave confessions under torture now waiting for execution outside," she said as she glowered with stern disapproval at the Council members, Judges and four Wardens. "I have demanded they bring them back to the court." She said as those who left earlier returned and sat in the back under enforcers' guard.

"Your laws state torture nullifies any confession, even if there is evidence to support the accusation or not." She stopped, allowing what she said to sink in. "Therefore, you must strike the prior testimony from the official records. Why did no judge stop this farce before I arrived?" She stared at the paneled Judges as they squirmed in their seats under her scrutiny.

Nodding heads and loud talking swirled around the chamber. Ryakin sensed things turning in their favor, the earlier outrage over the condition of the accused back in full force. Faith in the Temple strong throughout the empire. No High Priestess in written history ever defended a non-temple citizen in all their history. Many shocked to silence by her attendance.

"This envoy will function as a witness. She nodded the direction of a short stout pasty white Helto citizen steps behind her acolytes. He will make sure this court adheres to the laws of GIA in a trial of this stature. This trial will have reverberations throughout the alliance," she said. The envoy pulled out a small globe which, when released, floated overhead. Ryakin sensed the tension rise in the court as murmurs circulated. The scrutiny of GIA's council, something no empire wished.

She demanded they go back over the information presented up to this time. The Priestess stood statue-still until the court scribe finished. She ambled with deliberate intent until she stood inches from Prince

Satoric, ignoring all others. Ryakin paid close attention to their interaction. He knew without a doubt his and the lives of the others depended upon the outcome. Prince Satoric rushed into the silence.

"I have allowed this unusual interruption of our courts, out of respect to the temple," he nodded her direction. "Yet might I remind you; you are not an Anunnaki citizen and cannot stand for those being weighed in judgment."

Angry renunciations towards Prince Satoric rose, and he ignored them. "If you have information, the empire's enforcers do not have," he said, glancing around, "and withheld this from them, you did so illegally." The slightest smile hovering on his lips. A shocked hissed of breath throughout the court overrode all other sounds, followed by loud cries of outrage from the accusation.

The High Priestess, with the lightest tap on the stone floor with her staff, caused a soft ringing to vibrate deep in Ryakin's bones. Silence fell. Without taking her eyes off Prince Satoric. Her voice no longer soft but iron hard, she declared. "Your laws, need I remind you, Prince Satoric..." She stared at him for several moments before looking at the others, resuming her speech.

"This court." She said, allowing the statement to sink in. "Voted to allow any temple priestess, the right to stand for any citizen of your empire, when events are grievous enough to weigh hard upon temple rights."

She waited till she had their full attention. "If you do not follow the law, laws I remind you," she regarded each one before speaking once more, "each voted every sar to renew in this council. An oath you also swore before me." All talking ceased, the only sound the soft scrape of shoes on stone and the slightest rustle of clothing before she spoke again.

"If you ignore the law. I shall enforce it. For you." she said in a reasonable voice. She struck her staff on the marble floor with a gentle touch. This time, a weird feeling of edginess flowed through Ryakin.

In through each side door flowed twenty Mekalam warriors of the temple, their radiant white uniforms and cloaks transforming by the second step into full battle armor. Wicked looking plasma rifles slung across their chest, their right hand resting on their low-slung handhelds, as they lined the outer walls.

Prince Satoric's words seconds later spat loud enough for those in the tiers to hear. "Votes coerced by a weak-minded emperor, controlled by his overly zealous wife and," he stared at the Mekalam warriors, "by force."

The spectators did not miss the implication.

The High Priestess waited, still as a statue, face calm. Waited for the murmurs and whispers to pass, before speaking once more. "Do you deny the temple the rights?" She said, as she turned towards the other judges. "However, Prince Satoric believes them acquired."

She turned towards the Anunnaki blooded in the rows and gallery.

Prince Satoric met her words with an icy stare. Ryakin detected the rage in his cold red eyes burning through the High Priestess and her two acolytes. *Prince Satoric must be one of the conspirators.* He appears determined to prove them guilty. As a Warden, he could persuade the council to appoint him as ruler later. From the expression on Prince Satoric's face, he realized the Hight Priestess outmaneuvered him. Moments later, the council and court judges took a vote on whether the High Priestess could defend the accused.

Prince Satoric and the first and third wardens voted against temple involvement. The second warden and all nine other judges and council members voted in favor of the High Priestess' right to defend the accused.

"Understand this trial is being pulsed across the empire, the temple, and GIA." She said as the acolyte on her right pulled out an isomorphic holo device, which rose to float next to them. She explained what transpired for those now watching before moving to present exculpatory evidence.

"One suspects, much will change in the court's views, and the public, by what evidence I present. Evidence disproving these lies," the High Priestess said. She let those words hang as pandemonium broke out. She motioned for six warriors to step next to the prisoners as protection from any threat from those in the court chamber.

"First, in response to the accusation against the temple, I presented the evidence sent to us from an unnamed source, the turn we received the package. We sent it to Ministry Seven's AC nine, guild Master of Law Enforcement. We have the sealed signature of receipt. She motioned for the acolyte on her left to give it to the court."

The judges reviewed it, declaring it authentic, adding it to the evidence. All eyes turned to where the Minister sat. Now an empty chair. Two Mekalam left at a gesture from the High Priestess. Ryakin hoped she sent them to catch the Minister before he got away.

"The first holo to present is from the Imperial gardens on the evening of the emperor's murder. I will wait while the court's forensic team verifies the meh as authentic and untouched."

Ryakin gazed at the Mekalam still as statues, not one restless movement since they stopped and stood to attention. The discipline impressed him, leaving him in no doubt about their lethalness. He scrutinized the blooded in their ranked seats and the spectators in the galley sections packed full. Their faces no longer hostile when they gazed his direction.

He worked to contain his hope. Forced himself to take deep breaths. He tried to shut out his thoughts, but they intensified against his will. The High Priestess of the temple, standing to their defense a strong influential factor.

Evidence now favoring them hurt neither. And implications of mishandling, or mismanagement of important evidence damaging to the court's declaration of guilt. Evidence making the onlookers re-think they're guilt.

The court now announced the holo presented as a true and unaltered recording of the night in question. Lights dimmed, and the holo erupted to life. One scene showed a heroic battle by Jynnalt, her paladins and their attackers. Till, a sonic cannon's blast blew them to the ground. They never rose. Her paladin's valiant stand, against all odds, trying to protect her made him ashamed of his attempts to demote them from her protection detail. Tears came to Ryakin's eyes. The darkness hiding the fact from those present. In the background, the battle and later murder of the emperor and the disappearance of the Empress into the alcove as the rest of the Eagle warriors died. Gasps of outrage as the events proceeded.

The holo panned to a conversation between two unknown males, too far away to pick up what they said, after the fighting ended. Those left standing easy enough to identify as assassins. The assassins rolled bodies into rugs in the distance where his wife and her paladins fought to the last, afterward loading them on a hovercraft. Explaining their disappearance.

It proved Jynnalt to be in the wrong place at the wrong time. The conspirators using her impromptu arrival as an opportunity to cast her as the villain. Before the holo shut down, they saw three figures besides the body of the emperor. Impossible to make out who they were as their backs were to the holo meh recorder. The clothing appeared to belong to wealthy ranking Anunnaki nobles. None of the three next to the dead emperor matched the accused stature or builds. Nothing in the holo meh though cleared Prince Anu, only the house of Ki and indirectly the house of Tc.

The court erupted in chaos. Many throwing accusations at Prince Satoric. He vigorously declared them guilty to any who listened up to this point. From the expression on some faces, they thought he might have a nefarious political reason for his quick judgement.

"Order!" The High Priestess banged her staff on the marble floor hard. An agony of pain shot through Ryakin's ears, followed by a bone-jarring vibration. When the courtyard quieted, the High Priestess spoke once more.

"The Temple is curious as to why you have not released the information to the public that only forty of those who participated in the riots were actual Anunnaki empire citizens."

All eyes turned towards Prince Satoric. "I have no idea how you discovered the fact, but we kept it secret to determine who and how someone achieved this. Now, though, everyone is aware and those guilty will rush to cover their tracks. I will say no more on this, as we are still investigating the event in question."

Prince Satoric needed to stem the accusatory glares and yelled accusations declared, "I believe the court members agree," he said. "We should defer this trial till we discover further evidence because of this latest information, reviewed as valid by this court, from the Temple."

He tried to dismiss the court. The second warden stood.

"I am sure the court, considering this recent information, finds in favor of Queen Jynnalt of Ki and her house, along with Prince Ryakin, her consort, of any crime. We release King Rualui and his house with no further investigation. Judgement falls in the accused favor and against the adjudicator Prince Satoric." He scanned up and down the row. All voted "aye," in agreement, though Prince Satoric and the two other wardens slower to cast their votes.

"However," Prince Iltasadum went on, "we shall require a vote on a provisional power to represent the emperor. Until we clear Prince Anu of all charges, and he is officially the heir to the throne." he paused. "Or found guilty. We agree he should have the freedom he always enjoyed, but not the political power, wherever he might be now." He gazed at the High Priestess with a questioning brow, to which she gave a slight nod before he proceeded. "The council will restrain Prince Anu from voting on any matter affecting his status under investigation. We release the accused guild members and commoners to the custody of the Temple." He bowed towards the High Priestess, "to assure no further... persuasions someone might use against them. All present will now vote yah or nay to the aforementioned articles."

The vote was unanimous.

"The next vote is the temporary replacement of the emperor's power to the four Wardens. This, the most logical as the provisional emperor's court duties in the council. Till such time as Prince Anu once more presents himself within the Empire."

Prince Iltasadum's voice stern, as he addressed the court further. "This is our safest course forward for now. Politically, this judgement adjusts the balance of power, as I am sure we are all aware. I implore the council to not make any drastic changes to empire laws or traditions. Allow the investigations into this matter to proceed with all parties. Let us settle the charges against Prince Anu.

Once more unambiguous ayes of agreement from the court.

Ryakin saw his uncle frown, lean over and whisper to Prince Jaui, who nodded, before turning his attention back to the proceedings. Ryakin sensed whatever his uncle whispered to Prince Jaui; did not bode well for his brother.

Prince Iltasadum, as the second warden spoke once more, "I bow to the council's position. We shall revisit the matter of the emperor once the evidence between the three agencies gathered and compared before making an irrevocable decision." The other council members agreed. Prince Satoric glared at the others, his face a thunder of murderous rage.

Slick. Getting the council to agree on holo forced them to include GIA and the Temple in the investigation.

The High Priestess left minutes afterward. As soon as she stepped out the door, the Mekalam warriors flowed from the chamber with precise coordination, their battle armor turning back to temple uniforms as they left. Their uniforms spotless white from head to toe, including their cloaks, except for the Sigil of the Temple on their upper left chest. A seven-pointed blue star, and the symbol of everlasting life, in titanium white, in the center.

Ryakin almost collapsed from relief and from the months-long ordeal. Family members rushed in to hug him and his brother. He glanced around and realized he would not die this turn. The sweet scent his sister by law wore reminded him of Jynnalt, and tears shined in his eyes.

Chapter 22

AN UPDRAFT OF AIR RUSHED over Jynnalt as she stood on the platform, cooling her from the turn's early warmth. The sky a cloudless wash of pale turquoise overhead.

She drank earlier in the morning after the herd beasts. Slobber still floating on the surface. She never thought she might be desperate enough to drink from a trough after animals. Now that mattered little. Water, life for both her and her child.

At a slight flutter in her belly, she placed her hand there and sensed the child. Tears formed, and a rush of relief flowed through her. Taking a deep breath, she relaxed, feeling lighter than these past fourteen turns. She still carried her child, who's kicking informed her the baby still lived. Thankfully, she only vaguely recalled her time on the ships, or the fact her life and her child's life hung by a thread not so long ago.

She remembered the hold of the ship which brought them here and the grav tubes to the canyon floor. The nightmare treks through the desert, a memory of blazing thirst and pain. Placing one foot after another, driving her in a mindless quest forward. Her lips chapped with dried blood and her feet raw, the blisters on her delicate skin exposed to the searing heat. She healed without infection.

She swore to do whatever she needed to do to survive, to deliver her child. If forced to beg, plead, or crawl, she would. At that thought, the guards came out motioning with hand gestures towards an empty platform which arrived by a cable system. Those to slow received the lash from their whips or a hard yank on their chains towards transom. Jynnalt, the first to step on the platform, preferring to face her fate, then sit here, hiding from what came next. No guards got on the transom platform with them. Once packed full of prisoners, their captors secured the waist-high door and stepped back.

At a wave from one of them, the transom lifted and moved towards the edge of the cliff. Ten of the beasts the guards rode here walked the opposite direction, harness and lines attached to the platforms. Jynnalt suffered a jolt as the floor beneath her lifted, and the overhead wires tightened, moving them forward and over the cliff. For a second, they hung suspended, swinging.

An expansive bay and estuary plains lay before her in either direction. The mesmeric panorama before her stole her breath, a magnificent sight. For a second, her thoughts stopped. The loud, aggressive rattle of Tavas' chains caught her attention as he stepped behind her, placing a hand upon her shoulder.

A sense of comfort filled her. For the moment, she was not alone. Four of her paladins still with her. She grimaced as the thought crossed her mind. Guilt flooded her at wishing this horror of slavery and an uncertain future upon anyone. She gripped the wood railing tighter. The sheer tranquility of the scene before her, so at odds with the trauma she endured since that fateful night. She leaned closer to the edge, trying to control her tears as Tavas gave her a comforting squeeze.

Without them, she was alone. She tried talking to the other females, but they did not understand her language nor appear to have an embedded translator. She spoke with those few capable of galactic. The common tongue for the Council of Nines alliance members. Few of the females, though, appeared from systems within CON's alliances. She understood them, yet they did not understand her. Her implanted translator working fine the decoder did not take long to turn gibberish into an understandable language of those around her. She gave up on speech with most and resorted to signing. Inefficient without a collective understanding of gestures.

PHOENIX RISING

From the platform's exalted heights, Jynnalt gazed at a city that covered at least a hundred standards surrounded by a high wall. The city set in three-step levels; each level divided by interior walls half the height of the outer. The outer wall as broad as a causeway. Citizens and transport of some kind traversing along its surface. From here, they appeared like insects. The outer wall crenulated with openings spaced an equal distance apart.

Taller than the surrounding wall stood a ziggurat, in the third-highest section of the city. The mid-city section of gorgeous glowing white marble buildings. Roofs a mix of gleaming gold and red inter-spiced with one glorious statue after another. In the upper western mid quarter section of the city, immense twin palaces faced a plaza which separated them with checkered black, red, and white squares. The lower section a confusing mass of dingy dark roofed tenements.

To the east stretching off into the distance a rich vibrant Delta which the canyon river-fed, the roar from the waterfalls reaching them this far away. To the south, straight ahead, a turquoise sea which blew the cooling winds from earlier. The Delta lands ran to the eastern mountain range, which decreased in size as it marched into the sea, the tops buried under waves.

The western side wall dropped ten stories to an ancient quay, then dropped an additional twenty stories to a dry sandy expanse reaching to the far-off outer wall thousands of flyers lived upon. A harbor, now long dry, bleached bones of ancient gargantuan sea creatures sticking out of the sandy bottom. Headlands on either side framed a colossal seawall holding back the hungry waves. This once a thriving seaport in antiquity. The distant screeching of sea flyers carried on the wind. Thousands of them lined the top of what appeared to be an ancient seawall. Others wheeled over the beaches to the west and the rocky promontories. A tantalizing salty tang of the sea arrived on the breeze.

The highest sections of streets laid out as if a giant computer board. The configuration connecting the greater and smaller ziggurats to each other and the central street, which led straight to the largest one. This city appeared designed to amaze both citizens and visitors alike. At the third-lowest section, closest to the beach, sat a giant open-air oval amphitheater. Small square pyramids adorned the outer four corners. On the Delta side, to the east, lay a panorama of rich rural patchwork of farms. Spacious areas of crops, orchard trees of various kinds and sizes shaded pasture lands between well-irrigated canals. Closer to the cliffs, spacious open grasslands with vast herds of foraging beasts dotted with sparkling lakes.

The male Malkuth standing next to her spoke. "See how the pattern differs from those used throughout the galaxy?" Without looking her way, he pointed at the upper north third section. "Yet, you can still recognize its basic use is for power production for the city, and most likely for the surrounding areas. From the size of the ziggurat, the output must supply an immense amount of power. The smaller ziggurats regulate and control the power flow. It puzzles me though why the power plant is off. The planet appears viable enough to still supply the necessary raw energy."

Jynnalt spied his brow furrow as he stared at the city spread before them.

"Why would they do that?" He asked in a rush of standardized common galactic from her right side, his pronunciations elegant.

"How would you know?" She asked as she glanced first at him, then at the city growing as they got closer to the ground.

"Examine how they lack the slight shimmer over their surface," he said as unconsciously he reached for Jynnalt's arm.

Before he touched her, he found his hand in a tight grip by Tavas's, the other three males pressed up behind him threateningly. His eyes widened, though he appeared less concerned than most if grabbed in such a manner.

"Sorry," he said as he tugged his hand from Tavas' grip.

Tavas released him, but the other three stayed close. Jynnalt amazed that he acted unfazed as he went back to explaining.

"They're polished white limestone, their capstones I'd bet orichalcum infused nanospheres. I bet those smaller ziggurats function as resistors and capacitors. The pattern appears far more complex than those we use."

Jynnalt could tell he filed away everything he perceived,

distinguished, or identified. He more curious about the science, as opposed to the view which captivated her for a fleeting time. She glanced back at the city and realized he was right. She detected the smallest one flicker and shimmer in a strange pattern. "That one over there is working, I believe," she said, looking back at him.

He stared for a few minutes before speaking. "Yes, I missed that," he said.

She ignored the antipathy in his voice. "May I ask your name?" Jynnalt said courteously. She sensed something familiar about him.

He glanced at her. "Kendo, I helped tend you on the ship. And was with you on Niuard during the troubles."

Now she realized the sense of familiarity. Disgusted with herself for not recognizing him right away. Jynnalt changed the subject, turning to her paladins. "I need you to do everything you can to survive. This means ignoring what I might endure," she said, glancing over at Kendo, wondering what he thought of her remark. *Pureblood Malkuth*, she'd bet. Under his breath she caught him snort before murmuring, "doubt they will stop trying to watch over you," he said quiet enough she sensed he spoke to himself.

She prayed he was wrong. She should have waited for Ryakin as Tavas requested. The two of them, together, might have prevailed. Her foolish rush to pass along the meh, entrusted to her when she found the dying operative, took them from their loved ones. Worse, she endangered her child.

Since captured, no one took her possessions. The incriminating meh and the brittle relic bag still on her person. When the chance presented itself, she needed to hide them. Odd. She did not remember taking the relic with her when she left to visit the emperor and empress, yet she must have. The night the assassins murdered the emperor, hazy, disjointed, and confusing, when she tried to think about what happened.

The citizens in the city enlarged, no longer resembling scurrying insects in a hive. Now she noticed the monuments and statues scattered throughout the city haphazardly. The second section's buildings of various shapes and sizes between a warren of streets intersected with plazas of open grounds filled with colorful tents.

"Tavas, you overheard my father speak many times of the mythical cities of the Murians. This place reminds me of some of his tales," she said, trying to lighten the dark reality of their situation for a few more minutes. When the platform touched the ground, she understood her life no longer hers.

Twenty minutes later, they arrived before a rough stone plaza behind the city. The guards unloaded them, or more like herded and moved them to where tents sat. The original group they'd paired her with now back together, minus one who died on the forced march through the desert. They chained them back together and left them with a guard.

Two turns later, over two thousand prisoners stood on the plains behind the city. By the second turn, a male, no longer hidden behind mis-matched battle armor, approached her in the tents they placed the slaves in overnight. She shrank back in reflex, but he grabbed her as another entered and unchained her from the others and dragged her out of the tent. She realized exactly who and what they were once out of armor.

In the academy, they showed images of this species. *Sabations.* The trainers taught they fled the galaxy when they lost the Great War three hundred sars ago. How did the Council of Nine miss the fact Sabations are the reavers? This must be the reason they left no living witnesses. To hide their presence.

Sweating from the heat and uncertainty left her weak. She stumbled, and the guard yanked her behind him. Flat wooden stands three feet tall on the massive stones of the plaza backed up to the north outer wall of the city. High ululating voices hawking the prisoner's value, creating a cacophony as patrons shouted to outbid each other. Screams filled the air from slaves being branded by their new owner's guards.

The male Sabations wore loose flowing pants of thick coarse material, black skin boots, and a half sleeveless tunic. They tucked wicked knives in their belts and projectile handhelds strapped within easy reach on their leg. Not a single energy weapon present. Females in the stands to the east covered head to toe in colorful flowing, long-sleeved robes, their hair, and faces covered, leaving only their eyes visible.

Anger boiled within her. Overriding her fear when she realized members from all CON's alliances, merchants mingled with outlaws and bandits from throughout the galaxy. They *have knowledge of* the Sabations' existence here, yet never leaked it. The outlaws and bandits she understood, being criminals, but the sight of the others enraged her. They used the Sabations to gain illicit goods and slaves. Which helped the Sabations to regroup and rebuild. Logic kicked in. Thinking back, she remembered those alliances attacked by reavers like the others in the galaxy. So, not the alliances, but criminal profiteers. Jynnalt did not doubt there might even be Anunnaki criminals present.

She glanced along the line before pushed by a guard on to the plaza, and the strange outer runic stones. A shock coursed through her for a second, along with a quick flash of green light before her eyes. It passed as quick as a flash of lightning. Then she caught sight of Kendo and her four paladins, the paladins three tents away from where Kendo stood. Kendo's face white as death. She glanced away, not wanting to imagine him so fearful as he faced his fate. Her anger still hot enough to burn away her fear.

The air a liquid heat which undulated before her, radiating from the stones. The second star now joined the other, rising off the horizon.

They sold her to a female in deep purple robes and coverings edged in gold thread. A guard pulled Jynnalt off to the side and branded her shoulder, handing her clothing, which covered little. The toga like item reached her upper thigh and exposed her stomach, covered her chest and unbranded shoulder. Open on the sides with a rope belt at her waist.

For some odd reason, they handed her the relic; the meh hidden inside the brittle bag full of ash. Afterward, they shoved her in a pen with other females crying and hysterical. Most other races and varied species present, though some Elohim like her. Straining, she recognized her paladins and Kendo also in pens languishing for the rest of the turn. She wished she could glimpse their brands. They led many slaves off towards the Delta plains or towards the east and sizable pens next to resting airships. Others taken back to the transoms and returned to the high plateau.

As the first star lowered on the horizon, the hair rose on her neck as if something sinister arrived. Glancing upward, she perceived a huge robed being standing on the wall high above, observing the slaves. Jynnalt trembled as dread gripped her. Jerked her head away, not wanting to draw its attention, puzzled at her reaction as she shivered with terror.

While at Ki, she met hundreds if not thousands of species. More in Agade. Some left her with disgust or unease, though none with outright fear. She glanced back up, but the strange creature no longer stood there. A brief time later, a male dressed in slave attire came and motioned for them to follow. Small silver bells chimed around his ankles and wrist. She swayed on her feet, faint from rising too fast when he tugged viciously on her chains. The chains answered with a loud rattling. The guard gave her a calculating look, then turned to gaze at the others, before motioning them to follow. She sensed a mad manner and a nervous behavior about him, which gave her little confidence in whoever bought her.

A jolt of relief ran through her as she realized her paladins and Kendo's brands matched hers. The additional guard's force marched them with other slaves up to a causeway gate. The gateway led to a quay of what once appeared to be a seafaring ship dock. Now a wasteland of dry sand. They headed toward the western entrance gates to the city. Two hundred slaves in less than an hour disappeared through the five-story tall arched gateways standing open.

Warriors stood outside the gate, watching, and checking those unchained seeking entrance to the city. The visitors from earlier, originating from various spheres of influence as they moved past the slaves, heading inside. After a check by the guards of their persons and identified with physical paperwork, they gave them entrance. Actual paper, not metal sheaf. Her mind raced. She realized not a single device that required electrical or plasma energy appeared to work.

The guards no longer using stunners. They used crude whips and curdles. Moments later, a thought came to her. A dampening field. Must be. Then she remembered her translator still worked. She understood the conversations of the Sabation's by the end of her second turn, and the visiting merchant's species. For now, she let it go, exhausted, and leaned against the wall, closing her eyes as the baby kicked.

Even this far away from the beach, the soft swishing sounds of waves reached her. A gentle breeze blew her direction, full of the sharp tangy odors of salty sea spray underlay with whiffs of fish, decay, and death. The discordant screaming of screeching flyers covering the seawall the only thing keeping her awake as the heat and distant waves lulled her. The wall against which she leaned soared ten stories high. On the other side of the quay, a twenty-story drop to the dry cove's seabed. Now only long-dead sea creatures left as bleached skeletons half-buried in the sand. In the far distance, a rocky premonitory stretched out to meet the seawall.

The screeching flyers made rest impossible, so she examined the carvings. The limestone facia carved with frescos along the base. Citizens in striking clothing, most likely the original owners of this place, frozen in time. Part of the frescoes faded out colors of what appeared Elohim along with strange creatures. They reminded her of the meh's her father showed her of Murian cities and their mythical beasts. She realized one panel displayed prominently the Phoenix. Time and neglect though took their toll on the scenes. The city, from the pictographs on the wall frescoes, once a place of abundance, wealth, and comfort. Now. A civilization forgotten, its inhabitant's dreams and ambitions dead. Swept away in a flood of blood and fire or by the slow bitter death of immorality and decadence. The city itself left to decay, becoming this shabby body. Denied the dignity of fading away gracefully to curious ruins explored by future questing academics as they squabbled endlessly over whom the inhabitants once were. Squatters, now the only residents.

A chill yanked her out of the comfortable doze she fell into after another hour passed. Somehow, she sensed the being in the robes from earlier. Straightening, she glanced around before tilting her head back to scan the top of the granite wall. A small group of Society members, hoods covering their heads in this heat, stood high overhead. Moments later, she spotted the creature once more staring at the slaves before gazing out towards the plateau. She watched as the creature pointed a clawed fingernail out toward the seawall. She turned and shaded her eyes, trying to discover what interested the creature. Flyers screeching and hopping, taking to the air in enormous groups, agitated.

The Sabation warriors patrolling high above stopped and stared the same direction. Others standing by rapid-fire projectile guns, referred to as RFP's, versatile and cheap to produce, stepped away from them, pointing.

Now others on the wall pointing the same direction. The guards with the slaves turned and scanned the horizon. Those in front pushed the slaves faster through the gate. In the distance, a thin line of foaming white on the harbor spread out fast. Water spilled through an opening in the seawall which must have cracked open, widening as the sea rushed in to reclaim the cove.

The crack of whips snapping filled the air as yelled orders no one understood sought to move them faster. No guards now protected the gates. Those in front raced forward in panic.

A churning mass of bodies blocked the gates, her paladins shoving and pushing to get her through before the wave washed them away. A roaring sound built behind, as if a terrible beast approached. At the last moment, she and her paladins broke through to the inside. Pushed left towards an alleyway that ran along the inner wall packed full of panicked slaves. Other slaves crushed in around them. The gate closed before the water crashed through, forced shut by forty guards. Sounds of screams and begging of those left outside became muffled yet still carried to those inside the fortress. Minutes passed before the screams and pounding stopped and the roar of rushing water subsided.

Tavas held her tight as she shook. After a time, she straightened and asked, "How many do you think got caught by the wave?" She asked subdued, staring at the gate.

"Listen to me. They could do nothing. The seawall must have broken. This city ancient thousands of sars ago. I believe the Sabations do not understand how to repair anything here or even care. They will use the city up before they move on. My grandfather told me that is why the Great War started. Sabations believed they could move wherever they wanted. Use up the resources of those territories. They provided nothing in return. Leaving devastation and waste as they moved to the next system. Void locust is what he called them," Tavas said, watching the guards as he spoke.

"You also believe these are Sabations?" Jynnalt asked, staring at one moving their direction, whip cracking. He nodded.

Kendo, looking towards the others for confirmation, inquired, "Has anyone else detected a dampening field? I think the range is to the plateau. I realized when they got to a certain point, they stopped and put away all their energy weapons and replaced them with whips, knives, and the small rifle RFP's. No one's translators are working. The slaves, who don't know galactic, can only speak with those of their native tongue."

"Mine works."

All five turned to stare at her, making her uncomfortable. "At least my translator works. I can't say anything about the rest."

Kendo appeared to think before saying, "when Jynnalt stepped on the stone plaza's runes, she glanced my direction." He paused; his brow furrowed before stating. "Her eyes glowed, and the torq she wears pulsed a rich golden green light for a second. The stones glowed various colors in response around the entire court's edge. Few realized they did. Just flashed of a second, so I thought I imagined it."

The crack of a whip ended their conversation, forcing them back to their group with others of the same brand. She thought about what Kendo said as their guards marched them through the winding streets. She did not observe fear on his face earlier but astonishment at what he thought he witnessed. When they passed the massive amphitheater, the guards separated the males, moving them off towards a small gate leading inside the lower Coliseum. For all her brave words on the transom the other turn, her throat tightened, and her heart raced. The whip cracked, and she flinched at the bite across her arm, raising a welt from which blood welled. She did not linger, following those in front.

They filed through a squalid maze of jammed together buildings, buildings which, from the distance of the transom, appeared mesmerizing. Up close, nothing but crumbling tenement houses lining sprawling alleys and streets. Streets filled with tradespeople, vendors, and pedestrians. Now and then, an occasional piece of masonry, both small and big, crashed to the ground, becoming sharp shrapnel.

A piece cut one female severe enough the guards stopped, one tied off the bleeding and threw her over his shoulder before they moved forward. Other times, food and body waste splashed over them before running off into the gutters. The guards fought off starving Canis, big and small, that hunted the streets. They attacked citizens for the smallest piece of food or those who might be an easy prey to strike. They passed five of them and three sizeable Felix snarling and fighting over a Delaxtion body. Or rather the remains of one as they tore away decaying flesh and ran off with their prize, before another snatched the piece away. Visions of Niuard rose in her mind.

They passed beneath dark covered passageways before reentering the light of uncovered streets. Passed round open tavern doors showing gloomy interiors where giant kegs of drinks served to patrons by slaves barely clothed. A female bent across a table as a male ground away from behind while others yelled encouragement, a vacant expression in her eyes. Jynnalt's face heated, and she stared straight ahead at the roadway. Deafening as the street noise appeared, the unmistakable sound of slave's bells a discordant symphony underneath.

One time, they turned a corner and came upon a makeshift arena where a sizable impromptu fight stopped their progress to their destination. Sabations in tattered, grimy tunics, and various spheres of influence's visitors jeered and howled with laughter. The slaves forced to fight for their masters, betting on them. If they lost, their mangled carcasses dumped into street carts and hauled away like refuse. In the ring's center, limbs lay in pools of slick, tacky blood. Blue, brown, red, and black splashed across the stones from the various species. A strange creature two feet in height and nine feet long displayed a long snout full of sharp, wicked teeth. A long muscular flat tail, its back armored with embedded bony plates, lurked at the outer edge of the circle. The beast dashed in and fought off a canis before dragging one corpse leg off into the shadowy alley across from them. Other than the newest slaves, no one paid any attention.

Sabations, Society members, outlaws, pirates, and rebels along with privateering merchants along the path they traveled. Visitors from every corner of the galaxy, scribes from Grekia, pleasure servers from Paithi, and slaves from every galactic sector together in the street's crush. Animal trainers and sellers, unsworn warriors, bards, and taletellers filled the open forums and plaza's they passed as the streets got steeper.

An hour later, after their guards fought their way through swarming streets, they stopped before ornate gates leading into a walled section.

From the twisted turns along the way, she lost track of where they were, confusing her as to their location. When they entered the open plaza with black, red, and white squares, she realized they stopped at the plaza between the twin palaces.

They marched to a covered portico with massive double doors. Then down ten flights of stairs. Each level leading off from its landing too long hallways with curtains covering doorways.

The guards stopped at level eight, walked her down the hallway before opening a curtain. This she figured her new living quarters. Cramped, filthy, damp, a windowless chamber with no running water. A stone block covered with a thin pillow and even thinner blanket. A small chest at the end of the bed and only a curtain to separate the chamber from the outer hallway.

The guards showed them where to go for their personal care and needs. Communal chambers which both males and females used at the same time. Next, the guards took them to a metalworker who attached delicate silvery bells to their ankles and lighter chains between their wrists and feet. When they took her back to her chamber, they attached her to a ring next to the bed, letting her reach the doorway yet go no further. The future she expected, as a Queen and wife, ran out. This future which lay before her, terrifying.

Chapter 23

THE KINGDOM OF SANISUTIM possessed little resources, making tithe by turning their minor kingdom into a giant junkyard selling off parts they salvaged. For travelers, this passage a nightmare of unmarked derelicts floating throughout the systems, each a hazard to a passing ship. Smaller pieces, parts, and bubbles of floating fluids increased the dangers further.

Ikath was resting. Assured by Riurrel, he can navigate better than him through this potential minefield. Earlier, he locked Ikath out of a few minor control systems. Ikath, though, kept the primary override commands in his head as a precaution. Still, he figured a sulky Riurrel was harder to deal with and chose not to use them. He decided getting rest before the meeting might not hurt. Of late sleep, a luxury.

Halfway through, Riurrel flew right into a huge floating globular of engine fluids. Riurrel freaked, his coolant exchangers clogged, choking him.

Ikath rushed forward, passing lights blinking on the systems minor control consoles. When he entered the cockpit, every single system light was flashing with red warnings. Riurrel did not respond to Ikath's voice command. He worked fast, finding the problem. They flew right in to floating Ritalin fluid. This was bad, the fluid suffocating Riurrel's heat exchangers, robbing him of power as each second passed.

Without scanners, he did a visual check for a planet, praying one was close. His eyes narrowed, and relief washed over him. Ahead on his port side, a brownish-red planet with reflective white patches filled the screen. He almost missed the planet as the sludge blended with the planet on the viewscreen. The white patches, though, caught his attention.

"Riurrel listen. Make a steep entry dive to the planet ahead on your port side."

"*Whhhhhhhy?*"

The weird, slow response chilled Ikath. He broke into a sweat. "Listen, Riurrel. Just this once. Dive now! If not, it will be too late. You will miss your window and shoot past the planet."

He was not sure he could get Riurrel to turn if they missed this opportunity, with the systems failing fast. Riurrel would be non-functioning soon. The ship would become a piece of junk, like those they flew through for the last three turns. The likelihood of rescue nil. Ikath would join the junk as a dissected corpse floating grotesquely around the cockpit.

Seconds later Riurrel responded sluggishly, but he altered course, entering the planet's atmosphere steep enough to burn off the fluids. For the first five minutes, he was a flaming ball. Three minutes afterward, the flashing lights stopped and lit up blue steady. Ikath breathed a sigh of relief. They leveled to a proper angle and Ikath released fire foam coating on the hull, putting out the fire before further damage occurred. Seconds later, he realized Riurrel intended to land in the white flats of a desert.

"Riurrel, the fluid's cleaned off and the fire's out. What are you doing?"

"*Need recoveryyyy timmme.*"

That sounded bad. "Okay."

For the next two hours, Riurrel sat powering his solar systems batteries with the furnace blast of solar energy from the desert star overhead. Ikath did an in-depth system check to find out if they damaged anything beyond what might be repairable while here, including the outer hull. Scanner readouts reported the atmosphere was breathable and the radiation within tolerance for his species. The ramp exit opened, and a blast of furnace heat invaded the cool interior. Ikath's hair felt seared to his head. Worse, the oxygen mixes far from optimal. Riurrel was right, his systems were still not one hundred percent. He went back inside for air breathers, and as a precaution stripped and stepped into the radiation protection spray shower. Moments after the shower, he grabbed a radiation suit and the air ventilator, better prepared to attempt the outdoors once more.

Outside, he checked the horizon for life forms, detected no movement or moving blips on his scanner either. Relaxing, he called a hundred of the small spiderdrones outside to clear any fluid left in the exchangers and to check and do temporary repairs on the hull. He needed a full-service station or dock for full repair. Four hours later, he double-checked the spiderdrones work, re-calibrated the exchange system and replaced important parts with spares to be on the safe side.

Before he finished, he was down to only his underclothing. The radiation suit far too hot as sweat poured off his body. As soon as he stepped inside, a blast of freezing air hit him, and he headed straight to his quarters for a towel. He stood shivering as he dried himself, before stepping once more into the radiation scrubber before sickness overcame him. He quickly dressed and headed back to the cockpit, double-checking the minor controls on his way forward. Last, he checked the power system. The command gage showed the batteries to the control boards full.

"Riurrel, time to go." In response, the systems shut down around him, one after another. "What are you doing? Command override Ikath 67894-001." Nothing happened. The cockpit controls remained dark. How the *helc* did Riurrel figure out the override codes to disable the controls and lock him out of command? Something to worry about later. A bigger problem threatened them. If Riurrel refuse to leave out of fear, he would strand them till a passing ship responded to the emergency beacon. That presented an immense problem. He took the back lane to stay off the Igigi's tracking. The frigate's bow wave small enough to avoid registering.

For the next three hours, Ikath pleaded with Riurrel, to no avail. Ikath took the one shot left to him. Appeal to his sense of superiority.

He calculated three months of provisions on board, six if he was careful.

"Arguing with me got us in this predicament. I always piloted better than you. You just won't admit it."

Seconds passed with no response. Tense moments later and a small light flickered on and Riurrel said one thing. "*Fock.*"

"Nice one. Is that all you got? Are you admitting to my superior flying skills? At least I didn't fly us in a patch of fluid the size of a station."

The control board lit up. "Never, you are heavy-handed. You might crash me into something the size of a battleship. Fluids are more difficult for my sensors to detect floating in space. No one expects fluids floating in space. This is the only reason the abominable stuff attached to me."

"The *stuff,* as you call the fluid, did not attach to you, you flew right through center. I think I should fly us. You're recovering and need to rest your circuits."

"I am fine." Riurrel shot back.

The snappy come back let Ikath know Riurrel was getting back to his old self.

"Then why this hesitancy about leaving? Afraid. The boneyard is still there. You might make another mistake. Ten minutes later, they lifted off, back on to their original destination. They arrived at the Traveler Station, Cirealia, behind schedule. This entire sector the seedier region of the Sanisutim in the Curses Run gate section nineteen. He was eight hours late for his meeting. The docking computer tried to take over Riurrel's guidance system, and he outright refused to relinquish control. The dock operator called to ask if there was a problem.

Riurrel sent a shock back along with the comms. Ikath heard a deafening howl of pain through his console's comms. Riurrel took advantage and commandeered the docking computer before the control operator recovered from the electrical spike. Ikath heaved a sigh of relief this the Riurrel he knew. "Give over the docking command controls to the station."

"Fine," he said as he released control.

"Behave, I need to come back here and words gotten out you're a jinx, not terrific when we are dealing with superstitious outlaws. They barred us from the last station. Claimed unless I fix the ship's glitches, referring to you, I was not welcome back. They suggested I should buy another ship and scrap you. *Helc*, they even offered me several others at low prices."

"Stolen, I checked their transponder idents. They tried to erase them. I turned them over to GIA's enforcers and their locations. Don't worry, I made sure the trace points to his oh so mighty nasty dock master. They are being raided at this moment."

His smug pat on the back tone made Ikath wish at least once he would follow a command like any normal Ai. They took orders and did as directed by their handlers. Someone somewhere screwed up royal when they coded Riurrel's program.

"That dock was filthy and disgusting. You recall I defended myself because you did not answer me when I told you what they were doing."

"Ahh, if you recall, I was being chased by some rather unsavory criminals. They wanted blood. Mine."

"I can't forget, you forced me to kill those thugs trying to ship jack me. The ships were collateral damage."

"Me?" Ikath said, outrage clear in his tone, but changed the subject. "How did you do that? I forgot to ask, trying to save my skin and all with no help from you worried about your lock being scratched."

"Produced a black hole to amplify my power output from the tractor tech."

Ikath sensed Riurrel dismissed his ability, shrugging off such a powerful and technologically advanced capability. *Weird.*

"The station boss was rather unhappy you killed his thugs. Forced me to replace his ships and reimburse him for the three killed for losing labor, plus an additional amount. He stated he might let me go without killing me if I paid on the spot. Otherwise, he would put a rather large bounty on my head. You cost me a fortune by your stunt."

"Those three wanted to ship jack me. They broke the outer lock, which you, by the way, replaced with a cheaper one from the original *top of the line* one. *You* wanted to make me appear less affluent. Why didn't you inform them you stole me to explain my superiority to their ships? So yes, all your fault."

Moments passed as neither said a word. Riurrel at last spoke, his tone sulky. "Besides, I did not mean to kill them. Bios are delicate, no idea how you dominate the galaxy."

"You damaged the surrounding ships, so they are just as delicate." Ikath shot back.

"They did not die," Riurrel said.

"They are not alive. You are using a false argument. Stop trying to pull a fast one. You know if they were Ai's, your little stunt would overload their systems, which would kill them. You told me yourself. So where is your defense now? Hmm?"

Five minutes passed without a word between them, then Riurrel said, "my lock still needs fixing. Besides, you are the one who did not return when I told you those three were damaging me. I took care of those bags of water with no help from you. So, blame yourself and not me, we are no longer welcome."

Ikath rolled his eyes and took a deep breath. *Please, by all the demons and gods, let the temple recall Riurrel and replace him with any other ship, even a simple computer-controlled one.*

"Why did you feel the necessity of reporting the incident to the temple priestess? They might recall us from the field and assign me to transport duty. Far beneath my capabilities."

"I am required to inform the temple of any deaths during my investigation. Especially if caused by me or, in this case, my out-of-control Ai."

Riurrel cut in, "*Our* investigation."

Ikath ignored the remark. Something he became excellent at doing. "You know that. Besides, I remember you reporting me for theft, claiming it was your duty, to be honest." Ikath said. Silence met his remark.

Ikath discreetly investigated other users of Riurrel before him and found no complaints. None. He requested Riurrel's systems checked out three separate times, explaining to Riurrel he needed to make sure he was functioning at full capacity.

Riurrel went for the diagnostics without complaint. And got a clean pass on his codes and systems. Ikath asked the priestess to investigate for personality anomalies. Hours later, they informed him they found nothing to show any of the symptoms he described. He dropped the subject after the shipwright priestess and priest suggested he join a mental health center to resolve his problem.

Riurrel spoke up again. "Why is an Ai not in charge? Why so few capable Ai's? Why are inferior bags of water in charge at docking stations? Look, this thing is bringing me closer to the edge. I am taking control. This idiot will do more damage to my hull than you since assigned to this mission." Ikath let Riurrel do as he wanted. For now, if he felt endangered, he became defensive.

At one temple he visited a crazy scholar theorized life forms might exist in deepspace as pure energy. He knew he did not imagine Riurrel's behavior or responses. Riurrel displayed a genuine personality. He believed the ship sucked one in and the AI and life form merged.

"Make sure you are discreet. I do not need attention brought to us here. I would like to keep this as a fall back hideout."

Time passed interminably and silently, and he thanked the gods as his thoughts turned to this meeting. It took twenty minutes for the outer bay slip door to close with a groan and clanging bang of old docking doors. Twenty more minutes for their bay enclosure to decompress and fill with an appropriate oxygen mix. Twice the time of the worst stations run by outlaws.

"I promise no trouble." Riurrel said. His tone neutral.

After they touched down, Ikath admitted to himself the landing was superb, but he would never admit such a thing. Riurrel's ego gigantic enough.

He entered the dock and noted four other existing ships. Gloomy lighting making deep shadows around edges. "Riurrel, check for anyone who might appear suspicious."

Riurrel responded seconds later.

"No one appears to be skulking around, waiting to take you by surprise. None hiding. No jamming or listening or tracking devices active."

One thing he trusted. Riurrel's sensors. Ikath moved towards the inner station entrance door. The one marked for oxygen/nitrogen mix breathers. The scanner over the door checked his breath and indicated which bio-nanite decontamination canister he should use. He grabbed the masked breathed deeply before stepping through the entrance door. A rush of tingling flooded through him as the nanites inundated his system.

"I would appreciate a thank you for guarding your safety. And an acknowledgment of my skills. If I were an ordinary Ai, you would not work me so hard. I would not be capable of helping as much."

"True, but they are far less annoying and would leave me to do my work in peace."

Ikath regretted the words as soon as they came out his mouth. Riurrel would make sure he paid for the remark, so he tried to soothe him by saying, "I'm sorry, ignore what I said. Lacking sleep and all."

"Not true. You forget I monitor your waking and sleeping biorhythms."

He figured best not to say anything else. Then wondered about the contact. Who they sent this time? He discovered the last agent tortured in ways he could not imagine when he accompanied his Lordship, Riciad, to his new fortress dungeon. His stature elevated by those calling themselves the Three Pillars. They informed Lord Riciad they obtained nothing from him. He killed himself with a poison, destroying his spirit meh before they tortured him further. What they did to the whisper agent horrifying.

Rounding a corner, he stopped before he ran into someone blocking his path. His heart drummed a quick beat, till he realized the person was the Ghost Walker. The one who sent him on his mission during Nibiru's attack. The mission which allowed him an inside connection to the criminal organization he was investigating and now worked within.

"I need you to give me the information for the whisper agent you were to meet. You're eight hours late. He left twenty minutes after your meeting time passed. I can get this information to the correct... Priestess."

He held out his hand. Ikath hesitated. A moment later, he handed over the missive. The Ghost Walker possessed the correct ident codes when he first met him and Riurrel recognized him. Ikath rarely trusted anyone, yet he did this Ghost Walker.

"I came here to enlist your aid after your meeting. However, you were late. There is a different, more urgent assignment for you. Take this to the Citadel Gate," he said. Handing over a cheap appearing necklace common throughout this area. "Once you arrive at the proper coordinates, the instructions will activate, and you are to put in the directions. I'll pulse you what you are to do when you arrive. This is all I can tell you. For now."

Ikath took the necklace and slipped it into his pocket.

"What caused you to be late?"

Ikath followed the Ghost Walker over to a table outside a feasthall called Labu's Tears on the causeway. A holo server popped up between them on the table, asking what interested them. Both requested honeyed mead produced by the locals. The cheapest item on the menu. The built-in replicator to the side of the table produced two tall ice-cold mugs. And they both paid with a fourth of a Beka coin. Coins untraceable.

Ikath explained what happened and how he found overriding Riurrel's systems harder with each turn.

"Trust Riurrel, he is temperamental, silly and, yes, even arrogant, but he has a good heart. Believe it or not, he is your best resource. Don't fight him all the time." The Walker said while leaning back relaxed, one hand on his mead, the other resting on his leg.

"I sent him for a diagnostic. And checked the records from other operators. The others claimed he's normal. No problems. Why me?"

The Ghost Walker shrugged without glancing his direction, "I find the situation strange as well. You're right, he's never interacted with another operator until you came along. He must find you interesting or challenging."

"So, you know about his personality. Why don't you tell the Temple coders?"

"Because I designed and built him for the Temple."

Shocked, Ikath stared at him before declaring, "I thought CON and the Temple forbid the ability to code an Ai with free will."

"Who says he gained free will?"

Ikath started to respond, but something caught the Ghost Walker's attention across the causeway. Curious, he gazed the direction the

Walker did, trying to figure out what caught his attention. He caught a flash of light out of the corner of his eye. When he turned back the Ghost Walker, now no longer in his seat; the mug of icy mead untouched as frosty air flowed around the glass.

He glanced around, wondering if he could still get a glimpse of him as he left the merchant's square. He appeared to vanish into thin air. Ikath frowned. Once more he thought about the rumors of Ghost Walkers, yet remembered nothing about them disappearing in a flash of light. Swords yes, exceptional fighting skills, yes, great stealth and tracking skills, yes. This Ghost Walker went far beyond normal stealth. The temple trained Ikath to pay attention for signs of stealth usage. He detected none of the normal signs when around this Ghost Walker. Last time he met him Riurrel stunned him, so he chalked his lack of ability to catch the stealth to still recovering. Yet, here he also vanished in a blink of light.

He shook his head before walking back to Riurrel. Few ever met a Ghost Walker. Low-ranking Temple Priestess almost never warriors in the Temple either. Sometimes operatives got help from them, however they usually never met them personally. They would receive information left at various places on their ships. Part of the reason, they tracked the most dangerous criminals of the galaxy for the Temple and the Council of Nine. Keeping their identity secret was paramount. Like the Society, criminals, and pirates in public, they kept their hoods over their heads when hunting. At least those are the rumors citizens and Temple folks passed around. This Walker did not appear to worry much about concealing himself.

Arriving back at the bay, he overheard Riurrel's voice coming from the ship's outside comms.

"Hey, you two lazy bones, shift change does not give you the right to ignore your duty to a paying customer. I understand the station is old and at a minimal level of functioning. Maybe if you did your jobs, the place would not be so bad. I understand how you got a forty-three for a station rating. Shame on you. How about fueling my ship? The ships already sitting here disgraceful, no mag locks to keep them parked securely. I comprehend the flashing from the refueling hoses means disconnect them and I am not a dock worker. Are you water bags blind? Do I need to explain this means the ships are full, and dangerous to leave those hoses in, idiots all of you? The pressure builds and can rupture. That means fire. FIRE onboard a STATION."

Three workers moved out to the bay. Sullen, angry expressions on their faces as they glanced over at Riurrel.

"May I remind you they pay you more than enough to do your jobs? Disconnect these hoses properly and straighten out the mess of wiring and equipment scattered across the bay. Where are your supervisors? They should dock you all a turn's tithe or two."

"*Drog, helc, sheat*," Ikath cursed under his breath as he rushed towards Riurrel. "What the *helc* are you doing?" he demanded through his cybernetics. "I said discreet, *remember*?" This *droging* ship would be the end of him one of these turns. *Asset his arse.*

As he came abreast of the dockworkers, he said, "Sorry, my father's senile, thinks he's a boss everywhere we go. I thought I secured and locked him in his chambers before entering the station. Now and then he gets out. Just ignore him. Don't worry, I can fuel my tank. I don't need help. Sorry, he's been a bother." He waved them off and studied them as they walked away, indolent and surly despite his explanation.

"You are back earlier than I thought you would be. Was the whisper agent gone?" Riurrel asked, acting as if nothing untoward just occurred.

"No. Your friend showed up and took over this one."

"He did not stop to visit me. Is he coming by later?"

Ikath discerned the hopeful tone in Riurrel's voice. "No, he is sending us on an important mission," he said, feeding Riurrel's ego to distract him. He brought the necklace with the hidden meh close enough for the wireless system to connect. Afterward, for a few minutes, he went through the preflight checklist. Once ready, he started the engines and called for clearance. Riurrel, more discreet this time, took over the guidance computer as he rose from the bay floor.

At the last second, Ikath spotted a dockworker-run out from underneath the ship as the landing gear retracted into Riurrel's belly.

"Hey, one of my struts almost got caught by a mag lock, which would have ripped it off. I think the worker did that on purpose."

"Maybe he was just checking on something. And if he was messing with it, you brought this on yourself. That's what you get for being so bossy with the dockworkers. Not smart to piss them off when they have such intimate access to you. I would think about that next time," he said, a slight grin on his face.

Chapter 24

THE SERENITY OF THE beach sustained her, gave her a moment of tranquility and a sense of rest and control. Without these times and her son, Jynnalt, would have withered and died. Ossa, her guards, with her female slaves, including Jynnalt, would arrive at this beach at every turn as the star peeked above the horizon. Red gold light shimmered across cerulean blue water. A golden streak to the horizon as the star rose to fill the vista. Small white-capped waves lapped with a soft, whooshing sound across the white sand. Flocks of feathered flyers, which she dubbed wheelers because of their habit of circling, burst hysterically into the air, their cries scolding them for invading their territory. Her son, a small toddler, raced after them, laughing and giggling loudly with joy as she supervised him. A small replica of his father, with little of her in him.

A cool breeze blew in from the azure water, contrasting with the soft scorching sand, and made her shiver with pleasure. She focused on those sensations as she listened to the whisper of the foliage from the tropical plants at the edge of the beach. A dazzle of riotous colors of pinks and yellows, reds, and blues scattered throughout the dark green leaves. She inhaled the exotic scents from the flowers, dancing to the slightest whims of breezes coming in off the sea. Soothing her with its similarity to the beach her family visited every hot season on Kestrel. This is where she practiced her sword dancing routine even in the most severe weather, if allowed by Ossa, her owner. Time faded into the background as Jynnalt danced the warrior's dance. The dance lacked the silvery flash of a sword or the deadly melody as it sliced through the air, emphasizing her movements.

Tall, thin trees with long purple fronds at the tops swayed in the wind. Bunches of brown hard-shelled nuts nestled beneath which Ossa's slaves collected before heading back. The Sabations refused to eat the nuts, disliking the sweetness of the inner meat and milk. She ordered them collected to give to her slaves. They added a rich source of nutrients to their diet.

The scene skewered to somewhere new. She now stood on a vast, empty plain. Ossa between two strange trees that shimmered as blood ran in rivulets off her and her son. Jynnalt stood frozen before them, unable to move. They faded away as she reached out to grab her son.

A loud bang startled her. The clink of chains jerking her to a sitting position. Disorientated by the stink of mold, sewage and a bitter body odor gagged her. She tried to recollect where she was. She leaned against the stone wall behind her and gazed around at her prison. A clammy, icy stone floor and cell bars in front. There were no windows to allow light in to judge time, only soft dim torch lights to aid the guards. She wore the same ragged clothes from when they arrested them.

Her life changed for the worst. She thought over the time since she arrived here as a slave. Ossa, her owner, the daughter of the warlord, did not mistreat her. She was a kind and caring mistress of her slaves. But she still owned her. The odd thing the slaves owned before she and the newest ones arrived shied away from Ossa. They stared at her with a deep hatred and fear. Jynnalt figured a natural occurrence of being owned by another. Her life now comprised waiting on another under threat of the lash and spending time with her son in their small assigned quarters.

Once her son was born, Ossa demanded she received a larger chamber and to leave her unchained at night. One time she spotted Kendo entering the warlord's palace, running errands, but she could not catch his attention. Since the turn, the Sabations sold them like herdbeast and separated them. Jynnalt did not know if her paladins were alive or dead.

The city drastically changed since she arrived. As if it'd been waiting for something slumbering. Whatever happened, the device controlling the water turned on. Loud screeching and screes of metal to metal for turns. Then quieter. Now no sounds came from the machinery. Once the harbor filled, the water controls inside the city sprang to life.

Twenty turns later, strange drones appeared. They resembled a variety of small insect-like creatures, and in the night repaired the damage and daily wear and tear. The former glory of the city semi-repaired after only five months since she arrived. Every night since, the drones repaired damage or vandalism done from the earlier turn.

The harbor, now full of crystal-clear waters, filtered by a mechanism in the walls. Inside the city, fountains filled with freshwater. The plumbing now repaired gave clean running water inside buildings. Tree's, herbs, and edible plants brought inside and planted by the drones, yet no one ever detected them outside the walls. Or where the plants came from. The city bloomed a riot of colors. A cool paradise as the nuts and fruit bushes and trees' sweet scents mingled with the stench pervasive in the lower sections. The mechanized systems to maintain and repair the city appeared controlled somewhere from the upper section. Still, only the city-controlled equipment and the strange insect like drones functioned. The dampening field denied outside energy sources.

Once she overheard Ossa and her father arguing about a race, they called the Heliosag's. The Society introduced them to the Sabations. Ossa trusted neither of them. "father your chieftains take their gifts, believing in their powers and promises. These outsiders are trying to provoke war. They promise to restore the clans to their former glory." Ossa said, as she motioned for Jynnalt to bring more drink and pour for them before she spoke once more.

"The reason they defeated us was our arrogance and disregard for other's property. They considered us a scourge. We have a home here and live well. Why can we not stay and trade instead of steal? This system has enough resources to support our clans. The difficulty of navigating the nebula gives us protection from outside raiders."

It amazed Jynnalt, listening as she sat in a corner in attendance. Ossa's father agreed with her. He explained to his daughter his chieftains did not think the same as he did. The Society's enticements of treasures and power overcame their common sense. He also told her someone worked in the background within their own clan with the outsiders. Soon he would discover who the traitor was and punish them. Uncomfortable speaking to his daughter of such matters, he changed the subject. The rest of the night, they talked about family and other important clan issues, letting Jynnalt learn about Sabation's life.

A door banged close by, jerking her back to the present. She watched as Ossa's father Hatian enter. He walked over to the cell holding his daughter, motioned the guards to let her out. As soon as they did, they retreated, given them privacy.

"I should have given you more protection. I fault myself. You understand, even I cannot defy our laws. You know this." The sadness in his eyes made Jynnalt realize he loved his daughter.

"I will not shame you, father. I will not beg."

Jynnalt saw tears form in his eyes.

"I know you will not shame our clan. You are more a warrior than all your brothers put together."

Jynnalt remembered the night which brought them to this impasse. Ossa refusing the offer of mating to the Warlord's most powerful chieftain's son. That night during a festival he paid off her protectors, and with eleven warriors broke into her chamber. Ossa did not beg when they attempted to rape and murder her. Ahapesh stood before her, explaining what they intended to do. He did not expect it when she slashed him across the face with a small knife. Jynnalt jumped into action, killing three, before one threatened her son, forcing her to relinquish the knife she took from the first warrior she killed. Ossa's father burst in with his warriors right then.

Ahapesh maintained she released her warriors from duty when he arrived. Claimed she accommodated him until he realized she set a trap and meant to kill him, pointing to the deep slash across his face for emphasis. Ossa claimed Ahapesh paid off her guards, which left her defenseless. Her guards sided with Ahapesh and claimed she released them for the night.

Clan law forced the Warlord to arrest his daughter. Unless someone cleared her of the crime of attacking a chieftain's warrior, let alone the chieftain's son, clan law demanded he treat her as any other. The sounds of Ahapesh and his warrior's laughter still rang in Jynnalt's ears. Ossa and her imprisoned for the last month since the attack.

Jynnalt overheard the guards saying the clan's Chieftains demanded a trial. If Ossa's champion lost in the arena, Ossa and her slaves would die, taunted and tortured, before given a horrific death.

Jynnalt befriended a female slave a month after she arrived, who could speak galactic and now sat in the cell next to hers. She informed Jynnalt of the customs of the Sabations in these types of matters.

"They will auction off her slave's children to outsiders. Their laws and superstitions forbid selling them to other Sabations or their clans once there is a judgment against their owner. They are superstitious, but they are also pragmatists. The tithe a slave child brings to a clan is worth too much to sacrifice."

A sense of relief washed over her when she overheard this. She would die, but her son, though a slave, would live. The Sabations would sacrifice the adults one by one for the amusement of the crowds in the arena. Crowds of Sabations, criminals and the decadent bored thrill-seekers from outer empires and kingdoms came here illegally to enjoy the live games. The criminally and morally depraved. Those who hungered for brutality and horrific deaths of others. The more gruesome the sport, the more the spectators cheered. They craved this horror, bored by False Reality and the knowledge of deaths in those games false. The carnage a farce. A craving bubbling up within the vilest members of society, lacking in morality. Entitled beings believing their wants and horrific obsessions of more value over innocent lives.

Something civilized society did not offer. They lusted after actual death in their entertainment; outlawed throughout the galaxy by the Council of Nine after the defeat of the Sabations three hundred sars ago.

A warrior approached Ossa's father, Hatian, and whispered in his ear. Hatian's shoulders slumped as he nodded his acknowledgment, his eyes shimmering. As the warrior passed Jynnalt's cell, he stared at her as if she was a strange and aberrant creature.

Ossa peered at him and waited. Finally, he spoke. "he came to inform me about the outcome of the vote of the clan. They declared the trial a challenge contest. The chieftains have chosen your defender," he turned towards Jynnalt. "It's this slave. Ahapesh wants revenge for the death of his three warriors she killed."

To Jynnalt, the gods intervened, giving her a fighting chance. If she died, she would not be helpless before a jeering crowd slaughtered for their pleasure.

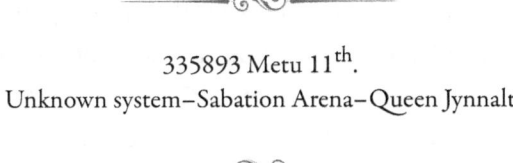

335893 Metu 11th.
Unknown system–Sabation Arena–Queen Jynnalt

GUARDS CAME FOR HER while the other prisoners slept. The bang of the doors startling her from a sound sleep. Groggy, she staggered to her feet as the key turned in the lock. Ossa rose in her cell, her face sad, full of fear.

They took her to a bath chamber and left her to bathe. Afterward, she braided her hair, then found a thin leather strip dropped in a corner to tie off the bottom ends. She gazed around for her clothing and realized they took hers and left others.

Sarc skin boots that came up over her knees with built-in metal shin guards. A short skirt also of Sarc skin, slits of strips one inch thick which reached to her mid-thighs. A thick belt with metal rings, a metal breastplate which fit a little too tight, straps which went over each shoulder with metasteel studs. Thick wrist and armbands of plain steel metal and no helmet. Nothing more.

This is not armor, its ceremonial wear pretending to be armor. She doubted there were a lot of female fighters who fought in the arena ring games, wondering where they got the little female armor she now wore.

When she left the bath chamber, one of the Sabation's stepped in front, and two to her side. Then marched her through dim corridors as shadows danced and reached for her on the walls in the gloom.

There were doors every few feet till they came to a dead-end facing petrified wooden double doors. Strange creatures fought legendary heroes from ancient times carved across them. They opened the doors and motioned she was to enter.

When she stepped inside, she realized the chamber was full of swords and shields from ancient to newer times. They strewed the weapons throughout the cavernous stone chamber in a manner that spoke of contempt. Countless stunning ornate swords littered about, most fine for show and ceremony, useless in battle, so she ignored them.

She tried the long, deep curved swords and despaired of finding at least a semi-balanced one, which was not too long or too heavy. The Sabation's talked amongst themselves or laughing as she wandered the chamber. The larger one remarking, "as if a female recognizes the true worth of a sword."

One guard did not laugh. "She grasps how to use a knife, don't forget, she killed three warriors, and she ignores the pretty swords. Unlike the few females brought here to choose a weapon," he said. "I'd bet on her. Ahapesh is arrogant."

The others took him up on the bet, laughing hard and remarking about the ease with which they earned their tithe this turn. Jynnalt ignored the guards, concentrating on her search. Now they paid more attention with a bet riding on the outcome. While the guards argued, she walked past countless numbers of flashy swords. When she picked none of those, they paid more attention. She didn't care. Jynnalt trained her entire life with a sword and knew what she needed to give her a fighting chance.

She lifted and assessed those which appeared promising, yet each time put it back disappointed and dissatisfied. In a shadowed corner, something drew her attention. A sword with a slight curve, a single-edged blade with a small circular guard and long grip to accommodate two hands. She trained with both one-handed sword and shield and the traditional two-handed swords of Ki. This one fitted as if forged for her.

The finish a black mirror like metal she did not recognize. She swung the sword in a figure-eight pattern, feeling its balance. A soft, humming whistle sounded as the sword sliced through the air with no effort. She sensed an odd, imperceptible vibration in the handle. The cross-guard itself a small collar of an intricately carved beast that fit against the edge of her hand in a comfortable grip. The sword alive, an extension of her. She experienced a connection deep within.

The slightest flare of faint ripples of energy flowed along the edge, then vanished, and she shook her head. Now only seeing a superbly forged sword. This was the sword she either killed with or died by.

Kill them and flee.

A microsecond of a thought. She understood the results as soon as she thought about them. Her son likely tortured and killed within the arena. The thought of endangering his life chilled her to the bone. Ossa, who treated her with dignity during her enslavement along with her household slaves, would die without a chance. Jynnalt their only opportunity for life. Besides, there was nowhere to flee.

If she lost, they intended to sell him for profit. The tithe going to the winner. Sabation's blood tithe. If she died in the arena. He'd live no matter the outcome. As long as she fought. She handed over the sword.

Once they left the chamber, they entered a warren of long hallways as dim as the earlier corridor. Stone cells facing the hallway covered by bars. After a half-hour of twist and turns, they came upon the cells which held her four paladins.

Surprised, she hesitated till the guard behind pushed her forward. Tavas's voice kept calling out her name as she walked away. The sound of rattled bars and desperation receded till they turned a corner, and his voice no longer carried to her. That all four still lived gave her solace.

They stopped before a door, which opened into a square chamber. Large ornate gates leading into the arena gave her a full view of what transpired. Revulsion overcame her as the morning progressed. The screams and pitiful moans of the dying, their blood splashed across the arena from the games or executions, sickening. A contrived spectacle for those in the stands who jeered, cheered, and screamed for blood, staggering in its lack of empathy. The amount of cruelty and acts of depravity amongst the Sabations inconceivable in her former life.

She stood before the gates to the arena sands, her guards observing her every move. Forced her to turn back when she tried to turn away. As they executed the slaves, maimed, or abused for the most minor offenses, to their owners in gruesome manners.

The Colosseum arena reeked with the bitter odor of despair, death, and fear, mingled with the coppery sweet scent of blood. An odd, musky scent radiated off the blistering bloody sand. Sometimes they only maimed offenders, allowing them to live. Legs and hands dismembered because of a minor crime declared before the crowds. Other times handed over to groups of favored fighters and abused before the catcalls of the crowd.

Afterward, the arena tenders pushed the gored, bloodied sand towards the outer edges. Strange insects, the Sabations called sand feeders, cleaned the sand to a pristine white. A vague memory assailed her from the march here. The slaves were careful to stay out of their reach as they spread the cleaned sand. One careless slave got close to the edge and three insects attacked, spraying him with fluid. His body dissolving as they pulled him down into their pit; his screams of agony filled the air.

The crowd laughed, joked, and jeered high above in the stands. Here there were no resurrection vats. No cloned bodies. Children born in captivity did not have a bio spirit meh chip embedded into the brain to achieve resurrection, even if the vats existed.

They brought out her son, along with Ossa's entire household, for special bidding. Not waiting for the fight of judgement. The assumption clear.

"*No.*" Her heart hammered against her ribcage. Her body trembling violently. She pushed up against the bars, her knuckles white as she gripped the metal. Because of the quality of the slaves, the bidding started high, then progressed fast and furious. One dressed as a Rider rose from a group far across the arena with a prohibitively expensive bid ending the auction. Relief flooded through her. She never realized the Riders kept slaves. Her son at least removed from amongst the cruelty of the Sabations. She could not figure out the reason the Rider bought them, but thanked the gods they did. Craning her neck, she tried to see and memorize the pod markings on their belt buckle, but the bidder was too far away.

An hour later, after more open sales of other slaves, the guards next to her handed her the sword and motioned for her to follow out the gate into the arena. When her foot touched the sands, she froze as terror seized her. She forgot everything. Sars of training disappeared in the blink of a moment. The sword no longer lightweight but an immense stone dragging at her arm. Till a guard shoved her forward. She thought the armor left her exposed with next to nothing of protection. Somehow, she managed to walk forward. Trembled as the world around her slowed. Cocooned her in silence and time.

The crowd's jeers and taunting high above her only muffled background noise. Glaring white sand, blinding. A piercing cry from a raptor circling high overhead caught her attention. She glanced skyward. Caltac's voice spoke. *Fear cuts deeper than any blade. If you fear to lose, you have lost.* He told her after one of their grueling sessions when she pulled back from a strike. The correct responds, to step in and block. The world snapped back as catcalls and jeering, an overwhelming sudden roar.

They stopped her before the Warlord's stand and forced her to her knees. Ossa's father high above stood and stretched open his arms. A blast of deep bass horns sounded, and seconds later, the arena fell silent.

"This is a contest of Labbu's judgment. Ossa of the under clan Ha'ti daughter of Warlord Hatian, demands justice sought from the warrior Ahapesh. The claim. He entered her sanctum without permission, attacked her property, and attempted to take which an un-mated maiden holds of value."

Jynnalt sensed from the chieftain's reactions, the Warlord insulted the chieftain's son, and his clan, by not naming them. Nor did he address the other side of the accusations. Angry murmurs rose from the chieftain's section.

Ignoring them, he called Ahapesh to appear. He demanded he and his clan swear to abide by the laws of Labbu's judgment. A resounding yes echoed through the arena. The Warlord sat, and the guards left the arena.

She faced the warrior. Yellow-eyed and stocky. His build bulky, not with fat, but muscle as he swaggered towards her. Contempt and amusement on his face.

A mutter went through the crowd. Catcalls from outer sphere patrons with little understanding of the difference to this fight from earlier shows. The patrons wanted the games to move to a more exciting contest of death and gore, actual fights. Battles between warriors. Not one with a female. Ahapesh turned three sixty, his arms spread high above his head, grinning before facing her.

Her son and Ryakin's flash through her head. Something clicked, settled. Her training rushed upon her. She stood facing him; the sword held before her in a fighting stance.

He grinned at her, saying, "I shall feed your body to the sea wheelers and your bones to the sand feeders."

"Come, try to kill me." She spat at him in galactic baring her teeth. He stared at her in confusion for a second before throwing his head back and laughing. He may not have understood her words, but he sensed their intent.

Her sword flashed, drawing a thin red line along his arm. His eyes widened in surprise as he sidestepped, barely dodging the killing blow. Jynnalt spun before he recovered and drove the knife-edge of her foot through his guard into his jaw. She slammed him backward, his arms windmilled as he fought for balance. She lunged forward, placing a kick to his kidney missing as he dove to the side. First blood belonged to her.

Rolling to his feet, amusement no longer on his face. His visage enraged. Bored conversation filled the arena overhead, fueling his anger, his eyes narrowing. He made a sloppy rush at her. With ease, she side-stepped. Too late, he realized her maneuver and threw himself back. Her sword kissed his shoulder, cutting deep. For several minutes, she parried the flurry of blows from him with skill and finesse.

His greater strength and longer reach forced her back towards the edge of the arena and the sand feeders.

The resounding ring of frenzied metal on metal, flashes of light glinting off swords as both parried furious blows. The crowd's attention now focused on them. Jynnalt received nicks and cuts, all slight and stinging. Streaks of blood on the warrior's face and arms proving she inflicted wounds on him. The outer edges of the sand rippled; the insects, maddened by the blood now dripping from both opponents. Liquid fire slid along her left arm when her attention wavered towards those rippling sands.

The armband kept the cut from going to the bone. He whirled and sliced out again. She intuitively dropped to her knees, arching backward, her head not far off the sand. The whistle of his sword passed a whisper above her body.

She came up fast, leaped forward and rolled, putting distance between them and back towards the center of the arena. The warrior followed close behind. Pressuring her. Still, her blade drew blood more frequently than his. Forcing Ahapesh to slow his attacks. To become cautious.

That gave her breathing room. She met the warrior's gaze without blinking as tension hummed between them. The conversation above quieting as the speed of their furious movements and flashing sparks from swords drew attention.

Cheers rose from patrons above when one of her slashes drew a long razor-thin line from which blood flowed. The screeching scream from the raptor overhead came as the warrior moved fast and low, with a vicious kick at her knee.

She slid her leg back, avoiding the strike, then snapped forward. Her heel struck hard on his weight-bearing knee. His knee buckled. Faster than she expected, he came back up with a strike.

She parried the move, but her grip on the sword slipped, slick with sweat and blood running down her arms. Her sword flew out of her hands and became planted in the sand an arm's length away. She lunged for it, but a slash from his sword just missed her hand as she jerked it back. She backed off, breathing hard as she faced him. Loud boos and jeers filled the air. His breathing as hard as hers.

They circled each other. Cognizant of the others fighting style. Jynnalt unarmed gave Ahapesh the advantage. His confidence surged. He rushed in, pressuring her, forcing her once more towards the outer edge of the arena.

At one point, she stumbled, and he landed a cut on her thigh. Blood flowed in a stream down her leg. The intense pain demanded her attention. She ignored it.

Ahapesh turned towards the crowd, raising his sword high.

Jynnalt shook her head. Loss of blood made the arena spin. The raptor circling overhead screamed in fury. She glanced upward and her head cleared. *Focus. Focus or you die.* She took a long deep breath and collected her strength while Ahapesh played to the crowd

She realized he was confident of a win. Taking a slow walk around the arena, sword held high above his head. The crowd booed and jeered. When he turned towards her, his expression pure rage.

Ahapesh charged, his face red. Fury and victory written on his face.

She tried to sidestep, stumbled. Her brow slick with sweat and splattered blood as rivulets from a scalp laceration ran across her face and under her armor.

He stayed inside her reach, no longer allowing her to use her legs to place punishing kicks. Yet, he could not take a blow killing strike either. She slapped away the sword, taking minor cuts each time. A wrong calculation on her part and she would lose a finger or a hand.

He struck her face with the pommel of his sword. Her sight exploded into white light. Blood from her lips and nose splashed across their chests.

Shock and pain hammered her with explosive force. Instinctively, she threw herself backward, rolling away from his punishing blows. Coming up to her feet, facing where she thought he last stood, blinded by blood in her eyes.

She swiped her arm across her face, clearing the blood in time to leap away from his intended killing blow, the blade sliding past without harm. Now, he was off balance from her unexpected move. She kicked out, sending him sprawling on the sand. He rolled sideways and jumped to his feet before she stomped his neck.

Then he whirled to face her before staggering two steps as he backed away, gasping for breath himself. He no longer mocked her. His mouth twisted in anger. His eyes, cold, grim.

Pain tore through her with every pulse of her heart.

The slash on her thigh bled profusely, running into her boot. A cut above her left eye burned. She wiped sweat and blood out of her eyes once more, her strength ebbing fast. She understood if she did not get her sword soon, she'd die on these sands. Looking around, she realized they'd circled back to where the blade stood. She kept moving in such a way as to get closer while keeping his mind on her movements, not her sword.

He followed, attempting to bring the fight to a quick finish. She sensed her chance. She waited for him to rush in.

When he did, he let out a curdling scream meant to freeze her in place. Before he struck, she rolled in under his guard and came up, sword in hand. Rising to her full height, she held the sword two handed. An electric jolt of power flashed through her. With every ounce of strength, she sliced from his shoulder to his opposite hip before she spun away. Stopped three steps off in a ready stance facing him.

The upper half of the body slid to the ground. Gouts of blood sprayed across the pristine white sand. Each pulse less, feeding the sands in an ever-widening pool. The lower half took one step forward before falling. Blood gushed in a fountain, spraying Jynnalt as the body fell, jerking.

The chieftain's son blinked twice, the eyes staring at her for an endless moment of disbelief. Arapesh's life fled within seconds. His eyes glassed over, becoming a dead stare. Covered in blood, she dropped to one knee, head down as exhaustion and pain consumed her.

One hand clinging to her sword, the other planted in the ground before her as she swayed to a hot gush of wind. She kneeled, gasping for breath, blood dripping off her face to the sand. Silence filled the arena. Her world, the blurry growing pool of red sand before her.

Her hands trembled uncontrollably. *Get up. Stand.*

A scream from the raptor high above.

She forced herself to her feet by sheer willpower. The brilliant turquoise sky above with scattered, scant fluffy clouds, stark against the dark black gore and red blood splashed in a great arced across the white sands, held her in its grip. She staggered as the fight's end rushed in on her. The crowd's roar of unbelief quivered in the surrounding air. Fiery heat from the furnace of the sand caressed her. A searing breeze, drying the sweat, gore, and blood on her body. She shivered. Her limbs lead. The rasping sound of her tortured breathing thunder in her ears.

Numb, she gazed high overhead where the Warlord stood. A blurred image of color. Three long gongs sounded. Silence fell. Patrons stayed on their feet, waiting for the judgement.

The wind blew another blast of heat across the arena, and the raptor overhead screamed in proud defiance. Somehow, she found herself next to Ossa, who held her gore covered arm high above her head. The only thing keeping her on her feet.

The blood and gore tacky on her body in the intense heat. She heard Ossa cleared of any wrongdoing and the Chieftain's son faulted. The sands of the arena raced towards her.

Chapter 25

RYAKIN FLEW IN WITH six of his most trusted paladins and three co-pilots. The Corvette, Ki's newest state-of-the-art weaponry, a balance between energy and kinetic firepower. The corvette's electronics just below the capabilities of a phantom class signal ship, unheard of in a craft this size. A faster than luminous engine or FTL combined with pulsed plasma thrusters and back up hydrogen, giving faster response and maneuverability when needed at subluminal speeds. They also sported the most sophisticated shields one this size could have. One of its unique accomplishments, a stealth field capable of stealthing, under fire. On larger ships, this failed because of the immense power requirements.

Ki's engineering guilds and shipwrights working on this and other projects for the market before the murder of Emperor Lahamu.

When Queen Jynnalt disappeared, Kalmia, during the confusion, moved Ki's various research and manufacturing guilds to secret bases to continue their work. The results. These Corvettes and several capital fleet ships. They finished twenty-two prototypes of Corvettes and eighteen capital Dreadnoughts, which were in use by ranking members of the militia, now considered loyalists.

The most important feature of the smaller craft, a beacon layer skip engine. Under normal circumstances, they would have handed those improvements over to the merchant guilds of Ki. The guilds forwarding them to GIA for approval for market. Now, these ships stood between the destruction or survival of the loyalist. Developed in secret by the ever-paranoid Kalmia of Ministry Fourteen, she made sure what they worked on stayed secret. Along with their production runs and prototypes.

The cockpit's pulse beeped three times, landing control demanding their identification. They squawked their ident codes.

"Hailing frequency," Ryakin said, "sending now."

"Control tower acknowledges." Directing them to their assigned docking space.

As soon as he landed and disembarked, he saw Tayoshi exiting his ship and waved him over.

The bay displayed the intricate style of the Anunnaki empire, the others he visited lately throughout the galaxy a neutral gray, utilitarian and bland with zero styles. Distasteful to most Anunnaki, including himself.

Tayoshi, a friend from the academy, joined the loyalist eight months ago, and Ryakin made sure he got one of the proto class Corvettes. Tayoshi hid the ship on a small island in his home systems third world Kaatina. Though they stayed connected through entag encrypted holo pulses, neither met in person during the last sar and a half. Ryakin careful not to taint his fellow friends with his presence.

The seventeen dreadnoughts protecting this station new prototypes. For now, kept out of sight and only crewed by those vetted heavily.

There were no identifying marks, sigils, or silks. Nothing on the inside to identify them either, or the crew's uniforms. They did a DNA signature sweep every thirty-six hours, destroying any trace of who crewed the ship if captured.

The loyalist hidden shipwright docks churning out ships, still not fast enough. Kalmia hid them in false worlds and moons. Hidden from untrusted, prying eyes of Ki.

When Jynnalt and he arrived here on progression, sidetracked to this secret base by Kalmia, who informed him, this was the oldest station Ki built, over five hundred sars old. As time passed, Ministry fourteen gained control of the station. In fact, this is the Ministry's first base off system. Refitted over time, the floor was a mix of older metals with newer composite materials. Worn-out parts no polishing hid, offset by newer replacement's gleaming brightly. The contrast between old and new stark. The station crews, a different story. Disciplined and sharp.

Tayoshi, a grin on his face, said, "the conquering hero of the Anunnaki empire. Ten decisive battles and you broke the siege of Riik. Chakian mothers must use your name to make their children obedient."

Ryakin frowned. The thought of his battles viewed in that manner disquieting.

Tayoshi laughed, slapping his back, "forget I said that, I was only teasing."

"Their politicians at the palace would have required the Riik citizens to starve rather than surrender. They forced me to do something before their citizens paid for their folly," Ryakin said, his pulse pounding at his temple, his lips tense.

A moment passed, Tayoshi, who was his friend since childhood, knew when to keep silent. Something Ryakin appreciated about him. The so-called Pillars assigned Prince Ryakin's fleet to the worst battlefront after abandoning any pretense of peace with Chakian. Most agreed the Three Wardens hoped Ryakin died or disgrace himself. Instead, he became a heroic figure to the empire's commoners, guilds, and titled alike. Ryakin changed the subject as quick as possible.

"How's your family?"

"My sisters are fine. They keep asking when I will bring you home for a visit. Mother is her normal sweet hypochondriac self. Father works long hours at the ministry, avoiding her as usual."

"I thought there was a younger brother, wasn't his name Thianor," Ryakin asked? The laughter and good humor drain from Tayoshi.

"My youngest brother served on the Nean." They walked on in silence till Tayoshi said, "by the dark daemons, you made them pay for their treachery when they found your fleet. Rumor says Nemesis took out the Kolnari."

Ryakin perceived the steel and rage underlying his friend's voice. Something not there in his genial friend and the fact saddened him.

"I grasp I should not celebrate, but I did. That you destroyed him made it sweeter. Our family will never feel the same after his loss. I am hoping this truce holds, and the treaty accomplishes the promised peace. No family should suffer such a wrenching loss. On either side, as my mother reminds me so often. They walked on in silence, Ryakin thinking about the cruelties of war."

Minutes later, Tayoshi and he walked through the open blast doors into the meeting chambers. Packed full of blooded peers and lamane's, along with the loftiest titles in the empire and guilds. Total he estimated approximately two hundred and eighty-two males and females filled the chamber. The swirling metal maw slammed shut with a reverberating clang behind them. The chamber quiet for a second before the sound of voices resumed as those already here went back to their conversations.

Ryakin stopped a step beyond the blast door and glanced around for his brother. Spotted Rualui as he came through the door on the other side of the chamber. Before Ryakin headed over to his brother, he turned towards Tayoshi. "Let's not allow so much time to pass before we see each other again. You and your family are always welcome wherever I am." With that said, he hurried off to catch his brother before the meeting started.

When he reached Rualui, he indicated they would talk later as he strode to the center of the chamber and stepped on the raised dais of the central platform. His brother waited a moment for the noise to die off. Rualui gazed around the chamber stating, "I believe all are here who are coming. Let's start the meeting," he said. His voice carried throughout the chamber's natural stone, amplifying sound to the farthest seat for those attending. Attendees still standing moved to their seats.

The blast doors at the back of the chamber swirled open and Prince Iltasadum strode in amongst gasps and whispers. Several upper ranking council members rose. Intending to leave. Rualui called out.

"We should let him speak. He earned the right to speak for all his faithful sars of service. At least listen to what he says," he said. Iron in his tone. "You aren't aware of this, but Prince Iltasadum is the one who organized us. He went through me knowing you might not trust a Warden." The others sat, though, at the edge of their seats, ready to leave if what he said did not agree with them.

Prince Iltasadum glanced around at the distrustful faces. "Yes, I'm guilty of helping the wardens to displace the power of the throne. But I did so because they convinced me the action temporary. The loyal council members informed the decree would last only till the enforcers and the temple cleared Prince Anu of the taint of regicide. I worked to make sure the ruling temporary. They duped me, like many others. Most afraid to speak out now. They declared the law designed to keep the government functioning until they crowned Prince Anu. I fell for their words, like others, some here now. Months later, I discovered, they have no intention of allowing Prince Anu to live. They never did. They only adapted their original plans when forced to by the intercession of the Temple. I now fear for his life. I suspect the other Three Wardens are behind the attempts. Two assassination attempts on temple grounds, which did not go well for the assassins," he said, pausing at the angry voices. After moments passed, they quieted.

"I applied to move him in secret, this time and the Temple and GIA agreed against the wishes of the other three Wardens. Our whisper agents discovered the false riots of ninety-two, specifically engineered by the Society, to allow an assassination attempt against Prince Anu. They wanted to remove him without the bother of a trial or the political fallout." He glanced over at Rualui and seemed to hesitate before commencing.

"The Temple though approved my relocation request for Prince Anu to Temple grounds for asylum two turns prior to the riots. Still, we needed to move him without the knowledge of the council. Difficult, as he was under arrest. When the riots began, we took that as the perfect opportunity. Ghost Walkers moved in and removed him from Anunnaki custody. The Temple well within their rights to do so under GIA's by-laws. The disappearance caught those now proclaimed the Pillars off guard. He moves often, leaving those hunting for him scrambling."

Prince Iltasadum waited for the chamber to quiet before speaking again. "In the past, many of you here trusted my judgment. Trust me once more," he said as he stared at those assembled. Even for an Anunnaki, he was old. Deep laugh wrinkles represented his sense of humor. Pink eyes full of wisdom though slightly milky white, his hair translucent with age. Still, somehow, he kept up with many younger than himself.

"The other three wardens are passing laws, making every citizen an indentured slave. They intend to erode our rights turn by turn. I do what I can. One against three accomplishes nothing in voting, politically they decrease my position at every turn. Those three and a small circle of their cronies will soon control everything and emasculate the power of the ranking blooded. They intend to outlaw the temple, claiming they interfere with proper governance, then destroy our traditions and history by claiming them as harmful or false. Grim times are upon us. Not just here, not just our empire," he said, his voice ringing throughout. "Ripples of conflict increase throughout the galaxy every cycle."

A young male stood, his clothes rustling in the cool artificial breeze as the automatic air circulators kicked in as body heat increased the chamber temperature. Ryakin's eyes narrowed. *Why did he mop at his brow as if sweating from intense heat?* Ryakin could not place him. *Promoted after the disaster?*

Prince Iltasadum acknowledged him by title and name. "My Lord Tount Apason. You've something to say?"

Ryakin noted he wore his battle uniform rakishly, something trained fleet officers never did. Ryakin's jaw tightened in disapproval. Lord Apason glanced over at Vice Dukian Ahimelek, who nodded his head in encouragement.

"You benefited from recent events. I accuse you of trying to force the other three wardens out. You want the throne for yourself." He said, as noisy hisses circulated through the chamber.

Iltasadum, after a second, said, "Prince Anu is our true sovereign. The three warden's usurpers. You either believe those facts or you do not. If you don't, why are you here?"

Tount Apason glanced once more at Ahimelek before proceeding. "Maybe, ahh, maybe," his face scrunched up, then lightened, "so later you can kill Prince Anu."

To Ryakin, he sounded as if he tried to think up an excuse when caught with his hand in the treat jar so many mothers kept in the kitchen. Remaining quiet, he waited to see how Iltasadum managed this accusation.

The chamber erupted into a loud argument about what Tount Apason said. Minutes later, Rualui shouted for quiet. Once they settled, he introduced Kalmia. "Before anyone decides one way or the other, you need to hear this information."

Prince Iltasadum left the stand, going to sit in an adjacent seat.

Kalmia wasted no time on niceties. "Our agents learned the three wardens have allied with the Visage empire bordering the Chakian's. You understand the Visage long desire access to the wealthier trade lanes. Prince Satoric will offer them a small portion of the lanes on the side closest to them in return for an alliance. Though a small empire, they have formidable fleet ships with well-trained crews."

Tount Apason rose. "That is preposterous. Why would he give away what we are fighting for from the Chakian's?"

Rualui told him to sit, as he did not hold the floor. A third of the chamber blooded nodded at his remarks. Others demanded a further explanation from Prince Iltasadum.

Kalmia demanded silence and proper order. "Prince Satoric never intends to hand over even a small portion of the trade lanes. He will use this temporary alliance of convenience before he turns on them." She said, motioning, and the chamber lights darkened. A holo map of the Anunnaki empire and its spheres of influence filled the center of the chamber.

"Focus here," the map zoomed in to the area she pointed at, "we discovered the Visage empire is building ships along the Chakian border. This is where they are massing their forces. They sent a message through operatives who we intercepted. We allowed the message to proceed to the destination. Proof for later." She said, stopping the holo for a moment.

"The person who received the missive caught by one of our best whisper agents on a recording holo." She turned the holo back on. They watched the exchange by the courier and a figure dressed as a Society High Priest hood covering his head. The figure melted into the crowd after the exchange, the whisper agent deftly keeping the figure in sight. The agent spotted him as he entered a public barge area. As he entered the loading platform, he lowered his hood and, with a flick of his wrist, turned his cloak inside out. He must have thought he fooled anyone following him. He turned and gazed at the crowd as if looking for something. Nodded to his left, then followed the crowd boarding. Gasps of outrage filled the chamber. The person. Prince Satoric.

Kalmia turned the holo off, ignored the sounds, and proceeded with the briefing, ignoring the shocked remarks.

"We believe they hid a large number of their fleet size from Prince Satoric's. Why, we are unsure, but suspect they did so to double cross the Anunnaki empire later." She glanced around. "Memie's domain is where they are amassing, which sits between Visage and Chakian, as you all know. What you may not realize is Memie allied itself with the Visage against GIA's council's strict admonishment. An uneasy truce held in place between the Chakian and Memie because of the iron grip of GIA. Memie's kingdom unhappy since GIA ruled against them."

Prince Iltasadum walked to Kalmia's side. "This is fact. I've seen Prince Satoric's memos and plans." His bass voice rumbled throughout the chamber. His oration skills highly effective in the council throughout his sars of service.

A chorus of consternation greeted the news. The Visage species quick to anger and formidable enemies. A war-centric culture.

Saques Aitil of Tc stood. "The Visage empire is never wise to betray. They've long memories and short fuses. If what you claim is the truth... Prince Satoric will take us from one war to another in a brief time. Draining off the wealth of the empire."

Prince Iltasadum waited a moment. "We must stop Prince Satoric before he entangles us in events we cannot recover from."

Sarl Thinda of Golson stood. "If what you claim is true, this is madness. I'm not here for this. Helping the rightful heir, Prince Anu, regain his rightful throne is one thing. A war council, another." He said, a nervous expression on his face before sitting.

Ryakin figured the next time this council called upon his support; he would decline. Would he keep quiet about this meeting, or would he try to garner favor with the three wardens? Something this council needs to think about soon. He glanced around, checking the faces of those present. They sat at the half circle-shaped tables four levels high. Commoners and guild members and apprentices at the lowest level. The highest seats held in reserve for the Kings, Queens and Dukians. For now, the emptiest row. Only the four outer borders, along with Tc and Da inner kingdoms, were close to full. He represented Ki as the legitimate Consort.

Prince Iltasadum's voice rang true. "is anyone ever prepared for war? Even those who train a lifetime." Nodding heads of those who fought on the front lines of the Chakian war for the last five months seen throughout the chamber.

"We can end this war. We can take back what is ours. Put the rightful heir on the throne. If, and only if, we stand together." More nodding occurred. Loud arguments broke out throughout the chamber.

Both Tount Apason and Vice Dukian Ahimelek stood claiming pressing matters and excused themselves. Ryakin ordered Ki's whisper agents to put a tracker on their ships before they left.

"Find out where they go from here. And who they meet with."

Next, he ordered the officer in charge of the station to start the star skip engines. Most in the chamber unaware of what he was doing. "Prepare for skip to another star system, I will relay the coordinates after the meeting," he said as quiet as possible. Seconds later, the subtle vibration of the engines came through the floor. Other fleet officers present realized the fact as well. They glanced his way with a speculative look. Ryakin glanced at the two empty seats. They grasped the reasons for the precaution.

Kalmia took over once more, banging on the stand to bring order. "We gained this next piece of information through the death of many of our operators. This relates to the taint on the kingdom of Ki and what happened to Queen Jynnalt." The chamber quieted, and all eyes turned towards the holo.

Ryakin took a deep breath. He did not believe Jynnalt lived. But somehow, without his acknowledgment, he refused to believe her dead. Leaving him in a state of confusion. He tensed, expecting the worst.

The holo showed Tavas, the commander of her paladins, carrying Jynnalt's body on to a Free Empires Federation slaver ship. A stranger, and five of his henchmen holding a weapon on him and her three other paladins. Ryakin shocked to his core at her condition. A rush of intense sensation choked him, yet he could not tear his eyes away.

The stranger negotiated with the slaver, who checked that the female was still living. Ryakin, for a second, did not realize he rose to his feet, waiting for the answer. The slaver crew's life tender moved to check her condition.

Ryakin sucked in his breath at the damage to her back, black like hit by a sonic cannon. How flesh appears turns afterward if they survived the hit. The slice across her front from her shoulder to her hip made him explosively exhale. That was not a normal thing seen on battlefields anymore in modern times, yet every warrior in the chamber recognize a sword cut when they spotted one. The gash on her head might be from a projectile weapon.

The life tender nodded in the affirmative and an explosive burst of air left his lungs. His heart hammered at the amount of damage she took and still lived. Amazed, she survived long enough for Tavas to carry her unconscious on to the Free Federation ship.

Kalmia stopped the holo at this point. She avoided his eyes. "We caught up with the slave ship sometime later. Nothing but debris spreading through deepspace." Ryakin's knees buckled, and he sat. For one second, hope flooded through him. Hope she lived. His brother laid his hand on his shoulder. He brushed it away.

Kalmia once more continued, "later from another whisper agent, we received this meh. A strange, rusty hulled transport popped into view. Moments later, the interior. Citizens of all species and races piled inside a massive bay. High above them, strange pod-like shapes stacked row upon row. Ten citizens appeared injured, others dead, the rest listless. Outlaws wearing mismatched battle uniforms of various empires came down into the hold. One moved to where, unbelievably, a filthy Jynnalt sat. His heart stopped. Jynnalt. He was positive. Her hair matted with dried blood, clothes in tatters, dirt under her fingernails, sitting up drinking. Keif, one of the missing Paladins, held the cup for her. To Ryakin, she appeared gorgeous, breathing, alive. She finished drinking and rose with help from Keif and moved out of view of the holo. Seconds later, the holo ended. In sudden violence. Smashed to the ground with whoever was holding the recorder meh.

Kalmia said, "we discovered later the whisper operator who sent this died. Lucky for us, he set the recording to send automatically on a timer."

His heart still hammered from seeing Jynnalt walking with a little aid, surrounded by her paladins. Her skin a more normal tone, the gash on her head scabbed. The lights came on in the chamber and the holo projection winked out. All eyes turned to Ryakin. Some with shame for thinking the worst of her, others with triumph. Those who always believed her innocent; yet dead felt justified.

"That is the last information we received of Queen Jynnalt's whereabouts. We did not retrieve the last location." Kalmia turned to give the stand over to Prince Iltasadum.

Ryakin's internal command comm's opened. "Commander." Knight Tijal, a young ambitious officer Ryakin left in charge of the newest fleet dreadnought, the Night Raptor, said in his cyberware. "We detected a warp bubble a few minutes ago that fizzled out. Then another, which did not. Scanner officers verified the occurrence not natural. Small signature non-fleet. Could be a sightseeing citizen. I set a red alert. In case. And notified docking personnel in the station to prep your Corvettes for takeoff."

That cut his euphoric feelings short. "Keep me informed."

Other Fleet Commanders, he could tell by the blank expressions on their faces, received the same information via their cyberware. He sensed the tension in the chamber rise. Kalmia leaned over, whispered something to Prince Iltasadum. Ryakin figured she informed him of developing events. Kalmia motioned him towards the back-blast door. He shook his head and sat. An expression of frustration crossed her face. She turned back to the assembled council.

"This last bit of information I need to convey is very important." She turned on the holoprojector and it flared to life. "These worlds here and here." Kalmia pointed them out on the three-dimensional holo map floating above them. "Are vulnerable. We uncovered indications the other three Wardens might set them up for a false attack by the Chakian's. We believe to stop the peace treaty."

Loud murmured voices circulated in the darkened chamber as the systems she was pointing out showed in enormous relief.

"Worse, once the false attack's over and the truce declared finished, they will send a force deep into the Chakian territory. Prince Satoric wants to make a point to the Chakian Empress. He can hit the heart of her empire any time he wants."

Rualui stood, and the lights brightened. "We cannot let that happen; this will destroy any chance for the peace treaty to go forward. It will force GIA to vote in favor of the Anunnaki empire. The Chakian's will never stand by the ruling. They will proclaim their innocence and the war will be back on. If this happens, the ruling will destabilize the entire sector once more."

Prince Iltasadum stood. "We all want to survive this coming war." he paused. "Many of us won't. *Whether we win or lose.* Our citizens rely on us to do the right thing. Not save us by betraying them."

Rualui stood. "Those of you here," he stared at each one before moving to the next. "Have a choice to make. Are you going to allow our empire, paid for in the blood of our ancestors, ripped away from our citizens who we swore an oath to protect? Or do we stand and fight? Fight for our values and what belongs to us. Or do we allow our enemies to enslave us, deny us our religion? Let them cast our empire into depravity and decadence? Think long and hard on your answer. This will define you and your house." His brother strode to the empty seat next to Ryakin. He realized for the first time how heavy a burden his brother's Kingship was.

"We will pay an exorbitant price, make no mistake," Rualui whispered. "The laments for the dead loud, lasting a long time."

Kalmia once more took the stand. "Loyal councilors and blooded you must recognize a civil war will soon be upon us."

Right then, an emergency pulse information announcement tone sounded, interrupting her. The station chief in charge said, "I believe you will all want to see this." Their screen went blank, then The Three Wardens together in the throne chamber popped on. Apparently, they missed the start of the pulse.

Prince Satoric stared out from the recording holo's a somber frown upon his face. "The Chakian Empire is desperate. They fear us growing strong enough to take back what once was ours. We struggled against the Chakian's attempts several times to end the truce before we could reach the treaty conference. A truce only works if all parties abide by the rules. From the moment they struck at helpless citizens, citizens with paltry defense against their attack, citizens of our empire, we, the Three Pillars, consider the Truce irrevocably broken. No more," Prince Satoric declared, "our patience's over. The Chakian's crossed the truce-line along with the Citrea kingdom. They attacked the system of Aage on our inner border. Less than three hours ago."

"Did anyone else spot the term three, not four wardens?" someone called out.

"War is upon us once more," Prince Satoric exclaimed. "And will continue until the Chakian empire bow before us. The pulse turned to scenes of strewn bodies of innocent children, females, and males. Entire cities burned to their foundations. Herd beasts by the thousands lay in fields, unmoving as carrion feasted upon them.

"We appealed to GIA's council for relief, to no avail. They declared in council to not censor nor demand reparations from them. Worse, they did not demand a cessation of hostilities from either of the aggressors. Because of this, we, the Three Pillars, and the great council have declared GIA as no longer recognized and are recalling our envoys. They abdicated their authority to protect us from a predatory empire. Despite provocation, we worked hard to keep the Truce. This transgression broke our resolve."

The other two wardens stepped up beside Prince Satoric. "The Malkuth abandoned the treaties of GIA and withdrew from several key areas because of their own internal unrest. They refuse to enforce the truce between us and the Chakian, leaving the burden upon us. We shall not allow these incursions into our sphere of influence to go unanswered. Do they think us weak? Do they think we cannot and will not answer their insults to our empire?" He said, pausing for a moment. "We now announce the Truce of Chakian and Citrea invalid."

Those in the chamber viewed the news pulse with growing horror.

We're too late. Ryakin stared at the shock on the faces of those gathered. A message beeped from his direct link to Nemesis in standby mode at the Phoenix Gate. He excused himself and went out to the hallway.

"Scanner officers confirm there are ten Imperial Dreadnoughts exiting the gate. They skipped to the Gishulum Empire system in a holding pattern. Over."

The same rush Ryakin always got before battle, commingled fear and excitement, engulfed him. They were on a collision course with the Imperialist. Outnumbered and outgunned. He notified the protective ring of dreadnoughts to prepare for skip, their engines already spun up because of the earlier alert, holding in the gas giant's outer ionosphere.

He stood and roared over the hysterical questions about the treaty announcement. "We must leave now. Ten full Imperial dreadnoughts are about to skip on top of our location."

Pandemonium broke out amongst the non-warriors. Fleet officers taking the events in stride rounded them up and hurried them out in a semblance of order back to their ships, prepped and ready to go.

Ryakin reached his Corvette at the same time Tayoshi did. Both waited for those who arrived with them to load. Tayoshi yelled across at him. "Remind me, lingering here may not be such a promising idea." Ryakin chuckled. At least Tayoshi never lost his sense of humor no matter how dangerous the surrounding events were.

Ryakin listened to the comm's as calls came in. The Imperial dreadnoughts skipped in just out of firing range of the dreadnoughts. Indicating they knew their location. Like a puffball mushroom releasing its spores, they discharged their deadly cargo of support fighting ships to the surrounding area. More incoming skip signatures coming across comms. Skip signatures, outer edge of asteroid belt; two hundred and eighty-two degrees upper. Six ballistic Satires and two Cires heavy bombers. The odds against them stacking up fast.

Once the last of the loyalist groups loaded into the twenty-two corvettes Ryakin loaded.

"Skip signatures five standards out from bay doors. Ident. Drone assault spiders." Ryakin tensed. DAS's were fast and lethal.

Discordant horns blared out a three-minute warning. Notifying workers in the bay, the outer doors to deepspace prepared to open. Those without protective gear warned to move back to pressurized areas. Red lights flashed as the bay crew rushed to finish their tasks, pulling away anchor bolts and disconnecting fueling hoses, before racing to safety in the surrounding chambers. Amber lighting strips to the outer gate turned green. The doors groaned, then opened a crack. Massive doors big enough to handle deepspace battleships of the line responded to the powerful hydraulics.

Launch bay doors bent in. Hit with a sonic blast. All the deepspace crews still in the bay in protective gear assisting the launch blown backward. They slid across the floor till they slammed up against a wall, or struts, of one of the Corvettes. Their environmental suits doing little to protect them against the assault. None rose from their twisted prone state on the floor, their suits magnetics' keeping them in place. He stopped his preflight check and fired the engines. Crew members ran to gun positions.

Seconds later, eight drone assault spiders burst in as they finished blasting the massive airlock door open. Landing, they transformed into eight-legged precision killing machines. Lasers and kinetic weapons firing at inner control booths. Ignoring the corvettes loaded with the attendees from the meeting.

A red split tailed scorpion on a backdrop of gold adorned the battle drone's breastplate. The insignia of the Imperial house of Zu. Eight heavy leg struts clanked to the floor. Seven other drones coming in close behind the first, rapidly spreading out, firing. They stood half the height of the bay doors.

The Corvettes fought their way out, firing as they flashed past the drones. The destroyed drone smoking ruins. They exited straight into the newest Imperial shadow dancers, deadly and fast. The fighters did not expect the weaponry and maneuverability of the corvettes. The group of Corvettes destroyed a third of the fighters before they reacted, yet not all escape unscathed.

Seven loyalist ships with sections of their hulls open to deepspace from the deadly lasers and missiles. The shimmer of shields the only thing keeping the ships intact. *Those won't hold for long. Three minutes, five if lucky.*

Across Ryakin's comm's Nemesis's voice cut in.

"Prepare for displacement ripples. Advise free flow status. This will allow the ship to ride the wave instead of being torn apart." Without question, Ryakin relayed Nemesis instructions to the other pilots. A gamble, making them vulnerable for seconds, but they were out of options. The fighters, seeing them slow punched their engines to max speed. Their first and last mistake.

Nemesis exploded out of the skip window between the corvettes and the chasing enemy. Shadow dancers became instant debris that flew in all directions as they hit Nemesis shields.

Warp bubble accelerators encircling Nemesis, pulsing faster and faster. Nemesis kept the warp bubble building as the corvettes raced towards the ship.

"Bay doors open for emergency landings." Nemesis voice came across his comm's.

All twenty-two-corvettes landed.

Three slid along the floor of the bay, taking out anchor bolts or fuel lines, producing smoking sparks flying from underneath their torn and shattered bodies. Others with holes and chunks missing from hulls, their inner shields between them, and disaster achieved a semi-acceptable landing. A warp bubble sprang into existence around Nemesis as missiles raced towards them. A streak of light and Nemesis warped a. Seconds later, command informed Ryakin the base took minor damage. The enemy focused on the escaping corvettes ignored the station momentarily, giving them time to open a skip window before the major attack fixated on them.

The civil war began.

Chapter 26

335893 GGS Cava 15th
Outer Border Kingdom Unknown System–Prince Ryakin

RYAKIN STOOD ON THE battlements of the fortress, staring out across the valley, covered in whitefall. The turn a dismal gray with scudding clouds overhead, his battle cloak dancing and snapping to the whims of the wind. Ice crystals landed and froze, riming his shoulders and arms milky white.

High above, blue and green bands of the gas giant dominated the sky. Nothing registered. He fought to quiet his mind. Tried to block out his need to drop everything and find Jynnalt. Yet his mind refused to submit. The knowledge Jynnalt lived, injured, and enslaved somewhere out there gnawed at his gut.

Thoughts and questions about what he should do and where she might be at this moment consumed him. A nagging background noise every waking moment. *How did she burrow so deep under my skin? What is it about her that is impossible for me to let her go?* His paladins far enough away to give him privacy, yet close enough to protect him if needed. No longer a separation between fleet duty or off for paladins. Death stalked even from within the fleet since the split with the Imperialist.

His entire life he believed nothing to impossible to solve. Decide on a plan and have the fortitude to follow through. Simple. Uncomplicated.

Yet, the loyalist faced insurmountable odds. Odds that overwhelmed him. Left him incapable of changing the direction events headed. In the past, he scoffed at others, unable to see the way before them and act. Yet, here he stood. Lost. A victim of his own arrogance. Unable to direct the circumstance as everything careened out of control around him.

Hunted by the Imperialist for the last three months, the members of the first meeting, which they barely escaped, moved continually. The three Wardens now calling themselves the Three Pillars of the Anunnaki Empire. Obvious to all, they seized the throne. Fear did not allow those words spoken out loud within the empire. They attacked the loyalist fortresses, murdered innocent citizens and commoners, unleashing a fury of fear and hatred upon them.

The outer cold matched his feelings. Innocent blood sat heavy upon his conscience. Clouded his judgment. Logic told him the so-called Three Pillars responsible, yet guilt still assaulted his every waking hour.

Loyal ground troops fought still in six of the attacked strongholds, not yet defeated. Ryakin's warrior's training foresaw the end. Defeat without support from an inter-orbital fleet. Still, the Imperialist fleets faced months of ongoing battles to quell the last strongholds of the rebellions in Tc and Da.

In the end, they will win through attritions and overwhelming numbers. Guerrilla warfare would follow. Waged by loyalist, creating unrest and chaos for the occupying forces. Not a winning strategy.

The outer border systems kingdoms another matter, where despite their earlier success, the outcome of ongoing battles less certain for imperialist fleets. Their citizens far more warlike, their ground forces better equipped and trained. The border kingdoms only required Tc and Da's fleet support to push the Imperialist out of their kingdoms. A third of Tc's blooded houses follow his brother and a quarter of Da, their King, to add to Ki's fleets that joined them.

Support those who joined feared, claiming if they lost their fleets, it'd be catastrophic.

Some arguing, Ki and the border kingdoms could not produce fleet ships fast enough to fill their losses if they engaged the Imperialist. Ki's shipwright guild claimed they could, yet many doubted the truth of the statement.

Caltac' and N'lari joined him. Stood silent next to him for a few moments before Caltac' said, "In three hours, the council will meet. Your brother sent me to find you and let you know," his tone neutral.

Without looking at Caltac' Ryakin said, his breath misting from the icy air, "in Tc, the ground battles might take months to shift in the Imperialist's favor. Months of deepspace bombardments weakening the city's shields turn by turn. The shields will fail. I used that tactic against the Chakian's. The difference is they will slaughter the herd beast and destroy crops. Wonder which will happen first. The failure of the city shields or the starvations of citizens?" Ryakin heeded the defeated sound in his own voice and shook his head. Looking over at Caltac' and N'lari.

N'lari squarely looked him in the face. "I once knew someone like you. Smart, brave, capable of seeing what others did not during battle. Able to act when fear held others back. He also blamed himself for things out of his control after they finished the battle. For decisions others made. This cost him his life at far too young an age." Ryakin could hear the sorrow in his voice and wondered who this stoic warrior mourned.

"I would prefer you not meet his fate before your time," N'lari said, then bowed his head and left him and Caltac' standing in the storm. Something struck Ryakin as odd when N'lari spoke earlier. He could not figure out exactly what bothered him. He examined him as he left, shrugged before going back to his thoughts. Moments later, Caltac' also left. He found himself once more standing in the storm by himself.

The temporary docks came into visible orbit high overhead. A speck of black against the blue band of the gas giant. He wondered about what N'lari told him. Ryakin thought about the sorrow in his voice. Surprised, since N'lari appeared tougher than anyone he knew. Yet Ryakin sensed he deeply cared for those around him. With a deep abiding loyalty, he extended to Jynnalt and himself. Half an hour later, his brother found him on the battlements. Caltac' must have informed him where he hid from the others.

Once his brother got within earshot, he called out over the wind. "This came in on the pulse a half hour ago," his brother said breathlessly.

Ryakin wondered if his brother happened to be out of breath from the news he rushed to impart. Or the physical trek up the stairs.

"The Three Pillars one turn ago declared the Temple an enemy of the Empire. They declared they were to vacate the lands and hand them over to the Anunnaki Imperial empire.

The truth, they made a surprise attack, *four turns earlier,* before the actual announcement. They altered the holo's time frames to fool the citizens. Kalmia's Ministry analyst claim. The problem for the Imperialist information bards is ten priestesses told the commoners about the attack three turns prior to the news feed.

Publicly, the Three Pillars made their false announcement of offering them a chance to leave without bloodshed. The Priestess disputed this, which spread like wildfire amongst the faithful. Pulses now show the Imperialist forces in control of the high Temple of the Anunnaki Empire. They showed no Priest or priestess bodies, out of fear of the faithful's reaction. Now there is speculation about what happened to Prince Anu.

The anger in his brother's voice did not surprise him. He and his wife were ardent supporters of the faith.

"Information is pouring in from other channels that Prince Anu is dead, or possibly in custody, which is the same as a death sentence. They cannot allow him to live. They might keep him alive for a brief time to torture him for his control passwords," Rualui said. Rubbing his hands together, trying to warm them, his breath white misty puffs when he spoke. The mist from his brother's breath caught Ryakin's attention, and his brow furrowed.

"Are you paying attention or staring at me in disbelief?" Rualui asked with a curious expression.

Ryakin shook his head, ignoring the question. "What's the location of Prince Ea? As his father's heir, they might decide he is a danger."

Whatever caught his attention earlier now slipped from his mind. "We might still rally the citizens around him as a legitimate heir and ruler. These three wardens are cunning and greedy. They overreach. We can use that against them, but only if we have Prince Ea's backing for our cause, if his father is dead."

"What is the purpose behind telling me something I already know?" Rualui asked.

In frustration Ryakin said, "if we do nothing. We become outlaws, not rebels. This," he flung his arm to encompass the whole above and below, "is all we will be. We must support those fighting on the ground, *now*, for this cause, or we've lost. Right here. Right now. We become cowards," he said. Thinking about N'lari's remark before he left.

"I agree. This is not the time for diplomacy or fear," Rualui said, holding up his hand. "Before you run away with the thought, listen. We need the other's fleets. Prince Satoric declared his daughter Princess Tesiskel, Queen of Ki, hoping to quell rebellions with this move. He believes her status as Jynnalt's mother will help their cause. Instead, it fueled the fire. Ki is now in open rebellion against Jynnalt's mother.

"Our operatives along with Kalmia's say she's never been popular among the upper Kierian ranks. Her reputation is even worse amongst the peers and commoners. In the guild halls, she's reviled. If a Guild Master wants to teach a guild member a lesson. They send them to work for her or her vyzier Duurua," Ryakin said, looking out over the pristine white valley. Bare trees stood stark, silent, slumbering, ignoring the death of the world to the surrounding deep freeze of the harsh winter.

"I will argue to go back and defend Tc and the Temple grounds. This news scared them. We cannot let the Temple fall; or those here will believe they cannot withstand imperialist forces either. We must convince them to act. Many are talking of moving their fleets farther away, out of the Anunnaki Sphere of Influence. They believe without Prince Anu, there is no legitimate claim." Rualui said.

"You meant to say they want to keep hiding. How many of their commanders agree with their blooded lords?"

"From what I can tell, none." His brother turned towards Ryakin, "listen, do not create a mutiny. It will taint you and any who join you." Rualui grabbed his arm. Ryakin shook off the hand and faced his brother.

"I would not do such a thing. I may be quicker to act than you. But rarely do I act without thought of consequences." He stared out at the valley before glancing at his brother and seeing relief on his face. Anger washed over him.

"I am taking my forces, legitimately under my control, to back up those on the ground at the outer edge of Ki. Our intel says the Imperial forces are heading towards Peistis. The newest colony system in Ki. I will not leave my citizens for slaughter like those in Tc and later Da."

As soon as he said it, he regretted his words from the stricken expression on his brother's face.

"You realize I did not mean it the way it sounded. I spoke without thought, angry you would think I would do such a dishonorable thing." He rushed to say, "you always do what is best for Tc, for me, and others, before yourself. I never thought you abandoned your citizens. None of us foresaw what the Imperialists intended. I would have made the same decision in the same circumstances."

Rualui's expression furious when he spoke. Ryakin realized, thankfully, not at him. "When I try to sleep at night, the scenes from those pulses run in an endless loop through my head. I will support any decision you make at the council. We need to head to the chamber to arrive on time. It took me forever climbing those stares. Probably why you come here. To avoid us bureaucrats and politicians."

Ryakin laughed, "you need more exercise. Maybe you should join me more often."

"Don't start. Jena harps enough for you both." He smiled.

The smile, the first from his brother in months. Ryakin glad he put it there after his earlier senseless remark.

On the first floor, Ryakin and Rualui passed by rows of tall arched clear metacrystal windows. They overlooked the long, expansive valley stretched out far below. Whitefall fell faster, building up on window ledges. Dancing through the air to the whims of the storm, reducing visibility. Ryakin shivered from the chill in the air. The fortress owned by a low ranking and quite poor blooded Cer Tolaj Ondeltz'Leedar of the Riven kingdom. This the reason the fortress lacked more modern accommodations, like heat in the stone hallways.

When they entered through the thick double doors of the Adsullata Fire tree wood, a confusion of arguing voices met them. Rualui slammed the door behind himself as he entered. All conversation stopped as those present peered their direction. Ryakin detected most appeared uncomfortable at the sight of the brothers.

Lord Talif, a Hiomite of Da, with a belligerent attitude, stepped forward to the center dais.

"I am surrendering the ships under my command. Prince Satoric sent through the public pulse that any who surrenders within the next five turns will receive a full pardon from all actions and crimes. Besides, we agree, Prince Anu is most likely dead or in a dungeon. He is the *only* reason we fought against the Imperialist."

Ryakin's face tightened as he stepped up close to the blooded Lord.

"Crimes against the *throne*. None here committed any crime against the *throne*. We are fighting for the legitimate heir. That is not a crime. It's our *duty*." Ryakin saw heads nodding as he spoke and took more heart. "Do you forget what the Imperialist did to one of Da's systems citizens? Do you trust those three usurpers will ignore the fact you rejected their claim to the throne originally? There is no information since Prince Iltasadum's capture on whether he is alive or dead. They may not punish you now, but they will. Later, they will bring false accusations against you. Do you want to live under the edge of the sword, never knowing when the death blow drops?" Lord Talif's eyes widen at the taunting contempt in Ryakin's voice.

Ryakin's eyes narrowed, and he stood straighter, "I will not." As he paced in front of the benches saying, "I will stand with my citizens or I shall fall with them. *I shall not run and hide... anymore.*"

Rualui stepped up behind him. "I was wrong to leave my citizens to the Three Pillar's mercy. I thought they would treat them with honor and respect. Remember what they did to Tc and Da's capital systems? *Where was their honor?* Tc's capital surrendered. Under my orders, I wanted to spare them from the label of conspirators. I trusted Prince Satoric's and the other so-called Pillar's keeping their word. Make sure no harm came to those innocents of any crime. They made an example of my citizens. They bombed them from deepspace with Dreadnoughts, leaving smoking ruins where a city of over seven million citizens and their children lived. *After* they lowered their shields and surrender. Remember? *Honor. Mercy. Trust.* You are fools if you believe a single word uttered by them. Afterward, they destroyed every city, slaughtered their herd beasts, leaving Tc's capital planet a ruin. My brother is right. We must either fight or become outlaws along with our families." Rualui left his last remark hanging in the chamber.

Ryakin spoke. "The Imperialist drop warriors receive support from their fleets. If we do not send help soon, what's left of Tc's ground forces are finished, the Imperialist will overrun them in less than a fortnight. The false Queen, Jynnalt's mother, will surrender Ki. They won't attack there, as the surrender will be unconditional. Without a shot fired," he said. Fleet officers nodding. "That was always Prince Satoric's end plan for the Kierian Kingdom."

"I fled with the fleets of Ki which follow me, with the rest of you three months ago, even though I voted against doing so. The Imperialist hunt us, and we run. Each time farther away from our kingdoms. Their tactic is to cut us off from supporting our citizens while they decimate and destroy our kingdoms and homes. As our citizens look to the heavens, praying to the gods for us to arrive and join the fight. Our Kingdoms. Yet we fail them. Ignore their suffering under the heel of oppression." Ryakin said as he stopped a moment to let what he said sink in.

"Brave. Loyal. None of our actions of late proved either. Our commoners and guilds keep their oaths to us. Yet we are less than honorable." He stopped to take a breath and to gauge the reaction of those in the chamber. N'lari was right. The death of those murdered in the opening salvos of the war was not on him.

"Blame the Three Pillars who murdered innocents when they surrendered and were helpless. Blame them for holding out the hand of peace as they hid the knife behind their backs. We here in this chamber must take the blame for our inaction. For running and hiding. For protecting our interest and not our kingdoms. We will lose in a month if we don't fight back."

Now Rualui spoke, "justice has gone awry. Laws twisted. Our traditions and religion are being torn from us. For what? So, the corrupt can steal our citizen's wealth, take away our freedoms, freedoms our ancestors fought for. Will we abandon the innocent to pay the price? Think you can wash your hands of their deaths after deserting them. Safe someplace, hopefully hidden from the Three Pillars assassins," Rualui asked?

Ryakin looked around. All but Lord Talif were now nodding in acquiescence.

A freezing gust of wind entered when the door behind them opened and a shocked look appeared on those gathered before Ryakin and Rualui. Both glanced at the doorway. Surprise caught them off guard before bowing their heads. Prince Anu stood before them. The High Priestess of the Anunnaki Temple behind him.

Both stepped into the chamber. "We obtained information, more like a rumor. They executed Prince Iltasadum earlier this turn. Intelligence says they will pulse the information later across the empire's news channel. The high priestess said with no introduction.

Questions erupted throughout the chamber.

"We thought you were dead. What happened?" Council members asked, all at the same time creating an uproar within the chamber.

"Ghost walkers uncovered the plot to attack the Temple. We evacuated before they arrived." Prince Anu said with an unpleasant laugh. "Hours before their dreadnoughts skipped in the last of the Temple, along with their tithe and goods skipped out. I would love to have seen their faces. Still, they forced us to take a circuitous route to here, hence the delay in arriving."

Ryakin spotted the ministers of sector fourteen exchanging glances, a significant amount unspoken in the terse expressions they gave each other. He would inquire about the reason from Kalmia later. For now, he left for Nemesis to prepare a battle plan. Before he left, he sensed the atmosphere in the chamber different from when he entered. The loyalist charged with hope. He realized Lord Talif missing, yet never saw him leave.

Chapter 27

335893 GGS Cava 30th.
Unknown Location Sabation Arena–Queen Jynnalt

THE AIR WAS SULTRY, turgid, and cloying as she entered the arena. *At least this next to nothing armor won't induce heatstroke.* As she walked toward the center of the ring, she kept her opponent in sight. Jynnalt learned much in her fights since that first time. Survival a better teacher than training alone. As the only female fighter ever to win consistently, she was worth a fortune to Ossa's father, the Warlord who now owned her.

Important guest arrived, and the Warlord of the Ha'ti clan Hatian wanted to show off his best fighters. He tasked his overseer of the games to present a Grand Spectacle to impress and awe them. As she and her opponent walked towards the warlord's stands to pay their respects, the sandstorm horns shrieked out a warning, followed by ear-splitting sirens. She jumped, surprised by the sound. Both she and her opponent scanned the sky, expecting to see the retractable cover rise over the Colosseum. Nothing happened. Questioning voices rose and grew louder throughout the crowd. She noted the Warlord sent warriors scurrying off towards the direction of the coliseum control chambers. Most likely to investigate why the slaves were not working the manual pulleys to raise the cover.

Patrons throughout the Coliseum stood pointing skyward. The scuffling, stamping sounds of feet and movement grew as groups headed towards exits. An ominous sense of something wrong overcame Jynnalt. Her heightened senses kicked into overdrive. She glanced upward, as something on the periphery to her right caught her attention, and she glanced that direction. *Ustrix.*

She realized two of Ustrix's friends were trying to pull him back before he fell over the edge. He leaned too far over the side to wave his cloak; she assumed to catch her attention. Her heart pounded as a rush of adrenaline raced through her, forgetting her opponent and the sirens as she franticly looked for Ryakin. He was not with them.

Other Anunnaki crowded around Ustrix in the lower stands section reserved for foreigners. They also waved cloaks.

A whining, sizzling sound, followed by an intense flash, blinded her. She jerked away from the glowing red-scorching sand beside her. Her unprotected sword arm burned as if on fire. She sprinted back towards the gate as plasma bolts tore her stunned opponent apart where he stood. The sharp odor of ozone mingled with burning flesh. A scent she was intimately familiar with as burning slaves alive in the arena as punishment for disobedience, a common event.

The throaty roar of a blackraptor behind Jynnalt forced her to dive sideways, coming up on one knee, her shield above her head. The fighter flashed overhead before shooting straight up after strafing screaming patrons. Two more came in tight, firing fuel-bombs into the Warlord's family stands. Before she reacted, an explosion rocked the Coliseum. Blowback threw Jynnalt hard into the sand of the stadium. White-fiery agony shot through her shoulder and she tasted blood. Moments later, the ringing in her head stopped. Rising, she glanced towards the Warlord's family stands while keeping an eye out for the return of the blackraptor.

Fire and roiling black smoke rose high into the sky as wreckage and rubble from the destroyed stone stand met her gaze. Chaos erupted as the chieftain's families closest to the destroyed stands, still alive, fled shrieking. Clothes blackened, blood flowing from wounds while fire engulfed others. Spectators pushed and shoved, mindless of whom they trampled, injured, or killed. Onlookers, now attacked by an unknown enemy, pushed or shoved others over the sides in their panic to get out of the stands. Those who fell devoured as screams rose while the sand feeders fought over bodies.

Two heavy Largin hover fighters flew into the open space of the Coliseum. Seconds later, they opened fire. They circled, firing on patrons, running, and screaming as they struggled to escape the lethal rounds of explosive projectiles. The fighters were firing small electromagnetic railguns in a steady stream of tracers and deadly rounds into the crowds. They slaughtered citizens and slaves, females, and children indiscriminately.

Jynnalt scanned the sky before spinning and Razing towards the gate, using the fighters above to shield her from the blackraptor's lethal guns. Two circled the outer edge of the Coliseum, looking for a chance to move in for a kill shot. A burst of electric whips lit up a tunnel to her left. For a second, she stood confused. Plasma whips? Someone figured out how to overcome the city's dampening field. Who? Did it matter? This was the chance for her and her paladins to escape during the confusion and chaos. The glint of steel from swords flashing back and forth and stuttering sparks from the whips showed the scene at the gate in a strange staccato tableau.

She sprinted for the gate's entrance as streaks of plasma bolts threw gouts of sand in front of her. She slid to a halt. Jynnalt realized the Largin's were withdrawing after destroying the upper level stands completely. The circling blackraptors turned in for the kill. She scrambled towards the entrance; her only chance to survive. One of the Largins circled back to cover the fighter, firing its cannons. The Coliseum stands section above the gate collapsed in crashing stones, dust, fire, and smoke. The entrance blasted to pieces by the blackraptor, cutting off her escape. When the dust cleared, stone debris blocked her exit out of the arena.

She glanced around in desperation, then spotted an observation window blown open from an earlier hit, the stubs of the bars still red hot. She sprinted for it. At the last second, she dived through the window, allowing herself to free fall ten feet to the floor. She rolled, coming up on to her feet. Plasma fire followed, raising a slight burn where it grazed her shoulder. The far wall sizzled, the stones red hot with a sizeable hole in the center. The chamber collapsed as she leaped into the hallway.

She choked on stone dust and mortar till the tunnel cleared, allowing her to catch her breath. Grimacing with pain, she squatted close to the floor, probing her shoulder to see if she dislocated it. She flexed her arm; the shoulder painful yet functioning.

She stood and assessed her surroundings. Smoke drifted in from the far-left intersecting tunnel. Straight ahead, empty. Her eyes burned as more smoke-filled the hallway. To her left, screams of agony and the snapping pop of Sabation plasma whips. Voices pleading for mercy, followed by guttural curses from Sabation guards. Jynnalt headed toward the sounds. Heart pounding, she gripped the sword tighter. Tense, her breath rasping in her ears, remembering those killed unjustly and in cold blood for the smallest offense by overseers and their masters.

She peaked around the corner and saw two Sabation overseers. Slaves cowered on the floor before them. Her pulse quickened as she snuck up behind the warrior's, sword held to her right. Neither realized she was behind them. With a single motion, she slashed off their heads, which fell forward, tumbling to the floor with surprised expressions on their faces. Victims of the razor-sharp edge of her sword. The bodies followed, crumpling to the ground, blood spraying across the slaves.

Those murdered before she arrived littered the tunnel ahead of the decapitated bodies. The ones still alive glanced around, their eyes wide and glassy as they stared at her uncomprehendingly. The blood pooled around them from the beheaded overseers. Jynnalt motioned towards the tunnel exit several times before they jumped up, jostling each other to sprint away.

The hallway filling with smoke as she kneeled next to a dead body, ripping off material from his clothes and wrapping the cloth around her head. She tucked her hair underneath. While she worked, she kept an eye out for any warriors or guards. She stood, taking a moment to orientate herself. If her memory served her, she needed to make a left turn at the next tunnel intersection. She placed her hand along the wall and felt ahead, making sure not to miss her turn in the smoky haze.

Relief filled her when the distinct sounds of clashing swords and the sizzling pop of Sabation whips reached her. She was close by the exit tunnel for the pit fighters before they entered the arena. Kendo and the others should be there. Curses, grunts, and screams of agony got louder the closer she got to the intersection. Those not killed from the earlier blast still fighting.

Were the Warlords enemies attacking the guards? Or the arena ring slaves? She moved cautiously, alert, listening.

There were Chakian fighters, Anunnaki blackraptors, and Memie Largin bomber fighters. Most likely stolen, like other ships the Sabations acquired.

Who was challenging Ossa's father, Hatian? Other system Warlords? Or his rebel chieftains? The Warlord and his family were dead. No one in the Warlords stands survived those bombs. *Why still fight?* Sabation law declared all a Warlord owns, along with his clan warriors, to anyone who defeats him in battle.

She moved towards the sound of fighting. The last place she spotted her paladins. She prayed to the luminous ones to keep them safe.

Muffled sounds of bombs dropping throughout the city reached her this deep underground. A noise caught her attention, and she moved towards the sound. The smoke bringing tears to her eyes as the caustic stench burned her nose and throat. Her eyes blurry. In this hazy smoke, split-second decision needed to decide who might be a friend or foe.

The sound of running footsteps reached her too late. Before she reacted, a Sabation male ran out of the side tunnel and plowed into her, knocking her off her feet. Her sword flew out of her hands as they both slammed to the floor, the breath knocked out of her. She rolled towards her sword, grabbed it, and rose to face him. He was already up and running, fleeing towards the exit, ignoring her. She moved forward, slick with sweat from the heat, as she stopped for a second when cool air blew her way. The lights overhead flickered and went out. *They hit a power grid*; the emergency lights came back on after a second from backup generators somewhere, casting an eerie green glow in the smoky tunnel. More proof the damping field either did not work or turned off.

The smoke ahead cleared for a moment, and she glimpsed one of the Sabation overseers forcing slaves into a cell. She got ready to attack, but smoke closed around him, thwarting her. A grunt and scuffling noises came from where she last saw him, and she moved with careful deliberation towards the fighting. Jynnalt jumped back as a body fell with a thud on the floor in front of her. She dropped into a fighting stance, prepared for whoever took out the overseer.

Ossa walked forward out of the smoke, stopping upon seeing her. "Are you friend or foe?" she asked in Sabations of Ossa as she held her sword, ready to act. She moved closer, hoping not to have to kill her.

Ossa froze with a sudden intake of breath, fear in her eyes. She stepped away, blurting out as if trying to convince herself. You... you cannot speak our tongue. Ossa's eyes narrowed as she stared at her.

"Sorry to inform you, but I can. The others cannot. Their translators are not working."

"Translator? What is that?" Jynnalt watched as she realized the truth. "You understood all those times I spoke aloud to myself. I——"

Whatever she said drowned out by a fusillade of sharp concussions. The walls and floor shook. Stone plaster from the ceiling showered both as if a giant shook the tunnel.

Jynnalt moved towards the sounds of fighting before stopping to look back. We can discuss this later. For now, I am going to find my paladins. Understand I will kill you if you try to stop me. Jynnalt waited for Ossa to say something.

When she did, it surprised her. "I'm trying to save these slaves from my father's three traitorous chieftains. They will kill them or re-enslave them. I will not allow that to happen."

Jynnalt nodded. Ossa appeared calm, yet full of nervous energy.

"Your family is dead," Jynnalt said, without blunting its force.

"I know. The first wave hit when you were in the ring. I feared you died," she said, nodding the direction Jynnalt was heading. "My father's enemies are fighting our overseers ahead over the valuable pit fighters. They are worth a fortune. I cannot help them; they would have sent their best warriors to capture them. I stabbed this one in the heart when he grabbed me. He realized I held a hidden dagger, too late."

"Any idea about getting out of here? Suggestions?" She looked away as she spoke before turning back to emphasize what she said next. "After I find my friends."

She moved closer to Ossa, staring the same direction as the sounds of fighting got louder. An idea hit Jynnalt as she stared at the dead overseer. She yanked off his key. "We allow the slaves trapped in their cells to fight for their freedom. Wait here. If I do not come back soon, leave with those you already have, don't wait around."

Moving into the smoke, she followed the sounds coming from ahead. She moved along the hall, unlocking cages. Whispering to occupants to make a run for the exit. She moved as fast as possible in the smoke-filled tunnel; sword held at the ready. Five cells further, Jynnalt found Kendo. He and the other slaves in the cell copied her, stripped the bed's materials, and wrapped them around their heads and face. Kendo pointed to his head wrap as they opened other cells before they moved on to the next. He hoped they understood the message. Pit fighters, as soon as released, grabbed the weapons from the cache for the arena.

They fought past two warriors and an overseer, killing them before moving on and releasing more slaves. She found Tavas and the other paladins killing the last of the Sabations they were fighting and helped them wrap their heads before moving out. Jynnalt led them back to where she left Ossa. She was still waiting. A relieved and anxious look crossed her face as they emerged from the smoke.

Jynnalt motioned for everyone to follow her and Ossa. Her paladins and the pit fighters on each side of the females and slave children, Ossa, collected while she waited. They found the exit to the stairs to the upper city. They did not run across any enemy warriors or guards along the way. When they stepped up on the causeway, a menacing wall of brown sand stretched high across the horizon as far as they could see.

From Jynnalt's experience, the sand wall was less than ten standards away, giving them only minutes. Ossa came up beside them, behind her thirty house slaves and twice the number of children, along with the twenty-two pit fighters they released. "Ossa, can we get to the landing pads unseen? Before the storm arrives. This is our only chance to escape. We can't wait for the storm's end. Jynnalt stepped in front of her.

My father built an underground hidden escape tunnel for our family if attacked. We can use the tunnel to reach a secret landing pad where my father anchored his best private ship. The ship is fast, has a full complement of weapons aboard and the best navigation instrumentation of those he received as tribute. It's a short distance back inside the tunnel. From here we are ten minutes away to reach the hidden doorway leading out to where the ships docked.

Kendo and the others stared at Jynnalt. "Let's not discuss this now." she said, then hurried to catch up to Ossa as she rushed ahead. Jynnalt prayed the trust she was putting in Ossa did not end in her leading them into a trap.

Ossa held up her hand to stop them. Jynnalt behind her heard muted talking. The voices coming from the left tunnel.

"The secret tunnel entrance is there." She whispered loud enough for Jynnalt to hear while pointing the direction the talking came from. Kendo moved up from behind, listening.

Two spoke with the lyrical accents of the Anunnaki, the others three or four Sabations, their guttural language easy to recognize. One spoke in a strange barking, cough like language. A language one of the Anunnaki appeared to understand. The speech punctuated with coughs and short growls even more strident and unpleasant to her ears than Sabation, though similar.

"You have yet to deliver the slaves we paid you for. Our acquaintance here paid you in engines that can withstand your sandstorms for the fighters. *Those engines* allowed you to fly in these gods forsaken storm. We also notified you of the storm in time to take advantage. And my master jammed the damping field. We gave you the element of surprise, along with an enormous investment in tithe to pay warriors willing to betray their Warlord."

The unmistakable sound of a sword unsheathed echoed in the hallway. "He demands the male Malkuth slave, the Warlord owned. You know, the one my master wants. Beware of not delivering." One of the Anunnaki said, followed by throaty growls and grunts.

Another Anunnaki male spoke. "I and *my* master paid you a hefty sum for the only fighting female on the planet. Tall, red hair, strange green eyes, remember her. I believe she killed your son." Jynnalt heard the rasping curse of the chieftain whose son disgraced his family by losing to her in the arena.

"I prefer her alive, although dead will suit my master's purpose. You can have the Sabation Warlord's daughter and all the slaves. If you can't accomplish this, we will revisit our deal."

One of the three Sabations spoke too fast. Her translator did not grasp the exact meaning, but Ossa stiffened next to her. Then his speech slowed enough for her translator to interpret him.

"What will you do? Restore the Warlord from the kingdom of the dead?" All the Sabations laughed. The sound of a sword whistled through the air, followed by thuds.

The Anunnaki speaker said. "I believe our friend has made his point."

Jynnalt stuck the tip of her sword out to see those in the hall ahead. Slaves behind her shushed others who were restless, feeling exposed and nervous in the hallway. Jynnalt froze, holding her breath. Moments passed, and those in the hallway ahead appeared to not detect their presence. She thought she recognized one of the Anunnaki from somewhere but where eluded her. The other's Anunnaki's back was towards her. Something about that citizen's voice caught her attention. For now, she worried about how to get past them.

She recognized the chieftain, whose son she killed in her first fight in the arena. The one next to him always by his side. A Sabation body on the floor cut in half she did not know. The grim wound staunched by what she presumed was a plasma weapon of an unknown type, leaving no blood splashed across the wall or floor.

Kendo gasped at the sight, forcing Jynnalt to pull the sword tip back fast as the rest of them froze. She held her breath as one of the Anunnaki called out, "Show yourselves, or we will fire." Heavy footsteps moved their direction.

Jynnalt and the others prepared to fight. Then a loud pounding sound from the other hallway caused one of the Anunnaki to call out, "This way, they ran across the hallway over there. This must be a diversion. Follow me." The footsteps moved away, and she relaxed a little. Jynnalt realized she was holding her breath.

"Quick, before they come back." Ossa motioned them forward, running halfway before looking back to assure herself they followed, then stepped over the upper half of the body still lying on the floor. She pushed on the stones in a pattern on the wall. A small doorway opened. Ossa and the slaves rushed through as Jynnalt, Kendo, and her paladins covered their retreat. She noted Kendo acting strangely as he took several steps as if to follow the enemy.

Once the others were in, Jynnalt and her paladins followed. She witnessed Tavas pulling Kendo through the door right before the door slammed shut. Leaving them in pitch darkness for a moment till pale green glow lights flared to life. Jynnalt followed the rest, leaving Kendo's strange behavior for a later discussion. When they're safe and no longer in danger, she would ask him about what happened back there.

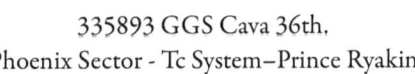

335893 GGS Cava 36th,
Phoenix Sector - Tc System–Prince Ryakin

OVER THE LAST FOUR turns, they listened to desperate calls coming over the command comms from their loyalist fleets in the kingdom. Inbound rescue fleets discovered too late, the Imperialist gained entrance through the Titan spawn defense, encircling Tc's systems without challenge. Ryakin focused on the battles closer to his position on the holo haptic projector in the DCIC with his upper command officers.

The loyalist ran into heavy resistance across Tc's kingdom. For now, he and his bridge officers stood by the holo battle map. They listened as fifteen light and heavy battlecruisers, and ten destroyers from Tc's ninetieth fleet engaged two Imperial deep battleships. The battleships from the third Imperial Warden Prince Jaui Ti*Ho's fifty-third fleet. They caught them as they exited the system with the evacuees and planetary ground troops. Sending a full wing of shadow fighters after the transports loaded with a precious cargo of citizens, seeds, and livestock. The Imperialist shadowers turned back to protect their battleships, engage with loyalist light battlecruisers and shadowers, making suicide attacks against them. Tc loyalists fought fiercely with inferior armaments but stronger shields and maneuverability against the battleships, buying time to allow the transports to reach deepspace and warp away.

When the battle finished, the loyalist lost eight hundred and fifty of their shadow fighters, one transport, and eleven heavy battlecruisers and every last destroyer. Now nothing more than smoking ruins. The horrendous scene of detritus and bodies floating in deepspace testament to the fierceness of the battle. They fell to the deadly rain of rail guns, cluster bombs, and small plasma cannons from the Imperialist battleships. Tc loyalist losses catastrophic. Planetary entag sky-eyes relayed the battle, showing the glow of fires still raging inside the interiors of the transports as they died a slow death. The shadower's and battlecruiser's heroic fight gave the other fourteen transports time to produce a warp bubble and escape.

The fact commanders called a strike against a transport full of innocent's citizens, especially by Anunnaki commanders, sickened and appalled Ryakin. If it's the last thing he ever did, those commanders would pay for their barbaric act.

"Open a channel to headquarters. As soon as they come through, I want you to send the message to my command chamber. Notify the Knight commanders. I want a meeting at the twenty-sixth hour on the flag's DCIC deck." Ryakin turned and strode towards the doorway to his private conference chambers.

"Yes, Commander." The officer adjusted the signal, blocking out the sounds of other ongoing battles throughout Tc's kingdom as he sent the call through to HQ.

"EC Kirud, Knight Ankak, Knight Jal. With me." He said.

When he reached the door, it slid open with a whoosh as he entered, followed by the other three. His ready chamber comfortable and large though not as luxurious as other kingdoms high ranking blooded. A command desk and chairs for him and his officers, the only furniture. The usual holo pads spaced throughout the chamber for meetings between his command fleet knights, and the private one next to his desk.

They took their seats as Ryakin poured drinks from his stock of an expensive smoky Alitiara whiskey; he gave each one a chalice and sat across from them. His expression tightened. He sat swirling his drink for a moment, then regarded the officers.

"Of all the major screw-ups so far, not changing Tc's Titan spawn codes is the worst. We're all to blame. I sent the information along to Kalmia. She acknowledged and sent back they would reset Ki's."

Restless, he raked his hand through his hair, taking a deep breath as he glanced over at his newest EC Kirud. "However, that will do little good unless we wrest Ki from the false Queen. For now, she controls Ki, including the Titan spawn defenses. Kalmia informed me they were working to find a way around Tesiskel's control. For now, I prefer the Titan's remain inactive."

"Excuse me." His EC, Kirud, said. A young ambitious officer on loan from Tount Abushita from Da. He was Ryakin's third replacement EC after Ustrix left to join his brother. On the Imperialist side. Kurid was not afraid to speak his mind, even when he shouldn't. Too many times, he overstepped his authority. Ryakin wondered if the Tount loaned him his EC to rid himself of the haughty little *sheat*. Ryakin's discerned his disdain as he glanced around his quarters. A wall of meh's of history and science, along with ancient to modern battles and tactics, lined one wall floor to ceiling, while on another wall, philosophies. The opposite wall was a well-crafted wood cabinet full of fine liquors and wines.

The derision in his voice hard to miss, "I thought Queen Tesiskel ruled Ki? Didn't she declare you and your crew," he stared at the others, "outlaws. How are you able to have the codes reset to keep out the Imperialist without her permission?"

Ryakin opened the battle map on the wall across from him, working to contain his anger. His two Kierian Knight officers felt no such restraint and spoke in unison.

"She is not the Queen." Jal said, a challenge in his voice, "if the Phoenix armor is not ash, Queen Jynnalt is alive; somewhere. No faithful Kierian will obey Princess Tesiskel's orders over Prince Ryakin's, her Consort, till that happens. Even then, the Phoenix armor needs to accept whoever is next in line for the throne, or the people will reject her."

"Her? Are there no male heirs in the bloodlines?"

"Only a Queen can hold the throne. The faithful will not obey a male King," Ankak nodded towards Ryakin, "though for now as her consort, he holds the throne. No one else." The tight set of both the Kierian Knight's lips and the stoniness of their faces dared Kirud to defy their assessment of the situation.

Jal leaned forward, saying, "I would love to see her face and that slimy rodent Duurua when Queen Jynnalt arrives and takes her rightful place. Or the council members who sided with this false Queen. Loyal Kierans know who the traitors are. Their betrayal will cost them. Those wardens who declared themselves the Three Pillar's, don't understand Ki or the outer borders, if they believe they can replace our Queen with someone related to her."

"I'm confused. She is Prince Satoric's daughter, making her of higher rank since the death of the emperor and the ascension of her father to his present position. She could order Queen Jynnalt to do what she wanted." Silence greeted him as Kirud glared at them, waiting for an answer.

Ryakin staring at the small holo battle map held his tongue. An idea hit him mid-thought, distracting him. *Could Kirud be a spy?*

He spoke before his two officers did, "true. If you're not Kierian, those facts make sense. To Kierian's they ignore any idea from the Anunnaki Empire, which does not allow them to follow their proven Queen. Yes, she is Queen Jynnalt's mother. None of those facts will change who the Kierian's bow the head for."

Kirud moved as if to rise, then turned towards Ryakin, a belligerent expression on his face. "So, is the Temple seeking her also? Or just Ki's investigators."

The question got his full attention, "Why this interest in my wife and the Temple, Ki is not your oath kingdom, and I'm told you're not particularly faithful? What does any of this matter to you or whether the Temple is looking for her?" Leaning back into his chair, he stared at Kirud for a moment, slammed back his Alitiara whiskey. The rich smoky flavor burned as it went down, clearing his head. He rose to pour another. The whiskey came from the Alitiars system in the Malkuth Kingdom. Only the Temple priest and priestess know the exact recipe. Making the whiskey prohibitively expensive.

He sat. "Everyone we can spare is trying to find her," he said, watching Kurid, alert for signs of deceit. "Once more I'm asking why so interested? You're not Kierian. Why does this matter to you? Your oath is to Da and your Tount?" Ryakin sipped his drink, studying him. Waiting for an answer.

The signal officer chimed. "Commander, headquarters pulsed, would you like me to send it to your chambers?"

"Put the pulse through."

Rualui's semi-translucent holo'haptic form popped up before him. Consternation, bitterness, and grief underscored the steel in his eyes.

"They're sending out news pulses to Tc's citizens stating that they're blooded betrayed them. The Three Pillars are telling the loyalist if they surrender without a fight, they'll exonerate them. The Igteirctell system was the first to agree and laid down their arms and shut off their shields. They jammed our signal. I tried to warn them."

His brother stood silent for a moment. "Our scientists are not sure how they did this as Imperialist are still sending over the normal pulse channels." Someone outside the holo's view handed him a chalice, and he took a deep swallow before he spoke again.

"This is how the Imperialist treated them." The look on his brother's face warned him to prepare for the worst. After what happened on the capital planet. He knew what that worst might be.

"We gained this holo from an operative in orbit."

Like any trained warriors, Ryakin was callous towards enemies in battle. Yet, amongst warriors existed an unspoken code of honor, at least in the Anunnaki Empire. Rules they rigorously followed, held to with fierce tightness. For that is their sanity and their souls. Watching the scene, he stiffened.

They lined up the planet's defensive ground troops out on the plains in parade formation. Normal protocol to surrender your forces. Those watching knew what this meant when the Imperialists rushed away in their vehicles. The fighters circling farther out than prudent in case those surrendering turned on those disarming them. His unease rose. His stomach clenched when he realized the Imperialist did not take the ground troop's weapons or accept command control from the Govingshin's son of the blood house of Nabunazir. He'd met him from the times when they came to court. Happy easy going, not a mean bone in his body. A little too easygoing by Ryakin's thoughts, still not someone he disliked. His breathing increased as his nostrils flared.

Eighteen Deep Imperial Battleships in orbit bombed the area with Star Killer neutron bombs. Four hundred and sixty-eight thousand perished in an instant. The sharp intake of breath from those in the chamber spoke volumes about their reaction, which mirrored his. The pounding of his heart hammered blows in his ears as his fist tightened, his knuckles white.

They moved on, destroying the power ziggurats and shield generators of the outer areas before someone might turn them back on. Next, the fighters circled in over the smaller surrounding cities. Drop command centers rained down in typical landing zone patterns, disgorging their ground troops by the thousands. Older atmos shadower dancers strafed anything moving ahead of the landing troops. Honorable battle laws ignored entirely. The tans and browns of walls painted obscenely with gore and blood. Afterward, bomb whalers came in, obliterating the smaller yet elegant cities to rubble. Dust for now obscuring the destruction. When the holo finished, a rage of silence resonated throughout the chamber.

His brother spoke once more in a tight, controlled voice, as if the gods themselves tried to hold him back. "They massacred the city's citizens. Every... last... one... of... them."

"They then showed that to the other cities, telling them if they did not capitulate, they would meet the same fate. Leaving out the fact the city surrendered. They implied the cities refused and fought."

Prince Anu stepped into the holo's view. Ryakin bowed his head, Anu acknowledging him before saying. "We cannot leave our citizens to the *mercy* of the Three Pillars. They will pay for what occurred this turn. But for now, we evacuate our people. Our forces are not strong enough now to take them on. I sent this holo out to every single loyalist ship. I still have access to the entag fleet channels. They have not figured out how to remove my codes. I doubt Prince Satoric and the other two realize the fury they unleashed. This was a horrific and deliberate annihilation of innocent blood, not some accidental collateral damage."

His brother all business once Prince Anu handed over the channel. "We pieced this together. From our sky-eyes and ghosters in strategic positions and our whisper operatives on the ground, that survived." Tc's sphere of influence popped up before them, Anu's voice in the background, the map filling their view.

"The Imperialist spread out in a curving line on all three sector levels, going system by system. Their Dreadnoughts are holding at each system's capital cities." He pointed to several places on the map which enlarged, showing the hostile dreadnaughts, "at these strategic points. They are controlling and directing the battles. They send out their battleships and carriers to engage the locals before moving on, leaving the mop up to the ground troops drop warriors. Tc's ground forces augmented by small loyalist commoners' groups are fighting hard to hold them off while ships and transports attempt to evacuate civilians. The problem is we don't have enough ships."

"So far, we defended and evacuated two hundred and fifty-eight systems with heavy casualties. GIA and the Temple fleet are on their way to assist but ran into an ambushed at the Forges Fire gate and are still engaged. There are one hundred and forty-two systems left to evacuate."

Swirling the amber-gold liquid in the crystal chalice, he listened to his brother. He noted the three officers with him and those on the holo pads, gauging their reactions. Kirud he discerned intent, but more with excitement than revulsion, making him uneasy. The other knights and commanders sickened and horrified. Many beyond shocked, which is what he expected. These were not outside vicious enemies; these were ranking Blooded and crews they knew and once trained or fought with together who committed these cruel acts.

"To even accomplish this much, our fleets are taking heavy losses. Ga's one hundred and sixty-second lost sixteen dreadnoughts, half its complement when they ran into Prince Jaui's fifty-third and fifty-fourth fleets. They also lost fifty-seven battleships. Only one is still operational. Fifteen reached Tz's border repair docks, damaged too bad to send back out. They also lost a full third of their support ships. Two of their largest dropships now wrecks rotating in deepspace. All hands lost."

Ryakin cleared his throat before speaking. "We could ask the commoners and private guilds of the outer borders to help. If we can get in and out fast enough, we can stay one step ahead of their fleets. I can take the seventy-ninth, eighty and ninety and keep them busy. This will take two turns to accomplish. Hit and run tactics will force them to move forward slowly. I'll put each fleet to a level. My task force will take the middle and coordinate the attacks to the others while doing the same ourselves. This should save more of our ships, where we're outnumbered."

"Agreed. I will order the Kierans council to confiscate all the private and guild ships," Prince Anu said.

"With all due respect your Grace, in the border kingdoms I've learned one thing which is absolute. No King or Queen remains one for long if they rule by heavy-handed administration. Their guilds and commoners necessitate a lighter touch. Or they do not remain seated on the throne. At least not for long. I would ask for the needed help. If you allow me to do so. I guarantee you will receive what you need."

Anu stepped away. Then appeared moments later, "The border Kings did not take my demands well. I will leave it up to you to acquire those ships." Prince Anu's holo winked out, but not before the frustrated anger showed upon his face. Ryakin dismissed the Knight Officers present on the holos pads and left the command chambers for the bridge, followed by his EC and Knights.

Chapter 28

335893 GGS Goem 3rd.
Phoenix Sector - Tc System–Prince Ryakin

THREE TURNS LATER, after a strange lack of response to the start of their rushed evacuation, the Imperialist Dreadnoughts were on the move once more. Intel showed them redeploying seven full fleets from the Chakian front to Tc, heading right towards Ryakin's fleets.

"Commander, a pulse from headquarters."

"Put it on the holo in DCIC," Ryakin said where they were reviewing a battle plan on-board Nemesis. His brother popped up on the pad. "Ryakin, you need to listen to this." The channel changed to a standard news holo'pulse. Prince Alalus announced, as the new vizier to the Three Pillars, all kingdoms and Empire fleets are now under Imperial control. Any action taken without an order from the Three Pillars is an act of treason. The channel switched back to Rualui as soon as the announcement finished.

"No mention of Prince Iltasadum? Prince Anu is correct. The intel they executed him in secret, most likely correct. So, per the council and the now newly appointed Three Pillars, any action taken by our fleet is illegal. That's the reason they stopped advancing for three turns. They wanted the council's vote of approval for control over all the kingdoms fleets."

The scanner officer called out, "two spatial contacts on the DSD's heading our direction. Readout from whisps shows a recon patrol, three

Battleships, two carriers, and five heavy battlecruisers."

"Red Alert. Move all ships into the upper thermosphere of Orlistean, ion drift thrusters only." Ryakin ordered while alarm klaxons blared throughout the fleets. Crews responded with reflexes honed by constant drills and lifelong training. The Varl and the Kiarn destroyers clipped each other in the tight corridor they maneuvered within. Helms officers misjudged the distance because of the havoc played on sensors by the electromagnetic interference (EMI) from the planet. Both reported incurring minor damage.

The last ships moved deeper into the outer thermosphere of the frozen blue gas giant. After tense moments, he let his breath out, not realizing he'd been holding it as the patrols passed without changing course. His scanner officers picking up faint pings. They were hunting. For them.

"Notify all ships we will hold here. Call a holo meeting between the Knight Commander's in thirty minutes."

Later, when his Knights were present, Ryakin laid out his strategy. The plan bold and aggressive entailed making a surprise offensive against their flagship dreadnought, the Reef Skimmer. Prince Iltasadum's flagship. One thing bothered him. *Who's commanding?*

With the thought in mind, he explained his plan. "Hit them hard, lure them back into the mines. We will fight a hit-and-run battle and exit as soon as they complete the evacuations. This will give our loyalist fleets," he glanced up at his commanders, "time to snatch victory out from under the Imperialist. We *must* keep them focused on us long enough for the final evacuations of the Tc's systems. This is vital."

"When I give the order, you are to disengage and make a checkered retreat through here." He pointed to the narrow channel between the mines the fleets feverishly laid during those three turns. Dreadnaught Commanders you need to be extra careful, not a lot of room to maneuver. The mines created a choke point. We can use that, decreasing their advantage of numbers. He gazed at his Knights, fear, and excitement on their youthful faces, which they worked hard to hide. He knew the emotion, felt it now. Experience hid the fact better. But over the fear was a determination to do their duty.

"I know the numbers arrayed against us superior. But we have the advantage. Whoever is in command of the Imperialist fleet is using textbook maneuvers. We can use that against them. Confusion, surprise, and their arrogance, our most important weapons. They are counting on their higher numbers. Remember, the Imperialist sent the border kingdoms to fight the Chakian's during the first half of the war. They held back most of the inner Kingdoms fleets for home defense. We all know the home systems participated in zero action." He stopped and considered their reactions. Their heads nodding, their expressions intent.

"You and your crews fought live engagements. In battles with the Chakian's formidable fighters. Before the war, you fought off pirates, reavers, and bandits. Don't sell yourself or your crews short. Reputations are just that till proven to be accurate. From what we have been able to gather from their actions is this: whoever is in command of the late Prince Iltasadum's task force has little or no experience other than FR games. That counts against them." Once more, nodding heads greeted his remark.

"Now let's get down to work." Ryakin said as he scrutinized their focused expressions.

Ryakin enlarged the battle map as he explained his strategy; the commanders, concentrating intently as he spoke. "This is our end game. This line of retreat," a glowing bright amber line pointing towards a funnel which narrowed towards a corridor between two bright red areas. "Red is the mines our screening ships laid the last three turns." The line turned bright yellow, showing the retreat section. "Our retreat is the trickiest. This is the linchpin of the entire plan." He stood and walked around the commander's holos before focusing on the map once more.

"At this point here, carriers and battleships will load our fast attack and support ships. The dreadnoughts will hold the line just outside this area, covering your retreat."

Nobody wanted to state the obvious. The fact plenty of space available. Many ships would not survive the battle. "Squeeze them in even if you must stack them up. Make room for any ships who reach you. Don't worry about which ship they are from. The Ai's will have the hardest part coordinating a warp to skip retreat. Up to that point, they will maintain their normal battle duties," he paused for a second, "till retreat is sounded.

His commanders stared at him before looking around, unease on their faces. The youngest, with the least battle time, spoke. "I'm confused. If we're retreating, how are we going to warp to skip in groups? Never overheard discussions about fleets doing this or attempting to do this in battle."

"Why not go to warp for retreat one ship in order like normal?" Three of his older, trusted fleets commanders spoke in unison.

He stepped back, allowing Nemesis's robotic avatar to step up to the holo-map. "I will let Nemesis explain as the Ai's in the fleet worked this part out." He waited for the uproar to quiet before saying, "first listen and consider the facts. Don't let your bias hinder your ability to think with the clarity you will need if we are to survive this battle.

"We can hit them hard, make them pay for what they did. This gives us the advantage of less loss to our fleet. If, and I mean if, we pull this off, the loyalist will receive a needed morale boost. What they did to the Igteirctell system was deliberate. Meant to demoralize us. We need to return the favor."

Nemesis stepped forward. "The advantage of this maneuver is warp trails can be tracked. Skip can't. If this works, they would have no way of tracking us to our fall back location. We Ai's studied how Queen Jynnalt accomplished this during the disaster. The problem, the immense power demands. We believe we have found a way to overcome this."

As Ryakin regarded those in the DCIC, he wondered who'd be the first to object. No one did. Before he said anything else, the comm's officer chimed him.

"Commander Knight Elgar request to come aboard."

"Permission granted. Send him straight to my commander's chambers as soon as he boards." Ryakin turned towards the others. "take a quick recess. Be back here thirty minutes from now and please think about listening to what Nemesis said."

He turned off the holo pulse pads and left for his command chamber.

When Elgar entered, Ryakin was ready with Altaian whiskey. The two sat sipping whiskey in comfortable silence before Elgar spoke. "We got a lead on four males and a female of blooded quality." Before Ryakin asked questions, he held up his hand. "We lost the trail. And the Dagger of Cineuian."

Ryakin choked on his whiskey. "How the *droging helc* can you lose a dreadnought?"

"Well, that is another thing. Cineuian ah, stole ah... herself."

Ryakin choked once more. After the burning in his throat passed, he put his drink on the table carefully, as if it might bite. "*Fock*," he stood and went to the cabinet, and grabbed the expensive bottle of whisky. He sat, placing the bottle between them.

"Go on, I'd like to hear how a ship's Ai out vulped you."

Elgar sat. "Cineuian claimed one of her power plants got damaged from an earlier ion storm. I ordered us to put into the nearest repair station. The closest one in the vicinity was an automated drone dock. You know all living crew must disembark. As soon as the last crew member stepped off to the dock station, Cineuian pulled away. Claimed she'd find her without us and warped off. She caught me with my pants around my ankles, not a pleasant sensation at my age and experience. I should have put her in sleep mode before exiting the ship, per fleet protocol. No actual commander does in the field. Well, except for those who pretend to be commanders. I only do so at base dock. Nothing to do afterward but come here. Note, I need to follow that protocol. After the Igigi responded to the Stranded in Dock signal. I headed straight here." He grunted. "Her slug of a highness would throw me in the dungeon if I arrived without the ship. Worse, she could justify her actions. No worry about an uprising. No, Commander worth his stars would lose a dreadnought."

"Outsmarted by an Ai, huh. I believe we shall keep this between ourselves."

Elgar slammed back his whiskey. "I know war, not investigations. That banita slug of a mother wanted me out of the way. This chasing around the galaxy kept me out of her hair. Besides, Kalmia told me her agents would track the ship down and put whisper agents on board once they locate Cineuian. I couldn't bring myself to notify the Ministry of Nine. An Ai going rogue, their purview. The old girl and I have fought too many battles together to betray her in such a way. Now it's up to you to decide what to do with her. And me."

He threw back the whiskey and drank before placing the empty crystal on the table and nudging the chalice Ryakin's direction, a not-so-subtle hint.

Ryakin, silent, thinking, paid no attention. Elgar kept his own counsel waiting.

Moments passed before Ryakin said, "maybe this is not so terrible. Who would suspect an Ai Dreadnought and some whisper agents of looking for someone?" He leaned back, staring at Elgar before speaking again, "when informed you were here, I was hoping to add her to the other Dreadnaughts. I'll have a message sent to Kalmia and the council saying I ordered Cineuian to continue the search on my authority. The orders will say I demanded your presence here for this battle and all the crew you could spare. I will leave out the fact there is no crew on board. I can't afford the Ai's in an uproar, and they would be if informed I sent Ministry Nine to hunt her down. Never ends well, for the Ai. Jynnalt would kill me if something happened to Cineuian," he said. Ryakin realized against all odds, he somehow thought she would one turn be back where she belonged. He changed the subject to the battle plan, pleased when Elgar nodded his head with approval.

"Downright sneaky of you, son," he said. "Still, the storm will hinder your fleets as well. How do you expect to counter the effects?" His tone questioning as he nudged his empty chalice once more in Ryakin's direction.

Few commoners rose as high as Elgar. He did because he was a brilliant tactician, and Ryakin valued any input from him. He grabbed the bottle and refilled their chalices'.

"Our ghosters have dropped whisps in projected static pockets for them to use when the storm rolls through. And our support ships for the last three turns set mines creating a narrow escape lane here." He showed him the map. "We used every DDRUMS's the fleet has to give our scanners a boost during the storm. Won't be one hundred percent, but will be more than the other side has. They will also have to spread out to keep their ships from slamming into each other from the gravitational waves generated at the trailing edge of the storm. Also, the storm will force them to pull in their whisp, as they are too fragile for this storm."

"Son, the slightest advantage can win an engagement. And never forget the Avatar of Random Events. I'd like to stick around and see how this one pans out. Do I have permission to stay aboard?"

Ryakin chuckled. "I was trying to figure out how to ask."

"You couldn't tear me away. Call your Knights back, let's get this done." His tone became reassuring, "Ryakin, if Jynnalt's alive, Cineuian will find her. Focus on this battle. You need to have a Kingdom for her to come back to rule."

The deepspace storm rolled in two hours later, playing havoc with signals and scanners. This forced the enemy fleet to deploy their ghosters. Ryakin called for battle stations on the general fleet pulse net. "It's a go for sleight of hand."

A quick yet well-organized urgency took hold of the fleet's crews heading to their post.

The loyalist unleashed their full wings of fighters and interceptors. Followed by complements of ghosters.

They will feel the pain of Igteirctell.

Ryakin would strike at the heart of their fleet. The flagship dreadnought Reef Skimmer and her capital ships. Task force, two and three sent to engage the rest.

Like clockwork, the interceptors took out their picket drones and the enemies' ghosters forced out by the storm but unaided by DDRUMS's. Each time they took out an enemy ghoster, theirs moved in, re-syncing the signals, mimicking the Imperialist ones they replaced. The few seconds delay should not worry their signal officers as they would attribute signal loss of a few seconds to the storm. Their interceptors aided by two ghosters hunted the shadow fighters' patrols. When they found them, they eliminated them with exacting precision.

So far, their luck held. As per fleet protocol, outer view port sensors shut down on the Imperialist ships to minimize damage. This left them dependent on their ghoster's signal as their outer eyes. They would not detect pressure waves from destroyed ships in the storm's havoc. Ryakin ordered his fleet to move throughout the enemy's outer lines after the interceptors called phase one completed. Unseen, silent, as ten ghosters and interceptors led Nemesis, a dark shadow slipping silently past ships, through the lines towards the Reef Skimmer. The quiet buzz and beeps of equipment the only sound on the bridge. The attack group slid past the outer edge where earlier their interceptors destroyed picket drones, replacing them with their own.

A half-hour later, without warning, *helc and death* descended on the Reef Skimmer and two of its attending carriers. Ryakin unleashed everything along with five wings of shadowers, three wings of interceptors and two wings of whale bombers which blew the central shield towers and deflectors. Anchor shields collapsed in seconds. Afterward, the interceptors split off, going after any fighter trying to launch from the damaged bays. Fleet members roused from meals or sleep into battle on the Imperialist ships, slow to respond. The Reef Skimmer hit with the full ferocity of a dreadnought and its complement of capital and support ships doomed before capable of firing back.

Nemesis slid along the Reef Skimmer's port side, unleashing Adramelech missiles, formidable gravitational shockwave weaponry. The Reef Skimmer veered hard to starboard, as the devastating blasts of the broadside fusillade from five of Nemesis missiles struck dead on target. The Reef Skimmer capsized into the carrier next to her as the shock waves hit hard, tearing the dreadnought from her anchor moorings. Nemesis energy cannons firing furiously destroyed the incoming Star Killer missiles from the Imperial carrier, the Augire. Nemesis sent out interceptors and bombers destroying the Augier's firing towers, putting her out of commission. The attack brutal and swift on the Imperialist forces around their flagship. The decompressing ship showed explosion as fire tore through the interior, outpacing its automatic suppression systems. Unable to contain the raging internal fires. The battle shield's failing as the Reef Skimmer fell astern of Nemesis, peripheral raking plasma cannons and Black daemon energy sappers bleed her power off fast.

Ryakin kept pounding the Reef Skimmer and the two capital carriers flanking her with Storm Furies. The thunderous reverberations from the formidable weapons felt underfoot on the battle bridge.

They caught the Imperialist by surprise. First strike theirs. Ryakin knew with seven to three odds the battle would not favor them for long.

"Recall all wings and ghosters." He ordered. There were less than forty minutes before the Reef Skimmer blew. The carriers next to her moving away, desperate to escape the blast radius. Both flanking carriers damaged beyond the ability to fight back signaled surrender.

Watching, Ryakin felt the rise of gratification and elation. Wanted them to burn.

Is this who you are? To become what you abhor? To lose decency and rational thought to rage?

He hesitated, fighting with his conscience against his earlier anger.

Ryakin turned away from the viewer. "Move in closer to the Augire and the Lunar Arrow. Offer to skip them out with us. Send a general broadcast to all Imperial ships in the blast radius. They have fifteen minutes to reach us and lock-down before we skip. We will release any non-loyalist ship when we reach our exit area. Order all returning wings to pick up any escape pods. Get me the commander of the Reef Skimmer."

Seconds later, the holo from the bridge of the Reef Skimmer appeared before him. Ryakin, shocked without thought, stepped towards the viewscreen as Knight Commander Rel's image stood before him. Once he'd considered her for a marriage contract. His brother did not approve, for unknown reasons, but afterward, they stayed friends. "Rel what the *helc*, move to your command escape pod. I am diverting a team of my fighters to pick you and your staff up. Abandon ship before it's too late.

"Sorry. Wish I could. The Reef Skimmer's destruction will cause the Three Pillar's to look for someone to punish. You do not understand what is going on in the empire under them. Save my crew and, if possible, please, I beg you save my family from their vengeance. Promise me. Understand this is the reason imperialist crews are not acting with honor. Our families held hostage against our obedience to the orders giving by the Three Pillars and their warrior's council. At least it was you and not someone else. I am sending over the Imperial entag codes. Use them however you can to best aid your cause."

A sick sensation rose in his stomach as he promised to do everything possible to save her family. One last time he begged her to abandon ship, to no avail. She cut comms.

Knight Elgar watching nodded his head in his direction before looking away.

Ryakin stood still for several seconds, staring at the blank viewscreen. Cleared his throat before saying, "as soon as nineteen minutes have passed, skip to the set coordinates." His voice steady, though his eyes shined as the subtle hum of the skip engines coming online rumbled through the floor. Nineteen tense minutes later, they skipped with a full complement of carriers, support ships and escape pods, both theirs and the Imperialist. As they exited on the far side of the battlefield, a searing light lit deepspace. The Reef Skimmer's death. Sudden. Final. Along with Commander Rel and her bridge crew, who refused to leave her side. He gave a salute of honor towards the death of the flagship and her courageous bridge crew. Grief something for later, in private.

Dropping the enemy ships, they skipped five minutes later. An unheard-of maneuver, so close to their last skip. The Kierian shipwrights made those improvements in secret. Still, the maneuver punished their skip engines. They left the enemy ships to tend their wounded and move out of the field of battle on their honor.

Nemesis came out of skip and almost collided with the dreadnought, the Neshu, bearing down on the Cygnus. The Cygnus, an older Dreadnought of Ga, incapable of outrunning the Neshu or out-gunning him either. Ryakin acted ordering. "Turn aft, fire all plasma cannons on the Neshu."

Cannon gunnery crews opened fire. Forcing the Neshu to break its pursuit and maneuver to engage. Nemesis unleashed Phalanx and Star Furies' missiles, followed by Black Daemon energy sappers on the Neshu, draining the energy shields. The attack unexpected, the Neshu scrambled to maneuver into position while taking heavy damage before turning into firing range to get off a shot.

Not fast enough. Its shields, still forward to cover incoming fire from the Cygnus, now switched covering her aft, leaving her bow exposed. The distance between them close enough to allow Nemesis's plasma cannons to make a swift and pitiless assault. The Neshu took a direct hit to the battle bridge. On her starboard side, a gash opened two feet wide from stem to stern. Nemesis and the Cygnus, which turned to fight, pounded her with raking broadsides.

The ships' officers were dead or maimed beyond doing their job. The battle holo showed internal fires raging. Seconds later, the ship's interior lit up like a glow globe, lighting deepspace around them. For tense moments, Ryakin waited. The Neshu slowed, fell out of battle, and drifted away. Her power cores ejected, removing any further explosions. Ryakin turned his attention to the rest of the battlefield. Nemesis reported thirty Gyps Fulvus scavenger ships skipped into the field of battle. Ryakin swore. How the *helc* were they so fast to find the battlefield. EC Kurid asked if he wanted to send in their shipwrights to deny them as much loot as possible.

"No. I won't endanger them. Let the Gyps grab what they can. If they get in the way, treat them as enemy combatants."

"Commander, scanners picking up ten full wings of fighters and a complement of bombers heading our way, released from the Neshu minutes before she went dark."

"Bring the griffins online." Hatches burst open and three hundred brutal Griffin railguns extended. They tracked the fast-approaching ships, the last gasp of the dying Neshu. Each colossal Griffin, fury and rage personified. A strike cruiser came into range. Nemesis gunners hit them with three feet long explosive munitions, firing five hundred and fifty rounds per second. The strike cruiser turned to instant glittery detritus and dangerous shrapnel. Punished hard for its insolence. More Griffin hatches across Nemesis slammed open. The screening ships of the seventy-ninth carriers and deepspace dreadnoughts in the thick of battle turned back to protect Nemesis, their flagship.

Two whale bombers from the Neshu got close enough to drop their bombs. Forty shadowers of the Neshu sacrificed themselves to take out one of Nemesis's tower cannons. Knight Elgar was conferring with Master Guild Officer fourth class on the wireless entag channel when a scatter bomb burst through three of the upper griffin gunner's sections. Mangled griffin railguns sucked out to deepspace by decompression spun away seconds before the emergency shielding engaged. A Chief third-class Journey's upper half of his body blown across the chamber to the floor. Dark blood pooling beneath the lower half, held in place by his magnetic decompression boots. Other warriors writhing in agony, arms or legs torn off. Life drones detached from walls, enveloping them in life repair transport units, or inserted meh chip removal devices before disappearing out the door with them. The damaged sealed before full decompression. "Evacuate those areas, close the blast doors and seal the sectors affected," Elgar said before looking back at the battle map. The Orvaf attacked by two Imperial Dreadnoughts and overwhelmed.

"Ghosters, give them a peek at Nemesis and the seventy-ninth battleships. Make us the bait. We need to pull them off the Orvaf. Notify them to be ready to turn and fire." Ryakin commanded, watching the battle map.

The commander of the Imperialist dreadnought the Kalla of the fifty-third took the bait, turning his full fleet their direction. He redeployed his ships into an anti-fast attack screening formation. Then ordered a textbook general attack, the thing Ryakin counted on. The commander of the Kalla split his fleet into divisions, ordering them to attack independently.

Ryakin order Nemesis to retreat. Needing to pull them closer to the killing field of mines. Three times the Ghosters allowed a peek at Nemesis and her screening ships. They were playing a vicious game of predators vying for control of territory. A game with only one winner.

"If you pull them to here," Knight Elgar said, pointing just outside the leading edge of the minefield. "You can have the ghosters blind them as we pull off to the side here." Now he pointed to the edge of the red line. "We will need every ghoster out to give a false image of us heading into the minefield. The signal won't hold for long, so hope they race right after the ghost images."

Ryakin nodded, agreeing. Tense moments passed as they executed the maneuver.

The Kalla took the bait. Followed the false signature, adjusting formation and speed as they attempted to intercept Ryakin's task force two, increasing speed to one hundred thousand standards per second.

Screening frigates, cruisers, destroyers, and battleships vanish one after the other as they hit the mines. The Kalla applied starboard bow thrusters' full power, trying to avoid the mines ahead. Turning directly into a larger grouping of mines which ripped her lower hull apart, taking with her the accompanying support ships caught in the blast radius.

Holes opened in the tight formation of three of the carriers and their support ships still intact as they scrambled to escape. Providing clear shots for the seventy-ninth, moving in fast while flanked by the Orvaf. They overwhelmed three of the Imperialist battleships with punishing broadsides, which forced them to slow before falling out of formation while internal fires and decompression ripped open their sides. The Imperial deepspace Dreadnaught the Geilild and three cruisers fell to their attack. Spewing clouds of atmosphere and debris, along with blasts of plasma balls of energy, rolling across the blackness of deepspace. The Geilild hit three more mines and exploded stunningly. Lighting up the entire battlefield.

Within twenty minutes the loyalist destroyed the Imperialist fifty-third fleet's capital ships. A third of its fast attack destroyers and heavy cruisers, their only ships left. The Imperial fifty-fourth also damaged beyond combat effectiveness. Their battle commander ordered a withdrawal of the forces from the field, loading both theirs and the fifty-third's smaller ships and skipping away seconds before incoming missiles struck.

Skip scavengers complicated the battlefield. Skipped in, grabbed pieces of unexploded or non-damaged armaments from the battlefield till they filled their holds. Skipped out to come back as soon as they offloaded their loot to their cargo ship's father away.

The sound of information flowed around the bridge in the background. From his crews or crews on other ships. Hectic calls laced with screams or orders, yells, or panicked cries for help. Others calm. Now and then, one of the Knight commanders of Dreadnaughts would pop up on the holo pads with an appeal or with information. Damaged equipment or broken bulkheads behind them as repair crews and spiderdrones raced to keep the ship battle effective.

Ryakin replenished and redeployed the eightieth loyalist carriers and their fighters for attacks. Returning Imperialist fire with starburst, black daemons, sappers and gigantic Phalanx cannons. Griffin railguns pounded away at incoming fast attack ships. Their own fighters taking them on head-to-head.

Ryakin in DCIC ordered the tactical commanders of his support carriers to "Open fire with your Griffins. Choose an enemy vessel and keep them under fire as soon as they come within range to apply pressure. Keep your bigger cannons in reserve for now."

The Destiny of Vropi fired on the strike cruiser Itallita and registered eight direct hits, one amidst the superstructure causing internal explosions, taking the ship out of the fight early. The Ria targeted the heavy battlecruiser Oprian, claiming a hit on the cruiser's shield turret, a second to the central cannon. She fell out of battle, going dark seconds later. Yiahal sighted the cruiser Tealion and claimed three hits. Golden Savian reported hits on the carrier Talon, two between the superstructure and forward deflector and another on the leading cannon turret.

On Nemesis DCIC battle map they witnessed Imperial ships chase loyalist fast attack ships and carriers. Their ships making sharp turns ahead of the minefields. The larger imperialist support ships realizing too late to avoid the mines as smaller ships blew apart around them. The devastation instant and horrifying. Loyalist fighters swarmed the few Imperialist ships who raced out to supposed safety. Imperialists left less than one-sixth of their screening ships to cover their fleets of capital ships and remaining Dreadnaughts. Odds now favored the Loyalist.

The Loyalist destroyer, Skeneksoian, closest to the enemy, turned to attack. On his own initiative, Knight Barashakushu steered his outclassed ship into the Imperial carrier the Cephius at full speed. Fired ten starburst missiles at the heavy battlecruiser Dark Diwas, damaging her enough to force her to fall back out of the line, protecting the Cephius. Seeing this, Ryakin ordered, "all screening ships follow the Skeneksoian," sending the rest of the squadron into the fray. The eightieth sent twenty destroyers to attack with desperate determination, drawing fire and disrupting the Imperialist formation as ships turned to avoid their starburst and Star Fury missiles.

Enemy ships continued to attack the Farr, and the Eitill took massive hits, both drifting off silent and dark. Detritus and burning atmosphere trailing behind them. After spending every torpedo, the Skrof continued to fight with its griffins until silenced by a group of twenty destroyers who converged upon him. Ryakin ordered sixteen of his escort carriers in his three task units to launch their shadowers, equipped with whatever weapons loaded. Even if these were only small griffins or scatter burst bombs. Collectively, ten wings of shadowers from the carriers at Ryakin's disposal. Although these were older models, such as the Ritins and Xicatha class, their close-range missiles and griffin railguns still caused extensive damage.

The Eewoiian, one of Ryakin's heavy battlecruisers off Nemesis middle starboard, exploded, hit by three Imperial destroyers. Nemesis's gunnery crews took out two. The third hit by debris from the one next to it slammed into their side, exploding. Nemesis shuddered hard from the impact. Smoke and flames poured through corridors while sirens wailed, and blast doors slammed shut, cutting off crews. Automated fire and smoke systems kicked on, and emergency decompression shields covered the damage. Replicator nanites tubes spewed out temporary repair hull sealant.

"Send emergency engineering teams to deck eighty," EC Kurid ordered.

Three of Ryakin's task force ghosters exploded, hit by stray missiles streaking around as they engineered false signatures. Knight Commander Vizlos order the rest to move away from the battle groups. Losing the three ghosters allowed the enemy close by to acquire scanner locks, no longer blinded. Knight Commander Vizlos called for the eightieth capitals to fall back, along with his screening ships, as he moved one of his ghosters to cover a larger sector. The effectiveness though decreased, this the best he could accomplish while maneuvering his fleet to the fallback position.

Ten loyalist screening destroyers vanished in seconds across the battle map. Fifty cruisers and two carriers from the 90th flickered, becoming brilliant expanding white spot on the holo. A loyalist cruiser spun out of formation, shields, and propulsion systems damaged, other ships close, frantic to maneuver clear of its path.

Ryakin appeared impassive. However, each loss ate at him. Seconds later, the Sul dreadnought headed straight for Nemesis. Before long they were exchanging broadsides in dueling passes, filling deepspace between them with missiles, railguns munitions, plasma trails, and black daemon sapper drones. The screening ships battling around them. A few found targets, the kinetic weapons absorbed by a fast flurry of covering energy shields. Each side weakening from the sappers as exterior hull drones worked with alacrity to destroy the attached sappers on hulls.

Five plasma hits strafed across the bow of Nemesis. The shields almost depleted yet holding. A heavy battlecruiser blew apart, identified as the Hiotia caught between Nemesis gunnery crews. The Hiotia's mistake was getting in reach of Nemesis deadly griffins. Still, the Hiotia got revenge with a direct hit before dying. Its bombs ripped into the ship's gunnery placement, spewing deadly shrapnel across the internal weapons on deck ten, killing the entire gunnery crew.

Plasma cannons from the Sul broke through weakened shields, opening eight holes in a straight line on the outer hull. None punched through the resilient outer skin to the inner bulkheads. Nemesis's damaged hull outer layers got an instant reaction from the replicator nanites tubes. The cold of deepspace immediately solidified the material to form a hard-temporary shell. The process the same as a biological body heals a wound. For the ships, a liquid mix of composite crystalline metallic nanite matter.

Across the battlefield, small and medium fast attack ships pounded the enemy with continuous fire between the fleets, dreadnoughts, and carrier's as they passed each other exchanging broadsides. Each side using fast attack fighters taking out firing towers and black daemon sappers. Or hoping to manage a lucky shot before their shielding engaged to cover the hull.

Interceptors and whale bombers, protected by shadowers, scanned for high-value targets. Outer deflectors, dishes or an array's shield towers, as they swarmed over the ships like insects around a herdbeast in the hot season. Launching Firestorms missiles or tactical nuclear bombs.

Knight Elgar pointed to the one sixty-second's dreadnought, the Star Shine in desperate need of cover. Damaged too bad to fight back against the Thrall and ten heavy cruisers and a half a wing of Raven interceptor bombers moving in for the kill.

"Star Shine, retreat to the channel. We will cover you."

"Acknowledged." Knight Commander Kepshar said. The Star Shine limped away, chased by enemy ships, their scanners missing the Nemesis group heading to intercept. Once they were within five hundred standards, Ryakin order every plasma cannon to open fire. The Thrall never knew what hit them.

One of the plasma beams broke through its weakened shield, shredding the ship's thick hull like it didn't exist. They got in a lucky hit, taking out the Thall's power plants. A moment later, he vanished in a massive explosion, a gravitational shockwave spreading outwards. Its surrounding screening ship engulfed in an instant, few escaping the devastation.

Ryakin turned his attention back to the holo-map. Halfway across the battlefield four Imperialist carriers, two Dreadnaughts, and four battleships flickered and vanished, engulfed when the loyalist dreadnought Airfyn exploded. The dreadnought Raemur of the ninetieth burst through the debris, followed closely by her screening ships. Knight Commander Raius, thinking fast, saved them by extending his shields around his smaller screening ships. Smaller Imperialist vessels further out who survived unscathed made a fast retreat to regain formation with the only remaining carrier of the Imperialist sixty-fifth fleet.

A massive invisible heat storm tornado, caused by the battle, tore through space, striking Nemesis before they were aware one existed. The ship shook violently as the internal artificial gravity field tried to compensate for the disruptive forces. For a moment Ryakin thought Nemesis would tear itself apart trying to compensate. Lights flashed as bridge stations dimmed, and the floor rocked forcefully under him. Their holo-map and scanners blinked out. Seconds later, the lights stabilized, and the battle map holo station projections came back. As it did, they spotted two battleships closing on them.

The heat tornado tore through the Imperialist ships as they opened fire. Rotated towards each other by the powerful tornado. Both fell victim to the other's fire, falling back once they regained control as the tornado passed. Out of range of Nemesis, they warped away, too damaged to stay and fight. Nine cruisers and five destroyers and a few interceptors caught in the heat tornado's edge applied full power, trying to outrun Nemesis before he reached weapons range. Information incoming from headquarters to the loyalist fleet saved them.

"Commander, the last transport ship of the evacuation has skipped. We're ordered to disengage all actions and retreat. Now."

Ryakin called out the order, "disengage and fall back. I repeat. Disengage and fall back."

"Acknowledge," responses came over the general battle-net, from the ships still functional.

Ryakin gave the order for the Ai's starting their plan. "Give over control to Ai's and implement Fleets End. Repeat. Implement Fleets End. Ignore all Imperial forces attempting to engage."

Something never did before on the battlefield as the Ai's implemented a handshaking protocol between the ships linking their warp and skip engines. This allowed grouping of the retreating ships the ability to warp, then skip out together.

Knight Asalluh Nemesis helms officer took manual control of the ship. The ship shuddered as he applied too much power to a section of the thrusters before throttling back a cringed look on his face.

The live feed displayed each group as they disappeared into warp. Ryakin's tension eased a little each time.

"Nemesis spins up our warp engines. Once the last ship clears, the channel engage warp, not before." Officer Asalluh struggled with the controls for several more moments while simultaneously checking readouts and maintaining helm. He appeared nervous, Ryakin figured most did not manually take the helm for warp without an Ai's help since the academy. They regarded the tattered remains of the eightieth and the ninetieth as they moved into the channel under heavy fire and warped away with no further losses.

Fifty-two carriers and their screening ships of Ryakin's seventy-ninth turned toward the mouth of the channel, retreating through fire and missiles, their shields holding.

The carrier Eye of Krefira, at the rear of the formation, became the focus of the dreadnoughts, the Syiru, Tir, and Utan. He sustained multiple hits before decompression blasts tore his sides out and the Eye of Krefira went dark. Two other carriers took damage from the starboard explosion yet still escape into the channel along with the Silver Daemon. The Imperialist learned their lessons the hard way earlier and fell back as she reached the semi-safety of the inner mouth of the channel. Three loyalist dreadnoughts covering her retreat, making the area too hot for the enemy.

Ryakin took Nemesis in close to the Eye of Krefira for rescue operations. He examined the display as internal fires burned and explosions ripped the ship to pieces section by section, escape pods blasting away ahead of the damaged sectors.

"Send collector drones over. We will hold off any incoming ships from here as we retrieve the pods," he said as scanner crews noted the cores ejected safely.

Something caught Knight Elgar's attention and Ryakin realized what a second later. The leading edge of a ship rising behind the dying carrier. Seconds later, the backside lit up as plasma streaks tore through the port side. The Eye of Krefira's aft section decompressed instantaneously, taking out escape pods as a quarter section of the ship blew outward. The heavy Imperial cruiser Spikohau rose over the destroyed hull, its shields on full force.

"Brace for impact!" Ryakin shouted. Seconds later, the ship shuddered around him, and something hit him hard in the head. A gush of warm liquid poured down the side of his face. A sharp bitter scent of electrical fire mingled with vital ship fluids filling the chamber with the smoky scent. The horrifying crackle and intense heat blasted him as plasma fire raced through burning bridge equipment. Those caught in the flames roiling in agony.

The warp bubble finished forming, forcing them into warping out microseconds after the Spikohau got off a direct hit to the bridge. They could not stop warp at this point. Two minutes into warp they skipped.

Nemesis engaged the shields to the bridge as he did. Spiderdrones flooded the bridge, ignoring screaming writhing officers as they went about attending to their job of repairing the ship's battle bridge. Life drones rushed to the injured, working fast to place them in repair units. The units placed the injured in suspended animation before they whisked them off the bridge. Half the crew disappeared into repair units in a blink of an eye, whisked away by the life drones.

Wiping blood free from his eyes, Ryakin called out, "Nemesis, can you control our exit speed with this damage?"

If they did not stop in time, they'd come out of skip too fast and hit the leading wall of the gravitational pull of the local vortex. For an undamaged ship, if they applied the braking thrusters and made a hard turn starboard or port as they came out of skip, no problem. For a brutally damaged ship, the maneuver would be harder to execute, as they may not have enough thrusters to maneuver. The vortex a natural phenomenon in this location. The tension on the bridge increased at Nemesis's answer.

"Sixty-three percent chance." Seconds passed before they exited and slewed too fast towards the vortex. The tugs, though, were prepared and set gravitational nets to help slow their forward speed. Nemesis plowed through three of them before slowing and going to drift speed.

Tugs moved off, dragging them to the temporary dock. Ryakin gazed out at the field of ships which survived the battle. Torn flapping ring accelerators bobbed up and down. Ships drifting or spinning without control as tugs, life and resurrection ships, raced towards them. Smoke poured out from holes, trapped between the shields, and hulls the smoke slid beneath the bright shimmer of emergency shields. Shipwright tugs loaded with repair drones worked in an efficient and quick manner.

A third of the ships he started in battle with missing in action or destroyed.

Chapter 29

335893 GGS Goem 10th.
Sabation Planet Under Attack–Chief Paladin Cer Tavas Tz^a*Seaborn^c

AS THEY EXITED THE tunnel, earsplitting explosions assaulted him, and the ground trembled beneath his feet in response. The agitated sensation of the shifting sand added to the other escaping slave's nervousness. Debris rained around them in a vast circle as the shield overhead gave protection from the deadly showers. Inside the protective bubble, calm reigned. Outside, the raging storm swarmed around the shield, attempting to batter its way inside.

The shields extended only far enough to encompass the frigate and ramp, the generator, and the hyper core injection casing and the mouth of the tunnel entrance. *Not much space to do outer preflight checks.* Tavas assessed Ossa for deceit. He did not trust her. Something seemed off about her. Not only because she was Sabation. Tavas, during his time spent amongst them, learned to read their body language. Her body language reminded him of those who connive and lie. Jynnalt never was an excellent judge of character. She lacked the ability to recognize those who practiced deceit regularly. This, to him, was always her worst weakness.

"Tiarn, Keif, Aidral, check the outer hull systems, afterward join us on the bridge," Tavas said. He followed the others up the ramp, stopped, taking one last look back. Outside the shield was an unsettling haze of brown. Dark grotesque shapes showing through now and then; illusions of the storm. To Tavas, the storm represented this world. He hated this desert, its citizens, and creatures from the first time he stepped upon the plateau. His hatred grew each turn. Forced to fight and kill for the pleasures of a crowd. No honor, no reason. Pure, animalistic survival. Even amongst their own, their culture and customs brutal.

For now, the shield appeared strong enough to hold back flying debris within the storm. Inside the ship, the howls of the storm decreased to a haunting moan when they entered the bridge. Tavas jumped into one of the four seats at the half circle-shaped consul before a viewing window. The symbols resembled the graffiti Tavas first spotted in the city. He bet these also Sabation.

He glanced up and regarded Jynnalt staring out the viewscreen. Storm lightning blending with the enemies' plasma flashes, impossible to tell one from the other. He caught glimpses of fighters swarming over the city and outlying desert. The ship's bridge was ten stories off the ground at the top level of the frigate. Obscured by the sandstorm, the city and outlying desert.

A stony expression on her face as she stared out. She lacked the hatred he expected to see. He realized she hid her thoughts, unlike when they first arrived. Before the cruelty and brutality of the Sabations games. Before fighting in the unholy killing grounds of the arena. He prayed the good in her not destroyed by what they forced her to do in the games. Twice she defied them. She refused to do their bidding and kill her opponent once, defeated and unarmed. Each time, the Warlord reluctantly spared her and her opponent. In those moments, he saw the iron strength of her. Prayed the Phoenix Armor still stood vigil, declaring her worthiness.

Tavas turned back to the controls, paying attention to every move Ossa made while trying to decipher what he viewed as graffiti before him. Intent on not missing what she was doing as she initiated the startup sequence with her codes before stepping back.

When she spoke to Jynnalt, he understood nothing, which frustrated him. He did not kill Ossa here and now because he swore an oath to serve Jynnalt. She declared Ossa under her protection. His oath tied to his honor. That part of himself he kept. He never gave up trying to save her and escape to go home. Home to his wife and children. When captured, he was too old and nanite bound to change. Dishonor worse than death. Much longer in the games and he might have fallen upon his sword.

Jynnalt being able to understand this Sabation piece of *sheat* puzzled him. Once he'd never believe he could so hate a species or race. Now darkness stained his soul. Jynnalt turned towards him at the sound of Ossa's guttural tones. He stared at the console, not wanting her to discover his shame. His hatred of Ossa and what she represented to him. Slavery, brutality, cruelty, and arrogance.

"She says she cannot do anything more; Sabations do not teach females to fly. Besides, they expected her father's warriors to be here with her. However, only the immediate family holds the ignition codes."

The lights flickered off and back on. The moan of the storm turned to a howling rage as an influx of wind buffeted and rocked the ship. Keif called up from the outer ramp's wireless. "Hey, the shield flickered off for a moment. A ton of sand poured in around the frigate. Keif grabbed one of the ramp stanchions before getting blown away."

"The ramp protected Tiarn and me," Aidral said.

Ossa spoke in rapid-fire towards Jynnalt, who translated.

"She is saying her father, angry with a slave for suggesting the need for more generators, claimed no one can attack during a sandstorm it'd be suicide. He executed the man for attempting to waste the clan's resources and for arguing with him."

"Explains a lot," Tavas said as he turned back to the ship's controls. "Murder the one who is the expert because you're an arrogant savage. If we don't have enough power during a critical phase and the generator kicks off, it will force us to start over. If the generator blows from an overload, we're stuck."

"We can hide here till the storm weakens, then head back towards the landing zone we arrived at. I believe three turns walk from here," Kendo said, intent on the controls, examining Tavas and what he did. Like Tavas, he waited for Jynnalt to translate the symbols as Ossa explained them to her.

Sweat popped out on his brow. Shields and lights flickered off and on three more times. Tavas prayed to the gods and daemons both. Whoever answered was fine with him. If they answered.

He listened to a rapid-fire exchange between Ossa and Jynnalt.

"She says the control panel is hard-wired to the ship. There is no haptic interface. And no Ai to calculate the skips. The Sabations view Ai's as daemons. We will have to depend on the computer for calculations."

Tavas's hobby in his younger sars, Star yacht Razing. They allowed no Ai's. Skip calculations by computer were nothing new to him. For the next ten minutes, Jynnalt explained what Ossa told her. To him, even though in Sabation, the controls still followed standard frigate galactic controls and procedures. He suspected they stole the ship and overlaid the Sabation symbols. As soon as he figured the sequence out, he understood how the controls worked.

As experienced pilots, none of them took long to grasp the meanings. The lights still flickered, but the power to the core was steady and rising. Tavas relished the feel of a physical control stick. They reminded him of happier times as an adolescent male.

The other three finished the preflight checks on the outer hull equipment and joined them on the bridge. Tavas explained what each control was and what they did. He moved over to the bridge's translucent metal viewing window. He listened as Jynnalt told the others where she wanted them.

She pulled up the schematics of the ship and pointed out where three of the ship's cannons and weapons chairs were on the frigate.

"Be alert. The storm will hide an enemy heading our way, on foot or in ships, till the last moment."

Her voice held the strength of command, lacking before this ordeal. Tavas, not sure he changed for the better. Not sure he could overcome the darkness now within. Too self-honest to lie to himself.

"The ground ladar and sensors will not function well during the storm. Listen for enemy ships. The ships will let off a deep, thrumming pulse from their anti-gravity engines. You will hear the sound over the sandstorm. That will be an incoming fighter. You won't have time to zero in, just fire in the general direction." They bowed their heads before leaving.

Tavas caught movement out of the corner of his eye in the

sandstorm. Someone exited the tunnel. He was sure.

Someone other than Ossa possessed information of this ship's location.

The others paid little attention when he said he would check on those below. Except Jynnalt. She stared at him a moment, grabbed her sword, and stepped to his side.

They entered the bridge tube while Kendo coaxed the engines to life without overtaxing the single generator.

"Wait," Kendo said, as he rose from his seat.

Tavas stopped the door from sliding shut.

"Jynnalt, you stay here and bring the engines online. Tavas and I can stand sentry after checking on the others. We can't afford a roving band of warriors searching for escapees from the city to find us in case the generator blinks at the wrong moment."

"No." The command sharp and swift. "Tavas and I often fought together in the arena. We fight well together and know each other's moves." Jynnalt softened her voice, saying, "We need those engines online and you're already half through the process."

Tavas shook his head. Kendo hesitated before sitting. He would not have Jynnalt's newfound command undermined.

Jynnalt turned to Ossa and told her to come with them and find a seat with the others. He was uncomfortable when Ossa stepped into the tube. Jynnalt released the door, which slid shut.

As soon as they arrived in the passenger compartment, he said, "I'm heading to the ramp."

Jynnalt nodded, not paying full attention. "Be right with you."

He stepped to the ground from the bottom of the ramp, scrutinized for ominous forms in the storm. From here, he examined the shadowy forms of fighters swooping in and out over the beleaguered city. The sandstorm giving the plasma bolts an eerie afterglow. A burst of brilliant blue-white lighting arched overhead, allowing him an instant snapshot of the city in the distance through the sand. The enemy fighters blew an immense hole in the outer wall for three-quarters of a standard.

Beyond, buildings loomed with gaping wounds and tangled pylons. Stark witness to violent assault. Vague shapes of vehicles lying on their sides or on their tops, crumpled as if thrown around by a giant's tantrum. Fractured service pipes in a jagged array out of the ground, the broken bones of the city. Craters pocket marked the causeways and alleyways from bombs.

Jynnalt joined him as the tortured city landscape lit up once more. She shuddered, and anguish crossed her face. He realized with sudden insight she mourned the innocents, even the Sabations. He gazed back at the city, his eyes blurred, and a weight lifted long hanging over him. His fear, Jynnalt, would become twisted and hate-filled, which did not happen. Jynnalt, through all the suffering, kept her decency. This ordeal did not break her. A true queen. He should have trusted the Phoenix Armor.

Movement caught his attention to his left. A black shape appeared and disappeared in the sands. The movement did not appear to be panicked slaves trying to escape during the chaos of battle. *Maybe a war band heading this way.*

Tavas motioned to drop and stayed put. Alert, waiting. Both tense.

Moments later, he noted the pained expression on her face. He grasped why. If the generator stuttered, it'd expose them. If the patrol walked into the shields, they still were in trouble.

"I'll check if they came back around. Stay here." Tavas gave her a stern expression before heading to the other side of the frigate.

After glancing around, he headed back and shook his head, showing he spotted nothing.

Jynnalt cried out, "behind you,"

He spun. He caught a flash of gray temple robes. Instinctively dropping into a fighting stance. His opponent hit him hard from the side. He fought, grappling with him to the ground. Tavas came up to his knee's fast. A sar of fighting for his life in the pits honed his senses and his skills; formidable before fighting in the ring. His opponent movements like a Ghost Walker. He could tell from his eyes he'd give no quarter his body language spoke volumes of his intention to kill Tavas. They circled each other, both respectful of the other's skills. This must be who followed them out through the hidden doorway. Who Kendo appeared aware of his presence.

The sound of the vibration of the thrumming antigrav engines as a fighter scoured the surrounding area, searching for escapees coming in fast. Bright flashes of lightning streaked overhead. Above him a blaze of white-blue streaks blinded him, the rapid staccato of griffins shook the ground under him, the roar deafening overhead.

The shield failed. The raging storm yanked him and his opponent apart moments before something slammed into him.

Next thing he grasped was Kendo and the others yelling. The sound close, yet far away at the same time. He was having trouble piecing together what was happening. Sounds of steps by his head and not on the ground confused him. Oppressive weight on the bottom half of his body restricting his breathing caused him to panic.

The sound of lifting and scraping noise. Followed by intense pain ripping through him. He screamed, opening his eyes. He understood his circumstances as soon as he did. A crashed blackraptor fighter destroyed by the Griffin's rapid-fire pinned him, trapping him beneath the wing. Only the upper half of his body from his waist up was free.

Kendo kneeled next to him. He felt the sting of an injection in his neck. His body relaxed. Relief for a moment slid through him. "I can't give you much. You are losing too much blood. We are trying to find something to leverage the wreckage and pull you out."

Before he lay back, the vision arose in his head of Jynnalt thrown through the air before everything went dark.

"Where's Jynnalt?" The despair in Kendo's eyes alarmed him. He frantically glanced around, his heart Razing as Keif kneeling over something caught his attention. "Jynnalt."

Keif said loud enough for the others to hear, "she is unconscious; so far the scanner found a concussion and a nasty sprain in her shoulder along with a lot of bruising."

He forced himself to stay calm. Tavas called over the other paladins, "move her inside. Take her off this gods-forsaken planet with or without me. Let me speak to Kendo alone for a moment." The other three paladins lifted her and moved her into the frigate.

Tavas grimaced, trying to get comfortable, an impossible feat.

"Kendo, you must do whatever is necessary if she comes around to keep her on the ship. If you don't, she will try to save me. You and I can't let that happen." He grabbed Kendo's arm. "Promise me. You put her on the frigate and take her away from here."

"I promise, though we have not given up on getting you out from under the wing," Kendo said.

Tavas foresaw the futility of the situation in Kendo's eyes. "Do your best, but don't sacrifice the others for me." They both recognized the truth.

"The city is still under attack. The ship still powering up. We have time. I believe the fighter got lost in the sandstorm," Kendo said

Thirty minutes of struggling, they realized they were not getting Tavas out from under the wing. They needed heavy equipment and life tenders on hand if they did. So did Tavas. It was in their eyes.

Jynnalt's voice, weak, came from the frigate's doorway, demanded what they were doing.

Too late to keep her from discovering the truth. He nodded to the others, saying, "Please, stop. I want time to speak with Jynnalt." His eyes pleaded with Kendo. "Please, I beg you, give me this time to say goodbye." He fell back, his voice weak. Kendo motioned for them to stop work and move away. Tavas scrutinized Ossa as she helped Jynnalt down the ramp. When they reached the bottom, Jynnalt spotted him trapped and broke away, stumbling his direction.

He held out his hand. She staggered over, dropping to her knees, and grabbed it. Her hands trembling. His throat tightened as a tear slid down her face.

"I want you close for a moment. You've always been like a daughter. I am proud of who you are. You became all I hoped for. Not as a Queen. But as the citizen you became. I know your heart aches from the loss of your son. I believe he is alive and well. Riders keep no slaves. There must be another reason they bought him and the others."

Jynnalt sat close, saying nothing. Her face soaked in tears while precious moments passed and the storm quieted.

Blood trickled from the corner of his mouth and lined his lips as the pain crept back. The earlier injection wearing off, yet he needed to tell her something, and he did not want another injection as Kendo moved towards him.

"Listen Jynnalt."

She leaned closer.

"Do not let the darkness of what happened here consume you... Almost did me. The hatred would have taken away that which I cherish. My soul. My honor. Hatred replacing it. I perceive this now. Do not punish innocents for the deeds of the wicked and brutal. Punish those who deserve it. You must promise me this." Tavas' eyes locked on hers.

Jynnalt kissed his cheek. His hand tightened on hers as she promised.

He forced a smile as his other hand rested on the wing. Through his agony, the sound of her sobs cut deep.

After a moment, she took a deep breath and sat back, rubbing the tears from her face. "There has to be away."

There was a determination in her voice. Her eyes pleaded with him. "Don't give up. Once you're out from under the wing, the ship's life bay can sustain you till we find someplace with a resurrection vat. I bet we are only five skips out from the closest civilized empire."

"Shh... look at me, Jynnalt. They tried..." he labored hard to breathe. "You ... unconscious. I prayed... you would not regain... consciousness to spare you... this pain." He waited for a moment as his breath got stronger. "Tell Tiashari and my girls I never forgot them, thought of them every turn. Tell them I love them."

Now hard to breathe, forcing him to stop. Time for him like the sands in an overturned bottle running out. A deep freeze rose within him even as sweat poured off him. No one needed to tell him what this meant as a pool of blood formed beneath him. The pressure of the wing kept him from bleeding out too fast. He wanted her gone before that happened. His wife and daughters grew brighter in his mind. As he remembered Tiashari's soothing touch, her sorrow whenever he left home. The vision faded, and he realized Jynnalt's tears dropped on his face. He needed to warn her and gathered his strength. *Do not trust Ossa.* He did not know if she heard him, his voice a bare whisper. Yet he lacked the energy, for now, to speak.

Tavas prayed for Kendo to come back. He could not hold on much longer. Jynnalt's face glistened with tears, warming his cooling skin for a second. Tavas shifted his position, lava poured through his body. He gritted his teeth and grimaced, not wanting her to comprehend the pain and agony this small movement cost him.

He placed his hand on one side of her face. "When your father died, I tried to fill his shoes. You have been a daughter, not a job." With his thumb, he wiped at her tears. "Remember me." He earnestly whispered. His hand became too heavy to hold up and dropped to the sand.

She sobbed. "Forget you. Never. I promise to care for your wife and daughters. I swear by everything I hold sacred."

He took minutes to gather himself. His breath labored.

"Take this," he held out, his hand wavering weakly and trembling in her direction as he tried to put a small microchip into her palm.

Gently, she took it.

"Promise... me... deliver... Tiashari..." he trailed off. His breath more ragged. A burst of lightning shot through the dwindling storm clouds as the winds died off.

It lit the surroundings before fading out, leaving behind a vivid afterimage in her mind of the devastated and ruined fighter.

Jynnalt realized the futility of rescuing him, yet her eyes darkened, and determination lit them. She stood, walking around the wing.

Tavas understood how stubborn she was, how indomitable her spirit was. Even when others did not. She did not appreciate her own tenacity. The things he admired about her would keep her here to die with him. She'd fight to her last breath to save him; he would not allow her to sacrifice herself for him.

A tremendous explosion lit the sky from the city and seconds later, the ground trembled with a rumbling sound, causing the wing to shift, pinning him tighter.

The cockpit of the fighter high above exploded. Flames shot upwards and out of the jagged, broken holes. The outline of the pilot writhed for what seemed an eternity. He must have been alive, but unconscious. Moments later, the form hung halfway out of the cockpit, a blackened smoking ruin.

Fire tore through the fighter. The crackling pop and hisses from nearby sparks and embers as they blanketed the surrounding ground added to the danger.

"The ammunition exploded. I think," He said.

Jynnalt rushed to his side. A quiet sob escaped her. She understood the wing shifted for the worst.

"Jynnalt," his voice came out a bare whisper as she kneeled to take his hand.

"I am here. If you stay, I do," she was not seeing him. She stared at the wing pinning him in place.

"They... tried... can't... Stop acting... irrational," he said. He understood her panic and determination. This would be the second time someone important in her life died in her presence. Her essential need to stop the inevitable, like when he found her holding her father and smoothing back his hair with her small hand. Pleading with the gods to save him. He knew she could not stop his death, either.

In the distance, streaks of plasma fire shined through the lightly blowing sand as the storm lost its power and ferocity. He tightened his grip on her hand. Jynnalt stared back at him, tears streaking her face. The coppery taste of blood welling in the back of his throat told him the sands of his life were now only a few grains.

"We have time."

Tavas understood the lie and desperation in her voice as the tears flowed. "Please... don't... cry. Your... breaking.... my heart."

"I'm not crying." She swiped furiously at her face. "Sands in my eyes, making them water. I am not leaving you here," she said, and he perceived the fierce determination in her voice. He understood Jynnalt, tried to hold back her sobs and failed. "We'll get you out," she said as lightning burst across the storm outside the shield, showing every line of her agony to him. The sound of the ship's engines roared to life along with the growling startup of its lift-off antigrav engines.

"Listen Jynnalt, don't allow this to destroy you. Grieve, but don't let it consume you. You grieved too long for your father." He stopped for a moment to catch his breath. "Give me your promise." He waited for a moment.

Seconds passed before she leaned over and kissed him on the forehead before whispering, "I promise," she rested her forehead on his chest. Her tears mingling with his sweat and blood.

"Go," Tavas said. "You can't help."

She did not move, her head still resting on his chest.

"Jynnalt." He stopped, attempting to breathe. Blood filled his mouth once more, choking him. Tavas coughed and blood splattered across Jynnalt's hair and face. He monitored Kendo as he approached, the hypo needle hidden at his side. Relief flooded through him. Tavas nodded once, acknowledging the time arrived.

He knew Kendo. Understood the strength of will this took for him to do as Tavas requested. Jynnalt turned unbelieving towards him when she felt the sting of the injection. He viewed her eyes start to glass over as the drug took hold.

"Jynnalt," she turned her head slowly in his direction, "I am sorry," Tavas said, letting her know he made Kendo do this. Her eyes shimmered with tears, and the depth of her pain ate at him. Seconds later, the drug claimed her. Kendo lifted her crumpled unconscious form and strode to the ramp for a moment, glanced back, nodded at Tavas, and disappeared into the ship.

His upper limbs became heavier and the fear, agony, and pain disappeared. Peacefulness engulfed him as he felt his surroundings slipping away. Before the blackness took him, he detected a shimmer like heat waves in the desert at mid-turn next to him. A figure seemed to form within. Everything faded to nothing.

335893 GGS Goem 27th.
Planetary Anomaly Sabation sector–Queen Jynnalt

AS IF COMING OUT OF a black hole, she became semi-aware of her surroundings, a ceaseless roaring in her consciousness. She was lying on a hard-uneven surface, digging into her back. Cold seeping into her bones. How long she laid upon the ground eluded her, or even where she was. Somewhere close the subdued sound of crackling followed by a sudden hiss and pop. An odd odor assailed her. All at once, she realized what the smell was. Ozone and burning electrical mingled together with all the other ship's fluids. Her nose stung as the scent strengthened.

As soon as she tried to sit up, fiery throbbing throughout her body and head stopped her. She fell backward, her skull pounding fierce enough to rob her of thought as she shivered in the chill air. Various aches and sharp stabbing pains.

She opened her eyes. At first, hard to focus. A blurry image rose before her. After several moments, her eyesight cleared, and the image coalesced into a massive wall. Behind which a city climbed into the clouds clinging to the mountainside.

Smoke curled upward in tendrils off to her left. She glanced the direction and realized the ruined upper half of the frigate lay in a deep furrow. The wings now only stubs ripped off as they crashed through the forest treetops. Long control linkages trailed along the ground behind the bridge of the destroyed frigate. She remembered struggling to bring them in for a landing. An anomaly hit them as they exited skip. Plunging them down into its gravity well before they reacted.

Thirty yards away a curtain wall to a city bathed blood-red, the early rays of the star rising washed across it. The city behind the wall silent. No movement except for flyers rising or landing on various buildings. Stonework of lattice styled architectures and zigzagging causeways. She stared, trying to figure out exactly where the *helc* she was. The chill of the morning air forced a shiver out of her, and pain grated along her nerves like an aching tooth.

Roaring sounds came from the silvery cascade of waterfalls. They turned into a churning white mist as the waterfall fell from the high reaches to the next lower level in steps within the metropolis. The roar of the water, the noise which dragged her out of oblivion. The frigate dominated the surrounding grassy area, its nose and parts of its bridge section broken apart feet from the city's immense enclosure wall. She stood, ignoring the sharp pains as she tried to figure out where she was.

A moan drew her attention over to her right. Kendo sat up, his hand holding his ribs on his left side. She checked him out. Other than a possible cracked rib, he appeared okay. Helping him up, she glanced around for her paladins. They were on the bridge with her before the crash. Relief engulfed her when the three of them came hobbling around the superstructure's stanchions, heading their direction.

"Thank the gods," she said, unaware of how tense she was at the thought of losing more of her paladins.

Downhill from them on the vibrant green grasslands, the passenger and cargo section of the frigate lay on its side. On the horizon, the glimmer of fire and gray black-smoke rose skyward. Most likely where she blew the bolts to separate the engine and power plants from the rest of the ship.

Behind the passenger compartment, an alpine forest sloped further down the side of the mountain they crashed upon.

"Amazing, somehow, you landed us clear of the trees. Thought you'd take out half the forest when you came in so shallow."

Ignoring Kendo and his remark, she gazed at the gentle slope of what must have been grazing land in front of the city. She changed the topic. "Look," she pointed to where figures exited and wandered around the passenger compartment below, "Ossa and some others are already outside. Ossa pointing to places as the slaves exited the ship."

Off to her left, something fluttered. Turning, she spotted a life tender drone coming towards them, one of its arms flapping at each lunging step forward, the arm hanging by a filament. Halfway to her, the drone stopped, stalling out as sparks flew. Shrill clacks and clicks filled the air.

"The first casualty of the crash," Kendo said, walking towards it, "shame I bet we will need them. I hope at least one life tender drone survived in the passenger section."

"Wait here. I will scavenge what I can from the bridge. Afterward, we'll head downhill to the others. Ossa appears to have the situation in hand. For now." She glanced that way once more before sparks erupting from the consoles high above caught her attention.

"Be careful," Kendo said with his normal worried visage before glancing up at the arcs sparking across what the crash left of the bridge as she climbed the frame.

She found a medical kit. The heavy pack aggravated her injuries. Yet she ignored the pain. Something she learned when fighting. Survival's painful. She figured what they might need and dropped the items below before climbing out. The five of them joined the others down the hill.

The major passenger's section's crash gel saved the passengers except for a female Dakitian and two males of unknown origins. Ex-slaves, pit fighters and Ossa were helping the rest out before they climbed back in for supplies and meds. They found a life tender drone, functional but trapped inside, unable to climb the emergency exit ladder and too heavy for the others to lift. They also discovered one food replicator in working order.

Most found clothes stuffed in a container. The oddity being they were not Sabation; they represented every conceivable alliance or federation in the Council of Nine. Made from the finest cloth. Jynnalt spied eight battle uniforms, nanite cubes with the Sigils of Iallful, and ten with the Purian Sigil from the inner Anunnaki Kingdoms. Most likely stolen. She grabbed one of the Iallful cubes. Proper nanite armor. She found a nanite booth in a different container. Struggled to set the booth upright, then stepped inside. Three minutes later she stepped out in full nanite uniform, helmet, boots, pants, shirt, wristbands, and full cloak of Iallful and winced, wishing for a Kierian one.

Her paladins were doing the same. Many pit fighters avoided the nanite cubes, unsure what they were until Tiarn showed them how to open them and use the booth. Soon they were digging around for their own.

Tiarn called over to her, "have you seen how many things are from the Anunnaki empire?"

"Ossa? How come there are so many empires different clothing" Jynnalt asked, pulling out a nanite cube for one of the ring fighters. She realized the corner damaged and threw it back in.

"They designed this vessel for our families escape and as we might have to take refuge in the outer galaxy, these clothes were to help us blend in. At least till my father regrouped and took his revenge on his enemies." Tears filled Ossa's eyes and her lips trembled.

Jynnalt gave her time to collect herself. For the Warlord, she held no sympathy. But Ossa protected her, was kind when she might have been cruel. She turned towards the paladins, still going through the clothing.

What they did not take for themselves, they placed in a pile for others in the camp.

"Kendo, there's nanite armor over there. Do you know how to use it?"

"Yes, though I will warn you, I am not a warrior." He shrugged. "I'm proficient enough."

"The slaves with us. Do you know how many were born one?"

Aidral answered before anyone else. "About a third, I think." He rubbed the back of his neck. "I found most languages easy. Learned about ten. Some, though, were beyond my physical abilities to recreate the sounds, but I understood what they said. Sabation one of those beyond my capabilities. I found languages fascinated me about how different they sounded without a translator. Fuller, richer, with more nuances."

"They have little information about normal civilization. Translators, nanites and so on. Sabation's forbid them knowledge of such things. Though arrivals like us did, you know what happened if we tried to teach them," Keif said, glancing around, not wanting any others to overhear. "If we find a way back. Where are they going to fit in?"

Jynnalt glanced over at him. "I will guarantee we care for them for."

"Before anyone decides their fate, maybe they should make their own choice." Keif walked to where she stood. "Being enslaved taught me how precious our freedoms are. Let's not deny them freedom to choose. Let them decide."

"I believe you are right. Still, they will need advice and information, so they won't regret their decision later." Seeing a dagger encased in a decorative Kierian sheath, she picked the sheath up and slid the blade halfway out. Kierian metasteel. She slid the blade in the sheath, glanced at the Sigil's markings. A fish half in and half out of three wavy lines for water, the house of Ahikilim. She stuffed the knife through her belt and changed the subject to one more at hand. "They seem to have raided Ki's sphere of influence a lot from the number of items here compared to others," she said as they went back to work.

"This was the Warlord's personal frigate. He took the best quality goods. Speaks volumes about Kierian production in my mind and less who they raided the most."

The rest of the midturn, they worked together to remove the life tender drone. They rigged a sling between them and hoisted it out to those waiting below in the impromptu camp. They set the drone to treating the children and females' injuries suffered in the accident first. Three hours later, the drone finished with the last of them and started to treat fighters and Jynnalt and her paladins. Kendo declared he required a pain killer nothing more.

"One tender out of four is more acceptable than nothing." Kendo said to no one in particular. He checked the supplies they loaded the tender with and calculate on average how long their supplies of medicinal aid might last. Six months at best, two or three at worst.

The earlier chill gave way to warmth as the star rose high above the horizon. Taking whatever protein bars and water canisters they found, they split amongst those working. Sweat ran in rivulets down her side, and her hands became clammy with the work. Blisters rose in spots from the long hours of strenuous exertion, getting necessary supplies hoisted up and out of the four stories to the escape hatch. Looking around, she figured they stripped everything useful for their immediate survival. She ordered them to hoist out the last item and join the others in their encampment. Next turn, they would check again to make sure they missed nothing.

As she exited, a brisk breeze cooled her sweaty face and set the purple, red and golden yellow leaves quivering throughout the surrounding forest. From her vantage point, she stared at the stunning vista before her. In the distance jagged icy mountains covered in whitefall redden by the now sinking star, their peaks disappearing high into the clouds. Far below, a hazy mist flowed like a river in a deep valley. Now and then giving her a peek at the distorted leafless trees and barren ground before once more disappearing under the thick mist.

The shadows lengthened and stretched as the star sank behind the twin peaks of the mountain on which the city rose before them.

She glanced towards the wall, soaring upward. The broken bridge of the frigate still smoking to the left of the massive closed barred gates. She glanced to her right, hoping she might find a breach somewhere making entry possible to enter the city. Nothing. *Drog, shame, the compartment landed sideways, otherwise, the hull would make excellent shelter.* The ex-slaves could not climb four stories to enter and exit with so many females and children. Climbing down to the camp below, Jynnalt saw a flash of light which caught her attention. She climbed back up and transformed her nanite suit into battle armor, taking advantage of the built-in long-range vision. Seconds later, with the enlarger imager, she spotted a small imperceptible door in the wall.

"Hey, guys, I see a doorway in the wall off to our right. Let's do a quick recon of the area. Might be we can slip into the city through there. I do not want to stay exposed out here longer than we must. Keif, Tiarn, Aidral, and Kendo with me."

"The rest stay here and prepare to move as much as you can in case we find a way inside. Those fighters who have weapons guard the women and children."

She wondered about the wisdom of leaving Ossa with them. "Ossa, maybe you should come with us." Jynnalt gazed at the fighters. Ossa glanced around and saw the ex-slave fighters armed and got the point, nodded, and joined up with them. Ten minutes after they got closer to the wall, Ossa's shook hard.

"What's wrong?" For a second, Jynnalt thought she would not answer. Something slithered away from the wall in the tall grasses, catching her attention till the sound disappeared in the distance.

"The miasma in this entire systems sector is impenetrable to our scanners. Long ago, when we took refuge in this nebula, our scouts attempted to investigate every world and planet exploring for those habitable to settle. The ones who came here," she took a deep breath, and her shaking eased a little, "They never came back. Sars passed and Warlords kept sending scouts..." she paused before going on, "to never be seen again. Except for one. He claimed daemons lived here. He died turns later after arriving back with his clan. His body dissolved into a green and black puddle of liquid. I'm telling you, this city's cursed."

Taking the threat to heart, Jynnalt told the others, "We know nothing about the fauna. Let's take no chances, go to battle armor, and engage comms. Ossa, walk between us." She pulled the gauss rifle she took earlier from the supplies around to her chest, giving her quick access. Other weapons built into the suit would appear at a thought through the suit's cyberware. The feeling once more of being in battle armor, with effective modern weapons, calmed her nerves. The suit fully loaded, the systems in working order.

Whatever they scared away from the wall her thermal's saw was a long, oddly shaped body as wide around as she was tall, still fleeing fast for the tree line. No other creatures fled before them. Five minutes later, they reached the door. Tiarn grabbed the small handle and pulled with the strength of the battle suit, expecting the door rusted shut. He fell backward, landing on his arse when it opened with ease. She held back a guffaw of laughter. The others not so kind as belly laughter from them rang out in the quiet settings. Keif and Trian, she doubted, would let him forget anytime soon. He rose and dusted the dirt off, giving the others a dangerous look. Kendo ignored him and moved to examine the hinges.

Screams filled the air, coming towards them fast.

"Ossa, stay by the door, keep it open. Get everyone through fast."

Ossa nodded and swallowed convulsively, her eyes huge.

They dashed past those Razing towards them as they topped the slope. Behind those running past them were giant insects. The insects lanced two of the males with front barbed appendages, who were defending the females and children, Razing uphill.

The spear-like appendages went through the nanite armor as if normal cloth, the slaves unaware of its shield capabilities and how to engage them. "Cover," they dropped to a knee and fired. Their familiarity with the weapons effective enough to take out the leading creatures swarming their direction as a burst of thousands of rounds disseminated the leading insects. Others stopped to devour their own dead, buying those fleeing time.

The stragglers and defenders both rushed past the five of them, Razing for the door. "Grenades." A launcher appeared on her rifle, and she fired. Gore and body parts of bugs blew into the sky as the five of them lobbed the swarm with explosives.

When the insects finished with the dead, they turned their attention on them once more. She was out of grenades. "Rapid-fire, retreat." Kendo tapped her shoulder; she stood and ran halfway towards the door then turned, kneeled, and fired, covering the next.

They did this in a leapfrog manner until they reached the wall and raced through to the other side. The sound of the thick door slamming behind her released her tension. After the fury of sound and chaotic action, the quiet calm on this side hit her with a sonic blast. She gazed around, stunned. A vast swath of grassland was between the outer wall and a shorter inner wall to the city proper. Bedded down for the night was a pasture full of herdbeast and split hooves as far as she could see. Soft, quiet mooing mixed with bleating and bahahas upon their arrival from various species of herdbeast.

The sound of a splash to her right caught her attention. Ripples of silvery light moved across the surface. Her helmet melded into the shoulders of the armor, refreshing air cooling her face.

Exotic night-blooming flowers, intoxicating, alive, vibrant, mingled with familiar scents. The strong loamy odor of rich ground floated on the twilight's chill air. Punctuated by the soft calls of herdbeast disturbed by their frantic race through the doorway.

"Let's move further in and find someplace we can make a temporary camp. We can wait till morning star rise to check out the area. Find out who is here if anyone."

Ossa moved towards her. "We should stay out here. Avoid the city. When the warrior came back, the only thing he kept repeating were daemons and city. Nothing else." Jynnalt understood the city terrified her, but they would not survive long without proper shelter. She gazed at the looming city, dark and forbidding shapes rising high above them.

"Daemons or not, it's our only chance. Most of the gear we scavenge from the wreckage most likely destroyed and unusable. Our packs have basic survival gear for a few turns."

Campfires flared to life around them from fire starters in the various packs. "Get some sleep. First light comes early."

She stood sentry for the first half. A silvery moon high above before Keif came and relieved her. Muffled snores from around the campfire, along with the crackle and pop from glowing embers, and loud sounds from night insects eventually lulled her to sleep.

Restless dreams haunted her. In the beginning, she held her son in her arms, felt the softness of his skin against her face, the innocent clean scent of him. At one point she was at the beach with Ossa and Ryakin and his son, both of their white hair full of glimmering starshine. The dream changed. Now her son gazed up at her from the floor. Playing with toys Tavas carved for him while enslaved, he somehow smuggled to her. When her son stared up at her, his mischievous grin, and the crinkle around his eyes so like his father as to make her breath catch. Now, she stood somewhere, nowhere as gray fog encapsulated her, a place without sound, only a strange sensation she was alone. The faint sound of her son's helpless crying came to her, causing a frantic sense within her. She tried to call out to him yet could not, torn apart by his helpless crying. Now she stood in pitch blackness as grief, fear and terror crashed in on her as something shook her. She sat straight up, gasping for breath. Groggy, she stared up into a flat face with a large scar going from the top of his forehead and disappearing into his shirt. Three front teeth missing and the rest yellow or black. Without thinking, she recoiled from the fetid stench which poured from his mouth.

She rolled up to her side, hoping he did not detect her reaction. The turns dawn a soft lavender and gusting winds as high clouds scuttled overhead, Razing to other places at the demanding whims of the winds.

After everyone was up, including the children, she called a meeting. An hour later, she and the agreed-upon groups turned towards the city resolute.

Time to discover if daemons lived within or not.

Chapter 30

SHE ROSE FROM THE DISHEVELED camp bed in the tent she shared with Ossa and the other females, following a restless night of broken sleep. The screeching cries and screams from the forest on the other side of the wall invaded her dreams throughout the night, sending them in weird and unintelligible directions. She stepped into the only nanite booth left to them with the cubed nanites of her battle suit. She dressed in quick practiced movements before heading to the tent set up as a feasthall. Desperate for a strong cup of false Kalach before any food. Overhead, twinkling stars still filled the indigo sky. The horizon outlined in a thin band of gray behind the mountains in the far distance. The chill of the dawn making her shiver and her breath a mist.

Each time she went with the others to check the wreckage for things to salvage the broken treetops and shredded branches, a stark reminder of their arrival. Turns after their crash, and the first attack by the giant insects, Kendo, curious about them, realized when the star rose, they disappeared. He even took quick jaunts along with Keif outside the walls. Keif never left without wearing his armor, or without his grenade launcher and his gauss rifle. At first, Aidral and Tiarn covered them from the doorway. Nothing happened. All they heard was chirping flyers and the rustle of creatures in the forest, along with the soft hum of normal insects greeting them.

After ten turns, desperation set in as the little purified water available in the packs ran out. The lake waters unusable as they could not assess the water for impurities. Kendo and Jynnalt convince the rest to chance going back to salvage what they could from the wreckage.

No equipment was missing, and only a few pieces smashed. The ship's hull peeled back like a figiata fruit skin. Kendo surmised the insects must eat only flesh. The evidence pointed out by him as the bodies of those who died in the crash gone. By the second turn of salvaging, they got lucky.

They found the replicator, the control pad and power source still in working condition and undamaged. It took them two turns to retrieve the unit. They cautiously decoupled the hoses and moved the replicator along with its power source to the camp. Another two weeks of hauling the full storage canisters with a sars worth of food, water, and various supplies.

At the cockpit bridge, they found the emergency beacon flashing, its power indefinite. Little chance for help, unless they overcame whatever anomaly caused them to crash.

For now, their essential needs taken care of along with basic tents and blankets. So far, the turns weather mild. The nights, though, frigid. This took a toll on the youngest.

Ossa's stories left few ex-slaves wanting to move into the city. Jynnalt hoped to prove the city not as sinister or dangerous as she claimed before the cold season arrived. Over time, she convinced them to assign groups to search the ruins to discover the truth. Cover from the coming cold is more important than ghost stories.

"We have plenty of weapons and ammo. Our medical supplies, though, are a different story. We're running short of necessary antibodies for the dangers of this planet. With all but one of the life drones destroyed, we're in danger of catching a disease we cannot overcome." She said, explaining to the others her worries if they stayed camping outside as the cold season descended upon this planet.

She thought of how impatient she used to be to have to spend an hour in the acclimation center in orbit or dockside. Now the lack of such units worried her. The immunization units took care of exposure to new microbes throughout the galaxy in this way before disembarking to a natural planet or world. It gave foreign passengers protection against exotic biologicals to them, ground side.

Seven of the children were running high fevers. This spurred the others to agree to investigate. To see if they might find medical supplies from other shipwrecks.

Jynnalt's group assigned to look for supplies stashed in the city in places past survivors might have taken refuge.

Kendo inclined to hunt for meh's or information storage devices, which might lead to helpful medical fauna. He explained those are the bases of all medicines for each world or planet.

Kendo decided to search for the medical area's in the city. He told Jynnalt he hoped they were devices which did not deteriorate.

He rushed in, ready to start the exploration, forcing her thoughts back to the here and now. Any time something new or interesting appeared, Kendo showed up champing at the bit to check the area out. He ignored the fact there were deadly creatures outside the wall as he collected items to take back and study, while others kept him safe by standing guard.

"Didn't you, more than once, inform me that patience is a virtue? I remember being lectured more times than I can count by you on the issue, and I can count pretty high." She said, with a raised eyebrow to punctuate her point as he settled next to her on the wooden bench.

Kendo grabbed a piece of herd beast meat from the replicator along with black bread from the local grains, stuffing the food into his mouth without a second thought as he spoke.

"Really?" The disgust in her tone from his lack of manners difficult to miss. The tent flap ripped open with a snapping sound, making them both flinched as the wind increased.

Ossa walked in with the children moments later. Jynnalt aware, none here resented her amongst them. They knew she was the one who saved them. Didn't hurt she neither refused duties assigned to her nor ordered others to do her work. Jynnalt scrutinized her as she helped the children. Wondered if other Sabations might not be the cruel monsters they first appeared. Or were only the males cruel? She studied Ossa as she pondered the idea, sipping from the steaming cup of false Kalach she enjoyed at the start of each turn. The roasted and brewed fruit of a plant comparable to the properties of the real Kalakh. They named the plant for the common one used throughout the galaxy. The bean, though far more bitter, the energizing effects stronger.

The star rising above the treetops, the sky now a light lavender, with bands of orange-red bathing the land in blood hued colors. She watched the exploration teams fill their packs with food and water. Collected their scanners and weapons, before heading over to the feast tent to grab a bite to eat.

By now, most of the lower levels investigated. Fighters backed up those exploring. Everyone, though, carried a weapon. The former fighters with the experience stood guard. Each turn, they sent out seven teams, based on having only seven semi-working scanners salvaged from the wreck. Six of the battle armors were glitchy, not as dependable because the turn's hazards took a toll on the only nanite repair unit they saved from the crash. So far all went well and the fears amongst the ex-slaves were lessening as each turn the teams returned with nothing unusual occurring.

Twenty minutes later, Jynnalt, her paladins and Kendo fixed their packs, grabbed a scanner, and headed out together. Jynnalt scheduled them to check the eastern sector.

The city was a massive construction connecting the structures with delicate arches overhead and walkways spanning broad causeways. Houses roofing overlapping, making them appear like one massive building. Along the way, they passed small garden areas overgrown and wild, no longer cared for, fed by the waterfalls throughout the city. They entered one of the lower buildings and when she stepped towards a door; it stuttered in the track before slowly groaning open.

Jynnalt started to step through the open doorway. Keif stepped in front, stopping her as he shook his head and went in first.

She leaned in and remarked, "I doubt anything can live in here other than dust mites and spiders," glimpsing only empty cobwebs in the corner. "I take back the part about spiders," she said before stepping through the door. "I'll check the windows to locate us in relation to the camp. The rest spread out and check doorways closest to here. Stay within earshot of each other. If you find anything interesting, call out."

Everywhere was an eternity of thick dust. A blanket of gray covered everything as far as she could see. Which muted any colors underneath, yet showed a tantalizing hint of what might be there.

Thick cobwebs covered the chambers, windows, and corners. A row of odd-shaped, possibly decorative item, hanging from the center of the ceiling, spaced throughout the chamber.

Everything in perfect order. Someone cleaned, straightened, and covered the items with care. This did not appear to be a hasty retreat. Whoever the citizens once were, they intended to come back.

Nor did the actions appear to be those of a last remnant of citizens leaving after a harrowing disease took its toll. All covered to keep out dust, weather, and insects.

A strange sense so strong as to enthrall her. The sense this was familiar, she couldn't shake. Ghostly visions of tall, elegant citizens in dazzling clothes filled the hall, eating and conversing, though no sounds accompany the words. She blinked and everything before her once more dust and white coverings. Jynnalt shook her head, peered around, but the vision did not reappear. A priestess would tell her the vision of another lifetime's memory. She leaned more towards her own vivid imagination. As a child, this sort of thing plagued her. The local priestess declared her blessed to see her past. She thought it more a curse as her mother punished her for making things up all the time.

"Let's move on. Mark the area on our maps as a gathering hall. The space is sizeable enough for winter. The location is well within the buildings. Note, no one's been in here in a long time. Those stranded in the past must not have used this area."

They moved on, following the central passageway ending in what appeared to be a carrier tube. Reluctantly looking at the dust, they decided maybe best to find stairs. There must be emergency ones somewhere in case of power failure. As she turned away, a light blinked, then a door slid open. Disturbed dust from a wall of white billowing clouds blowing their direction filled the air. Thick and choking.

Coughing and hacking through watery eyes, she realized the interior tube was dust-free. She motioned them to enter to catch their breath. Tiall the last to step inside, an unsure look upon his face when the door whooshed shut. No controls, at least none she could see. *Possibly voice controlled.* "Open." Nothing happened. "Door open." Same result. *Stupid, you do not know the language they spoke.* She realized how she expected her translator to make languages available. The ones unable to translate. Long dead and those without formation of repeating syntax.

An apparition of an ethereal female appeared. Not quite a solid form. A hint of a long flowing dress, each movement exposing an arm or back or shoulder as if appearing and disappearing like segmented holo frames. Her shoulders bare, her arm bands fierce Phoenixes with long flowing sleeves attached. The sheer material falling almost to the floor. Everything glimmered and sparkled as she shifted. At one-point, Jynnalt caught a hint of white long curly hair flowing down her back. The image shimmered as if made of crystal dust. Her features delicate with intelligent, strangely glowing turquoise eyes.

"Welcome Queen. Elder. Paladins. You have reached your destination. Please disembark." The voice a strange echo in her head. Spoke to her in Galactic. How? This made no sense. Uneasy, she glanced over at the others. Realized she spoke to them also from the expressions on their faces.

Jynnalt never sensed the slightest movement from the tube and expected to step out into the same hallway. The door whooshed open, and the image turned and stepped off, showing the dress gathered at the base of her back. A cascade of crystal-like dust flowed behind her as she moved away. The FR image faded as she walked further down the hallway.

The apparition at first startled her, but she recovered quick enough when she realized the sight a holo and harmless. She leaned forward and peeked into the hallway outside the tube. No dust. Glancing at her scanner, she realized it was blank. *Drog.* She attached the scanner to her belt. And pulled her rifle to the ready position. "Someone or something is maintaining this area. Stay alert."

Kendo stepped off and turned back towards them. "An invitation?" He stared down the hallway for a moment, an expression of deliberation on his face. "From whom, though?" He shrugged with a thoughtful frown as he stared at where the ghostly image disappeared. "I sense avoiding them is not the way to get the information we want to obtain."

"Easy enough for you to say, scholar. You won't be the one dealing with them if they're hostile," Tiarn said as he stepped out of the tube and raised his rifle, pointing down the hall.

"Tube might be on a loop." Kendo threw back over his shoulder as he headed the direction the apparition vanished. "I would get off before the door closes and goes somewhere else separating us. We are here to explore. Well, let's explore. Could be castaway's like us."

Keif, Aidral, and Jynnalt stepped out. Silence. They moved forward with caution, alert to any movement as they followed Kendo.

"I sensed no movement or directional pull on the tube. Did any of you?"

Shaking heads greeted her question. At one of the intersecting halls, sweet scents of ripe fruit permeated the cool air with the softest touch ruffling her hair. "Stop. Can't you smell the fruit flowers or feel the breeze?"

Kendo walked back towards her, a strange expression on his face. "This place responds to your presence more than ours. Why don't you lead?"

"Let's go this way, then. Find where the draft is coming from. Try to locate our position again by looking out a window as my scanner keeps glitching."

Three minutes later, they came to the end of the hallway. A sizeable double door faced them. Closed. The scanner incapable of reading inside the chamber. She stepped closer, and the doors opened.

As they entered, three buttons on a panel to the left of the door caught her attention. Each button a distinct shape. One triangle, one square and one round button. Curious, she touched the triangular button on the panel.

The wall facing them from floor to ceiling appeared to be a metacrystal window, which became translucent. As they entered, and the power came on in the chamber.

"Must have power somewhere to get the Metacrystals to work,"

Kendo said as he peered at the control panel.

She and Aidral walked over to the window. A stunning view of the city. Forest, grasslands, and the far distant fog-enshrouded valley spread before them in a perfect tapestry. A walled orchard of at least a hectare far below where they stood with purple leaves, bright green flowers, and sizeable hanging fruits of blood red.

Keif and Tiarn held back close to the doorway. Jynnalt wondered where the breeze from earlier came. The window dissipated, causing Jynnalt standing at the edge to leap backward, arms flailing. Aidral reached out a steadying hand, and she caught her balance.

The cheery chirping of small flyers, insects and the distant muted roar of the waterfalls mingled together in the wind. The early golden starlight on the horizon of the tree line and the surrounding forest of the air a refreshing coolness. In the far distance, a grim line hinted of a storm moving their direction. For now, the early morning skies overhead cloudless tinged a pale azure.

Jynnalt stood enjoying the fresh breeze of dawn blowing into the cool stone chamber. Tension eased from her shoulders, and she relaxed. Till she remembered the breeze from earlier must have come from here. Yet, no one was present except for them. The door closed when they discovered this chamber, this open window also closed when they entered. *Could this be FR with full sensory hepatic feedback?*

"This might not be real. This might be an FR chamber. Maybe the entire floor is." She blurted out. "Could be how the female on the tube could speak to us. Maybe tied to our thought patterns. There are scientists working on fully integrated mind immersion FR in Ki. I am sure other places are as well."

Kendo, on the other side of her, asked. "Jynnalt, what were you thinking as you stood there looking out?"

"I was wondering about the breeze from moments ago and where it came from."

"Think of something else."

Who is here?

An ancient female dressed in vivid red robes in white trim and gold edges appeared in the chamber with them. She resembled the ancient holo's from the Book of Priestesses from olden times. Stooped as if from a thousand sars, she held a Priestess staff of power. Her head swiveled their direction as if she knew they spotted her wizened face, her mouth caved in from a lack of teeth.

The apparition turned back towards a pile of ash and cackled, "Not long now, the Queen comes to take her place."

The image vanished in a blink. She looked over at the others and realized they also witnessed the image by the shocked look on their faces. An interesting pressure gripped her. Drove her. Find the Priestess. Seconds passed. A beeping noise made her flinch. When she glanced at the scanner, the viewscreen showed where they were and the area above in seamless detail. A faint thermal image of a living being six floors above them. She presented the scanner output to the others. "Let's find who's here."

Two hours later, they arrived at where the thermal dot on the scanners was. In the chamber just ahead, through a park-like setting, ornate double doors across the garden in a compact marble building. They went through the garden courtyard, their heavy boots clanking footsteps on the polished pure white marble floors.

White, grey veined marble columns offset and supported a crystal lattice roof. Crawling vines and downward drooping, bell-like flowers hung from overhead. The garden infused with a rich, sweet, hypnotic scent. A multitude of flyers sang, chirped, and whistled from the roof, vines or artfully arranged small trees while the splashing sounds from fountains mingled with the songs.

As they approached, the double doors opened before them. "I believe we have arrived. And received an invitation." Kendo at the rear walked forward next to Jynnalt. A massive chamber stretched before them. Jynnalt stepped back out and considered the dimensions of the building. Then back inside. They did not match. Confused at the discrepancy, unease took hold.

"This appears just like a Phoenix chamber, precisely like the images in the Holy Book of Queens."

She overheard the wonder in his voice. Realized he was breathing fast with excitement. "The Holy Book of Queens are only for the High

Priestess, her acolytes, and the Elder of the Malkuth."

Kendo didn't bother to glance her way. "Says who? Priestess of the High Temple? The Elder Malkuth? The acolytes? I can assure you they were not the ones who banned the book. The Book of Queens was available to all six hundred sars ago, along with the other books in public worship. Why was the book banned by the High Priestess Carna? Temple scholars have not discovered the reason. What purpose did this serve? Why did the High Priestess herself oversee the removal personally? She never gave a reason other than claiming the book was dangerous to the galaxy's peace. Now only the High Priestess and her acolytes and the Elder have an old copy kept well hidden. Others are illegal collectors who have outlawed replications. Some claim the books have missing or altered parts in them. Until they can find and restore the original, each High Priestess still enforces the ban. Not wanting to present possible falsehoods."

Her paladins uneasily brought their weapons to bear before moving into the chamber, Keif forward, Tiarn and Aidral left and right. Keif shot back, "is this fool a heretic? Or talking *sheat*?"

Without looking at her, and ignoring the other's remarks, Kendo replied, "The secret society of the Phoenix is searching for the accurate book. The deceased Arch Dukian of Ki, through his sister, when she died, gained an extensive library of rare and Apocrypha books. He allowed us to examine some of the books. Those books were a great aid to us in our search. He informed us he hid them in a chamber. Only one true blooded of his house is aware of the location. No one is aware who the person is or might be. He claimed he hid them in this manner in case anything happened to him. I suspect his oldest daughter holds the key. Now the Queen of Ki. Though many looked for the chamber after his death, they never found the hidden library."

Her heart hammered as an urge to attack Kendo developed within her. Taking deep breaths, she tilted her head back, looking at the upper reaches hidden in darkness. She struggled to regain control of her emotions, unable to speak.

Strangers, guests in her home pilfered through private chambers looking for something her father valued and hid from prying eyes.

Citizens in an illegal secret society she now understood Kendo belonged to from his remarks.

She did not believe her father belonged to this group Kendo referred. Her father, kind and curious, might have allowed one he trusted to view the books. She doubted he understood how the information might fall into the wrong hands. Her aunt might have belonged to this group. Might be the reason no one spoke of her. The house's tragic secret. They must have gotten their information about the book's existence from her aunt before she died. She wondered if her father's murder involved someone in their search for those books.

Star rays burst through the windows. They cast a golden glow around the edges of colorful images in stained crystal windows high above. Each scene a dazzling display of rich colors and splendor on the pure white marble floors in the massive hall before them. Serenity depicted in the reflections on the floor filled her with a profound sense this place was sacred. Mystical. Where gods presented themselves to mere mortals. Her outrage against Kendo dissipated. Without thinking, she stepped further into the chamber. To each side, rows of females dressed like the art holo's she'd seen of Phoenix Queens in ceremonial robes. Fire rose from their feet, reaching greedy tendrils towards their waist. Both rapturous joy and intense sorrow on their faces. The females standing upon a pile of ash. High above their heads, a Phoenix hovered over them, wings spread out towards the shadowed upper reaches. The images alive, as if judging and weighing her.

The ancient crone from earlier appeared out of nowhere next to her as if she dropped out of thin air, startling her. Once she recovered, Jynnalt reached out and touched her, making sure she was not an apparition resembling the one from the carrier tube.

"The Elder speaks in wisdom. An evil wind of one of the god's avatar of destruction's minions took the book from public view. Now the winds blow otherwise. A haze descends upon time and space."

With that, she turned, ignoring them, and stepped towards the crystal door at the end of the Grand Hall. She stopped throwing back over her shoulder, saying.

"You cannot deny your destiny, but your fate is in your hands. You must choose." She moved back closer to Jynnalt and peered into her face. "Ah, that explains it. I know your father and mother."

"My father is dead. Where exactly did you meet my mother?"

"Wrong, little one. Your father breathes and your mother walks amongst the ancestors."

Her brows furrowed as she thought about what the crones said. *She has me mixed up with another.* An idea struck her the next second. The crone must be able to come and go as she pleased. "Is their someway off this planet? Can you help us?"

"No, I will live here for eternity. I never leave. I am the Guardian and High Priestess of the ashes." She cocked her head, "Someone close to you walks with the lost. Deeper into destruction as the avatar fails."

Ignoring them, she went towards the door with a slow and dignified step. A cackling laugh, and the rhythmic bang from her staff echoing as the sound floated back to them. With each step she took, she stood straighter and taller, moved with more fluid grace as a blue aura brightened around her.

"That makes no sense. I believe her solitude amongst FR apparitions has unhinged her mind," Tiarn muttered, though not loud enough for the ancient to hear.

For a second, Jynnalt sensed the power this crone possessed. Immense. Unlimited. "Come, Queen, time arrived and demands your presence. You must raise the dead." Her cackle held the stink of insanity.

Somehow, Jynnalt found she stood before the door next to the crone, yet did not remember walking there. Her stomach queasy and her limbs weak as if she lacked control of them as she stood next to the ancient priestess.

Right before a rainbow of starlight engulfed her, she saw a blank space in the row of images right next to the crystal door. The aura around the crone now a blinding blue radiating from her. Another odd skip in time. She found herself before an altar with gleaming metallic ash. It resembled the ash from the bag the priestess died for on Niuard. She remembered she intended to return the relic to the Temple, yet it never happened. She reached for the bag she always kept. It still hung at her side. Yet when she opened it, all that was there was the meh which got her into this mess. No ash.

At that moment, a streak of lightning crashed through the chimney and surrounded her and the altar in dancing blue plasma fire. Blinded and in agony, every nerve in her body stabbing pain. The pain vanished in a blink. Something was licking at her face. Claws and beak pulling on her as her head cleared. Looking at the altar, a colorful flyer stared back at her. One clawed leg held tight to her arm.

Her brow furrowed as she wondered how she got here and why she felt fear seconds earlier. This tiny, harmless creature? Or the unknown? She shook her head. Everything shifted for a split-second, and she detected a click like sensation and sensed the universe set right. Without thinking, she reached out and picked up the small colorful flyer and put it on her wrist, as if compelled to hold the creature. The strange flyer, cold and wet to the touch. She jerked as a razor-sharp claw raked across her palm. The creature's beak dipped forward, and its tongue darted out, lapping at the welling blood.

Wherever its tongue touched, sealed the wound and removed the pain. Yet, left a golden scar on her palm in the symbol of fire. Bewildered, she tried to put the creature back on the altar. The creature, however, held a different idea and hopped up along her arm to stare her straight in the eye. A soft, lyrical, echoing voice sounded in her head. *Mine.*

It was an emphatic statement. Before she responded, the creature spoke again. *Starstorm.* Jynnalt noted the plumage was now dry. Various shades of gray and black, with two longer iridescent black feathers on the top of its head, which curled over its back.

Its feet resembled felises paws with sharp talons, unlike any flyers she encountered. A long sinuous neck and heavy beak made the beast appear gawky and weird. The tail feathers reached past her knees with deep black tips.

The creature Starstorm shifted. She realized the feathers were iridescent as flashes of greens, blues, and yellows, along with reds, rippled as the flyer moved. Strange, no longer the size of her palm, but the size of a small Kieran raptor from her home planet. Its talons gripped her arm tightly without digging into her flesh.

Starstorm. Rise now. The creature's voice in her head said. Tilted its head upward and pushed off with graceful and forceful wing strokes rising in the chimney leading to the outside before disappearing.

Jynnalt jolted out of her connection to the creature by a flash of lightning overhead. Her chest hurt, and a strange heaviness overcame her, leaving her light-headed and confused for a second. The floor shifted and everything blurred around her before coming back into focus.

Where once a crystal door stood, now only a broken frame of rotting wood hung sideways. The wind blew through open gaps in the walls and the collapsed open roof overhead.

"Did you see it?" The desperation in her voice obvious.

"Yes." The answer came in unison. Fear and wonder, something Jynnalt never considered hearing in her paladins' voices.

"We have to go. Now. Something's not right," Kendo said as he glanced around at the ruin within which they now stood.

The promised storm of earlier arrived in a ferocious booming of thunder. The elegant garden of earlier gone, now only thick moss climbing broken walls while dirt and weeds covered the marble floor. They went back the way they remembered, stopped at a tube they swore was the one that brought them here. But no boot prints marred the floor's surface, and eons of dust covered the interior. Thirty minutes later, they finally found some stairs and descended. She was careful, as there were empty spaces where stone walls once stood. Crashed and broken far below. The stairwell area's thick with dirt, other spots of dust depending on if the walls still stood.

Frigid air blasted through empty windows frames. Frost forming around the edges. The now missing roof showing black clouds climbing high, obliterating the turn's earlier golden rays. Gusts of freezing winds blew in through the collapsed walls and the start of icy raindrops hit them, making splashing patterns in the surrounding dirt and dust.

Jynnalt stumbled on a broken stone sticking up and caught her balance on the only piece of wall left standing. Lightning danced across the heavens, followed by the rumble of thunder. Darkness fell fast. The chamber they just passed in stark relief of ruined stonework and overgrown weeds and hanging vines as lightning flashed across the sky above. Close by, the humming sizzle of striking plasma energy. She thought a leaf blew past her in the wind as they raced across what once was a chamber now open to the elements. She realized a small creature raced to leave the fury of the storm for cover under a broken stone wall.

Exhaustion hit hard. At least they were down to the exit to the pastured grasslands. She would be happy once out of this god's cursed place.

"We will not tell the others what occurred this turn. We can say this section of the city is unstable and unsafe. Off-limits from now on," she said. She gazed at the others. "won't be a lie." Silence greeted her. She sensed they agreed. Finally, they stepped out into the open. Above them blazed the fury of multiple streaks of lightning which lit the sky. Concussive thunder pounded her eardrums as the ground trembled. Then, as if unleashed from the heavens, a torrent of icy rain drenched them.

She stopped dead. No herdbeast anywhere and wild tall grasses reaching to her chin thrashed in the wind. The protective outer wall, no longer solid, shocked her. Tooth gaped and open in big stretches with piles of stone tumbled down the steep hill towards the forest at each open section. The forest snarled twisted trees and hanging vines.

Helc and daemons.

Chapter 31

335893 GGS Elec 31ˢᵗ.
Ki Border with Ga Undeveloped planetary system–Prince Ryakin

THE RUINED BODY OF his brother's royal barge sat at the bottom of a crater created as the barge skid across the land before coming to rest world side. The deepspace barge dominated the land. A leviathan captured from the heavens. In deepspace, the royal barge considered sleek, capable of carrying only two hundred citizens and crew.

A scar four standards long stretched across the land. Ending where the barge slid to its ultimate resting place. Smokey dark mountains peeked above the ruined barge in the distance. The open rosy sky behind held scattered clouds in long, thin bands.

They found the wreckage three turns after his brother did not show up at a critical meeting with the Chakian's. For the last five turns, they sifted through the wreckage, trying to discover what happened while looking for survivors. So far, they discovered the crew at the crash. Dead. Yet not one of the ranking blooded. Or the king of Tc or Da bodies or Dna signatures anywhere in the wreckage or the surrounding areas.

The recovery and investigation camp sat at the edge of the undamaged forest in a sizeable meadow. Ryakin stood outside his temporary shelter as he viewed the utter devastation before him. Colorful native flyers chirped, chittered, and sang a greeting to the morning star. Golden rosy light streaked out between the long shadows from tall hardwood trees of the wetlands to his left. Cool air and sweet scents of heady flowers wafted on the morning breeze throughout the meadow. The early turn cool but comfortable.

Violent thoughts raced around in his head; his arms crossed over his chest, staring at the destruction. Ryakin listened as reports came through his comm's. The breeze changed direction and blew the stench of death his way gagging him. This was his first physical recovery site, and he was learning hard lessons. At the sound of a challenging screech overhead he glanced up. Carrion raptors circled high overhead waiting for the chance to land and feast upon the ruined decaying flesh.

A concussive explosion shook the ground. Startling, but not dangerous at his location. His team of engineers set the camp far enough away to avoid any problems during recovery. The chatter over comms. One of the injection cores blew before the engineers removed the core from the aft sector. On a barge, they were not as huge or dangerous as the smallest frigate of the fleet. Still, the explosion fearsome in the surrounding area.

Flyers by the hundreds burst from trees in alarm, darkening the sky. They flew further back into the forest, away from the turmoil in the area.

Burning flare-ups occasionally seen from the interior as electrical systems, ignitable fluids, and smaller plasmas injection cores burned. Those standing a safe distance away and watching or collecting information got afterimages of the flickering blue plasma fire eating at the body of the ship. While specialized engineers worked relentlessly to contain the damage. Dead strewn along the scar and in the crater around the wreck added to the horror of the scene.

The hum of collection drones checking for meh chips, which still functioned blended with the surrounding insects. The effort a long shot. Too much time passed before they found the wreckage, turns past the acceptable recovery of spirit meh's for vatting. The drones recovered no viable chips so far. Still, guardians from Ki's Temple collected the meh chips from the drones, hoping to recover memories which might not have deteriorated. They could get an idea of what occurred, though not resurrect them.

This world is months away from colonization, after two generations of terraforming. The system located between the borders of Ki and the kingdom of Ga. All involved parties agreed this appeared the best place to hold a secret meeting with Chakian officials to discuss an alliance with the loyalist. The list of personnel with access to this meeting short.

At that moment, something about a male to Ryakin's right sifting through the debris caught his attention. His actions appeared somehow odd and secretive to him.

The roar of a shuttle landing pulled his attention away as a shuttle came to land to the right of him in the meadow. Elgar and Kalmia exited as soon as the ramp lowered. The heat from the ship's cooling engines exhausts fans saturated the air with a distinctive metallic ozone odor as the air around the ship shimmered with liquid heat waves.

They both approached Ryakin. Elgar never lost his commoner's crassness after sixty sars in the fleet or his habit of stating what he thought. Ryakin glared at him, daring him to say something. Elgar ignored the warning glare.

"Listen, if your brother is alive, he will need you to keep your emotions in check. Send tracker operatives after them, use Ki's Information Collection and Retrieval unit."

Kalmia's spoke. "My whisper operatives are the empire's best."

Ryakin ignored Elgar, going straight after Kalmia. "Like how your operatives found Jynnalt?" He stared at her, waiting for her to say anything in ICaR's defense.

She stared back, and he gazed away when she said, "Your accusation is unfair."

A movement out of the corner of his eye caught his attention. The same suspicious male, his actions off somehow. Elgar cleared his throat, bringing his attention back to their conversation.

"Ok, a cheap shot, I admit," Ryakin said, running his hand through his hair. "I know you, and your operatives worked overtime on Jynnalt's case. Worse, hampered by her own mother's cease and desist orders," he said. He glared about him burning with frustration, his nails bit into his palms as he fought to control his temper at the thought of Jynnalt's mother.

"On the subject of Jynnalt, I received more information. I am informing you Cineuian did not leave the shipwright dock without a crew. My division sent two hundred of my best operatives. I ordered Cineuian to take that action."

Ryakin's head turned Elgar's direction. "Did you know this?"

"Nope, I suspected. Thought she might have when she said she would send whisper agents to catch up and board her." Both swung back towards Kalmia, waiting. Moments later, she said.

"Ki needed Knight Elgar back here. On the battlefront. For the loyalist not chasing down leads. Also, this is the reason Princess Tesiskel sent him. She wanted his expertise unavailable to the loyalist. My operatives are better equipped to follow leads. They ran into a few pirates along the way. Short skirmishes in which Cineuian made quick work of them. Fleet Ai's learn about tactics apparently from their Commanders. Knight Elgar commanded Cineuian for a long time now. They seized twenty-three of the pirate's ships. Got some interesting information."

Ryakin opened his mouth, but a slight shake of Elgar's head and he waited.

"Smart choice." Kalmia nodded. "To go on, those answers led them to the fact there are planetary systems deep in the anomalous nebula of the Aephroltiays. The pirates claim the reavers live within the area. This is how they disappear after attacks. The reavers go to ground somewhere within those systems inside the nebula. We believe two hundred, probably more uncharted systems, are their home bases. The anomaly is off-limits to CON empires because of the dangerous conditions of the area and the fact the area is uncharted. For excellent reasons, the area lacks beacons, Trade lanes, and skip markers. Hence, why we have not discovered them before now?"

"Cut to the chase." His heartbeat pounded in his ears as his frustration rose.

"They found her imprint."

"What..."

Kalmia held up her hand. "Cineuian and my operatives arrived in a habitat system during a full-fledged battle. The battle was on the biggest planet between what we think were two rival clans. A massive sandstorm covered most of the battlefield, a strange technology blinded Cineuian for a bit, making the problem of recovery harder." She gazed off into the distance. Ryakin could not tell if she was thinking or remembering something.

"They sent down five agents, their best. Attacked before they reached Jynnalt's location. The assailants, an unknown species of extraordinary size. I can show you the image later along with the Dna signature," she said as she stopped and waited, as if gauging their reactions. "The kicker, the Temple list, no species matching the signatures. None. Not even emerging species."

"I believe you will be as shocked as our experts were, but for now, I will leave it at that. Another agent *claims* he spotted a Ghost Walker heading towards Jynnalt's location before attacked by said Walker. We received a blurry image, though not clear enough to identify if this attacker was an actual Ghost Walker. And because of the scrambled scanner's planetside, neither could we discern the individual's signature.

"I contacted the Temple for information about who they sent to find Queen Jynnalt. They reported to us they assigned no Ghost Walkers to such a mission or sent any for other reasons to the area."

Elgar stared at her; his brows drawn together. Ryakin thought the same sentiments mirrored on his face. "We lost another operative. She sent information back to Cineuian as she lay dying. This agent captured a meh of the same strange species from earlier entering a small frigate, which appeared to be from the empire of the Citrean. The ship's identifier listed as stolen in a raid two sars ago."

"Before you rush to any conclusions, understand the Temple suspected there are traitors in their midst? This might be a rogue. I notified someone I trust. She will... discreetly investigate. She was more shocked than I."

"Like the Imperial Master Zioria." He noted the annoyed expression on her face. "I read the report you sent my brother. Your conclusion is Master Zioria murdered the operative himself, attempting to retrieve the meh before the female officially delivered the evidence through the proper channels, exposing him. That missive got Jynnalt kidnapped, and the Emperor murdered."

"They always meant to murder the emperor and empress." Her expression grim. "At the time, there was no reason to suspect one of our highest Imperial officials in the Ministry to be a traitor. We since discovered Master Zioria's penchant for children in a manner best not described. Combined with his enjoyment of sadism at illegal pleasure houses outside the empire to avoid our laws. All this made him vulnerable to blackmail. We are investigating how he fooled the falsehood detection booth."

"I warned Jynnalt not to involve herself with this matter. If I thought she would not heed my warning, I would have asked another. Its importance required someone high enough to request the writ without question. At the time, it appeared best. Believe me, I regret the decision." She walked towards the wreck for several steps, then faced them.

Ryakin caught Kalmia watching him as he glanced over at the male from earlier. However, she ignored his lack of attention and proceeded.

"I received Intel which shows the loyalist have traitors in their midst. We discovered some by their connection to the Society."

Ryakin stared at the barge. "That would explain this," he flung his hand towards the destruction. "I will hunt down whoever did this." He left the rest unspoken. Moments passed as he stood still, his neck ridged with tension. Glared at the barge as if the ruined ship personally betrayed his brother.

"Son, listen. Find where your brother is before you take Ki's fleets chasing a dragon's tail."

"They told me the same thing, including my brother, after they released me from prison, and I wanted to search for Jynnalt. She is still missing. You found her once you lost her again. Now my brother, along with the king of Da and their entourage, is missing, most likely captured. I will not leave others to search for him. I will find him. Alive or dead. This time someone will pay. And I bet they will be the same people who kidnapped Jynnalt, murdered the Emperor and Empress and imprisoned my brother and myself."

"Agreed, however first discover his whereabouts, then stage a rescue," Elgar spoke as usual with common sense. "Find out if the Chakian's will help, then work on approval from Prince Anu. You can't fight the Imperialist, the Chakian's and the loyalist all at the same time."

Ryakin spotted the strange male staring at Kalmia as if he witnessed a malevolent spirit.

Kalmia asked, looking in the direction Ryakin was, "what is it about the worker over there you keep watching? You keep looking his way."

"Not sure. Just a feeling. He caught my attention acting odd earlier. I've noted his behavior on and off since. He has a nervous behavior about him. As if he's afraid or hiding something." Ryakin sighted the male in question once more glance their direction. To Ryakin, he seemed shifty. He moved off towards the edge of the forest, glancing back now and then.

"I want enforcers here now. Take into custody a male moving to the forest to the east of the wreck. Close to my location," he said into his comm's as he started towards him. After a second, the male broke and ran. His escape hindered by a patrolling whirlwind pilot who responded upon hearing the command and blocked his escape to the trees. Five fleet enforcers closed in along with Ryakin. A roar and backwash from a shuttle smartly landed in front of Ryakin, forcing him to skid to a stop. The shuttle set down, and the ramp lowered. Seconds later, EC Kirud stepped out. Minutes later, fleet enforcers came around the shuttle with the struggling male in custody. Ryakin started towards him, but an iron gripped grabbed hold of his arm and did not let go.

"If you beat him to death, you won't find the answers you need. Hand him over to Kalmia. Let her division acquire the information. They're trained on Intel retrieval." Ryakin yanked his arm out of Elgar's hold. Glared at the enforcers as they dragged the male behind them. His breathing slowed and his tension subsided a little before he stiffly nodded.

"Commander, we found these two items on him. Not sure what they are, but one appears to be a signal device, the other," the officer shrugged his shoulders and handed over the items.

He glanced at Elgar and then Kalmia. "EC, I want this prisoner taken back to the ship and thrown into the brig. He will stay there until Kalmia leaves. At which time she may take him with her."

"Commander," Kirud said, "because of your signal blackout you ordered while you are here, I came to inform you there is a Chakian fleet heading this way. Doubt they will take kindly to their ambassadors' disappearance. Our Dna signature is all over this scene."

"Listen to him. You can't afford a standoff or skirmish with a Chakian fleet. Not while Prince Anu is trying to negotiate with them for the loyalist. Send a message you were attempting to discover your brother King Rualui's whereabouts at the crash site, but moved off to let them investigate. Say you will share any information you discovered. And do so. Leave the rest of the diplomacy to Prince Anu. If you don't, you will squander any chance of an alliance between the loyalist and the Chakian empire. This is not just about your brother. Or you. The entire empire and her citizens are at stake," Elgar said.

"How long before they arrive?" Ryakin asked. As he moved back to where Kalmia stood, Kurid and Elgar walking with him.

"Approximately one turn, they are moving at full skip with a brief interval in between and no warp bow waves detected. They are coming fast."

Ryakin stared at his brother's destroyed royal barge before turning to Kirud. "Get the tugs and engineering teams down here now and remove the barge. Send the wreak to the nearest loyalist dock in Ki, order collection drones to gather the bodies which are ours and send them back for proper burials. All ships in the area are to load and prepare to skip out as soon as the tugs leave. Make it quick."

The guards, along with the prisoner, loaded the shuttle minutes earlier. Kirud boarded, and minutes later the engines roared to life. Ryakin regarded the shuttle lifting off, his clothing plastered to him from the strong blowback, before turning his attention to the destroyed barge. Seconds later, someone yelled and pointed skyward. The shuttle halfway to the outer atmosphere wobbled before banking steeply, then plunged in a straight dive towards the forest, disappearing. Seconds later, a thunderous sound and a ball of fire and black smoke poured skyward. Ryakin stood stunned, staring in that direction.

335893 GGS Caldr 27th.
Anunnaki Empire: Yilitria Travelers Station–Prince Ryakin

THE TRAVELER STATION took control of the barge's guidance system. Three times they lost the lock. The sharp jerk, when re-engaged, jolted him hard enough to leave bruises from the seat restraints. Elgar and Ryakin's five paladins, all dressed as commoners, suffered the same pain from the grimaces on their faces.

Nemesis, acting like the Star Captain of a small commercial barge, appeared unconcerned. He downloaded two turns ago into the revolutionary new body style he now occupied. The plans arrived in secret to the Kierian scientist and the shipwright's guild, delivered by a Temple priest, who would not reveal where the plans and new codes came from. This newest model next to impossible for scanners on casual passes to detect Nemesis's status as an Ai.

With no actual background, they created one. Ryakin realized every sensation as a new one for the Ai. The older approved bodies by galactic standards did not allow for sensory feedback, nor a fleshy outer skin, metal the only approved exoskeleton. Ryakin understood during war; the smallest innovation might make the difference between winning or losing. Still, he was slightly uneasy with the arrangement. He agreed to allow his ship's Ai to evaluate the system for the Temple.

Ryakin reached for the controls from the co-pilot seat. Stopped himself as his hands hovered over them. Use to landing his own craft as a fleet officer and pilot, this ordeal was aggravating.

Elgar peered over at him. "Traveler stations don't allow piloted entrance to their bays by non-fleet. As a civilian pilot, you would know this."

As they got close to the bay doors, which appeared to be opening to slow, the barge coming in too fast, he tensed. Without thinking, he reached for the controls. Elgar next to him stopped him with a hand over his and a shake of his head.

After what seemed an agonizing time, they moved through the outer airlock, almost grinding the sides of the ship on the doors. An hour passed as the doors ground shut. The station's controller moved them to a slip assigned to them, almost scraping the sides of two other parked ships. When the light turned green, the operator dropped them as if managing an offensive piece of garbage. This last insult of the ship landing, he was sure, giving him whiplash as he rubbed at his neck. Time passed interminably as he waited for the inner airlock door to close with a screeching clang. Once the barge was on the deck and powering down, he glanced around as he waited for the green light to debark.

Next to him, Elgar harrumphed. "They should shoot whoever is in charge. The condition of this bay is criminal."

To Ryakin's trained eye, the surfaces appeared as if a hundred sars of layered dust-coated them. Deepspace dust brought in by landing ships was flammable because of the attached hydrogen particles. His sense of outrage rose. Accidents in the fleet were minimal because of strict adherence to regulations. As he peered around, he itched to take the tenders in hand.

"Remember, you are not a fleet officer. You are a snobbish, bored, and lazy disenfranchised blooded who spent the talons of his inheritance. You're having to work as a co-pilot is beneath you. But earns you enough to eat, and a place to sleep with just enough left over to visit the gambling and pleasure houses." Elgar said, a warning note in his tone.

If someone told him places like this existed three sars earlier, he'd laughed at the assertion. In other empires, in GIA or CON, but not in the Anunnaki Empire. The empire enforced strict laws and codes against neglect and shoddy work with honest inspectors to prevent these sorts of critical conditions. Now spending more time in offbeat locations, in the empire as a loyalist trying to lie low. Out of sight of enforcers and legitimate writ inspectors, he was discovering the shadowy underbelly of the empire.

Inefficient lazy workers ambled around the bay. They ignored broken anchor locks and leaking hoses with utter contempt. Worse, they ignored vital safety details as if they did not matter. Albeit the station was old and required extra upkeep, but that was no excuse.

He worked at keeping his temper in check as the conditions of the bay strained his attitude. The effect not enhanced by the two tenders on duty ignoring them, till he blew his warning horn causing them to jump. Ryakin, now in a foul mood, would bet his suit's nanites they arrived at shift change.

Exiting the ramp, he spotted different tenders enter the inner chamber to start their scheduled oncoming shift, confirming his earlier verdict. One of the two original tenders working on connecting anchor bolts to their landing struts and the other connecting fuel lines. Both refused to look at them. Both technicians moved slower, casting sullen looks their direction.

Forced to ignore the station's negligence because of a jab in his ribs by Elgar. He could not resist a parting shot. Turning to two bay technicians working on the barge, "clean the outer hull of the dust." He demanded, scowling at them. "The ship's coated with deepspace impurities. Played havoc on our nav system." Afterward, he hurried to catch up with the others exiting into the registration center. Passed a tender who stared at him as he left. Ryakin figured he was trying to intimidate him. He stared right back as he passed.

After taking many wrong grav tubes, they wandered through concords full of businesses selling products in back chambers, illegal items throughout GIA and CON. Passed loud feasthalls with enticing entertainment, or FR stations to interact with non-oxygen breathers in other parts of the station or enter the games; if they spent enough tithe to play. After a while, they discovered a working directional holo.

They stepped out of the grav tube into a location any decent denizen of the galaxy avoided. The inner sections next to the interior apparatus controlling the gravity and life support and all the other myriad workings of a station. Where the cacophony from machinery and Cilithium waves interfered with scanners and other high-tech equipment sensitive to the waves.

Every Sense tingled, alert to danger. His armor disguised as low-level co-pilot's uniform of a private passenger line. Only fleet acquired battle armor. His nanites sensed his heightened state of adrenaline. In reaction, the armor kept trying to morph. He struggled to control his temper at the pure sloth and laziness of the station's workers, the evidence everywhere. He glanced over at Elgar and the paladins. They appeared alert yet collected and unaffected by their surroundings.

Enforcers avoided patrolling this sector, leaving criminals to go about their business unhampered. If nothing spilled over to the reputable parts, they behaved as if nothing illegal occurred on the station. For this station, their reputable side resembled the underbelly of other stations, making him wonder what type of criminals met in these establishments.

As they stepped off the grav tube, the door whooshed shut, and the tube shot away with an imperceptible hum. The stomp of their feet on the faux stone floor echoed loudly, broadcasting their presence.

Small pools of light fought against the darkened area. Ryakin realized seventy percent of the glow globes did not function. A group of three shady-looking patrons passed, disappearing into darkened areas. Minutes later to reappear further down in a pool of light or not at all. Derogatory symbol's defaced walls and businesses. He wrinkled his nose at the stench of garbage from disposal units no longer working.

A crash of glass caught their attention, followed by loud angry voices from an open doorway down to their left. Bellowed curses followed by a body that flew out the door and skidded to a heap, unmoving for seconds, and groaned before rising and scuttling off into the darker section.

It took another thirty minutes to find the Dragon's Plat feasthall. Thankful the feasthall was dim and the patron's the sort who minded their own business. His paladins entering before him with a discreet practiced flick of their wrists released swarms of hardened micro reconnaissance drones. Their cloak's hood covering their faces.

They spread out, going to separate tables spaced in such a way as to allow them to monitor who came and went. While the drones went through their handshaking protocols, allowing them more observations of the patrons and outer hallways leading here.

The odor of fetid decay emanated from three Wasuimings from the Free Solar Federation, filling the air. Unusual this far out of their territory, he noted. The surrounding area was conspicuous for the empty tables in the crowded feasthall.

Elgar, he, and Nemesis moved towards the back, away from the small bit of light from the entrance. They paid no attention to the paladins who entered minutes ahead of them, passing shadowy forms of various species, tall, short, or squat with fur, feathers, or skin. With diverse types of appendages in assorted colors of their native planets. The most common was the Elohim scattered throughout the hall in tight groups.

Background conversation merged with the jarring sound of machinery, which followed them in blending with the music from the live Ethitic bards. He moved away from the entrance into the darker recesses towards an empty table for five in the back corner. Ryakin and Elgar sat with their backs to the wall.

Two minutes later Nemesis spoke up, "The table replicator's broken," disgust permeating his voice.

A small server drone hobbled towards them with a broken strut, giving it a lopsided wobble. Requested what they wanted. Took their orders for three mugs of mead before hobbling off towards the bar. Ten minutes later, the drone arrived with their order. Taking his mug, Nemesis sniffed the beverage before taking a deep swallow, then scrunched up his face in a disgusted expression.

"Bad code, huh? Like you told me once when I tried to explain about our senses?" Ryakin said, monitoring the surrounding patrons.

"I now understand why there are things disliked immensely by biologicals. Your feedback systems are intense and not always pleasant. I will discuss this with the other Ai's so they can code my findings." He stared at the chalice as if it would reach out and attack him.

Ryakin was not sure if Elgar would spit the disgusting liquid out. His face a grimace of distaste before he swallowed, placing the mug on the table as if a bomb. From the other's reactions, he ignored his drink, watching those in the feasthall.

The ones they were waiting for arrived. No biomorph armor showed on the scanners, nor any unusual spikes in tech-signatures, no additional drones in the area either. Their military-grade hardware drones apprised them.

He put a false smile on his face as Ustrix approached his table. He did not stand, merely leaned back, and gestured for him and the male with him to take a seat. Pretended to take a deep drink before placing the chalice on the table, allowing a sizeable amount to spill out. "Were you followed?"

"No, and you?"

Ryakin ignored the remark. "I came out of respect to our past friendship to see what you wanted to say," the tone of Ryakin's voice made clear to all what he thought. The tension between them obvious to the others.

"Is your input time better now with your brother?" Nemesis asked curiously. Ryakin glanced his way and gave a slight shake of his head.

"You talk like an Ai," Ustrix said as he cocked his head. "Who are you?"

Ryakin cut in, "I did not agree to meet with you to have you interrogate or insult those I trust." The implication is clear.

Ustrix leaned back ignoring Ryakin and stared straight at Nemesis. "for those with past ties to loyalist under the Three Pillars is a nightmare," he rushed on, "not my brother, but the council. They watch us around the clock. Anyone associated with loyalist from the past better make the right connections. They keep us under constant surveillance. Lord Riciad..."

Ryakin interrupted, his fingers wrapped around the mug turning white, though he appeared relaxed. "He holds a false title from an illegal council, at the approval of three traitors." He paused, taking a deep breath, fighting to overcome the urge to grab Ustrix by the throat and pull him across the table. "Only my brother can approve a blooded to a higher rank or demote them as the King of Tc. The Sans Dukian of Tc, the one who followed my brother, still holds the lawful title."

Reaching for the mug in front of him, Ustrix took a swig, then spewed the brew across the table, his face turning green. "*What the helc*," he took a moment to catch his breath, "are they poisoning their customers, so they can rob them later?" He said as with great care he placed the mug on the table, realizing why the others were not drinking.

"The truth, I feel like a prisoner, humiliated and angered by the way they treat us," said Ustrix, bluntly not mincing words. "My brother also, but he must do what is best for our house as the Sans Dukian. Our oath house sided with the Imperialist. Would you prefer he broke his oath? Smear our house's honor?"

Guilt washed over Ryakin, a sensation he was becoming more familiar with than he cared. He understood what happened to an oath breaker's house. He understood what Ustrix was trying to tell him. Knew from personal experience the honor of any titleholder was something they dare not throw away with impunity. A House's reputation took generations to recover once ruined by a careless titleholder. He relaxed, somehow lighter. Watched as the tension left Ustrix and his old snarky smile flashed across his face.

"Are your personal problems concluded? Petty fights and arguments are not important. Save them for later."

"This list is crucial to Prince Anu and the loyalist movement. Temple and whisper agents died to acquire this information. The only reason I risked bringing this myself. *It's vital*," he said as he leaned forward and frowned at them. "When they banned the temple and seized their property and territories, they banned their operatives. If I'm caught working for the temple, they will execute me." The stranger with Ustrix said.

Ryakin knew he'd met him somewhere, but for now, where eluded him.

"This is Ikath. He is helping the temple is all you need to understand for now," Ustrix said, his tone aggressive

"Hours, before we left the Three Pillars along with the council, voted to withdraw from *both* GIA and CON officially agreeing with the Three Pillars announcement. The Anunnaki Empire is now an independent empire," Ikath said, letting out a harsh breath as he stared at the others.

Ryakin mused aloud. "What is the purpose of leaving GIA and CON? Now they have no protection from other possible predatory empires. Both can deny them future technology discovered by other empires.

"The temple will not aid them, either. After kicking them out of the empire, this might help our cause if we negotiate to bring them back if we win," Elgar said, shaking his head.

"Peace treaty with the Chakian's," Ustrix answered.

"We did not hear about a peace treaty." Ryakin exchanged a glance with Elgar, who, from his expression, was thinking the same as he was. *Droging* backstabbing *sheat's*. "Anu needs to be told right away. Before meeting with the Chakian's. Wonder if the delivery of Prince Anu will be part of any agreement?" He glanced back at Ikath, narrowing his eyes leaning forward.

The Bartender turned up the public pulse. The news bard speaking said the Three Pillars vacated the absolution by the temple and GIA of King Rualui, Prince Ryakin, and Queen Jynnalt. All three declared traitors to the empire. A bounty of five million talons in tithe paid upon their delivery. Alive or dead. The Three Pillars as of this announcement reopened the investigation. All their properties and titles held by the Empire till the trial finishes by either a guilty or innocent finding of the Greater Court Council.

"My brother received no official notification for chambers. Which is your fault?" Ustrix said as he leaned back in his chair.

"Mine, what the *helc*. You can't possibly blame me for what the Three Pillars do." He reached for the mug, then sat back, resting a hand on the table, the other on his belt as he glanced around, alert for betrayal.

"You destroyed the Chakian's largest task force, shattered them in fact, then you occupied two of their largest cities and blockaded Citrea. Before becoming a loyalist, you did your job too well, handing the Three Pillars a near defeat of the Chakian empire. The Chakian Empress wants your head. And Prince Satoric is happy to oblige. He fears your abilities in the field too much to allow you to stay alive. He fears more will follow Prince Anu if you're his Fleet Commander."

Ikath spoke. "The Three Pillars wanted to force the Chakian's over trade lane rights and Citrea. The Chakian's refused, waiting for a vote from the GIA's council they thought would go their way. They claim the war declared by the Anunnaki empire's council illegal. By the Anunnaki's own laws, only the Emperor or Empress can declare war. They sent their demand the Anunnaki remove their occupying forces in an appeal to both GIA and CON."

"Now if the Chakian's gain a favorable vote, it won't matter, because the Three Pillars withdrew from both alliances."

Ikath handed over the meh with the list. Nonchalant Ryakin attached the decryption devise given to him by Kalmia to verify the information. He tensed as he thumbed through the parts the decoder worked. He stared incredulously at a few of the names. Stiffened the further he read before he stopped.

"As you can see, the rot starts at the highest levels. Backed by proof. Believe me, what we brought to you is only the rim of a black hole of corruption. You comprehend from their behavior but can't see where the action comes from."

"There is an entire nest of traitors, agents, and spies working within the midst of the empire for a long time. This, we believe, is only a minimal amount. Worse, this list grows daily. The hard-working classes and guild members are rejecting their lies, forcing the Three Pillars to clamp down harder."

"How were we so blind?" Ryakin glanced around at the others at the table.

"We were all fooled," Ustrix said. "No one saw this coming."

"Not true." A tall stranger walked up, grabbed an empty chair, spun it around and sat.

"I am not your enemy." He nodded towards Nemesis. "Ask him, and Ikath."

"I collaborated with him a few times in the past," Ikath said in acknowledgment. "He is the one who sent me to warn Prince Anu of an ambush. So far, he has not steered me wrong."

"In the data sphere, the information is he is tracking those involved in trying to bring down the Anunnaki empire and others throughout the galaxy. I trust him." Those at the table stared at Nemesis.

"Data sphere?" Suspicion crossed Ustrix's face once more.

Before he asked any more questions, the stranger spoke. "Please call off your paladins and let me explain a few things. I am sure you are aware they are moving this way; I would hate to hurt them."

Ryakin stared at the stranger for a moment as his paladins closed in, the stranger's relaxed stance and self-assurance worrying. *He's stupid or unaware of my paladin's abilities. Or he can do as he claimed.* They could not afford a scene, and he preferred to not assess the stranger's claims, for now. Besides, he got an odd impression, as if this stranger understood more than he cared, yet did not appear older than himself. "All clear, I repeat, all clear." The paladins moved indifferently back to their tables and sat nursing their untouched drinks once more.

"Good, now drink up. We have to go." No one reached for their drinks. "No, then okay, in the next couple of seconds, the bay you are all docked at will explode."

Ryakin pulled out his handheld under the table while trying to make his uniform morph, but nothing happened. Looking around, he spotted the others also trying with no results. Their uniforms remained in a passive state.

"Your battle armor will not do you much good. Their ships in orbit put a damper field in place to prevent their use. Just in case. I guess they were right. Five million talon of tithe is the richest bounty in history."

"Who are they?" Ryakin asked. "And how do we tell you're not one of them?"

"You must decide whether to trust me or kill me now, as the freelance hunters arrived for the bounty on your heads twenty minutes ago. They will destroy your ships, leaving you no way off the station. At least this is what they believe."

Ryakin nodded as Elgar pulled out his gauss handheld and placed the weapon on the table. Ikath rose from his chair, a strange blank look on his face, before he sat. Ryakin recognized cyberware communication. Any fleet officer worth their stars would.

"Yes, Riurrel left and is standing by stealth'd next to Vith. Inform your protection. We are fighting our way out of here in the next ten seconds. Move when I tell you. They offered a reward to any who will help them on the station. No one here betrayed you, so stop looking at each other. The betrayal is from a loyalist at your highest level. Worry about who later. Right now, work on staying alive."

"I sent the map of the station and the layout to your pulses. I marked our escape route." The Dragon's Plat shook, rattling the mugs, the sound of smashing glass and the groan of strained metal as the floor trembled.

"Now." They rose smoothly with practiced ease, took down patrons as they reached for weapons.

The server drone scurried behind the bar in a strange hopping skip. "Don't shoot me." Repeated several times.

The paladins killed five in quick, efficient movements as they retreated. Then backed out the door, joining the others. Leaving the interior feasthall a chaos of moans and screams as various colored blood mingled before a thin stream flowed out into the corridor.

Staccato booms echoed as three shots ricochet off the wall behind them. Shrapnel hit Ryakin and Ikath both with deadly spray, cutting deep across their arms and back. The stranger threw something on the ground, creating a thick black smoke screen between them and those chasing them before he sprinted away. The rest on his heels, yells, and calls behind them as they followed.

Ryakin knew the hunters did not have the use of their morph armor either. Disabling there's also disabled their own. He spotted Elgar falling back, limping, and ran to help him.

"Go, I will hold them here. I will just slow you down. The list and you are more important than this old shell."

"Not happening." Ryakin's heart pumping hard as he fought to catch his breath. Out of nowhere, the stranger appeared, taking the other side. Between him and Ryakin, they caught up with the others.

"Get on the grav tube."

"But..."

"Now, do as I say."

They jumped on, weapons at the ready. Ikath tried to make the tube turn on, to no avail. "No power, they must have turned all the station's tubes off at the control center. We have to move."

Before they did, the stranger stepped up, slapped a small device next to the controls, and the doors slid shut. The tube whisked away from the platform faster than normal. The hunters and patrons firing as they disappeared down the tunnel. One shot hit the window, shattering the glass, spraying razor-sharp pieces towards them.

For several hours, they fought running battles, always heading in the direction the stranger led. Twice the hunters thought they trapped them, but the stranger produced unfamiliar devices allowing them to escape.

Half of them dragged along by the others by the time they arrived at the location the stranger indicated originally. Exhaustion was taking its toll. Ryakin knew they needed to reach safety; soon. The stranger stopped before an outer wall, attaching one of his devices.

Part of the wall disappeared, showing an airlock leading to a ship.

The airlock somehow drilled through the thick hull of the station. They rushed through as fast as possible. Ryakin gazed back as the stranger removed the device and the wall behind them appeared solid once more.

They stumbled and fell into the ship as the stranger followed by Ryakin rushed by, heading to the cockpit.

Once in the cockpit, the stranger gave a terse command, "Vith, now," he threw himself into the command seat and strapped in, Ryakin jumped in the seat next to his.

Exhausted, the others found seats in the back and strapped in.

Moments later, Ryakin jolted as they disengaged from the impromptu airlock. Pushed away faster, aided by decompressing atmosphere which escaped out from the hole before emergency shielding temporarily covered the breech.

The ship was larger than Ryakin expected as he glanced at view screens of the passenger area. He realized drones moved amongst the group, tending the wounded, the worst ones removed to repair units. One paladin bad enough. The drones removed him to a repair unit and wheeled him off into the depths of the ship.

Twenty minutes later, Ustrix and Ikath arrived in the cockpit. The stranger pointed towards seats as he concentrated on piloting. He opened a skip window as three energy sapper missiles raced their direction. They skipped a hair's breadth ahead of the inbound missiles.

Hours later, Ikath and Ustrix loaded onto the ship called Riurrel, still attached to Vith. Ustrix said before leaving, "One last thing. I'm sorry about your brother."

Ryakin froze. "How do you know what happened to my brother?"

"Right before we left the Three Pillars, paraded him and the others caught with him through the city. They declared them traitors and decreed they will execute them in ten turns. I thought you knew."

Blind rage choked him, at the galaxy, at his father, who left his brother to carry the house's shame. Forced his brother to always try to do the honorable thing, the right thing, while ignoring risk to himself. Ryakin should have been the one to go on the mission to meet the Chakian's. His brother, as usual, claimed as the ruler of Tc's this is his duty, his task alone.

Before the stranger dropped them off at a loyalist base Ryakin, list in hand, demanded he informed him who betrayed them.

"Kalmia will explain." Refusing any further conversation, the stranger left.

Chapter 32

RYAKIN STOOD SILENT as the waking world washed over him, soothing his tumultuous emotions. The morning's light making his and Elgar's uniforms glow a layered red gold over their house's colors. His mind on the latest information about his brother and Jynnalt.

Their agents sent back information the trial of the traitors postponed once more because of the unrest of the commoners. Cineuian with the Kierian whisper agents on board, still in the anomalous nebula searching. A heavy sensation overwhelmed him. Something lately he was familiar with. Loss. Regret. An insidious tiredness engulfed him.

"War makes the young old long before their time," Elgar said as he watched the shuttles arriving from the loyalist blooded and their knights from their flagship Dreadnoughts. Anchored in orbit of this small unnamed system, which for now served as their headquarters.

Ryakin's hodgepodge fleets on patrol and high alert. Ki's fleet hunted haphazardly. Tesiskel enraged at the lack of effort on Ki's Knight Commander's at catching the rogue fleets. Ryakin realized the enemy sensors should spot their fleet, yet they sailed past as if blind or changed direction. Eight separate times support ships from cruisers and destroyers to bombers held back, then quietly joined up with their fleet. Their knights surrendering their ships to Ryakin. Eighty percent of the Kierian fleet was now under his control. The latest to join was the

Dreadnought Spawn's Demise and all her support ships.

Prince Satoric sent half his fleet to supplement those lost to Jynnalt's mother Kierian's call the usurper.

Turning towards him, Ryakin asked, "Why do you mention this here now?"

"You need to keep your mind focused on your mission. Let the rest go or you will make a critical mistake. At the wrong time."

"I see why Jynnalt's father trusted you enough to make you her guardian."

Elgar chuckled, "there is more to the story. The truth is, he abhorred that gorgon he married. The house of Airal at the time was almost bankrupt, and what the Imperial House of offered in the contract made the match appealing even with the scandal. They despised each other on sight. I never understood her outright hatred for her daughter. There is a story behind why he once told me, but he died before he apprised me of what."

Ryakin doubted spousal disagreement as the actual reason for granting him the guardianship, but did not pursue the subject for now. To leave a prominent blooded position of power, to one with an exalted fleet rank, yet a commoner by birth, he never heard of before he met Elgar. Something else, something of extreme importance, was at play. If he survived this war, he intended to discover why, even if his wife and child became lost to him, he wanted to understand. They stood for the next few hours in comfortable conversation, waiting on Prince Anu's shuttle. Neither wanting to join the others. Both uncomfortable with so many operatives of the shadowy whisper arts of Ministry fourteen present.

The star rose higher, caressing the surroundings with a pleasant warmth. Prince Anu's shuttle arrived with his entourage. Trailed by the Eagle Paladins, who abandoned the Three Pillars and joined Prince Anu, who they considered the emperor. Wasting no time, he headed straight for the council chambers. Too many times they escape by the slice of an atom. This meeting would be quick before they skip the false world to another location just within range of a gas giant in Ki. The power requirements to maintain the station immense. This one reason they orbited gas giants. The station siphoned off gases and gravitational waves for power. The other reason, gas giants uninhabitable.

He, Elgar, and Prince Anu's entourage entered the chamber where the council members gathered. They waited for the quiet murmurs of voices to become silent as they moved to their assigned seats. Waited for Prince Anu to sit before they did.

After the obligatory formal openings, Prince Anu called upon the supply division for an inventory over the next sar for their fleet's needs and other essential and boring matters.

Kalmia startled Ryakin out of his musing while the various master's voices droned on in a monotone reading from their ledgers. She leaned next to him and whispered in his ear, "follow me outside, so I can speak to you in private."

"Can this wait? I'm trying to figure out how to convince Prince Anu to allow me to rescue my brother and those captured with him. I have a plan. One I want to submit for consideration to the council."

"No," Kalmia's voice was adamant.

He swiveled his head towards her. One look at her face convinced him, and he rose and followed her out. Other heads turn their direction. He ignored them.

Their footsteps echoed in the massive base. Tall buildings reached toward the black abyss of the roof, high overhead like pillars. In all directions, the buildings disappeared off into the distance in a checkered pattern. Broad walkways of polished black gold veined marble between them. The sense of being insignificant amongst the buildings intense. The silence, other than the clack of their footsteps, unnerving.

They hid this base within what was a small, pristine world. A false image. This was a small Traveler's station covered deep with dirt to grow flora and support fauna with crystalline aqua green seas and large blue lakes. The station housed a full-time staff of Ministry's fourteen operatives, who lived and worked here on behalf of Ki. One of many such hidden Kierian bases. Bases Tesiskel and her newest council, unaware, pledged only to the true Queen of Ki.

They walked in silence till Kalmia held up the meh, he retrieved from Yilitria's Station.

"Before I show you this meh, I need you to allow Nemesis to jam all signals in the area. Discreetly. I don't want the other Ai's knowing what he is doing. Nor do I want the operatives who work here to know either. I'm told he's capable of doing such a thing?"

He overheard the questioning tone and realized she was guessing based on rumors. Rumors from whisper agents.

"I'll ask him. I'm unaware of such capabilities." His face blanked out a second while he used his cyberware link to Nemesis.

"Something he gained from the stranger on your trip from retrieving this meh. Or something in his new operating system. An operative I trust passed on this piece of information." Kalmia said as she waited.

"He did as you requested. How, I am not sure. Are you referring to the strange Ghost Walker who saved us at Yilitria's Station? You claim he gave Nemesis additional coding?" He asked, his annoyance flashed to the surface. That information classified. Once he left here, he would start an investigation of who leaked the information to Kalmia.

"Now what is this about? I want enough time to present my plan to rescue my brother and the king of Da."

"Hold off till you see the information retrieved from that meh, only the names of provable traitorous acts left un-encrypted. My operatives are still decrypting the rest. Afterwards, we will follow up with in-depth investigations." She led him toward a towering building closest to them. The echo of his footsteps taunting amongst the massive buildings.

When they first arrived, she'd placed the meh on a holoprojection receptor next to where he sat. The display opened and rows upon rows of names and the evidence of their perfidy laid bare to his disbelief. As he read each section, his anger built. An organization, the one called the Society, was inciting this civil war. The Societies Order appeared connected somehow to whoever's behind everything which occurred since they arrived in the Anunnaki Empire. Jynnalt and he fought too many times over how dangerous the Society was. Jynnalt viewed them as a threat. He ignored them as a harmless cult of citizens, their behaviors on the dark edge of morality. Shunned by normal citizens. He now understood how wrong he was.

Five names grabbed his complete attention. Without turning

towards Kalmia, he asked, "Do you believe this information to be accurate?"

"The proof is there. We did not include a name without enough proof to make a legal case. The other half of the meh of names we deciphered are under suspicion, the rest we are still working to decrypt. I felt it best not to show those till they're cleared or proven guilty; I removed those names for now. When, or if, we acquire enough proof they are guilty, I shall warn you. For now, I shall allocate operatives to gather the proper information on their movements and actions."

He heard her footsteps behind him and after looking at the list; he tensed. Names on their he'd never suspect.

"I trust the source of this meh," she said from off to his side and slightly behind. "We validated all those on the list against times and places. The names I wanted you to see are on the next page."

Afterward, he sat stunned. Battled by the urge to recoil from the truth. The reason they were always on the run. All their meetings and plans were never a secret. They might as well have broadcast them over the pulse.

Rage boiled up, stormed through him, blinded him. Ryakin enraged at himself also for his blind acceptance of those in power. Names appeared on the list he trusted, even admired. A sinking sensation filled him as he read each name. Moments later, he took a deep breath and rose taut, yet in control. There were still a lot of names he respected, not on the list. Thank the gods.

"Give the list to Nemesis as soon as possible. I want to go over each name in the privacy of my ship's chambers."

"Understand, I will send you the proven traitor's names. I *will not* send those names, which are unproven." Kalmia stared at him with an enigmatic look on her face. A look which did not bode well. Later, he would investigate why she balked at his request. For now, he lacked the time.

When he thought of the proof of wrongdoing held in his hand, bitterness filled him. Information provided by the empire's *faithful* operatives, working in deeper shadows. *Indefensible proof.* Most information for now unusable. Except for five names. Five traitors here on this station. At this moment.

As he re-entered the chamber, he spied Arch Dukian of Da Syka, pull a meh from his robes and place it upon the central dais's holoprojector.

"I received this meh from King Shullat with an offer from the Three Pillars. An offer of peace."

The hall erupted. Loud uproars of arguing overrode any further remarks he might have said.

Minutes passed while Arch Dukian Syka waited before raising his voice and saying, "agree to the Three Pillars peace offering in good faith. They will give you reasonable terms." He spoke loud enough to overcome the noise.

"Everyone in this hall understood what you said," Ryakin strode straight to him, "and everyone here rejects any *supposed* peace offer. They rounded up blooded families, high ranking Guild Masters, and those of the Peerage. Last in their net, the commoners Lamanes. Afterward, they handed their houses over to those who testified falsely before the court, then murdered them through execution. Seven or eight even gained control over houses without being of the bloodline. The only thing required to gain a house title was being a crony of the three traitors or ranking council members supporting them. To us, the only peace treaty acceptable is if the Three Pillars declare Prince Anu Emperor. Then turn themselves over to his authority for investigation in the attack upon our Empire and their traitorous actions afterward."

Arch Dukian Syka stared his direction with an expression of pure hatred. Washing away the last visage of doubt in his mind, the information on the meh he still held tight in his hand was true.

Prince Anu stood from his chair above the others. "Let him speak. I will not allow us to throw out procedural laws of the council even in these times. The floor is his and the right to finish what he wants to say. Agreeable or not."

Ryakin bowed his head towards Anu, "my pardon, your grace," he addressed him with what should be his proper title, the reference not lost upon Prince Anu. Ryakin discerned the smallest lift in the corner of his mouth before vanishing. He moved back to his seat, his steps measured, tense. His face stony. *My turn will come, and you will wish you stopped speaking when you could, Syka.* Kalmia, from the back of the chamber, nodded her head his direction.

Arch Dukian Syka spoke once more. This time, he turned and faced Prince Anu, ignoring those behind him, punctuating his speech with expert acumen. "To show good faith, order those who followed you to lower their Silks."

The chamber exploded as members rose to their feet in protest. Ryakin remained seated. He realized the reason for this show of conciliatory rhetoric. The Three Pillars framed the words in a manner the loyalist would decline. Prince Anu rose to his feet. "Silence." The roar of his voice brought instant quiet. "We will not act like savages. Once more, the floor is his." He sat. His face expressionless. "Proceed." He nodded towards Arch Dukian Syka.

"You must swear you will end the civil war; one you cannot win. As for your wealth and your property. They will drop the charges against you if you give up any further claims on your titles." He turned back to the chamber, ignoring the angry faces. "This is draining the empire of its resources and setting house against house. My King captured, as you all know, along with the King of Tc, and awaiting trial for acts against the lawful government. Yet, he did not choose this path. Those with a clever tongue and those who took a blood oath bond to him coerced him."

He sauntered with haughtiness around the chamber. "My King suffered because of his decision. His citizens suffered. You have seen the destruction for yourselves." He paused. Brought on by us here in this chamber.

Ryakin waited for someone to speak. Respecting Anu's wishes. No one did.

"Yet, the ones who started this war forced you all to aid them in protecting their wealth. Their positions are the only ones to gain." Indistinct murmurs arose. He waited till they quieted. "The Imperialists outsmarted and out-gunned you in every battle. Do you believe, after we lost a third of our fleets, and they have captured two of our six commanding kings, in the foreseeable future, things will get any better?"

Prince Anu, still his eyes impassive, listened to the rhetoric of Syka's speech ring through the chamber. Syka moved closer to where Ryakin sat staring his direction.

"Who convinced you to join? Tell me who gains the most? Think about how your kingdoms got dragged to the brink of destruction?" Now he turned towards Prince Anu. "I ask you to answer on your oath. Did you start this war? Or were you pulled into this like these others, convinced the Three Pillars would assassinate you for your title and wealth? Who convinced you they were trying to steal the throne?"

Silence filled the council chamber as minutes passed. Calm, with no rancor in his voice, Prince Anu leaned forward. "Are they acknowledging my legal right to the throne?"

An Awkward moment passed. "That is out of their hands. The commoner's riot in the streets at the mere mention of placing you upon the throne, making the idea impossible, for the time being. They will not accept you unless given proof you did not murder Emperor Lahamu. To do that, you must turn yourself in and stand trial." To emphasize the point, he showed pulses from various riots. "The commoners tied the Three Pillar's hands with their demands," he spread his hands apart, "therefore, they reopened the investigation to help prove you innocent of any charges. However, in a show of good faith, you must surrender yourself. The citizens' faith in GIA and the Temple failed them in their hour of need. When and if the investigations clear you, they have every intention of going back to fulfilling their positions as Wardens."

Ryakin understood he lied about the Temple and GIA. Their whisper agents reported the riots occurred because they suppressed the citizen's faith and freedoms. And their exit from GIA. If Anu submitted to their authority, he would prove their power to any who doubted them. Worse, the surrender of Anu would demoralize the faithful, loyalist and citizens alike.

"So, why would they demand I renounce all claim to the throne?" Anu said as silence filled the chamber. Syka gazed at the hostile faces. "The council will vote on the next emperor as there are no blood heirs left, except for your line and you lack an acceptable and legitimate heir. *If* cleared, the taint of the accusation will always be upon you. They will allow you to take the title of the fourth warden. Ascending the other wardens over you. There is one demand they will not negotiate. One loyalist surrendered to them unconditionally."

"What are their other requests?" Anu asked, strangely composed despite their demands.

From here, Ryakin could see the throbbing of his temples. Yet, he appeared relaxed otherwise.

"All loyalists must acknowledge titles already removed and awarded to others by The Three Pillars and the council. They promise a healthy pension from the Imperial coffers to compensate for lost income. They will allow contracts between the original titleholder with a breedable female to a comparable heir in the bloodline of those now holding under the Three Pillars. The rest who still retain titles must forfeit them. With the same stipulations. The only other option left to any of you if you refuse this offer is to become an outlaw."

Roars of outrage from those present as they rose to their feet filled the chamber. Ryakin stayed quiet in his seat. At the back of the hall, he glimpsed the Tount of Da Abushita rise and make what he thought was a casual exit. Followed shortly by the Caiscou Urzat of Tc. Next, the Nibilis Ezisen of Tc. Followed by Nibilis Uzzieu of Da. Ryakin glanced back at Kalmia. She touched the back of her ear, communicating through her cyberware. Kalmia must have agents standing by for orders. A thought came to him, clicked into place. Tount Abushita did not loan him Knight Kurid to help him when Ustrix left to join his brother. He wanted a spy in Ryakin's command.

"I require one more question. If, as you say, the Three Pillar's will give up their positions they now hold, how are they going to accomplish all this?"

"They will do what they said before they step down, before handing over power to whoever the newest Emperor the council votes for."

Prince Anu stood after allowing ten minutes of arguing and rage vented by those present before he spoke. "You will sit and conduct yourselves with proper decorum, or I shall remove you, and anything voted on in this chamber will be out of your hands."

The threat made them sit, though angry murmurs still circulated.

Prince Anu sat once more. "How can you prove to those present Arch Dukian Syka what you say is true?"

"The meh placed on the holoprojector earlier. Shall I play the entire thing? I am sure the Ministry in charge can authenticate the meh for you."

Prince Anu nodded his permission. Arch Dukian Syka turned on the holo and let it play, stepping out of the way of the full-sized holo of King Shullat, who reiterated what Syka said earlier as he pleaded with them to heed his words before the holo ended.

"King Shullat omitted what happens if they find me guilty."

"I am only the messenger for my King. I cannot speak of information. I am not privy."

As if indifferent, Anu asked, "Are the Three Pillars and the council, they illegally appointed, giving back the Temple their property, and the territory owed them? Will they allow the Temple to hold mass for the faithful without harassment?"

Syka stuttered. He did not miss the reference to the legality of the council. "Once again, I cannot answer those questions."

Prince Anu's voice rose the slightest bit. "Appears; there is much you cannot answer. Tell me, who does the Three Pillars demand handed over, you mentioned earlier? Neither you nor King Shullat stated who the citizen is so far. Before I can take a vote, I need the name."

Ryakin tensed. He sensed what name Syka would say and rose to his feet. "Your Grace, I request the floor. I have something of importance to say before he divulges the name."

"Denied. I suggest you sit and allow this council to proceed in a manner fitting to a civilized empire. You *shall* have your moment."

Ryakin sat seething till he glanced at Kalmia. Something was up. He sensed it. Spotted Prince Anu's posture and realized he was playing the Arch Dukian and relaxed.

"Prince Anu. King Shullat thought this far wiser if you decide. Give you the chance to save the empire you say you love. Be the emperor you claim you are. Renounce your crown. Do what is right for your citizens and blooded."

Those who left earlier returned and sat.

"The name." Prince Anu demanded. His voice now held a subtle threat.

"I will do so after you bring up the force shield so the said party can't escape."

A slight smile hovered at the corner of his lips before Prince Anu nodded to his Eagle paladins. One pressed a button on the wristband of his armor. The shimmer of a force field enclosed the chamber along with the buzz of energy.

"The name?"

"Ryakin Tc*Airal of Ki. I now yield the floor to Prince Anu." He said. Making no reference to Ryakin's titles, or a nod to Anu, before moving to his seat with what he thought a dignified walk.

Prince Anu motioned for the meh on the center dais collected. He handed the meh over to his head Eagle paladin. "This meh is my response to the Three Pillars. Do not turn this on just yet. Before I play this meh, who wishes the floor.?" He focused on the surrounding chamber, ignoring Ryakin. The holographic display system in front of Prince Anu lit up with the Sigils of Houses requesting to speak. None lit for the house of Da. He called upon the Blood house of Aos.

Arch Dukian Rialum stood. "*That* was not a peace offer. *It* was a demand of *surrender* wrapped in honied platitudes. The Imperialists spread like a plague over Da and Tc kingdoms, stealing everything of value while enslaving commoners, guild members and slaughtering any who fight back. No one spared if they give the slightest offense, young, old, females. I say again, we ought to fight back, stop running."

"Our fleet is too weak at the moment," King Aurcari of Ga said loudly.

Arch Dukian Rialum turned towards the King. "What would you have us do? Surrender our blood houses, lay down our arms? Give up our fleets?" His tone held the slightest contempt as he stared at King Aurcari.

"For now, we're safe within the Titan's Defenses. They cannot bring their full force against us while they fight a war with the Chakian's."

Another spoke up, one Ryakin did not recognize, "Then explain how the reavers raid through our Titan Defenses with impunity? Something I wonder about a lot of late."

No answer was forthcoming.

Prince Anu allowed this exchange without interfering. Then he spoke, and silence fell. "I forgot to introduce my guests. Ambassador Viceroy Bolice Tipal from the GIA council. He would like to address this council before we proceed further."

Ryakin viewed the five traitors, blanch.

The ambassador rose and went to the center dais. "GIA's council voted in the case brought before them of the Anunnaki Empire's civil war. The vote was unanimous. We will not take sides as this goes against the charter to do so. Neither will GIA interfere. There is a freeze on any further legal matters from the Anunnaki Empire dealing with the civil war." Cries of disappointment echoed throughout the chamber. "It will still weigh other prior legal matters of the Anunnaki empire. The Anunnaki Empire can still bring a vote before GIA's council for those agendas. However, that appears unlikely for the Three Pillars as they exited the pact officially as of this turn. We will allow Prince Anu to represent the Anunnaki Empire in this matter. He reaffirmed the Anunnaki's entrance into GIA this dawn."

The smallest smirk of a smile float across Arch Dukian's Syka's face, and Ryakin wanted to punch him. Others smiled at the subtle acknowledgment from GIA. He sat impassively, his jaw stone under the light shadow of his tight-cropped beard. He sensed a trap. But for whom? Once more the names of those enforcers and whisper's operatives or those of rank came to mind. *Can I trust Kalmia or is this a setup*?

Prince Anu introduced the other standing next to him. Slender old hands threw back the hood. A gasp filled the chamber. It was the Highest Holy Priestess of the Temple. Standing next to her, the Anunnaki High Priestess also removed her hood so all could see her.

"I am here to give the blessings of the High Temple to Emperor Anu."

The reference not lost on any in the chamber. They bowed their heads.

"By the Book of Law, the High Priestess may declare for an emperor, King, or Queen. The Temple sworn to defend those denied their blood rights, or any rights in their own sphere of influence. We have cleared Prince Anu of offenses or suspicion in the murder of Emperor Lahamu. The Temple declares he is the rightful heir of the Anunnaki Empire by all rights invested in the Temple.

Five members in the chamber, faces drained of color, the five Ryakin aware of guilty of treason. Ryakin understood Prince Anu did not intend to surrender to the Three Pillars and their false courts under their control.

The High Priestess was still speaking, and he turned his attention back to her.

"Laws must be just and not demand one forego the essence and foundations of civilization. Family, traditional culture, and worship. The true three pillars of civilization. They deny these rights in the Anunnaki empire since the murder of Emperor Lahamu."

After her speech, she turned and left. The Anunnaki High Priestess walked with casual dignity to the stand and turned on the meh placed there earlier. King Shullat strapped to a table as tubes from his major arteries drained his blood into a clone. The Three Pillars, along with the five sitting in this council, on the list of traitors overseeing the operation. Everyone in the chamber horrified as the Arch Dukian Syka and four others present in the holo joked about the lights going out as life left the King's eyes. Gasps of outrage rose. The clone rose, a perfect copy of the King Shullat. Prince Satoric then ordered it to repeat what he said, and it did. *They made a golem.* A heinous crime throughout the Council of Nine's sphere of influence. A crime which carried a death sentence.

All five raced for the doors, only to slam into the force field.

"Thank you for giving me an excuse to raise those shields earlier. I was trying to figure out a reason to do so without raising your suspicions." Prince Anu said as he nodded their direction.

Arch Dukian Syka, though once he realized the trap did not act worried till Prince Anu looked at him. "I would not count on rescue by the Imperialist, this time they shall not arrive. We jammed any outgoing messages before you stepped foot on this station. We did, though, mimic your signals, sending the Imperialist fleet trailing on a wild tramarl chase. You shall be here for a long time. *A long, unpleasant time.*" Agents came behind the traitors, arresting them.

"Ryakin, you may take the floor. I hear you're working on a plan to rescue your brother and give the so-called Three Pillars some payback."

Ryakin stood and bowed his head before lying out his plan. "We can't hit them in our territories, not here, not now. But we can take the fight where they least expect us to and where they are the most unprepared. Their biggest fleets are on the Chakian front or patrolling in Da or Tc, trying to maintain control. Leaving only reserve's patrolling Nibiru."

For the next couple of hours, the rest of the meeting became a war council. The Anunnaki Temple declared they would add their fleet to Prince Anu's.

Hours later, Ryakin left for Nemesis, battle plan in hand, with the full blessing of the council and Prince Anu.

Chapter 33

335893 GGS Galle 20th

Planetary Anomaly Sabation Sector–Queen Jynnalt

AS THE RAYS OF THE star struck the lower area around their high camp on the ledge, Jynnalt and her paladins killed one of the slowest retreating insects. Kendo wanted the body to dissect. He was looking for a weakness to exploit. Three terrifying months passed since the city transformed into the ruins which stood there now. She and Kendo theorized the city's system for a fully integrated haptic feedback False Reality presentation. Ruins. That's what the city was. The true appearance of the city's ancient stone outlines. Crumbling walls everywhere. And stones strewn about the hillside. The wall deteriorated to an eon of weather and time. Something or someone shut the feedback system off, or the entire thing failed. Either way, awful luck for them. She believed a power, unsure whether good or evil, existed here with them. A force that viewed them as intruders.

Kendo believed this the home of a formidable ancient. If true, the ancient might be an insane one. She pressed her lips together. She did not believe in ancients, myths, and fairytales. Her fascination with them died with her father. Supernatural beings invoked to bring order to a brutal time. One fact remained. Their situation turned from dangerous to disastrous.

One hundred and eleven turns ago, they exited the ruins to chaos. The others outside that turn fought their way from the camps to the crumbling city entrance. Better protection than out in the open grasslands. Those wearing suits and carrying weapons fighting the insects. Females and children sprinting for safety, like their first contact with the horrific insects.

Jynnalt and her group ran, placing themselves between the insects and the others. They launched grenades at the Razing; horrors, the explosions killing the voracious advancing line. This bought them time as the insects stopped to cannibalize the bodies of their fallen.

She and her paladins caught up to the others, covering the rear before they found a semi-defendable spot. A chamber with three standing walls. They fought throughout the dark of night, killing thousands before star rise. Their own numbers dwindled as five males and three females caught by the insects before anyone realized what was happening. They lost three more females when the insects ripped them off their precarious ledge. Over the following turns, they searched from star rise to star set, despairing of finding something easier to defend during the times of darkness. Exhaustion from fighting through each night taking a toll. They lost two males in the fights since then. Kendo discovered the massive cave high up a sheer cliff face by accident, looking for new plants. A sizeable stream ran through the back area, creating a small yet deep crystal-clear pool before disappearing into the depths of the mountain. Perfect for their needs. They risked drinking from the pool of water from the stream running through the cave, as they had little choice.

When the star lowered on the horizon, those out hunting or collecting plants to eat or for medicine retreated to the cave. Out of reach of the monstrous insects.

The slaves without bionanites sick often, but as time passed, their bodies adjusted. Kendo's insatiable curiosity amassed a significant knowledge of the flora of the planet for cures combined with his skills in medicine helped.

She thanked the gods the bugs did not climb or fly. Otherwise, this refuge might not protect them for long. This dawn she rose before the rays of the star reached the cave entrance. Kendo and she scheduled to explore the ruins, hoping to find answers, yet the odds were against getting any.

She sat enjoying her rising meal with a steaming mug of Kalakh. The beans freshly roasted yesterturn. She studied the scurry of activity; amazed at the resilience of life. For all the past abuses at the hands of the Sabations. Followed by the crash and horror of carnivorous insects stranded on a mysterious planet. Those still alive fell into familiar patterns of duties. Each one doing what was necessary for them to live and survive. Everyone depended on the others.

Two of the females came from developing systems, far from space faring, or civilization, their societies primitive in the hunter-gather stage still. Societies still tribal without cities, only nomadic family groups. They fared the best, as this was a familiar lifestyle for them.

The two slaves showed the others how to skin, clean, and prepare food. Later, they taught them the means to preserve the meats and foodstuff.

The first time the hunters brought back a kill, one female threw away the carcass, scolding them. "She's claiming the creature's a predator, not good to eat," Jynnalt said. "She says you need to look at the teeth." The female kept pointing at the mouth of the creature.

The next turn she and Kendo, along with her paladins, scanned for herbivores, cataloged what they found close to the ruins before inputting the findings into the other's scanners. At first, they took one scanner to a hunting party. Now they did not bother. Three months later, they grasped what to hunt and where. Between all the hunters, they never lacked for fresh meat. The others gathered berries and fruits.

Starsoaker and Leafcatcher stretched out their branches and opened their young leaves, drinking in the rays of the rising star. She realized they sent their taproots deep into the ground. Their sighs of pure pleasure, a singsong worship to the rising star, drifted her way. For a flash of time, she enjoyed the moment. To be one with everything. The sensation rare, the last couple sars struggling to survive. She never regretted rescuing the two sentient plants. One night, while on guard, weird screaming sounds traveled on the wind while she stood on the ledge. She grabbed their last working scanner, not taking any chances an unknown creature found them and was climbing up the cliff face. Two small sapling trees on the pathway up to their makeshift elevator. The insects tearing at their branches, the star an hour from rising. One tilted back its top branches, and she saw a face looking up at her as pitiful wails emanated from what appeared to be a mouth.

Thinking quick she grabbed a rope and threw it to them. Wiggling the rope in front of what she assumed were their faces for minutes. They grabbed the ropes with small pliable branches, and she and the two other sentries pulled them up, blasting the insects trying to hold on to their prey.

The ex-slaves afraid of them, at first. But their gentle natures overcame any objections soon enough. And the fact they inform them about the plant's properties of whether medicine, edible, or poisonous increased their odds of survival.

The smell of scorched ground, underlaid with a scent of bitterness, floated her way upon the breeze, making her wrinkle her nose as her earlier feelings disappeared. At least the odor was not that of feliscu urine the two trees exuded when wet. She realized they'd grown a foot since she rescued them. Her father once told her such things as sentient Tree Species called Treeialics existed, but she thought he was teasing her. Proof now stood before her very eyes.

This system's starlight appeared good for them. Still, the two saplings, she hoped, were growing at their normal rate of growth. She should ask Kendo, he might know. They saved over six hundred pods full of seeds. Rescued from the crashed transport, which to her appeared like a behemoth tree with stumps instead of branches. They stored them far in the back of the cave, out of starlight and in the coolest section.

She, Kendo, and her paladins collected everything Starsoaker and Leafcatcher asked them to salvage and spent turns recovering the items and storing them in the cave. The Treeialics explained how their pod of a hundred seeds broke open in the crash landing outside, which forced them to sprout. Both the only survivors of those hundred. In the ship itself, they found thousands of pods burned to a crisp. Both saplings lamenting for their unborn brethren poignant. Afterward, Kendo always found something for them to do outside the ship while they collected everything within. Still, they retrieve six hundred undamaged pods. Each one with approximately one hundred seeds.

The saplings always enjoyed exploring with Kendo. The two came back into the cave after their morning worship. Headed straight for her speaking as they came, "the ancient one's say, water one's left planet, infested harvesters."

"Are the harvesters the giant insects?"

They stared at each other, speaking in unison, "Trees not happy, water one's left."

"Ah, are the giant insects, the harvesters?"

They kept going on the same track. "Water ones tended cared them. No one cares. They want water ones to care. We told them you keep own branches. They sad. We say we care?" She gave permission but demanded they be back before the star set. Not sure why they asked her. They spent more time with Kendo. *How the helc does he get a straight answer from them?*

She gazed at them, her eyes half-closed as they headed out, her mood relaxed. Moments later, she became edgy. Yet didn't understand why.

A movement caught her attention. Kendo. He must have risen earlier than normal. Too many dark nights he stayed up late reviewing what he learned during the turn while the rest of them slept. Trying to find useful information. Half the night passed before he fell asleep most of the time. His studies saved them time after time. No one complained at his explorations and investigations, while others hunted, gathered, or did the other laborious myriad things necessary for survival. The replicator destroyed when dropped as they attempted to raise the unit to the cave high overhead.

Kendo kept his theory about the planet to himself, not wanting to get anyone's hopes up. In the meantime, he searched for useful plants for food and medicine with the scanner and the additional help of the saplings.

Kendo entered yawning, stretching his arms above his head, then grabbed a pack. Stuffed a scanner and various recording meh's and a laser torch into the pack, he took nothing else from the rest of the space reserved for specimens. Last, he grabbed a wicked knife and tucked it into his belt before heading straight for her. She couldn't resist a grin, her earlier mood passing. Besides, he appeared excited to have someone to talk with, other than the young saplings, with him in the ruins this turn. She nodded towards the insect they dragged up to the cave from their earlier kill.

"What you asked for, accomplished and delivered." She said, making sure not to inform him they almost lost Tiarn in the battle with the creature.

"After star set, I will dissect the insect and see if I can find any weakness." He moved to the gruesome corpse and covered the thing before sitting once more. He reached over and poured himself hot Kalakh, gulping fast. Then wiped his arm across his mouth.

"You appear off this morning. Is something wrong?"

"I despised this helplessness. I sense someone or something is here. Playing a joke on us. When we crashed and found the grasslands behind the high wall, we believed we were safe. The truth, we were never safe. The crone made me think escape was possible. To get home, perhaps a working ship stashed someplace. Or a signal strong enough to break through to the outer great currents and hail a passing ship or a lone Sailor traveling through."

A gust of wind caught the flap of the canvas from the makeshift covering across the cave opening. The flap snapped against the canvas like staccato rifle fire, making her jump, burning herself with the Kalakh. "*Helc, daemons, sheting gods.*" She jumped up, grabbed a cloth off the table and patted dry the spilled Kalakh.

"You can curse the Gods all you want, it will not help," Kendo said as he stuffed food into his mouth.

"True, but it makes me feel better."

The hunters, now ready to leave, broke into groups, grabbed food, and headed out. Jynnalt advised them to be careful and wished them luck.

Ossa and the others fixed breakfast for those still here. Later, the females would head to the lake to fish or gathered berries, fruits, and herbs. Others cleaned clothes, letting the children play for a while before they taught them their lessons. Kendo, during his wanderings, discovered a plant in the forest's undergrowth that made an excellent soap. Other plants he distilled into medicines for the fevers rampant amongst the children and adults.

The nanite material of the battle armor was not washable. Only a nanite unit could clean and repair them. They only recovered one from the crashed cargo section. Because of the size and weight, they spent ten turns to haul the unit up to the cavern. They gave priority to armor damaged the worst during each turn. After a while, battles with insects and other wildlife took a toll, leaving many wearing damaged armor as they only repaired the worst damaged suits in the unit. Three of the original suits were beyond repair, their nanite cubes heaped in a corner, cannibalized to help repair the other suits.

Dead here was dead. No vats. Not much different from when enslaved by the Sabations or fighting in the pits. They traded one dangerous place for another. The difference. Here, they made their own decisions. Decisions they lived and died by.

A week after they discovered the cave, they lost two other hunters who stumbled into the greenish-yellow fog in the valley. Discovered too late, the mist was gaseous chlorine, the reason the valley appeared shrouded in an eternal mist. The rescue party found them dead at the edge of the gas. Kendo understood what the mist was and ordered the others back. The next turn, Jynnalt Kendo and her paladins entered the area in the best battle suits, protecting them from the gas. Discovered that the insects retreated to there at star rise. They burned any nests they found, taking satisfaction in the explosions as they eliminated thousands of insects. This decreases the numbers which arrived with each star set.

Three turns later, two females and three of the males did not arrive on time at star set. The fighters grabbed weapons and proceeded back out after them. Too late. In the distance, a full hive speared and tore them apart before they moved close enough to rescue them. They raced to safety while the insects feasted in a feeding frenzy, blood spraying over the other hive members as they attacked each other in a chaotic fight.

Another five lost out hunting during the turns light. A search led to fresh blood splatters in the areas they were mapping. No bodies, no footprints. Nothing. An unknown creature must have killed them, adding one more danger to their already extensive list of threats.

After the others left, she and Kendo got their stuff and headed out.

Kendo talking as they headed towards the ruins. "I went back up to what I believe was the crystal tower chamber. The pile of ash the creature arose from gone. Only dust and dirt upon the altar. Ash has a unique signature. I did not find the slightest evidence of any."

Changing the topic, he said, "I realized the other turn you no longer carry the old worn bag."

She ignored him. "It's a false reality. An excellent one, I give you that. You admitted this by the proof of what you said. There is nothing real here, this is nothing more than the carcass of an ancient city, dead long eons past. *Helc,* even the priestess, was an illusion."

He grabbed her wrist before she reacted and turned her hand over, palm upward. Held her wrist in a tight grip. "What is this, then? I know of no false reality that can leave a physical mark." Pointed to the faint golden-red outline of the symbol the Temple used to depict a Phoenix Queen. "Think about this. The priestess might have been waiting for the right person."

"Or maybe the technology is far more advanced than ours. The FR might pick up our thoughts without a direct hook in, which would explain what I thought I witnessed and sensed. Whatever the being is, perhaps the crone picked up my desperation to get home."

"Oh, the Phoenix reminds you of home?"

She forgot how quick he was to latch on to anything said when he was hunting for information. "My father told me tales as a child of the ancient mythical Queens and their formidable Phoenix's." He stared at her. She could tell he was trying to figure out if she spoke the truth or not. She ignored the look and kept walking. Moments later, he caught up with her, silent for now. They entered the ruins and started up a set of semi-whole steps. She changed the subject, knowing his analytical mind jumped to questions she might not be able to answer.

"The power needs of a false reality on a scale the size of the city with such strong hepatic feedback as to be able to leave a physical mark must be enormous. Why did our scanners not note the immense output after we crashed here?"

She stopped, enjoying the view as he caught up to her. A brisk cool breeze set the colorful leaves quivering throughout the ancient, deformed forest. A sense of wrongness hit her like a sledgehammer, rocking her on her feet. She sensed something, *but what?*

Her heart hammered against her ribcage with such force, she trembled. Something compelled her towards the forest. She forgot why she was here, forgot Kendo. Forgot everything.

She rushed downward on the broken stairs, driven by what she did not comprehend, cloak swirling and snapping out behind her. A chill wind blew through the section where the walls fell away. She raced towards the lower levels, a dangerous warren of twists and turns. In a frenzy of compulsion, climbing downward.

At one point, she lost her balance and reached for a stone sticking out from the stairs. Missed and tumbled. The breath knocked out of her as a fire of agony from her shoulder to her elbow burned through her. Now the earlier sensation became a call in her head. The sense of frightened terror engulfed her. Drove her to get up, to press forwards towards whatever called her. She found herself at the edge of the forest, following an old animal trail.

The path took her farther eastward, away from the cave and safety as the star rose high on the horizon. Desperation and terror tore at her, drove her forward. The trail opened out to a narrow valley, sitting above the writhing chlorine vapors less than a half standard away on the hill. Dominated by a crystalline lake that appeared to be on fire beneath the surface.

As she broke out of the forest, Jynnalt came face to face with the largest raptor she'd ever imagined. It towered above her. A sense of relief washed through her, confusing her.

A soft keening came as intelligent eyes glanced her direction. Other than the size, the raptor reminded her of the paintings of a Phoenix. Albeit exceedingly tiny. The Raptor's right claw tangled and trapped in a web of vicious roots that tightened while Jynnalt stared. An angry scream filled the air as the raptor tore at another deadly root, trying to wrap around its other leg. Black orca blood pooled on the ground with the root in fast retreat.

The raptor, black with subtle iridescence colors that rippled through the feathers at the creatures' slightest movement, studied her with enormous emerald-green bright eyes.

At first, she took cautious steps one at a time while planning her approach. After the raptor made no threatening moves, she got braver. Somehow, she sensed the creature meant her no harm. She reached the raptor and kneeled to examine its trapped leg to see if possible, to break the creature free. If the raptor wanted to harm her, now was the time, as she was in a position for the creature to be able to rip her apart with its beak.

Startled when the raptor dropped its head and nudged her. She heard Kendo moving towards her seconds later. The creature lifted its head and delivered a furious hiss before once more lowering its head and with a gentle stroke rubbed along her side. As if to reassure her of its intentions. Each time Kendo attempted to approach; the cruel beak slashed towards him.

"Stay back." Jynnalt threw over her shoulder. "It does not seem to like you."

"How would you know, whatever it happens to be, doesn't like me?" She heard Kendo call out, prudently, farther away than moments ago. She figured he stepped back out of reach of the beast's vicious beak. Jynnalt snorted, hearing the sarcasm in his voice.

"It finds you less of a threat, smaller, female, more helpless. This beast might like me if it knew me." Jynnalt snorted, hearing the slight fear in his voice. For her or himself, she was not sure.

Jynnalt ignored him afterward as she tried to figure out how to release the creature. Frustrated, every move to pull the roots away made them tighten their grip. Then she remembered the laser torch in Kendo's pack.

"I think I know how to cut the foot loose from the roots. I need the torch," she glanced over her shoulder, "and the knife at your belt. The problem is, I doubt I can do this myself." She peeked back at Kendo.

"Seriously! You expect me to come over there?"

Kendo's head shaking in the negative as he viewed the raptor as if it'd devour him where he stood.

"Don't rush in. Approach slow enough for it to see you. Make yourself smaller." Jynnalt went back to examining the roots. She wished

Starsoaker, or Leafcatcher, was here. They might talk the tree out of its meal. A meat-eater. This tree must trap animals, then wait for them to die to soak up their nutrients from the liquefying flesh and bones. She remembered those who died, yet they found no tracks or marks left from an animal. This must have been what happened to them.

"How do you suggest I make myself smaller?" Kendo called out before taking a step towards her and the creature. The raptor once more lashed out at him with its dangerous beak, screaming a warning. "I believe your friend here is having zero to do with your idea, or me, for that matter. Ignore my earlier assurance, to the contrary. You are on your own. Sorry."

He did not sound sorry to her. She rose to her feet, and the creature gave another soft keening sound, lowering its head to rub its beak along her arm. Fascinated, she reached up and stroked the head before scratching above the eye. The raptor purred with pure pleasure. "Throw me the torch and knife."

He did, and she went to work burning and cutting away the roots.

After burning three of the roots, the tree attempted to grab her; she applied the torch, and the root retreated. She ignored everything around her but the injured, trapped raptor. Intent and careful not to burn the beast. Not being able to have Kendo's help forced her to concentrate entirely on what she was doing. With a scream of challenge, the raptor broke free and leaped into the air as the last root released its meal and the entire tree vanished underground. Jynnalt moved away to go stand next to Kendo.

Her head thrown back, awestruck as the raptor flew upwards, flashes of color rippling across its back. She did not realize how long she took to free the raptor. The last dying rays of starlight lit its plumage as the raptor gave a fierce scream, then burst into fiery flames and vanished before her eyes.

"Did you see that?" Jynnalt turned towards Kendo. He stood rigid, his back to her, staring towards the woods.

"Jynnalt."

Before she answered, she spotted four strangers with plasma rifles held their direction.

"Stand where you are." A tall thin male off to the side of Jynnalt called out, his accent Kierian. She took one last look at where the raptor disappeared before turning back towards Kendo. No longer sensing its presence.

Cineuian, in her robotic form, strode out of the forest straight for Jynnalt. Lowered her head before declaring, "Your Highness," then grabbed her and hugged her, startling Jynnalt, the metal embrace biting into her skin.

"Your Highness," Kendo said as an eyebrow shot up.

Tears welled in her eyes, and she hugged Cineuian back. The star stood halfway on the horizon, bathing the landscape below blood red. Seconds later, a deafening silence fell, the herald of the turn's death. The local creature's instincts for self-preservation well-honed.

Panic hit her as she realized what the lengthening shadows across the valley and the rapidly lowering star brought. Amazed how adrenaline changed her priorities. She glanced at Kendo.

Both gazed around for a defensible spot.

"Call in your team's. Now." She spotted a rocky outcrop, and the darkness beneath implied the under area might be deep enough to fit the group. Kendo saw the ledge at the same time. In the background, she overheard Cineuian obeying her order without question.

"*Sheat, drog, helc.* Whoever is with you, call them in." She sensed the panic in her voice as she hurried toward what might become their last stance. "We need to prepare for a fight. A fight I fear we might not survive."

"This is our best defensible place. How far out are the rest of your team? Any not here by star set is dead."

"All are here. We stayed in the woods. The beast appeared to trust you and you appeared not to want the creatures harmed. So as not to startle it, we waited out of sight. My databanks have no information on the creatures of this planet." Cineuian glanced skyward, "are you afraid the flyer will come back to attack us?"

"No. Something far more terrifying. In enormous numbers. I'm not sure we will be alive by next star rise." She realized the warriors with Cineuian lacked armor. Their weapons formidable, but without armor, most would die in the first swarm.

"The others should be inside the cave by now," as if to prove her wrong, her paladins came running out of the trail into the valley. They must have tracked them. She waved her arms, and they raced her direction.

"Kendo, sorry I got you into this situation."

Three temple ghost walkers appeared out of nowhere. Bowed deeply towards Kendo. "Elder, as our assigned mission is to recover you, dead or alive, we joined these searching for the same group we were."

Jynnalt grinned. "Elder, huh? I believe we are even. You must be an important council member for them to send Ghost Walkers to find you, no less. I'm impressed." Then she sobered and glanced around, preparing to fight. "We have been in worse situations, though the odds of ending up dead over getting out alive would be the better bet. If I gambled."

The sound of the buzzing grew louder, resembling the roar of an engine out of synch, Razing towards them. Jynnalt, Kendo, and her paladins understood the shock the others would experience when they realize what they faced. The first twinkle of stars shone overhead.

Right before the line of Razing insects reached them, a black form swooped down from the sky. Bright blue plasma flames charred the onrushing insects. Powerful wind from wing strokes pushed them back as they tried to leap forward toward the overhang, back into the destructive flames.

Moments later, a shuttle called by Cineuian touched down. They raced for the ramp. The raptor screamed a challenge at the insects before disappearing, then once more diving in and burning swaths, forcing them back. A flaming beacon before vanishing into the dark. The shuttle lifted off, rising out of reach as more of the voracious insects arrived, Razing towards the shuttle, over the smoking bodies on the ground. Once the shuttle became airborne and out of reach of the insects, the raptor vanished.

Chapter 34

335893 GGS Droe 8th.
Ga Kingdom Capital System–Prince Ryakin

"HOW LONG DO YOU THINK, before Knight Frelliz realizes, we fooled him, and he is blockading derelict ships?" Ryakin asked as he and Elgar moved up to the DCIC dais where Nemesis stood.

"About now. I would bet a herd beast's feast for the crew. He counted on the Three Pillars granting him a title. He understands they required a lot more action than a blockade on his part to gain a title."

"Did you observe how loose the blockade was? He held his reserves where he thought our fleet whispers somehow might miss them, youngsters," he said, shook his head and chuckled. "Think they came up with something new. The fleet's used those tactics since before his daddy fulfilled his contract."

"Bet he thinks our fleets are cowards for not rushing out to engage, giving him a big win," Ryakin said. For a few more minutes, he checked over the plans on the holo map, memorizing the battle plan.

"I leave Nemesis in your capable hands. Take care of him." Ryakin moved to leave.

Nemesis regarded him as he stood by the DCIC tactical map. "I heard that. I will take care of your crew. Elgar will aid me."

Ryakin gaze at Nemesis, a worried frown crossing his face. "Don't get smart. I'll call our friend and ask him to reset you to your original programming." His voice hardened. "Elgar is in full command. You will follow his orders. Or I will decommission you."

"Order received... Commander," Nemesis said, a slight pause before he acknowledged Ryakin's rank. The normally muted background beeps and whistles from the bridge filled the gap. Nemesis turned back to studying the tactical display.

Did he make a mistake allowing the temple Ghost Walker to alter Nemesis code? It gave him fewer constraints in his coding interactions and a physical body style undetectable as an Ai.

Could Ai's be dangerous? Would they always turn on the biological species who created them if given enough freedoms? The war of five hundred sars ago with the Ai's came to mind before he shook off the thought.

N'lari spoke, "Nemesis, you and I shall talk later."

Nemesis appeared chagrined. The modulated voice of the onboard ship's computer noted, "window to launch Basum's five-minute countdown, starting now."

They would use the gas giant in Nibiru's system's gravity as their slingshot into Nibiru Proper drift thrusters only, tricky, but possible. These were the best pilots in Ki's fleet.

The maneuver would move them past the sky eyes defensives network system in orbit around the planet. Without Igigi controllers, they might pull this off. Ryakin turned to Elgar once more, "Command of Silks transferred." Elgar nodded crisply.

He scrutinized the crew. Nemesis seemed to sense his attention and glanced up, snapping to attention. Nodded as smartly as Elgar. Ryakin glanced at the tactical command map, memorizing the positioning. It ran through Ryakin's mind uneasily once more wondered about whether Nemesis was trustworthy before he turned and left the bridge, heading to launch bay one.

Five minutes later, ten APAX Basum's launched. "The Kraken is loose."

Twenty minutes afterwards, the APAX pilots started the first dangerous turn into the gas giant's gravity for the slingshot maneuver.

The Basum's carrying the ten APAX rescue teams, with Ryakin leading, executed three quick burns. They came out of the slingshot pushing them to drift speed eight, heading into Nibiru proper. They flashed past the non-functioning Igigi sky eyes. Basum three came close to clipping one, but the pilot rolled away a split-second before hitting the sky eye and fought to regain control before rejoining the formation.

As they entered the atmosphere, they engaged their antigrav engines for three seconds. Then shut down and plunged downward in free fall with half a standard separating them in a v pattern. Upon reaching an atmos altitude, the pilots fired their fuel engines, which flared to life. The Basum's dropped from the bright starlit cloud tops into the heavy turbulence of furious winds and whitefall.

Ryakin listened over general comms as they passed through the upper atmosphere of Nibiru Proper in full stealth mode at supersonic drift five, heading in fast.

The modulated and controlled voice of the Nemesis computer came over the comms, "Action Stations. Action Stations. This is not a drill. Set Condition Red. Repeat, this is not a drill. Set Condition Red."

"Actual One speaking. Operation Nibiru is a go. Repeat. Operation Nibiru is a go. All fleets, weapons hot."

Nemesis scanner officer confirmed, "Incoming fighters, and interceptors."

Followed by the launch bay officer, "All Fleets advised, launch all wings. Ten minutes to intercept."

Over the next fifteen minutes, calls came across the comm's as each fleet reported contacts and launched their bombers and fighters. Their screening ships maneuvered to intercept patterns, protecting capital ships from incoming enemy fighters, rail fire, and missiles.

These Basum's the latest created by Kierian shipwrights and scientists. Sleek and agile, unlike most kingdoms Basum's, designed as combat gunships command dropships which transform into atmos whirlwinds. They were a good deal larger than the general-purpose atmos whirlwinds ground defenses. The size offset by the lightweight material of the nanites and the stealthing compounds.

As their speed dropped from atmospheric friction, their wings altered shape to the proper size and angle to increase lift and atmospheric control. Weapons burst forth from protected gun ports. Inscribed on the flanks of the Basum's were the markings of the Kierian Kingdoms elite assault team: an attacking Phoenix in blue flames.

The pilot called out, "fifteen minutes."

Moments later, they mimicked the signal of the ground defense troops, patrol fighters as they moved in for their designated landing zones. The frequency acquired from a whisper operative two turns ago.

"We gained our window, but it won't last long." The pilot said over comms. Turbulence bouncing them around, forcing the ten APAX Basum's farther apart.

The red warning light flashed inside the underbelly deployment section where Ryakin and the other warrior's prepared to make the drop as the ship got close to the ground. A jerk on his harness as the floor opened beneath him, accompanied by a harsh warning tone when the underbelly door slid open. The slight grinding vibration underfoot felt through the severe buffeting of the storm. Nine other Basum's with Ki's formidable teams preparing to drop two standards apart in meadows along the outer northwest city wall backed by forest and grasslands.

Each pilot came over Cyber comm's acknowledging they dropped their warriors. Team six's pilots came on last. "Package dropped." Seconds later. "Six going down. Repeat. Six going down."

APAX six's luck ran out. Their drop zone manned by an experienced warrior, not a city enforcer. As soon as he spotted the pattern of whitefall swirling against the wind, he guessed a ship's presence in stealth mode. And set the weapons to blanket the surrounding area with auto fire.

"Going down, repeat going down." Team six pilots called over comms.

Ryakin sent a go command to the other eight teams tactical heads-up display map in each warrior's helmets, with new coordinates. "Hold at checkpoint one."

This put them a half standard inside the city walls at the edge of the first courtyard along their route.

"Kraken team will assist team six and rejoin at checkpoint one."

Advanced cyberware connected their helmets, allowing information to flow between them as critical events happened, responding instantly to orders from their team leader. With the ability to reassign commands as necessary in the field. As they moved, their internal scanners updated terrain ahead, giving them their best route to the objective. The other teams moved out. Ryakin's team moved to aid team six, now pinned down from automated anti-craft cannons, rapid-fire plasma placements, and small anti-personnel griffins mounted on the outer walls.

They worked their way over to team six's position to give backup. Their Basum, now transformed to a whirlwind, followed thirty feet behind and ten feet above. The blades designed for silent flight, the outer edges pointing downward. Its hull made of the same chameleon stealth technology as the APAX team's battle armor. The winds buffeted the Whirlwind without mercy, challenging the pilot.

They arrived as APAX team six's Basum's exploded. Its fuel tank hit by explosive nanite neutralizing auto anti-craft shells. The railguns ammunition blew, sending shrapnel in all directions. An intense blast drove his team to the ground while those of team six's warriors violently tossed through the air towards them.

Ryakin's Kraken's sniper took out the guard. A second later, the auto projectile guns, along with the plasma cannon. His coil rifle's metal shaft loaded with powerful electromagnetic tips. A direct hit on the defenses, guns outer shielding knocking out their electronics' controls.

Ryakin rose and realized the rain of fiery debris killed three of team six warriors. The pilots and co-pilots blackened forms inside the burning hulk of the Basum. The stink of blood, death, and the bitter odor of fuels blended with the sharp ozone of whitefall. Burning ship pieces, body parts of stark red painted across the once pure whitefall of team six's drop zone.

Ryakin took a deep breath. Inside the confines of his battle armor, the acoustics of the helmet gave the sound an enhanced hissing. The team's APAX armor designed for close-range fast engagements loaded with the most advanced combat systems and utilities to conduct their mission. Biologicals to keep them in the fight, impervious to many types of damage. This was one of them. "Collect their spirit meh from those on the ground and pull the pilots out and take theirs when finished. We move out. Team six will link up with Kraken."

Their mission required their advanced chameleon camouflage to allow them to close in on their objective, unseen and unheard. Basum six's explosion changed those dynamics.

Thunderous reverberations and rattled building combined possible it alerted enforcers. They had to move faster than planned. Take more risks.

He checked the map. Noted the locations of observation drones along their routes. He stared at the destroyed ship and team's six dead as he decided his next move. The whitefall coming down heavy, the burning ship ate by the flames fast. Team's one and six's life tenders lending aid. Those not dead Ryakin combined with his team.

They cut through the gate and entered, following back alleyways and less traveled streets, joining up with the other teams at checkpoint one. As soon as they arrived, they moved the team's snipers to either Overwatch on rooftops or covering from behind. Their heads-up display pinpointing in red outlines enemies or dangers, yellow as unknown and green non-hostile.

Their battle armor masked their signals and blended with their surroundings, making them almost invisible. They passed entrances to guild halls and private compounds of master guild holders without detection. So far, only green outlines appeared on their heads-up displays as they moved quick and quiet. Their camouflage working. The security drones the only worry to the plan, yet wherever they passed, unrepaired drones lay. *Strange.* It made him uneasy. *What happened here? Why would the guilds not fix their damaged security drones at once*? Drones helped the enforcers with Intel. Lack of intel caused mistakes; mistakes led to a lack of enforcement or deaths.

They now moved through the Imperial Emperors Court's guild outer buildings. As they moved through the city, he spotted more observation and security drones damaged in the merchant terminal docking and lift-off areas. The citizens of Agade prided themselves on being cosmopolitan. This invited unsavory galactic denizens. The enforcers, swift to respond to criminal events, which allowed them to keep crime under control. Because of this, law-abiding citizens and tourists alike enjoyed the city without fear. Observation and security drones, the key to quick response times.

Team seven reached their outer destination five minutes ahead of schedule. They expected to find the court's warehouses of meh's the scribes maintained closed for Restturn. They found an abandoned warehouse full of dust and broken meh's. Broken and unrepaired holo machinery walls with graffiti of bizarre patterns and shattered metacrystal scattered on the floors. Worse than what was happening in the outer causeway's courtyard. At least worse for their mission.

"Team leader seven. Arrived at checkpoint ten. Sending image."

"Kraken received."

When Ryakin regarded the image, he understood why team leader seven thought it important.

"Team leader seven, there's a crowd gathering on the courtside of the building. They appear nervous, angry. There are eleven enforcers in the tower standing the upper cannons with coil rifles and two gauss handhelds holstered on each leg. There are thirty enforcers and forty ground fleet stationed throughout the courtyard and under the court's porticoes. Standard issue weapons."

"Acknowledged. Sitrep team's status."

The teams called out as they arrived at their checkpoints. They relayed back the same images of an abandoned guild court buildings around the courtyard, all derelict, unfit for use. The crowds increasing as they moved towards the Imperial inner causeway.

The teams calling out yellows and greens for contacts, other than those noted by team seven. This smelled like a setup. His team was still two minutes out. Raggedly dressed commoners and guild citizens congregated in the streets ahead of them. Hundreds cowered in doorways in tattered clothing, pitiful piles of goods at their feet, children hiding behind adults. A crowd of commoners, in worse condition, heading the same direction they were going.

That movement forced them further off the prearranged route. Tensions rose as they worked their way to what should be the scribe's major records building. Most likely in the same condition as the others. "Check for FR signatures."

"Acknowledged." Each team reported back in the negative.

"Team leader eight. There's movement by the tower gate. Ten enforcers are lining up between the court and courtyard. They appear as if they are preparing to bring out prisoners."

"Team leader seven. They are bringing out someone; wait, ten more enforcers are surrounding them. *It's* Prince Iltasadum, his wife, heir, and their other three young children. I now see King Rualui and Queen Jena holding her son, and their family, including his mother and sisters. They are leading them to the executioner's stand."

The warrior forgot those were Ryakin's family.

"Our Intel's been wrong about several things," team leader seven said.

Anunnaki's laws forbid work or official business, including courts to function on Restturn. Our intel said the Imperial courts scheduled the trial to occur the following Firstturn. Their plan intended a jailbreak without crowds. This changed everything. He thought fast as a crash of metacrystal windows breaking filled the courtyard.

Each team saying, "citizens are breaking windows in the buildings at our location,"

The rooftop snipers stated, "citizens are climbing on the roof at our position. Reposition?" Each acknowledged they were still unnoticed, their camouflaged working.

The citizens on the roof still showed green. If action occurred from them, it would be hand to hand with knives. Their weapons designed to lock against use on a green target. Yet another strange anomaly; those on the roof moved to the building's edges, broken pieces of metacrete along with rocks in their hands. They went from green to yellow as the armor now assessed them as a marginal-level threat.

Ryakin realized not a single blooded was in the crowds or under the portico, and no scribes were in the area. The mood was restless, angry. When they spotted the prisoners, rage like a flash fire ignited the crowds, now yelling obscenities at the enforcers.

One of the APAX warriors from team six brought him four public broadcast meh's he'd found on the floor. Curious, Ryakin ran them through his holo in his wrist projector.

One was a proclamation banning the Temple. The second, a decree by the Three Pillars that anyone caught worshiping, ordered publicly flogged with a hundred lashes. And half of what they owned taken as forfeiture for the crime of false worship. The third announcement a prohibitive price increase for vatting. Now expensive, even for the wealthy amongst the empire. The fourth decree declared no mass gatherings allowed. Citizens only allowed outside of their dwellings or sectors from star rise to star set. Those caught outside from dusk to dawn, arrested as aiding sedition.

The worst horror. Children caught praying declared punishable with the same severity. Ryakin knew few adults survived a flogging of a hundred lashes. The cost of vatting now a prohibited expense. With half their income seized as punishment, commoners, and lower-ranking guild members, if they paid the vatting fees, ended up homeless on the streets begging. Explaining much of what they'd seen on the way here. How could any decent person punish a child so severely? Let alone in so heinous a manner? A muscle in his jaw twitched.

He gazed out the broken window. He figured the punishment courtyards filled up every turn with those who disobeyed the decree. The Three Pillars misjudged the unshakable reservoir of faith amongst commoners and guilds. Or the ranking blooded.

Power constraints forced team members inside to turn off their stealth masking. A child so dirty and ragged, he could not tell if it was a male or female entered the building. Glimpsed their Sigil badges and melted back out the doorway. Vanishing as effectively as if stealth'd. Poverty was never this wretched in Nibiru Proper. *Who is gathering our Intel? Why not inform us of these conditions?*

"Kraken to teams three and four. Move within striking distance of the tower. On my mark, move in and remove the prisoners from custody. The rest of the teams prepare to create a diversion. Three and four exits back to their Basum's when package acquired. Team Kraken and the other's will cover your retreat.

"Three. On the move."

"Four. On the move."

Seconds after they were in place, the crowd roared. The deep, throaty sound of a wounded beast.

His teams would not acquire Prince Iltasadum in time. *Another piece of false Intel.* Too many enforcers and fleet guarding the prisoners and spread throughout the courtyard. Too many innocent citizens. They led

Prince Iltasadum up the steps to the Execution box. On the platform before the box, the executioner announced his crimes against the Three Pillars and the council. Foremost, the accusation of Treason.

"Team leader five to Kraken. Examine the east upper-security wall."

Prince Jaui and Prince Jabutia stood there, two of the Three Pillars.

Seconds later, the executioners forced Prince Iltasadum into the booth, chaining him in place. A minute later, the bolt shot through his head and out the other side. The bolt designed to destroy the meh chip, permanent death. Iltasadum's body went limp. His wife screamed, reaching for him as she fell to her knees. The enforcers yanked her back to her feet.

"Kraken to all teams, stay alert. Unarmed or not, the guards are about to lose control of this crowd *soon*."

Right then his comm's squawked. "Actual One to Kraken." The voice was not Elgar's. It was Ankak's, Elgar's second in command.

Something's wrong. Ryakin's frown turned into a grimace as Ankak relayed the information to him.

"The Three Pillars moved half the warden's fleets back to Nibiru Proper. The Imperialist hid within the gas giants' outer layer with three full fleets of ships of an unknown design. They are not transmitting transponder codes, nor do they display any identifiable markings. They flank us between the Imperialist and the unknown fleets. At this point, we need an avatar of creation to win."

Someone betrayed them. Who, he was not sure, but if he survived this turn, he would find out?

Ryakin ordered Ankak to transfer the crew to the Wayfarer dreadnought. Once Ankak finished moving the crew to the older ship, he relayed the holo of Nemesis. A burning shell against the black of deepspace. The Wayfarer now flashing Airal's Sigils and Silks as Ki's flagship.

"Knight Elgar?" Ryakin said, his voice tense.

"Eukiof, a low-ranking knight in the signals' division, stabbed Elgar when he caught him sending the Imperialist our control transponder codes. Knight Jal showed up in time with enforcers to stop Elgar's murder and cut off the flow of information. Not fast enough. Nemesis came under direct attack. Knight Elgar is critical. I transferred him to the Light, a Life Tender.

Ryakin understood they now faced an experienced battle fleet. A vastly different pulsar from system defense fleets. He found himself trapped between wanting to stay and rescue his brother and family. Or turn the mission over to his second and return to the fleet and take control.

The next thing Ankak said took away any choice in the matter. "Heavy battlecruisers and Taiguh's are blocking the path back to the fleet. Three Imperial transports, with troop Basum's, are heading into Nibiru Proper. Eta twenty minutes. You need to either complete your mission soon or abort and find a way out."

"Kraken, acknowledge." The line cleared.

Another roar caught his attention, this one louder, angrier, full of rage, came to him from outside the building. He stepped to one of the broken windows. Prince Iltasadum's wife hysterical and fighting to keep the enforcers from forcing her up the stairs to the booth and chaining her to the posts. With his enhanced vision of the suit, the pure terror on her face tore at him.

The sniper teams reported the roofs were becoming crowded with not just metacrete wielding citizens. Others on the roof held slingshots and dangerous implements of their trades. Ryakin sensed the tension in their voices. Even elite warriors faced with a mass of enraged citizens feared the worst.

Like a quasar, an idea came to him. "Kraken, to all teams, hold. Mission change. He informed them of the alternative plan. He allowed each the opportunity to head back to the Basum's and find a way out. None did. Nor did the pilots standing ready to do their part.

"Prepare to engage on my mark."

Chapter 35

KNIGHT COMMANDER Pymic C'Kvuoj of the twenty-seventh Imperialist Fleet Dreadnought the Keek sat basking in the warmth of revenge. Earlier, he testified against his brother on the official court pulse. He stated his brother and family were staunch followers of the Temple. Eminently true. What he lied about was claiming he caught them in hidden worship when he visited the other turn. An outright lie. One easy to disprove, yet it did not matter. Prince Satoric, of the Three Pillars, supported his claim. He never felt this ecstatic in his life; *ever.* The sensation of winning, and his brother's failure, washed away all his past losses to him in one fell swoop.

He sat blowing on his scalding drink of expensive Voag in peace as he reveled in his brother's downfall. He did not intend for the torture to end there. Slow, bit by bit, he would use his position with the Three Pillars and the Imperialist warrior's guild to tear his brother's life to pieces. To make him pay for each slight and perceived insult. He wanted to receive a title to shove into his brother's face. Once the Three Pillars granted him one, he intended to destroy him entirely along with his family. Wipe them out of existence. He arrived an hour earlier after watching the public flogging. Their children included. He was close enough for his brother to see him. Enjoyed the rage and hatred on his face.

He rarely fulfilled his duties as Knight commander, leaving his duties to his EC and second. The exception was when ground forces requested an orbital strike to quell the rebellious Kierian commoners. When these calls came, his weapons officers targeted the location. With pin-point accuracy, they wiped an entire camp off the map while doing slight damage to the surrounding land. His standing orders never do an orbital strike on a camp without his presence on the bridge. He never explained the order to his bridge Knights or Officers. Each time, he would imagine the camp as his brother's. After the strike, King Duurua moved his loyal followers into the area to reward them. Commoners who recognized his authority as King. However, hundreds of camp areas went unoccupied. Ninety percent of commoners still rejected his claim to the throne.

"Commander," his annoying EC interrupted his private time, turning his pleasure into aggravation, "there is a strange skip window forming." Pymic frowned at the holo, then sighed. "Can you not manage this yourself? Should I be considering a more competent EC? Determine friend or foe and take appropriate action."

A battle klaxon sounded, and the ship lurched hard. Thrown from his chair, Pymic smacked his head on the edge of the table. Dazed, he rose to his feet, then stepped on the holo command pad.

"What the *fock* is going on? What hit us?" No one answered back. He pulled up the command ship's overlay and saw a smoking hole where the bridge should be. The battle viewer went live rerouting DCIC to his quarters, showing the fleet under attack. By Kierian warships. Impossible. How? The only Kierian warships left not locked in dock, the traitor Prince Ryakin controlled. And they were about to be ambushed in the Nibiru system. The Three Pillar's would finish the loyalist in one fell swoop. Then his mind kicked in gear. The Ai sounding a discordant warning klaxon. "Power supply critical. Time till explosion fifteen minutes, life systems critical and failing, antigrav systems critical failure in ten minutes."

He did the only thing he thought prudent. He activated his command escape pod, climbed in, and hit eject.

❧

335894 GGS Droe 8th.

THE DAGGER OF CINEUIAN skipped in-system. Right into the center of The Three Pillars twenty-seventh, sixty-seventh and the sixty-ninth fleet. Sent to assist King Duurua to maintain order and help keep control over the rebellious commoners and citizens. The Kierian fleet deemed traitorous. Their Knight Commander's and crews awaiting trial and execution. Jynnalt deployed her complement of ships in a matter of minutes. Chaos ensued throughout the Imperialist fleet at rest. A chaos Jynnalt and her Knight Commander's took full advantage. Twenty minutes later, hundreds of Imperialist capital ships, detritus, and debris. Smoke poured from others, trapped between the hull and the outer shielding as internally they glowed with raging fires. Fourteen Imperialist dreadnoughts destroyed in a blink. Hit hard by their Adramelech cannons pressure waves. Dreadnoughts crashed into battleships, rendering them inoperable in minutes. The Imperialist ships docked too close to each other. Lazy and inept. A mistake which cost them the battle before they ever fired a shot. They could not recover before, torn apart by a barrage of Storm Fury missiles. Explosions tore apart the crew. Pieces of bodies left rotating in space.

Jynnalt ordered her fleet's full complement of fighters released. Minutes later, they were taking out any enemy fighters as they exited damaged bays. Enemy fighters ran straight into a hail of ferocious griffin's fire, turning them to instantaneous debris. The Imperialist support ships retreated before the fury of the onslaught, warping out. Yet, unable to. Titan's defensive platforms activated by Kalmia on the system side. The anti-warp and anti-skip field, along with the immense shielding, would keep them within the system trapping them.

Nine Dreadnoughts and thousands of support ships surrendered to her crews, who boarded and took control. Ki's trained boarding crews of specialized engineers worked quick. They ejected the power plants before they could go critical on salvageable ships. They deployed collection drones to the bodies floating in deepspace to collect their chips.

She scanned her crew. These, the ones who remained faithful. Imprisoned in their dock barracks for refusal to bow to the false King and her mother.

Kalmia, when informed of Jynnalt's return, snuck rebel warriors through forged orders which put them in the outer defensive barracks far away from prying eyes. Willing commoners replaced those in the dungeons. They did this under the occupying enemy's forces noses. The occupiers paid little attention as they viewed the encryption codes unbreakable while docked. Encrypted with King Duurua's personal codes. They also locked the ships Ai's in sleep mode. Leaving only the major computers online. The lackadaisical attitude of the Imperial officers and absence of professionalism by King Duurua's warriors and enforcers in this matter bordered on criminal. This sloppy attitude benefited the Kierian rebels and Jynnalt.

Now she needed to move her plan forward. A plan she and Kalmia worked out over the last couple of turns as she hid in plain sight on the Travelers station, The Rogue of Fire. Well-versed by Kalmia of her assessment of the enemy's fleet, their ground troops, their temperament, experience, and anything else she needed to know. Kalmia notified Ki's rebel ground warriors, who still fought hit-and-run battles. Their morale improved once their Queen, Jynnalt, was safe. The armor, no longer grey but a glossy black, told the truth.

All Imperialists grumbled about everything, the food to coarse, inferior quality goods, antiquated or difficult to run equipment, and the lack of the supposed competence of the outer border's guilders.

The Imperialist guild workers, the false government imported, lost control over various minor systems. Unable to regain control, they requested the Kierian's coders assist them believing this a glitch. They claimed the system far inferior to the systems they normally worked with. The Kieran guild coders informed them the glitch would work itself out by the end of the week and to ignore the problems.

Word spread like wildfire. The Queen arrived. Fighting planetside increased in ferocity as they took back territory and sections of various cities. Jynnalt's battle in the heavens provoked fierce battles planetside.

Once they gained full control over the invading fleet of Prince

Satoric, Jynnalt announced to the Kierian citizens, "This is Queen Jynnalt. I hereby take control of Ki by right as Queen. A right granted by our laws and the Phoenix Armor,"

It pulsed the message with her DNA signature throughout the kingdom. On every planet and every world, on Travelers Stations and platforms and manufacturing moons. She signed off and glanced over at Keif, now her head paladin. "Tell the others to be ready to go planetside. To the throne chamber," she said before stepping towards her EC, "Knight Eidira, I transfer the Silks to your command. May you serve honorably."

He nodded, earnest. This would be the first time he held a full command. She understood his determination. He would not dishonor her or her faith in him.

"Knight Jeid, I place you in command of the drop troops. Guard your back. There are traitors amongst those fighting planetside."

"Ossa, Cineuian, Tiarn, Aidral, you're with me. Starsoaker and Leafcatcher. I need you to stay on board." The sudden consternation on their faces almost made her laugh. The seriousness of the matter kept her from doing so.

Kendo spoke up, "*Ah,* mind if I joined your party?"

All eyes turned towards the Ghost Walkers, Kendo's constant attendants. She hesitated, not wanting to endanger a valuable ally. Yet, she sensed he'd find a way even if she said no. He defied the Malkuth council when they demanded him to go back home. She since learned he was not any council Elder; he was *the* Elder. The ruler of the Malkuth. In frustration, the Malkuth requested additional walkers from the Temple, which they sent without hesitation.

Jynnalt eyed them now. Not an awful idea for them to join her party if they must fight their way out of the throne chamber.

"You are welcome to come along. At your own risk," she added. "I'm taking back Ki." She strode off towards shuttle bay one. "I am not sitting here safe while others endanger themselves for me."

To *helc* with Kalmia's cautions, she of all people should understand.

"The citizens need to see me planetside. To know I will fight for them. I listened to the horrors done to my people under my mother's pet vyzier. Time, I saved them from this false King." *And my mother.* Something she wanted to avoid yet understood was impossible to do.

She ordered the tow and salvage crews to the wreckage as soon as workable. She wanted none of the debris raining down on the planet. From what they told her of late, the citizens subjected to enough terror from the heavens. On the way to the surface, her shuttle passed the fleets tugs and salvage ships heading to repair docks. Damaged ships in tow.

As they came in for a landing, information came across the comm's. The citizens of Ki rose en mass when they heard Queen Jynnalt's announcement. Sporadic battles became ferocious, full-fledged ones. Ki no longer under threat from orbital strikes. Loyal commoners, guilds and the ragtag rebel forces who escaped during the purge of the ground defense units fought back with a fury. Jynnalt's rebel forces wrested control from the usurpers step by bloody step across the planet.

The first thing she did was head straight to the prison where her mother incarcerated her loyal paladins. Her mother sent them there because these warriors refused to disavow her as their Queen, refused to swear to the False King. Now she would reward them for their faithfulness. Later, the faithless would meet their punishment.

A half-hour later, she strode up to the ornate double doors to the throne chamber followed by her official, if now ragged, royal paladins.

Kalmia notified her the council and her mother retreated there when they realized they were under attack. The royal throne chamber never once breached by an invader.

Their group approached the gates and imperialist palace guards attempted to stop them. They fell before the rage of her paladins and the skill of the Walkers. Fast.

The doors locked along with the slightest shimmer of shielding. For a second, her old uncertainty rose. *What if they don't unlock at my command? What will I do then?* She took a deep breath. *Time to find out.* "Unlock." The distinctive clanging sound of the inner mechanisms sliding back as the doors unlocked echoed loudly in the hallway. She let out the breath she realized she'd been holding. An empty throne chair greeted her; the consorts chair occupied by her mother.

"Look at you. Back from wherever you hid, like a coward. You dare enter the King's throne chamber with weapons," Tesiskel scoffed. "Is that a sword handle?" The incredulous tone of amusement clear. Then pure outrage as she realized an Ai accompanied her. "You dared to bring that... *that thing* here expressly against the law."

"This is the *Queen's* chamber, and I learned to dare much, *mother*. This sword kept me alive, allowing me to return and reclaim my throne. Which you stole." She said as she gazed around the chamber.

"It appears you dare much. As well," she said as she strolled towards the throne. "Piece of advice, mother," she said, approaching, without challenge from the automated drone plasma cannons located high above.

Her mother's face blanched as she realized the fact.

"It is never wise to leave the officers and crews locked in their loading docks barracks." She said, no longer looking at her mother but the council sitting frozen. "Do you know why?" She paused before looking back at her mother. Silence filled the hall as her mother refuse to rise to the bait.

"Hmm," Jynnalt paced back over to the now cowering council members. "Can any of you *knowledgeable* council members tell my mother what I am referring to?" She strode closer and stared for a long moment at each one. "No. Then *I* will." She walked back to the center, only feet from the throne.

"Because if they escape, they can access those ships." She waited. Knowing her mother. She was not disappointed.

"The ships in encrypted lockdown mode. Why bother wasting tithe and effort to imprison them elsewhere?" Tesiskel spat back. "I am sorry. If you are counting on using them, you will need King Duurua to give you the release codes." An expression of malicious triumph crossed her face. "Not even I have those codes." She glanced over at the empty throne before looking back at her eldest. "My advice to you. Leave while you can. As my daughter, at least I owe you a warning. Prince Satoric's warriors will arrive soon. So, leave while you can. Someone's head will roll for allowing you to sneak past the defenses. A traitor, most likely. You only achieved your capture by coming here."

"Are you done? Mother?"

Her mother sat up straighter, her eyes narrowed before she relaxed and leaned back as if unconcerned.

In the back chamber, messengers came and went, speaking with Kalmia and someone Jynnalt did not know by the door. She ignored them. "Where is Duurua?"

"He is his highness to you."

"No, I do not believe so. I declared him a criminal of Ki. For the moment, it is beside the point." Stepping up to the full sized holo pulse pad, she ordered the earlier battle between her fleet and Tesiskel's father's replayed. The outcome clear quick enough. When finished, it blinked out.

"I did not *sneak* back into *my Kingdom*." The expressions on the faces of the older council members told her they understood. She walked back over to them.

"I recognize none of you except for one. I hope you treated my council with kindness when you stole their rightful places." She stepped closer. "You shall share whatever fate you decided for them."

One of the younger members rose, pulled his official robes around himself, lifted his head and turned his back on her before walking towards the council member's doors. Jynnalt waited for him to reach his destination before she called out.

"Lock council's throne chamber's back door." The sound of the locking mechanism thundered in the chamber's silence. The first sign of fear passed over Tesiskel's face.

"How did you do that?" Tesiskel glanced at her council, a frown of worry on her face. The oldest, the only council member Jynnalt recognized, his manner calm.

"Our history states Ki was founded because of a betrayal of the heir to the newly founded Anunnaki Empire. Betrayal of their eldest son. Ki's founding couple, Anki and So'listra.

"Lies. Anki never contracted, not even provided offspring by his concubines. Records show he was impotent. Nor was he ever married or even contracted. What does this matter? Here? Now?"

"Anki married. His rightful wife was So'listra a Malkuth princess. When she became pregnant with twins, his younger brothers conspired together against him. They murdered Anki, heir to the throne, as their father lay dying. So'listra escaped with help from Anki's mother. Her father was the Elder of the Malkuth and awarded her this kingdom and all its wealth, including the breeding grounds of the Sailors," he said, stopping for a minute to take a drink before proceeding. "And the most cherished possession of the Temple. The Phoenix Armor."

"What does a backlane border's kingdom unfounded myths have to do with any of"

"Patience has never been one of your virtues, mother. Let him speak. You might learn something."

"Because of the betrayal. Ki's kingdom's officials set our control systems up in such a way that if the legitimate Queen or heir still lives, they have complete control over every system. Any usurper who attempts to steal the throne can't overcome the legitimate Queen's codes with their own encrypted passwords. It means, by the atoms, Princess Tesiskel, our Queen and no one else, is in control of every system throughout Ki. Encrypted or not. The control systems until her death became permanently and physically locked to her Dna signature. Able to override any others. The Phoenix armor is the key."

Her mother stared at the councilors, enraged. "You are aware of this."

"We tried to inform you." A chorus of voices said.

"Father told me you threw a fit and informed everyone you couldn't care less about our backlane myths and legends. Nor the workings of our government. Too bad you ignored his advice." She said, then paused, looking around. "Duurua realized what this meant when the systems locked out his lackeys, as he is not present. Did he run like a coward when he realized I arrived? That's a statement, no need to answer. Tell me how long he has been absent. Three, no wait, four turns. Funny you're still here. Did he leave you to face me alone?"

Jynnalt stared at her mother. "Lockout any prior users of the systems since my last presence in the palace. I give authority to Kalmia, to allow *only* vetted loyalist users for the next week."

"I can tell you begin to understand. Mother." The elders never moved when the younger one attempted to leave. They realized exactly what Jynnalt's presence here meant. Their faces showing their fear and shock.

"I regret mother, you despised the Kierian citizens, and your late husband, my father, so much. You never attempted to understand the simplest laws or rules of the kingdom. To your detriment," she said, walking closer.

Her mother's face betrayed her hate and spite towards Jynnalt. The elder council member, the one who told the tale, rose. "Your contempt and disgust for your contracted kingdom has never been far from the surface long before your betrayal."

"Duurua should have removed you when he begged me to allow him to. However, I thought we needed to keep at least one of the past council members to legitimize this council. How wrong I was. Did you betray us? Pass along whisper information. There is a word for what you did. Treason. You shall pay the price for your actions." She said before turning towards Jynnalt, "You have much to learn about secrets, *my daughter*, and one of those secrets will be your downfall." she said and leaned back, pure hatred on her face.

Before anyone could say anything, Jynnalt spoke up. "Yes, another mistake you made. Though if I were you, I would be careful of what threats you throw around, tread with a light foot in this matter. Especially when you accuse another of your crimes. Mother," she walked up to her and leaned in close and whispered, "remember, I was there when they murdered Emperor Lahamu. Saw the guilty paying the pirate and the three standing by the body of the Emperor. Believe me, on this I will make sure everyone involved in the Emperor's murder pays for their treason."

Her mother's eyes widened.

"The lead assassin when I capture him, and I will, I promise. He will pay for the crimes he committed. But first, he will testify against those who hired him." Stepping back, she moved away. She did not expect her to answer. Her mother's stony face and tight-pressed lips said all she needed to know.

Her mother stood; each word spit her direction. "After they destroy the fleets your husband stole from Ki, and his drop warriors, they will turn their attention your direction. My father will not take well the destruction to his fleets sent to keep the peace." Her mother's spite clear, "those my father trusts betrayed your precious husband. My father's devoted followers embedded high in the loyalist ranks. He will crush this rebellion. These barbaric outer borders *will bow* before him. After he executes their upper ranks and fills them with those faithful to him."

"So, not the Three Pillars, just your father?" Her mother's expression, her answer.

Leaning forward, a subtle smile upon Tesiskel's lips said, "your husband along with the loyalist fleets will be defeated. The council and I observing the battle on the holo before you so rudely burst in. And for your information, King Duurua is there helping to destroy this petty rebellion. Father will compensate him for his participation. Enormously."

"I will bite." She turned towards the holo-pad. "Pulse on for the Nibiru's system."

A different battle filled the space between the throne and the upper chamber floor. The expression of surprise by her mother told her the battle was not going as she expected.

Minutes later Jynnalt said, "you underestimated me, mother. The fault lies in me for my past behavior. I thank you for the information about the battle. Shut off holo," she said.

"You will not wait for it to finish?"

The taunt not lost on her. Though it might not be going as her mother liked, neither did it favor her husband and the loyalist fleet. She learned since arriving, a civil war raged between those who supported Prince Anu, the legal heir, called loyalist, and rebels. Those who supported the rule of the Three Pillars, the Imperialist.

She turned away to speak to Cineuian, who stood silently this whole time.

The double doors to the throne chamber crashed opened and a group of enforcers entered. She tensed till they bowed their heads in deep respect.

"Your Highness, Kalmia told us, you required our service. How may we serve?" She recognized the commander of the Enforcers from before, older, and far more worn, but still faithful.

Kalmia made a slight nod of her head when Jynnalt glanced her way. "Arrest those sitting where my council should be. Call a scribe to scourer the records, find my loyal council members and restore them to their rightful places. If you discover any officially murdered, I want the information noted. Also, who testified against them and who sentenced them?"

"Cineuian, which fleet took the most damage in our retaking Ki?"

"The Command Dreadnought of the one hundred and fifty-first, along with three others in its fleet, took the worst beating. The rest of the fleets barely scratched.

"Assemble the others and inform them to once more prepare for battle. Leave the one hundred and fifty-first to protect against any attempt to retake Ki."

Taunting laughter from the throne reached her. "How do you think you will reach them in time? The trade lanes require a royal traveler's writ. However, even with one, the Chakian's are blockading the lanes. The Igigi are sticklers for their rules, they will not interfere with battling forces. They must maintain their neutral stance throughout the galaxy. For the other routes, you would have to battle your way through Imperialist forces from here to Nibiru. You can't possibly arrive before their eventual defeat."

"Open a pulse channel to the Chakian Queen and the High Temple Priestess." The holo sat blank.

"Oh gracious, did you think either would talk with a disposed Queen from a small back-lane kingdom like yours?"

"Yes, mother, I did," she said. The expression on Tesiskel's face became worried. Everyone in the chamber could hear the tone of authority unmistakable in her daughter's voice.

Then the holo popped up, split in two. One side a wizened ancient of unknown sars, hunched and bent yet dressed in the rich clothing of the empress of the Chakian empire. The other old yet not as ancient in the plain robes of the Highest Holy Temple Priestess.

"I am asking for a favor. As Queen of Ki, of the Anunnaki empire, in return, I will acknowledge your legal status within Ki and all entailed," she said to both.

Both responded, "Listening."

Jynnalt laid out what she needed. Both agreed to her terms before signing off.

Ignoring her mother's gasp of astonishment, she once more requested a channel. "Open pulse channel to the commanding Igigi of the Trade lanes within the Anunnaki Empire."

When an Igigi answered, he bowed in respect to her, before asking how he might be of assistance. With careful respect, she made her request and received an affirmative answer. The pulse blinked out as soon as she finished.

"Mother, I leave you to languish in the company of your council. I hope they might explain things to you better during your stay in the cells in the bowls of the palace. Kalmia, I leave Ossa in your care. She made it possible for me to be here, treat her with respect. Cineuian with me. Kendo, you can join me or go your way. If you want to head home, Kalmia can arrange your transportation. At my expense.

"I have come this far; I will go with you."

"You understand this will mean another battle? One we might lose."

He shrugged. A smile tugging at his lips.

"At this point, what is one more, and any battle carries the risk of failure," he said than shuddered, "at least they are not carnivorous insects, either giants or of the sand-dwelling sort."

She left as she entered a wild storm full of contained power and fury.

Chapter 36

335893 GGS Droe 8th.
Nibiru Outer System–Queen Jynnalt

JYNNALT CALLED THE Silks before sending her officers and Cineuian up to the Dreadnought to prepare to leave. While they assembled, she went to the palace courtyard where the Phoenix Armor stood.

She wanted to stand before the armor and see if she was still acceptable. When she arrived, a sense of tranquility overwhelmed her, bringing a glimmer of tears to her eyes.

This time, she was sure the Phoenix statues bowed to her. She wondered if the armor would accept her if she stood the test this turn. After all, she did in the arena. The screams of the dying rang in her mind along with every wrong decision which brought about her downfall. Proper decisions she failed to do. Somehow, standing before the armor healed a hurt deep inside. Nullified the soul-destroying hatred building towards herself. Once ready to leave, she bowed with respect before heading out. The armor gave her something precious. Peace with herself.

She froze. Visions of her son, older, still chubby of face, flashed before her, laughing. Her eyes shimmered. The scene blurred, then disappeared. Why show her this now? Was the vision real or an illusion? She took a deep breath to steady herself. Somehow, she would find him. She swore this. She put him out of mind and concentrated on the immediate future, shaking her head before heading to her waiting shuttle.

Now forty minutes out from the exit tower to Nibiru, she called a battle council with her commanders and officers. Her Knight commanders pulsed in for the meeting. She pulled up the holo map from Nibiru's exit.

Eager to aid the beleaguered fleets, and Ryakin, her patience worn thin, she got straight to the point. During her enslavement, her need to see him kept her alive. Only to arrive and find him in a life and death battle was not how she envisioned their reunion.

Prince Anu, the other three border Kings and Queens, and the Kieran fleets along with Ryakin led the Task Force to rescue King Rualui, and King Da's, and their heir's and family. Slated for public execution. These executions allowed the Three Pillars to steal their thrones and dangle them before others. Blooded who were faithful to them.

Kalmia did not hide the fact that the fate of the Anunnaki Empire and the border kingdoms hung on the outcome of this battle. Information she learned about the degree of betrayal from within horrified Jynnalt, yet somehow did not surprise her. Outnumbered, the loyalist fought with furious determination. They made the Imperialist pay for each ship lost. What little she witnessed in the holo in the throne chamber made her realize the skill of her fleets and though she did not show this, she was proud of them. She paced; afraid they would not arrive soon enough. Restlessness drove her as she thought about Ryakin.

"They informed me our Queen returned; some claimed from the dead. I chalked the information up to hopeful thinking once the tide of battle went our way. I also wondered if Kalmia, crafty as ever, spread the rumor to boost morale," Re Dukian Aulauc said from his flagships Dreadnought the Weyisa on the holo-pad.

"When the Commanders pulse in, we will start the meeting." She said, halting any further remarks he might make. Once they were present, including all their EC's and seconds, the reaction was the same. Relief, incredulity, and hope.

"All present," Cineuian said. "Recording of the meeting started." She stepped away from the DCIC holo-pad to the lower steps.

"Your Highness, may I speak."

The voice a familiar one. The tone held no hint of censor. No hint of Jynnalt's distance from her when she became Queen. Kalmia informed her Racin in her position as Arch Dukian of Ki was the highest title to refuse to repudiate her. Tesiskel imprisoned her, and when they could not get her to break, they scheduled her execution. The execution set for the end of this week. Tesiskel awarded the title, and all entailed to Skyta. Jynnalt's eyes narrowed, and her lips tightened at the thought. The long imprisonment took its toll on Razin, shocking Jynnalt at her first sight of her. They denied prisoners by the orders of Duurua replacement nanites or repair units. Thin to the point of gaunt, her hair lackluster, black circles under her eyes though still shining with intelligence and determination.

Warmed by her presence and appreciative of her friendship, she nodded, unable to speak, the full-size holo of Racin before her blurry. She realized how she missed her friendship and her staunch loyalty.

"From this moment forward, all can speak without asking permission."

"Great timing. Your arrival will ruin Skyta's turn. Now she can't keep her ill-gotten title. Can't wait to tell her the news."

Laconic, as always, the remark broke the ice between the two. Jynnalt could not stop herself from chuckling before saying, "so you forgive my awful behavior? Besides, I owed you a rescue." She shot back, and both smiled at the inside joke between them. "I'll allow you to break the shocking news to her. She does not get to keep what she helped steal. I doubt she will like her next accommodations."

Racin nodded, then changed the subject, jumping right in with what she wanted to say. "There are three principal advantages to this idea. First, we can use the maneuver you used at Kiestrial. Impressive, I will say. The sudden chaos of unknown ships skipping in during the heat of battle will rattle their best commanders. Also, the unexpected attacks will take an instant toll. They will waste valuable time trying to figure out who just skipped into the middle of their battle. Friend or foe."

Second, our actions will force the enemy to scramble to reorganize; ours won't. We can send a flash signal to the loyalist fleet. We will skip amongst them. This will give them the upper hand and prevent any friendly fire. We can then give cover for their hardest hit ships to warp out of the boxed-in positions they are in now.

A female she did not recognize spoke. Her badge showed her rank as Sarl her Sigil, the blood house of Spahn. "We can also reduce the chances for the Imperialist ships to escape and reform without being engaged. We should be able to break the battle into a disorganized one for the Imperialist, but more controlled on our side. Depending on whether our intel is correct, and whether there are ships of an unknown empire fighting."

Jynnalt held up a hand before anyone else spoke. "I recognize who those unknown fleets belong to. The Society, crewed by a combination of Society members, Sabation warriors, and an unknown species of a bi-pedal reptilian, the Sabations called Heliosags."

Gasp greeted her account, some staring at her as if she lost her mind and others demanding where her information came from.

"I assure you I am correct. We can discuss how I am aware of these facts later. For now, I wanted you to understand what you are up against." Silence greeted her, but only for a few moments.

Another Knight chimed in, "We need to force them into single ship-to-ship actions, in which we excel and take the momentum from them. This will give us a chance to prevail over their larger numbers. Even with our fleets added to those in battle, the Imperialists and their allies outnumber us. This battle needs to be swift and concise. There's no time for niceties. Make no mistake, this battle will be brutal if we are to prevail. We must prevent reinforcements from arriving before we break them, and they flee or surrender."

Racin broke in, looking around at each of them. "You know, once in the heat of battle, exchanging broadsides ship-to-ship, everything comes down to guts, instincts, and experience. Larger numbers, though, can overwhelm the best fighters. We have the guts, instincts, and experience, we lack the numbers. Be smart about your choice of targets."

"I doubt our destruction of their Overwatch fleet at Kiestrial reached the Imperialist yet. If not, they do not understand. This fleet is even here or exists. Still, a surprise will only go so far. We must route them fast, or we risk losing everything," Knight Commander Kummu said.

Re Dukian Aulauc spoke, "I'd bet a war beast they don't know. Kalmia took care of that problem before you arrived. She jammed all incoming and outgoing signals prior to your attack. How, I don't want to know, or even open that mug of Banita crawlers. However, we won't be able to do that here."

Another male spoke up, who Jynnalt did not recognize. His Sigil badge belonged to the blood house Yia. His rank Saques. "Let's say they're informed somehow. They will expect you to follow normal fleet tactics. Expect you will want to strengthen your hold on Ki before making a move. So even if they know, I doubt they will expect an attack from you."

"The rout of the Imperialist fleet at Kiestrial fired up our warriors. Their morale is another advantage. The Imperialist crews since the Three Pillars took over control of the empire, shoddy training, and no morale. Commoners and Guilders forced into service overseen by arrogant, recently appointed Knights and Blooded. The fact officers who bought their commissions combined with no idea how to command balances out their numbers against ours commanded them."

Another Knight spoke up. "None of the home defense commanders graduated from the warrior's academy. Intel says when the warrior's council complained, they removed them and replaced them with those loyal to the policies of the Three Pillars. Political appointments with no warrior training." He said, shaking his head. "The only way now to gain command is through the council. When the loyalist split off in the middle of a war with Chakian, the Imperialist lost a good portion of their fleets. Many of their best commanders and officers with the most experience in the field joined us."

"Agreed, but we need more than morale to defeat the forces arrayed against the loyalist already in battle. Don't forget the Societies fleets' nobody thought existed, The Society, and their warriors of Sabations and those being's our Queen called the Heliosag all allies of the Three Pillars. We lack intel about their training, ships, or command. They fielded a sizeable force. Any intel about reserves in the area?" Knight Commander Triitle, a friend of Elgar's, of the Dreadnought the Fire

Dream, interrupted. "Anyone aware of the capabilities of their ships or commanders?"

Blank stares and shaking heads met the question. A whisper agent present spoke. "The agency lacks intel from around the galaxy. We do not understand how they could field a single fleet. Let alone the several at Nibiru in battle. How they kept this secret we are trying to discover."

"I do, however once more, this is not the time. Get with Kalmia once this battle is over. I gave her all the information I know. To answer Commanders Knight Triitle's question, they are vicious fighters with no honor. Expect none, give none in return."

Commander Triitle looked at the agent, "Does the Temple have any answers about their abilities in battle? Where the *helc* they got a Task Force the size of this one with no one realizing the fact?"

"Temple command does not share information on what they know. I can guess, but this is neither the time nor the place, as Queen Airal pointed out," the whisper agent said.

Jynnalt broke in, "I believe our chances best to go after the Societies fleet first. Focus on them first, disabling or destroying as many as possible. We can let Ryakin's Task Force concentrate on the Imperialist. There are ships with crew members on board collaborating with the loyalist. Let's not kill or destroy any Anunnaki ships if possible, other than the Societies."

She let the thought hang in the air for a second. "These imperialist's crews are Anunnaki citizens, most of them conscripted by the Three Pillars government."

Re Dukian Aulauc spoke, pointing out a glaring problem to a surprise attack, "They will place recon cruisers on the periphery of the battle along with ghosters and whisps. How do we keep the scouts from notifying them an enemy fleet is incoming from the exit tower gate?"

She looked around at those present and those on holoprojection. "We will skip from inside the Tower gate."

Loud arguing broke out as they all tried to speak at once. Most agreeing with each other, it was a terrible idea. She allowed the dissenting voices to go on for a bit, letting each speak their piece. Then she raised her hand. Silence fell.

"Our fleets are equal or superior to any in the galaxy. Even the other borders." This brought a faint smile to her commanders for a second. "Your crews and you shown your metal in battle, time over, with reaver's, and from what I understand, your battles with the Chakian empire. And in our history, the Kierian fleets of the Anunnaki were the most feared by the enemy. Our gunners are fast and accurate, our fighters and bombers eager and brave. Our bridge officers better trained in all areas from navigation, scanning, and helms. *Helc,* our academy, still teaches helm and navigation, minus Ai aid." She stopped talking, looking them all in the eye before saying.

"All those are not the reason we are the best. We are the best because our commanders are daring, take risks, don't take the straightforward path, backing all this up with their crew's experience. Your crews will follow you to *helc* and back. That is why we win." A moment passed in total quiet.

"Well now, that you stroked our ego's what's the plan, and how in the *helc* and *dragon eggs* are we supposed to pull this off?" Racin asked.

Loud laughter broke the tension. She felt a fleeting smile. After this battle, if they survived, she would take the time to meet with Razin, as a friend, not a Queen.

"The Igigi agreed to close the lane when we arrive. They will divert power from the Tower to our ships, allowing us to skip from the gate to the beacon sitting outside the gas giant. My helm and navigation officers did this once before. With no Ai's help, with their help, this should be a breeze. Cineuian will send over the coordinates and information on how and where. The other Ai's will coordinate with her for the skip. You must first give them a battlefield command so they can override the signal from the beacon. Declaring capital ships illegal to skip in. It will put us right in the battle's center. Warp directly from there to the coordinates given to us by the loyalist Task Force. Warp rings out during skip. Believe me, we can do this."

Silence met her announcement. Till Racin spoke, "skipping in from the trade lane it is."

The others nodded in unison, stunned at the help from a source they never expected. The Igigi.

335894 GGS Tuiu 15ᵗʰ
Nibiru Proper Outer Agade–Prince Ryakin

ACROSS COMMS, RYAKIN got ready to send in his teams. "On my mark, prepare to—-"

The crowd rushed the executioner's platform as others produced weapons and attacked the enforcers and fleet crews. Sudden. Swift. Unexpected by the Imperialist guards and him.

Thinking quick Ryakin called out, "Kraken to team eight. Take Prince Jaui and Prince Jabutia now. As soon as you acquire them, move back to your Basum's. The rest take out those firing on the crowd, give them support. It's a rescue attempt by those in the crowd."

The chatter of their weapons and the flash of plasma fire added to the turmoil. Precise, taking out the warriors attempting to hold the crowd back. This created panic amongst untried fleet warriors who broke and ran for cover.

The prisoners disappeared into the crowds. He glimpsed Prince Iltasadum's heir and Jena with his brother before someone threw a commoner's cloak's over them and hustled them away from the courtyard.

His comm's crackled to life, "Actual to Kraken, twenty Kierian incoming dropships to outer Agada plains. LZ coordinate sent. *Situation has changed.* Repeat. *Situation has changed.*"

Thirty minutes later, his APAX team's joined forces with the drop command. Prince Jaui and Prince Jabutia now in their custody. Prince Satoric's location unknown for now.

Commander Meikia tried to transfer command to Ryakin, who refused. He intended to go after Prince Satoric with his teams as soon as their intel pinpointed his location. In the last twenty minutes, the temperature plummeted to well below zero, adding worse conditions to fight under. Yet the earlier blizzard moved away. The sky now turquoise, the star overhead bright, the reflection off the blanket of whitefall blinding, his visor responded darkening.

The battle in the heaven's unseen groundside. Taking place on the dark side of the gas giant in Nibiru's systems. The battle planetside bloody. Civilians and warriors lay sightless, staring at the firmament overhead. Smoking ruins of war tanks, artillery batteries, destroyed from overhead by atmos fighters and whirlwinds. The broken parts scattered across the landscape as fires blazed in buildings within the city.

The staccato chatter of weapons, along with a loud whirring sound and concussive explosions, sounded close to where they stood. Two Society fighters overhead raced towards them, firing, bullets kicking up dirt off to their right. Loyalist fighters took them out with direct hits. The enemy fighters becoming two fiery streaks. Seconds later, distance explosions mushroomed to rising fireballs high in the sky.

Ryakin stood next to Commander Meikia's fleet repulser battle barge, small gauss mounted cannons on each side capable of firing a thousand rounds a second. Their ground forces joined by the hodgepodge regiment of loyal rebel fighters. All waited before the largest outside gates to the city. Next to the three giant spider tanks, the repulser attack skimmer Ryakin rode appeared tiny. The loyalist ground troops moved through Agade's commoner city unimpeded. Both prisoners captured earlier sitting cuffed and guarded in the back of a light strike vehicle. Ryakin called Basum one to pick up the prisoners and rejoin the fleet. If they won this turn, the Pillars would stand trial. If they lost, he intended the APAX warriors to take the two back to Ki's secret base for information.

The Imperialist's newest class of dropships and jackstrikers, along with an unknown class of fighter escorting them, flashed overhead, chased by loyalist fighters, which fired three hellbore missiles. Imperialist air defense took out the loyalist fighters, which moments later exploded as fiery clouds rose skyward to Ryakin's left. Other jackstrikers zoomed past before slowing as they headed for Agade's Imperial fleet terminal.

Shimmering shields covered the walls and gates. The blasts from the spider tanks did not damage to the gate. Without warning, the shields dropped. Seconds later, the concentrated fire from the spider tanks left the gate sitting at an odd angle, melted metasteel dripping from their edges.

Smaller tanks moved forward, grappling the gate to pull them further open, allowing their forces to move through to the city. Ryakin felt a trickle of warmth slide along his ribs, but ignored it. During the battle with the Imperialist blocking their path to the city, he took a hit in his side at the weakest area of the nanite material.

The nanite armor did an automatic infield battle repair, but the armor was now thinner than before at that spot. Pain meds took the brunt of the burning sensation away, and bionanites sealed the wound. His heads-up display listing the wound as non-fatal.

"Kraken to team five and eight rejoin me at the mark on your maps. The rest assist ground troop commanders."

The mark just outside an access door to the tunnel system for the power grid and reclamations waste maintenance. Ryakin intended to reach the palace through here, bypassing the fighting and enter unseen.

Intel arrived, claiming Prince Satoric and the warrior's council were directing the battle from there. If they captured Prince Satoric and the council, this civil war ended. Here, this turn.

The loyalist moved into the city. The roar of bloodthirsty and terrifying battle accompanying them.

Ryakin requested a map of the power, water, and waste tunnels from Duac, a leader of the most effective rebel group planetside and an old friend from the academy. Ryakin was looking over the plans as Ustrix arrived informed by Duac where to find him. Ustrix brought a guide, a guild worker, instrumental to the few rebels' successes inside the city proper. The maps were useless and outdated; the worker told them. They sealed tunnels shut and then rerouted recent ones to cover those areas, yet never put them on the map's layout. Ustrix explained to him the guide helped them use the tunnels' underground as he worked in the waste reclamation guild. They could take those passages to the palace. Unpleasant, but the safest and fastest way to stay alive and complete their mission.

Ryakin scrutinized the guide as he checked something in his helmet before nodding. "This is the door. The palace is upward and northeast of here."

Fifteen minutes later, they reached the bottom of a long stairwell and stood in a small, accessible area. Tunnels led off in different directions. Every so often, as far as he could see, were doorways with actual handles to open them.

"Weird. I would never imagine all this was here. Under my feet, as I walked above," Ustrix said. Something slithered over his armored boot. He yelped, jumping back. "Is there anything dangerous down here?"

"Allosauruses, various scavenger rodents, and night flyers." The guide shrugged. "If you leave them alone, they won't bother you unless they are hungry." He jerked his head upward toward the tunnel ceiling.

Thousands of night flyers were in one of the three tunnels ahead, clinging to the ceiling, hanging upside down high above. Not the small ones, either. These are the larger species. The APAX warriors looked up, then back toward the tunnels, saying nothing.

"This way." The guide took off into the tunnel the night flyers occupied. After a few steps, he stopped, looking back, "well?"

They followed reluctantly. The further they went, the more the stench became an unbearable odoriferous smelling water full of garbage. Putrefied and festering effluent and a hint of sulfuric hideous rotten eggs and waste odor wafted towards them. Forced them to shut down the scent sensors on their helmets to keep from gagging. Except for their guide, who wore no suit, and appeared not to care.

At each junction carved into the stone were directional indicators. Though not much help, covered in slime and dirt, making them unreadable. This forced them to trust the guide to get them to the palace safely and in one piece. One time, their heads-up display showed danger outlined in red as a huge Allosaurus swam languorously past. To their relief, it kept going. All weapons trained on it.

They trudged through the subterranean system, following the guide through twists and turns. Ryakin's built-in planetary positioner showed them steadily moving towards the palace. He did not trust the guild worker yet could not say why, so kept his unease to himself. Without exact records of the tunnels for their maps to use, they needed his experience down here. Ahead of them, a broad crack opened all the way to the surface level. Earlier, the tunnel shook around them. This the reason why, he guessed. A bomb strike which penetrated deep enough to open a part of the tunnel to the upper causeway. Smoke and dust filled the tunnel as their suits switched to dual vision. Scanners showed the debris didn't block the passage, but it'd be tight to cross. Ryakin, at the rear, regarded the others as they disappeared into the smoke. He followed, coming out on the other side. Ustrix waiting for him as he emerged from the swirling smoke. A relieved expression on his face.

"The next turn ahead will take you straight to the palace underground entrance in less than five minutes. I will take you as far as the exit stairs."

Ryakin nodded, "I'll be glad to get out of these daemons' spawned tunnels." Minutes later, they reached their destination, and the guide pointed, before heading back in the direction they came. Ryakin considered the guide's actions as he stopped for a moment by a door before moving into the dimness and disappearing around a corner.

Ustrix looked back over his shoulder. "Any idea of the location of Prince Satoric?"

"Our intel claims he's in the warrior's council directing the battle." The sound of a plasma rifle charging behind chilled him as he reacted, pulling his rifle up to the ready position. The APAX warriors also turned towards the sound; too late.

Heavy nanite-piercing rounds with tracers filled the tunnel. A blast from a sonic grenade slammed Ryakin into the wall next to him. His helmets heads-up display flashing before going black. A second later, it felt like hammers raked across his chest as agony hit him like a sledgehammer.

Next thing he knew, someone said something in the distance,

"He's lost a lot of blood."

He clawed his way back from the black well. Fighting not to slip back down into the engulfing darkness. Somewhere in the distance, once more, voices called his name. The voice was frantic. Wanting to reassure the familiar voice, he opened his eyes and raised his head.

A bolt of pain exploded, and the sound of a groan echoed in the surroundings before he grasped the sound came from him. A face leaned over him, blurry, out of focus. Red hair. The face solidified into Jynnalt, with tears running down her face. He reached up, wanting to touch her, to make sure he was not dreaming.

The apparition seized his hand and held tight. Not a dream. His heart stuttered in relief, stronger than his pain. Pushing himself to a sitting position helped by Jynnalt, he said, "Took you long enough to come home," his voice came out whispery in a croaking sound.

He tried to rise with her help. Pain exploded like a living, vicious thing. Gasping, he stopped for a moment. A sting in his neck and the pain subsided seconds later. This allowed him to think clearer. Slow and careful, he rose to his feet, using the wall next to him and Jynnalt's hold on his arm to steady himself.

Ten feet away, life tenders were working on Ustrix. Farther up the tunnel, drones collected meh chips from his APAX warriors. All dead.

Jynnalt shook her head. "When we landed, we got an anonymous message which said someone set an ambush for you in the tunnel entrance to the palace. So, I came to back you up," she glanced around at the others, "a little late."

"The fleet battle. What is happening?" He asked as he gathered himself.

"The Society's fleet retreated, abandoning the Imperialist as soon as we engaged. They warped out, then went to skip without a single shot fired. As they fled, we got direct hits on five of their ships, but we could not ignore the Imperialist fleet. Prince Satoric's flagship abandoned the battle minutes afterward, following the Societies. No idea if he was on board. Our scanners did not locate him planetside, though. We have not checked the Traveler's Stations yet. My guess he escaped. I doubt he is with the council."

Ryakin took a step forward, staggered two steps more than walked towards Ustrix. "How is he?"

A female life tender answered without looking at him. "Critical, but stable for now. Most likely, we won't vat him." She stood and motioned for them to move him to the waiting life pod. They sealed him inside. She worked various controls, waited for the pod to show his vitals, nodded, then punched the coordinates to the temporary Life Center set up outside on the palace grounds. He sensed Jynnalt's concern as she helped to keep him standing.

"We arrived as you fell. Your attackers committed suicide. I wanted to get at least one alive or recoverable. Whatever their suites injected into them not only killed them but destroyed their meh chips beyond recovery."

"They were waiting in those chambers behind us. The guide unlocked the door as he left. I wondered what he was doing. We need to find him. Find out who paid him to double cross us."

The female life tender standing next to him scanned his vitals and motioned for a pod and the other tenders to come her direction.

"I am fine, for now." He recognized the expression on Jynnalt's face. He ignored it. He hoped she'd not make a scene. She didn't.

For the next couple of minutes, he checked out his armor and found it was not good for more than reclamation. His helmet destroyed, hung in a tangle of melted nanites cloth hanging half off his left shoulder. Morphed somewhere between the uniform and the battle armor. He spotted Jynnalt, her back turned away from him, nodding towards a female he did not recognize. Then she commanded, "grab those weapons. Our research guild will want to examine them. Small rifle fire should not be able to shred nanite armor the way these did."

"Prince Anu arrived half an hour ago. He requests our presence in the throne chamber. Can you walk on your own?"

"Yes, like your timing, though earlier would have been better."

Her expression told him she was not sure if he was being humorous or sarcastic.

Fifteen minutes later, they arrived at the throne chamber amidst arguing and yelling. Ryakin spotted his brother first thing as they entered, and relief flooded through him. The strain of uncertainty melted away. Everyone he cared about was here except for Ustrix. And his chances of recovery excellent.

"It's done. Legal and binding. You must obey the law. If you do not, then you will be no better than those you overthrew this turn."

Ryakin did not recognize the speaker. But his ceremonial robes decreed he was the High Elder of the Great Council. He recognized Prince Alalus, who was the acting Lord Vyzier to the Three Pillars. He was not sure what his title was now. Prince Alalus' wife stood next to him and a young female, he guessed from her appearance, was their daughter.

Behind Prince Alalus stood the newest blooded which gained titles, illegally, under the Imperialist Three Pillars. On the other side stood Prince Anu, behind him, stood those who rebelled against the Three Pillars, the loyalist.

Prince Anu turned to them as they entered. "The prisoner's?"

"Dead, unrevivable your Grace," Ryakin said. "I received a message the transport ship they were on hit and destroyed right before we arrived in the hall, your Grace."

"I see," Prince Anu said before turning back to the council, "I propose a compromise I will abide by; *If Prince Alalus will.*"

The High Elder stepped forward before Alalus could speak. "Will the council hear the proposal?"

All said aye, and he nodded towards Prince Anu, cutting off Prince Alalus' attempt to stop him from speaking. "The law says he has the right, if made during the first turn, to challenge your claim. Are you going to ignore the law?" The threat plain to those assembled here. The elder could declare for another during this time.

"No, I grant the chamber floor to Prince Anu."

"I propose I take back my position as the cupbearer to the crown." Prince Alalus started once more to object, and once more, the Elder silenced him.

"On the condition that my son Prince Ea marries Prince Alalus' eldest daughter Damkina. If they produce a male offspring, I will concede the Cupbearer title and the position to my grandson once he becomes old enough to hold the title. I will keep this covenant as long as Prince Alalus acts in the best interest of the Anunnaki Empire and her citizens."

Disappointment crossed his brother's face and those of the other loyalists. He realized the same look was upon his face. His wife appeared more interested than concerned. For a second, resentment rose before subsiding at the memory of the holo and the sight of her battered, unconscious form taken aboard the strange ship. The enemies who stood here also deeply wounded her. She fought battles, just not the same ones.

Lord Riciad leaned forward and whispered in Prince Alalus' ear. Differing emotions passing over Alalus face. Anger, hatred, then odd enough resignation.

"I will accept the terms. Prince Anu will regain his prior duties as Cupbearer and all the entailed rights. The wedding held here this turn and sealed with the full approval of the High Council. Or I will not agree."

The council will now take a vote. Within minutes, the undisputed vote came back. "Accepted. The earlier decree destroyed as void. We agree on all terms. All parties come forward."

Twenty minutes later, Prince Ea and Princess Damkina married by the Anunnaki High Priestess officiating, making the ceremony legal and binding. Prince Anu reinstated and given his articles of title. Alalus became the official Emperor of the Anunnaki Empire. Anu once more regulated to cupbearer.

"As my first act, I demand all the commoners punished for the riots during Caldr eighth. They shall lose half of all their profits for this sar."

The silence of shock filled the chamber.

Jynnalt spoke up with the ring of authority. "Kierian civilization bases enmity and criminality towards an individual's actions, not a group. The Empire's laws are the same. Is your first act to be to punish an entire class not by their individual actions but by the actions of others? If so, you're already a tyrant by Anunnaki standards." She said as she paused, looking around at those gathered. "I believe you gained the throne by those you intend to punish. And... that proclamation would break the oath moments ago that you swore to rule in the best interest of *your citizens. With your first command.* Ryakin sensed those within the chamber, waited along with her for his answer. Moments passed in silence at her challenge to Emperor Alalus.

He looked around and realized the hostility on the faces. "I see your point. To punish all for the actions of others would send a dishonest message. My apologies. I must admit this turn a trying one."

"I'll give you this warning. If you punish any who helped bring down the Three Pillar's, you shall break this covenant. You swore this turn. Leaving me no choice but to back any claim Prince Anu makes afterward.

And I'll give you a piece of advice. I would seek a Vyzier who can guide you, wisely. As Emperor, I suggest you think first before you speak."

A soft gasp rippled through the chamber, along with quiet laughter. Ryakin caught the rage in Emperor Alalus' eyes flash for a second before they narrowed, his face stony.

"Are you finished chastising *your Emperor*?" Alalus asked, his tone silky, with an undertone of threat towards Jynnalt not lost upon those present. "Where is King Duurua? I don't see him here." The sly tone not missed on those assembled.

Jynnalt walked toward the throne. "There is no King Duurua." She stated flatly. Moments passed and tension sizzled between those assembled.

Riciad leaned over and again whispered in his ear. Emperor Alalus said, "once more, I apologize for my hasty tongue. You are right, I must learn to think before I speak."

Ryakin realized Emperor Alalus would never let his wife embarrass him before those assembled to go without punishment. He feared it would not bode well for her or Ki.

She spoke once more, "I arrived here to deliver a message to the ruler of the Anunnaki Empire and skipped right into the middle of battle. Imagine my surprise. I believe they mistook us for their enemy, so naturally, we defended ourselves."

Ryakin and the others gathered in the chamber stared at her. Confused looks on their faces.

"I forgot to explain Ki's new status concerning the Anunnaki Empire." Jynnalt strode forward and handed the great council's scribe an official meh holo'writ. Signed and sealed by the Council of Nine, GIA, and The Holy Seer Temple of Radiance and the Malkuth. He realized the ex Anunnaki High Temple Priestess stood behind her along with an envoy to the Malkuth empire and an envoy to the Council of Nine and GIA.

"Read the decree," she said in a pleasant tone, as if unconcerned.

Pride flowed through him as she stood defiantly before Emperor Alalus. No longer the unsure female he married.

Alalus nodded toward the scribe who placed the writ on the

chamber's holo-pad and four images popped up, each in their own sections. "The Council of Nine approves the request of Ki, passed already with the approval of GIA, for withdrawal from the Anunnaki Empire from this moment forthwith." There was a pause before the holo proceeded.

"We request the Malkuth and the Holy Seer Temple recognize the full rights of Ki as an independent kingdom. Per the original agreement. This states Ki has the right, at any future date, when the interest of the Kierian kingdom to stay within the Anunnaki empire is no longer acceptable to the Kingdom to leave. The petition to leave through GIA, CON and the High Temple and by the Malkuth approved. We award the Kingdom of Ki the rights of secession." The holo'writ blinked out. Indistinct murmurs rose in volume through the chamber as those present discussed the matter.

Emperor Alalus stood and roared, "Silence." The chamber fell quiet. "I'm told the Malkuth Elder is missing and by their own laws, unless declared dead and another heir ascends the throne, their council cannot sign an agreement. That makes this... writ... invalid," he said, spittle foaming around his mouth as he spoke.

Ryakin tensed as she stepped towards the throne. Prince Anu appeared ready to support her, even with the blood still drying on the crowns' agreement he signed. Then a figure grabbed her arm, pulling her back gently behind him as he threw back his hood and stepped forward. A gasp echoing in the chamber.

"As the Elder of the Malkuth stands before you, I assure you I added my seal of approval. Your objection carries no weight. The writ is valid. I also formally demand you submit to the Temple and GIA how you were aware of my status as missing. Our highest orders in the Malkuth empire are the only ones aware of the fact." Emperor Alalus face blanched.

Ryakin would inquire later of Jynnalt how the missing Elder of the Malkuth came to be with her party. A story for a later time, he was sure Elgar would say.

He swayed on his feet as dizziness assailed him. Jynnalt moved back to him, stepping close. "Wrap your arm around my waist as if in affection." He did so, though he did not fake the feelings.

"Your grace," she said Emperor Alalus' direction, though she did not bow her head, "I and my consort and our parties are leaving. This is no longer our affair. You may send envoys to Ki with my permission to work out trade deals... or not."

Jynnalt subtly helped him as they walked slow but with dignity out the ornate double doors of the Anunnaki Empires emperor's chamber.

"It is time we go home, husband and rest."

"If I understand anything about Prince Anu, this will not be the end of this affair. For now, his position is too weak to take the throne. He is just biding his time."

"Maybe, maybe not. I just want to go home. This is something to worry over at a different time."

"Agreed."

Home, both forced to fight along different twisted pathways. For now, there is peace. Ryakin wondered for how long. Now he wanted to rebuild and restart. To watch the star rise and star set with Jynnalt by his side. Nothing more.

Chapter Epilogue

335894 GGS Tuiu 26th.
Kiestrial Royal Palace.

THE SEARCH FOR HER son followed myriad trails, yet none acquired any information as to his whereabouts. Kalmia used Ki's vast resources at her disposal with no results. Jynnalt, pregnant with twin daughters, hid her sorrow from those around her, desperate for normalcy. Peace for a time descended upon the Kierian kingdom. Jynnalt and Ryakin no longer took a single turn for granted.

Emperor Alalus, after eight months, bent enough to start discussions on a trade deal with Ki as the Chakian empire won their case against the Anunnaki in GIA. Both the Council of Nine and GIA kept fleets patrolling the trade lanes to enforce the treaty. Still, Emperor Alalus declined to reenter the Galactic Interstellar Alliance or the Council of Nine.

Unrest ferments across the galaxy and the Temple's unease grows as more empires and kingdoms fall and sphere after sphere of influence defeated by the Society and Sabation coalition. The Anunnaki Empire, harbingers of the taint spreading throughout the galaxy, waiting to engulf them all as a new danger hatches.

About the Author

Raised as an Air Force military brat, I later married a military service member in the Army. I have traveled the world and the USA.

As a young person, I worked a winter at Mt. Hood ski lodge. Later, a stable hand for two prestigious stables in Oregon, that led to the desire to own land and have a ranch.

I worked in the field for a petroleum geologist company in Ventura, California. Fished for salmon in Alaska on the Kenai peninsula. Worked for Pinkerton as an armed and unarmed security officer. Worked security while in Germany for the University of Maryland. Also worked on base in Mannheim, Germany as a telephone operator. Back in stateside, I earned my Criminal Justice degree while working full time once more for Pinkerton, which later became Securitas. Then to the streets as a police officer. I now own land in Colorado.

I grew up a Star Trek, and later a Star Wars fan, as an older adult, a fan of Stargate SG-1 and Stargate Atlantis. Spent long nights listening to Art Bell on coast to coast and later George Noory. Love the unique aspects of the History channel.

I have two beautiful girls now grown with children of their own, and seven intelligent, beautiful, and inquisitive grandchildren. I live on the Eastern plains of Colorado with the company of my two dogs, Sadie and Lilly and my family.

This story was a journey for me. I always wrote, especially in times of stress, though not professionally. Science fiction an easy love for me. But then I read one man's life's work regarding academia and Ancient Gods, which led my imagination to flow, thinking.

What if this could be real? What if tales of rumored ancient civilizations and gods held truth? How did it all fit together? It awoke something exciting; a story to somehow make the Ancient Gods become real, their history deeply intertwined with our history. I hope to take you on a similar journey of imaginary what if's..

Don't miss out!

Visit the website below and you can sign up to receive emails whenever C.S. Wade publishes a new book. There's no charge and no obligation.

https://books2read.com/r/B-A-MQBL-ITIGB

BOOKS 2 READ

Connecting independent readers to independent writers.

About the Author

Raised as an Air Force military brat, I later married a military service member in the Army. I have traveled the world and the USA.

As a young person I worked a winter at Mt. Hood ski lodge. Later a stable hand for two prestigious stables in Oregon, that led to the desire to own land and have a ranch.

I worked in the field for a Petroleum geologist company in Ventura, California. Fished for salmon in Alaska on the Kenai peninsula. Worked for Pinkerton as an armed and unarmed security officer. Worked security while in Germany for the University of Maryland. Also worked on base in Mannheim Germany as a telephone operator. Back stateside I earned my Criminal Justice degree while working full time once more for Pinkerton, which later became Securitas. Then to the streets as a police officer. I now own land in Colorado.

I grew up a Star Trek, and later a Star Wars fan, as an older adult a fan of Stargate SG-1 and Stargate Atlantis. Spent long nights listening to Art Bell on coast to coast and later George Noory. Love the unique aspects of the History channel.

I have two beautiful girls now grown with children of their own, and seven intelligent, beautiful and inquisitive grandchildren. I live on the Eastern plains of Colorado with the company of my pup, Sadie.

This story was a journey for me. I always wrote, especially in times of stress, though not professionally. Science fiction an easy love for me. But then I read one man's life's work regarding academia and Ancient Gods, which led my imagination to flow, thinking.

What if this could be real? What if tales of rumored ancient civilizations and Gods held truth? How did it all fit together? It awoke something exciting; a story to somehow make the Ancient Gods become real, their history deeply intertwined with our history. I hope to take you on a similar journey.

Read more at cswadebooks.com.

About the Publisher

Platinum Oak Publishing is a new small press for Indie authors who work hard to put their best efforts forth. We help guide and direct new and experienced authors towards articles and companies that are helpful. We have many directions to grow while serving the Indie Authors community. Come grow with us.